Praise for *The Map of Time*

"A brilliant and breathtaking trip."

—Scott Westerfeld, *New York Times* best-selling author of *Leviathan*

"A singularly inventive, luscious story with a core of pure, unsettling weirdness. With unnerving grace and disturbing fantasy, it effortlessly straddles that impossible line between being decidedly familiar, and yet absolutely new."

—Cherie Priest, author of *Boneshaker*

"Palma makes his U.S. debut with the brilliant first in a trilogy, an intriguing thriller that explores the ramifications of time travel in three intersecting narratives."

—*Publishers Weekly* (starred review)

"Readers who embark on the journey . . . will be richly rewarded."

—*Booklist* (starred review)

"Lyrical storytelling and a rich attention to detail make this prize-winning novel an enthralling read."

—*Library Journal* (starred review)

"Palma is a master of ingenious plotting."

—*Kirkus Reviews*

"A big genre-bending delight."

—*The Washington Post*

"Palma uses the basic ingredients of steampunk—fantasy, mystery, ripping adventure, and Victorian-era high tech—to marvelous effect."

—*The Seattle Times*

"A thought-provoking and entertaining read."

—*The Boston Globe*

Praise for *The Map of the Sky*

"The unreal becomes real, fantasy becomes history, and the reader is thoroughly entertained by an unending parade of bafflements and surprises. This book is a complete delight."

—*K. W. Jeter, author of Infernal Devices*

"A top-notch sequel . . . Fans of intelligent science fiction as well as historical thrillers will be rewarded."

—*Publishers Weekly* (starred review)

"The wondrous Palma genre-hops to great effect in this worthy sequel."

—*Booklist*

"*The Map of the Sky* keeps the reader guessing, checking, and thinking, all the while providing many sidelights on the literary history of sci-fi itself."

—*The Wall Street Journal*

"A cross-genre masterpiece."

—Associated Press

the MAP of CHAOS

the MAP of CHAOS

A Novel

FÉLIX J. PALMA

TRANSLATED BY NICK CAISTOR

ATRIA BOOKS

NEW YORK   LONDON   TORONTO   SYDNEY   NEW DELHI

ATRIA BOOKS
An Imprint of Simon & Schuster, Inc.
1230 Avenue of the Americas
New York, NY 10020

Copyright © 2015 by Cronotilus, S.L.

First Atria Books hardcover edition June 2015

ATRIA BOOKS and colophon are trademarks of Simon & Schuster, Inc.

For information about special discounts for bulk purchases, please contact Simon &
Schuster Special Sales at 1-866-506-1949 or business@simonandschuster.com.

The Simon & Schuster Speakers Bureau can bring authors to your live event. For
more information or to book an event, contact the Simon & Schuster Speakers Bureau at 1-866-248-3049 or visit our website at www.simonspeakers.com.

Manufactured in the United States of America

10 9 8 7 6 5 4 3 2 1

Library of Congress Cataloging-in-Publication Data
    Palma, Félix J.
        [Mapo del caos. English]
        The map of chaos : a novel / Félix J. Palma ; translated by Nick Caistor.—
    First Atria Books hardcover edition.
            pages cm
        Includes bibliographical references and index.
        1. Wells, H. G. (Herbert George), 1866–1946—Fiction. I. Caistor,
    Nick, translator. II. Title.
    PQ6666.A3965M3313 2015
    863'.64—dc23

                                                    2014030620

ISBN 978-1-4516-8818-4
ISBN 978-1-4516-8820-7 (ebook)

*To my parents and their literary
work, whose pages continue to grow.*

Do I believe in ghosts? No, but I'm afraid of them.

— *Marquise du Deffand*

If we could somehow control these probabilities, one could perform feats that would be indistinguishable from magic.

— *Michio Kaku, Parallel Worlds*

Lord knows what it was that I dreamed, experienced, and then dreamed once more, until I am no longer able to tell dream and reality apart.

— *Eric Rücker Eddison, The Worm Ouroboros*

CONTENTS

the MAP of CHAOS

WELCOME, DEAR READER, AS YOU PLUNGE INTO THE PAGES OF OUR FINAL MELODRAMA, WHERE FRESH ADVENTURES AWAIT YOU EVEN MORE ASTONISHING THAN THE LAST!

BEFORE EMBARKING UPON THIS STORY, BE SURE TO GO TO THE END OF THE BOOK, WHERE YOU WILL FIND THE CAST OF CHARACTERS WHO WILL ACCOMPANY YOU.

IF TIME TRAVEL AND MARTIAN INVASIONS WERE NOT ENOUGH TO QUICKEN YOUR PULSE, YOU ARE INVITED TO VENTURE INTO A WORLD INHABITED BY GHOSTS AND OTHER MONSTERS OF THE MIND.

YOU MAY WISH TO RECONSIDER BEFORE READING ON. HOWEVER, IT IS MY DUTY TO WARN YOU THAT IF YOU LOSE COURAGE, YOU WILL NEVER DISCOVER WHAT LIES BEYOND THE WORLD YOU THINK YOU KNOW.

HE DEBATE WAS DUE TO COMMENCE IN FIFTEEN minutes when they glimpsed the Palace of Knowledge silhouetted against the golden canvas of twilight. The tiled domes of the vast edifice, soaring above the pointed rooftops of the London skyline, fragmented the sun's last rays into myriad shimmering reflections. Bloated zeppelins, aerostats, ornithopters, and winged cabriolets circled around like a swarm of insects, bobbing amidst the clouds. In one of those very carriages, gliding majestically toward the building, sat the eminent biologist Herbert George Wells, accompanied by his lovely wife. Or should I say, his intelligent, dazzlingly beautiful wife.

At that moment, the biologist looked down from his window. An agitated crowd thronged the narrow streets that snaked between the lofty towers studded with stained glass windows, and connected by suspension bridges. Gentlemen in top hats and capes prattled to one another through their communication gloves, ladies walked their mechanical dogs, children whizzed by on electric roller skates, and long-legged automatons made their way through the torrent of people, stepping over them with calculated agility as they went diligently about their errands. From the waters of the Thames, gilded by the sunset, tiny *Nautiluses* manufactured by Verne Industries would occasionally rise to the surface, like globefish, to disgorge their passengers on both banks of the river. However, as they drew closer to where the palace stood in South Kensington, the teeming anthill appeared to be moving in one direction. Everyone knew that the most important debate to be held in the

Palace of Knowledge in the last ten years was taking place that evening. Just then, as if to remind the ornithopter's passengers, a mechanical bird flew by announcing the event with pompous enthusiasm before gliding toward the nearest building, where it continued its refrain perched on a gargoyle head.

Inside the flying machine, Wells took a deep breath in an attempt to calm himself and wiped his clammy hands on his trouser legs.

"Do you think *his* hands are sweating as well?" he asked Jane.

"Of course, Bertie. He has as much invested in this as you. Besides, we mustn't forget that his problem makes it—"

"What problem? Oh, come now, Jane!" Wells interrupted. "He's been seeing the best speech therapist in the kingdom for years. It's high time we stopped thinking he has a problem."

As though considering the matter closed, Wells settled back in his seat and gazed absentmindedly at the rows of sunflower houses colonizing Hyde Park, turning on their pillars in search of the sun's last rays. He wasn't going to admit to Jane that his rival suffered from that insidious problem (which, if necessary, he fully intended to make use of), for if the man trounced him, his defeat would be doubly shameful. But Wells wasn't going to fail. Whether or not the old man had his *little* problem under control, Wells outstripped him as a speaker. If he gave an inspired performance that evening, he would beat the old man hands down, and even if he didn't he would still triumph. Wells was slightly concerned that his opponent might win the public over with some of the syllogisms he used to spice up his rhetoric. However, Wells trusted the audience would not be blinded by a vulgar fireworks display.

Wells smiled to himself. He truly believed that his was the most significant generation to have walked the Earth, for, unlike those that had gone before, his held the future of the human race in its hands. Right or wrong, the decisions it made would reverberate through the centuries to come. Wells couldn't hide his enthusiasm at belonging to this exhilarating period of human history, when the world's salvation was to be decided. If all went well, that evening his name might be recorded for all time in the annals of History.

"It isn't vanity that makes me want to win, Jane," he suddenly said to his wife. "It is simply that I believe my theory is correct, and we can't waste time proving his."

"I know, dear. You are many things to me, but I have never thought of you as vain," she fibbed. "If only there were sufficient funding to back both projects. Having to choose between them is risky. If we're mistaken—"

Jane broke off in mid-sentence, and Wells said nothing more. His was the winning theory, he was certain of that. Although there were times, especially certain nights as he observed the lights of the city through his study window, when he wondered whether finally they weren't all mistaken; whether his world, where the quest for Knowledge controlled everything, really *was* the best of all possible worlds. During those moments of weakness, as he referred to them in the cold light of day, he toyed with the idea that Ignorance was preferable to Knowledge. It might have been better to allow Nature and her laws to remain shrouded in darkness, to carry on believing that comets heralded the death of kings, and dragons still dwelled in unmapped territories . . . But the Church of Knowledge, the sole religion on the planet, whose Holy See was in London, brought together philosophy, theology, politics, and the sciences in a single discipline. It ruled men's lives from the moment they were born, encouraging them to decipher the Creator's work, to discover its components. It even compelled them to solve the riddle of their own existence. Under the Church's auspices, man had transformed the quest for Knowledge into his reason for being, and, in his eagerness to unravel each of the mysteries that made the universe beautiful, he had ended up peeping behind the curtain. Perhaps they were now simply paying the price for their recklessness.

A red carpet had been rolled out in front of the palace doors, and on either side a noisy crowd was brandishing every sort of placard while a dozen bobbies tried to contain their fervor. Since its construction, the cathedralesque building had been the stage of great symposia regarding the dimensions of the universe, the origins of time, or the existence of the super-atom, all legendary debates whose most memorable phrases and parries had passed into common usage. The ornithopter circled the palace towers, hovering for a moment before alighting on a clear area of street cordoned off for that purpose. The cleaner-spiders had made the windows gleam, and the mechanical pelicans had devoured the garbage in the gutters, leaving that part of the city spotless and crying out to be sullied anew. When the ornithopter had finally landed, a liveried automaton went to hold open the door for its occupants. Before stepping out, Wells glanced at Jane with a look of combined resolve and fear; she responded with a reassuring smile. The crowd burst into a unanimous roar of jubilation as he emerged from the vehicle. Wells could hear shouts of encouragement mixed with the booing of his rival's supporters. With Jane on his arm, he crossed the gauntlet that was the red carpet, following the automaton and waving to the public as he tried hard to project the serenity of one who considers himself far superior to his opponent.

They walked through the portal, which bore an inscription in huge bronze lettering: "Science without religion is lame, religion without science is blind." Once inside, the automaton led them along a narrow corridor to a dressing room and then offered to take Jane to the VIP box. It was time for them to part. Jane went over to Wells and straightened his tie.

"Don't worry, Bertie. You're going to be fine."

"Thank you, my dear," he mumbled.

They closed their eyes and gently joined foreheads for a few seconds, each honoring the other's mind. After that intimate gesture, with which couples conveyed how necessary and enlightening the other's company was for them in their collective journey toward Knowledge, Jane looked straight at her husband.

"Best of luck, my dear," she told him before declaring: "Chaos is inevitable."

"Chaos is inevitable," Wells repeated diligently.

He wished he could leave his wife with the slogan used in his parents' day: "We are what we know," which so faithfully summed up the aspirations of their generation. However, since the discovery of the dreadful fate that awaited the universe, the Church had imposed this new slogan to raise awareness that the end was nigh.

After saying good-bye, Jane followed the automaton to the VIP box. As Wells watched her walk away, he admired yet again the miraculous sequence of genes that had created this woman, slender and lovely as a Dresden figurine, a sequence he had been unable to resist secretly unraveling in his laboratory, despite feeling that there was something oddly obscene about reducing his wife to an abstract jumble of facts and formulas. Before she disappeared at the end of the corridor, Jane gave him a final smile of encouragement, and the biologist experienced a sudden desire to kiss his wife's lips. He instantly chastised himself. A kiss? What was he thinking? That gesture had long been obsolete, ever since the Church of Knowledge deemed it unproductive and subversive. Gloomily, he resolved to examine his response at length once the debate was over. The Church encouraged people from an early age to analyze everything, including their feelings, to map out their inner selves and learn to repress any emotion that wasn't useful or easily controlled. It wasn't that love, or passion, or friendship was forbidden. Love of books or a passion for research was heartily approved of, provided the mind was in charge. But love between two people could take place only under strict surveillance. It was possible to abandon oneself freely to love (indeed, the Church encouraged young people to mate in order to perpetuate the species), but it was also necessary to spend time analyzing love, examining its hidden motives, drawing diagrams of it and comparing them with those of a partner, presenting regular reports on love's origin, evolution, and inconsistencies to the local parish priest, who would help scrutinize those treacherous emotions until they could be understood, for understanding was what made it possible to control everything. And yet, none of those emotions survived such scrutiny. The more you understood them, the fainter they became, like a dream fading as you try to recall it.

Wells couldn't help admiring the Church of Knowledge's ingenious solution to this thorny issue. By insisting love be understood, it had created the perfect vaccine against love. Prohibiting love would have elevated it, made it more desirable, capable of fomenting uprisings, wars, and acts of revenge. In short, it would have brought about another Dark Era, which would only have stood in the way of progress. And what would have become of them then? Would they have gotten that far had they allowed their feelings to govern them? Would they have amassed all that Knowledge, which as things stood might prove their only route to salvation? Wells didn't think so. He was convinced that the key to the survival of the species lay in the judicious act of bridling mankind's emotional impulses, unshackling humans from their feelings just as thousands of years before they had been freed from their instincts. Yet there were times, when he watched Jane sleeping, that he couldn't stop himself from having doubts. Contemplating the placid abandon of her lovely face, the extreme fragility of her body momentarily deprived of the admirable personality that infused it with life, he would wonder whether the path to salvation and the path to happiness were one and the same.

Brushing aside these thoughts, he entered the dressing room, the tiny space where he must spend the last few minutes before walking out onstage. He stood in the middle of the room, choosing not to sit on any of the chairs. The door opposite led to the auditorium. Through it filtered the excited roars of the crowd and the voice of Abraham Frey, the celebrated moderator, who at that moment was welcoming the various dignitaries attending the event. Soon they would announce his name, and he would have to go out onto the stage. Wells ruefully contemplated the right-hand wall. He knew that on the other side of it, in the adjoining dressing room, his rival was doubtless listening to the cries of the audience resounding through the amphitheater with the same feigned determination.

Then Wells heard his name and the door opened, inviting him to abandon his sanctuary. He took a deep breath and strode forth onto the back of the stage. Seeing him, the crowd burst into feverish applause. A couple of the recording orbs floating above the auditorium whirled over and began circling him. Wells raised his hands in greeting as he gave his most serene smile, imagining it being reproduced on the communication screens in millions of homes. He walked over to his lectern, which bore the stem of a voice enhancer, and spread his hands over its surface. One of the spotlights located above the stage bathed his puny figure in a golden glow. Five or six yards to his right, his opponent's lectern stood empty. While acknowledging the applause, the biologist took the opportunity to examine the stalls, separated from him by the pit, where a mechanical orchestra had started to play an evocative melody. Music creates order out of chaos, he thought, recalling the words of a famous violinist who had received the Church's blessing. Amidst the audience, Wells noticed banners and signs sporting his image as well as some of his famous sayings. Up above the rows of seats, beneath an enormous pennant with an eight-pointed star emerging from two concentric circles, Queen Victoria sat on her wheeled throne, in which she traveled everywhere of late. Next to her, on a less sumptuous throne, sat Cardinal Violet Tucker, the highest authority in the Church of Knowledge, who would preside over the debate. Her entourage sat in a cluster on her left, a flock of bishops and deacons with stern, embittered faces, who, together with the cardinal, made up the Budgetary Commission. That gaunt old lady, dressed in a black robe with gold silk buttons, and a sash and beret likewise gold, the color of Knowledge, would ultimately decide his fate. Wells noticed the goblet cupped in her right hand, which if the rumors were correct contained her anti-cancer medicine. On either side of the theater stood the boxes reserved for the authorities and prominent attendees, most notably Jules Verne, the French entrepreneur; Clara Shelley, the heiress to Prometheus Industries, a leading manufacturer of automatons; and various members of the scientific community. Wells could see Jane in the VIP box. She was talking to Doctor Pleasance, the wife of his rival, a handsome woman of about forty who, like Jane, worked as project director in her husband's laboratory.

Pacing up and down the stage between the orchestra pit and the lecterns was Abraham Frey, who wore a bronze helmet that had a voice enhancer projecting from its right side, leaving his hands free to perform their characteristic gestures. At that moment, he was introducing Wells's opponent, listing his many achievements over a long life devoted to the service of Knowledge. Inundated by this torrent of information, Wells was able to make out the words "Knowledge Church College," in Oxford, where his rival had given his celebrated lectures in mathematics and physics, and where Wells himself had studied. There, conversing between its ancient walls and strolling across its verdant meadows, the two men had forged an inspiring teacher-pupil relationship, and although Wells had finally chosen biology over physics, they had continued to meet regularly, incapable of renouncing a friendship they had both deemed fruitful enough to pursue. No one could have imagined that, in years to come, fate would make rivals of them. While in private this was a source of amusement to them, it in no way diminished the ferocity with which each defended his position during the many debates they had engaged in prior to the one taking place that evening, in which the Church would decide which of their projects was most likely to save the world.

"And now, Your Majesty, Your Eminence, leaders of the Church of Knowledge, ladies and gentlemen, please welcome the distinguished physicist and mathematician Charles Lutwidge Dodgson."

Followers of Wells's rival broke into loud cheers as their idol's name was announced. The tiny door to his dressing room opened, and an elderly gentlemen of about sixty emerged, waving to the public as he approached his lectern, just as Wells had done moments before. He was tall and thin, his white hair meticulously groomed, and his face possessed the languid beauty of a weary archangel. As he watched him, Wells couldn't help feeling a sense of compassion. Clearly, Charles Dodgson would have preferred to be spending that magnificent, golden evening on one of his habitual boating excursions along the Thames rather than arguing with his former pupil about how best to save the world, yet neither man could shirk his responsibilities. They greeted each other with a stiff nod, and each stood quietly at his lectern, waiting for the moderator to begin. Frey called for silence, stroking the flank of the air with his hand.

"Ladies and gentlemen," he exclaimed in the baritone voice for which he was famous. "As we all know, our beloved universe is dying. And it has been for millions of years. Ever since the universe burst forth amidst a blazing cataclysm, it has been expanding at breakneck speed, but it has also been cooling. And that same cooling process that once nurtured life will eventually snuff it out." He paused, plunging his hands into his jacket pockets, and started pacing up and down the stage, staring at the ground, like a man on a stroll daydreaming. "Subject to the three laws of thermodynamics," he went on, "the galaxies are flying apart. Everything is aging. Wearing out. The end of the world is near. Stars will burn out, magic holes evaporate, temperatures will descend to absolute zero. And we humans, incapable of continuing our work in this frozen landscape . . . will become extinct."

Frey gave a woeful sigh and began to shake his head silently, drawing out the suspense, until at last he exclaimed, almost in anger: "But we aren't plants, or helpless creatures that must resign themselves to a tragic destiny. We are Mankind! And having assimilated this terrible discovery, Mankind began to wonder whether there wasn't a way of surviving the inevitable, even the death of the universe itself. And the answer, ladies and gentlemen, was yes! But this does not mean we should challenge chaos like a suicidal warrior, defying Nature . . . and God. No, such a display of bravado would be absurd. It would be enough . . . to flee, to emigrate to another universe. Is that possible? Can we leave this condemned universe for another, more hospitable one and begin once again? And if so, how? Formulas have been scrawled on the blackboards of all the world's laboratories in an attempt to find out. But perhaps our salvation depends on one of the two exceptional minds here with us today."

Wells contemplated the audience, who were loudly applauding the moderator's speech. Placards and banners waved about like buffeted trees. Everyone there had been born into a world under sentence of death, and although they might not be around to experience the end Frey had so starkly depicted, the so-called Day of Chaos, they knew that their grandchildren or great-grandchildren would. All estimates now spoke in terms of a few generations, because the cooling of the universe was happening more quickly than had first been predicted. And was this the legacy they wanted to leave their descendants, a frozen universe where life was impossible? No, of course not. God had thrown down the glove, and Man had picked it up. The first thing Wells's mother had told him when he was old enough to understand was that everything he could see (which at that moment was the backyard of their house in Bromley, but also the sky and the trees peeping out from behind the wall) would be destroyed, because the Creator hadn't made the world to last forever, although he had been kind enough to give man a short enough life span so that he could have the illusion that it would. Like most young men and women of his generation, Wells had devoured countless books in his compulsive pursuit of Knowledge, spurred on by a romantic ambition to save the world. Could there be a more noble achievement? And perhaps, that very evening, what had once been a child's naïve dream would become reality, for Wells was the leading proponent of one of the two most important theories about how to save humanity.

According to the lots they had drawn, the chairman invited Dodgson to open the debate. Before speaking, he took a sip of water. His old professor had never been one of those ruddy types brimming with energy and enthusiasm, but Wells could see how old age had blurred his features, giving him an air of painful fragility. He looked incapable of frightening a mouse. Finally, Dodgson balanced his glass on the lectern, gave the usual formalities, and launched into his speech:

"Since receiving the dreadful news that everything we love is destined to die, a single question has been floating in the air: Is it possible for us to engage the powers of science and flee this lost world for another? I say yes, dear audience, it most emphatically is. And I am here this evening to tell you how."

Dodgson was talking in a calm voice in order not to set off his stammer, doubtless on the advice of his speech therapist. That would render his discourse a little subdued, Wells reflected, whilst he himself could deliver his speech unhampered, thus endowing it with that theatrical vehemence that so easily roused the masses. Wells let the old man continue, waiting for the most opportune moment to interrupt him.

"As many of you know, on the evening when, in this very auditorium, following a memorable debate, it was established that the universe was dying, I was busy trying to find ways of injecting methane into Mars's atmosphere. My intention was to produce an artificial greenhouse effect on the red planet, raising its temperature and melting its surface to create lakes and rivers in preparation for a first human colony, so that if a meteorite struck Earth or we experienced another ice age we would have somewhere safe to go. Needless to say, the news about the end of the world changed the course of my research, and even my life. I forgot all about Mars, which was doomed like the rest of the universe, and, along with every conscientious scientist, I devoted myself to investigating ways of emigrating to a younger universe whose fate was not hanging in the balance. Ever since the illustrious Newton enlightened our minds"—at this the audience thundered "Hurrah for Newton!"—"we have all known that ours isn't the only universe, but, as countless studies and experiments have shown, it is simply another bubble in the ocean of infinity. Any law or equation that contradicts this truth is doomed to failure and humiliation. Equally, we know that in this eternal ocean, bubbles are continually created and destroyed. Whilst this may bode ill for those of us who find ourselves in a dying bubble, it also provides a glimmer of hope, for as I speak, myriad universes are being born. And somewhere waiting for us out there is a luminous new world, the ideal place for an exiled civilization to build a new home. But how will we get there? How will we achieve what would undoubtedly be the greatest escape of all time? It is very simple: through the traditional method of opening a tunnel, something with which even the most ignorant convict is familiar. As I have discussed in my numerous articles, the universe is riddled with magic holes that possess an infinite gravitational force that sucks in anything around them. Is it not possible that these holes exist for a reason? Perhaps they are simply the Creator's subtle way of telling us how to free ourselves from his own snare. But what lies behind these holes? There are many theories, an infinite number, if you'll pardon the pun. But I am convinced that at the center of each is a tunnel connecting to another identical hole in another universe. Unfortunately, we have no way of traveling to any of those holes, because they are too far away from our planet, and their environment is too unstable. But that needn't be a problem, for what I propose to do is create a magic hole artificially in my laboratory. I am certain that in a controlled environment . . ."

"But, my dear Charles, your hole would be too small," Wells interrupted him at last. "I can't see the whole of humanity passing through it one by one. Even the Creator would lose patience. Besides, I can't speak for the audience, but personally I have no wish to be devoured, by a magic hole or anything else. You know as well as I do that the sheer force of gravity would make mincemeat of us. We would be sucked into its center and crushed to death." He paused for dramatic effect before adding with a mocking air, "In fact, the only use for your hole would be to dispose of the evidence of a crime."

Wells's quip, which he had rehearsed a hundred times in front of a mirror, elicited the predictable laughter from the audience. Charles, however, was unfazed.

"Oh, have no fear, George. None of that would happen if the hole was spinning, because the centripetal force would cancel out the gravitational force. So that anyone going into it, far from being crushed to death, would be sucked into a neighboring universe. It would be a small matter of balancing the two forces to prevent the hole from fracturing. And once I achieved that, naturally there would be no need for the whole of humanity to pass through it. We would simply send ahead a few automatons, with the genetic information of every person on the planet codified in their memories. Once they reached the Other Side, they would construct a laboratory and implant the aforementioned data into living cells, thus replicating the whole of humanity."

"By the Atlantic Codex!" Wells feigned astonishment, although he was well acquainted with Charles's theory. "All I can say is I hope those puppets don't make a mess of things and we all come out with frogs' heads . . ."

A fresh round of laughter reached them from the audience, and Wells noticed Charles beginning to twitch nervously.

"Tha-Tha-That way the whole of humanity could pass through an opening the size of a ra-ra-rabbit hole," he attempted to explain.

"Yes, yes, only first you must create it, my friend." Wells assumed a weary air. "But tell me, isn't this all rather complicated? Wouldn't it be better if each of us were able to leap across to that universe for himself?"

"By all means, George, go ahead. Leap into another universe and bring me back a glass of water; mine's empty," Charles parried.

"I'd like nothing more than to quench your thirst, Charles. However, I fear that for the moment I am unable to oblige. In order to leap into another universe I need a grant from the Budgetary Commission."

"So, what you are saying is that today you can't take that leap, but tomorrow you can?" Charles inquired with a wry smile.

"Yes, that's what I'm saying," Wells replied cautiously.

"Then I fear you are bound to fail, my dear George, for there is no 'tomorrow,' only 'today.'"

The audience howled with laughter. Wells cursed himself for having walked straight into it but was undeterred.

"What I mean is I will succeed the day the Budgetary Commission awards me a grant." He pronounced the words slowly, after making sure he wasn't leaving himself open to any more of Charles's retorts. "For as you know, I am busy developing a miracle serum, a virus I have called 'cronotemia' in tribute to past experiments, when men from our Age of Enlightenment believed we could travel in time. Once injected, the virus will mix with our blood and the hormones secreted by our brain, producing a genetic mutation that will enable us to reach the other universe without the need to be taken apart and reassembled on the Other Side. I am on the brink of perfecting the virus, of finding a stable solution that will reconfigure almost imperceptibly the molecular structure of our brains, allowing us to see what was hitherto invisible. As our learned audience doubtless already knows, all matter originates from the birth of our universe, and the atoms that make up our bodies are connected to other atoms on the far side of the cosmos. And if a particle floating around at the far side of the universe can communicate with us, then perhaps we can peer into that abyss, see what is behind it, and leap. Whether we like it or not, we are joined to those other worlds by an invisible umbilical cord. All we have to do is find the way to switch that connection from an atomic level to our macroscopic reality."

The debate went on for the remainder of the allotted hour amid witty asides, abrupt or barbed comments designed to ridicule or bamboozle the opponent, and even a few outbursts from Dodgson, who became increasingly flustered as he realized his ex-pupil was starting to win over the audience. In contrast, the biologist kept his cool throughout, smiling to himself as his rival became more and more excitable and his stammer began to render his speech almost unintelligible. Finally, just before the debate concluded, Wells uttered his much-rehearsed closing statement.

"A pinprick, a mere pinprick, of my serum is enough to make us superhuman, supernatural beings capable of living in any dimension. Trust in my project, Your Majesties, allow me to transform you into gods, and let us leave my dear opponent playing with his rabbit holes."

Charles was about to reply but was stopped short by the bell. The debate was over. The voice enhancers retracted into the lecterns, and Frey's voice could be heard celebrating their thrilling contest and inviting the Church of Knowledge to deliver its verdict. The orchestra struck up another evocative tune and the clerics conferred in whispers among the audience, but Cardinal Tucker immediately rose to her feet with the aid of her staff, and silence descended once more upon the auditorium.

"Having heard the two applicants for the Save Mankind Project Grant," she announced in her faltering voice, "we have come to the following decision: notwithstanding Professor Dodgson's celebrated wisdom, we believe that the task of saving us all must rest in the hands of the promising biologist Herbert George Wells, to whom I hereby extend my congratulations. May Knowledge guide your path, Mr. Wells. Chaos is inevitable!"

Wells felt his head spin as the theater exploded into triumphant roars on hearing the verdict. Hundreds of pennants bearing the Star of Chaos danced about like waves in a stormy ocean. He raised his hands, into which the fate of humankind had now been entrusted, saluting the excited audience, which immediately began chanting his name to loud cheers. He saw Jane and his team applauding and embracing one another in the box of honor, while Charles's wife remained in her chair, hands folded in her lap, oblivious to the surrounding uproar. Her eyes were fixed on her husband, who had lowered his head in defeat. Wells would have liked to comfort him, but the gesture would have been tasteless. Frey signaled to Wells, who walked over to him and allowed the chairman to raise his right arm as the audience cried out his name. Above the clamor, only Wells could hear Charles muttering angrily behind him:

"Eppur si muove."

Wells chose to ignore the reference to Galileo and instead gave a beaming smile, basking in the adulation of his supporters, who had started to descend from the rows of seats. A group of young girls climbed onto the stage and asked him to autograph their science textbooks. He did so with pleasure as he located Jane amid the crowd gathering to congratulate him in front of the stage and gave her a conspiratorial smile. Wells did not see Charles turn from his lectern and walk toward the dressing room door, nor did he notice the huge man who intercepted him before he was able to slip away. He was too busy drinking in his success. Charles could say what he liked, but Wells was the one who whose task it was to save mankind. That was what had been decided.

It took Wells eight months to hit on the magic potion that would enable the human race to flee to a neighboring universe without the need to dig any tunnels. Eight months, during which he and Jane and the rest of the team worked day and night, practically camping out in the state-of-the-art laboratory they had set up with the Commission's money. When at long last they thought they had synthesized the virus, Wells asked Jane to fetch Newton, the Border Collie they had acquired three months before. Wells had decided they should give a dog the honor of leading mankind's intended exodus rather than a rat, a guinea pig, or a monkey, for whilst the intelligence of the latter was more celebrated, everyone knew that dogs had the most developed homing instinct of any species and could find their way back even over great distances. So, if the leap was successful, there was a slight possibility the dog might follow its own scent and leap in the other direction, and if that happened, they would be able to study any unforeseen side effects of the virus, as well as the physical toll it might take on the animal. Jane had regarded as less than scientific her husband's belief in the popular idea of canine loyalty, but when she first saw the puppy cavorting in the shop window, with its eager little eyes and an adorable heart-shaped white patch on its forehead, any doubts she had melted away. And so, little Newton arrived at the Wells's house, with the mission of vanishing into thin air a few months later, although before that happened nothing prevented him from being simply a pet.

When Jane appeared with the puppy, Wells placed him on the laboratory bench, and, without further ado, pinched his haunch and injected him with the virus. Then they shut him in a glass-walled room designed for that purpose, and everyone on the team observed him. If they weren't mistaken, the virus would travel through the bloodstream to the puppy's brain, where it would pierce the cells like a needle, introducing new elements that would heighten the brain's sensitivity to the point where, to put it simply, the dog would be able to see the thread that joined it to that other part of itself drifting on the far side of the universe.

They took turns doing six-hour shifts outside the glass-walled room, although Jane preferred to keep watch inside, playing with the puppy and stroking it. Wells advised her not to become too attached to the animal, because sooner or later it would disappear and she would find herself caressing the carpet. However, the days went by and Wells's ominous warning didn't come true. When the time limit they had set for the leap to occur ran out, they entered the phase where the likelihood of error began to grow exponentially, until one fine day Wells realized that continuing to wait in front of the window for the puppy to disappear was a question of faith or stubbornness more than anything else, and he announced that the experiment had failed.

Over the following weeks, they retraced one by one each step they had taken in engineering the virus, while Newton, freed from captivity, frolicked at their feet, showing no sign of physical decline, nor any sign of performing the miracle that would send shock waves through society. It had all looked foolproof on paper. The damned virus had to work. So why didn't it? They tried tinkering with the strain, but none of the modifications they made had the stability of the first. Everything pointed to that being the correct virus, the only viable one. Then where was the error? Wells searched in vain, becoming increasingly obsessed with finding what had gone wrong, while it began to dawn on the others, including Jane, that the theory on which everything was based had been incorrect. However, Wells refused to accept that conclusion and would fly into a rage if any member of the team hinted at it. He wasn't prepared to concede defeat and determinedly kept up his research, growing increasingly irritable as the days went by, so that several members of his team were obliged to decamp. Jane watched him working feverishly in silence, ever more tormented and isolated, and wondered how long it would be before he conceded that he'd wasted the Church's funds on a misguided theory.

One morning, they received an invitation from Charles Dodgson to take tea with him at his house in Oxford. During the past months the two men had corresponded occasionally. The professor had benignly inquired how his ex-pupil's research was going, but Wells had been evasive. He had decided to tell Charles nothing until he had succeeded in synthesizing the virus and had shown that it worked by injecting Newton. Then he would write to him, or call him through the communication glove, and invite him to his house, bestowing on him the privilege of being the first scientist outside his team to discover that mankind had found a way of saving itself. But since Newton had not disappeared as he was supposed to, that call had never taken place. Two exasperating months later, Wells received the invitation from Dodgson. He considered refusing it but didn't have the heart. The last thing he wanted was to have to admit to Charles that the virus did not work. Jane told him he might benefit from his old friend's advice. Besides, Charles still lived at Knowledge Church College, Wells's alma mater, and perhaps the memories associated with those noble edifices would inspire him with new ideas, not to mention allow him to take a walk in the beautiful surrounding countryside, for it never hurt to get some fresh air. Wells agreed, not so much because the idea appealed to him, but in order to avoid an argument with his wife. He didn't even raise an objection when Jane suggested taking along Newton, who when left alone at home would amuse himself by chewing up cushions, books, or other objects accidentally left within reach of his jaws. And so, one cold January afternoon, an ornithopter left the couple and Newton in front of the college gates, where Charles was awaiting them, his carefully groomed hair mussed by the downdraft of the vehicle's propellers.

When the ornithopter had taken off again, Wells and Charles regarded each other for a moment in silence, like two men who had agreed to take part in a duel at dawn. Then they burst out laughing and embraced affectionately, slapping each other vigorously on the back as if trying to warm each other up.

"I'm sorry you lost the debate, Charles," Wells felt compelled to say.

"You mustn't apologize," Charles admonished. "Just as I wouldn't if you had lost. We each believe the other is mistaken, but provided you think me brilliantly mistaken, I don't mind."

Then Charles gave Jane the warmest welcome and excused his wife, Pleasance, who was busy giving a lecture. If her students didn't keep her too long, she might see them before they left.

"But what have we here?" Charles exclaimed, addressing the dog, who instantly began wagging his tail.

Before Wells could explain that it was a constant reminder of his fail- ure, Jane said: "His name is Newton, and he's been living with us for the last five months."

Charles stooped to stroke the tuft of white hair between the dog's eyes while uttering a few words to it, which only Newton appeared to understand. After this exchange of confidences, the professor, smooth- ing down his tousled hair, led his guests through a small garden to his chambers near the cathedral spire. In one of the larger rooms, where the wallpaper pattern was of sunflowers the size of plates, a domestic autom- aton was arranging a tea set on an exquisitely carved table, around which stood four Chippendale chairs. Hearing them come in, the automaton swung round, placed its metallic palms on the floor, and walked over to them on its hands before reverting to the normal hominid posture and greeting them with a theatrical bow, doffing an invisible hat.

"I see you still can't resist reprogramming your automatons, Charles," Wells remarked.

"Oh, I'm just trying to give them a bit of personality. I can't abide those tedious factory settings." The professor grinned, and then, ad- dressing the automaton, he added: "Thank you, Robert Louis. No one can balance the cups and saucers on the sugar bowl quite like you." The automaton acknowledged the compliment and appeared to blush, doubt- less the result of another of Charles's additions to its original program- ming. Wells shook his head in amusement while Robert Louis, knee joints creaking, went over to the door to await further orders. Wells's domestic automaton was also an RL6 Prometheus, but it would never have occurred to him to give it a name using those initials, much less open up its skull and rearrange its wiring to give it the soul of an acrobat. Charles, on the other hand, was unable to accept things as they came; he had to put his stamp on them, and that was precisely why Wells had learned to appreciate him more than his other professors.

While Charles and Jane finished laying the table, Wells took the op- portunity to stroll around the room. Alongside some of the most tech- nologically advanced appliances (Wells saw a food warmer, a writing glove, a heat transmitter, and even a dust-swallowing mouse stretched out on a pedestal table, its innards exposed, as though Charles were halfway through performing a dissection) was a different type of object that offered a glimpse into the professor's more eccentric side, including some antique toys and a collection of music boxes. Wells walked over to where they were stacked on a shelf and stroked a couple of them the way he would a dozing cat, but he did not venture to open them, refusing to unleash their music and the minute ballerina that might lie squashed inside. At the back of the room a heavy curtain separated the formal part of the room from the *terra incognita* of the professor's laboratory.

Then Wells studied the walls, adorned with several of Charles's own drawings, illustrations from his textbooks on mathematical logic for children. Notwithstanding the playful spirit in which they were written, the Church, accustomed to indulging Charles's foibles, had given his books its blessing, for they were thought to help children develop their intelligence from an early age. Even so, fearing his reputation as a scientist might be compromised, Charles had taken the precaution of publishing them under the pseudonym of Lewis Carroll. He had written most of them whilst sitting on the banks of the river Thames, in the honey-colored spring light, for the professor was in the habit of boating on the river, gently cleaving its waters with his oars. More than once, when Wells was still his pupil, he had enjoyed the privilege of accompanying him.

"Come and sit next to me," Charles had said to him one afternoon on the riverbank, "and try to imagine a perfectly useless object."

"A perfectly useless object," Wells had repeated, sitting down with his back against the tree. "I'm afraid I wouldn't know how. Besides, what would be the use?"

"Oh, it's more useful than you think." Charles grinned and, seeing that his pupil was still puzzled, added, "I have something here that might help you."

He produced from his jacket pocket an ornate porcelain pillbox. He opened the lid by pressing a spring, the same as a pocket watch, revealing a tiny mound of golden powder. Wells raised his eyebrows.

"Is it . . . fairy dust?"

To Wells's astonishment, Charles nodded. It would never have entered Wells's head that his professor might take such a substance. It had been banned by the Church for more than a decade, because they thought it stimulated the brain in a negative way, inciting people to imagine unproductive things.

"Take some, and then try doing what I said," Charles exhorted, taking a pinch himself and raising it to his nostril. Then he offered the box to Wells, who hesitated.

"Oh, go on, George, be a devil. Why do you suppose humans have noses, to smell the lilies of the field?"

At last Wells took a pinch of the fairy dust and snuffed it into his nose as his professor smiled at him approvingly. Once the ritual had been consummated, Charles put the pillbox away, leaned back against the tree, and slowly closed his eyes.

"Now let your mind drift, George," Charles ordered in an excited whisper. "Find out how far you are able to go."

Amused, Wells grinned and leaned back as well, closing his eyes. For a few moments, he tried to do what Charles had said and imagine a perfectly useless object, but he couldn't stop his mind from reflecting about whether it was possible to diagnose a person's illness by analyzing his breath, as was done with blood or urine. It was something he had been speculating about for days. Vaguely disappointed, he thought of remarking to his professor that the fairy dust hadn't worked on him, but he decided to sit still with his eyes closed and wait for Charles to stir. He didn't want to interrupt him in case the professor was making his mind fly the way children flew kites. Wells concentrated on enjoying the delicious cool breeze riffling the water, amusing himself by trying to discover a break in the constant buzz of insects in his ears, and presently he started to feel drowsy. In his sluggish state, he noticed his mind begin to reel, and his thoughts rolled around in his head as they slowly began to lose all logic. He was momentarily seized with panic as he realized that each idea he formed instantly floated away, like a ship adrift, but he managed to calm down, telling himself that nothing bad was happening to his brain, that his altered state was an effect of the fairy dust, and he abandoned himself to it with a sense of curiosity rather than fear. A flood of nonsensical images, as impossible as they were suggestive, began filling his head, swirling and intermingling to create outlandish configurations. He saw Martian airships flying toward Earth, invisible men, and strange creatures, half pig, half hyena. And he felt a stab of excitement. This was like riding a wild horse bareback. Mesmerized, he let the feeling intensify to see if he might not be able to ride a dragon, too. Wells had no idea how long he remained in that state, creating and demolishing stories, with only the logic of delirium as his guide. He assumed Charles was doing the same at his side, but when it began to grow cold and he opened his eyes, he discovered his professor gazing at him with a wry smile.

"What you've been doing is imagining, my dear George, and although there are many who believe it has no use, I can assure you it does. We are what we imagine," he declared, rephrasing the old motto. "You'll find out for yourself soon enough."

And so he had. That very night, while Jane was asleep, Wells had shut himself in his study and donned his writing glove. Only this time not with the intention of penning any essays or articles that might help advance mankind's understanding of the world. This time he was going to write down the tales inspired by the images he had glimpsed under the influence of the fairy dust. He took a deep breath and tried to conjure them, but it was as though his mind, having reverted to its natural state of rigidity, refused all attempts. After hours spent trying to regurgitate them, he gave up and went outside onto the patio. The night sky was swarming with dirigibles, but Wells had no difficulty making out the *Albatross*, the airship bristling with propellers commissioned from Verne Industries by one of the richest men on the planet: Gilliam Murray, known as the Master of Imagination, because, while his business card described him as an antiques dealer, everyone knew he was involved in the manufacture and sale of fairy dust. That rotund braggart controlled his increasingly vast empire from his flying fortress, without the ecclesiastical police ever having succeeded in infiltrating his impenetrable web of bribery, threats, and extortion. And so, immune to the world's highest authority, the omnipresent *Albatross* cast a tainted shadow over the London evenings, reminding men that if they wished to explore the limits of their imagination, all they needed to do was take a pinch of Gilliam Murray's golden dust.

Wells had never imagined he would one day go in search of the substance manufactured by that despicable individual, and yet, not without a sense of shame, this was precisely what he found himself doing the following day. Not wishing to importune his professor, he made his way to Limehouse, an area of the city inhabited by so-called Ignorants, those who had decided to turn their backs on Knowledge. Wells had been told it was easy to get the dust there, and he was not mistaken: he came away with a full pillbox. During the night, he locked himself in his study, snuffed a pinch of the powder, put on his writing glove, and waited. His mind soon began to reel, as it had on that golden afternoon he had spent with Charles. Three hours later, with only a vague memory of his fingers flickering incessantly over the paper, Wells discovered that he had managed to fashion a story. He repeated the ritual the following night, and the night after, and so on, until he had a pile of stories invented on a playful whim. He had no idea why he wrote them, only to let them molder in his desk drawer because he dared not show them to anyone, not even to Jane. He didn't consider them worthy examples of a craft capable of producing useful insights. The protagonists of his tales were scientists caught up in strange, unwholesome experiments that contributed nothing to society, ambitious men who used science for their own ends, who sought invisibility or turned animals into humans, and he doubted the Church would give them its blessing. Perhaps that was why he enjoyed writing them.

However, the guilty knowledge that he was deliberately and regularly producing something sinful began to plague him during his waking hours, especially when he encountered an ecclesiastical policeman in the street. Indeed, his anxiety reached such a fever pitch that one night he gathered up those stories, which he had begun to realize contained more wisdom than all the dry essays he wrote, and threw them on the fire. That pile of ashes put an end to several months during which he had acted like a madman, and not like the acclaimed biologist he was. From then on, he was content to behave the way society expected and scrupulously avoided spending any more golden afternoons with his professor.

Nine or ten years had passed since those rapturous nights. During that time, Wells had imagined nothing. At least nothing that wasn't related to making things work, such as the accursed virus, cronotemia.

Wells shook his head, ridding himself of those memories, and went over to the table to lend a hand. When they had arranged the tea things, the three of them sat down and began a pleasant conversation about this and that, which Wells followed with a mixture of wistfulness and apprehension, aware that it was only a polite preamble before Dodgson ventured to ask about the thing that really interested him. When at last the conversation appeared to run out of steam, and a hush descended on them, Charles cleared his throat. Wells knew the moment had arrived.

"T-Tell me, George, how is your r-research going?" Charles asked, trying hard to control his stammer. "Y-You don't give much away in your letters."

Wells glanced at Jane, who nodded, encouraging him to come clean with Charles.

"Oh, excellently," Wells replied, with unerring enthusiasm. "I assure you it is progressing in leaps and bounds."

Charles looked at him skeptically.

"I-In leaps and bounds, you say? Is that a fact? I know you well, George, and from your tone of voice and posture, not to mention the fleeting look you just gave your dear wife, I would say the exact opposite is true. Look at you bolt upright in your chair, legs crossed, one swinging to and fro like pendulum. I-I'll wager you still haven't achieved any satisfactory results."

Wells looked slightly shamefaced and shifted in his chair, glancing once more at Jane, who nodded more forcefully this time. Then he turned to Charles, who was still smiling at him, and at last gave a feeble sigh.

"You're right," he confessed with a defeated air. "I'm at the end of my tether. We managed to synthesize the virus, only it doesn't work. I tried it on the dog"—he pointed to the constant reminder of his failure lying on the rug—"but without success. We've been over everything a thousand times but I still can't see what went wrong."

"A thousand times? Coincidentally, the same number of pieces a cup always breaks into when dropped on the floor . . . ," Charles jested, but when he saw that Wells made no attempt to laugh, he adopted a solemn expression, before adding, "Although I do understand, my friend. I sense you are on the verge of giving up."

"Absolutely not, Charles! That is unthinkable!" Wells declared, contemplating his wife's forlorn expression, which merely strengthened his resolve. "I assure you I shall carry on my research until I have discovered my mistake and put it right. The Church has given me the task of saving mankind and I have no intention of letting it down. If I did, I'd never be able to look myself in the face again."

"Y-You'd have great difficulty shaving if that were the case, George. But let's not be overdramatic. Perhaps you are right," Charles said reassuringly. Wells raised his eyebrows. "You must retrace your steps one by one, discover your mistake, and put it right." He gave a mischievous smile. "E-Even if that means going farther back than you thought, right?"

Wells remained silent.

"It's true, Bertie," Jane said softly. "Perhaps the time has come to accept that . . . Charles's theory is the correct one."

Wells looked at his wife and then at Dodgson, who was waiting for a reply. Charles had drawn him into a trap, but he still wasn't prepared to surrender.

"I'm afraid I can't pronounce the words you wish to hear, Charles," he replied with as much grace as he could muster. "My failure is only a temporary setback. My virus may not have worked, but I remain completely convinced we are on the right track. And that you could never succeed in creating a magic hole even if you had all the funding from the Budgetary Commission."

Charles looked at him calmly for a few seconds, but then a smile gradually appeared on his lips.

"Is that really what you think? I wouldn't be so sure if I were you."

"What do you mean?" Wells asked uneasily.

"Much as I adore your company," Charles said, looking at the couple with affection, "it isn't my only reason for inviting you here. There's something I want to show you. Something you say is impossible to create."

Wells stared at him, bewildered. Charles gestured to the automaton.

"Would you mind drawing back the curtain please, Robert Louis?"

The automaton walked over to the curtain, on its feet this time, took hold of one end, and, moving in reverse, began to draw it back, revealing what was behind. Wells leapt from his chair as if someone had just screamed "Fire!" and Jane's cup clattered into its saucer. Even Newton stiffened on the rug. It took a few seconds for them to understand what they were seeing, for it wasn't something that was easy to grasp. Somebody had sketched a hole on the fabric of reality, an orifice measuring roughly two yards in diameter, which appeared to be gyrating slowly. Around it was a ring of shimmering, grainy mist, slightly ragged at the edges, while the center was an absolute black, a frozen blackness like the one threatening the existence of the universe. Right next to the hole, reality seemed to bend as though wanting to pour through it. The hole was hovering about eighteen inches from the floor, above a metal stand bristling with levers and valves, and was surrounded by various complex constructions that seemed to be holding it in place.

"What the devil is this?" Wells spluttered.

"It's a magic hole, George," replied Charles.

Wells edged his way toward the phenomenon, closely followed by Jane, while Charles watched them from his chair with a satisfied grin. Wells let the purr of the machines calm his stupefaction and, keeping a safe distance behind the invisible boundary of the curtain, studied this rent in the air. The edges appeared to be made of gas, and because the hole curved slightly inward, it gave an impression of depth, although no sound came from within and all that could be seen was a dense, smooth blackness.

"You've done it . . ." Wells was incredulous.

Charles stood up and went over to join them.

"That's right, my friend: I've done it."

"But how? Where did you get the money to pay for all this?" Wells pointed to the machinery shielding the hole. "There's at least seven hundred thousand pounds' worth of equipment here."

"Eight hundred thousand, to be precise," the professor corrected him.

"But that's more than the entire Budgetary Commission grant!" Wells exclaimed, with mounting astonishment. "Unless you've inherited money from a string of rich uncles, I don't understand how you laid your hands on that amount . . ."

"My dear George, just because the Church has no faith in my project, it doesn't mean nobody does. A lot of people thought I was right—which is more than I can say for my friend and ex-pupil Herbert George Wells. And one of them happened to be wealthy enough to fund my research," Charles added enigmatically.

"Who the devil might that be?" George stammered.

A smile flickered across Charles's face for a moment.

"Gilliam Murray."

"You mean the Master of Imagination? Did he lend you all this money?"

Charles nodded, and Wells raised his hands to his head in disbelief. This was more incredible than the magic hole itself. Gilliam Murray . . .

By the whiskers of Kepler, what had Charles got himself into? Everyone knew that Murray was one of the richest men on the planet, and the last person anyone should do business with.

"Are you out of your mind, Charles?" he cried. "You know what a reputation that crook has! I doubt very much he actually believes in your theory. And even if he does, do you really think he would use your magic hole for the common good? My God, Charles, your naïveté outweighs even your ingenuity!"

"What did you expect me to do?" Dodgson protested. "After the Church turned its back on me—thanks to you, *my dear friend*—Murray was the only hope I had of being able to continue my research."

"But at what price, Charles, at what price?" Wells said reprovingly. Dodgson pursed his lips in resignation. It was plain he, too, was unhappy about the action he had been forced to take. Wells felt sorry for the old man before him, who was shaking his head as he looked down at his shoes, like a child ashamed of its latest act of disobedience. Wells gave a sigh and inquired in a calmer voice: "When do you have to pay him back?"

"Well . . ." Charles hesitated. "A couple of weeks ago."

"What!"

"But that doesn't matter now, George!" Charles hastened to reassure him. "What matters is that I did it. I created a magic hole! Look, there it is. I was right, George, not you! Still," he added, contemplating Wells with a serious expression, "I didn't invite you here to crow over you but to ask you to put in a good word for me with the Church. The hole needs perfecting. It is stable enough to send simple objects, but I don't know what would happen with something as complex in information and energy as a man."

Wells looked at Dodgson, who was clasping his arm with a frail hand and gazing at him beseechingly. Then he glanced suspiciously at the hole.

"What do you suppose might happen?"

"I have no idea," Charles confessed. "I expect anyone who tried to pass through it would be crushed to death. But if you could convince the Church to back me, I'd be able to finish perfecting it, and I wouldn't need to worry about finding the money to pay Murray back, because I'd have more than enough to last the rest of my life. Will you do that, George? Will you help me? You can't deny my theory was the correct one."

Wells cast a weary eye around Dodgson's laboratory. Gathering dust in a corner, like a symbol of his ancient hopes, was the discarded model of the colony Charles planned to establish on Mars, east of Mount Olympus. Then he contemplated the hole, and Newton, still slumped on the rug, symbols of the ominous present.

"You're right, Charles," said Wells, nodding dolefully. "Your theory was correct, not mine. Have no fear. I'll talk to the cardinals."

"Thank you, my friend," Charles replied. "I'm confident that in three or four months the hole will be ready. I only need to make a few slight adjustments."

"A few slight adjustments? You don't know how glad I am to hear it," a voice behind them said.

Surprised to find they were not alone in the room, Wells, Charles, Jane, and even Newton turned their heads as one. Three men were standing in the doorway. Only the one in the middle was unarmed, yet he seemed the most threatening of them all. His splendid, bullish physique was hidden under a luxurious overcoat that almost swept the floor, and a self-satisfied smile played on his fleshy lips. The man on his left was a redhead, almost as tall as he was, and looked strong enough to juggle oxen. On his right stood a much younger man with a jutting jaw and a penetrating gaze. He looked agile rather than strong, capable of dodging all the oxen the redhead might throw at him. Both men were holding guns, marking them out as hired thugs of the man they were flanking, who in turn was pointing a strange device at Robert Louis. The automaton was standing next to the wall, where it had gone after drawing back the curtain, slumped forward like a rag doll, its arms dangling at its sides and the red light of its eyes extinguished. Wells supposed that, if pointed at an ornithopter, that thing could bring it down, and he couldn't help wondering about the circuitry it contained.

"Mr. Murray, how nice to see you again!" Charles pretended to be pleased but made no move to approach him. "You've arrived in time for tea; please sit down and join us, if you wish."

The Master of Imagination put his device away in his coat pocket and, remaining where he was, studied Charles for a few seconds, smiling at him almost affectionately.

"You're too kind, Professor, only I didn't come here to drink tea with you."

"Naturally, naturally," Charles said, glancing uneasily at Wells and Jane, who were standing close to each other only a few yards from the hole, scarcely daring to move. "I—I imagine you came for your money. I—I'm aware the payment was due a fortnight ago, but we scientists are the most absentminded people on the planet," he laughed, twisting the hem of his jacket between his fingers. "Although you were kind enough to remind me in your amiable and not in the slightest bit intimidating telegram, which makes my lateness all the more inexcusable . . . However, let us not dwell on that!" Dodgson declared excitedly. "As you can see, the m-magic hole is almost finished, and it is going make me extremely r-rich, so that I shall be able to pay you back double the amount you generously lent me. For any trouble I've caused—"

"Is that so?" Murray grinned from the doorway. "You are truly generous, Professor. Unfortunately, I'm not interested in your money."

With that, he walked over to the shelves containing the pile of musical boxes, wearing a smile of feigned curiosity. Despite his heavy build, his movements were effortless and possessed an almost sensual elegance. Charles, struggling to overcome his bewilderment, watched Murray run his finger over the lids of a few of the boxes.

"Do you have any idea how much I am worth, Professor?" he asked, lifting the lid of an ebony box and setting off a jingle imported straight from childhood. He let the melody float in the air for a moment before imprisoning it once more. Then he looked at Dodgson, who shook his head. "You don't? Neither do I: my fortune is incalculable." He pressed his lips together with an air of disappointment. "And yet, even with an incalculable fortune, I am unable to have everything I want. Alas, there are many things I cannot buy. Can you imagine what they are, Professor? No, I see that you can't . . . Perhaps that is because you have never needed them. I'm referring to dignity, admiration, respect . . ." Murray gave a chilling laugh while Charles contemplated him with mounting unease. "You look surprised, Professor . . . Perhaps you assume that a man in my profession wouldn't care about such things. But you see, I do care, I care a great deal." He sighed theatrically. "I'm tired of the hypocrisy of this world. You and countless others like you consume the drug I produce . . ." Dodgson and Wells exchanged worried looks. Like everyone else, they knew Murray had not amassed his fortune through being an antiques dealer, and yet, like everyone else, it suited them to pretend they didn't. However, the cards were on the table now, and the Master of Imagination's sudden display of honesty did not bode well. "The Church denounces me from its pulpits the world over," Murray lamented, "and yet conveniently looks the other way, allowing my business to enjoy the necessary impunity. Indeed, it often does more than look the other way . . . But I'm fed up with being the Church's scapegoat, and that of Cardinal Tucker and her entourage of putrid old fogies," he declared in a sudden outburst of rage. "They need me because they *desire* the power I give them over the people, and the people need me because they *desire* the happiness I give them. And yet, to all of them I am *undesirable*! The devil incarnate! Ironic, don't you think?" he asked them, putting on a sickly-sweet smile.

Wells swallowed hard. He no longer doubted that this scene was going to end badly for them, and yet he couldn't help considering Murray's impassioned speech with a sense of fascination, for what he had just said confirmed a surprising fact: the Church was covertly involved in the fairy dust industry. It was easy enough to go one step further and realize that the Church had devised a cunning plan to repress man's imagination, the same way it had his capacity for love: it knew that preventing people from imagining would only make them want to imagine more, and so it had decided to make them doubt their capacity by creating a substance that artificially enhanced the imagination, and then making it illegal, so that it became at once fascinating and dangerous. Thus mankind had become addicted to fairy dust, convinced they needed it to be able to imagine, even though they had doubtless always possessed that gift. However, the Church still had to supply its devotees with the illegal substance, for it didn't wish to eradicate entirely that quality in man, which, like love, could lead to Knowledge. Only in order to reap the benefits without losing control over its subjects, the Church had to transform it into a sordid, clandestine addiction. And that was where Murray, the Master of Imagination, came in: by having him traffic in the illegal substance, the Church remained untarnished. Murray wasn't the first to have played that reviled but necessary role. The Church had produced other shadowy figures embodying everything that was despicable about the world, for each new generation. But it seemed Murray was to be the first to rebel against his fate.

"I'm tired of doing the dirty work for that bunch of old busybodies," Murray went on, "while they go around pretending to despise me. I've had enough of grinding up fairies with my pestle and mortar so the world can go on imagining." He gave an embittered laugh. "I don't want to continue being the Master of Imagination. I don't want to be remembered as the villain of the story when I die. No, I can think of a far better sobriquet. I want to be remembered as the Savior of Humanity! Could there be any greater achievement?" He grinned, his eyes moving from Dodgson to Wells, then back to Dodgson. "So, Professor, despite all your wisdom, you are a complete fool if you think I am simply going to accept your money and discreetly step aside so that you can take all the glory. That's not how the story is going to unfold."

Murray looked into his eyes, waiting for a response.

"And h-how is it going to h-happen?" Charles replied at last.

"I'll tell you," Murray said calmly, still staring straight at him. "It will happen like this: the eminent Professor Dodgson will blow his brains out on the afternoon of the fourteenth of January 1898—that is to say, this afternoon—after battling with depression for months, having been defeated in a crucial debate by his former pupil"—here Murray grinned at Wells—"to see who would save the universe."

"My God . . . ," Jane murmured, moving closer to Wells, who wrapped his arms around her as he observed with dread Murray's thugs, their bodies gradually tensing as their boss went on.

"It will be a great loss," Murray continued, a sardonic smile playing on his lips. "A terrible shock, Professor, but after a few months everyone will have forgotten. And then the millionaire Gilliam Murray will announce that his team of scientists has succeeded in creating a magic hole in their laboratory, just as the great Professor Dodgson had planned to do—a hole through which humanity will be able to escape its dreadful fate."

"What!" Charles exploded. "But the hole is *my* creation! I—I won't let you steal it!"

"Listen, Charles . . ." Wells tried to calm him, as he saw the two thugs raise their guns and aim at Dodgson.

"You won't *let* me?" Murray gave a hoarse, rasping laugh while Charles fidgeted nervously on the spot. "In case you hadn't realized, Professor, I didn't come here to ask your permission. I am Gilliam Murray, and I take what I want." He gestured to the redheaded giant. "Martin, please. Aim at the temple. Remember, it has to look like suicide."

The killer nodded and strolled over to where Charles was standing, unable to move. Wells made as if to help his friend but was stopped by the other man pointing his gun at him. Wells put his arms around his wife once more, and the couple watched the redheaded man press his gun against the old man's temple with theatrical delicacy. Dodgson, too bewildered and scared to do anything else, shifted his weight from one leg to the other.

"A few last words before you leave, Professor?" asked Murray, amused.

Charles scowled and tilted his head slightly, as though leaning against the gun that was about to kill him.

"W-When you don't know where you are going, one path is as good as any other," he replied.

Wells swiftly placed a hand over his wife's eyes, and everything went dark. Jane didn't see what happened; she only heard a blast, followed by the muffled thud of a body hitting the ground. Then silence. A few seconds later, cracks appeared in the darkness as Wells moved his fingers away from her eyes, and Jane saw Murray gazing impassively at Dodgson's outstretched body while the redhead stood over him, holding a gun with a wisp of smoke rising from it.

"My God, Bertie . . . ," she sobbed, burying her head in her husband's chest.

Murray turned to the couple.

"I have to confess, Mr. Wells, I wasn't expecting to find you here, accompanied by your wife, and"—he looked at Newton, who had started to bark ferociously—"your pet dog, so I'm afraid there is no part for you in my little play. But as I'm sure you'll understand, I can't let you live. And after I've killed you, I shall throw your bodies into the hole. As you said yourself, a magic hole is the perfect place to dispose of the evidence of a crime."

"Damn you, Murray," Wells hissed in disgust as he held on to Jane tightly. "I hope your *Albatross* sinks under your vast weight and crashes, preferably into the Church's Holy See."

Murray gave a loud guffaw, then signaled to the thug whose weapon was trained on Wells.

"Go ahead, Tom. It doesn't need to look like suicide, so you can shoot them anywhere. Oh, and kill that damned mutt while you're at it."

The young man answering to the name of Tom looked at the picturesque trio he was supposed to execute. He decided to start with the man. He cocked his pistol, extended his arm, and aimed at Wells's head. But Wells did not flinch. Rather than beg for mercy, close his eyes, lower his head, or improvise some last words, he stared straight at the youth. And for a split second the two men looked at each other in silence. Wells's bravery seemed to take the lad by surprise, or perhaps he was laughing to himself at this stupid display of courage, but in any event he delayed pulling the trigger. Wells guessed that, despite all his experience, the killer had never had to shoot someone who showed such dignity when helpless, moreover with the addition of a sobbing wife in his arms and a faithful hound at his feet. Realizing that the time it would take for the lad to pull the trigger was the only time he had in which to act, he wheeled round, grabbing Jane by the arm and pulling her toward the hole. If they were going to go through it, better alive than dead.

"Jump, Jane, jump!" he cried, shielding her body with his as they bridged the short distance between them and the hole Dodgson had managed to tunnel into the air.

Wells feared he would receive a bullet in his back at any moment, but as he lunged forward and his body started to go through the hole, he knew the killer would not have time to shoot. Newton followed them, leaping through just as the orifice folded in on itself with a deafening roar. Then what could have been a gust of cosmic wind swept through the room, accompanied by a flash of white light that blinded the three men left behind.

After the thunderous explosion, a heavy silence fell. Murray blinked a few times and finally saw that the hole had vanished. All that was left of it were a few strands of mist hovering above the metal stand. It took several moments for him to realize he no longer had anything to trade in, and that he would never be the savior of mankind.

It seemed History wasn't going to happen the way he had imagined either.

"It seemed History wasn't going to happen the way he had imagined either," Jane read. It was a good way to end a chapter, she reflected with a satisfied smile before blowing on the paper to dry the ink. Leaning back in her chair, she observed with delight the freshly cut roses on her desk. She had picked them from the rosebush that very morning as the sky chose the colors of dawn and the cold night air still lingered on their petals.

At that moment, Wells tiptoed into her study with his habitual reverence, as though afraid his manly presence might disrupt the delicate feminine atmosphere floating in the room. He spent a few moments contemplating the charming orderliness around him, whose enchantment was so alien to him, and his eyes flashed as he caught sight of the scribbled pages on his wife's desk.

"What are you writing, my dear?" he asked with feigned nonchalance.

Ever since his wife had told him she wanted to turn one of their unoccupied rooms into a study, Wells had resolved to spend part of his extremely limited and valuable time trying to find out what his wife was doing in there. Direct questioning had failed, because she merely replied with a shrug. Joshing hadn't worked either. "Are you drawing pictures of animals in there?" he had once asked, but Jane hadn't laughed the way she usually did when he said such things. Her silence was tomb-like, and since torture was not an option, Wells had been forced to resort to surprise incursions. Thus he had discovered that Jane went into her study to write, which wasn't much of a discovery, as he could almost have worked it out without having to go in there. She was hardly likely to use the room for breeding rabbits, practicing devil worship, or dancing naked. Besides, she had half jokingly threatened him with it. Now all he had to do was find out *what* she was writing.

"Oh, nothing of any interest," Jane replied, quickly hiding the sheets of paper in her desk drawer, the lock of which Wells had unsuccessfully tried to force open. "I'll let you read it once it's finished."

Once it's finished . . . That meant nothing. What if it was never finished? What if for some reason she decided not to finish it? What if the world came to an end first? If it did, he would never know what Jane had been doing during the three or four hours she spent in her study every day. Was she writing a diary? Or perhaps a recipe book? But why be so cagey about a recipe book?

"One of the things I most hate in life is couples who keep secrets from each other," Wells said, being deliberately dramatic.

"I thought what you most hated was the fact that no one has invented an electric razor yet," Jane chuckled. She went on talking to him as she took his arm and led him toward the door, trying not to give the impression she was getting rid of him. "But don't be such a grouch. What does it matter what I write? Your work is the important thing, Bertie, so stop wasting your time spying on me and get writing."

"At least you know what I'm writing," he grumbled. "I let you see everything I do, whereas you're . . ."

". . . an unfathomable mystery to you, and you can't bear it, I know. I already explained it to you once: this is the only way of keeping your interest in me alive. I have to stop you from deciphering me, dear. Because if you understood everything about me, you would soon tire of me and start looking for other *mysteries,* and your crowning work, your true masterpiece, would never be written . . . So go back to your study and leave me with my *trivial* entertainments. They're not important. They aren't even as good as your earlier stories."

"Don't you think *I* should be the judge of that?" Wells retorted, surprised rather than annoyed at suddenly finding himself on the other side of the door. "But I suppose you're right, as always. I should get back to my work and—"

"Splendid, dear."

Jane gave her husband a parting wink and withdrew into her sanctuary. After shrugging, Wells went down to the ground floor, where he hid away in *his* study. Ensconced in his chair, he glanced wearily around him. Despite having placed all his books and knickknacks on the shelves as carefully as Jane, his room only gave off an atmosphere of sterile sedateness. However much he changed things round, the room never felt warm. Wells sighed and contemplated the sheaf of blank pages before him. He proposed to record on them all his hard-earned wisdom, everything he had seen. And who could tell: perhaps that knowledge might change the fate of the world, although Wells couldn't help wondering how much he was driven by altruism and how much by vanity. He reached for his pen, ready to begin his "crowning' work, as Jane had called it, while the sounds from the street and the neighboring park seeped in through his window, noises from a world that went by immersed in the smug satisfaction of believing itself unique . . .

PART ONE

1

 HERE WAS NOTHING INSPECTOR CORNELIUS Clayton would have liked more than for the dinner Valerie de Bompard had organized in honor of the successful outcome of his first case to end in a sudden attack of indigestion on the part of all her guests, himself excluded, the sooner for him to remain alone with the beautiful countess. And why should such a thing not happen? he mused, raising his fork mechanically to his mouth. After all, such unfortunate incidents fell within the bounds of the possible, especially since the castle cook already had experience in these matters, having three months earlier almost poisoned the entire domestic staff by serving them rotten food. However, the guests were already well into their second course and none of them showed signs of feeling the slightest bit queasy. And so Clayton resigned himself to having to endure the wretched dinner to the very end, telling himself he might find it more bearable if he forgot about the countess momentarily and simply enjoyed the praise lavished on him by the other guests. Did he not fully deserve it? Naturally: he was there as assistant to the legendary Captain Angus Sinclair, head of the mysterious Special Branch at Scotland Yard, but it had been his ingenious plan, and not the vain prestige of his superior, that had finally freed the town of Blackmoor from the terrible curse that had been hanging over it for months.

They had been assigned to the case after the first human remains were discovered, so brutally savaged that even the London press had printed the story. The grisly murders had begun to take place at each full moon, a few days after the cook had nearly poisoned the servants at the castle. Hitherto, the bloodthirsty fiend had been content to disembowel a few cows and sheep, as well as an occasional forest creature. But the beast's ferocity, previously unseen in any known predator, caused the inhabitants of Blackmoor to live in fear of the terrible day when it would finally decide to feast on human flesh. Perhaps that explained why Valerie de Bompard had found it so difficult to engage replacements while her own staff was convalescing. The majority of youngsters in the village had declined the offer, not only because the countess did not pay as promptly as one might expect of such a wealthy lady, but because the thought of working in the castle buried deep within the forest terrified them. Clayton could only sympathize when confronted for the first time with that sinister mass of stones that seemed to have been transported there from some infernal nightmare.

But he soon discovered that the inside of the castle was more daunting still. The dining hall, for example, was a gloomy chamber with lofty ceilings so immense that the fire in the hearth, above which hung a portrait of the countess, could scarcely warm it. In that imitation crypt, lined with tapestries and dusty coats of arms, the vast oak table not only made the guests feel somewhat isolated but forced them to project their voices like tenors on a stage. Clayton studied the four men whose unremarkable biographies could have been written on the back of a playing card: the stout Chief Constable Dombey, the cadaverous Father Harris, the prim Doctor Russell, and the corpulent town butcher, a Mr. Price, who had led the packs of hounds through the forests of Blackmoor. The day Inspector Clayton and Captain Sinclair had arrived from London to take charge of the case, none of these men had made them feel welcome, and yet now, three weeks later, they seemed anxious to help them forget this by smothering them with praise. Clayton glanced toward the end of the interminable table, to where the only person whose admiration he really wanted was sitting. The Countess de Bompard was studying him, an amused expression on her face. Did she consider him arrogant for accepting their praise with such disdain? Ought he to appear indifferent to his own exploits? How was he to know? He always felt terribly vulnerable when exposed to the countess's scrutiny, like a soldier forced during a surprise attack to leave his tent without his full armor.

Clayton glanced at his boss, who was sitting beside him, hoping to find some clue in his demeanor, but Captain Sinclair was busily devouring his roast beef, apparently oblivious to the conversation. Only occasionally would he shake his head distractedly, a stray lock falling across the sinister lens on his right eye, which gave off a reddish glow. It appeared that the veteran inspector had decided to remain in the background, abandoning Clayton to his fate. Clayton couldn't help cursing him for maintaining this stubborn silence now, when throughout their investigation he had talked endlessly, airing his wisdom and experience at every opportunity and adopting a new muddled theory each time a fresh aspect of the case arose. The worst moment of all had been when the captain gave Clayton advice on romantic matters, giving rise to a scene of paternal solicitude the inspector found excruciatingly embarrassing. All the more so because Captain Sinclair, who was incapable of plain speaking, had employed so many metaphors and euphemisms that the two men had ended their conversation without ever knowing what the devil they had been talking about.

"In a nutshell: young as you are," Chief Constable Dombey was summing up, "you have a remarkable mind, Inspector Clayton. I doubt that anyone sitting at this table would disagree with that. Although, I admit that, to begin with, your methods seemed to me, er . . . somewhat impetuous," he declared, smiling at Clayton with exaggerated politeness.

The inspector instantly returned his smile, only too aware that the chief constable was unable to resist ending his speech on a critical note, making it clear to everyone present that although these two gentlemen from London had succeeded in solving the case, they had done so only by resorting to unorthodox methods, which he considered beneath him.

"I understand that my actions might have appeared impetuous to you, Chief Constable," Clayton said good-naturedly. "In fact, that was precisely the impression I wished to give our adversary. However, everything I did was the outcome of deep reflection and the most painstaking deductive reasoning, for which I am indebted to my mentor, Captain Sinclair here. He deserves all the credit," Clayton added with false modesty, bowing slightly to his superior, who nodded indulgently.

"Why, I understood that from the outset!" Doctor Russell hastened to declare. "It is with good reason that a doctor uses science on a daily basis in the pursuit of his work. Unlike the chief constable here, I didn't allow your youth and apparent inexperience to put me off, Inspector Clayton. I know a scientific mind when I see one."

The chief constable gave a loud guffaw, causing his enormous belly to wobble.

"Who are you trying to fool, Russell!" he protested, jabbing his fork at him. "Your scientific approach consisted in systematically suspecting all the townsfolk, including old Mrs. Sproles, who is nigh on a hundred and confined to a wheelchair."

The doctor was about to respond when the butcher piped up.

"Since you're mentioning everyone else's failings, Chief Constable, you might recall your own and apologize for having so readily cast aspersions on others."

"I assure you, had you owned a cat instead of that enormous hound, I would never have—"

But before the chief constable could finish, the countess spoke up from the far end of the table. Everyone turned toward her in amazement, for Valerie de Bompard's tinkling voice had risen above theirs with the delicacy of a dove amid a flock of crows.

"Gentlemen, we are all understandably exhausted after recent events." She had a hint of a French accent that gave her words a charming lightness. "However, Inspector Clayton is our honored guest, and I am afraid we risk making his head spin with our petty squabbling. You will notice, Inspector," she addressed Clayton with an almost childlike zeal, "that I say 'our,' for despite having arrived in this country as a foreigner only a short time ago I already feel I am English. Not for nothing have the good people of Blackmoor clasped me to their bosom as if they had known me since birth." Despite the countess's friendly tone, her mocking words fell upon the gathering like a cold, unpleasant rain. "Which is why I should like to thank you once more, on behalf of everyone here, for what you have done for us, for our beloved Blackmoor."

She raised her glass between slender fingers, so daintily that it looked as if she had willed it to levitate. The others instantly followed suit. "Gentlemen, these have been evil and terrible times for all. For two years now, we have been living in fear, at the mercy of a bloodthirsty beast," she went on in a theatrical tone like a storyteller before an audience of children, "but, thanks to Inspector Clayton's formidable mind, the nightmare is finally over, and the evil creature has been defeated. I don't believe anyone here will ever forget the night of the fifth of February 1888, when the inspector freed us from our curse. And now, for God's sake, gentlemen"— her mischievous grin twinkled irreverently behind her raised glass—"let us once and for all drink a toast to Cornelius Clayton, the brave young man who hunted down the werewolf of Blackmoor!"

Since they were too far away from one another to clink glasses, they all raised their champagne flutes in the air. Clayton nodded graciously at the countess's words and forced himself to smile with a mixture of smugness and humility. The chief constable promptly proposed another toast, this time in honor of their hostess, and it was Valerie de Bompard's turn to lower her gaze with that shy expression that always made Clayton's heart miss a beat. It might be worth pointing out at this juncture that the inspector did not consider himself an expert with the ladies—quite the opposite, though he did pride himself on knowing enough about human behavior to be able to claim with some authority that Valerie de Bompard had nothing in common with the rest of the female race, or indeed with humanity as a whole. Every one of her gestures was a fathomless mystery to him. The shy expression with which she had greeted the chief constable's toast, for example, reminded him less of the decorous behavior of a lady in society than the deceptive calm of the Venus flytrap before it ensnares the wretched insect alighting on its leaves.

As he sat down again, Clayton recalled the unease he had felt the first time he saw her. It had been as if he were in the presence of a creature so fascinating, it was hard to believe she belonged to the tawdry world around her. On that day, the countess had worn a sky-blue silk ensemble with matching gloves and had set it off with a wide-brimmed hat trimmed with an elaborate sprig of leaves and berries into which the milliner, in keeping with the fashion of the day, had tucked a miniature stuffed dormouse and several orange-winged butterflies, which seemed to embody the rebellious thoughts that must be bubbling inside her head. No, Clayton had not known what to make of the countess then, nor did he now. He had only succeeded in falling madly in love with her.

"So tell us, Inspector," said the vicar, interrupting Clayton's daydream. "Was it clear to you from the start which direction your investigation should take? I ask you because I imagine that, when dealing with the supernatural, one can choose from an almost infinite number of possible theories."

"Infinity isn't a very practical concept to work with, Vicar, unless our salary were to be augmented accordingly," Clayton replied. This brought a few laughs from his fellow guests, including, he imagined, the sound of tinkling bells. "That is why, when confronted with events like the Blackmoor atrocities, which are difficult to explain in terms of the established order of the natural world, we must first eliminate all possible rational explanations. Only then can we deem something supernatural, an idea to which my department is clearly open."

"That is what we should have done!" the doctor remarked ruefully. "Used a bit of common sense. Only, as in all small towns, Blackmoor is full of superstitious people, and we all know—"

"Oh, stop pretending you are any different, Russell!" the chief constable rebuked him once more. "I happen to know that you were more scared than anyone. Your maid informed mine that you were melting all your spoons to make a silver bullet, because you claimed it was the only thing that could kill a werewolf. Where on earth did you come up with such a silly idea?"

The doctor was going to deny it but then chuckled instead.

"Well, I'll be damned, the cheeky little gossip! Yes, I confess to melting the teaspoons. And if you'd listened to a word I'd said during these past few months, Chief Constable, you wouldn't be asking me now how I came up with such a silly idea." He turned away from him and addressed Clayton in a more measured tone, as if speaking to an equal. "The fact is, Inspector, a French colleague of mine, with whom I correspond, told me about a gruesome animal that terrorized the region of Gévaudan in the last century. Many claimed it was a werewolf and that they only succeeded in shooting it down with silver bullets. That is why I melted nearly all our cutlery, much to my wife's displeasure."

"Well, you got a telling off for nothing, Russell," the butcher laughed.

"I am aware of that," the doctor snapped. "But who would have imagined that the werewolf terrorizing our town was in fact Tom Hollister dressed in that ridiculous disguise?"

Everyone looked toward the corner of the dining hall where the doctor was pointing, and a gloomy silence instantly descended on the room. Clayton watched the other guests shake their heads, each immersed in his own recollections as he gazed at the enormous wolf hide draped over a wooden easel, gleaming in the light of the candles dotted sparingly about the room. Sinclair had displayed it there like a trophy so the guests could examine it as they came in. And they had, with a mixture of horror and admiration, for the disguise was a work of art, worthy of an expert taxidermist. The enormous skin, which at first sight they had thought belonged to a giant wolf, was in fact made of several different pelts that had been carefully stitched together and then cut accordingly, with sections of it stuffed with hemp and straw to give the impression of a huge beast with bulging muscles. The forelegs had been stretched over a framework of jointed wooden bars until they vaguely resembled human limbs covered in thick fur, and each had tacked onto its end a glove that bristled with clawlike blades. The ensemble had been crowned with a wolf's head whose mouth had been fixed into a hideously ferocious growl. It came as no surprise that Hollister, who was sturdy enough to support the cumbersome disguise, could transform himself into a terrifying werewolf in anyone's eyes by draping it over his shoulders, fastening it to his arms and legs with special leather straps, and using the animal's head as a helmet. Especially if he only appeared during the full moon, arching his back grotesquely and howling like a wild animal.

Clayton had also been taken in when he first saw the creature standing before him, huge and terrifying, and as he and the others chased it through the dark depths of the forest, his blood pulsing in his temples, his heart pounding in his chest, it was the certainty that they were pursuing a real werewolf that had mitigated his suspicions. Yes, it was a werewolf they were pursuing because, despite Sinclair's evasive answers when he had joined the Special Branch, Clayton knew that such fantastical creatures did exist. But the monster had turned out to be a hoax. Inspector Clayton could not help but feel that this cast something of a pall over his triumph, and he was no longer sure that joining the Special Branch had been the right decision. Perhaps he had been too hasty in accepting Sinclair's offer, having done so in the belief that a world closed to other mortals would open up to him. And yet his first "special" case had consisted of hunting down a yokel wearing an assortment of animal skins. Not to mention falling in love with a woman who lived in a sinister castle.

"How is it possible that the thing scares me even now?" the doctor admitted suddenly, breaking the silence.

He rose to his feet and, doubtless emboldened by drink, shuffled over to the disguise with a penguin-like gait.

"Be careful, Russell; take a silver teaspoon with you just in case!" yelled Price, waving his in the air.

The doctor dismissed the butcher's advice with a drunken flourish that sent him tottering toward the animal hide.

"Look out!" shouted Sinclair, leaping from his chair like a nursemaid watching over her wards at play in the park, his mechanical eye emitting a buzz of alarm.

The captain planned to take the disguise back to London, to the Chamber of Marvels in the basement of the Natural History Museum.

This was where the Special Branch stored evidence from cases passed on to them because they defied man's reason. He wanted the skin, which he saw as an important part of their division's history, to reach the museum in one piece. When he saw the doctor regain his balance with no other consequence than the hilarity of the onlookers, his face relaxed and he smiled benevolently, although, since he was already on his feet, he decided to go over to the costume himself. Chief Constable Dombey instantly followed suit, as did Price and Harris. Doctor Russell then launched into a scientific exposition of the methods used to create that handiwork, while the others, including Sinclair, felt obliged to nod diligently as the quack continued to show off his knowledge.

And while that impromptu conference was taking place around the disguise, back at the table Clayton finally plucked up the courage to look straight at the countess, from whom he was separated by a generous expanse of solid oak. Throughout all the weeks of his investigation, whenever he and the countess were together, whether in a room full of people or in a garden maze, Clayton's eyes would invariably end up meeting hers, those eyes that seemed to have been waiting for him forever, and whose mystery had begun to haunt his nights. For the inspector, who prided himself on his ability to read a man's thoughts from the way he knotted his tie, was utterly incapable of deciphering her gaze, which might have been expressing gentle adoration, the cruelest disdain, or even some unimaginable private hell. Perhaps all of those at once. And it was in those same eyes that Clayton was drowning now as he admired the countess, and she allowed herself to be admired as always with a smile, enveloping him in her dark, bewitching beauty, which transformed the voices of the other guests into a nonsensical babble, the dining hall into a hazy backdrop, and the entire universe into a distant, possibly imaginary place.

Clayton had never seen Valerie look as magnificent as she did that evening, or as painfully fragile. She was dressed in black and silver: her dazzlingly pale neck rose out of a velvet bodice that emphasized her proud breasts and matched her long calfskin gloves; her silver skirt fell in billowing folds that revealed a constellation of tiny diamonds. Seeing her seated there, illuminated by the shimmering candles, Clayton could not help thinking that, regardless of her indeterminate age, she resembled more than ever a girl queen, childish and capricious, cruel only by birthright. Realizing he was clutching his glass more firmly than usual, and fearing he might break it or do something even more stupid, like leaping onto the table and sprinting frantically toward the countess, swept along on the current of his confused desire, Clayton averted his gaze, and the room regained its movement, its sounds, its stubborn solidity.

"The fact is, the more I look at it, the more I admire it," he heard the doctor say. "A truly splendid piece of work, gentlemen. Look at this. The hide is perfectly tanned and uncommonly soft." He leaned forward and sniffed one of the feet. "I'd say it was preserved using a mixture of arsenic and chalk, like in the old days."

The butcher, to whom Doctor Russell's explanations were beginning to sound like a lullaby, nodded and gave a deep sigh.

"That's all very well, Doctor, but I can't help wondering how a fellow like Hollister could make a costume like this and, more to the point, why he killed those three people. Alas, due to his tragic demise he will never be able to answer these questions. However," he said, turning to Clayton, "you promised us you would, Inspector, and I think we are all so anxious to know."

"With pleasure, gentlemen." Clayton grinned, aware that the moment he had been waiting for throughout the meal had finally arrived.

He stood up from the table, avoiding the countess's gaze, and gave a cursory glance at his audience, which was standing in front of the costume as if posing for a group photograph, a look of intense expectation on their faces.

"Well, I assume you want me to begin with the first question: How could someone as unsophisticated as Hollister produce this outstanding piece of taxidermy? There is a very simple answer to that, gentlemen: through books. As you know, once we discovered Hollister was the werewolf, Captain Sinclair and I searched his shack, where we found books on taxidermy, bestiaries containing images of werewolves, and a variety of substances and tools used in taxidermy. But why would anyone go to such lengths to commit a murder when there are many easier ways of doing it?" Clayton clasped his hands behind his back, pursing his lips ruefully, as if to say he didn't know the answer to that either. Captain Sinclair smiled to himself at his subordinate's weakness for theatrical pauses. "Let us consider for a moment what we know about Hollister's character. Before he threw himself into the ravine, all of you considered him a harmless clodhopper, with just enough brains to resent the unlucky hand life had dealt him—something he used to complain about whenever he drank: he was forced to quit school because his parents died when he was still a boy, leaving only a mound of debt and a few acres of stony soil he would struggle to grow anything on. He was also an extremely good-looking young lad, although alas none of the ladies he courted, all of them of noble birth, deigned to show any interest in him. Apparently a poor wretch like him was aiming too high. Now, let us take a closer look at his victims: What did Anderson, Perry, and Dalton have in common?" Clayton observed his audience with a grin. "Their land was adjacent to Hollister's but, unlike his, theirs was fertile. Thus my inquiries led me in that direction. And so I discovered that Hollister, in his eagerness to make money, had attempted to purchase their lands, but that his neighbors had never agreed to sell. Indeed, two of them, to whom Hollister's father had owed money, even threatened to seize his property if he didn't pay up. That must have been when the lad, at the end of his tether, cooked up his plan. A brilliant plan, in my view: he would kill his stupid neighbors in a manner that would not only divert suspicion from himself but would also compel the dead men's families to sell their land quickly and at a reduced price. Why? Because it was cursed. Because a terrible monster had begun prowling there, exacting a life at each full moon. But turning into a werewolf was beyond his capabilities, and so he resorted to using a costume, which, in order not to arouse suspicion, he was forced to make himself. And that, ladies and gentlemen, is how poor, honest Tom Hollister became the werewolf of Blackmoor."

There was an awed silence. Even Sinclair, who was familiar with Clayton's exposition, seemed delighted by his performance. Satisfied with the outcome, Clayton looked straight at the countess and thought he glimpsed a fresh sparkle in her eyes.

"Brilliant, Inspector Clayton." She smiled. "An exposition as intelligent as it was entertaining. I have no doubt that a bright future awaits you at Scotland Yard."

Clayton acknowledged the compliment with a slight bow, preferring not to say anything that might break the spell of the unanimous admiration he had conjured around him, and wondered whether he hadn't at last managed to impress the countess. He had never been confronted by a woman like her before and was ignorant of the basic rules of refined courtship: after all, he was no more than a humble policeman, perhaps too lowly for her, or too young, or too unsophisticated, doubtless too much in love. He was not even sure whether it was possible to seduce a woman like Valerie de Bompard with his intellect, or what she might want from a man like him. A night of passion, a moment's amusement, a respite from loneliness, or perhaps an eccentric noblewoman's mere whim? He was hoping for a great deal more. But it was pointless to surmise. Very soon, the expectations Valerie de Bompard had been sowing in the air around him would either become a reality or would vanish forever. Because the case had been solved, they had caught the werewolf, and the next day their carriage would depart for London . . . although perhaps with only one detective on board. Everything would depend on what happened once the dinner was over.

Clayton would have been happy to remain trapped in that instant for all eternity, his gaze intertwined with that of the countess and glimpsing in her smile the promise of a happiness he had never believed existed, but at that very moment the servants, who had doubtless been waiting outside the door for him to finish his speech, burst into the room carrying trays piled high with cakes, fruit, cheese, and bottles of liqueur. The inspector tried to conceal his irritation as he watched the guests heading for their places, more excited by the prodigious array of desserts than by Clayton's brilliant deductions, which moments before they had so passionately applauded. Accepting that he had been defeated by a pile of cakes, the inspector walked back to his seat with an ironic smile. As he passed the countess's portrait, he could not help glancing at it with a look of frustration. But no sooner had Clayton clasped the back of his chair than something deep inside made him turn toward the portrait once more. He took two strides and found himself standing before the canvas, indifferent to whether his sudden interest might puzzle the countess or the other guests. Suddenly, the rest of the world had disappeared beneath a veil of fog. All that remained was him and the painting, which had produced a stab of anxiety he found impossible to explain.

As the flurry of plates and glasses continued behind him, he strove to examine every inch of the canvas, which showed Valerie de Bompard in all her majestic beauty, standing beside a large table piled with neat stacks of books and papers. The day they had arrived at the castle, Captain Sinclair had praised the portrait to the skies, and afterward the countess had informed them it was the work of her late husband, the count de Bompard, a man of many talents, one of which, it seemed, was painting. In fact, the countess had posed for the portrait in her husband's study, and now Clayton could make out in the background, purposefully made hazy by the artist, a vast library whose uppermost reaches vanished into the odd-looking shadows that enveloped the ceiling. Thick, exquisitely bound volumes lined the shelves, alongside an array of objects that Clayton scarcely recognized save for one or two. There was a gilt telescope, a collection of flasks, bottles, and funnels arranged in order of size, an enormous armillary sphere, and . . . It took him a few moments to take in what was next to the sphere. When he did, an icy fear ran though his body like snake venom, while in his brain the whisperings of comprehension began to grow louder and louder.

The servants left the dining hall and Clayton returned to his seat, fearful his knees might buckle under him. What he had just discovered in the painting had turned his solution of the case upside down, and he could only watch in astonishment as the elements began to reconfigure. Clayton leaned back in his chair, each new puzzle piece like a stabbing pain in his entrails. When at last it was complete, he had to acknowledge with a mixture of surprise and dismay that this new configuration made more sense than the last one. His amazement nearly spilled forth in the form of a hysterical laugh, but he managed to contain himself. He took a long sip of brandy, followed by several deep breaths. The liquor calmed him somewhat. He must not give way, he told himself. He had to regain his composure, assimilate the discovery he had just made, and act accordingly.

Fortunately, the guests were still engaged in a trivial conversation about how delicious the meal had been, allowing Clayton to emerge gradually from the stupor into which the revelation had plunged him. He discreetly wiped the beads of sweat from his brow, and even managed to recover his smile, as he pretended to follow the conversation while avoiding everyone's gaze, in particular that of the countess. When Valerie had first shown him the Count de Bompard's painting, Clayton's eyes had focused on her image. The countess eclipsed everything around her, as she did in real life. But now he had seen all the details. The details . . . they were what decided the outcome of an investigation, even if as in this case it was something as ludicrous as a circle of mice holding hands and dancing.

"Imagine how long it must have taken Hollister to make that costume," Price was saying, "to hunt down enough wolves, and to stitch their pelts together alone at home! And all that without arousing the slightest suspicion! A terrifying thought, isn't it? I knew the lad quite well. He used to help me sometimes in the shop, and we'd often have a chat. All the same, I'd never have imagined—" He broke off in midsentence and shrugged.

Everyone nodded, sharing in the butcher's bewilderment, except Clayton, who, struggling to overcome his fear, was looking straight at the countess, anticipating her response. Valerie de Bompard, who was nodding like the others in a gesture of regret, caught the inspector's eye and as always held his gaze unflinchingly, a mischievous smile playing on her lips. Clayton knew he must first decide how to act on the information he had just stumbled across, then try to work out a plan before the end of the dinner. But, confronted with the countess's smile, he couldn't prevent a feeling of anger from welling up inside him. *I have no doubt a bright future awaits you at Scotland Yard,* she had said to him, and the same words that had gladdened him before became like shards of glass piercing his heart. He felt his blood begin to boil.

"People are never what they seem," he heard himself say as though it were someone else's voice, his gaze still fixed on the countess. "We all have our secrets, and yet we're always surprised when we discover that other people do, too. Wouldn't you agree, Countess?"

Valerie was still smiling, but Clayton thought he perceived a glint of confusion in her eyes. Not fear—not yet. That would come later.

"Naturally, Inspector, we all have a hidden side we don't show others," she replied, making her crystal glass sing as she ran her finger round it swiftly but delicately. "However, if you'll allow me to make a distinction, there is a world of difference between the almost obligatory lies we all tell to protect our privacy and possessing the dual personality of a murderer."

Clayton nodded, as did the other guests, but he made sure the countess noticed the sardonic veneer to his look.

"In any event, there is something diabolical about the zeal with which Hollister embarked on the study of taxidermy," the vicar said, wandering off the subject, his cheeks ruddy from the alcohol. "All that sinister knowledge hidden away in his house: jars filled with strange, noxious substances, books on alchemy, medieval treatises . . . It brings to mind tales of witches and pacts with the devil. Even though the explanation for those dreadful murders has turned out to be human, I can't help seeing the mark of the Evil One imprinted on young Hollister's actions."

"The devil? Oh, come now, Father!" the chief constable spluttered, alarmed nonetheless.

"Unfortunately, Father Harris," Captain Sinclair interjected in a loud, clear voice, "I'm afraid that the hand of the Evil One in this matter is too far-fetched even for our jurisdiction."

The remark elicited a few chuckles, which Clayton ignored, leaning back in his seat, his gaze still locked with that of the countess. There was no question but that the inspector's manner had aroused her curiosity. No sooner had the laughter subsided than she turned to Sinclair.

"I couldn't agree more, Captain. The Evil One . . . I refuse to believe that men shun their natural goodness and the word of God for a creature like that billy goat that presides over witches' covens. In fact, I have always resisted the idea that everything is exactly as it is depicted in folk tales. That is why I find your work so intriguing: it must be fascinating to investigate monsters and discover what lies behind them, the genuine truth about myths, their legitimate fantastical nature. Talk to us, Captain, tell us about your work."

"Er . . . I'm afraid that's impossible, Countess," Sinclair apologized, slightly startled. "Our work demands confidentiality and—"

"Oh, don't be so coy, Captain! This isn't a convention of sage old druids; we're in Blackmoor! Go on, make an exception, please," the countess implored, pouting flirtatiously. "I'm sure we'd all love to know about the workings of your remarkable division: Do you use new, revolutionary techniques, or on the contrary do you go out armed with crucifixes, holy water, and stakes carved from ash wood when you hunt down vampires? They say such creatures can turn themselves into bats or even mist."

"And can't set foot on consecrated ground," added the vicar.

"And have certain deformities, such as a protruding tailbone," interjected the doctor.

"And that they are born with the mother's placenta wrapped around their heads, like a turban," said the chief constable. Everyone burst out laughing.

When the guffaws had abated, the countess went on, contemplating the captain mischievously.

"Are all those things true, Captain? Personally, I find it hard to believe such creatures can be warded off with garlic, or that they have forked tongues," she said, poking the tip of hers suggestively between her lips.

"Well"—Sinclair cleared his throat, trying to hide his unease—"I'm afraid to say, Countess, that most of those things are no more than superstitions."

Everyone stared at the captain, expecting him to elaborate on that interesting topic. Sinclair gave a resigned sigh and sat up in his seat. Realizing that his superior was going to inflict on those poor people the same speech he had given him when he had joined the department, Clayton settled back in his own chair, silently thanking the captain for prolonging that interminable dinner. All of a sudden, he didn't want it to end: what awaited him afterward no longer seemed so enticing. He hoped the captain would go on talking until the next day, or the next month, to give him enough time to order his thoughts and decide what to do. For the moment, the only thing he knew for sure was that he had no intention of sharing his discovery with Sinclair. He wanted to interrogate the countess alone, so that she would be able to answer all the questions bubbling inside his head, even if the majority of them bore no relation to the case.

"As you know, gentlemen, our department is responsible for looking into the supernatural, everything that is beyond man's comprehension," Clayton heard the captain explain as he ran his fingers over his dragon-shaped lapel pin. "Alas, as on this occasion, most of our investigations turn out to be hoaxes. This is something Inspector Clayton is starting to learn, isn't it, my boy?" Clayton felt obliged to nod in agreement. "But even the cases we can only explain by resorting to the fantastical show us that the supernatural rarely coincides with popular folklore. Werewolves are a perfect example. They first appeared in Greek mythology, but it wasn't until the Middle Ages that stories about werewolves began to proliferate. Our files contain a cutting from a German gazette dating back to . . ." Sinclair frowned, trying to recall the date.

"Fifteen eighty-nine," Clayton said wearily.

"Yes, precisely, fifteen eighty-nine. And it gives an account of children whose guts were ripped out by a supposed werewolf in the town of Bedburg. It is the oldest account we have, but by no means the only one. There are countless such stories. Hundreds, nay, thousands of cases that have only helped the werewolf myth grow. And yet myths are simply facts that have been filtered through the popular imagination, which has a tendency toward theatrical, nauseating romanticism that ends up distorting reality until it becomes unrecognizable. Thanks to those myths, and to penny dreadfuls like *Wagner the Wer-Wolf* or *Hugues the Wer-Wolf*, most people today think of werewolves as wretched creatures who at each full moon are transformed into wolves against their will and, overwhelmed by a terrible bloodlust, are driven to kill indiscriminately. Among the many other foolish notions, the power to turn into a werewolf is said to be obtained from drinking rainwater accumulating in wolf tracks, or from wearing a belt made from wolf hide, or from being bitten by another werewolf. Since you can verify the fallacy of the first two for yourselves, allow me to demonstrate the impossibility of the third by means of a simple calculation: if werewolves, like vampires, turned all their victims into creatures like themselves by biting them, before long the entire world's population would cease to be human. Reason allows us to refute the other fascinating traits with which folklore has endowed those creatures. The moon's influence, for example, is an idea that originates in the myths of southern France. I am sure you will all agree that running through a forest during a full moon is much easier than in the darkest night, making it likely that the first time a murderer was branded as a werewolf, it was for the sake of mere convenience. In any event, we have known about the moon's influence since ancient times; its effect on the tide, the weather, men's mood, and, er . . ."

"Certain female complaints," Clayton suggested.

"Indeed, certain female complaints. And so, if werewolves did exist, the effects of the moon on their behavior would undoubtedly be the least fantastical aspect of their nature." Sinclair paused and then turned to the doctor with an ironical smile. "As for silver bullets being an infallible weapon against werewolves, Doctor Russell, I'm afraid that is something that, for the moment, only you and a handful of others know about. Perhaps one day it will become just another indisputable characteristic of those creatures. For that to happen it would suffice for authors to decide to use it in their novels. Although, frankly, the idea is so outlandish I doubt they ever will."

"So, are you saying werewolves don't exist?" asked Price, a man who preferred simple, definite conclusions.

"I didn't say that, Mr. Price," replied Sinclair, adding to the butcher's puzzlement. "I wouldn't presume to claim that something doesn't exist simply because I haven't seen it. All I'm saying is that if they did exist, they would bear little resemblance to the ridiculous creatures myths have turned them into," he concluded, pointing to the costume adorning the corner of the dining hall.

Of course not, thought Clayton, glancing at the woman seated at the head of the table.

And with that the conversation soon lapsed into a series of humdrum commentaries. Finally, the countess, encouraged by the inebriated Doctor Russell's raptures over each of the dishes served, summoned Mrs. Pickerton from the kitchen so that they might all congratulate her in person. The woman accepted their compliments with relief, saying she had been concerned the guests might have found some of her food bland, because a few months earlier a thief had raided the castle pantry, making off with several sacks of salt, which still had not been replaced. Everyone had to assure her heartily, almost swearing on Father Harris's Bible, that they had noticed no such lack, to the greater credit of her skills as a cook.

When Mrs. Pickerton had left the way she came, Clayton began thinking to himself. The salt had gone missing . . . This last tidbit came as an unexpected gift, which he duly registered. Now there was no doubt in his mind that he had solved the case. Until then, he had held on to the faint hope that he might be mistaken, but that hope had evaporated. He almost had the impression that everyone there could hear his heart breaking, like a walnut crushed under someone's boot.

2

A S THEY WERE SAYING FAREWELL, CLAYTON had the awkward knowledge that he did not deserve the guests' parting congratulations, while alongside him Sinclair accepted them with evident satisfaction. Clayton couldn't help contemplating him forlornly: the poor captain had no idea their case was only just beginning. When the guests had finally departed, the countess and the two inspectors, slightly inhibited by the sudden silence, were left standing in the castle's vast entrance hall, at the foot of a magnificent marble staircase.

"Well, I think it's about time for bed," the captain announced. "We have an early start in the morning. The dinner was splendid, Countess, and so is your kindness for offering us your hospitality for so many days."

"It has been my pleasure, Captain," replied Valerie de Bompard, smiling genially. "Two of the most intelligent men in the land staying under my roof! I assure you I'm unlikely ever to forget it."

She stretched out one of her gloved hands, upon which the captain planted an exaggeratedly chaste kiss. Then she offered it to Clayton, but the inspector made no attempt to kiss it. He simply stood motionless, like a man suckled by wolves who knows nothing of how to behave, watching silently as her hand hovered in the air.

"You go on ahead, Captain," he said at last, looking straight at the countess. "It has been an eventful evening, and I am far too excited to go to sleep. Perhaps the countess would agree to have a nightcap with me."

The countess's hesitation was fleeting. She instantly gave a sly grin.

"Why, of course, Inspector. I have a superb bottle of port that I keep for special occasions."

"This is undoubtedly one of them," replied Clayton, gazing at her even more intently.

Sinclair was obliged to clear his throat in an attempt to break the spell.

"Er . . . in that case, I'll say good night," he said. "We have a long journey ahead of us tomorrow, and . . ."

Sensing their lack of interest, Sinclair left his sentence unfinished. He began slowly ascending the staircase, like an actor reluctant to leave the stage in the middle of a crucial scene. The countess finally looked away from Clayton and, with a loud swish of silk, made her way back to the dining hall. The inspector followed, but had scarcely advanced two steps when the captain's voice held him back.

"Inspector Clayton . . ."

Clayton looked toward the top of the stairs, where the captain's burly, imposing frame was scrutinizing him through the semidarkness, only faintly illuminated by the candelabra in the entrance hall.

"What is it, Captain?"

Sinclair peered at him in silence for a few moments, the red glow from his artificial eye intermittently lighting up his face, as if his thoughts were made up of light and blood. Had he guessed there was something amiss?

"You've done a fine job, my boy," he grunted at last. "A fine job . . ." And, turning around, he went off to his room.

Not without a sense of relief, Clayton remained gazing up the staircase until the captain disappeared, swallowed up by the darkness. He recalled the captain's advice on affairs of the heart offered to him in recent days under the assumption that it was all nothing more than a harmless flirtation. But the captain hadn't the slightest inkling of what was really about to happen in the dining hall, no more than the countess herself in all likelihood—or, if he was honest, than Clayton himself. There was no telling what direction the conversation would take once he showed his hand. He might even need his gun, he told himself, and quickly felt one of his jacket pockets to make sure it was there. Heaving a sigh, he approached the dining hall, bumping into one of the maids, who had just finished clearing the dessert things away. Valerie de Bompard was standing in front of a small mahogany table, pouring two glasses of port. The fire in the hearth played over the thousand sparkles on her dress, casting a golden glow over her arms and back and transforming the decanted liquid into gold.

"Inspector Clayton!" she exclaimed in her mocking French accent. "For a moment I was afraid you had been refused permission to stay up late and were on your way upstairs, clutching your nanny's skirts."

Clayton went over to the countess, whose eyes met his as she handed him one of the glasses. The inspector felt himself once more teetering on the edge of the dark, fathomless abyss of her gaze, and for the umpteenth time it occurred to him that it was not only the perfect combination of Valerie de Bompard's features and proportions that made her beautiful but something much more profound and difficult to describe. She was incredibly beautiful because she had decided to be so, because that was her desire. And Clayton was convinced that nothing in the world could stand in the way of anything she desired. Taking the glass, he returned her smile with a casually sophisticated air.

"My nanny's skirts . . ." He grinned at the image of Sinclair squeezed into a governess's outfit. "I confess that anyone who ordered me to bed dressed in a gown as lovely as yours I would be hard put not to obey. You look stunning this evening, Countess."

"Is that the only compliment you can think of?" she chuckled. "Frankly, I was expecting something more from a man of your exquisite intellect. And besides, you shouldn't try to flirt with me, Inspector. I'm a dangerous woman. I thought you'd realized that by now."

"Why ever would I think that?"

She clinked her glass against his and then took a sip.

"Oh, come now, Inspector, there's no need to pretend with me!"

"I . . ." Clayton swallowed.

"I find it hard to believe you haven't heard the gossip circulating about me in the town!" she exclaimed. "The Countess de Bompard, that Frenchwoman with a murky past! A fortune hunter who married the old Count de Bompard for his money and position and who, when he disappeared under mysterious circumstances, fled her native France to avoid the scandal and the dreadful rumors that began to assail her! I'm sure you heard all that and more during the course of your investigation."

"You are well acquainted with your neighbors' opinion of you," Clayton simply replied.

"And don't you think them cruel? I was nothing but a poor widow wanting to mourn in peace. But I soon realized that would be impossible: evil tongues have wings, and my undeserved notoriety followed me here . . . Damn it! The moment I arrived in this godforsaken place to take possession of the count's English castle, the first thing all the women did was lock up their husbands . . . As if I could possibly be interested in any of those yokels!"

Clayton had to admit he had never heard any woman curse others in quite the same way. Possibly some of the women of ill repute in the London slums, but certainly no lady. After this charming display of vulgarity, the countess took another sip from her glass and seemed to calm down.

"No, I prefer intelligent men. Like Armand," she went on in a gentler voice. "Or you."

She tilted her head back slightly, studying Clayton through narrowed eyes, and an ethereal smile played on her lips as she gauged the effect of her words on him. Clayton tried to prevent any emotion from registering on his face. After a few moments' silence, the countess gave a derisive smile, as though she found his efforts to resist her amusing. So hypnotic was her gaze that the inspector had to remind himself that no matter how much he wanted to taste her lips, she was not what she seemed, and their encounter could not end pleasantly. He stepped away from Valerie and walked over to the portrait hanging over the white marble mantelpiece, underneath which two plush armchairs languished. Staring at the ironical smile with which the countess surveyed the world from the canvas, he told himself it was time for the game to commence.

"Tell me about him. Tell me about Armand."

The countess gave a soft laugh behind him.

"About Armand? Why, Inspector, I assure you, you have much to learn about the art of seduction. Asking a woman to tell you about another man is hardly appropriate."

"I'm not sure I agree, Countess. Nothing defines a woman better than the men who have loved her. So tell me about him," he demanded with deliberate brusqueness. "He painted this portrait, didn't he?"

There was a silence, during which Clayton could imagine the bewilderment on the countess's face. After a few moments, her voice rang out.

"Very well, Inspector, if you insist, I shall tell you about him. Armand was a man in a class of his own! Honorable and wise, extremely wise. I suppose intellectual pride was his only weakness, if you can consider it as such. He loved to paint me . . ." Clayton heard a sorrowful sigh. "He did my portrait many times. He used to say I had an unworldly beauty, and he was the humble chronicler whose sacred task was to preserve it for posterity." The inspector heard her take a few steps forward until she was standing beside him. "However, this portrait is particularly dear to me, because he painted it days before . . . well, you already know about his tragic end." Valerie's words caught in her throat, as if she were on the verge of tears.

"It was painted in his study, wasn't it?" Clayton asked, insensitive to her pain.

"Yes, that was where he did all his research."

Clayton pursed his lips with a mixture of anger and sorrow as he recalled his surprise at discovering a haven of secret knowledge in Tom Hollister's humble, dilapidated abode, amid the rats and piles of refuse. The man had spent a long time poring over the numerous manuals on taxidermy neatly lining the shelves in order of size and even color. These stood next to endless rows of substances in jars and some alarming-looking implements: skull scrapers, pincers, colored powders, cotton-wool balls, containers filled with glass eyes, like macabre sweets . . . All meticulously arranged, to the millimeter, composing a cocoon of harmony amid the confusion that reigned in the shack.

"What were the count's areas of expertise?"

"Everything," the countess replied with evident pride, increasingly intrigued by the inspector's sudden interest. "All areas of knowledge and art. He was a brilliant scholar and a scientist far ahead of his time. Centuries ago he would doubtless have been burned at the stake, but fortunately we live in a different age. Nowadays, those who are different or superior merely have to endure envy and slander," she concluded.

"Did you love him?" the inspector asked, still not looking at her.

The countess hesitated.

"I felt a profound admiration for him. And I was deeply grateful for—"

"But did you love him?" Clayton repeated abruptly.

Valerie de Bompard remained silent for a few moments.

"I could tell you to mind your own business, Inspector," she replied softly but firmly.

"You could. But all I want to know is whether you are capable of love," he replied, mimicking her tone as he turned to face her.

"I didn't love him, Inspector. But that doesn't mean I can't love others." The countess smiled, her small white teeth glistening like precious pearls. "You must understand that the relationship between Armand and me was never that of a normal couple."

"I see."

"I don't think you do." She laughed. "I was terribly young when I met Armand, Inspector. You might say that I was a feral child, without a shred of education, who lived in darkness, and that Armand kindled in me the flame of knowledge. He educated me, not simply to be a young lady, but to be an equal, like a man. He taught me everything I know, including, when the time was right, about love and pleasure. For, according to Armand de Bompard, if someone hasn't experienced love and pleasure, they cannot aspire to true knowledge. And so I don't know whether he married me because he was in love with me or simply because he couldn't imagine my education being complete without the mastery of love, the highest of the arts. But the fact is, he completed his masterpiece by making me his wife. And you ask me if I loved him? Why, I'm not even sure *he* loved *me!*" The countess bit her lower lip and looked defiantly at Clayton. "No, I don't suppose I loved him. But perhaps what we had was greater than love."

A silence ensued, which they both allowed to continue as they regarded each other intently.

"Well, I've told you about Armand," the countess said at last. "If your theory is correct, you should know me better now than you did five minutes ago. So, tell me, Inspector, who am I?"

"I'd gladly give any part of my anatomy if it helped me to discover who exactly you are, Countess."

She laughed sarcastically.

"Well, I shan't ask that much of you, Inspector. But no more talk of the past. Or of Armand. Tonight we are celebrating," she said, recovering some of her vivacity. Realizing her glass was empty, she went back to the table to refill it. "You don't know how grateful I am to you for having caught that idiot Hollister. He always seemed to perpetrate his crimes whenever I threw a ball. It was becoming something of a habit for the chief constable's men to burst in and silence the orchestra, loudly informing their superior of bloodied corpses and spilled entrails. Can you imagine anything more tasteless? Despite all one's efforts to look beautiful and make a grand entrance that enchants one's guests, such interruptions are enough to ruin any ball. It's hard to continue enjoying oneself after something like that. You were at the last one, so you could see for yourself." She sashayed back over to Clayton. "Although, I must confess, my real regret when Hollister interrupted my party by killing dear Mr. Dalton was that he did so just at the moment you appeared to have plucked up the courage to ask me to dance. What a pity. Still, at least you used that courage to catch the killer and solve the case."

The countess contemplated him, waiting for his response. Clayton lifted his glass and emptied it in one go, steeling himself for what he was about to say, which was very different from what she was expecting.

"No, Countess, you are mistaken: I solved the case only this evening. And it was Armand who gave me the clue."

She looked at him, amused.

"What do you mean?"

Clayton stepped away from the countess with a sigh and motioned to the portrait with his chin.

"Third shelf on the right. You can't see it unless you look hard, but I have a bad habit of noticing the details."

The countess glanced at him uneasily. He motioned toward the portrait again, inviting her to examine it more closely, and she finally obeyed, approaching the fireplace more dazed than intrigued.

"Next to the armillary sphere. What do you see?"

The countess looked at the spot in the painting where Clayton had pointed.

"Three mice dancing in a circle."

The inspector nodded dolefully.

"Quite so. Three stuffed mice, whose charming pose reveals the extraordinary skill of the taxidermist."

She said nothing, still not turning toward him. Clayton realized she was trying to retrace the chain of his thoughts since he had noticed the mice, to see where it led. Only, of course, it was not simply the accursed mice.

"They're scarcely visible, aren't they? I'll wager it's the first time you've noticed them. And yet they are there. They have always been there. Brown mice, standing upright on their little feet . . . As adorable as they are incriminating."

"I'm afraid I don't understand what you are insinuating, Inspector," she said evasively, turning to face him.

"Really? You needn't worry, I can explain it to you step by step." Clayton gave a wry smile. "Do you recall the explanation I gave over dinner?

Well, now forget about it. You'll find this one much better. After hearing it I'm sure you'll have no doubt about the great future I have ahead of me at Scotland Yard." She remained silent. "Good, let's start with the day we first met," Clayton went on. "Do you remember the hat you wore? You don't? I do. Unfortunately, I never forget anything. It had a wide brim and was adorned with butterflies and a little brown dormouse. I also remember that when Captain Sinclair remarked on how exquisite it was, you told him it had been sent over from America. Something about your reply troubled me. I've always had a wide range of interests, and I happen to know a little about zoology. I am scarcely more than an amateur, but I couldn't help noticing that the butterflies on your hat were of the monarch variety, which are typically found in the United States." Clayton clasped his hands behind his back and began pacing in circles around the point where he had launched into his speech, with a look of concentration on his face, as though suddenly he had forgotten the countess, the room, and even himself and were sweeping through the passageways of his own mind, where his thoughts hung in neat rows, like the wash on a line. "However, the *Muscardinus avellanarius,* or common dormouse, is native to the British Isles. And that was what bothered me. I didn't give it much importance at the time: I assumed that in a fit of originality you had asked your milliner to revamp the hat by placing an English rodent alongside some American butterflies. But now I know you can't afford to employ a milliner, because during our inquiries we discovered the difficulties you are having in inheriting your husband's French estate due to the ongoing investigation of his disappearance. Which means you must have done it yourself . . . And this evening those little mice told me it couldn't have been very difficult, because you were initiated into the art of taxidermy by a great teacher . . ."

Clayton gestured toward the portrait above the fireplace.

"Naturally, you also created that disguise that so impressed the doctor," he said, pointing to the werewolf costume. "You did so, unless I'm mistaken, a little over three months ago, and that explains the disappearance of the salt from the castle pantries. You used that to tan the hides. I have no need to search the cellars to deduce that your laboratory is down there, close enough to the servants' quarters for them to be overcome by the fumes from the arsenic and other noxious substances you were obliged to use. You had a mask for protection, but I'll wager you suffered burns to your skin, or perhaps you stained your fingers with some indelible substance, which is why you always wear gloves. But let's not digress. What drove you to make the costume? The answer is simple. Until then, for whatever reason, you had been content to kill domestic animals and a few head of cattle. But you knew that diet wouldn't be sufficient and you would soon have to start murdering your neighbors. Fearing those deaths would eventually incriminate you—which is doubtless what happened in France, forcing you to flee the country—it occurred to you to create a fake werewolf, a monstrous beast capable of inflicting on its victims the terrible wounds you yourself would cause. Tom Hollister, the greedy, strapping young lad who had supplied you with the hides, seemed perfect for the part. Seducing him must have been child's play, persuading him to confess his disappointments and desires to you, and then coming up with a plan you devised whereby he could get his hands on the land he coveted. For it was you, not poor Tom Hollister, who conceived the plan I described earlier as brilliant. Hollister was merely your puppet. Doubtless you offered to kill his neighbors as proof of your boundless love, convincing him you would both have the perfect alibi if he appeared in the forest wearing the werewolf costume on the evenings when you threw your balls." Clayton shook his head in disbelief, as though he himself was astonished at the ease with which all the pieces fitted together. "Balls that always coincided with a full moon, and which, on the pretext of making a grand entrance, you always arrived at late, after you had committed your bloody crimes, probably slipping back into the castle through one of its many secret passageways. Thus, when the latest murder was announced, you only had to look horrified like the others, surrounded by witnesses that included the town authorities and, at your last ball, two Scotland Yard inspectors.

"But everything changed the night Hollister threw himself into the ravine. When news reached the castle that we were trying to retrieve the body of the so-called werewolf, whose mysterious nature would soon be revealed, you instantly realized that, unable to believe that an ignorant peasant could have produced such an elaborate outfit, we would naturally suspect the existence of an accomplice. And so, while we were attempting to retrieve the body, you hurried over to Hollister's shack, where you planted the necessary evidence to prove he had acted alone. However, the habits we learn in childhood are stronger than the most powerful survival instinct, and you couldn't help arranging everything neatly. It was that neatness I noticed this evening in Armand's painting. That scrupulous, almost fanatical orderliness of the sage who loves his instruments and his books. The same love he undoubtedly sought to instill in his pupil. That was your mistake, Countess. Although, if it's any consolation," Clayton added scornfully, "I expect the count would have been proud of you . . . at least in that respect."

During the inspector's brief summary, Valerie de Bompard's haughty expression had given way to a look of animal intensity, and a terror bordering on madness.

"I doubt it," she replied. "It was a stupid mistake. And Armand despised stupid mistakes."

"And yet he made the stupidest mistake of all. He fell in love with you," said the inspector. "As did I."

Silence descended on the room once more. The countess was staring at Clayton intently. She looked like a panther caught in a snare, beautifully furious, bathed in the light of the stars. Everything about her posture screamed out that no hunter deserved to trap such a splendid specimen.

"You succeeded in making me so eager to impress you," Clayton said at last, "to win your admiration, that I stopped listening to the voice inside me crying out each time something wasn't right. You succeeded in making me care only about the moment when I would stand before you like a hero. You succeeded in making me approach this textbook case as if I were blind and deaf, ignoring all the details, or the numerous coincidences. Because of you, for the first time in my whole career I was no longer guided by my fierce urge to solve a mystery, but rather by the desire to see a flicker of emotion in your eyes that I could fully understand. But tonight the scales have fallen from my eyes. I have seen you for what you are."

Valerie de Bompard said nothing. She walked over to the mahogany table and with trembling hands poured herself another glass of port. Then, tilting her graceful neck back sharply, she drained it in one go. She remained lost for a few moments in the maze of her thoughts before slamming the glass down on the table, tearing off her gloves, and flinging them at Clayton's feet. The inspector could see that her hands were covered in scars, red blotches, and hideous welts, and although he had already guessed as much, he could not help feeling a strange pang in his chest. He looked at the countess and felt his head start to spin. The Countess de Bompard smiled bravely, attempting to muster her usual mocking disdain, but the tears were trickling down her cheeks.

"Congratulations, Inspector Clayton. As you can see, you have indeed solved the case this time. And you should be doubly satisfied, because, unlike Hollister, I am the real thing."

The inspector gazed at her sorrowfully.

"What are you, Valerie?" he almost whispered.

"Do you really want me to tell you? Are you sure you are ready to hear the answer?"

"Almost certainly not," sighed Clayton. "But I still need to know."

"Very well, then, I shall tell you a story, a beautiful story. A story of damnation and salvation. The story of my life. And perhaps, after hearing it, you will be able to answer that question yourself."

She began speaking softly, like someone reciting a lesson well learned, or an ancient, unforgotten prayer.

"One fine day, a French nobleman was leading a hunt in the forest surrounding his castle, when his horse suddenly bridled, almost trampling a dirty, disheveled girl who was wandering through the woods, muttering to herself in a foreign tongue. The Count de Bompard and his men assumed she had been abandoned by the band of Gypsies who had set up camp in the area during the previous week. Seeing that her skin was covered in sores and she was severely malnourished, they decided to take her with them back to the castle. I was that girl, Inspector. When I mentioned just now that Armand had found a feral child, it was no flight of fancy. By the time my health had been restored, the count had grown fond of me and decided to keep me with him, under his protection, as his ward. I have few recollections from my first months at the castle and none from the preceding years. I have no idea how I came to be in that forest, or whether I am in fact the daughter of Gypsies. I simply don't remember. I had no life before Armand and would have had none after had he not decided my fate, for I would never have survived in that forest, or become what I am today."

She fell silent for a few moments, as though searching for the right words with which to begin the next chapter of her story, the one for which Clayton was possibly unprepared.

"Armand gave me everything, Inspector. Everything except deliverance from my curse. That was impossible, even for him. He was content to share my terrible, dark secret: he was my friend, my companion, and my fears became his own. Others like me have been less fortunate . . . But one day Armand had to go away. He didn't say where or why, he only swore that it was his duty and begged me not to ask questions. I obeyed him, as always. And after that, I was left alone. Alone to face the truth of what I am. And when the thirst came upon me, all the promises I had made to my husband before his departure meant nothing. You cannot possibly imagine what it feels like to be me, Inspector, the indescribable torment of being alive. Nor can you imagine the dreadful loneliness that devours me in this world to which I do not belong, which considers me accursed . . . Do you think I don't want to die? Every day I wish I were dead with all my heart . . . But I promised Armand I wouldn't kill myself, that I would stand firm, that I would find a way of living with my curse. And I assure you I tried. Oh, yes, I tried with all my might, but I failed . . . At first, I endeavored to survive by killing livestock and small animals, as you deduced, but I soon realized that wouldn't fend off my craving for long, and that very soon I would have to track down the sustenance I really needed . . ."

Clayton looked at her impassively, saying nothing.

"It would all be a lot simpler if I were just wearing a belt made of wolf hide, wouldn't it? Because I would only have to burn it. Unfortunately, what changes me into what I am is also part of me." The countess tried to make light of the situation. "But I promise you, that isn't the real me. No, that isn't me. Believe me when I tell you that each of those deaths weighs on my conscience."

"Assuming you have one," Clayton muttered.

The countess smiled weakly.

"But the thing I shall never forgive myself for is failing the man who gave me everything," she went on, ignoring the inspector's remark, "the man who considered me beautiful, despite knowing what I was, who made me feel, not like a monster, but like a worthwhile being—the most worthwhile being in the entire universe . . ." Her voice faltered and her eyes filled with tears. "And you remind me so much of him . . . The first time I saw you, I felt I was looking into my husband's eyes anew . . ." She edged toward Clayton, reaching out a hand to touch his face. The inspector could feel the scorching heat from the fire on his back, and yet the countess's fingers burned more than the flames themselves. With neither the strength nor the will to resist, Clayton let her run them over his cheek in an ardent caress, scarcely brushing his lips before withdrawing her hand. "You have the eyes of an old man, Inspector, eyes that view the world from somewhere remote and unassailable, that endeavor to understand it whilst remaining outside of it. And yet . . ." The countess moved her face closer to Clayton's, who could smell the salty aroma of her tear-stained skin. "Your lips are made for love."

Clayton gripped her wrist, restraining her.

"Don't even try," he warned. "You cannot prevent me from doing what I have to do. I am going to arrest you, Countess. It's my duty. I shall deliver you to Scotland Yard handcuffed, in chains if necessary . . .

and may God save your soul," he murmured, giving an impression of coldness that belied his true feelings. "I shan't deny that I feel a sense of horror at your tragic fate. Our scientists will strip off your splendid clothes, strap you naked to a chair, and examine you as if you were an animal. They won't stop until they discover what sort of monster lives inside you, and afterward they will lock you in a cage for the rest of your life."

The countess simply smiled at him, the way a man would smile when recalling the stories that frightened him as a child. It was then Clayton saw, from close up, that the countess's eyes were not totally black: a fine ring of gold, like a solar eclipse, encircled her irises.

"What you said earlier is true," he heard her say, her lips within kissing distance of his. "I manipulated you. I used my smiles to cloud your thinking. But all the time I was dazzling you . . . I was also falling in love with you."

"You're lying," Clayton said between gritted teeth.

The countess pulled an amused face, as if he were joking.

"Do you know why you love me, Clayton? You love me because you don't understand me, because I am a riddle to you. I intrigue you, I trouble you, I keep you awake at night, and I take away your appetite. You want to solve the puzzle I present you because that is the most powerful form of possession there is. And I confess that for the first time in my life I feel the same way," she said, her breath quickening. "It's true, from the moment I saw you I felt the need to discover what lay behind your eyes . . . Believe it or not, I fell in love with you, Clayton. But I forced myself to struggle against those feelings that were growing stronger and stronger. I am a monster and cannot permit myself the luxury of falling in love. But I don't want to struggle any longer, Inspector. Not now. I, too, deserve to know at least once in my life what it feels like to love. So, I am begging you, Inspector, let's forget who we are just for tonight and give way to our desire. I promise you that tomorrow we will go back to being a Scotland Yard inspector and his prisoner . . . But the night is still young."

As she spoke, Clayton felt her hot breath on his face, he smelled the sweet fragrance of her hair, and he noticed the blood pulsing fiercely in her slender wrist, still firmly clasped in his hand. And, perhaps because at that point it was his only way of resisting, Clayton squeezed that part of her as hard as he could, hoping to cause her pain, to hear her fragile bones snap in his grip. The countess groaned, but that didn't stop her. Her smoldering lips slid across his cheek toward his mouth.

"I only want to know what it is to love, before the day dawns and everything comes to an end . . . ," she whispered to him before her lips melted in his.

Clayton slowly released the countess's wrist, opening his fingers almost without realizing it, like a tree letting the fruit it has been cradling for months fall to the ground. For a few seconds his arm hung in the air, orphaned, purposeless, until at last the countess flung her arms around him. After a moment's hesitation, Clayton clasped her by the waist with a fervor he had never imagined he could feel. A mysterious, powerful desire raged through him like a fire, searing his veins and setting his reason alight, threatening to rip open his body from the inside, to blow him up like a keg of dynamite. And in his urgency to smother that fire, Clayton pressed his body hard against hers, as though he hoped to break through the frontiers of her flesh and plunge headlong into the muddy depths of her soul. He knew he wanted to possess her, to put an end to the sudden hunger overwhelming him. The countess pulled her mouth away from his and Clayton felt her run her lips excitedly over his neck, nipping him with her teeth. Incapable of thinking rationally, Clayton pushed her from him, ready to throw her down on the rug and make her his, take her roughly until he had extinguished the flames of desire burning him up. At that moment, their eyes met, and the inspector was jolted out of himself. The countess's gaze wasn't what he had expected. A cold, calm light flickered in her eyes, belying the abandon of her body.

"I can't let you arrest me, Inspector," he heard her say, as if her voice were reaching him from far away. "Armand de Bompard's finest creation cannot end up in a dirty cage. Nor can I destroy you, my beloved Cornelius, because I love you as I've never loved anyone before. So there is only one thing for me to do . . . Forgive me, I beg you."

Clayton reacted swiftly, but he was unable to dodge the blow. He only succeeded in preventing the poker, which the countess had taken from the hearth while they had been kissing, from hitting him square on the head. Reeling, he tried to grab her to stop his fall, but only managed to slide his hands languidly over the countess's hips before sinking to his knees and slowly toppling over, in an almost absurdly voluptuous manner, onto the rug where seconds before he had wanted to take her.

3

ORTUNATELY, THE VIOLENT BLOW HAD NOT
been hard enough to plunge his mind into the fog of
unconsciousness, and, sprawled on the floor, Clayton could hear the
countess's footsteps as she fled the dining room and the subsequent tapping sound in the hallway, like a tune interspersed with silences, as she
walked across the rugs. His head throbbing, still too befuddled to order
his body to stand up, the inspector heard her leave the castle, and in his
imagination saw her descending the castle steps, holding up her skirts,
running away from it, plunging into the forest that lapped at its doors
like a sinister ocean. He realized if he didn't go after her immediately, he
would never catch her. With a supreme effort of will he rolled over painfully and, placing his hands on the floor, began to heave himself up. A
violent wave of nausea forced him to remain on his hands and knees for
a few seconds, head lolling between his shoulders, as though bowing to
some ancient idol. At last Clayton managed to stand and, propping himself up on the furniture as he went along, left the dining hall.

The yawning castle door exhaled the ghostly breath of night. Clayton strode through it, his resolve growing as the cold air cleared his
head. He was surprised to find the countess's shoes and jewelry strewn
haphazardly over the steps. Apparently she had cast them off as she ran.
If this was part of some erotic game, Clayton found it almost unbearable.
He took one of the lanterns illuminating the bottom of the steps and
plunged into the forest, following the tracks left on the ground by the
countess's bare feet.

He walked on for a while, guided by her footsteps. He was shivering with cold, and yet his head was burning, especially in the spot where the countess had aimed her treacherous blow, which was throbbing painfully. From time to time, his vision became blurred and he had to lean against a tree while he tried to focus again. Then he resumed the chase, jaw firmly clenched as he sharpened his senses as best he could, listening for the slightest sound coming from the forest. Like the bow of a violin, the wind drew languid whispers from the branches of the trees. The darkness crowded in on him, as if trying to smother him. Suddenly, on the ground, Clayton made out what looked like a black puddle reflecting the starry sky. Holding the lantern aloft, he discovered the countess's glittering dress lying among the dead leaves. Kneeling, he clasped it in his hand reverentially. The exquisite robe still exuded the countess's warm fragrance, but it was torn in several places as though she had ripped it off clumsily. Clayton rose to his feet and cast a bewildered look around as the cold grip of fear began to settle over him.

He continued walking, trying not to panic. After a while, he noticed the countess's footprints had begun taking on a strange shape and the distances between them were growing longer. At first he thought he had lost the trail, but advancing a few yards he stumbled upon it again, only to lose sight of it once more. In spite of this, he pressed on, guided by instinct more than anything else. Now and then, he would come across a lone footprint in the middle of the path, a footprint that no longer seemed human, or a tree with its branches broken. All this brought fresh doubts to Clayton's mind, but he resisted the temptation to speculate in order to stay sane as long as he could. All of a sudden he recognized the path the countess was taking. He himself had followed it with a few men from the town two nights before . . . It led to the ravine where Tom Hollister had plunged to his death.

He couldn't help seeing himself once more leading that group of townsfolk through the impenetrable darkness of the forest, heady with the excitement of the chase and the fantastical idea that they were pursuing a genuine werewolf. But things had changed. Now he was tramping alone through that accursed forest, feeling terribly naked, surrounded by menacing trees that seemed to conspire against him. With an overwhelming sense of regret he realized that the world he knew had vanished forever. The enormity of his loss almost took his breath away. He carried on along the path like a sleepwalker, knowing it would never lead him to where he wanted to go: to the past, to the reassuring, rational past, precisely to the day when the legendary Captain Sinclair had invited him to join the Special Branch, so that he could turn him down, inform him that he wasn't the slightest bit interested, that he preferred to carry on living in the bland but comforting universe whose workings he understood so well and where supernatural beings never escaped the pages of bestiaries. For there was always a risk you might fall in love with one of them. Now it was too late for that, he reflected forlornly. There was nothing for it but to follow Valerie de Bompard's tracks and perform his role in the insane performance it was his destiny to take part in.

With his free hand, Clayton had unwittingly begun stroking the key that hung round his neck, nervously fingering the two tiny wings of the angel that adorned it. The key opened the Chamber of Marvels in the basement of the Natural History Museum, and since it had been entrusted to him less than a month before, Clayton had come to see it as a sort of lucky charm, a symbol of that supernatural world hidden in one of reality's folds, toward which he seemed to be heading that night. But now he was convinced that the knowledge awaiting him was something for which he considered himself ill prepared, knowledge capable of destroying a man forever.

Trying desperately to make his mind go back to thinking with its reassuring logic, Clayton wondered why Valerie de Bompard was guiding him to that place. For he was sure of one thing: the countess was leading him exactly where she wanted, as she always had, as she always did with everyone. And he had no choice but to answer her call.

Suddenly the night was shattered by a long, mournful howl coming from the ravine. Clayton, his face twisted with fear, grabbed the gun from his pocket and ran toward the sound, holding the lantern up in front of him and drawing back the veil of darkness as he went. Gasping for breath, he came to a small clearing in front of the gully. Once again, he made out a pair of strange-looking tracks. They appeared to approach the edge, then vanish. Clayton put down the lantern, swallowed, and drew closer to the ravine. He steeled himself to look down, unable to fend off the image of Valerie de Bompard's beautiful body lying smashed to pieces on the rocks, unsure if that was the worst thing he could discover. But the foot of the ravine was plunged in thick darkness, and he could see nothing. Even so, he lingered at the edge for a few seconds, peering stubbornly into the blackness, his clothes whipped by the icy wind arising from those depths like a noiseless cry of despair. Finally, mystified, he retreated a few yards. And it was then that he heard a low-sounding growl behind him, so faint that for a moment he thought he had imagined it. Very slowly, he swiveled round, pistol half raised, as though still not wishing to admit his danger. Atop a small, rocky outcrop, a she-wolf as imposing as an ancient sphinx was observing him. The animal's soft golden pelt shone in the moonlight as if it were sculpted in bronze.

"Valerie . . . ?" he whispered half unconsciously.

The wolf tilted its head to one side and gave another low growl, as though laughing at Clayton. Suddenly, the inspector felt the weight of the gun in his hand. He was almost surprised to discover he was armed, that the cold, metallic object he was holding was a weapon: a device man had created in order to take the lives of his enemies and preserve his own. Still, Clayton made no attempt to aim at the she-wolf. He was content to wait, and for an infinite moment man and beast stared at each other in silence the way Clayton and the countess had in the dining hall at the castle, separated by the length of an oak table. Then the she-wolf bared her fangs and leapt at him.

The animal's heft knocked him to the ground, winding him. The gun slipped from his hand as if of its own volition. Before he had time to react, he felt the wolf's jaws close around his throat, pinning him to the ground, its sharp fangs pressing into his flesh, like a deadly snare

about to snap shut around his neck. Clayton didn't move. He awaited the
she-wolf's decision, quaking under its weight. The animal remained in
that position for a few moments, with Clayton at its mercy, as if to make
it clear his fate depended on a mere movement of its jaws. And then, as
swiftly and gracefully as when it had knocked him over, the wolf withdrew. Clayton breathed out, amazed that he was still alive. How was it
possible? Unsure whether the wetness he could feel down his neck was
blood or sweat, and hardly caring, he tried to sit up. The animal was
watching him from a few yards away, body tensed, ready to pounce again
at any moment. Clayton observed the wolf in silence, ashamed because
he could not stop trembling. Was this creature that growled like a wolf,
smelled like a wolf, and moved like a wolf really the woman he loved?
Part of him refused to accept such an outrageous idea, perhaps because
to do so would be to hurl himself into an even deeper abyss—that of
insanity. But the other part of him that was skilled at piecing things together had no doubt. Out of the corner of his eye, Clayton could see
the gun within easy reach, and he automatically started calculating. If
he rolled over fast enough, he might be able to grab it before the wolf
pounced again. Was that what she wanted? No sooner had he formu-
lated the question than the wolf suddenly gave a snarl and hurled itself at
Clayton like a bolt of coppery lightning. The inspector reacted without
thinking, stretching his right arm out toward the gun while raising the
other to repel the creature's attack. He wrapped the fingers of his right
hand around the gun butt just as the wolf buried its fangs deep into his
left forearm. Seized by an intense burning pain, Clayton pressed the gun
barrel to the wolf's enormous head but did not shoot. He remained motionless, his finger on the trigger. Man and beast looked deep into each
other's eyes, frozen in that position, which seemed to hold back the flow
of time. Clayton was so close that he could see fine rings of gold, like
solar eclipses, encircling the wolf's irises. And he had the impression the
animal was imploring him. But this time he had no intention of bowing to its desires. Not this time. The gun still pressed to the animal's
head, the inspector watched the blood begin to trickle from his trapped

limb, spreading out in a dark stain on the sleeve of his jacket. He felt a stabbing pain in his arm, but in the end it was a bearable pain. The wolf also seemed to perceive this and sank its fangs even deeper into Clayton's flesh, until he could feel them tearing through the muscles in his forearm. He clenched his jaw to stifle a scream but couldn't help an inhuman cry escaping from between his gritted teeth. There was a brief pause, and then the wolf's fangs bit into his flesh with renewed ferocity. Clayton's face twisted into an agonized grimace. As the pain intensified, so did his resolve not to pull the trigger. For if he did, it meant that she would have won. Then he heard a crunch of bones. A searing pain swept him like a flood to the brink of unconsciousness. In spite of everything, Clayton still did not shoot.

It was his survival instinct that finally fired the bullet. Astonished, he heard the sharp crack of an explosion, and the body that had been crushing him toppled gently to one side, like a lover after the moment of pleasure.

"No . . . ," he murmured.

He contemplated the dead animal stretched out beside him as the pain from his left arm spread through his body like molten lava. Despite the fog clouding his brain, he realized the pain was too excruciating to be caused by a simple wound. Mustering the last ounce of his strength, Clayton managed to sit up straight enough to examine his arm. What he saw horrified him: there was no hand at the end of his left arm. Only a bleeding stump, from which hung a snarl of tendons. His hand was a few yards away, lying on the ground like a piece of refuse, like something that bore no relation to his body. Stifling the urge to retch, Clayton gazed from the errant hand to the bloody stump that had supplanted it, trying to convince himself that the fleshy lump belonged to him, that the discarded hand was his own.

When at last he managed to tear his eyes away from the hypnotic vision, he turned once more to the wolf, sprawled beside him in the pool of light cast by the lantern. Clutching the stump with his other hand, he studied the animal at length and saw that its forelegs were flayed and scarred. But after having looked straight into the wolf's eyes, that clue seemed superfluous. The blood trickled from its right temple, and its eyes no longer possessed that mocking glint that the inspector had been unable to fathom. Now they possessed the absolute, incontrovertible aspect of death.

"You succeeded, didn't you, Countess? You got what you wanted . . . ," he heard himself utter in a plaintive voice, unsure whether he meant to condemn or applaud her actions.

The Countess de Bompard always got what she wanted, he thought resentfully. She had found a way of taking her own life without breaking the promise she had made to her husband, regardless of whether or not from now on Clayton had to live with his own curse. And, despite his anger, he had to admit she had been right when, just before hitting him on the head, she had told him there was no other way. Or did he honestly believe that their loving each other would suffice? What sort of life could they have had? He would not have been prepared to smile at her as if nothing had happened those nights when she returned home with a torn dress and the contented look of one who has sated her most secret appetite, nor would he have been able to stop his hand from trembling at breakfast the following morning as he read in the newspaper about some brutal murder, pretending there was no connection between the wretched victim and the woman he loved. No, he wasn't prepared for that. And perhaps Armand de Bompard hadn't been either. No doubt that was why he had left her, because he had realized that, in spite of all his knowledge, there was only one way to end her awful affliction. But Armand had loved her too much to do what Clayton had done.

He let out a terrible cry of rage, piercing the depths of the night with his suffering. He howled and howled until he had exhausted himself. It helped calm him a little. Almost out of apathy, he, too, thought of taking his own life on the spot. What did it matter in the end? All he had to do was press the gun to his head and pull the trigger. Again. His body would then topple over beside that of Valerie, and they would lie there, man and beast, shrouded in darkness, an unsolvable mystery. But instead, he began tearing at his jacket in order to make a tourniquet to stanch his bleeding stump. It seemed a futile gesture, like everything else he had done that night. He couldn't understand why he didn't simply let himself die, if what remained of his life wasn't worth living, if the succession of days, months, years yearning for Valerie de Bompard would only seem like torture. No, he couldn't understand why, and yet he wound the piece of cloth he had managed to tear off his jacket round his stump as tightly as he could.

As he did so, he remembered telling the countess at some point during the evening that he would give any part of his anatomy to understand who or what she was. Clayton smiled bitterly. Now he finally knew what Valerie de Bompard was.

4

CLAYTON'S LEFT ARM WAS EVENTUALLY FITTED WITH a hand fashioned from metal and wood, a sophisticated device with rivets and screws and bronze spokes extending from the wrist and tapering off into jointed fingers. It also contained a newfangled mechanism whereby each time the inspector tensed an arm muscle the gesture was translated into a movement of his mechanical hand. The invention had been a gift from Her Majesty, who had commanded her private surgeon, together with a celebrated master armorer and one of Prague's greatest automaton makers, to join their skills with those of the Special Branch's scientists to ensure that Captain Sinclair's most promising novice needn't go round like a useless cripple. Overwhelmed, Clayton had shown his gratitude the best way he knew how, by practicing for days on end to be able to clasp the monarch's hand with his shiny prosthesis before planting on it the customary kiss. In spite of all that, it hadn't been the most elegant of greetings, for his metal hand scarcely responded with the same precision as his original hand. And things had not improved much since then, he realized with regret each time he tried to carry out the simplest domestic task. He had just discovered he wasn't very skilled at sealing windows either. Still, in time he would learn to use the thing more naturally, he reflected with a sigh. If he kept practicing, he would soon be able to hold a beer glass without smashing it, or take a queen's hand without fracturing a couple of her fingers. After all, he had only had it just over seven months. Seven months since the Countess de Bompard had chewed off his real hand, leaving him mutilated in more ways than one.

"Are you all right, Inspector?" Sinclair asked, noticing Clayton gazing dreamily at the window it had taken him so long to seal.

"Er . . . yes, quite all right, Captain . . . This one's finished."

Sinclair gave a nod of satisfaction and went over to the window, where, as representative of the investigating committee, he added his flamboyant signature to the seal. Then he nodded to Clayton, and the two men approached the center of the spacious room, where the other members of the committee were waiting to take part that evening in the séance led by Madame Amber.

"Good. Everything has been set up so that we can verify the authenticity of the events under the strictest possible conditions," announced Sinclair, casting a stern eye over the gathering. "As you are aware, Sir Henry Blendell, architect to Her Majesty the Queen, whose integrity is unimpeachable, and the creator of the most celebrated secret passageways and trick furniture in history, having examined Madame Amber's mansion from top to bottom, and in particular this room where the séance is to take place, has signed a document stating that he has found no evidence of mechanical jiggery-pokery in this house. There are no trapdoors or hidden springs in this room, or in any part of the house, and no false bottoms or rotating panels in any of the furniture. As for the table we will sit at during the séance, it has been thoroughly checked over for wheels or pulleys or any other kind of lifting device. Furthermore, Inspector Clayton and I have boarded up the fireplace and sealed the only two windows in the room. We have likewise placed bells on the bottoms of the curtains and scattered sawdust on the floor, so any trapdoors that might have escaped Sir John's attention will be impossible to open without our becoming aware of it. Doctor Ramsey and Professor Crookes, both of whom are with us today, have set up their equipment around the room. These include recording thermometers, light-measuring machines, and infrared devices. In addition, the séance will be recorded on a phonograph, whose cylinder will be kept in our archives should anyone wish to consult it at a later date . . . In light of all this, I think it is safe to say that never before has the stage for a spiritualist séance been so thoroughly examined. I'm afraid that any spirits wishing to make an appearance here tonight will have to be genuine."

Everyone received the captain's words with nods and grunts of approval, and some even giggled nervously, unable to contain their excitement.

"Good, we only have to wait for the ladies to finish examining Madame Amber, and the séance can begin," Sinclair said finally, glancing toward the partition at one end of the room.

It was an exquisite Japanese screen made of mahogany and bamboo, about twenty feet wide and divided into four embroidered silk panels representing the four seasons. The gentlemen members of the committee were staring at it, not so much entranced by its delicate appearance as by the suggestive rustle of garments behind it. For on the far side of its panels one of those scenes was taking place that men usually had to pay to see: the only two lady members of the committee were busy undressing Madame Amber. Through the latticework running along the bottom of the screen, the medium's small, pale feet were visible, like two little white mice at play amid the women's hulking shoes.

Clayton was also observing the screen, almost without seeing it, though for quite different reasons. As he did so, he was imagining his voice as he unmasked Madame Amber being captured for eternity on the phonograph cylinder. He was fascinated by the idea that his words might endure so long, remaining imprinted on that roll of paraffined cardboard while he grew old and turned into someone who no longer resembled the youth who had uttered them. Assured that the cylinder would imbue his words with a modest degree of immortality, he merely would need to clear his throat and pronounce his accusations in a clear, loud voice, as though projecting from a stage. For he would succeed in unmasking Madame Amber, of that he had no doubt.

Given his intentions, Clayton could not help but feel his presence in the commission was rather deceitful, since someone at some ministry or other had suggested Captain Sinclair and his finest detective in the Special Branch join it in order to do exactly the opposite. Ever since the year 1848, when in a small American town called Hydesville the Fox sisters had contacted a spirit by means of a crude method of sounds and spirit raps, a veritable plague of mediums had spread all over the planet. So much so that toward the middle of the century there was hardly a soirée where the guests didn't clear the table after dinner, eager to try communicating with the dead. Indeed, around that time, according to what Clayton had read in *The Yorkshireman,* invitations to "tea and table turning" became all the rage in the United States, reaching the shores of England in the 1860s with the arrival of the medium Daniel Dunglas Home, who decided to settle in England to seek a cure for a lung ailment. At the time, Home was considered the greatest medium the world had ever seen. There were currently more than a hundred mediums in London alone: ferrymen without a ferry eager to transport the living over to the other shore so that they could communicate with their dead, for rather more coins than the single one Charon charged for the passage.

Because so many charlatans had taken advantage of the situation to try to make their fortunes at the expense of the credulous, it was inevitable that committees would be formed to separate the wheat from the chaff. The problem was that, although the members of such committees were noteworthy men and women, known for their moral rectitude, most had only one goal: to expose charlatans. According to defenders of the cause, this created a wall of negative vibrations through which spirits were unable to pass, resulting in some mediums feeling obliged to resort to trickery. To Clayton it seemed like the most childish excuse, yet he couldn't deny they were right about the attitude of most committee members. When they stumbled on the fantastical, they refused to recognize it as such, however much irrefutable evidence they were confronted with. Clayton had read a few of their curious reports, which alternated between an almost offensive disdain for the medium or a dismissive shrug of the shoulders when they failed to prove he or she was a sham. Occasionally, they would proffer explanations for some psychic phenomena that were even less credible than the involvement of spirits themselves. Anything was preferable to acceptance. Moreover, it was absurd to create a research group to study spiritual phenomena made up of people who were prejudiced against the subject they were supposed to be investigating. That was why he and Sinclair had been invited to join the committee: to act as a counterbalance to the intransigent skepticism of the majority of its members with their openness toward the supernatural as a possible explanation for such happenings, assuming there was no other, of course. After all, the assumption was that the two inspectors from Scotland Yard's Special Branch, who rode on unicorns and danced with fairies, were far less reluctant when it came to accepting the forays that spirits made into our world. And that was the position Clayton had decided to adopt. Until he saw for the first time the poster of the beautiful, ethereal Madame Amber inviting her clientele to visit her salon with a false air of dreamy innocence. From that moment on, he realized it was his duty to unmask her, to bring to an end her peaceful reign of deception; of parading through the smartest salons in London, leaving everyone in awe; of living like a goddess in the midst of the poor, foolish mortals, whose pockets she emptied with a smile on her face. Yes, it was his duty, because only he could see the cunning self-interest oozing from her beautiful eyes. Because only he could see the truth behind the pretty face of a woman who was always used to getting what she wanted.

THE INSPECTOR TOOK ADVANTAGE of everyone gazing at the screen to examine the other members of the committee once more. He had already checked their backgrounds, since it was common practice for bogus mediums to rely on accomplices during their séances. However, none of them had aroused his suspicions, since most of them had published an article or taken part in a debate that was critical of spiritualism. The various members consisted of Ramsey, a lanky doctor with a horsey face, who was not only a professor at the School of Medicine but also a celebrated surgeon, an eminent chemist, and a brilliant biologist who apparently had a penchant for cracking his knuckles at regular intervals; the burly, dynamic Colonel Garrick, in charge of sanitation at the Ministry of Defense; the discreet engineer, Holland; the frail Professor Burke, who lectured at the School of Law; an aristocrat turned magician who called himself Count Duggan, and whose eccentric presence in the group owed itself to the fact that the main psychic phenomena of the medium world could be reproduced artificially by sleight of hand; and last but not least a scientist with curly whiskers and a bushy beard named William Crookes, awarded a gold medal by the Royal Society in recognition of his numerous and valuable discoveries.

Besides the two inspectors, and one other member of the committee who will be introduced shortly, Crookes was the only one with an open-minded attitude toward spiritualism, although that hadn't always been the case. The eminent scientist had begun his research into psychic phenomena driven by the moral necessity of exposing the deceit they involved, a gesture that was much lauded by his colleagues, who were keen for someone of his stature to teach the members of that burgeoning sect a lesson. However, after investigating Home, Crookes had not delivered the hoped-for verdict. In an article he wrote for *The Quarterly Journal of Science,* he had conceded the existence of a new power, to which he had given the pompous name "psychic force." His conclusions had thrown the scientific establishment into turmoil, condemning Crookes to an icy professional ostracism. Only a few of his closest friends, like Doctor Ramsey, who was also on the committee, had remained loyal to him, although they chose to maintain a reserved silence with regard to his enthusiastic claims. But Crookes had seen Home float his armchair up to the ceiling and trace in the air a little girl's hand, which then plucked the petals from the flower in his lapel, and so what else could he have said?

However, the most shocking incident was still to come. After his studies of the celebrated Home were published, Crookes received a visit from the no-less-famous Florence Cook, a fifteen-year-old girl of humble origin who had gained considerable prestige as a medium thanks to her ectoplasmic materializations: more precisely, those of a spirit named

Katie King, who claimed she was the daughter of the legendary pirate Henry Morgan. For three years, Florence had been summoning Katie in front of numerous witnesses, and, as was frequently the case, the more miraculous a medium's exploits, the more the shadow of suspicion hung over him or her. Ridding herself of that shadow was what brought Florence to Crookes's elegant house in Mornington Road to make him the following proposal: if he could demonstrate that her powers were false, he was free to expose her publicly to the press; if on the contrary he proved they were genuine, he would likewise make it public. Crookes accepted the young girl's challenge and invited her to live with him and his large family for as long as it took to carry out the experiments. It was a bold gesture that had caused a stir, not only among the scientific establishment, but also in society at large, as one can imagine. Crookes spent three months examining Florence in his study and also organized several public séances, to which he invited half a dozen of his fellow scientists. The séances always followed the same course: young Florence, with her hands bound, connected to a galvanometer by a few slender wires, would lie on Crookes's study floor, her black velvet dress pinned down and her face covered with a shawl so that the light in the room would not distract her. A few moments later she would go into a trance, and to everyone's amazement a beautiful young girl dressed in white would appear, claiming she was the ghost of Katie King. With a coquettish laugh, Katie would agree to be photographed by Crookes using one of his homemade cameras; she would stroll arm in arm with him, recounting stories of India, where she had lived an earthly life full of adventure; and she would even perch on the laps of the most skeptical gentlemen, mischievously stroking their beards. As there were plenty who claimed that, owing to their striking resemblance and the fact they were never in the same room together at the same time, Katie and Florence were one and the same person, Crookes was obliged to carry out further experiments to establish a series of differences between them. Katie, unlike Florence, did not have pierced ears; she was also taller than Florence, had fairer skin and hair, and there was no small scar on her neck. One day when Florence was suffering from a cold, Crookes had listened to her chest with a stethoscope and discovered she had a wheeze, whereas Katie's lungs presented no such symptoms to his ears. As if that were not enough, Crookes convinced Katie to remain in the same room as the medium and be photographed beside her, and although he made no attempt to uncover Florence's face for fear it might bring her out of her trance, it was clear these were two different women.

Crookes's claims that Florence's powers were genuine secured the reputation of the young medium, although, unfortunately, the same could not be said of his own. However, this time it was not because the scientist had once more risked his credibility defending the existence of life after death, but rather because in his articles he couldn't conceal the fact that he had fallen head over heels in love with Katie King, the pirate's daughter who had been dead for many years. Crookes's descriptions of her, which Clayton had read with a wry smile, had more in common with the doggerel of a second-rate poet than the dry discourse of a scientist: "The photographs fail to do justice to Katie's flawless beauty, as words are insufficient to describe her allure. Her enchanting presence makes you want to kneel down and worship her." It was clear that the brilliant scientist, discoverer of thallium and inventor of the radiometer, had allowed himself to be seduced by the adorable ghost with whom he strolled through his study like lovers in a park. It made him the laughingstock of every salon in London, and his few remaining friends, including Doctor Ramsey, turned their backs on him in shame, weary perhaps of defending the indefensible, or simply afraid society would tar them with the same brush. But during the spring of 1874, Katie had made her final farewells to Florence and Crookes. She had fulfilled her mission, she told them, by proving to the skeptics the existence of the Beyond and was now able to rest in peace. Since then, Crookes had not seen or spoken of Katie again, and time, ever merciful, had finally silenced the mocking voices. Besides scandalizing half of London, it was obvious that the unearthly love affair had left Crookes heartbroken, but at least his prestige as a scientist had survived, and whilst his presence at any function still aroused a few pitying smiles, his discoveries continued to win him the admiration of his colleagues, and it was even rumored he might receive a knighthood in the not-too-distant future. However, it was enough for Clayton to note the intense look of yearning in Crookes's eyes to realize he still had not forgotten Katie King. The inspector would even have wagered his good hand that, for all Crookes's claims that his interest in spiritualism was purely scientific, his real aim was to find her again.

CLAYTON TURNED HIS ATTENTION from Crookes to the remaining member of the group, a frail old lady whose commitment to the cause of spiritualism he found almost touching. Catherine Lansbury was the only one who was not part of the committee but had been given permission to attend the séance thanks to her generous donations, which had replenished its empty coffers. That benevolent contribution had allowed her to participate in all of the committee's investigations. So far that year, according to Clayton's information, Mrs. Lansbury had attended no fewer than a dozen séances in London and beyond. That interest in spiritualism had puzzled Clayton, because, despite her apparent fragility, Mrs. Lansbury's eyes sparkled with a determination that had none of the benign befuddlement one expects in somebody approaching eighty. They radiated tenacity of spirit and a clearheaded intelligence, and it was no surprise to discover that she was the inventor of the Mechanical Servant, a device that had conquered the homes of the wealthiest English families. This was why Clayton found it all the harder to understand her decision to squander her fortune on something as dubious as spiritualism.

"I've been wanting to attend one of Madame Amber's séances," she had confessed to him excitedly during the brief exchange they had enjoyed on arriving at the house. "Her waiting list is so long I can scarcely believe I'm finally here. She really does excel at spiritualism in all its forms, but they say her materializations are second to none. Perhaps she is a genuine Maelstrom coordinator . . . It's a long time since I met one."

Clayton had no idea what Mrs. Lansbury was talking about, but simply said, "I hope she doesn't disappoint you."

What else could he say to her? Apparently, the old lady's mental faculties weren't as keen as her lucid gaze suggested. Clayton regretted the existence of unscrupulous people who took advantage of such people and was unable to prevent that regret from showing in his gaze. To his astonishment, however, he discovered Mrs. Lansbury staring back at him with a similar look of compassion, as if she had glimpsed behind his eyes his dark, barren soul and had realized that the ashes covering it were simply the remnants of the spectacular fire that had consumed him seven months earlier.

Professor Burke's voice brought the inspector back to reality.

"Ah, how I wish I could examine Madame Amber personally!" he whispered conspiratorially so that the ladies could not hear. "This might be our only chance to touch such a beautiful woman, don't you agree, gentlemen?"

The men all nodded hastily, except for Professor Crookes and the engineer named Holland—Crookes because his spectral romance appeared to have placed him above the temptations of the flesh, and Holland because one of the ladies behind the screen disrobing the medium was his wife.

"Undoubtedly, Professor," Count Duggan said dolefully, also in hushed tones. Then he appeared to reflect and added, "Perhaps I could offer to conclude the examination myself, because there is more than likely a hidden pocket in her undergarments. I say, Captain, don't you think that we ought to verify . . ."

"I'm afraid I cannot allow that, Count Duggan," Sinclair interrupted him rather coldly.

"But she's so ravishing!" moaned Duggan. "You gentlemen don't appreciate that, because, unlike me, you didn't see her close up at Lady Colesberry's ball. And I can assure you she is even more beautiful than in the photographs of her."

At this, Burke asked to be tied to his chair, for fear he could not control his actions, and they all laughed, rejoicing in their manly celebration of Madame Amber's loveliness.

"Let us not allow beauty to sidetrack us from our scientific experiment, gentlemen," warned Clayton, unable to conceal his disdain for those men who couldn't help giving in to their weaknesses.

A sudden commotion on the far side of the screen interrupted their conversation, and everyone watched as the two ladies from the committee stepped out from behind its panels. After pausing deliberately for a few seconds, the way an actress would to create a sense of anticipation among the audience, Madame Amber emerged. The luminescent strips sewn onto her gown by Mrs. Jones, head nurse at the Nightingale Training School at St Thomas's Hospital, and Mrs. Holland, the engineer's stout wife, caused the medium to glow as if she were made of strands of interwoven sunlight. She waited beside the screen for a moment, soaking up the admiration, a faint smile playing on her lips, then walked over to the gathering escorted by the two women. She wore a close-fitting silk gown, which, far from clothing her, seemed to leave her naked. As she walked, the fabric alternately hinted at and hid her small, pert breasts, like an intermittent spell. Her hair, so blond it was almost white, was parted in a zigzag, separating it into two strips that fell in graceful curls over the gentle curve of her shoulders. She was slender, not very tall, and the calculated languidness of her movements gave her childlike body an even more otherworldly appearance. She came to a halt as she reached the center of the room and greeted the committee members with a haughty smile, which Clayton assumed was part of the performance. She had such an air of lightness that in comparison her two escorts seemed hewn from heavy, rough stone. A scent of violets enveloped her, and her fine, pale features had the allure of virtue about to be corrupted. But more than anything, Clayton was struck by her huge, round eyes, which the Creator had colored an almost diaphanous blue.

"We have finished examining Madame Amber, gentlemen," Nurse Jones declared in a professional tone, "and can guarantee she has nothing concealed in her garments, mouth, or hair."

Sinclair nodded, half-entranced, half-satisfied, and was about to invite everyone to take a seat at the table to begin the séance when Clayton interrupted him.

"I'm sure your examination has been more than thorough, ladies, but let me remind you that a woman has other natural orifices in addition to her mouth," he said calmly.

The ladies stared at the inspector aghast; even some of the gentlemen were shocked by his words. Madame Amber looked deeply offended but almost instantly adopted the righteous smile of a selfless martyr prepared to undergo any sacrifice.

"Perhaps you wish to examine me in person, Inspector," she said with a childish pout, which caused more than one gentleman to loosen his necktie.

Clayton observed her impassively.

"Oh, I fear one of my hands is not delicate enough to do the job," he parried with a slight shrug. "I might hurt you."

"What if you only used the one made of flesh and blood?" She grinned suggestively.

"That is the one I was referring to," said the inspector. "With the other I would simply rip you to shreds."

He glanced at Nurse Jones with a hint of impatience. "When you're ready, Nurse."

Nurse Jones looked inquiringly at the group and, when nobody said anything, shrugged.

"Very well . . . ," she said, making no attempt to conceal the fact that she found the whole idea abhorrent. "If you have no objection, Madame Amber, shall we perform the task in your rooms?"

The medium nodded quietly, gave Clayton an icy look, and walked out behind the two ladies. The inspector watched her leave with a look of indifference.

"Good God, Inspector, aren't you being unnecessarily demanding?" said Holland, once they were alone. "Let's not stoop to indelicacy or rudeness, what?"

"I quite agree," chimed in Burke. "It was obvious Madame Amber felt offended by your insistence—"

"Gentlemen, let us not forget that this is a scientific experiment," retorted Clayton. "A woman can be completely naked and yet conceal a small object, such as a scrap of muslin, or even a rubber mask."

An abrupt silence fell. Even Sinclair appeared unable to come up with the appropriate words to salvage the situation.

"Inspector Clayton is right, gentlemen." Doctor Ramsey spoke at last, cracking the knuckles of each hand one by one. "Our only aim is, and always has been, to seek the truth, and in doing so we will inevitably subject mediums to certain, er . . . indelicacies."

"Even so, for the sake of decorum and our honor as gentlemen . . . ," Holland protested.

"Poppycock!" declared Colonel Garrick, who until then had remained silent. "Most mediums exploit our decency to carry out their infamous trickery, which is why we have to be as rigorous as possible. Remember, they are mostly charlatans, like that priest who calls himself Doctor Monck."

"Or that swindler Slade," added Count Duggan, referring to an expert in automatic writing whose trial for fraud had given rise to a spate of complaints and prosecutions against mediums. "I attended one of his séances myself, you know. He used to give them where he lodged at a boardinghouse in Russell Square, and he charged twenty shillings, though they barely lasted fifteen minutes. But that was ample time for me to—"

"Yes, Henry Slade was a true confidence trickster, doubtless the cleverest of all," Garrick interrupted. "Although it requires no special talent to convince someone who is gullible."

Hearing this, Crookes stiffened. "I'd like to think your remark wasn't directed at anyone in particular, Colonel."

"Only at whoever wishes to take it personally." Garrick shrugged.

There was flurry of laughter, which Doctor Ramsey swiftly quelled.

"Come, come, gentlemen . . . Let's not lower ourselves to personal insult."

"Oh, many thanks for your defense, Ramsey, *dear chap*," Crookes warbled, "although I fear it is a little late and quite unnecessary, for, as you know, lately I have learned to defend myself."

"For heaven's sake, Crookes, there's no need to take it personally," the doctor implored, producing a succession of deafening cracks with his knuckles. "You know my opinion about your studies. I regret that at the time you saw it as a betrayal, but I haven't changed my mind: few mediums are free of suspicion, and I'm afraid they don't include your sainted Florence, who as you are aware was exposed during a séance eight years ago."

"I wasn't at that tragic séance, and only fools speak of things they don't know about," Crookes retorted. "But I can speak of the miracles that occurred under my own roof, as can numerous others who witnessed them. And I have proof! The photographs I took are at the disposition of—"

"Those photographs prove nothing, Crookes. I saw them, remember? And I pointed out to you that in one of them you could see the edge of a black dress peeping out from beneath Katie King's white robes—"

"Lies!" roared Crookes. Then he looked at his friend in despair. "Oh, Ramsey, what the blazes has happened to you over the past few years? I appreciate your skepticism—I respect it, even—but I shall never understand your blindness: Do you honestly deny the possibility of life after death, despite there being reports of apparitions dating back to the days of Tertullian? The Hereafter exists, and I am sure it is an exact replica of our world, as affirmed by Swedenborg, the greatest medium of modern times."

"I have never denied or affirmed the existence of the Hereafter, whether it resembles this world or not," Ramsey insisted wearily. He remained silent for a few moments before adding, in a philosophical tone, "In the end, every reality is an imitation of itself."

"An imitation of itself . . . ! You don't know how right you are, Doctor Ramsey!" Mrs. Lansbury guffawed.

Ramsey glanced at her, somewhat surprised by her interjection, and then once more addressed Crookes.

"But you must admit, William, that those historical apparitions were vague and sporadic. And yet, if we believed all the recent cases, we would find ourselves confronted with an organized invasion, or dare I say it . . . with an epidemic. Besides, I was merely questioning Florence's honesty," he added, avoiding his old friend's offended, angry gaze.

"And don't forget, Crookes," Holland piped up, "that Margaretta Fox herself sent a letter from New York proclaiming that all her séances had been hoaxes. What further proof do we need that mediums are a bunch of charlatans who prey on people's tragedies and hopes in order to line their own pockets?"

"The press only know how to feed drivel to the public!" said Crookes with disdain.

"I have to agree with you there, Crookes," said Colonel Garrick. "Let's be fair, gentlemen: if a member of the public goes to any newspaper with a story about exposing a fraudulent medium, they publish it amid great fanfare; but if the same individual proclaims the truth of some supernatural phenomenon they have witnessed, it barely gets a mention."

Crookes gave a nod of gratitude, although it was clear from his stony expression that he hadn't forgotten the colonel's earlier remarks, or the hilarity they had produced.

"I agree that the press isn't what it used to be," complained Burke. "Look at the way they are treating the murders of those two prostitutes in Whitechapel . . ."

The conversation then turned to the two horrific crimes, whose grisly details the press had revealed without caring how accurate they were, thus hindering the police investigation, with the sole aim, Sinclair hastened to add, of satisfying their readers' morbid appetites. Everyone gave their opinion on the matter, apart from Clayton. Once he had finished investigating Madame Amber, he would study the reports on those ruthless killings written up by Inspector Reid of the Criminal Investigation Department and draw his own conclusions.

Like Ramsey and Garrick, Clayton believed that the majority of mediums were impostors, but that didn't mean there weren't any genuine seers capable of producing true miracles, as Crookes claimed. That was something he, who wore around his neck a key to a secret chamber full of miracles, was in no position to deny. Not to mention the fact that every morning he knotted his tie with a mechanical hand that constantly reminded him that the fantastical existed. Thus his misgivings about Madame Amber were not the result of any prejudice toward the supernatural: a certain countess had immunized him against that for life, although it seemed she had also prevented him ever again from believing in the innocence of a beautiful woman.

The door then opened, and the medium reentered the room, the humiliating examination to which she had just been subjected having failed to wipe the virginal smile from her lips. Seeing her appear like a delicate butterfly after its wings have been plucked by a cruel child, Captain Sinclair steeled himself and gave Clayton a meaningful look, silently ordering him, with the wrath of his one good eye, to think twice before inventing some fresh demand. Then, smiling gallantly at Madame Amber, he invited everyone to be seated at the table.

The séance would now begin.

5

OR SEVERAL MINUTES NOT A LIVING SOUND was heard in the spacious room bathed in the dim light of an infrared lamp, not even the breathing of the twelve people seated around the table. From the moment when Captain Sinclair had commanded silence and they had all obediently joined hands, no one dared to move or make the slightest noise. Even the captain's glass eye appeared to have stopped its habitual flashing and buzzing like an ember slowly fizzling out as it sinks into water. The twelve remained suspended in that silent glow as though frozen in time. Only two things betrayed life's unceasing flow: the placid hum of the phonograph working away in a corner of the room, its spinning cylinder oblivious to the wound inflicted on it by the stylus, and Clayton's eyes, which despite his motionless body flitted around the room, examining every corner.

Once he had checked that the various machines were functioning properly, the inspector contemplated the medium. She was sitting opposite him, her eyes gently closed, bound to her chair and with two short chains, each equipped with a padlock fastening her wrists to those of Doctor Ramsey and Colonel Garrick. As Clayton cast his gaze over his fellow committee members, he was unable to detect on their faces any trace of the skepticism they had shown moments before. Their fingertips touching those of their neighbors, they all seemed absorbed in an almost pious meditation, convinced something was about to occur that would shake them to the core, whether it came from this world or the next.

Sinclair's voice suddenly boomed out, causing them to jump out of their skins. Without warning, the captain had launched into his record of the séance, in a voice loud enough to be picked up by phonographs as far away as Paris. Having recovered from the shock, the committee members hurriedly resumed their frozen postures. Only the medium remained as motionless as a sphinx, deep in the supposed trance she had entered into as soon as the séance began. The young woman's lips were parted, and she was breathing slowly and deeply, her small breasts lifting at regular intervals, constrained by the fine silk gown, attracting the furtive glances of the men around the table like moths around a fire. Breathing too regularly, Clayton thought skeptically.

"Subject: séance of twelve September 1888. Time: nine o'clock p.m. Place: Madame Amber's residence, number twelve Mayflower Road, London. Monitor on the right side: Colonel Garrick; monitor on the left side: Doctor Ramsey. Assistants: Mrs. Holland, Mr. Holland, Professor Crookes, Count Duggan . . ."

And while Sinclair continued his breakdown of the rigorous scientific conditions under which the séance was being monitored, Clayton's eyes alighted on the three objects in the middle of the table awaiting telekinetic experiments: a small gilt bell, a gardenia, and a lace handkerchief. They were still immobile, and might continue to be, and yet the inspector had the impression they were charged with an air of anticipation, as if they had already secretly decided to move and were simply awaiting Madame Amber's command. He shook his head, attempting to rid himself of such an absurd idea, no doubt a result of his mind playing tricks on him.

Captain Sinclair's presentation ended as abruptly as it had begun, and silence once again fell on the gathering. Moments later, Madame Amber, her face still registering a look of intense ecstasy whose alchemy none of the mortals gathered around would ever comprehend, gave a succession of faint moans from her parted lips. Soon afterward, her lovely brow wrinkled, then gradually recovered its original smoothness, as though a light breeze had rippled the calm surface of a lake. This caused an almost electric shiver to pass through the human circle. Although everything about the medium's face appeared genuine, Clayton was certain that she was faking: something deep inside him insisted that a woman that beautiful couldn't possibly be honest, couldn't possibly be at the service of truth. No supreme power was whole and incorruptible, and was there any power greater than that possessed by a beautiful woman? He glanced around him and discovered four pairs of eyes belonging to four of the men around the table—including, to his astonishment, Captain Sinclair—descending lasciviously toward Madame Amber's pulsating cleavage. None of the men concentrated on monitoring the séance, unable to tear their gaze from the slow rise and fall of the medium's fragile, provocative, almost girlish breasts. His eyes then crossed those of Count Duggan, who gave him a knowing wink. Disgusted by the thought that this eccentric character assumed he was prey to the same lustfulness as the others, Clayton considered calling them to attention but then thought better of it. He didn't relish the idea of the cylinder preserving in time one of his admonishments, which might even offend the ladies. He frowned at the count and concentrated once more on the medium.

It was then that the little bell on the table started making a noise, emitting several short, loud tinkles. All eyes fell on the completely mundane object that had suddenly been transformed into a bridge between two worlds. Following the brief call to attention, the bell was silent again. Then Madame Amber resumed her moaning, arching her back and shaking her head violently from side to side; her platinum hair lashed her face like a seagull trying to peck out her eyes. At that moment the bell began to lift very slowly into the air until it was floating about eight inches above the tabletop, where it began to ring furiously, as though shaken by a relentless, invisible hand. At the same time, a series of loud thuds rang out quite clearly, although no one could quite make out which part of the room they were coming from. Clayton had read numerous accounts of loud noises, like huge fists pummeling the walls, but these sounded more like knitting needles dropped on a marble floor, only painfully amplified. As though competing with the thuds, the bell continued tinkling hysterically, and in the midst of that cacophony the gardenia began sliding toward the edge of the table, where it toppled into Nurse Jones's lap, causing her to throw herself back in her chair with a look of horror, as though a scorpion had just landed on her skirts. It was then that the lace handkerchief took to the air with a delicate flourish and began to float past the flabbergasted onlookers like a jellyfish.

In the meantime, Clayton's eyes darted frenetically around the room, checking the different monitors again and again. He was certain the bells attached to the curtains hadn't made a sound before the hubbub had started, although he had to admit that they were of no use now. If anything was moving the weighty hangings, there was no way he could have heard, or indeed seen anything through that bloodred half-light. However, from where he was sitting he could glimpse the record-ing thermometers, the infrared apparatus, and the other devices set up around the room, none of which appeared to detect any movement in their immediate vicinity. Leaning away from the table just far enough so as not to break the human chain imposed by his neighbors' hands, Clayton noticed the sawdust was undisturbed, as was the plank blocking off the chimney opening and the seals around the windows. As for his fellow participants, most of them had eschewed their role of strict ob-server and were gazing spellbound at the riotous activity of the bell, the leisurely progress of the handkerchief, or at Madame Amber herself as she writhed on her chair in a manner as lewd as it was hair-raising.

Where was the contemptuous skepticism they had exhibited only moments ago? Clayton wondered. When it was all over, these staunch disbelievers would doubtless pooh-pooh what happened during the sé-ance with one of those vague, disdainful phrases they had read in the newspapers, but there was no denying that at that moment they re-sembled a group of schoolchildren mesmerized by a fireworks display. Crookes in particular was exhilarated: his offended expression had given way to a beaming smile, and he even urged his colleagues to smell the handkerchief, assuring them the strong perfume impregnating it hadn't been there before the séance started. Clayton sighed inwardly. It seemed Crookes's broken heart was easier to mend than his own. Vexed, he tried to catch the captain's eye, but Sinclair ignored him. When the bell first started ringing, Sinclair had backed up Clayton's visual monitoring of the situation, but since a particularly violent spasm had caused Madame Amber's gown to slip off one of her shoulders, revealing the outline of her breast, pale and delicate as a snowflake, Clayton had given up on his superior. Of all the people around the table, only one seemed as poised as the inspector: Mrs. Lansbury, who was observing the scene with what appeared to be a cold, professional eye. Clayton studied the frail old lady, wondering whether her attitude was a sign of unflinching belief in spiritualism or bitter disappointment. It could have been either of those two things, and yet something told him the old lady shared his misgivings.

All at once, the thudding stopped so abruptly that the ensuing silence seemed to burst everyone's eardrums. A second later, the bell crashed onto the table, bouncing several times before finally rolling around forlornly on the same spot, as though lulling itself to sleep. The handkerchief floated toward Madame Amber, who had ceased convulsing and was staring straight ahead with glazed eyes, and settled on her face with the milky softness of a bride's veil. The effect of the delicate caress on her was overwhelming: her body tensed with such force that the chair she was seated on lifted off the ground, and her head snapped backward, as though someone had yanked her hair violently, and then forward, causing her mane to trace a silvery streak of lightning in the air as the handkerchief slipped into her lap. She remained motionless, her chin pressed to her chest, her hair obscuring her face like an ivory mask, while strange gurgling, rattling sounds came from her throat. Beneath the pale skin of her forearms, her veins and muscles appeared grotesquely swollen, as if her body were being subjected to some inhuman pressure.

"Good God, she's suffocating!" Nurse Jones squawked, her voice faltering.

But before anyone could react, the strange panting noises stopped. Madame Amber's body relaxed visibly, and behind her a new, startling phenomenon began to take place. A row of phosphorescent lights, like minute, inexplicably beautiful shimmering dragonflies appeared, hov-

ering above her head, then immediately started to move about, swirling in a tiny constellation, before melding into a luminous, effervescent
mass that began to grow more dense and to expand. The resplendent
cloud appeared to be feeding directly off Madame Amber's head, like a
phantom leech, or perhaps it was coming from there, as though distilled
through her hair. Clayton understood that Madame Amber was preparing to perform one of her celebrated materializations, the phenomena
that brought mediums the most prestige and whose complexity posed
one of the most dangerous challenges to a charlatan.

"Look, a face is forming!" Crookes exclaimed excitedly, blinking
again and again as though attempting to discern the features of the beautiful pirate's daughter through the mist.

Clayton saw that he was right. Amid that nebulous cloud he glimpsed
a vague shape emerging. However, disappointingly for Crookes, it appeared to be the three-quarter profile of a man. All that was visible of
him was his nose, whiskers, and fleshy lips, which looked as if they were
poised for a kiss or to start whistling.

"I can feel his breath on my hand!" Colonel Garrick, who was closest
to the materialization, declared half in terror, half in awe.

Two stark white hands then appeared on either side of the face; they
seemed more solid, less ethereal, than the face, and their fingers moved
with an odd grace, although at the level of the wrists they became more
vaporous, merging with the luminous cloud encircling the ghostlike
profile. Clayton studied the face and the hands with mounting rage. His
only desire was to leap to his feet and grab hold of those nebulous forms,
convinced the ingenious fraud would instantly be exposed. But he
forced himself to remain seated, for Sinclair had commanded that under
no circumstances should they interrupt the séance, no matter what suspicions they might have while it was going on. Their mission was limited to making sure the séance was correctly monitored, studying the
medium's modus operandi, recording the séance, and analyzing the data
on the various devices so as to be able to arrive at relevant conclusions,
which would enable them to decide whether or not to take any further

action. In short, they must be alert to everything that went on but were forbidden to intervene. That being so, Clayton had no choice but to be patient and hope that Madame Amber slipped up, or that one of the devices registered some anomaly that would allow them to bring her to justice. He sighed impatiently, focusing his attention on the wraithlike figure that had emanated from the medium, which suddenly started to dissolve. The face and hands gradually became elongated, distorting, as though the figure were melting, and in a matter of seconds it spilled onto the floor and vanished beneath the table like a gelatinous drizzle.

Everyone sat expectantly, watching Madame Amber in strained silence. She seemed to be asleep or unconscious, her head tilted slightly forward, her limp body apparently held up only by the two monitors. Doctor Ramsey and Colonel Garrick exchanged worried glances above the medium's blond locks. Just then, Madame Amber tried feebly to raise her head. Ramsey called her name gently, and she responded with a drawn-out moan, as though awakening from a deep sleep. After several attempts, she managed to sit up straight, blinking as she looked around her in bewilderment. She frowned, coughed a few times, and then slumped onto Colonel Garrick's shoulder, apparently exhausted.

"We ought to give her some water," advised the doctor, "and I'd like to check her pulse."

"The cords are chafing her skin," Colonel Garrick remarked in a tone far less professional than that of Ramsey, doubtless enchanted by the sweet weight of that head nestled on his shoulder.

"I'm afraid all that will have to wait," Clayton snapped.

"The water will have to wait," Captain Sinclair corrected calmly, glowering at his subordinate. "No one must leave the table until Clayton and I have checked the readings on the monitors. But you can start untying her, and by all means check the young lady's pulse, Doctor Ramsey, and perhaps see about, er . . . covering her up."

Clayton looked at the captain without responding, and at Sinclair's signal, the two men stood up at the same time, lifting their chairs so as not to drag them through the sawdust. In the meantime, Garrick and

Ramsey assisted Madame Amber as the others looked on in concern. While the doctor began untying her wrists, the colonel gently patted her cheek, encouraging her in the gentlest of voices to tell them how she was feeling. The medium tried to do as he asked, opening her mouth a few times, but was unable to utter a sound. She raised a pale hand to her throat and gave a faint smile, as though apologizing to everyone for her tiresome, inopportune exhaustion. And then her expression, which Clayton had been observing closely, became transfigured: the smile froze on her lips, and a sudden terror crumpled her delicate features like paper, twisting them into an unrecognizable mass. Bewildered, the inspector turned to where Madame Amber's gaze was fixed.

In a corner of the room, shrouded in the reddish half-light, stood the motionless figure of a man. He was clad in a dark suit, torn in places, beneath which a powerful body was visible. Due to the distance, and the opaque gloom, Clayton could only just make out a coarsely featured face, crowned by a pair of wild eyes, and underscored by a powerful chin covered in an unkempt beard. But besides his appearance, there was something else about the man that startled the inspector: his figure appeared not to possess the luminous, vaporous quality attributed to spirits, but rather seemed perfectly outlined and consistent, as if he were made of the same stuff as any normal human being, except in one respect: he was transparent. The man's body, although it gave the impression of being solid flesh and blood, seemed to let the light through, or in this case the semidarkness.

The supposed spirit did not say or do anything. His posture oozed menace, and his eyes glinted with an almost inhuman hatred. Clayton contemplated him with growing astonishment, then wheeled round to look at Madame Amber, who was quaking in her chair, her mouth open in a soundless cry of terror. Without knowing why, Clayton sensed this time that her emotion was genuine. The rest of the group was also staring toward the corner, without daring to rise from the table. They all appeared visibly alarmed by the apparition, but above all by the dense atmosphere of impending doom. Then Clayton noticed Mrs. Lansbury. Like the others, the old lady was contemplating the looming figure with terror, yet her eyes betrayed something different, something that looked like defiance.

"You! It's you!" the apparition suddenly bellowed, shaking with anger and pointing at one of the people at the table, arm outstretched.

They all looked at one another, scared and confused, trying to discover whom his words were intended for, all except Madame Amber and Mrs. Lansbury, who kept on staring intently at the stranger.

"I've found you! At last, I've found you! And this time you'll give me what is mine!" roared the apparition, his words giving way to a blood-curdling howl.

His rage was so intense it twisted his mouth into a hideous snarl, like a ferocious gargoyle, through which, absurdly, the pattern of the wallpaper was visible. Then, to everyone's astonishment, the diminutive Mrs. Lansbury stood up from her chair and confronted the figure, with only her trembling dignity as protection.

From then on, events took place at breakneck speed. The stranger yelled a curse and instantly charged at the group, flying past Clayton, who received a sharp blow to the shoulder. Then he leapt onto the table and hurled himself at poor Mrs. Lansbury, who had no time to escape. Everyone jumped to his or her feet, no longer worried about disturbing the sawdust. Some screamed, others uttered words of disbelief. Madame Amber flung herself to the floor and began crawling toward the Japanese screen. Clayton and Sinclair grabbed hold of the stranger, who had managed to seize the old lady by the throat. However, with an astonishing display of agility, the man jerked his head back violently, hitting the captain square on the nose. Sinclair fell to the floor, tracing a bloody arc that spurted from the middle of his face and dragging Clayton along with him. No sooner had the inspector landed on the floor than he leapt back to his feet, looking around for his gun, which had slipped from his hand. But he realized instantly there was no time for that: Mrs. Lansbury's life was ebbing through her assailant's powerful fingers, and so he hurled himself once more at the apparition. He managed to grip the phantom's powerful neck in a lock, hoping to force him to release his prey. Glimpsing his own arms through the body he was trying to overpower, which felt completely normal to the touch, startled him momentarily, but he quickly tightened his hold again. However, despite straining every muscle in his body, and no doubt inflicting great pain as he dug his metal hand hard into that transparent throat, the stranger seemed to possess the invincible strength of a madman, and the inspector could not make him release his deadly grip on the old lady's throat. Her face was turning purple, and there was nothing else he could do. The man was going to kill her before Clayton's eyes.

Then he heard a voice behind him cry out: "Get down, Inspector!"

Glancing over his shoulder, Clayton saw Colonel Garrick aiming a pistol at him. He instantly flung himself to the floor. He heard a shot ring out and saw the old lady's frail, seemingly lifeless body slump in front of him.

Then someone switched on the lights. Clayton hurriedly leaned over Mrs. Lansbury. To his relief, he discovered she was still breathing and did not seem to be seriously injured. He sprang to his feet, crashing into Nurse Jones, who had come to their aid.

"Try to resuscitate her!" he commanded.

Nurse Jones nodded and called out in a quavering voice to Doctor Ramsey, who was standing quietly in a corner, furiously jotting in a tiny book. Clayton looked anxiously around for the apparition. He saw a dazed Captain Sinclair, his face caked in blood, struggling to his feet with the aid of Burke and Crookes, who were holding him by both arms. The Hollands were clasping each other, both pale faced, close to swooning, although Mrs. Holland seemed to be the one holding her husband up so that he wouldn't collapse. From the other side of the table, Count Duggan was waving his arms frantically in the air, gesturing toward the screen, in front of which Colonel Garrick was resolutely brandishing his still-smoking gun. Clayton ran over to him, catching the pistol Sinclair threw as he hurtled past. He reached the colonel, who looked at him with a frown.

"I think the fellow's hiding behind there!" he whispered, nodding at the screen.

Clayton agreed, and, communicating their intentions to each other through gestures, the two men, weapons at the ready, proceeded with caution, each approaching one end of the screen. Then they heard muffled noise coming from behind it, like someone or something scratching a wall. As they drew closer, they made out a woman's voice repeating what sounded like a nonsensical prayer. Clayton turned to the colonel, signaling to him to pull back the screen carefully; but, judging from the violent kick he gave it, Garrick misinterpreted his gestures. There was a deafening crash as the screen toppled to the floor, and when the cloud of sawdust settled, the two men were confronted with a harmless clothes hanger, from which Madame Amber's clothes hung limply, in an empty corner. However, the mysterious noises went on, even more clearly now. There was no question about it—somebody was scratching at a surface— and Clayton thought he could hear Madame Amber's voice repeating the same desperate appeal over and over:

"Open up, let me in, open up, I beg you . . ."

The inspector went over to the corner made by the two converging walls and examined it carefully. He discovered that, thanks to a clever optical illusion, the wallpaper concealed a tiny crack—a small opening that hadn't been there during the exhaustive inspection they had carried out. But now it was. Inserting one of his metal fingers into the gap, Clayton discovered a tiny spring, which he pressed. The walls instantly parted, creaking on invisible hinges, proving they were mere partitions. And there, in the hollow concealed by that ingenious feat of carpentry, appeared Madame Amber. She was crouching, her face red from crying, scratching at the floor with bloodied fingernails as she repeated over and over the same demand: "Open up, let me in . . ."

As soon as the light revealed her hiding place, she began to scream, arms outstretched as though fending off the figure leaning over her.

"No, no, no! I didn't summon you! Why have you come back? Be off with you and never return! Go back to the hell from whence you came!"

Clayton grabbed her roughly by the arms and flung her at Colonel Garrick, whom Sinclair had now joined.

"Hold her!" the inspector commanded, his eyes flashing wildly, not realizing that he was issuing orders to his own captain.

At that moment, Clayton was only interested in the area of floor Madame Amber had been scratching moments before. He bent down, sweeping aside the remnants of sawdust, blood, and even a few bits of broken nail that the medium had torn off in the heat of her folly. He studied the parquetry closely but could find nothing odd about it. Granted, it was an exquisite piece of work. But the inspector already knew what was beneath it. He rapped on the floor with his metal fist.

"I know you can hear me!" he shouted. "This is Inspector Cornelius Clayton from Scotland Yard's Special Branch. In the name of Her Majesty, I command you to open the trapdoor and show yourself immediately. Whoever you are, come out quietly and with your hands up."

A dense silence ensued. Clayton's fist was poised to rap on the floor again when they heard a man's faint voice reply almost meekly.

"It won't open. The catch is stuck and . . . it only opens from the inside . . . I'm trapped down here."

"Who are you?" Clayton demanded, trying to match that timorous voice to the powerful figure he had grappled with moments before.

Silence. And then, at last, they heard from the depths: "My name is Sir Henry Blendell, architect to Her Majesty the Queen, gold medalist of the Worshipful Company of Engineers, honorary automaton creator of the Society of Watchmakers and Designers of Prague, renowned creator of the secret passageway in the castle at . . ."

Clayton was altogether too astonished to notice the growing murmur behind him. *The* Sir Henry Blendell? He conjured up the image he had of Her Majesty's architect, a corpulent man, in good shape despite his advanced years, of medium height and with white hair . . . Yes, it was possible that with the right disguise he might pass for the mysterious specter that had just terrified the wits out of them all. He glanced sideways at the phonograph, to make sure it was still working despite all hell having broken loose in the room. He placed both hands on the floor and, drawing closer, spoke in a stentorian voice.

"Sir Henry, do you confess to being Madame Amber's associate?"

"Please, I can't breathe . . ."

Clayton banged on the floor with both fists.

"Do you confess that you used your knowledge to aid the medium known as Madame Amber, that you conspired to contrive each and every one of the fraudulent spiritual séances she performed and knowingly certified the conditions in which said séances were carried out, and that you and she committed repeatedly and with malice aforethought the crimes of hoax, deception, and false pretense?"

"Yes, yes . . . But please, I beg you, lift the floorboards with a crowbar or a chisel. I suffer from claustrophobia . . ."

"Do you also confess to having rigged today's séance, on the twelfth of September in the year of grace 1888, at the residence of Madame Amber, located at number twelve Mayflower Road?" Clayton bawled.

"Inspector Clayton," Sinclair intervened, "for the love of God, is this really necessary?"

"Yes, yes . . . I confess to everything! But please, get me out of here . . . I'm suffocating."

Clayton straightened up, a slightly crazed grimace of triumph on his lips. His feverish gaze sought out Madame Amber's innocent blue eyes. He wanted to look straight at that her and spew out all his contempt, to tell her in no uncertain terms that her naïve attempts to beguile the public might have worked on pathetic little men like the one slowly suffocating beneath his feet, but not on Cornelius Clayton of Scotland Yard's Special Branch. I'm sorry, dear woman, he wanted to tell her, but you aren't as good as you thought, or perhaps you haven't been evil enough. One can't always get what one wants, and it was high time someone taught you that inevitable lesson . . .

But Clayton couldn't say those things to Madame Amber, for the simple reason that she was lying in a faint on the floor. Her head lay in Colonel Garrick's lap, and one hand was clasped between those of Captain Sinclair, who was trying to bring her round by tapping her gently on the back while crying out for a hammer and chisel.

6

DESPITE NOT HAVING SLEPT A WINK THAT night, Inspector Cornelius Clayton strode out early next morning toward number 3 Furnival Street. He hoped the chill air would clear his thoughts, or at least dislodge the niggling pain that had taken root at the base of his skull at some point during that endless night. After leaving Scotland Yard, he had decided not to take a cab and had instead made his way down to the river. The streets were shrouded in a damp fog that obliged him to turn up the collar of his coat and bury his hands in his pockets. He slowed his pace as he reached the Victoria Embankment, intending to stroll along the Thames as far as the Strand. He liked seeing the dawn lazily cast its light over the water, as though sketching it with an unsteady hand among the city's edifices. At that hour, still obscured by swirls of mist, the river allowed the first barges to cleave its waters, like derelict floating castles with their brimming cargoes of coal, oysters, and eels. A crowd of boats, sloops, and small vessels jostled on both banks of the river, disgorging onto its quays baskets filled with squid, shellfish, and other treasures snatched from the sea, whose foul odors the wind wafted through the neighboring streets. Before reaching Waterloo Bridge, which the dawn light outlined in greyish hues in the distance, Clayton crossed the Strand and wandered into Covent Garden market. Unconsciously, he adjusted his pace to the steady rhythm of the tradespeople who had been laboriously setting up their stalls since four o'clock and disappeared among the noisy labyrinth lined with barrows brimming with cabbages and onions, flower baskets, beer barrels and

•• 116 ••

fruit stalls, where, regardless of the early hour, a mob of ragged beggars, children robbed of their childhood, and picturesquely skinny cats were competing for the stall holders' scraps. Unperturbed by these sights, Clayton soon slipped through the gap between a stall selling shiny apples and one with gladioli, clashing in the breeze like fantastical rapiers. He stepped absentmindedly through puddles, where the reflections from streetlights glinted and were then extinguished as he passed, heralding another of those cold, dreary days typical of London in autumn.

Finally he crossed the Aldwych and drew near to his destination. However, despite his resolute stride, Inspector Clayton remained far away. In fact, he was still in the interview room in Scotland Yard, where for the past few hours he had been taking statements from Madame Amber, whose real name was Sarah Willard, and from Sir Henry Blendell, architect to Her Majesty, the most honorable, trustworthy man in the realm, at least until the ill-fated day when the beautiful medium with platinum-blond hair and deep-blue eyes had crossed his path.

For the umpteenth time, Clayton went over in his head the lengthy confession he and Captain Sinclair had finally dragged out of them. First they had put them in different rooms and, aiming to wear them down and unsettle them, had subjected them to the same cross-examination, over and over, laying small traps for them among the torrent of questions. They had even resorted to the old trick of assuring each of them that the other, in the safety of the adjacent room, had betrayed them to save his or her own skin. Then, just before dawn, they had confronted them both in the same room, in the desperate hope one of them would break down. But it had all been in vain. All night long they had repeated the same version of events, identical down to the last detail: they acknowledged their personal relationship and their criminal association; they confessed to having carried out hundreds of deceptions during the past few years, which had made them very rich; Sarah Willard possessed none of the powers she claimed to have as Madame Amber; she had possessed them as a child (she swore on the Holy Bible) but had lost them when she reached puberty and since then had been incapable of summoning spirits of any kind whatsoever, nor had she experienced any paranormal phenomena; however, inspired by the growing vogue for spiritualism, she had fraudulently resuscitated her childhood powers, determined that the memory of those past horrors should not only give her nightmares but also line her pockets with silver; she had decided to drag herself out of poverty by posing as a medium, and not just any medium, but the greatest and most famous medium of all times; she had planned it all carefully, including her seduction of Sir Henry, since she realized her beauty and talent for acting were not enough and that she needed an accomplice who could help her with the technical aspects; despite his unimpeachable personal integrity, Sir Henry had been far easier to seduce than she had expected; the poor old man had fallen madly in love after one kiss and had instantly consented to all her proposals, driven by an inflamed passion and his lustful desire to possess her (this was the only time during the interrogation where their two confessions diverged, for Sir Henry insisted he had acted purely out of a Christian desire to help a lost soul overcome the sufferings that afflicted her); the knight of the realm had placed the extraordinary wealth of his knowledge at her service, transforming her town house, and any venue he was sent to inspect, with a maze of ingenious hidden devices designed to evade any scrutiny: trapdoors, springs, pulleys, false floors, nylon threads, powerful magnets, tubes emitting fluorescent gas, stuffed gloves that resembled floating hands, rubber masks, imprints of ghostly faces and bodies. As for Madame Amber, she confessed to being an accomplished regurgitator who could use her stomach to conceal an astonishing number of objects, thus slipping past even the most thorough examinations, even those stooping to the outrageous discourtesy of violating her most intimate cavities; the previous night, for example, disguising what she was doing with violent spasms, she had succeeded in regurgitating a rubber capsule containing hydrogen phosphide, which she had then bitten; exposed to air, the gas had created the will-o'-the-wisps and the luminous cloud. After that she had regurgitated several yards of fine gauze, onto which a face had been painted, and which gave the appearance of a ghost as it wafted above her thanks to the current of air coming from a tiny pipe under the table (the ghostly breath Colonel Garrick had felt on his hand).

Until then, the interrogation had been plain sailing for the two inspectors, but once they reached that point in the confession, both Miss Willard and Sir Henry had proved obstinate. They were willing to sign a confession and prepared to face the accusations that would be hurled at them in the coming days; they would plead guilty to fraud and be publicly derided. But they had no intention of being tried for the attempted murder of Mrs. Lansbury. That was where they drew the line. The final apparition, the menacing figure that had tried to throttle the old lady, was none of their doing. They might be charlatans, but they were not murderers. They weren't responsible for that *thing*.

Clayton kicked a loose cobblestone in his path. The affair was fiendishly complicated. None of the pieces slotted together. Who, or *what*, was that figure he had managed to seize before Colonel Garrick fired his gun? He was almost persuaded that the sinister apparition was another trick of the performance. It had knocked into him and he had felt its muscles when he trapped it in a stranglehold, the texture of its clothes, the heat from its body, even the sour odor of sweat . . . It was true that for a moment he had the impression the apparition possessed a strange transparency or invisibility, but with hindsight he wasn't so sure. The stranger was completely human, that much was certain, and it could not have been anyone but Sir Henry, who must have been wearing a disguise. Or perhaps he had soaked his costume in some chemical or other, possibly ether, which had created that curious illusion of transparency. And then, for some unknown reason, he had threatened the poor old lady, fled through the trapdoor, and gotten rid of the costume somewhere in the house. Yes, all the facts pointed in that direction, although Clayton had to admit there were still far too many unanswered questions. So many in fact that it almost drove him to distraction. For example: If the fictitious apparition was part of the séance, why had they decided to include it? And why assault a defenseless old lady instead of sticking to their usual fairground act, which had brought them so much success? If it was simply another trick, why then deny it? Had things got out of hand, and were they now trying to limit the damage, or did they have some motive for attacking Mrs. Lansbury? But if that were the case, doing so in front of witnesses wasn't very wise. On the other hand, Clayton couldn't forget what had seemed to him Madame Amber's genuine terror. And was it precisely that terror that had made her force the trapdoor from the outside, thus breaking its delicate mechanism and throwing away many months' work? It made no sense . . . Clayton shook his head abruptly, like a dog irritated after a sudden downpour. He felt compelled to find the missing piece in the puzzle that would finally give it meaning.

If he accepted that Miss Willard and her accomplice were telling the truth, then who was the mysterious man who had appeared out of nowhere? A murderer who was pursuing Mrs. Lansbury and had decided to kill her during a séance where two Scotland Yard detectives were in attendance? The idea was absurd, and yet it tallied with the mysterious words the figure had addressed to the old lady, and above all with the expression on her face, for she seemed to recognize him, despite denying it afterward. But how could anyone have entered that sealed room without Madame Amber's or Sir Henry's help? Were all three of them involved in the attempt on the old lady's life?

There was one final possibility, the only one that would make the case worthy of being investigated by Scotland Yard's Special Branch: the apparition was a genuine spirit that had come from the Hereafter. But one spirit summoned during a fraudulent séance by a medium who possessed no supernatural powers? And yet Miss Willard claimed to have had them as a child. Should he then believe her version and accept that Sarah Willard's former talent had been restored that particular night, as the terrified young woman had assured him, allowing her to summon the evil spirit? As dawn approached, Sinclair had announced that, for the time being, this seemingly absurd theory was the least absurd of all, but Clayton had pursed his lips and said nothing. Old Sinclair was welcome to see ghosts on every corner if he wished, but in the recent past the inspector had learned many lessons, and foremost among them was never to underestimate the powerful combination of an ingenious disguise and an exceedingly beautiful woman.

Clayton scowled disdainfully as he recalled Sarah Willard's face when he had left her at dawn. The conceited medium, who had beguiled almost the entire male population of England with her beauty, had been reduced to a trembling little girl in the cellars of Scotland Yard. When the interrogation was over, she had grabbed the inspector by the lapels and, looking straight at him with her deep-blue eyes, had begged him to lock her in the darkest cell if he so wished, but please to keep the spirits away from her, not to let them haunt her . . . She had assured him, amid moans, that she couldn't face reliving the horrors of her childhood: the panic that used to seize her when she felt a cold, transparent form slip between her sheets, seeking the heat from her body as she lay completely still, reciting every prayer she knew while the phantom's icy breath on her neck made her shiver; and the mirrors—the horror when she looked at herself in a mirror and saw the pale reflection of a figure behind her, of someone gazing at her intently, even though whenever she turned around there was no one there; and the voices, the incessant voices . . . She had begged him in this way as she struggled to control the hysteria threatening to overwhelm her, and her voice had sounded so desperate that even the guard at the door had gulped. But Clayton had simply looked at her impassively for a few seconds and then, holding her wrists firmly, plucked her tiny clenched fists from his jacket. After sitting her down in a chair where she went on sobbing, he left the room without a backward glance.

She was lying. They were both lying, he was certain. Clayton didn't know whether spirits existed or not—he didn't have enough information as yet to arrive at any conclusion—but one thing he did know was that the figure in Madame Amber's drawing room was made of flesh and blood the same as he. Sinclair was welcome to go hunting ghosts if he so wished, but he, Clayton, knew exactly the direction in which to take the investigation: he had to find Sir Henry's costume, and if that meant dismantling Madame Amber's house brick by brick, then so be it. But before he started demolishing buildings, he needed to have a little chat with the old lady who had a penchant for spiritualism. Clayton sensed that Mrs. Lansbury knew more than she was admitting. He was convinced the key to unraveling the whole business lay behind those kindly yet mocking eyes that had so defiantly contemplated the apparition, and for that reason he had decided to go directly to her house, without even stopping off for a few hours' sleep.

Dawn had already materialized. At that moment, when the world was scarcely illuminated by the first rays of light, all was silent, and a brisk morning breeze caressed the slumbering city like an angel's breath, as Dickens might say. Any respectable person could now receive a visit, however unexpected, without it creating a stir. At last Inspector Clayton turned into Furnival Street and made his way to Mrs. Lansbury's residence, a tall, neo-Gothic town house with a turrets and narrow windows. Without further ado, he mounted the front steps and rang the doorbell. Adopting an aggressive stance, hands behind his back, legs slightly apart, he prepared to confront the icy disdain of a butler outraged at such an early morning visit. But even if he had to contend with an army of sullen domestic servants and go up to the old lady's bedroom to wake her himself, Clayton was determined to speak to Mrs. Lansbury, to force her to reveal what part she was playing in all this.

He was surprised when Mrs. Lansbury herself came to the door, and moreover that she did so almost immediately, as if she had been stationed behind it. However, he was still more taken aback by her odd appearance, and her equally odd behavior. Catherine Lansbury opened the door a crack, just enough to poke her disheveled head through the gap. Her immaculate chignon of the night before had completely unraveled, and a few grey strands of hair now hung limply over her eyes. She stood there, clutching the door with both hands, while Inspector Clayton quickly changed his threatening posture, doffing his hat and feeling suddenly ridiculous confronted by the old lady's startled face, which in a matter of seconds went from fear through disappointment to surprise, and then almost to appreciation. She seemed unable to find the right words to express the whirl of emotions and thoughts spinning round in her head. At last she seemed to rouse herself and, cutting short Clayton's timid greeting with a furious signal to be quiet, stepped cautiously outside, looked up and down the street, and, taking the inspector's arm, pulled him in, swiftly closing the door behind them.

Clayton followed her across the gloomy hallway, repressing the ridiculous urge to walk on tiptoe, until they reached a doorway, which they both stepped through. While Mrs. Lansbury was turning the key in the door, checking several times that she had locked it properly and then making sure the windows were also secure, Clayton took the opportunity to examine with interest the tiny study they found themselves in, which was much better illuminated than the hallway. It was a modestly furnished room with two windows that presumably overlooked the garden. Opposite them was a fine desk piled with scribbled documents, files, and writing paraphernalia, on the corner of which a vase with what looked like freshly cut roses had pride of place. At the center of the room was a rather forlorn pedestal table on which someone had laid out a dainty tea set. Mrs. Lansbury peered anxiously around the room like a frightened mouse, forgetting the inspector's presence until he was obliged to attract her attention.

"Ahem, Mrs. Lansbury . . ."

The old lady looked at him, her eyelids fluttering.

"Oh! I'm so sorry, I wasn't expecting you . . . ," she whispered.

"You were expecting someone else at this hour?" Clayton said with surprise, gesturing toward the tea tray and also speaking in a whisper.

"Oh, yes, yes . . . I was. Someone very important. I asked him to come a few hours ago. Perhaps I should have done so sooner. The moment I arrived home from the séance last night, I sent my faithful servant, Doris, to his house with an urgent message . . . begging him to come. But he hasn't answered my call, or even replied to my message. And my maid hasn't returned either . . . Oh, my dear Doris! If I am to blame for anything happening to her I shall never . . . She is my only servant, you see. I can't afford more staff; I spend all my money on . . . So Doris is the only one who looks after me. Perhaps I oughtn't to have sent her to fetch . . . But what else was I to do?" She looked beseechingly at Clayton. "Tell me, what else was I to do? I couldn't think of any other solution. He has found me, he knows where I am hiding, and now I have run out of time." The old lady glanced nervously about again, whispering to herself. "Yes, I've run out of time . . ."

"Mrs. Lansbury, I'm afraid I don't understand—"

"I forget your name, young man," the old lady interrupted, looking again at Clayton, who was struck once more by the look of determination in her eyes, which belied their owner's tremulous fragility.

"I'm Inspector Cornelius Clayton of Scotland Yard's Special Branch. We met last night at the séance . . ."

"Oh, I remember perfectly well where we met, young man! I simply forgot your name. I'm not a senile old woman. You're the young fellow with the broken heart. I know you a lot better than you think—oh yes, a lot better . . . But please, sit down. Would you care for some tea?"

Without waiting for his reply, Mrs. Lansbury sat down and began pouring the tea with an unsteady hand. Her lips were moving slightly, as if she was praying. Clayton sat down, taking care not to knock the table with his bony knees and send all the cups flying.

"Try one of these, young man," the old lady said, holding out a plate. "Kemp's biscuits. They are made with butter and aniseed, and I've never tasted anything quite like them. They're delicious, my favorites. They don't make them where I come from, you know. In any case, it's a shame I came across them so late, I've scarcely been able to enjoy them for a few years . . . You see"—she tried to give a cheery smile, but Clayton noticed she was shaking—"I'm afraid today will be the last time I eat them."

"And why is that, Mrs. Lansbury?" the inspector said, surprised.

She gazed at him in silence for a few seconds with that same appraising look, as though she were weighing up his usefulness.

"Because, young man, the Villain has found me," she replied at last, so softly that Clayton had to lean over the table to hear her. "And he's going to kill me."

"The Villain?"

The old lady gestured to him to lower his voice.

"Yes, the Villain. Any story worth its salt must have a villain, don't you agree? And ours had one, too," she said ruefully. "The most terrible villain you could ever imagine. And now he's coming to kill me."

"If you're referring to the man who attacked you at Madame Amber's house, have no fear: I assure you, he's behind bars," Clayton replied, trying to set her mind at rest.

"Behind bars?" The old lady gave a benevolent chuckle, as though touched by the inspector's naïveté. "No prison exists that can contain the Villain, son. Not one."

"What do you mean?"

"I mean exactly what I said! Do you think I'm speaking in riddles? He's going to kill me, at any moment. So don't say another word. There isn't time. Just listen to me," she commanded abruptly.

She brushed the crumbs off her skirt with a determined gesture, plucked a small key from her clenched fist, and walked over to the desk. After unlocking a tiny drawer she returned holding a book, which she held out to the inspector with a strange solemnity.

"What is this?" asked Clayton tentatively.

"Take it. Hurry!"

The inspector grasped the book. It was small, scarcely larger than a missal, its covers bound in dark leather. On the front, embossed in gold, was a star with eight arrowlike points. Underneath it, also in gold, was written *The Map of Chaos*. Clayton examined its pages with interest. All of them were handwritten, filled with what appeared to be complex mathematical formulas interspersed with strange geometrical diagrams. Puzzled, he looked at the old lady, who drew closer, placing her hand on his shoulder. She was trembling violently, like leaves in an autumn breeze, but her gaze was courageous and her voice serene when she said, "The key to the salvation of the world lies within the pages of this book.

Of the world as you know it"—she spread her arms, gesturing at their surroundings, before contemplating him in earnest—"but also of all those worlds you can only imagine. For I must warn you, young man, that the whole universe is in danger. So listen well, Inspector Clayton of Scotland Yard's Special Branch: the man who appeared at the séance yesterday evening is looking for this book in order to destroy it. He is an evil creature; he has killed before, and he won't hesitate to kill again. He murdered my husband"—her voice faltered for a moment—"but I managed to escape and keep the book safe . . . All this time, I've been trying to continue with the plan my husband and I devised to save the universe. But the Villain found me before I had time to put it into practice. Now everything depends on you."

"On me?" said Clayton, astonished.

The old lady nodded apologetically.

"I'm afraid so, my boy. I sent for the only person I could trust hours ago. But he hasn't come, I don't know why . . . and now there isn't time. I daresay I should have asked him to come sooner, years ago, when I first arrived. Yes, perhaps it was wrong of me not to. Perhaps my husband and I were mistaken to depend entirely on the Maelstrom Coordinates . . . We undoubtedly made many mistakes. But none of that matters now. We did the best we could, given the circumstances . . . What is important above all is to keep the book safe. Take it, Clayton. You must guard it with your life if necessary and give it to those who come from the Other Side and—"

"'Those who come from the Other Side'?" Clayton interrupted, unable to hide his impatience. "But . . . who are they? And what is this book exactly? And why is the universe in da—"

"Didn't anyone teach you that it is very rude to interrupt your elders?" the old lady scolded him. "Do you suppose I would give you something so precious without explaining what it is and what you must do with it? Didn't I tell you that we had a plan, young man?"

"I . . . forgive me," Clayton stammered.

All of a sudden they heard a resounding crash coming from the floor above. The old lady stared up at the ceiling with her eyes open wide, the blood draining from her face.

"He's here," she exclaimed in a faltering voice. "The Villain has come for me."

Clayton took out his gun as he got up from his chair.

"Not if I can prevent it," he reassured her.

Slipping the book into his coat pocket, and with the terrified Mrs. Lansbury close on his heels, he went over to the door. He unlocked it noiselessly, stepped gingerly out into the corridor, and closed it behind him, leaving the old lady alone inside.

"Lock yourself in," he ordered in a whisper, "and don't open the door until I—"

But before he could finish his sentence, he heard the old lady turn the key. Her extreme caution brought a smile to his lips. He turned around, gun at the ready, and confronted the hall stairs, which vanished into the thick gloom of the upper floors. He still did not know what to think of the eccentric Mrs. Lansbury, but one thing was certain: somebody had broken into the house, probably through an upstairs window. He himself had heard the loud clatter on the floor above. And if Doris was the old lady's only servant, which the thick layer of dust on the banister and the cobwebs draped between its rails would suggest, then only an intruder could have made that noise. Yet whoever it was did not know Clayton was there, and so he had the advantage of surprise. He began to climb the stairs slowly, trying not to let their creaking give him away. He soon realized he had no need to be so cautious, for a loud din of thuds and clatters reached him from upstairs, as if the intruder was ransacking one of the rooms. Clayton hurtled up the remaining steps and found himself on a landing that gave onto a corridor with rows of doors on either side.

Mrs. Lansbury must have moved around in the gloom with the ease of a blind person, since, with the exception of the study, the rest of her house was plunged in darkness. On the landing, the dawn light streamed through the stained-glass window into bands of blue, red, and green, allowing Clayton to move forward without the aid of a candle, but he couldn't see clearly enough to make out his surroundings plainly. Doing his best to avoid the furniture cluttering the corridor, he crept forward and soon found the door to the room from which the unearthly din was emanating. He stood to one side of it, switched his gun over to his metal hand so as to be able to turn the doorknob with his good hand, and slowly began to push the door open.

In front of him, a room inhabited by shadows slowly began to take shape. Judging from the vague outline of the furnishings, this must be the old lady's bedroom. But from where the inspector was standing, only part of the room was visible: the door itself blocked off the rest, where the intruder must have been. All of a sudden Clayton glimpsed the man's figure reflected in a mirror between the bed and a broken window. He watched in silence, unable to believe his eyes. The intruder had his back to the mirror and was busy rummaging through a chest of drawers. He seemed to have the same build as the man who had appeared at Madame Amber's house. But he himself had locked Sir Henry in a cell before leaving to come here. How could it possibly be him in that room? And if it wasn't him, then who was it? What most surprised Clayton was that, through the figure, he was able to glimpse fragments of the chest of drawers and even the wallpaper, though hazily at best, as if he were looking through a lace curtain fluttering in the breeze. In the meantime, the intruder was cursing through gritted teeth, becoming angrier and angrier as the old lady's possessions fell about his feet. Then, through a door that the inspector couldn't see, he moved into the adjoining room.

Clayton did the same, via the corridor. He found the corresponding door and began to turn the handle as cautiously as before. On the far side of the room, he could dimly make out the intruder's bulky figure busy with some task, and he stole toward him, training his gun on him. But when he was only a few steps away he could see from the light filtering in from the street that what he was aiming at was an object on wheels with two mechanical arms that ended in a broom and a cloth.

Before he could figure out that the intruder had switched on the old lady's Mechanical Servant, the heavy bookcase on the wall next to him suddenly began to topple over. Clayton raised his right arm to try to stop it, but it was far too heavy and came down on top of him, crushing him painfully against the floor. Just as he felt his ribs about to crack, a savage laugh rang through the room. And then: silence. For several minutes, Clayton remained motionless, dazed by the blow. Had it not been for the Mechanical Servant brushing his face persistently with its broom, he would have passed out. The brushing roused him, and he started trying to ease out from beneath the weighty bookcase. Cursing himself for having fallen into such a stupid trap, he pricked up his ears. After pushing the bookcase on top of him, the intruder had left the room and descended the stairs, and now Clayton could hear him roaring on the ground floor as he stormed through the house, angrily flinging open doors and slamming them shut.

"Where are you hiding, damn you? Haven't you understood yet that nothing can save you from me? You know what I'm after. Give it to me now and I might kill you painlessly!"

Terrified by the visceral rage in the intruder's voice, Clayton understood that it wouldn't be long before he came to the locked door, the one to the old lady's study. Fearing for Mrs. Lansbury's life, which he had sworn to protect, Clayton clenched his teeth and, despite the agonizing pain, continued struggling to free himself from the bookcase. At the same time, he was following the progress of the intruder, who appeared to be knocking over everything in his way. Finally, Clayton heard him let out a triumphant guffaw.

"So this is where you're hiding, you tiresome old woman! Open up!"

That spurred Clayton on, and with a supreme effort he managed to pull himself free of the bookcase and began crawling painfully along the floor like a newborn calf. Once he was clear, the inspector dragged himself to his feet, gave the Mechanical Servant an unceremonious kick, and hobbled into the corridor as though walking on stilts. Terribly dizzy, he started to descend the stairs laboriously, clinging to the banister rail, even as the intruder hurled himself at the old lady's study, alternately punching and kicking the locked door. Clayton had scarcely managed to negotiate a couple of steps when he heard the sound of wood splintering as the door began to give way, followed by Mrs. Lansbury's terrified screams. Realizing the intruder would finish breaking down the door before he had time to reach the bottom of the stairs, the inspector propped his elbows on the banister rail and aimed at the stranger.

"Stop!" he cried with as much authority as he could muster. "Place your hands above your head and turn around!"

But he was unable to make himself heard above the figure's inhuman roars. He cocked his gun and fired at the ceiling. That brought the stranger up short. The inspector watched his body tense as he realized someone was aiming at him from the stairs. But instead of turning round with his hands up, as Clayton had hoped, the intruder bolted toward the front door. The hallway was wide and long enough to allow Clayton to take steady aim from his vantage point. As if this were a target practice, he placed the gun sight level with the intruder's back and prepared to pull the trigger. Yet he did not want to kill the intruder, only to stop him from escaping, and so Clayton lowered his weapon before firing. The intruder came to an abrupt halt, reaching down to where Clayton's bullet had lodged itself in the back of his left thigh. Then, as though possessed by a monstrous fury that seemed to reduce the wound to little more than a minor nuisance, he resumed his escape, staggering and cursing as he went. Clayton went down the stairs, managing not to trip over, and ran across the hallway after him. He stepped through the wide-open front door and lurched down the front steps.

He looked to left and right, but to his astonishment could see no trace of the stranger. How had he managed to run the length of the street and vanish so quickly, and with a wounded leg? Clayton spun round a few times, until he was facing the old lady's house again. He gazed silently at the open door. Could the intruder still be inside the house? Then, on the top of the steps, a strange thing began to happen: a large bloodstain started to materialize out of nowhere, as though traced that very instant by an invisible hand. As if watching a magic trick, Clayton gazed in astonishment as it spread across the wooden threshold, finally taking on the shape of a squashed crab. Seconds later, another stain appeared on the second step, and then a third on the next, and suddenly a trail of red was moving toward him like a bloody fuse. It passed between his legs, forcing him to wheel round in order to follow the miraculous apparition. Then the phenomenon ceased as quickly as it had started, right in the middle of the street, a few yards from where Clayton was standing. He turned back to face the house and began to follow the bloody trail back to its source. A larger bloodstain in the hallway, together with some conspicuous spatters on a doorjamb, seemed to indicate the exact spot where the shot had hit him. Clayton could have sworn they were not there before. He shook his head and forced himself to forget the mystery for a few moments in order to concentrate on the old lady, who must be waiting in fear of her life on the other side of the half-demolished study door.

"Open up, Mrs. Lansbury," he said in a reassuring voice when he reached the study. "It's me, Inspector Clayton. The intruder has fled."

But there was no reply from inside.

"Mrs. Lansbury?" he called out.

Silence. Clayton repeated her name several times, and when she didn't answer, he demolished the rest of the door, which gave way easily. He burst into the room, afraid he was going to find the old woman's limp body sprawled on the floor, but there was no one there. Dumbfounded, he glanced around, examining every corner of the tiny room. The desk, the pedestal table with the tea things, the supposedly mouthwatering Kemp's biscuits—everything was in its place: only the old lady was missing. After checking that the key was still in the lock, and the windows fastened from the inside, Clayton strode desperately around the room in search of a hiding place where he might find her. To no avail. How had Mrs. Lansbury managed to leave the room? And who could have abducted her, if the door was locked from the inside?

Spinning slowly around, Clayton surveyed the room once more, certain he had missed something. Suddenly, the giddy feeling began to intensify and he realized it had nothing to do with the blow from the bookcase. No, this dizziness was different, although familiar. And he knew that it was happening to him again.

"No, not now . . . ," he cursed.

But before he could finish his sentence, he fainted away, dragging the vase from the desk with him as he fell. He lay sprawled flat in the empty room, ripped from consciousness, just as the rest of the world prepared to face the mystery of a new day.

This time, the darkness smelled of freshly cut roses.

7

UT THE SMELL HAD NOT ALWAYS BEEN AS sweet. The first time darkness had descended on him he had been enveloped in an unpleasant stench of horse manure, having passed out in a pestilential alleyway, cracking his head against the dirty cobbles. The second time the smell had spread over him with the leisurely rhythm of an old curtain, a mixture of musty fabric, wood, and polished leather, as he had fainted in a theater, sliding almost voluptuously out of his seat and onto the soft carpet. Eight more fainting fits had followed, all impregnated with different smells, until the aroma of the white roses. This was the first time he had fainted while in the midst of an investigation.

The first of those journeys (that was what he called them: journeys, not fainting fits) had occurred the same day he was discharged from Guy's Hospital, where he had been sent to recover from his terrible mutilation. Clayton had ignored the nurses' advice and left without even waiting for Sinclair, who had offered to take him back to his own house, where he could finish his convalescence under his wife's care. Once out of hospital, in a further act of revolt, Clayton had eschewed taking a carriage and insisted on walking back to his modest apartment on Milton Street. As he walked, he swung his truncated arm almost brazenly, oblivious to the compassionate looks of the passersby and the awful cold that froze his phantom fingers, fingers no glove could ever keep warm again. He needed to clear away the cobwebs clinging to his brain after thirty days of swallowing opiates, and also to stretch his stiff legs. But he soon regretted his decision: it was too cold outside, his legs ached, he had an excruciating itch where his severed hand had been, and he noticed he felt more and more giddy with each step. Then, as he cut down a side alley, he sensed someone following him. He knew this without needing to turn around or to hear a noise behind him. However, before he could do anything about it, he felt an icy hook pierce his stomach and jerk him upward. He wasn't aware of falling or hitting the ground. Only of the darkness, and the smell of horse manure.

That was the first time he ever dreamt about Valerie.

When a few sharp slaps on his cheek brought him round, he found himself face-to-face with a well-dressed gentleman who was gazing at him with a concerned look. He was a middle-aged fellow, with a pleasant face that might have appeared anodyne were it not for a very black goatee that looked like it had been colored in with a piece of charcoal, and a pair of flamboyant gold spectacles. The man introduced himself as Doctor Clive Higgins and explained he had been following Clayton for a few streets, alarmed by his sickly pallor and unsteady gait. But Clayton had fainted just as he was about to catch up with him to ask if he was feeling ill. Clayton mumbled something about his recent stay in the hospital and asked the doctor to let him continue on his way, assuring him he was quite all right and that he lived close by. Clayton was lying because he wanted to be left alone as soon as possible, the sooner to be able to relish the strange, beautiful images the dreams had left in his head before they vanished. Doctor Higgins let him go, but not without warning him, in an oddly serious tone, that he was in need of help that he, the doctor, could provide. Then he pressed a cream-colored card with gold edging into Clayton's hand. Underneath his name was printed the address of his consulting rooms and the puzzling title *Doctor of Neurology, Psychoanalysis, and Other Afflictions of the Soul.*

After promising to pay him a visit, Clayton hurried home. When he arrived, he emptied a triple dose of the sleeping pills he had been given at the hospital into his good hand, swallowed them down with a mouthful of brandy, and lay on the bed with his heart pounding, not even bothering to take his coat off. He was so desperate to resume his beautiful dream exactly where he had left off that he didn't care if the number of tablets he had taken meant that he never woke up again. But he didn't manage to dream about her again. He woke up a few hours later with a pounding headache and a feeling of anxiety produced by the overdose of pills.

He had to wait another twelve days before he dreamt about Valerie again, this time in the theater. The same icy hook in the stomach, the same sudden feeling of being hoisted into the air, the same dizziness and precipitous darkness. But also the same dream, so wonderful and vivid that when he awoke, for a few hours at least, everything around him seemed more illusory than any dream. A week later the same thing happened again, this time while he was making a cup of tea, which had ended up in pieces on the kitchen floor beside his unconscious body. And yet, he never managed to dream about her when he slept any other way. He had tried taking pills, alcohol, a mixture of the two, lying in bed all day reciting from memory tedious police reports, or stretching out on the sofa until the early hours. But it was no use. He never dreamt about her during his normal sleep. No, those dreams came to him only during those fainting fits.

And yet there was no pattern, nothing he could control. They were liable to happen to him at any moment, in the most unexpected situations, regardless of what he was doing at the time. It made no difference whether he was nervous or relaxed, standing or sitting, alone or in a crowd. They just happened: a slight dizziness followed by that sharp pull in his stomach that caused him to collapse suddenly. Journeys, he called them. How else was he supposed to describe them? In the end, while his body remained sprawled on the floor where he fell, his mind soared far away from there, always toward the same place.

Although he never felt happier than when he was having those strange fainting fits, they soon became a source of concern. They happened so often that Clayton had to admit he could no longer treat them as occasional incidents, but rather as an unmistakable sign that something inside him had radically changed, that his soul was no longer the same. His most recent journey alarmed him the most, because he had fainted in the middle of an investigation. He, the highly acclaimed Inspector Cornelius Clayton, had collapsed at a crime scene. What would Sinclair say if he found out? What would his superiors think? And how long would he be able to conceal those incidents? This time he had miraculously avoided being discovered unconsious in the old lady's study, enabling him to omit that shameful fact from his written report, but next time he might not be so fortunate. He dreaded to think what would happen if it were revealed that he suffered regularly from fainting fits. Doubtless they would put him on sick leave, send him to a doctor, and refuse to let him carry on working until they had discovered what ailed him. And what would become of him then, if he couldn't occupy his mind with other things? He would go crazy, that was certain. Work was the only thing that brought calm to his brain. Only when he was immersed in an investigation, fixated on the details of some case, juggling theories and conjectures, was he able to stop thinking about her. Almost.

While he had been working on the Madame Amber case, for example, he had all but forgotten about the countess. A routine case of suspected fraud had all of a sudden turned into an extraordinary mystery, a true puzzle for a mind hungry for challenges. Not only had a murderous spirit materialized during a fraudulent séance, but that same spirit had pursued one of the participants home a few hours later, apparently with the aim of stealing a mysterious book that, according to the old lady, contained nothing less than the means of saving the world.

And now Clayton knew the reason why Mrs. Lansbury's servant had never returned: poor Doris's body had been discovered by Scotland Yard detectives the following day in a nearby street, so horribly mutilated that even the hardened officers had been appalled. No message was found on her. Clearly the murderer had intercepted the maid before she had been able to deliver it, and so the intended recipient never knew how anxiously the old lady had awaited him and Clayton had no way of finding out who the devil he was. Subsequent inquiries revealed that Mrs.

Lansbury enjoyed no social life beyond her interest in spiritualism. The detectives had to limit themselves to interviewing the people who had bumped into her most frequently at séances, but none of them had any relationship with the eccentric old lady beyond the obligatory courtesies and were therefore unlikely to be the intended recipient of the message. Apart from that, she did not seem to have any family or friends. Catherine Lansbury had appeared out of nowhere in London society a few years before. She possessed a small fortune thanks to owning the patent for the Mechanical Servant, but no one had been able to discover anything more about her, except that she was a widow and came from a distant land, which seemed surprising given her impeccable English accent. Recent rumor had it that she had squandered her fortune on her obsession with the Hereafter and it was only a matter of time before her creditors caught up with her. Even so, the old lady did not seem to have relinquished her costly pastime, although, according to some of the statements, she never sought to make contact with anyone in particular during the séances, as was habitually the case. At no time had she asked to speak to her deceased husband, for example, and if some crafty medium declared joyously that he was in the room and wished to speak to her, Mrs. Lansbury would consistently refuse, waving her small, wrinkled hand in the air as though someone had paid her an inappropriate compliment before replying, "I don't think so: my husband knows perfectly well I have no wish to speak to him. Besides, he isn't the one I'm looking for. It is others I seek. I shall wait."

After that she would remain silent, in expectation of those who it would seem never turned up. Could they be the same ones she herself had referred to as "those from the Other Side," for whom the book was apparently intended? And who was the strange creature who had tried to steal it? How had he managed to appear during the séance, and how had he suddenly vanished in the middle of the street, leaving a trail of blood that had become visible only moments later? More important still, how had the old lady disappeared from a room that was locked on the inside? Too many questions without any answers.

Although they were frustrating questions, they distracted him, saving him from himself. He needed those questions because they were the barrier that kept at bay that other ferocious hoard of thoughts, which if they invaded his mind would end up destroying it. And so he had no other choice but to keep his fainting fits secret. None of his superiors must ever find out, not even Captain Sinclair. And if that also meant no more dreaming about Valerie, he would have to accept that, he told himself, as he fingered the gold-edged card that had been languishing in his coat pocket for the last six months like a treasure at the bottom of the ocean, until he had rescued it a week earlier.

The sound of a door clicking open and the gentle murmur of female voices announced that the session of the patient before him had ended. Clayton fixed his eyes apprehensively on the door of the waiting room. When he had arrived at Doctor Higgins's consulting rooms an hour earlier, a plump nurse had guided him there along a corridor lined with doors, inviting him to leave his hat on the stand and to take a seat in one of the small armchairs. Noticing his ashen face, she had assured him that no one would disturb him while he was waiting, as no two patients were ever asked to wait in the same room, thus guaranteeing absolute discretion. Afflictions of the soul were apparently very delicate matters, Clayton reflected when she had gone. After standing rigidly for a few moments in the center of the room, he finally took off his hat and ventured to sit down, wondering about his fellow patients in the adjoining cells, which seemed to stretch out forever, like a hall of mirrors: neurasthenic gentlemen overwhelmed by the intolerable pressures of business; ladies suffering from chlorosis, their skins a delicate greenish hue, like forest fairies in which some child had stopped believing; hysterical young girls in desperate need of a husband, or possibly a lover? What the devil was he doing among this display of deviant behavior? But now it seemed it was too late. The murmur of voices had taken on the habitual inflection of departures, and the sound of a door gently clicking shut told Clayton that Doctor Higgins was done healing that particular patient's soul. The tap of approaching footsteps followed, and the waiting room door opened, framing the nurse.

"You may go in now, Mr. Sinclair!" Clayton silently cursed himself for his complete lack of imagination when it came to giving a false name. "Doctor Higgins is waiting for you."

WHILE HE SPOKE, DOCTOR Higgins was in the habit of tugging his goatee between his thumb and forefinger, a gesture that possibly betrayed an incurable affliction of the soul, and which didn't exactly help Clayton to feel at ease. Indeed, it had the opposite effect on him, and so he had to take his eyes off the doctor and cast them around his spacious office. He studied the volumes lining the bookshelves, so thick they seemed to hold all the wisdom in the world between their pages; the engravings of body parts covering the walls; the uncomfortable couch; and the display cabinet in a corner, containing a few human skulls with deranged smiles lying on a bed of scalpels, syringes, and other sinister-looking instruments.

"So you would describe them as a kind of, er . . . *journey.* Is that correct, Mr. Sinclair?" the doctor inquired.

"Yes . . . more or less." Clayton fidgeted impatiently in the uncomfortable leather armchair, unable to find a position that made him feel more relaxed. He decided to cross his legs and lean forward slightly, fixing his gaze a few feet beyond his shoes. "I don't really know how to explain it. You see, the fact is, I know my body isn't there—even when I am completely unconscious I know that I'm not completely there—and yet somehow I don't feel I am dreaming either, and when I wake up I don't even remember it as a dream . . . It is as if that place really existed and I am able to travel there with my mind—or my soul." He shrugged, despairing at how all this must sound. "Does what I'm saying appear stupid to you, Doctor?"

Doctor Higgins smiled reassuringly. "If I devoted myself to treating stupid people I would have a full practice, and I would be a wealthy man."

Clayton gazed at him in silence for a few seconds but decided it was best not to tell him that, to judge by the nurse's excessive precautions, Dr.

Higgins did have a full practice, and by his watch, his ring, and his flamboyant spectacles, all evidently solid gold, he was indeed a wealthy man.

"So tell me, Mr. Sinclair, this place you dream of, is it always the same?"

"Yes."

"Describe it to me," the doctor said, removing his spectacles and placing them on top of one of the piles of books on his desk, where they perched like an eagle on a rock.

"Well . . . it's not easy."

"Please try."

Clayton heaved a sigh.

"It is a strange yet familiar country," he said at last. "In my . . . dreams, I arrive in a place that could be anywhere in the English countryside. In fact, I could be in one of those serene meadows with babbling brooks that Keats described, or at least that's how it feels when I am there. But at the same time, everything is different. It is as if someone had taken everything around me, placed it in a dice cup, and shaken it before throwing it over the world again. That place would be what came out. There everything is . . . all mixed-up."

"What do you mean?"

"Well . . . people aren't just people, or perhaps they are, people like you and me, but they are also something *else.* It is as if they had animals inside them, or maybe it is the other way round: they are animals with human souls . . . Sometimes I see them in their animal guise, and the next moment I find myself contemplating a woman, a man, or a child. The whole of Nature is mixed-up, merged: the creatures in that place are both animals and humans, and possibly plants too. There are bat-men, fish-women, butterfly-children, but also moss-babies and old people who are snow . . . Only when I'm there, none of that surprises me. Everything flows harmoniously and naturally; I never think it could be otherwise. I myself am many things, a different thing each journey: sometimes an animal, or wind, or rain . . . When I am wind, I like to blow on her haunches, rippling her coat, and she runs over the hill, turns, and passes through me; sometimes I am the dew on the grass, and I soak her fur when she lies down on me; other times I run with her; she is swift and I can only outrun her when I am a wolf too . . . and sometimes we talk and drink tea in her elegant drawing room, and she picks a piece of fruit from my arm and bites into it joyously, for I am a tree, and sometimes a bird soaring in the sky, and she howls with rage because she can't reach me—"

"You always dream about the same place, yet all your dreams are different," the doctor broke in.

"Yes," Clayton replied, both irritated and unsettled by the interruption. "I always go to the same place, and I always encounter the same, er . . . person."

"A woman?"

Clayton hesitated for a moment.

"She isn't exactly a woman. I already told you that the definitions we use here are impossible to apply there. Let's say she is . . . *feminine*."

The doctor nodded thoughtfully and stroked his goatee, a smile flickering on his lips.

"But each journey is very different from the others," Clayton went on, trying to change the subject.

"That's odd," mused the doctor. "Recurring dreams usually present few variations . . ."

"I already told you they aren't like dreams."

"Yes, so you did." The doctor gave his goatee a few gentle tugs, like an actor making sure his false beard is firmly stuck on. Then he glanced down at his notes. "You also told me they started approximately six months ago."

"That's right."

"And that nothing like this has ever happened to you before."

"No."

"Are you positive you never suffered from any childhood episodes of sleepwalking, or other disorders such as insomnia or nightmares?"

"Yes."

"And please try to remember: Have you at any other time in your life experienced any of the following symptoms: migraines, phonophobia, or digestive disorders . . ."

Clayton shook his head.

". . . apathy, fatigue, depression, loss of appetite . . ."

"Well, lately there are days when I feel tired and have no appetite—"

"No, no! I'm only interested in the period leading up to six months ago, before you started having these . . . dreams."

"Not as far as I can remember."

"Hallucinations, mania, dizziness . . ."

"No."

". . . sexual dysfunction?"

"I fear I have led a rather dull life up until now."

Doctor Higgins nodded and, giving his beard a rest, put on his spectacles before absentmindedly scribbling a few lines in his notebook.

"And what exactly happened to you six months ago, Mr. Sinclair?" he asked without looking up.

Clayton stifled his surprise.

"I beg your pardon, Doctor? I'm afraid I didn't quite hear what you said."

The doctor glanced at him over the rims of his gold spectacles.

"Clearly something must have happened to you. The sudden onset of this symptomatology with no previous history can't have come out of nowhere, don't you agree? Try to think back. It could have been something you considered trivial at the time: a slight blow to the head or some other seemingly harmless incident. Perhaps during a trip you ate some rotten food; blood infections can produce strange symptoms. Or was it something of a sentimental nature, a trauma that affected you deeply . . . ?"

Clayton pretended to straighten the cuffs of his jacket to gain time. For some stupid reason it hadn't occurred to him that he would have to speak to Dr. Higgins about what had happened at Blackmoor, even though he knew (he had always known, without any need to express it in words) that everything had started there. Something of a sentimental nature? Yes, you might say so . . .

"Seven months ago, something happened that . . . ," he began, "that affected me deeply. But that is all I can tell you. It is a professional matter of the strictest confidence that I am not at liberty to discuss."

"Of the strictest confidence?" The doctor glanced at his notes again. "I see you are a . . . locksmith by profession, Mr. Sinclair."

"Er . . . yes, that's right."

"And you lost your hand . . ."

"Due to that confidential matter that I'm not at liberty to discuss."

"I understand," the doctor said, leaning back in the chair as he observed Clayton patiently. "But, Mr. Sinclair, you must understand that I cannot help you unless—"

"Please, that's enough!" Clayton cried. His sudden outburst caused the doctor to look offended, and the inspector instantly regretted having raised his voice. What would he do if the man threw him out of his consulting room and refused to treat him? He didn't think he had the courage to find another doctor and submit himself to a similar interrogation. And so he took a deep breath and tried to speak calmly, but the words poured out in torrents. "Forgive me, Doctor, but I don't need more questions. What I need are answers. I told you I am not at liberty to discuss what happened to me. You will have to find out what is wrong with me without that information. Consider it a challenge, like a criminal investigation where there are only a few clues and the rest depends on your imagination. It isn't so difficult; in my work I . . . well, many of the locks I have to open are like that, believe me." The doctor regarded him in silence, as though considering his appeal. "Are there no other tests you can give me? Blood tests, for example? Prescribe whatever you want. I'm willing to try anything, I assure you. I'll be your guinea pig if you like. Feel free, I don't care . . ." Clayton ran his trembling hand over his face and then looked straight at the doctor. "Do whatever you want. But I need this to stop . . . I beg you."

Doctor Higgins continued to contemplate him for a few moments more, then stood up and went over to the cabinet on the opposite wall. While he was rummaging about in it he said: "Roll up your shirtsleeve, please, Mr. Sinclair. I'm going to take a blood sample, and then I'll test it for several things: creatinine, potassium, chlorine, sodium . . . and a few other things besides. I'll also do a red blood cell count." The doctor spun round with a grin, brandishing a syringe, which Clayton thought looked enormous. "Who knows, maybe we'll discover something interesting."

8

*I*NSPECTOR CORNELIUS CLAYTON CAUTIOUSLY turned up the collar of his coat, peering with a complete lack of caution around either side of the doorway, then plunged into the gentle jaws of the fog slinking along Taviton Street. But we are not going to follow him. Instead, we shall leave him to disappear among the crowded Bloomsbury streets while we remain in front of number 10, mesmerized by the soft golden glow of the X above the door, which, as on pirate maps, seems to mark the spot where we should dig for treasure. Moments later, our patience is unexpectedly rewarded, as Dr. Higgins hurries out of the house. Yes, despite having a full consulting room, he abandons his patients to their fate and dives into the freezing fog, taking the opposite direction to Clayton, which leads me to conclude that the reason why he has suddenly absconded is not precisely in order to trail the inspector. Where can he be heading in such a hurry? Let us follow him.

After crossing a couple of streets, doing his best to imitate the sprightly gait of a young colt, Dr. Clive Higgins hailed a carriage on Gower Street, gave the driver the address of the Albemarle Club, and slumped into his seat with an exasperated groan. Once inside, he unbuttoned his overcoat, tore off his gloves and scarf, and removed his hat. Fanning himself with the latter, he watched the carriage skirting Soho via Oxford Street while he continued to gasp for air, as though he were crossing a scorching desert instead of traversing London on an inclement October day. However, shortly before arriving at his destination, he put everything back on, assumed a placid air, and stepped out of the carriage. He proceeded to mount the steps to the Albemarle Club with the briskness of someone whose overriding desire is for a warm fire and a glass of brandy.

Once inside, having shed his warm clothes again, and pretending to shiver as he handed the damp garments to a solicitous attendant, he made his way with the same jaunty walk toward a table beside a large window, greeting with peremptory nods any members he passed. At the table, which stood next to the only unlit fire in the room, four gentlemen reclined comfortably in leather armchairs, smoking and chatting congenially among themselves. However, when they spotted Dr. Higgins walking toward them across the vast room, the four of them stopped conversing and watched him approach in expectant silence.

"Good day, gentlemen," the doctor said gruffly as he took a seat among them and gestured impatiently to the nearest waiter.

"You're late, Higgins," one of the men chided, smiling.

"My dear Angier, perhaps we are all too late," the doctor grunted, giving his goatee a few desperate tugs.

"Come, come, Higgins, what's eating you?" another of the gentlemen retorted in a mollifying voice, which you will recognize if you have been paying attention, for it was none other than Doctor Theodore Ramsey, the eminent physician so fond of cracking his knuckles. "We thought you might bring good tidings."

Higgins snatched the glass of brandy from the waiter's tray before the man had time to place it on the table and greedily swallowed almost half of it, closing his eyes as he did so. Then he gave a sigh.

"Forgive me, my friends. Please accept my apologies, Angier. I'm at my wit's end. My cooling system has been on the blink all morning," he declared, pulling impatiently at his beard as if to prove it. "I've been insufferably hot for hours."

The others gave him concerned looks.

"How ghastly! And you haven't been able to repair it?" asked Angier, fiddling with his right earlobe, visibly alarmed.

"I haven't had time. As you guessed, Ramsey, I bring tidings. I'm not sure yet if they are good or not, but I wanted to pass them on without delay. In any case, I expect I can hold out until this afternoon, and I think I have the means to fix the problem in my laboratory . . . I just wish it wasn't so damnably hot!"

"Don't grumble, Higgins. You're lucky it's the beginning of winter, the coldest season in their year. Imagine if this had happened during that inferno they call summer," remarked a third gentleman, who every now and then crossed his eyes in a most peculiar fashion as he spoke. "And things could be worse. For example, you could be having trouble with the neuronal circuitry that allows us to suppress the anxiety of randomness."

"You're right, Melford," Ramsey agreed vehemently, cracking his knuckles one by one. "*The anxiety of randomness* . . . A truly terrifying thing."

"Quite so. But a malfunction in the cooling system is still an absolute nuisance. It happened to me last summer," Angier added, flicking his earlobe gently, "and I had to beg them to send me a new mechanism as soon as—"

"Inferno? Did I hear you say 'inferno,' Melford?" the fourth gentleman, who had so far remained silent, interrupted in a soft voice.

He was a stout fellow with bushy grey whiskers that curled up like a bull's horns, and he wore a plain dark suit livened up by a florid waistcoat. The other men looked at him in surprise.

"I . . . ," stammered Melford.

"*Inferno?* Surely you aren't serious, any of you . . . You grumble about the climate? It is so obvious you haven't been to the Other Side recently! Have you forgotten what it is like there?" The fourth gentleman observed his companions one by one, his impressive whiskers quivering with rage, causing all of them, more or less swiftly, to lower their eyes contritely. "The minor discomforts we have to put up with here," the man went on in a lecturing tone, "pale in comparison. I say this as someone who has just come back from there. From the place where we have no choice but to suffer the insufferable." Satisfied with his admonishment, he settled back in his chair, relaxing slightly his harsh expression. "Gentlemen, I beg you not to trivialize such matters. On the Other Side, the Dark Time has begun. And they need us. Desperately."

The five of them fell silent for a few moments, eyes vacant as they became lost in thought.

"How are things back there, Kramer?" Ramsey ventured at last.

"It is getting colder all the time," the other man replied. "And there is no light now."

They all groaned quietly.

"Perhaps Higgins was right when he said just now that we arrived here too late." Melford squinted. "Perhaps nothing we do here has any meaning now."

"There is still some hope. Recent calculations give us ten years," said Kramer.

"By all the dead suns!" Angier gasped. "Ten years? I hardly think that is long enough."

"Calm down, Angier. You know very well that period refers to *their* extinction, not ours," said Kramer, gesturing with a nod at their surroundings. "Our torment could last a few more decades, but they don't have that long. And they are our only escape route. We have ten years to prevent their destruction. Otherwise, we will be doomed as well."

"And what do recent studies show about the possibility of opening other doors?" asked Melford.

"Nothing promising," Kramer replied ruefully. "I fear that won't be possible. Not in our current situation. This world is the only chance we have of saving ourselves."

"But they have only ten years left . . . ," muttered Angier.

Kramer raised his arms suddenly, like an odalisque sprinkling rose petals.

"These are rough calculations, gentlemen, although there is little margin for error," he said. "We have ten years, possibly a bit longer, to find a way of preventing the epidemic ravaging this world. If we fail, an apocalypse of devastating proportions will be unleashed. And we on the Other Side, like a drowning man whose fingers slip fatally from the flotsam to which he is clinging, will plunge forever into eternal darkness and oblivion."

They all remained silent and cast their eyes around the room. The Albemarle Club, founded in 1874, was one of the most prestigious and popular clubs in London. At that time of day, however, there were only a few clusters of armchairs dotted about, forming small islands, and a handful of gentlemen smoking their solitary pipes, absentmindedly cupping a brandy glass, or reading a newspaper with an air of boredom, content to have escaped from their suffocating homes for a few hours.

"Look at them . . . ," muttered Melford, with a sudden flash of animosity. "They haven't the slightest idea how sick their world is, or that it is nearing its end. On the contrary: they think they are in the middle of something. They think they are different from everything before and everything after. They think they are speeding toward some destination on one of their swift trains. They study, contemplate, marvel at one another. And yet they see nothing. They don't see that the end is coming, nor do they suspect that all possible trains will soon collide into a morass of eternal darkness, nothingness, chaos."

"But how could they, Melford!" Doctor Ramsey said, almost reprovingly. "They are so far from the Supreme Knowledge! At times I feel ashamed of having made my name as a scientist in this world, where all I can offer is baubles . . . but other times I can't help laughing at their monumental ignorance . . ." He gave a hollow laugh and took a sip of brandy to steady himself. "Although it is true that among them there are some whose intelligence shines out above the rest, and whose company can be a pleasant balm to us poor, lonely exiles . . ." Ramsey noticed his companions' stern looks and nodded, trying to sound cheerier. "Naturally, I am referring to a companionship that is productive and advances our sacred mission. As you know, thanks to my prestige as a scientist and my friendship with Mr. Crookes, I have been able to infiltrate spiritualist circles and to carry out various studies of countless apparitions that have been well received on the Other Side. Some mediums' ectoplasmic materializations offer plenty of answers! I assume you have read my latest report, where I elaborated an interesting table comparing the—"

"We are aware of your research into spiritualism, Ramsey. We also know about your friendship with that Crookes fellow, which placed us in such danger when you almost gave our mission away," Kramer scolded him severely.

"I never endangered our mission!" Ramsey protested fiercely.

"Settle down, my friend," Kramer warned with icy calm.

"It was only a moment of weakness . . . ," the doctor went on, instantly lowering his tone. "But in the end I did my duty. Crookes knows nothing, and he never will, I can assure you . . . And so it should to be. None of the inhabitants of this world should know the truth: they would never understand our mission. They would see us as menacing invaders. They would fear us as one fears the unknown. They would turn us into the stuff of nightmares and try to destroy us. We cannot trust them. Or feelings such as love or friendship that cloud our minds," he insisted. "I haven't forgotten that, gentlemen. Like Armand de Bompard, I never forget the wonderful world from which I come."

"Our world, oh, our wonderful world . . . ," Melford chipped in, with a nostalgia that wasn't entirely devoid of irony. "As we speak, on the Other Side, our miraculous civilization is cowering around the last remaining black holes. Our bodies, skillfully modified to survive the cold, dead ocean of darkness, will soon cease to function. And our minds will be capable of only the most sluggish connections, frozen in a long, dark nirvana. Until in the end we are converted into a lifeless cloud of dead particles. So it is written in the second law. A law we arrogantly believed we could escape. But the second law is inevitable. Chaos is inevitable!"

"Chaos is inevitable!" his companions intoned as one, taking out their fob watches, opening them to reveal the engraving inside: a star containing a tiny circle with eight arrows pointing outward and piercing a second, concentric circle. A star I am sure you are familiar with.

"Chaos is inevitable!" repeated Kramer. "You are quite right, Melford, and we mustn't forget that. But there is still a glimmer of hope. Do you recall not so long ago when we managed to open the tunnel to this side? For one glorious instant we thought we had succeeded." They all nodded, smiling weakly, a flicker of that distant hope in their eyes. "Wasn't it wonderful? The news spread like wildfire among our scientists. A stable tunnel had been opened! We had the chance of starting afresh in another world! A young world, full of light and heat. A universe where stars were still being born. A new, warm planet where we would inject the seed of our doomed civilization. Where we would be reborn, far from our inhospitable, dying home—"

"But that world was sick!" Angier thumped the table with his clenched fist, making the brandy glasses shake and a couple of members look up disgruntled from their newspapers. "I also remember the day we discovered it was ravaged by a strange epidemic of apocalyptic proportions, and that its end might even be nearer than our own. Yes, I also remember that. And how, in spite of everything, we kept our faith: we believed we could find a cure in time for the Great Exodus. But no one is certain we will succeed now, are they, Kramer?" he asked, each word loaded with anguish. "It's been a long time and we still haven't obtained any results. We don't know how the virus got here, or when the disease started. We don't know who was infected first. We have no idea how to cure it. And we still haven't produced a vaccine. After all this time, we continue to know nothing about it, Kramer. Nothing. As you said, there is hope, but it is rapidly diminishing . . ."

"We still have ten years left," Kramer retorted. "And the Executioners might provide us with an extra one or two."

"The Executioners!" Doctor Ramsey snorted, cracking his knuckles. "It is shocking that we have had to resort to those ruthless killers. By all the dead suns! We're a level QIII civilization, and have been for thousands of years. And now, having reached the end of the road, we high priests of Wisdom can think of nothing better than to order a slaughter. That will be our magnificent legacy, gentlemen. A slaughter of innocents, like the one perpetrated by their King Herod, only on a universal scale." He gave another joyless laugh. "When our end comes, our atoms will float in the eternal void, representing forever and for no one the image of barbarism—"

"The Executioners are a necessary evil for the time being . . . ," Kramer interrupted him sharply. "We created them because we needed more time. We never considered them the ideal solution, Ramsey. You mustn't become agitated, and that goes for you too, Angier. I won't say it again. Either you calm down or I shall be forced to report your excitable state to the Other Side. If it weren't for the Executioners, this would all have ended a long time ago. We are simply building a dam in order to try to contain the uncontainable, to give us time to investigate the sickness. If we still have ten years in which to do so, then it is thanks to their work, gentlemen. Although the fact remains that we all dislike them," he admitted, with a final shudder.

"They are monstrous," murmured Melford, echoing the other man's sentiments.

"Terrifying," reiterated Angier. "Do you know that the animals here can sense them? Horses rear up, dogs bark, and—"

"You needn't have anything to do with them if they repulse you so much. As you know, their orders come from the Other Side," Kramer reminded them. "But don't forget we still have a slim chance thanks to them. Think about it: a single instant snatched from the inevitability of chaos could be the precious one in which our scientists find the solution."

"And how will we know when the end has commenced?" Melford asked. "What do you believe will happen?"

Kramer sighed.

"I presume we will see wonderful and terrible things. Incomprehensible to all those who do not possess the Supreme Knowledge. Mankind's worst nightmares will come true . . . And by the time that happens, it will certainly be too late . . . In ten, possibly twelve years . . . But not much more."

"Then we had better hurry up," said Higgins, who had been silent for most of the conversation. "As I mentioned when I arrived, I have something to show you. For the moment, it isn't much," he apologized, rummaging in his pockets. His free hand made as if to tug his beard, but he immediately pulled it away with a vexed expression. Then he produced a small test tube filled with red liquid and showed it to the others. "But it could end up being good news."

They all gazed at the test tube, fascinated.

"Is that the blood of . . . ?" Melford whispered.

"Yes," Higgins confirmed triumphantly. "The young man mutilated by the Count de Bompard's whelp."

"You did it!" said Kramer excitedly.

Higgins nodded smugly.

"He paid me a visit today. But have no fear. I was very cunning. Despite his exceptional intelligence, he suspected nothing. In fact, he practically begged me to take a blood sample."

"Do you think this might lead us somewhere?" Angier asked hopefully.

"It's possible. The young man suffers strange episodes. His body is desperately trying to make the leap, but only his mind succeeds," Higgins explained. "It is as if something inside him, something he didn't possess before, and which she may have contaminated him with when she bit him, compels him to leap while at the same time firmly anchoring his body in this world. Sickness and cure, all in the same person. Armand always suspected that creatures like her might contain in their nature the key to a possible future vaccine. That is why for years his research took that direction, but despite all his studies he never found an answer. In the end, he had to admit to the Other Side that he had failed, and he was forced to abandon his creature in order to concentrate on other projects. But Armand overlooked something in his research. It is possible that the clue he was looking for in his wife's nature only became active when combined with the blood of *some* of her victims . . . Of course, Armand's mistake was that he fell in love with her." Doctor Ramsey opened his mouth to speak, but Kramer silenced him with an abrupt gesture. "Because of his feelings toward the young she-wolf," Higgins went on, with a hint of sarcasm, "he tried to teach her to control the deadly side of her nature, and his original line of investigation was never explored. Yes, we could be looking at the beginnings of a vaccine; it is too soon to say." He tucked the test tube away in his pocket. "I can't tell you any more until I have analyzed Farlow and Co.'s new reels, which are made of steel with an ivory spool, perfect for salmon fishing, and far superior in quality to any others I have tried."

They all nodded enthusiastically while one of the waiters, who had approached noiselessly, leaned over and said. "Forgive me for interrupting you, gentlemen, but a few of the other members have asked me to light the fire on this side of the room . . . it seems they are feeling cold. I hope it isn't inconvenient."

"I'm off—I have lots of work to do!" Higgins stood up, suddenly pale. "I promise to be in touch with the latest news, gentlemen . . ." Taking his leave of them all with a quick nod, he hurried away.

In the meantime, the waiter lit the fire, which was soon blazing pleasantly in the grate a few yards from the four men.

In the meantime, let us take this opportunity to leave the four gentlemen and return to Inspector Clayton. However, if you will permit me, I'll pass over the next ten years, since I am anxious above all to discover whether the Cavaliers of Chaos, aided by the evil Executioners, will finally succeed in saving the world. During those years nothing important has happened related to our case (or in the life of the inspector, in my opinion), and so you will not miss anything crucial if we leap forward to the first of August 1898, a date some of you may be familiar with. That is the day when our tale, after flowing underground for ten years, springs forth on the surface once more.

9

EN YEARS AFTER THE SÉANCE, THE WAX CYLIN-
der still preserved Inspector Cornelius Clayton's voice urging Sir Henry Blendell to confess. And as on many other occasions
during those years, the inspector's words, uttered in a different time and
place, were now being broadcast in the Chamber of Marvels, drifting
over the mermaids' skeletons, photographs of fairies, werewolf hides,
and stuffed Minotaur head stored in its confines. In one corner, elbows
resting on a table and lit up dramatically by a small lamp, sat the inspector. During the ten years that had passed, he had changed greatly
in appearance, and who hadn't? He was more wan, more haggard, more
stooped; in short, he had less sparkle. But those changes only affected
the outside. He had experienced the odd turmoil, but nothing on the
seismic scale of his first case; and, as time passed, his soul had begun to
resemble one of those much-thumbed volumes that always fall open at
the same page. It could be said that, contrary to what he had predicted at
the time, he still recognized himself in the disenchanted, arrogant youth
whose voice was recorded on the cylinder.

Perhaps the only noticeable difference was that he was far less eager
to understand the world around him, which had turned into an even
more absurd place over those years. There were many events that had
made his hair stand on end, throwing up connections as tangled as they
were futile for a mind such as his, alert as it was to that kind of detail:
after slaying five prostitutes, Jack the Ripper, as the Whitechapel murderer was called, had vanished without trace, taking with him the mys-

tery of his identity. Also, some years later his literary equivalent, Dorian Gray, had unleashed his depravity on London's poorest neighborhoods while his author languished in jail, convicted of sodomy—the same reprehensible activity Prince Albert Victor, the queen's grandson, had been discovered (by Clayton's colleagues at the Yard) engaging in at a male brothel in Cleveland Street. However, the queen's nephew hadn't been locked up anywhere, and the monarchy had chosen to divert the public's attention toward the conquest of South Africa, where heroic deeds no longer celebrated in storybooks still occurred, and where the English race could display its courage and heroism in all its glory by massacring poor Africans. Added to that was the continuous worker unrest, the suffragette demonstrations, and the wars in the colonies, or other events that are more germane to our tale: Margaretta Fox had retracted the statements she had made to *The New York Herald* condemning the spiritualist movement and confessed she had done so for money, and Professor Crookes, who as rumor suggested had finally been knighted, had confirmed in his address to the British Association the existence of that psychic force he had first championed thirty years earlier. And so, much to the displeasure of some, thanks to the abovementioned events and many others, during the ten intervening years the belief in spirits and their emissaries, mediums, had only intensified, something which is crucial to this tale, as you will soon discover.

Despite having surrendered to the world's complex mystery, Clayton still endeavored to bring as much order to it as possible, rather like the fastidious guest who upon encountering a wrinkled tablecloth can't help unconsciously smoothing out the part in front of him. And so he had gone on solving cases, some deadly dull, self-evident almost to the point of being offensive, others interesting enough to occupy his inquiring mind, thus distracting him for a while from the demons that forever plagued him. Although a few of those cases had confronted him once more with the realm of the fantastic, I will refrain from elaborating on them here, in order not to stray from the path I have set myself, possibly never to find it again. Suffice to say, not because it was one of his most exciting cases but owing to the relevance of one of its protagonists to our story, the inspector still felt a desire to investigate a company called Murray's Time Travel. For those of you who don't know, or have forgotten, the aforementioned company had opened for business in the autumn of 1896, shortly after the author H. G. Wells published his famous novel *The Time Machine,* with the aim of bringing Wells's novel to life. For the paltry sum of one hundred pounds, Murray's Time Travel boasted that it could take you to the future—to the year 2000, to be precise. There a battle for possession of the planet was raging between the brave Captain Shackleton, leader of the human resistance army, and his archenemy, the automaton Solomon.

Naturally, Scotland Yard's Special Branch had felt obliged from the outset to investigate the supposed miracle so as to rule out any possibility of fraud, although the reports given by the first time travelers to be interviewed had been so extraordinary that neither Sinclair nor Clayton could imagine anyone being capable of inventing such a brilliant hoax. From their accounts, it appeared that the travelers reached the nebulous future on a time tram called the *Cronotilus,* which traversed the fourth dimension, a pink plain inhabited by dangerous, time-eating dragons. As you will easily appreciate, the two inspectors were more than keen to climb aboard this remarkable tram, but Gilliam Murray, who owned the company, had become a very powerful man overnight and, sheltering behind an army of lawyers, managed to spare his company from inspection. Finally, after a laborious legal battle, a judge had approved the long-awaited warrant that gave Captain Sinclair and his future successor (no one at the Yard doubted that Clayton would step into his boss's shoes when he retired) complete freedom to snoop into Murray's affairs. But just then an unfortunate tragedy had occurred that plunged the country into a long period of mourning: Gilliam Murray, the Master of Time, the man who had opened the doors of the future to the inhabitants of the present, had passed away, devoured by a dragon from the fourth dimension. His company had been closed down and all that remained of Murray's Time Travel was a ramshackle theater in Soho whose dusty façade appeared to conceal no other mystery than decay.

Continuously echoing behind each of Clayton's investigations like the distant rumor of a waterfall was the unsolved puzzle of Mrs. Lansbury's disappearance. The inspector had not stopped thinking about it for a single moment: ten years of toying with the different pieces, rearranging them in a thousand different ways, trying unsuccessfully to make them fit together. And how often over the years had he longed to unearth a new piece that would make sense of the whole? But neither the old lady nor the transparent stranger, to whom she had referred as the Villain, had turned up again, dead or alive. Despite all this, Clayton had done his best from the outset to prevent that mystery from becoming an unsolvable riddle consigned to the dusty archives at Scotland Yard. Following the old lady's disappearance, he had ordered a team of architects and carpenters (including Sir Henry Blendell, who had agreed to collaborate in exchange for a reduction to his sentence) to search the house from top to bottom, in particular the old lady's study, convinced it must contain a false wall, a hidden trapdoor, or some other ingenious device whereby Mrs. Lansbury had been able to escape without unlocking the door. But the accursed room revealed none of those things. It was an ordinary, everyday study. The blood in the street, steps, and hallway was equally ordinary and had finally dried the way ordinary, everyday blood always did, regardless of the curious properties it had revealed to Clayton, proof of which was to be found only in his memory.

Lacking any sense of the direction the investigation should take, and tired of going round in circles with the handful of clues they had, much to Clayton's dismay his department had gradually shelved the case. Two years later, a wealthy merchant had purchased the old lady's house, and from time to time the inspector would pass by it on his way home, contemplating wistfully the incongruous family tableau glimpsed through its windows, in the warm interior where he had once grappled with a transparent creature. It was about this time that he began to accept that the case would never be resolved, that it would become just another drop in the ocean of mysteries engulfing the world. As time went by, the protagonists of those events gradually began to fade, until the whole episode became no more than a hazy memory. Madame Amber hanged herself in the lunatic asylum where she had been confined, unable to bear any more visitations by spirits, whom she claimed were the only ones that troubled to go and visit her. As for Sir Henry Blendell, after serving his sentence, cut short due to his collaboration as well as good behavior, he moved to a small town in New York State where no one knew of his disgrace, and there, according to the occasional reports that made their way back to Clayton, he ran a carpenter's shop that produced ordinary, everyday furniture for ordinary, everyday citizens who had no need of wardrobes or dressers with false bottoms. As I have already mentioned, neither hide nor hair was seen again of Mrs. Lansbury. As for the Villain . . . Clayton had not ruled out the possibility that he had used some kind of disguise or other device to perform the miracles Clayton had witnessed. But over time, he, too, had begun to believe that the creature was supernatural. Outlandish as that might sound, it was after all the simplest explanation, as Captain Sinclair had understood almost from the start.

And now, ten years on, Clayton seemed to be the only one making any effort to keep the memory of that case alive. He gazed distractedly around the Chamber of Marvels as the phonograph re-created once more the scene he knew by heart: the captain's monotonous voice initiating the séance, followed by a strained silence mixed with the participants' subdued breathing, then their gasps of surprise as the little bell, the handkerchief, and the gardenia came to life. Then Madame Amber's sensual groans, the loud thudding, Nurse Jones screeching that the medium was choking, Doctor Ramsey demanding she be brought some water, and finally, heralding the cacophonous sounds of the brawl, the Villain's voice, steeped in evil as though emerging from a putrid gorge.

"I've found you! At last, I've found you! And this time, you'll give me what is mine!"

What is mine . . . At least now he knew what the Villain had been referring to, reflected Clayton, stroking the book the old lady had entrusted to him. This was what the creature had been looking for, and he was not afraid to kill in order to get hold of it. Yet if he had wanted it so much, why did he not come back for it? At first, Clayton had expected they were bound to renew their half-finished duel, but as the years went by he realized the Villain could not have known that he was the one now in possession of *The Map of Chaos*. Doubtless the Villain had not gotten a proper look at him during their brief confrontation in the murky gloom at Mrs. Lansbury's house, and hadn't heard his voice either, and so was unable to recognize in that unexpected opponent the inspector who had thwarted his attempt to throttle the old lady during the séance. He must have mistaken him for a servant. And that meant he must be looking elsewhere for the book. Perhaps he believed it was still with the old lady, wherever she might be, or perhaps with the intended recipient of the message the Villain had intercepted. If so, that person was in grave danger, although there was little Clayton could do about it, as he had no clue as to who it was. He sighed with resignation and contemplated the book that Mrs. Lansbury had told him to guard with his life. And that was what he had done for the last ten years. He had hidden the book away in the Chamber of Marvels, a place that, as far as the world was concerned, did not exist, and waited for someone to come to claim it. But no one seemed to be aware that the book existed. And so, whenever he wasn't working on a case, like now, he would descend into the Chamber, turn on the phonograph, and spend hours poring over the map, wondering who had written it, what formulas those were, what extreme danger was threatening the world, and how that handful of scribbled pages could possibly save it.

Throughout those years, afraid each time that it might have fatal consequences, he had shown the book to some of England's most celebrated mathematicians, but none of them had been able to decipher the obscure formulas or the geometrical drawings, nor had they been able to tell him what the Maelstrom Coordinates to which the old lady had referred a couple of times might be, saying that they'd never heard of that expression.

Clayton cradled the book in his hand with a familiarity that had come with the years. He ran his finger over the eight-pointed star adorning the cover, and the tiny circle from which the ornate arrows sprang, then the second, concentric circle traversing them, which resembled a ship's wheel. He leafed through the pages, as always in the vague hope that this random search would reveal the meaning of it all, feeling the weight of responsibility the old lady had placed on his shoulders. Her words had become imprinted on his memory without the need for any phonograph: "The key to the salvation of the world lies within the pages of this book. Of the world as you know it, but also of all those worlds you can only imagine . . . You must guard it with your life if necessary and give it to those who come from the Other Side." And although no one had claimed it during the ten intervening years, Clayton only needed recall the burning passion in the old lady's eyes to be sure that sooner or later someone would. That someone might be the Villain himself, he occasionally imagined with a shiver, that transparent murderer whom bullets scarcely grazed, that ruthless creature who would go on killing until he got hold of the book.

The sound of the Chamber door opening made him start. Who could it be at that hour? he wondered, glancing at the tiny window in one of the walls through which the pale dawn light was beginning to seep. But he immediately had the answer as he saw, framed against the door, a stout figure with a flashing red light in place of one of his eyes. When Captain Sinclair discovered him leaning on the desk, he gave a sigh and weaved his way through the fantastical bric-a-brac that filled the room.

I am sure any of you would wager that during the ten years that had passed, the relationship between Clayton and the captain could only have grown closer, given the dozens of cases they had worked on, the dangers they had braved together, and the secret adventures they had lived through. However, anyone placing his bets on that card would lose everything down to his socks, because some souls are only prepared to reveal so much and will not allow you to delve any deeper, and both Clayton and the captain possessed that sort of impermeable soul. And so the relationship between them had scarcely evolved from what it was at the beginning of this story.

In some cases that lack of intimacy had worked in the inspector's favor. For example, it had freed him from the need to address in any depth the matter of his fainting fits, whose resolution is something you must all be wondering about, for when we left Clayton ten years ago he was sneaking out of Dr. Higgins's consulting rooms. You should know that Clayton was later informed that the tests our mysterious doctor carried out revealed no abnormalities, and although the inspector sought advice from a few other medical practitioners, he eventually gave up trying to find a solution to his problem because it ceased to be one, at least in his work, which was what most concerned him. And how was that possible? Thanks to Captain Sinclair deciding to ignore it. Yes, during those ten years, Clayton had collapsed dozens of times while on duty, mostly in full view of Sinclair. At first Clayton had explained these lapses away with a variety of excuses (lack of sleep, anxiety associated with the case they were working on, not eating properly . . .), but as soon as he realized that the captain accepted them with an impassive silence, he stopped justifying them and simply grinned idiotically when he came to, in whatever corner his boss had put him so he wouldn't be in the way. Clayton never knew if the captain had believed any of his excuses, or whether he had mentioned it to his superiors, but the fact is he was never called into anyone's office, leading him to assume that, regardless of the many problems it caused them, Sinclair had decided to overlook his eccentric habit of collapsing all over the place without prior warning. Despite the relative peace of mind this gave him, Clayton continued to be intrigued by the reasons for the captain's behavior—that is, until one afternoon when Mrs. Sinclair confessed to Clayton, during one of her frequent attacks of honesty over tea, that her husband's potent seed couldn't take root in her barren womb. In a voice dripping with melancholy, Marcia Julia Sinclair had described to him the long, arduous years during which they had struggled to produce an heir, the endless frustrations, and, above all, the enormous disappointment of discovering that, after a certain age, not even the hardest-fought battle of this kind had any chance of success. After that, the inspector was in no doubt as to why the captain had chosen to help him bear his heavy burden. Fate had decided that he filled perfectly the empty space left in his captain's marriage, and the immunity that granted him, although he had not asked for it, proved very convenient. He showed his gratitude to Sinclair every day in the only way their lack of intimacy allowed: mutely. The captain responded in kind, also using that coded language of awkward smiles, subtle nods, and significant raisings of the eyebrows, whereby each told the other he knew that the other knew. Thus Clayton's fainting fits ceased to be a problem and became something he had to learn to live with. As you will understand, he couldn't help feeling grateful that things had worked out that way, because it enabled him to go on dreaming about Valerie.

"Heaven knows why I went looking for you at your house, the club, or the Yard, when I know perfectly well you like to spend every spare moment shut away in here," the captain grumbled, more to himself than to Clayton, panting for breath as he came to a halt near the inspector.

The ten years that had passed had flecked his hair with white and added a few more furrows to his face, but on the whole Sinclair seemed scarcely affected by the passage of time, like those soaring cliffs whose erosion by the waves is so slow as to be almost imperceptible to the human eye.

"Good morning, Captain," Clayton said, hurriedly switching off the phonograph, like a child caught red-handed. "You're up early."

"Likewise, Inspector," Sinclair retorted, frowning at the book lying on the desk.

Clayton gave a shrug. Sinclair then observed his subordinate at length, nervously pursing and relaxing his lips, reluctant to speak.

"Perhaps you should stop brooding over that case . . . ," he said at last. "Stop brooding over everything, in fact. It isn't advisable in this profession to take your work home with you."

Clayton nodded with feigned indifference, wondering what his boss would think if he knew that the Countess de Bompard's portrait was hanging on a wall in the cellar of his home.

"You're still young. You have your whole life ahead of you," Sinclair went on, since that morning Clayton seemed ready to exceed his habitual quota of lengthy silences. "I shall be retiring soon, and you can rest assured I shall recommend you as my replacement. So take a tip from this old-timer: Don't let any case jeopardize your private life," he concluded, absentmindedly stroking the extraordinary monocle covering his right eye.

Clayton gave a sardonic smile.

"Thanks for the advice, Captain, but we both know you won't be recommending me and that I shan't hold it against you. My *little* difficulty will be far less trouble to everyone if you keep me in an office filling in forms instead of sending me out onto the streets with a handful of novices under my command." Sinclair opened his mouth, about to protest, only to close it again, conceding with regret that the inspector had predicted his own future far more accurately than he. "As for my private life, you needn't worry: I don't have one."

"Precisely," Sinclair retorted. "Don't you think we all need a bit of, er . . . feminine company come nightfall?"

Clayton smiled to himself. These brusque, clumsy assaults the captain occasionally made on his craggy heart, clearly at his wife's behest, never failed to touch him.

"I have no desire to frequent brothels, if that is what you mean," he replied with mock indignation.

"Good heavens, no, Inspector . . . I was referring to a less, er . . . ephemeral sort of companionship. I don't know whether you've noticed that my secretary, Miss Barkin, always remembers how you take your coffee, yet she always makes mine exactly the way I most detest it."

"Interesting. I think that needs investigating," Clayton said, feigning thoughtfulness as he leaned back in his chair and folded his arms. "Is that the new case you came here to have me embark on?"

"I shan't deny that neither Marcia nor I would object to your brooding over that case," the captain growled, finally betraying the fact that this was more his wife's doing than his own. He shrugged and gave a sigh. He had more than kept his side of the bargain by pointing out to the thick-skinned inspector the attentions his secretary lavished on him. It was time to move on to the real reason for his being there. "And yet something tells me that the case I came here to tell you about will interest you much more."

"Are you sure any case could interest me more than the vagaries of Miss Barkin's coffee making, Captain?" Clayton grinned, visibly relieved that the conversation had taken a different turn.

"I have no doubt whatsoever," Sinclair assured him, "since it involves that author you admire so much, the one who wrote the novel about the Martian invasion."

"H. G. Wells?" Clayton gasped, starting to his feet.

The captain nodded, pleased he had at least been able to provide his subordinate with a new toy to distract him.

"He lives in Worcester Park." Sinclair rummaged in his jacket pocket and handed Clayton a note. "Here's the address. Get there as quickly as you can."

Clayton read the note and nodded.

"What is it about, Captain?"

Sinclair grinned. He knew that this was the part the inspector would appreciate the most.

"A Martian cylinder appeared last night on Horsell Common," he explained. "Exactly as Mr. Wells described in his novel."

PART TWO

Are the manifold mysteries threatening the universe causing you to quake in your shoes, dear reader? Have no fear: as in all good detective stories, everything will be revealed.

But no reader can live on mysteries alone. So keep turning the pages of this disquieting novel and you will find yourself immersed in a love story that defies death itself. But do not forget that the most formidable villain you could ever imagine is searching for the very book you are holding. If necessary, guard it with your life!

10

ONTGOMERY GILMORE WOULD HAVE PRE-
ferred not to suffer from that irrational fear of
heights that made him go green around the gills. Up until then, it had
remained hidden, like a stowaway, and no doubt harked back to some
long-forgotten episode in childhood. A painful tumble from the garden wall at his parents' house? The angry admonishments of an overly
zealous governess? Who could say? Whatever the case, that seed, which
grudgingly took root in his soul at some point in his life, had continued
to grow surreptitiously, only to appear at the worst possible moment:
precisely when he found himself suspended at a considerable height in
midair, beneath an inflated hot-air balloon. Unfortunately for him, the
object was moving higher and higher, until it seemed they would touch
the sun itself, or at least that is what the man in control of it seemed to
wish to do. He was a taciturn fellow who responded to Gilmore's cease-
less questions (did he think they were on the right course, were they
flying at the correct height, was the wind speed adequate . . . ?) with a
shrug, switching the grubby toothpick he was chewing from one side of
his mouth to the other. Gilmore imagined strangling the man with his
bare hands, and the thought consoled him slightly, although he made no
attempt to act on it, if only because that would have meant letting go of
the side of the basket, and this was something he didn't have the stomach
for, not even so as to wipe away the sweat pouring down his temples. He
was content to remain jammed in among the crowd of acrobats filling
the tiny basket and jumping around like a troop of unruly monkeys as

they practiced their next routine, and to try to maintain a smile of aloof indifference as he wondered what the devil he had intended by wearing a bright purple suit, a top hat that weighed a ton, and a spinning bow tie he feared might slash his throat at any moment.

He had wanted to make her laugh, he told himself. That was his intention. The instructions in the letter had been clear. That was the reason why he was in that hot-air balloon that kept swaying perilously from side to side, dressed in that ridiculous, clownish outfit. And he was determined to succeed. Even if he had to die trying. He imagined himself falling out of the balloon, crashing onto the grass, but instantly rejected the idea as impractical: he hadn't taken the trouble of orchestrating the whole thing merely to sacrifice himself. And so he clung with renewed vigor to the sides of the basket, determined to arrive in one piece at Horsell Common, where in a few moments' time the most spectacular Martian invasion he had been able to stage would commence, allowing him to win the heart of the woman he loved. Or, if the Creator considered that too ambitious, then at least to make her laugh.

Because, unfortunately for Gilmore, the tactics he employed to win over other women didn't work on Emma Harlow. He had tried everything: he had presented her with thirty-seven hats, fêted her parents, and placed his immense fortune at her feet, assuring her over and over that he could grant any of her wishes, however impossible it seemed. But with his insistence he had only succeeded in making the girl, tired of his clumsy advances, throw down a challenge as cruel as it was unachievable: she would agree to marry him if he succeeded in reproducing the Martian invasion the author H. G. Wells described in his novel *The War of the Worlds*. Naturally, he needn't go so far as to destroy the Earth and all its inhabitants; he only had to re-create the beginning of the invasion credibly enough so that every newspaper in England picked up the story. If he succeeded, she would give him her hand. But if he failed, he had to admit that even he was unable to grant her the impossible and give up his ridiculous courtship of her once and for all.

When he heard her utter that whimsical request, Gilmore wasn't sure whether to laugh or cry. Wells. H. G. Wells. That fellow again. Once more fate was obliging him to joust with the author's imagination. Would he never be rid of that man? Would their lives be forever joined until one of them died, untangling the infuriating knot?

But despite realizing that the girl had only proposed that challenge to rid herself of her most relentless suitor, the only man she had failed to dissuade with her arrogance and animosity, Gilmore had taken up the gauntlet and traveled to London, ready to make the world believe that Martians were invading the planet, even though this time he was doing it for love. However, he soon discovered that reproducing a Martian invasion realistic enough to deceive the whole of England wasn't as easy as he had first thought. No matter how hard he tried, after various failed attempts, and with the time limit Emma had given him about to expire, Gilmore had been forced to appeal to the only person who could help him: H. G. Wells himself, author of the novel he was supposed to reproduce. He had been driven to it by despair, certain that, having read his letter, Wells would instantly screw it up and throw it in the wastepaper basket, although somewhere deep down he had a faint hope that Wells might reply, for Gilmore was convinced the author considered himself superior and would take every opportunity to demonstrate it to him. And so it proved. A letter with Wells's name on the return address had appeared in Gilmore's mailbox a few days later, as miraculously as a flower in the snow:

Dear Gilliam,

This might strike you as odd, but knowing you are in love has filled me with joy. However, there is little I can do to help you, except to advise you not to waste your time reproducing the Martian invasion. Make her laugh. Yes, make that girl laugh so that her laughter spills into the air like a pocketful of silver coins.

And then she will be yours forever.

Affectionately,

Your friend, George.

Yes! Wells, his biggest enemy, probably the person who most hated him on the planet, had written back to him! And not only that, he had also honored his love, offered him advice, and, most amazing of all, had signed off affectionately, proclaiming himself his friend. Gilmore couldn't have hoped for more, given everything that had passed between them two years before. Indeed, initially, unable to rid himself completely of his old mistrust, Gilmore had thought he glimpsed a veiled threat between those apparently harmless lines, above all when Wells had addressed him by his real name. Was the author warning him of the power he wielded over him now that he knew his secret? Was he intending to blackmail him later on, or, not possessing the torturer's patience, would he be content to destroy him by revealing to the world the true identity of the mysterious millionaire Montgomery Gilmore? What was Wells playing at? However, after that bout of suspicion, Gilmore had calmed down. His fears seemed absurd, especially as he himself had written to Wells confessing what he had probably suspected all along—a secret no one but his most loyal henchmen knew about: that Gilliam Murray, owner of Murray's Time Travel, the famous Master of Time, had not been devoured by a dragon on the pink plains of the fourth dimension, as the press had shouted from the rooftops, but had staged his own death and was in fact still alive, masquerading as the millionaire Montgomery Gilmore, no less. Alive and in love.

However, Wells had not given him away, but nor had he explained in his letter, as Murray had hoped, how to produce a Martian as credible as those in his novel. No, Wells had told him to make her laugh. That was all. As if he were sure that would suffice. And Murray had decided to follow his advice. Not that he had any choice. And that was why he now found himself in that accursed hot-air balloon full of acrobats who couldn't stay still.

A series of sharp jolts interrupted his reflections. Murray glowered at the acrobats, who were currently dangling from the sides of the hot-air balloon, until he realized that could only mean one thing: they were arriving at their destination. His heart began racing. He looked uneasily at the ground, and his suspicions were confirmed. Beyond the soft tree-tops over which they were now floating, he could see the green pastures of Horsell Common, where, under cover of darkness, his assistants had positioned the Martian cylinder. A noisy crowd had gathered around the object, and as the balloon began to its descent, Murray could smell the air thick with gunpowder from the fireworks display. (He himself had arranged for the first ones to be let off from inside the cylinder to inaugurate the spectacle.) He could hear the band playing below, and gradually he was able to make out the colorful procession of horses, elephants, dancers, conjurors, sword swallowers, clowns, and jugglers he had hired, which, as far as he could tell from above, were delighting the crowd. And, squinting, he could just make out the shape of the would-be Martian, a puppet poking out of a trapdoor in the cylinder and moving to the rhythm of the festive music even as it waved a banner, whose slogan Murray had no need to read from there because he had written it himself: "Emma, will you marry me?"

Just then, a crescendo of rolling drums made everyone turn around, eager to see what fresh marvels they heralded. The hot-air balloon descended another yard or so, though no one seemed to have noticed it yet. However, Murray was close enough now to the crowd to be able to see some of the faces turning this way and that. His heart skipped a beat when, peeping out from beneath a parasol that was continuously twirling, he made out Emma's face, expressing a look of charming astonishment. There she was, fearless as an Amazon, delicate as a blossom, honoring the appointment she herself had agreed to as the deadline for her challenge. On August first, Martians will land on Horsell Common, he had promised her. You have my word, Emma. They will come all the way from Mars just so that you marry me. She had kept the appointment, ready to see him fail in his attempt to achieve the impossible. And there she had found a cylinder, like a cornucopia from which had spilled an entire circus . . . Murray swallowed, unable to contain his excitement. What would the girl's reaction be when he climbed out of the hot-air balloon, revealing himself to be the person responsible for all that jubilation? However, before he had time to answer his own question, he spotted Wells standing a few feet beyond the girl. He had on a garish checked three-piece suit, which only he could wear with such naturalness, and next to him, looking for all the world as if Wells had used up all the colors, was a lanky fellow dressed in a plain dark suit. Despite his agitation, Murray couldn't help grinning when he saw him. Not only had Wells deigned to give him advice, he had come there to support him in person. Did his future happiness matter so much to Wells? The thought moved him more than if he had heard a whale sing, and he felt a sudden wave of affection for the author and, by extension, for the rest of the human race, excepting the unflappable hot-air balloon pilot. Overcome with emotion, he swore to himself that if he succeeded in marrying Emma, Wells would be his best man, and he would never again hate anyone as he had hated him, nor would he ever exchange blows with anyone again, or make another enemy so long as he lived. He would be the most generous man on the planet, someone whose happiness made it impossible for him to desire the unhappiness of others. A man cleansed by love, a pure altruist, a pure philanthropist.

It was then that the balloon's enormous shadow slid across the crowd, and a hundred faces turned and looked upward. Murray hurriedly recoiled from the edge. He didn't want anyone to see him until the basket had touched the ground and he stepped out with the grandiose flourishes he had spent the past few days rehearsing in front of a mirror. His arrival must be triumphant, he reminded himself, as the acrobats began to perform pirouettes, descending the multicolored ropes and dangling gracefully from the ends. When the balloon had reached the place where it was supposed to land, next to the cylinder, the acrobats leapt to the ground and, like the most outlandish collection of footmen imaginable, spread out across the grass, genuflecting gracefully as they prepared to welcome their master. Then Murray took a deep breath, activated the vapor machine inside his hat, as well as the device operating his rotating bow tie, and mustered his most dazzling smile: the moment had arrived for him to make his appearance in the spectacle he had orchestrated to make the woman he loved laugh.

However, if that was Murray's interpretation of the scene, Wells observed it through very different eyes. When the enormous shadow passed over their heads like the darkness of an eclipse, Wells and Clayton looked up and contemplated in silent awe the huge hot-air balloon descend toward the cylinder as it prepared to land. Wells, his mouth set in a pale line, watched the gigantic, brightly colored globe with its pompous, glittering "G." Suspended from it was a small basket, rocking from side to side, and although for the moment only the underneath was visible, Wells knew perfectly well who was inside it. He gave a sigh as he saw the troupe of acrobats dressed as footmen dangling from the basket. There was only one man who could have planned such a vulgar, ostentatious entrance. What Wells remained unsure of was whether he would have the stomach to contemplate Murray's contemptible face again after two blissful years of believing he was rid of him for good.

He was of half a mind to turn on his heel and leave, but finally he stayed where he was, because he wasn't completely sure in what capacity he had requested that Clayton accompany him. That skinny detective with the fake hand, who registered his astonishment at the spectacle by raising his right eyebrow, had arrived at Wells's house to tell him that a Martian cylinder had landed on Horsell Common exactly as he described in his novel. And had Wells not received a letter a month before announcing that madness, he would have taken him for a lunatic or a prankster.

The letter, the accursed letter . . . He had opened it tentatively when he saw the sender's name, but after he finished reading it, an almost savage fury had erased any other sensation.

Dear George,

    I imagine it will come as no surprise to you to receive a letter from a dead man, for we are both aware that you are the only man in all England who knows I am still alive. What will doubtless surprise you is the reason for my writing, and that is none other than to request your help. Yes, that is right, I am sending you this letter because I need your help.

Let me begin by not wasting time dissembling. We both know that our distaste for each other is unmitigated. Consequently, you will understand the humiliation I feel at having to write you this letter. However, I am willing to endure that humiliation if it means obtaining your help, which gives you some clue as to how desperate I am. Imagine me kneeling and begging at your feet, if it pleases you. It is of no consequence to me. I do not value my dignity enough not to sacrifice it. I realize the absurdity of asking for help from one's enemy, and yet is it not also a sign of respect, a way of admitting one's inferiority? And I fully recognize my own: as you know I have always prided myself on my imagination. But now I need help from someone with a greater imagination than mine. And I know of none comparable to yours, George. It is as simple as that. If you help me, I will happily stop hating you. Even though I don't suppose that is much of an incentive. Bear in mind I will also owe you a favor, and, as you know, I am a millionaire now. That might be more of an incentive. If you help me, George, you may name your price. Any price. You have my word, George.

And why do I need your help? you must be wondering. Well, at the risk of rekindling your hatred of me, the matter relates to one of your other novels, this time *The War of the Worlds*. As your brilliant mind has no doubt already deduced, I have to re-create a Martian invasion. However, this time I assure you I am not at-tempting to prove anything to you, nor do I intend to profit from it. You must believe me. I no longer need either of those things. This time I am driven by something I need more than anything in the world, and without which I will die: love, George, the love of the most beautiful woman I have ever seen. If you have been in love you will understand what I am referring to. I daresay you will find it hard, perhaps impossible, to believe that a man like me can fall in love, yet if you met her it would seem strange to you if I had not. Ah, George, I was unable to resist her charms, and I assure you her immense fortune is not one of them, for as I told you, I have enough money to last several lifetimes. No, George, I am referring to her charming smile, her golden skin, the savage sweetness of her eyes, even the adorable way she twirls her parasol when she is nervous . . . No man could be immune to her beauty, even you.

But in order to have her, I must arrange for a cylinder to land on Horsell Common on August 1, and for a Martian to emerge from it, just like in your novel, George. And I don't know how! I have tried everything, but as I told you, my imagination has its limits. I need yours, George. Help me, please. If I pull it off, that woman will be my wife. And if that happens, I promise I shall no longer be your enemy, for Gilliam Murray will be finally laid to rest. Please, I beg you, I implore you, assist this lovesick soul.

Yours,

G. M.

Unbelievable! How could Murray have the effrontery to ask him to help reproduce the Martian invasion from his own novel? Did he honestly believe there was the remotest possibility that he would agree? That was too much to expect, even for one as presumptuous as Murray. He went to throw the letter away, but before doing so decided to show it to Jane, assuming she would be overcome by the same anger as he and that the two of them could fulminate to their hearts' delight against Murray's pride and ingenuousness, over a glass of wine, perhaps, as the sun set lazily behind the trees. But no. Jane had considered Murray's idea one of the most romantic gestures anyone could make and had even encouraged Wells to help him. People change, Bertie, she had said. You are a very inflexible person, but the rest of humanity is more malleable. And it is obvious Murray has changed. For the sake of love! Wells burst into a cynical laugh. For the sake of love! Murray couldn't have chosen a better argument with which to convince Jane of that dubious conversion from Hyde to Jekyll. If Wells deigned to reply, it would merely be to inform him that nothing could expunge the loathing he felt for Murray, much less that outpouring of sentimental drivel. But he had no desire to embroil himself once more in a contest that brought him only bad memories, and so in the end Wells had decided it was best not to reply at all, convinced that indifference would be the greatest insult he could inflict upon Murray.

Indifference . . . Perhaps that should have been his posture three years earlier when that upstart had asked for his opinion about the little novel he had written. As some readers will recall, at that time Murray had not yet become the famous Master of Time but was an aspiring novelist with more delusions of grandeur than genuine talent, who sought the approval of the man he considered one of England's greatest authors. And the fact is that Wells could have talked his way out of it with a few pronouncements as affable as they were vague. But instead he had opted for overrated honesty, not just because he didn't think that ill-tempered ogre deserved any efforts at dissimulation, but because Murray's whole being was clamoring for a dose of humility, which he himself had given Wells the wherewithal to administer. Who could resist such an invitation? Clearly not Wells, who with unnecessary brutality had told the poor aspiring author what he thought of his novel, curious to see his reaction, and had thus unwittingly thrown down a challenge that would ensnare the two men in an absurd duel for years to come. Murray's attempt at a novel was a naïve futuristic love story set in the year 2000, where automatons had taken over the Earth and only a small group of humans led by the brave Captain Shackleton had the courage to defy them. The plot was preposterous and Wells had no trouble finishing off his merciless dissection of it by arguing that the future it described was totally improbable, and the work therefore a futile, forgettable pile of nonsense. Imagination was a gift that should always be at the service of truth. Any fool could imagine impossible things, but only a true genius could imagine the infinite possibilities that reality offered, and clearly

Murray wasn't one of them. After that dressing-down, Murray had vowed to himself as he left Wells's house that he would show the author how wrong he was, and a few months later Murray's Time Travel had opened to the public, offering the inhabitants of the nineteenth century a chance to visit the future, which, to Wells's astonishment, was exactly as Murray had imagined it in his novel. And for two years afterward, Wells had been subjected to that humiliation, receiving regular invitations from an increasingly wealthy, powerful, and (if there was any truth in the rumors circulating in the stevedores' taverns) dangerous Murray, to embark on one of his expeditions to the *improbable* future. Until one day the Master of Time decided to stage his own death, and at last Wells was able to breathe easily and try to pretend that the whole thing had been a bad dream.

But then, when he had almost succeeded, Murray's ridiculous letter had arrived in his mailbox. And although he hadn't replied to it, he hadn't thrown it away either. It was too beautiful. He would occasionally slip it out from between the pages of the book where he kept it hidden and relish the bit where Murray acknowledged his superiority. Although Wells had never doubted that truth, he nevertheless delighted in the fact that Murray had finally accepted it. The last time he had read the letter was that very morning, the last day Murray had in which to fulfill his beloved's wish. As Wells put the kettle on, he imagined Murray's frustration when he realized that, despite all his money, he had failed to reproduce a Martian invasion and that some things were beyond even *his* reach. And that thought both reassured and pleased Wells, for imagination was a sublime gift that raised man above the level of animals, opened the doors to awareness, to the evolution and advancement of the human race, and consequently should be protected from crass impersonators, talentless upstarts, entrepreneurs, and above all lovers exposing themselves to public ridicule.

It was then that Clayton knocked on his door to inform him that a Martian cylinder had appeared on Horsell Common. And, cursing Murray for being unable to admit defeat, Wells climbed aboard the inspector's carriage. What else could he have done? After all, if a Martian cylinder identical to the one he had described in his novel had landed on Horsell Common, it was only logical that Scotland Yard would require him to go there. What Wells found less logical was that the inspector seemed to believe this might be a genuine Martian invasion, possibly orchestrated by the author himself through his novel. Wells was obliged to show the inspector Murray's letter to persuade him that the whole thing was a hoax cooked up by the ex–Master of Time, who was given to this sort of prank. But, to Wells's surprise, the inspector had tucked the letter away in his jacket pocket. He confessed that whilst this opened up a whole new perspective on the matter, it was nevertheless the job of Scotland Yard's Special Branch to leave no stone unturned, and he could not rule out the possibility that Wells himself had written the letter and was hindering the investigation by pointing the finger at a dead man. Wells had been rendered speechless by such a wild assertion, and the two men had spent the remainder of the journey in strained silence.

"It is absurd of you to think that I might be in league with Martians simply because I wrote a novel announcing their arrival!" he had protested at last, unable to contain his rage.

"As absurd as someone re-creating a Martian invasion to win a lady's heart" had been the inspector's disdainful reply.

You see, Wells now thought to himself, glancing away from Murray's stupid steaming hat and grinning smugly at the inspector: apparently someone had orchestrated all this *precisely* to steal the love of a lady. Clayton clearly owed him an apology, and yet he seemed unwilling to do so.

"So the Master of Time is alive and kicking . . . ," he said simply. Wells had grown weary of telling him that repeatedly on the way there.

The author rolled his eyes and raised his hands, as though expecting a pair of doves to land on them. No, Gilliam Murray hadn't died. The brute who had stepped out of the hot-air balloon was certainly he— although Wells had to admit with all the weight he had lost, and that red beard obscuring his face, not to mention his ridiculous outfit, few would have recognized him. But those sly animal eyes capable of concealing anything, like a magician's hat, had not changed. And Wells noticed the old animosity he felt for Murray stirring inside him. There he was, making a mockery of him again, turning his latest novel into a vulgar fairground attraction, this time to further his romantic interests. And there was Wells, dragged out of his house halfway through his cup of tea, his shoes caked in mud, forced to witness Murray's pantomime in the midst of a deafening crowd—drawn as always by the magnetism of that man who snared everything in his path—and, furthermore, to defend himself against charges of espionage and treason on a planetary level. Would he never be rid of Murray? Would their lives be forever joined until one of them died, untangling the infuriating knot?

"Interesting, most interesting," he heard Clayton reflect aloud, his eyes glued to the spectacle. "This resurrection is very timely, as I happen to have a few unanswered questions I'd like to put to Mr. Murray concerning his business, questions that are no doubt still pertinent. A great many questions, in fact."

Wells looked in astonishment at Clayton, whose lips had twisted into a malevolent smile as he doubtless anticipated the moment when the Master of Time would finally be at his mercy, sitting in the interrogation room, forced to answer all his questions.

"I congratulate you on your good fortune, Inspector Clayton," Wells remarked disdainfully. "And since the absence of any Martians clears me of all suspicion, I beg you to excuse me, but I have far more important things to do than stand around waiting for the dénouement of this ridiculous melodrama."

Clayton nodded absentmindedly, hypnotized by the spectacle, yet Wells did not stir either. It was difficult for them to take their eyes off the sight unfolding before them. The crowd had begun to separate until a human corridor opened between Murray and the charming young lady with the parasol, doubtless the one for whom Murray had organized the whole charade. And as Wells looked at her more closely, he had to admit that, if anything, Murray's description of her in his letter did not do her justice. The girl was astonishingly beautiful: she possessed the delicate lightness of a soap bubble, her skin seemed to be coated in gold, and her eyes, despite being wide-open with astonishment, expressed that perfect blend of charm and high-spiritedness capable of turning any man's head. For a few seemingly eternal moments, Wells watched her remain motionless, nervously twirling her parasol, while at the other end of the corridor formed by the hushed crowd, Murray's bow tie was also rotating. It was the only part of him that was moving, for the man appeared frozen, arms flung open, the hat he had just removed clasped in one hand, a broad grin on his face, waiting, like a suspended jellyfish, for Emma to breathe life into him with a loving eye. But that wouldn't happen, Wells thought to himself, convinced the girl would turn on her heel and go back the way she had come, leaving Murray with his steaming hat and his rotating bow tie in the midst of the admiring crowd. What else could she do? Murray had failed to reproduce the invasion, no matter how hard he tried to make up for it with this gaudy display. And Emma Harlow seemed too intelligent to let herself be bamboozled by all that. But then, to Wells's astonishment, a smile began to flutter on the girl's lips, and although at first she tried to resist, she finally gave a charming giggle. A sigh of delight instantly spread through the crowd. Deflated, Wells watched the girl walk toward Murray amid the applause of the public, and he decided that he had seen enough.

He moved away from the throng, visibly annoyed, and went in search of a carriage that would take him back to Worcester Park, to the novel he was currently working on, and to that cup of tea abandoned on the kitchen table. To that ordinary, everyday life of his, so distant from the romantic nonsense Murray was accustomed to indulging in. Wells shook his head. He wished the couple all the luck in the world, he thought with disdain. The girl would certainly need it if she ended up married to that fellow. She couldn't be very intelligent, after all, if she believed a sense of humor was a sound enough basis for a relationship, he told himself as a voice in his head asked him how long it was since he had last made Jane laugh like that.

In any event, the couple's happiness would be short-lived, because the intrepid Inspector Clayton was intent on reopening the investigation into Murray's Time Travel. Finally someone was going to do what he himself had so long been hoping for. He gave a weary sigh, eager to get home as soon as possible and tell Jane everything that had happened so she could work her magic, bring her commonsense irony to bear on the matter, play down its importance, and invite him to view things in perspective, enabling him finally to store it somewhere in his head where it wouldn't importune him.

Wells looked toward the hill where the carriages were parked, trying to work out how far he had to walk, when all of a sudden a distant figure caught his attention. His crooked posture suggested an elderly gentleman, and although he was too far away for Wells to see his face, he had the impression that the stranger was observing him with equal interest. Suddenly, an intense feeling of unease overwhelmed him, and he had to stop and double over, as though he were about to be sick. His stomach was churning, and his heart felt heavy with grief. He hadn't experienced that feeling for so long . . . why now? All at once, the sensation vanished as suddenly as it had appeared, leaving behind only a vague, lingering melancholy, and no answers. When he looked up toward the hill again, he saw that the figure of the old man had also disappeared.

11

WHEN WELLS ARRIVED HOME, IRRITATED AND exhausted, Jane had just returned from London, where she had been lunching with the Garfields. He immediately launched into an account of the shameful spectacle he had been forced to witness on Horsell Common, describing to Jane each of the surprises that had emerged from the cylinder, in a tone of voice that made it obvious how farcical he had found the whole thing. And yet, as he spoke, Jane's face began to light up more and more, until, to his astonishment, he realized that Murray's amorous gesture thrilled his wife the way few things ever had. She opined that it was the most romantic thing a man could do for a woman, and this unreserved approval, rather than fueling his jealousy, depressed Wells, because it implied that his small acts of love were trifling in comparison. He hadn't stepped out of a hot-air balloon in order to win her heart. No, he hadn't. But what merit or effort did that entail, besides the logistics? Wells had won Jane's heart on their long walks to Charing Cross station, when he had charmed her with words, simply with who he was, without the need to employ fakirs and acrobats or wear a steaming hat. He had chosen the more arduous route, using only his amusing, enveloping oratory. In other words, he hadn't resorted to trickery. But Jane clearly didn't see it that way. In her eyes, not only had Murray organized that whole extravaganza down to the very last detail, but he had risked public ridicule to win that woman's heart. Would Wells have been capable of doing as much for her? Of course not, so he should start ridding himself of those old resentments, because he was building up so much hatred he scarcely had anyplace left for happiness, or even the simplest pleasures in life.

With that, she marched out of the little room and slammed the door behind her, leaving Wells by himself, high and dry. He hated it when Jane cut short their disagreements by going off in a huff to some other part of the house, not so much because it left him in mid-sentence, but because it prevented them from resolving things there and then, obliging him to argue in installments. He slumped into a chair, not yet in the mood to chase her around from room to room. Forget your old resentments, she had said, the same as when he showed her Murray's letter. Wells hadn't brought the subject up again since that fateful day, and as his wife hadn't either, he assumed she had ended up forgetting about it. But perhaps Jane hadn't forgotten about it at all, perhaps she was only pretending in order to keep the peace, and, like the corpse one thinks one has disposed of at the bottom of a lake, the matter had unexpectedly risen to the surface. Wells gave a sigh. Jane never ceased to surprise him. And yet he held no mystery for her, or so she never tired of telling him. It was as if he were transparent, his heart, digestive tract, liver, and other vital organs exposed to her scrutiny. In fact, his wife took advantage of any situation to come up with fresh theories about the workings of what she affectionately referred to as "the Wells specimen."

Only last week, she had shared another of these revelations with him. It could happen anywhere; Wells had no way of knowing. On that occasion, they were dining at a restaurant in Holborn, and for almost ten minutes Wells had been extolling the virtues of the wine they were drinking, without being able to persuade Jane to agree with him. She had been content to smile every now and then as she listened to her husband's rhapsody, more attentive to the ambience of the place than to his praise. And so Wells, who couldn't bear his wife to keep her opinions to herself, much less about something he had deemed excellent, was obliged to ask her directly if she disagreed with his opinion. Jane sighed, contemplating her husband for a few moments, as though considering whether to tell him what she thought or let it pass. At last, she shrugged, and entrusted herself to fate.

"The wine isn't bad, Bertie. But I don't think it as excellent as you maintain. Moreover, I would venture to say nor do you."

Jane's last pronouncement threw Wells, who insisted even more stubbornly on how pleasurable he found the wine, on how velvety it was as it slipped down his throat, the aftertaste it left in his mouth of a forest at dawn, and so on. Jane let him talk, making an irritating clucking sound with her tongue that succeeded in gradually dampening Wells's exalted speech. Finally, rather peevishly, he decided to listen to what his wife had to say. And Jane spoke with the authority conferred upon her by the many similar revelations she had made in the past.

"It isn't the wine itself you find excellent," she explained, smiling the way she always did when she began analyzing her husband, "but rather the situation."

And, with a sweep of her hand, she invited Wells to consider their surroundings. They were in a restaurant, which, as advertised, successfully combined the charm of a Parisian bistro with the silence and orderliness essential to the English way of life. In addition, there were few customers that evening, so the background conversation, far from being a nuisance, created a pleasant murmur. They had been seated at a corner table, from which they were able to observe their fellow diners discreetly from a distance. The waiter who had brought them the menu had even recognized Wells and praised his latest novel. The wine was served at the perfect temperature, in an elegant, tall-stemmed glass that was perfectly adapted to his hand and as light as a bubble. The orchestra was playing mellow music, he had enjoyed a productive day's work . . . need she go on?

"Any decent wine would taste excellent to you under these circumstances, Bertie. But you would have found the same wine unremarkable, and possibly downright bad, if they had given us a table beside the door and we had been forced to sit in a cold draft every time someone came in or left. Or if the waiter hadn't been so friendly, or if the lighting was too dim or too bright, or if . . ."

"All right, all right. But isn't that the same for everybody?" he had protested, rather halfheartedly, as though it were a formality he had to go through before yielding to Jane's new theory.

She shook her head.

"Nobody is as impressionable as you, Bertie. Nobody."

And Wells observed his habitual thoughtful silence following one of his wife's revelations. Then Jane began browsing through the menu, pretending to choose between the beef and the salmon, letting Wells muse at his leisure, aware that he was doing what he always did after she pronounced one of her judgments: recalling other incidents in his life to see whether that theory applied. When, after a few minutes, Wells saw the pointlessness of the exercise, he grudgingly accepted that she was right. And as they headed for home, he wondered whether Jane wasn't afraid that their love might be built on something as fragile as the random circumstances that had held sway the day they had met: the good humor with which he imparted his lecture, the black dress she wore because she was mourning her father's recent death, the light filtering through the window and setting her hair aflame, the boredom of the other students, which allowed the two of them to speak without feeling they were being watched . . . Perhaps if it had been raining that day, and he had been in a bad mood, or she had been wearing a different dress that didn't make her look so vulnerable, that dinner might never have taken place. But in the end what did it matter? he thought. The circumstances had been propitious, and, whether they liked it or not, here they were, happily together.

The sitting room door opened again, breaking off Wells's reflections, and from his armchair he saw Jane walk in holding the pruning shears, then take her straw hat from the stand. After putting it on, she left the room, giving him a stern look, as if it vexed her to see him slumped in an armchair instead of training a troupe of chimpanzees to dance for her. Whenever they quarreled, Jane would go out into the garden and vent her fury on the defenseless rosebushes, and for days the fragrance of freshly cut roses would fill the house. It was a smell Wells couldn't help associating with their squabbles, but also with their reconciliations, for sooner or later he would go to her with a submissive smile, the first of many steps he would have to take before Jane finally agreed to sign a peace treaty, which she always did. It was an unspoken rule that, by the time the roses wilted, Wells would need to have patched things up between them. And if out of apathy or indifference he allowed that deadline to expire, he might as well start packing his bags.

Before commencing the process, Wells couldn't help wondering once again if it was worth all the effort for a marriage he found increasingly stifling. Recently, for example, he had noticed within him the stirrings of desire for other women, for the newness of unknown bodies, for embarking anew on the forgotten adventure of courtship, of seducing a woman who wasn't yet aware of all his little foibles. He had felt guilty to begin with, but he soon realized that this intense desire did not affect the love he felt for Jane. He had no doubt that she was the woman with whom he wanted to end his days. It had taken them almost three years to get to know each other, and the idea of forging a similarly deep bond with another woman was unthinkable. And so, far from betraying Jane by experimenting with his desire, Wells felt he was betraying himself by trying to suppress it, advocating by his irreproachable behavior a virtue and honesty to which he did not subscribe. Whose bright idea had it been to force man into monogamy when it was so obviously not natural to him? Wells had needs his marriage couldn't satisfy. Perhaps he should speak to Jane about all this, he thought, explain to her that his soul craved more emotions than she alone could provide, and that if she allowed him to indulge in an occasional extramarital affair, he would promise never to fall in love and only maintain playful, fleeting dalliances that posed no threat to their marriage—something he preferred, in the end, for it would free him from the need to behave in the romantic fashion Jane was always complaining he lacked. Jane would remain the guiding light of his life, while those future lovers would only ever attain the pitiful status of stimulants, which as the years went by would become increasingly necessary if he didn't want the slow but sure road to decrepitude to plunge him into depression. However, no matter how reasonable that explanation seemed to him, he doubted very much whether his wife would understand or agree to a new routine whereby his controlled dalliances would be allowed to act as an aid to their marriage.

Wells rose from his chair and, eager for life to return to normal, went to find Jane and beg her forgiveness, which she conceded at about midnight. However, although on this occasion Jane appeared to have forgotten Wells's disappointing way of showing his love for her, or was pretending she had for the sake of keeping the peace, he was unable to. Not because of any grudge he bore, but because Murray was preventing him. In the days that followed, there wasn't a single newspaper in the land that didn't contain some sycophantic reference to his extraordinary, marvelous exploit, or a men's club where his audacity or daring was not the subject of a passionate debate. From the moment Murray made his unusual request for Emma Harlow's hand on Horsell Common, the couple had become the talk of the town. Hundreds of people with miserable lives contemplated them with adulation, happy that someone could achieve their dreams for them. Wells tried his best to avoid the astonishing display of public devotion toward Murray and succeeded for a while by avoiding newspapers and society gatherings.

But his luck could not last indefinitely, and two months later the two men's paths crossed at the opera. Wells had taken Jane to see *Faust* at the Royal Opera House and was comfortably ensconced in his seat, ready to enjoy that moment when all the circumstances seemed to coincide favorably (the chair was comfortable, he was close enough to the stage not to have to strain his eyes, he admired Goethe's work, the acoustics were excellent . . .), when all at once a disruptive element appeared. There was a general murmur, and people began to turn their opera glasses away from the stage toward one of the boxes, which Montgomery Gilmore had just entered, accompanied by his fiancée and her aunt. Realizing all eyes were upon them, Gilmore gave a magnanimous salute worthy of a Roman emperor, and motioned to Emma to curtsey gracefully, under the disapproving gaze of her aunt, that formidable-looking grande dame. A burst of enthusiastic applause rose from the audience. It couldn't be denied that happiness seemed to suit the couple down to the ground, and yet Wells refused to join in the noisy ovation. He remained with his arms folded, watching Jane applaud, and in doing so making it very clear that their difference of opinion over the matter would remain forever irreconcilable.

Once the curtain went up, Wells did his best to enjoy the opera; but, as Jane had predicted, the destabilizing factor of Murray's presence impeded him from doing so. He shifted in his seat, suddenly unable to get comfortable, while an almost visceral loathing for the genre began to take hold of him. He closed his eyes, blacking out the stage where the soprano was trying to decide whether an elegant Faust truly loved her. Wells opened his eyes and was preparing to close them again when Jane noticed the face he was pulling. She placed her hand gently on his, giving him a smile of encouragement, as if to say, Ignore this intrusion, Bertie. Enjoy the performance, and put all other thoughts out of your mind. And Wells let out a sigh. Very well, he would try. He wasn't going to let Murray's presence spoil his evening. He attempted to focus on the stage, where Faust, in a plumed hat and tight-fitting purple doublet, was walking in circles around Marguerite. But the sound of whispering a few rows behind immediately distracted him. What a beautiful young woman, he heard someone comment with admiration. Yes, and they say he asked for her hand by reproducing the novel of some chap called Geoffrey Wesley. Wells had to grit his teeth to prevent himself from uttering an oath. How long before that stupid opera finished?

OUTSIDE, ONE OF THOSE drizzles typical of London had set in where most of the water seems suspended in the air, unable to penetrate it. When the operagoers stepped out of the theater, they had the impression of plunging into an enormous fish tank. The footmen, splendid in their red and gold uniforms, strove to bring some kind of order to the chaotic procession of carriages slowly approaching the entrance to the Royal Opera House. The ladies sent their male companions—husbands or beaux—on the heroic mission of rousing their drivers to vie with the other carriages while they sought shelter beneath the portico, forming into selective groups and exchanging pleasantries about the opera, although most of them had given it but a fleeting glance. All anyone wanted was to arrive home as quickly as possible, take off their damp coats, asphyxiating corsets, and excruciating shoes, and put their aching feet up in front of the fire. And yet they all smiled politely, as if they wouldn't want to be anywhere else. In many ways it made far more interesting viewing than the performance they had seen in the theater.

One of the men exposed to the rain was Wells, who was doing his best to capture the attention of the nearest footman by tapping him gently on the shoulder, but to no avail, as the man was too busy barking at the sleepy coachmen. Tired of being jostled and apologized to by his male companions, Wells decided to return to the portico, where he had left Jane talking to an elderly couple called Stamford. Discreetly concealed behind one of the columns, Wells surveyed the sea of top hats and elaborate bonnets in search of Jane's modest hat decorated with pale pink roses, scarcely looking up for fear his and Murray's eyes might cross. Fortunately, there was no sign of his enormous frame protruding from the crowd like a bookmark. Perhaps he was one of the lucky ones who had found a carriage, Wells thought hopefully; or, true to his old habit of taking what did not belong to him, perhaps he had appropriated someone else's. He glimpsed Jane's chestnut hair a few yards away and walked over to her with a feeling of relief, but scarcely had he taken a few steps than a huge paw landed on his shoulder, threatening to hammer him into the ground.

"Damn it, George, I never thought I'd find you in this crowd!"

Wells turned around with exaggerated caution. And there was Murray. Standing in front of him. The late Master of Time. Smiling at him with the warm enthusiasm of one who has just bumped into a childhood friend.

"George!" he exclaimed again, clapping Wells repeatedly on the shoulder. "What a wonderful coincidence! Oh, no, please don't say a word: you must think me terribly rude, and you are quite right." Murray lowered his head in a gesture of remorse. "I'm a bounder, I know. Not a word of thanks during all this time, after what you did for me . . . Although I am not lying when I say I have thought of writing to you many times!"

Wells looked at Murray with the blank expression of a roast suckling pig, somewhat dampening his enthusiasm.

"Oh, come now, are you annoyed with me? Well, I suppose you have every right to be. What can I say in my defense? Only that during the past few months I have been floating on a cloud, that the Earth and everyone on it seems as remote and unreal to me as in a dream. But what can I say about love that you couldn't express far more poetically than I? Oh, George, George . . ." Murray seized Wells by both shoulders as if he were going to wring him out like a dishcloth, gazing into his eyes with such tenderness, Wells was afraid Murray's euphoria might end in an embrace. "But I shan't let you go on being annoyed! Why, I was going to write to you tomorrow to invite you to the reception I am giving next month at my residence, and I can tell you now that no excuse in the world is good enough to justify your not coming. However, it seems that fate has brought us together this evening and I am able to give you the wonderful news in person. Do you have any idea what I'm referring to?"

Wells could only shake his head feebly, dizzied by the frantic tirade of Murray, who was dragging out the suspense like a skilled conjuror.

"The charming Miss Harlow and myself . . . we are to be married!"

Murray smiled triumphantly, anticipating the other man's response. Until then, Wells had listened to Murray's prattle with a mixture of wonder and dread, like someone hearing a magic tree talk, but now he felt an age-old fury stirring inside. Wells took a step toward him.

"What are you playing at, Murray?" he hissed, almost choking with rage. "What the devil are you—"

But Murray didn't let him finish. He seized Wells by the arm and dragged him behind the column farthest from the crowd.

"Are you crazy, George?" he whispered dramatically, "You called me by my real name!"

"Let go of me, damn you!" Wells roared. "What do you think you're doing? And what the devil do you expect me to call you?"

Murray looked bewildered.

"You know perfectly well, George! Everyone calls me Montgomery Gilmore now. "

"Oh, yes, I know. But not me," Wells hissed between gritted teeth. "I know perfectly well who you are and what you're capable of, *Gilliam Murray*."

"Be quiet, George, I implore you!" the other man pleaded. "Emma might come over here at any moment and—"

Wells looked at him aghast.

"You mean to tell me even your betrothed doesn't know who you really are?"

"I—I . . . ," Murray stammered. "I haven't gotten round to telling her yet, but I fully intend to do so . . . Of course I do! I just have to find the right moment . . ."

"The right moment," repeated Wells sarcastically. "Perhaps you'll find it when she goes to visit you in jail. Assuming that she does, naturally."

Murray narrowed his eyes.

"What are you insinuating?" he asked menacingly.

Wells recoiled slightly.

"Oh, nothing."

"Do you know something about that accursed inspector who won't leave me in peace?" whispered Murray, seizing Wells's arm again. "Of course you do. I saw you with him when I stepped out of the balloon."

"Let go of me," Wells said firmly, trying to disguise the fear he felt at that flash of violence in Murray's eyes, which seemed to have risen to the surface from the depths of the old Gilliam. He was afraid now that the conversation would end in something less delicate than an embrace. "I said let—"

"You told him who I was, didn't you?" Murray interjected, clasping Wells's arm more tightly.

"Yes, damn it!" muttered Wells, torn between fear and rage. "I was forced to show him your letter. What choice did I have? He showed up at my house accusing me of having unleashed a Martian invasion. And for the love of God, Gilliam, if you wanted to go on pretending you were dead, do you really think the best way of doing it was to create a spectacle like that on Horsell Common?"

Murray remained silent, apparently engaged in some kind of inner struggle. Then he gazed with curiosity at his own hand clutching Wells's arm, almost as if it belonged to someone else. He instantly relaxed his grip, disgusted by his own gesture.

"Forgive me, George, I didn't mean to hurt you . . ." He rubbed his hands over his face, trying to take hold of himself. "I'm at my wit's end; that detective is driving me crazy, you know?" He contemplated Wells and screwed up his face. "Did Scotland Yard honestly think you had planned a Martian invasion? And was that long-legged pompous ass supposed to save us all? I'd like to see him fight a real Martian invasion . . . That pain in the neck is intent on investigating my old company, and he won't stop badgering me with questions . . . But have no fear. He won't find anything, because I have nothing to hide. And as far as I know, you can't be sent to prison for pretending to be dead, can you? What really worries me is that he is sparking rumors, and I couldn't bear any of them to reach Emma before I have a chance to tell her myself. Luckily, so far I've managed to hush them up."

"I can imagine how you went about it," Wells hissed with as much contempt as he could muster, rubbing his sore arm.

"Oh, no, George. That's not what I meant at all. I don't do that kind of thing anymore. As I told you in my letter, I'm a changed man. Money will hush most people up, if not everyone, but that detective seems immune to being bought off. He's like a dog with a bone. What the hell is he hoping to find?"

"The truth, I expect."

"The truth?" Murray smiled wistfully. "And what is the truth, George? Where is it written? There's nothing left of Murray's Time Travel except dust and cobwebs, because the hole into the future closed up."

"It closed up," Wells repeated. "But of course."

"That's right, George, it did. But you know perfectly well that the public, hungry for thrills, would never have accepted that. Which is why I decided to fake my own death, so that everyone would leave me in peace. And that's what I tried to explain to that detective friend of yours, but he doesn't believe a word I say."

"Can you blame him?" muttered Wells.

"What's the matter with you, George?" Murray sighed in dismay. "Why are you suddenly acting like a child? I don't understand! When you replied to my letter I thought that meant bygones would be bygones."

"What?" Wells looked at him in astonishment. "I never replied to your damnable letter."

"Of course you did," Murray said, bewildered.

"I tell you I didn't."

"Oh, come now, why deny it? It's true, you weren't exactly expansive, but at least you wrote back. You told me not to bother reproducing the Martian invasion, and that if I wanted to win Emma over, I should simply make her laugh."

Wells gave an incredulous snort.

"Have you lost your mind? Make her laugh? Why on earth would I advise you to do that?"

"I've no idea, George! But that's what you told me, and I followed your advice. That's why I put on that circus: to make Emma laugh. And it worked! It worked like a charm! You saw for yourself! Emma and I are in love and are going to be married, and all that happiness we owe in part to you, my friend." Trembling with emotion, Murray gazed into Wells's eyes. "And what else could I have concluded from your letter, other than that you had decided to bury the hatchet? But why are you trying to deny it now? Do you regret having written?"

"Of course not! I mean, I can't regret something *I never did*!"

"Bertie?"

The two men wheeled round. A few yards away, a woman in a hat with pale pink roses on it was gazing at them quizzically.

"Is something the matter, Bertie?" asked Jane, alarmed by the sudden silence that had descended between the two men. "I couldn't find you anywhere, and our coach is third in line . . . Are you all right?"

"Yes, Jane, I'm quite all right," he replied.

Wells scowled at Murray as he took his leave and walked over to his wife with the intention of taking her by the arm and leading her as far away as possible. But Murray bounded ahead of him. He planted himself in front of Jane and, before anyone could do anything, grasped her hand, and bowed.

"Mrs. Wells, allow me to introduce myself," he said, kissing her hand ceremoniously. "Montgomery Gilmore, at your service. My face might seem familiar to you. Perhaps I remind you of the man who went to your house a few years ago to ask your husband's advice about a novel he had written . . . However, let me assure you that you are mistaken: I am not that man. You have in front of you a new man, one redeemed by love. And in the name of that love, of which I declare myself utterly unworthy, I implore you to put in a good word for me with your stubborn husband."

Wells grunted. "It's time we were leaving, Jane!"

But his wife appeared not to hear him. She was gazing into Murray's eyes, her hand still clasped in his like a quivering bird. And she must have glimpsed something deep inside him, because, much to the despair of Wells, her lips spread in a gentle smile.

"You are quite right, Mr. . . . . Gilmore," she replied graciously. "Although this is the first time we meet, your face does seem familiar, but perhaps that is because your fame precedes you. I have heard much about you, not all of it good, I regret to say. However, I must tell you that the way you asked for your beloved's hand was the most beautiful, exciting, romantic gesture I have ever seen a man make to a woman."

"For goodness' sake, Jane!" Wells cried. "Have you gone mad? Why do you insist on calling him Gilmore when you know as well as I do that—"

"I call him by the name he used to introduce himself, Bertie."

"Enough!" Wells exploded. "This is the limit; we're going!"

He grabbed the arm of his wife, who managed to say good-bye to Murray with a fleeting, apologetic smile, and dragged her over to where the carriages were waiting at the curb. Murray blocked their way.

"George, I beg you, don't give me away," he said. "If you don't want to be my friend, very well, I understand. But please don't reveal my secret, at least not before I've spoken to Emma. I will reward you if—"

"Montgomery Gilmore!" a clear voice tinkled behind them. "Where on earth have you been hiding? All you had to do was inquire about our carriage. I trust you aren't thinking of hiring a hot-air balloon, for my aunt wouldn't like it."

Despite the playful tone in Emma's voice, the trio turned around with a start, like three conspirators caught in the act.

"Emma, my love!" Murray exclaimed, walking toward her with outstretched arms. "Where were you? I was worried sick. I was beginning to think you'd abandoned me!"

"Don't be silly! I'm the one who has spent the last fifteen minutes looking for you."

"Really? Why, I've been here all the time, chatting with my dear friends the Wellses," Murray replied, turning toward the couple with such a polished smile that Wells's gorge began to rise. "Mr. and Mrs. Wells, it is my honor to introduce you to my fiancée, Miss Emma Harlow. Darling, this is the author H. G. Wells and his charming wife."

"Mr. Wells! What a pleasure it is to meet you!" Emma exclaimed, pleasantly surprised. "I'm a great admirer of your work. I've read all your novels."

Wells kissed Emma's gracefully proffered hand, cursing Murray's aplomb and trying to suppress his rage. He would have liked nothing more than to unmask that impostor in front of the naïve young woman who had the misfortune to be betrothed to him. And yet, his sense of decorum, and above all his self-consciousness, far outweighed his sense of duty. But what if he dispensed with good manners and announced in a loud voice that Montgomery Gilmore was in fact Gilliam Murray, the deceased Master of Time? What face would Emma make then? Not to mention the obese lady clambering aboard her carriage clutching a miniature Pekinese to her ample bosom. Or the footman coming over to tell them their carriage was next in line, and the group of gentlemen next to them talking animatedly. Half of London society was crammed under the opera portico, jostling one another with genteel smiles. Wells was sure his revelation would provide them with a thrilling topic of conversation for the long, tedious winter season. And what could the all-powerful Murray do to stop him?

"Bertie, my dear, Miss Harlow asked you a question."

"What?"

Wells blinked, bewildered, but before he could apologize, he felt a painful cramp in his stomach. He couldn't help giving a drawn-out groan.

"Bertie, whatever is the matter?" Jane was alarmed.

Suddenly pale, Wells pulled out his handkerchief and wiped away the sweat glistening on his brow, wondering whether he might be suffering a sudden attack of indigestion.

"Are you feeling all right, Mr. Wells?" he heard Emma inquire.

"Yes, yes, I'm quite all right. It's just, er . . . my shoes are pinching me," he murmured, trying to straighten up. "Forgive me, Miss Harlow, what were you saying?"

"Oh, just that Monty told me you might not be able to come to the reception were are holding next month, and I wanted to know if there is any way I could change your minds. I am very persuasive when I want to be."

"Emma, my dear," Murray hurriedly intervened, "I'm sure that George and his charming wife must have a very good reason not to—"

"You're no doubt right, dear. But, as you must know by now, a good reason is something your future wife cannot help objecting to," replied the girl, smiling at the couple with the easy charm of someone used to getting her own way. "You see, Mr. Wells, as I'm sure you know, your latest novel played a pivotal, dare I say decisive, role in our romance," she declared, grinning at Murray. "Besides, Monty professes a boundless admiration for you. And as if that weren't enough, I am aware that the two of you enjoy a degree of friendship, about which, incidentally, my unforthcoming fiancé has told me next to nothing. Not that this worries me, for I feel sure I shall obtain more information from your charming wife. And so, as you can see, Mr. Wells, you and Mrs. Wells absolutely have to come to our ball."

Emma's beaming smile faded somewhat when she saw that Wells was no longer listening to her but was absorbed in contemplating something behind her. The young lady's exquisite manners prevented her from turning round, so she couldn't discover what it was the author was observing so intently. However, I can, and I have no qualms about telling you: Wells was staring at the back of one of the gentlemen who, having separated himself discreetly from his group, was almost propped against Murray's broad back, as if he were trying to listen in on their conversation. And the sight of those slightly sloping shoulders had aroused in Wells a strange feeling of unease, a profound melancholy that was as familiar as it was disturbing. Emma gave her fiancé a sidelong glance, to which he responded with a shrug.

"Miss Harlow," said Jane, who, despite the distress her husband's odd behavior was causing her, managed to sound quite calm, "George and I are very grateful for your kind interest, and I assure you we will do our utmost to comply with your wish—"

"I'm sorry, my dear, but I don't think we can do so," Wells cut in. Due to his malaise, his words sounded too abrupt to him, and, looking straight at the astonished young woman, he added in a more civil tone: "Please accept our apologies, Miss Harlow."

"Your carriage is waiting, sir," one of the footmen informed Wells. "Please follow me."

"Marvelous, marvelous!" declared Murray, visibly relieved. "What luck, George, there's your carriage. At last you can take the weight off those feet of yours. That's what I call a proper coachman. They don't make them like that anymore. You must give me the name of the agency he comes from, but not that of your shoemaker. You can't imagine the trouble I'm having with coachmen at the moment! My current one is a half-witted drunkard who spends all day boozing. And judging by the time he's taking, I'll wager he's at it again this evening. I can't even see the accursed carriage at the back of the queue. Well, it won't be the first time he leaves me high and dry, but by Jove it'll be the last! I shall dismiss him this very night. But hurry, George, get your skates on; don't make your charming wife stand around in this awful drizzle." Murray took Jane's hand and in his agitation kissed it repeatedly. Then he shook his hands at the couple, like an affectionate parent urging them on. "Don't stand on ceremony; get into your carriage. It's been a pleasure seeing you, George, as always." He made as if to clap Wells on the back but appeared to think better of it, and his hand made a vague gesture in the air. "Ah, and don't worry about the reception, you are excused. Emma and I understand that a famous author like you must have a hundred pressing engagements, isn't that right, darling?"

But before Emma had a chance to protest, various strange events began to occur in rapid succession: the carriage in which the stout old lady with the diminutive Pekinese was traveling pulled up short before leaving the rank, and its horses began prancing and snorting as they grew increasingly jumpy; almost at once, the strange anxiety that had taken hold of Wells vanished as if by magic, and he instinctively looked about for the gentleman who had been shielded by Murray's back. He caught sight of him scuttling round the corner of the building with the unsteady gait of an elderly man. Then the Pekinese began to bark uncontrollably, and, seemingly infected by the commotion, all the horses in the rank started to whinny and buck violently as the coachmen struggled unsuccessfully to calm them. All at once, before anyone could understand what was happening, the little dog leapt out of the carriage window and, seized by the folly that typifies that breed in moments of panic, went straight for the horses' legs, yapping ferociously and trying to bite anything that came near it. The dog's owner, her head poking out of the window, called it with strident little cries as she tried to open the door, but her attempts were thwarted by the sharp jolts the horses were giving the carriage. Then, seeing the distraught Pekinese venture into the deadly labyrinth of horses' legs, Jane tried to catch it before it was trampled.

Just then several people saw an incredibly tall man, wrapped in a long dark cloak and wearing a broad-brimmed hat, emerge from the shadows at the far end of the street. The mysterious figure stood still for a moment in the pool of light cast by one of the streetlamps before hurtling toward the portico. Those who had seen the figure would later describe to their friends how terrifying the image was, for the giant had been running impossibly fast, his cloak billowing menacingly behind him, and he was carrying a peculiar cane whose handle bore an eight-pointed star that shimmered like a magic charm. His feet, shod in heavy, studded black boots, made the ground reverberate at his approach. However, our friends, busy trying to rescue the Pekinese, did not notice the stranger until he passed through them like a whirlwind. Wells received a blow that sent him reeling. When he finally managed to regain his footing, still slightly giddy from the encounter, he glimpsed the figure as it disappeared round the same corner where the old man had fled moments before. All at once, a horrified uproar made him turn back toward the crowd. There, seemingly suspended in the streetlamp's amber glow, a ghastly tableau presented itself to his astonished eyes: Emma's face was twisted in a grimace of horror, the stout lady was gripping the rim of the carriage window with her fat fingers as she leaned out, the horses had reared up on their hind legs like majestic statues, and below them, at the mercy of their hooves, Jane, his Jane, lay sprawled on the ground. For what seemed like an eternal moment, Wells contemplated his wife lying there about to be trampled, as if he were studying the work of some heartless painter, feeling as if he might spend the rest of his life examining its gruesome details. Then a wave of fear sucked the air from his lungs and his soul from his body, and time breathed life back into the scene. Before Wells could move, a bulky figure swept past him and scooped Jane up like a force of Nature, snatching her from beneath the animals' hooves only seconds before they pounded the cobblestones.

When Wells finally managed to make his legs obey him, he ran over to his wife, with Emma close behind. Jane was still on the ground, protected by Murray's huge frame. Several men had grabbed the reins and were trying to steer the horses away from them, although the animals appeared to have calmed down miraculously, as had the Pekinese, which, after its display of bravura, had returned to its mistress's soft bosom. Wells and Emma knelt beside their respective companions, still shocked by what they had witnessed. Murray raised his head, and only when he was sure they were completely safe did he move away from Jane, freeing her from the makeshift shield of his body. The young woman's eyes were tight shut.

"Mrs. Wells, Jane . . . ," he whispered gently. "Are you all right?"

She nodded, slightly dazed, and then glanced about for her husband's face.

"Oh, B-Bertie, I was so afraid," she stammered. "The horses reared up, that man in the cloak pushed me, I lost my balance and fell right under . . . Oh, God, I thought they were going to—"

"Don't think about it, dear. You're safe now. It's all over."

They embraced tearfully while, next to them, Murray and Emma did the same, and the crowd that had gathered around them applauded excitedly. Jane's cheeks were wet with tears, and through her disheveled locks Wells's eyes met Murray's. Murray smiled.

"You damned fool," muttered Wells, "I don't know how you always succeed in stealing the limelight."

Murray gave a hearty laugh, beaming with happiness. And slowly the four of them, still shaking, rose to their feet, aided by the now solicitous footmen. As they brushed off their clothes, listening to the crowd congratulating Murray, Wells noticed Jane gesturing to him discreetly. No more than a slight bob of the head and a fleeting look, but he understood. He nodded with a sigh and turned toward Murray.

"Well, er . . . I don't think even I can find the suitable words to thank you for what you did this evening, so at least allow me to offer you and your fiancée a ride in our carriage, since your coachman seems to have left you high and dry, which in my opinion shows good judgment . . ." A discreet nudge in the ribs from Jane dissuaded Wells from continuing that line of thought. "Er, yes, allow us to accompany you to your respective residences. I am sure that some words of thanks will come to me on the way . . ."

The offer was graciously accepted, and the four of them walked toward Wells's carriage, the two men receiving the odd clap on the shoulder from the crowd. They located Emma's aunt, who had devoted the past half hour to the pleasurable pastime of criticizing her niece's insufferable fiancé to her friends, completely oblivious to what had been happening behind her back. The old lady screwed up her face as she climbed into the carriage, like someone entering a pigsty. Only when the three ladies had sat down did the men prepare to climb aboard as well. Murray smiled politely and stepped aside to let Wells pass.

"You first, George."

Wells smiled back sardonically and, stepping aside, replied, "No, please, you first. I'd rather not turn my back on you . . . Monty."

12

*I*S ONE OBLIGED TO BECOME THE FRIEND OF someone who saves the life of your spouse? What if that person is your fiercest enemy? These questions tormented Wells for weeks after that night at the opera, which he was having difficulty describing because of the changes in mood he had experienced that night. Jane kept insisting he thank Murray—Monty, as she called him—for saving her life. Shouldn't courtesy transcend resentment? Wells nodded glumly, like a child attempting to digest some grown-up truth, but was content to remain stubbornly silent until Jane stopped nagging him, and he assumed his passive resistance had finally won out over his wife's eagerness to be courteous. But again he was mistaken, because one morning, without any warning, he heard Jane say from the kitchen that Monty and his fiancée were coming to lunch that day.

The Wellses had moved to Sandgate, where the fresh air would be more beneficial to Wells's fragile health, and had rented Beach Cottage, which was proving less permanent than they had hoped, for it was too close to the sea and in stormy weather the waves would break over the roof. Nonetheless, at noon on that day, a coach with a pompous "G" on the door drew up at that cottage. Murray's new coachman, an old fellow who moved slowly, opened the carriage door, and Murray and his fiancée emerged, radiant and smiling, anticipating a pleasant day in the company of their new friends, the Wellses. Needless to say, the reception they got from Wells was rather frosty, but Jane, who had no intention of allowing her husband to spoil the lunch she had so lovingly prepared behind his back, took the couple by the arm and led them into the garden and began pointing out the virtues of the place. Disgruntled, Wells stayed behind with the coachman, who gave him an incongruously meaningful smile. Suddenly, Wells felt an overwhelming desire to cry—not to shed a few quiet tears, but to fill the oceans, because a deep melancholy had begun gnawing at his insides. Taken aback by that violent unhappiness, which not even Murray's presence could explain, Wells went back inside the house, afraid he would end up weeping on the coachman's shoulder. Once in the dining room, he thought it opportune to spend a few moments mulling over the sporadic attacks of melancholy he had been experiencing lately, but he had no time because at that very instant he heard the voices of Jane and their guests.

The guided tour of the garden and cottage, forcibly brief, ended in the dining room, where Wells was waiting for them with the brooding expression of a cornered rat. Murray promptly described the room as "cozy," making Jane glow with pride, since that morning she had filled the room with roses in an attempt to make it look less bleak. Wells, on the other hand, instantly made it clear that he had no intention of making his guests feel at home there. On the contrary, the first thing he did when they sat down to lunch was make a sarcastic remark about the "exuberant youth" of Murray's new coachman. However, ignoring his impertinence, Murray simply observed that the fellow was a careful driver and didn't drink, and that was all he asked. He was clearly much too happy to engage in a duel of words, and Wells's truculence soon proved as futile as it was inappropriate amid the festive mood that had settled over the table. Emma and Jane soon behaved with the ease of those who have known each other since childhood, and Murray, content to see his beloved having a good time, spoke casually about this and that, laughing at anything and everything, praising Jane's cooking and her and Emma's beauty, and, at every opportunity, lavishing his affection on Wells, who responded with growing irritation at the turn the lunch was taking. At one point, Murray slipped a great paw inside his jacket and conjured out of nowhere an invitation to his engagement ceremony. Jane insisted they would attend, but Wells merely made a vague gesture that could have been taken to mean anything, hurriedly slipping the invitation into his jacket pocket in the vain hope that everyone would forget it had ever been there. Later, when Jane whisked Emma away to show her the hibiscus bush adorning the back wall of the garden and the men sat down in front of the fire to smoke, Murray informed Wells, as if there could be any doubt, that he was the happiest man alive and that all that happiness he owed to the advice Wells had given him in his letter. It mattered little that for the umpteenth time Wells denied having written it: Murray was delighted by Wells's stubborn refusal to confess to that splendid gesture.

When the couple finally left for London, Wells reluctantly admitted to himself that Murray's enthusiasm had caused a tiny crack to appear in the façade of his hostility. But there was no reason for alarm: it was such a small chink it would take years to open up, and Wells had no intention of letting that happen. And yet, he soon discovered that what he thought or ceased to think had little bearing on his own life, for as they stood in front of the hibiscus bush the two women had already conspired to arrange another rendezvous for the following week, this time at Ascot, where the cream of English society would come together. Wells received the news with equanimity and during the intervening week made no objections, as he knew that arguing with Jane about it would be a waste of breath. He had already shown his reluctance to forge a friendship with the couple, for what he considered the most sensible of reasons, and the fact that his wife insisted on arranging those *unnatural* gatherings made it clear how little his opinion mattered to her.

On the afternoon they were to meet, Wells arrived at Ascot with his lips set in an expression of dignified defeat. Murray, who wore an elegant grey frock coat with matching waistcoat, was in high spirits as he welcomed them and guided them to his box, thanking them effusively all the while for having come. On the way, they were forced to pass through a sea of people, who glided from one side to the other like languorous ballet dancers, gauging each of their gestures to appear as dignified as possible. All the other gentlemen were dressed like Murray, in immaculate grey frock coats, with white flowers in their button-holes. The tips of their mustaches were waxed, and around their necks hung the obligatory binoculars. For their part, the ladies showed off their beautiful gowns, many with long trains it was difficult not to step on, strings of pearls, lace parasols, and huge, preposterous hats. Emma was waiting for them in the box. She had on a tight-fitting white dress with a black stripe down each side that enveloped her curvaceous figure from neck to toe. In keeping with the Ascot custom, Emma, too, wore a flamboyant hat with a large black-and-white-striped ribbon, a spray of white gauze, and two bright red blooms, which, like an oyster, seemed to enfold the beautiful pearl of her head. When Wells saw how warmly the two women greeted each other, and how Murray reveled in their company, he thought it best once and for all to cast off the role of resentful sarcastic fellow he had insisted on playing and to enjoy that splendid afternoon at the races along with everyone else. If he went on swimming against the tide, he told himself, he would only end up drowning. And so he pretended to blend in with those wealthy, stylish creatures, and he and Murray soon found themselves making fun of the mannered gestures of the gentlemen in the neighboring boxes and looking for comparisons among the ladies' impossible headwear.

"That one is shaped like a bell," said Murray.

"And that one resembles a shark's fin," Wells parried.

"And the one over there a toadstool."

"And that of her friend a bird's nest," Wells said, and then, before Murray had a chance to point out another, he quickly cut in, flaunting his superior inventiveness: "And the one that girl is wearing looks like a bowl of fruit."

Murray looked at the woman Wells was referring to and nodded silently, grinning to himself.

"Well, can you come up with a better comparison?"

"Oh, no, George, as always you have hit the nail right on the head. I was only smiling because I know that girl. And I assure you she is capable of far more fanciful acts than sporting such a hat." Wells looked at the young woman, intrigued. "Her name is Claire Haggerty, and the gentleman beside her is her husband, the son of a rich shipping magnate called Fairbank. We met them at a party last week. She didn't recognize me, of course, but I could never forget her."

"And why is that?" asked Wells, imagining some kind of romantic entanglement.

"Because she was one of the group who went on the second expedition I organized to the future," replied Murray. "And when I saw her climb aboard the *Cronotilus,* I swear I would never have imagined that bubbling away inside her little head was the mad idea of separating from the group and hiding in the ruins in order to stay behind in the year 2000. Luckily, we found her before she was able to get very far. I hate to imagine what might have happened if we hadn't discovered her in time."

"And why would anyone want to live in a ruined world?" Wells murmured, incredulous.

"I think she fell in love with Captain Shackleton." Murray smiled good-humoredly. Wells raised his eyebrows. "I assure you she wasn't the only one, George. You can't imagine the extent of some young girls' fantasies."

"Well, she seems to have found her hero without having to travel to the future," Wells said, noticing how the young woman doted on her affluent husband.

Murray nodded and, looking away from the couple, began rummaging through his pockets.

"Incidentally, George, I brought you something."

"Another invitation to travel to the year 2000 to add to my collection?" Murray's loud guffaw almost made the box quake.

"You should have accepted one of them, George," he said. "I guarantee you would have enjoyed the trip. But no, I'm afraid it's something else."

With a solemn gesture, he placed in Wells's hands the letter he denied having written. Wells opened it and at last was able to read the advice someone else had given Murray, to forget about reproducing a Martian invasion and simply make Emma laugh.

"Well, what have you to say now, George?"

A triumphant smile appeared on Wells's lips.

"This isn't my handwriting, I assure you," he told Murray, passing the letter back to him, "and I can prove it to you whenever you wish. As I told you, this was written by an imitator."

Murray folded the letter again and slipped it back into his pocket with great care. Then he studied Wells with an amused grin.

"Don't you think an imitator would try to reproduce your handwriting? Besides, how do you explain a stranger replying to a letter only you and I know exists?"

Wells shrugged. For a moment he imagined Jane replying secretly to the letter he hadn't wanted to answer but instantly ruled that out. Jane would never do anything behind his back. Besides, that wasn't her handwriting either.

"Do you know what my theory is?" said Murray. Wells shrugged again. "The letter is so clumsily executed it looks like someone crudely attempting to disguise his own handwriting, perhaps so that he could later deny his selfless act."

Murray concluded his theory with a wink that came close to rousing all the old resentment Wells had made such an effort to smother. And yet, knowing that this puzzling misunderstanding would one day be cleared up, he managed to contain himself and change the subject. Toward the end of the day, worn down by Murray's indefatigable bonhomie, Wells even thought it might only be a matter of time before, as the apocryphal letter announced, he would end up considering him his friend.

A week later, at the engagement ceremony, Wells was one of those who applauded the most. Somehow, he had grown used to the couple's mutual displays of affection and couldn't help feeling happy when he saw them formalize their betrothal. Murray and Emma agreed to marry in London, the city invaded by Martians that had joined their lives forever, but the wedding date was postponed until Emma's father, who had suffered the spectacular loss of all his hair, had recovered. Despite the couple's eagerness to tie the knot, they decided to wait until the bride-to-be's parents could cross the Atlantic, considering that they had already broken quite enough conventions.

Life went on regardless, and after the reprieve he had given Murray, Wells began to experience a kind of spiritual inertia, which to his surprise brought him a degree of serenity. Now that he had no great adversary who regularly upset him, who made him seethe whenever he thought about him, Wells felt oddly calm. If he stopped short of describing himself as happy it was because he had always been suspicious of such emphatic statements. As for his work, it had also begun to flow harmoniously, as though in accordance with his mood. Gone was his youthful zeal, the times when, in an attempt to find his own style, he would read his favorite authors with the methodical attention of a spy, as he dreamed of blazing a trail so original nothing hitherto published could be compared to it. And although critics had praised the imagination his novels exuded, the fact was that many of them hadn't evolved from his own ideas: he owed *The Time Machine, The Island of Doctor Moreau,* and *The Wonderful Visit* in part to Joseph Merrick, better known as the Elephant Man, with whom Wells had enjoyed a most inspiring meeting in 1888. But the novel with the strangest beginnings of all was undoubtedly *The War of the Worlds,* the work that had marked the start of his unexpected friendship with Murray. A stranger had passed the plot on to him when he was fifteen years old. At that time, Wells was apprenticed to the loathsome bakery in Southsea where his mother had sent him to learn a trade. Every afternoon after work he would saunter down to the jetty and stare into the black waters while he wondered forlornly whether drowning in them wouldn't be his only escape from the depressing future that awaited him. It was on one of those melancholy evenings that a strange fellow of about fifty had walked up to him and started to talk to him as if he knew him better than anyone else in the world. Despite Wells's initial mistrust, they had ended up holding a conversation, as brief as it was astonishing, during which the stranger had told him a terrifying tale about Martians conquering the Earth. After he had finished, he told Wells that the story was a gift: he could write it one day if he became an author, although if that happened, which the man seemed in no doubt about, Wells must promise to find a more suitable, hopeful ending. And his prediction had come true: that youth had gone on to become a writer and with five novels to his name had finally felt equal to the task the stranger had entrusted him with eighteen years before. In the end, he thought it had turned out rather well. As had occurred with *The Time Machine,* his readers, oblivious to the social message in his novel, had interpreted it as a simple fantastical tale, but Wells consoled himself by thinking that if the stranger on the jetty were still alive and had read the book, he might feel satisfied with the ending Wells had given it.

However, Wells paid less and less attention to the quest for surprising plots for his scientific novels, because in the past few years he had decided to change course: he would abandon the fantasy fiction that had brought him such success and instead use as his narrative material his own experiences and responses to life. For the moment, he had managed for better or worse to finish *Love and Mr. Lewisham* and almost without coming up for air had submerged himself in *Kipps: The Story of a Simple Soul,* a comic novel in the Dickensian style, with a host of amusing characters going about their ordinary lives. And the fact was Wells seemed to have discovered an inexhaustible mine within himself. Moving to Sandgate had undoubtedly proved a great success: he had more ideas in one day there than in a whole week in Worcester.

And so, five months later, when it became abundantly clear that the air in Sandgate agreed with him in more ways than one, the couple moved to Arnold House, a semidetached dwelling, less exposed to the elements, where the sea lurked at a safe distance at the far end of the garden. Murray and Emma were frequent visitors, and their neighbors, the Pophams, a couple of private means and sophisticated tastes, soon proved the perfect companions. They read a lot and so could discuss with them their latest reads and their favorite works, and they were also keen athletes. Together they helped teach Murray to swim, fixing a raft thirty yards from the shoreline so he could swim out to it.

Overnight, without anyone planning it, Arnold House became the center of a vibrant cultural universe, where meetings of leading members of the Fabian Society took place as did endless discussions about art and politics, but also about cookery, sport, or any subject worthy of serious or lighthearted debate. Many writers and thinkers lived nearby, and as everywhere was easily accessible by bicycle, a network of houses soon sprang up, like the one the Blands had at Dymchurch, through which a stream of writers, actors, painters, and others possessed by the Muses would pass, partaking in lengthy social gatherings, many of which led to heated debates about this and that, which occasionally ended in a game of badminton. After dark, those discussions would turn into impromptu parties that went on until two or three in the morning, and the next day a haggard group of guests would emerge with hangovers from their bedrooms to guzzle the usual hearty breakfast of bacon and eggs, punctually served up in the hosts' dining room at noon.

Wells, who thanks to the success of his novels no longer suffered the past hardships, could also abandon himself in a controlled way to that placid and deceptively carefree existence. Above all, he enjoyed seeing Murray and Emma comfortably integrated into their circle of friends. He was proud to have introduced them to that stimulating, creative world that they would otherwise not have had access to, and—why deny it?—he felt thrilled to arrive at those gatherings accompanied by the famous millionaire, to introduce him to his acquaintances as he might a species of exotic bird, leaving everyone to puzzle over how their paths had crossed and the extent of their friendship. Occasionally, in the middle of one of those gatherings, Wells would pause during a conversation and observe with delight how Murray endeared himself to the others with his sardonic remarks, or how within minutes he managed to make everyone forget he was a millionaire by rolling up his sleeves and helping out with the chores, whether it be pruning hedges or fetching logs.

But the one thing Murray really enjoyed was conversing with the authors who would turn up from time to time. Thus he met Bob Stevenson, Robert Louis's cousin, Ford Madox Ford, and Józef Teodor Konrad

Korzeniowski, a diminutive, unassuming Pole who had abbreviated his name to Joseph Conrad for the benefit of his English readers. Murray had read all of them and at the least opportunity would give them his brutally honest opinions without provoking an outcry, much to the astonishment of Wells, who had warned Murray about the fragile vanity of authors. On the contrary: many of them would smile as Murray painstakingly pulled their works apart, and some even ended up agreeing with him and asking his advice on some creative problem. Wells was never sure if his colleagues' submissive attitude toward Murray was a result of the protection of his immense fortune or the extraordinary insightfulness of his remarks. Whatever the case, Murray seemed more at ease in their company than Wells did, possibly because he had produced no body of work and so was not open to attack, unlike the unfortunate Wells, who would go on the defensive whenever there was any talk of the exact mode of expression or the most suitable word.

One of the things that most irritated Wells, for example, was Conrad's insistence on discovering what his true aims were when he set about writing a novel—a question to which Wells could give no clear or satisfactory answer. Yet it was the Pole's very stubbornness that allowed Wells to realize that during those past few months Murray had become one of his closest friends.

This was how it happened. Wells and Conrad had been lying on the beach at Sandgate one afternoon, discussing how best to describe a ship that had appeared on the horizon, and after a couple of hours during which neither had managed to convince the other, Conrad had withdrawn with the air of a swordsman who has just won a duel. Then Murray had gone over to Wells, had sat down beside him and tried to lift his spirits, telling him that Conrad only wrote about the horror of strange places and only enjoyed the favor of the critics because of the inevitable exoticism the Anglo-Saxon mind always imagined it perceived when a foreigner used the English language. Personally, he found Conrad's prose as exasperatingly elaborate as a piece of Indian carving. Murray's comparison made Wells burst out laughing, and before he knew it, he found himself admitting that more than once he had asked himself whether his own lack of attention to style didn't make him less of a writer. Murray was shocked. Surely he wasn't serious. Of course not! Wells simply wasn't like Conrad and other authors who were adept at grandiloquent prose, and why should he be? His only aim when starting a novel was to finish it, employing the simplest vocabulary possible to describe his vision of the world without too much fuss. He only sought to create entertaining stories with which to criticize what he thought was wrong with the world, in a language that didn't distract the reader's attention. Wells was astonished by Murray's accurate definition of him as a writer, and he remained silent, looking out to sea, where the contentious vessel still cleaved the waters. Then he glanced at Murray, who was still sitting beside him, smiling as he watched Emma cavorting with Jane down by the water's edge. Wells stifled a sudden urge to embrace Murray and instead heard himself saying that as soon as he could, he would introduce him to James Brand Pinker, his literary agent, who would help him publish his novel, the futuristic love story that had sparked their now-distant enmity. Wells's offer came four years too late, but Murray thanked him for his tardy gesture without alluding to that and wagged his head. He no longer had any interest in publishing that novel, nor did he intend to write another. He didn't need to. He was quite content to do nothing now except bask in Emma's love. And with that Murray stood up and strolled jauntily down toward the two women. Wells felt a slight pang of envy as he watched him. There went a man brimming with happiness who asked nothing more of life except perhaps that no one should take away what he had.

13

ND NOW PERMIT ME, AFTER RIFFLING through those last two years like a cardsharp shuffling his deck, to choose one from the pack and place it on the table for all to see, because it behooves our tale to describe the events that follow in greater detail. Let us then take a closer look at one frosty February afternoon in 1900, when, in an unprecedented gesture of altruism, Wells had invited one of the most celebrated authors of the day to Arnold House as a surprise for Murray, who was a keen admirer of the man's work.

At the agreed hour, the carriage with the pompous "G" announced its arrival with the slow clatter of hooves imposed by its old coachman. When it finally reached the entrance to Arnold House, Emma and Murray stepped out, enveloped in that happiness they had that never faded. The Wellses came out to welcome them, and after the usual polite greetings they walked toward the house. But the coachman detained Wells with a question.

"You don't happen to own a dog?" the old man asked, gesturing with his chin toward the garden gate, which stood ajar.

"I already told you I don't," replied Wells impatiently.

The peculiar melancholy he had been experiencing recently seized him once again, confirming his suspicions that it was somehow related to the coachman's presence. The idea was so absurd he could scarcely believe it, and yet he had realized over the past few months that every time the old man came he brought that uneasiness with him.

"Of course, of course . . . It slipped my mind. The trouble is, you see,

•• **215** ••

I have an irrational fear of them ever since I was bitten by one as a child," Wells heard the coachman explain as he tried once more to engage him in conversation.

"Then it must be difficult for you to work for Gilmore, as he has a rather large one," Wells retorted, looking at the man suspiciously.

"Er . . . yes. It is, rather. I spend all day avoiding Buzz. For some reason he insists on sniffing me all the time, as if he were inspecting me." Wells smiled to himself at the name Murray had chosen for his old dog, Eternal. "Look, this is the scar I got from the dog that bit me when I was a child," he said, extending his left arm.

Wells showed no interest in examining it. Instead, he used the opportunity to ask the old man what he had been burning to know since the day when, somewhat taken aback, he had noticed the coachman's other mutilated hand.

"What about the fingers missing on your right hand? Was that from a dog bite as well?"

The coachman looked at the hand Wells had referred to, and his face took on a sad, inscrutable look.

"Oh, no, that came from fighting a rather more formidable foe . . . ," he said, before going back to the subject that he really seemed interested in. "But I already showed you my scar, didn't I? And you said you'd once been bitten by a dog, too, isn't that so?"

"No. Actually, I told you I never had," Wells replied blankly. "Both times you asked."

The old man looked straight at him.

"Never? Are you certain?"

"Yes," replied Wells, no longer trying to hide his annoyance at this absurd exchange, "despite how convinced you seem to be of the contrary."

"So you have no scar on your left hand . . . But you do have one on your chin, whereas I don't . . ." The coachman smiled, as though talking to himself.

"When I was fifteen I fell down some stairs," Wells replied, raising his hand to touch the scar with a mixture of puzzlement and irritation.

"I see. Whereas I didn't. I was always very careful with stairs."

Wells looked at the coachman in silence and considered asking him why, if indeed there was a reason, he insisted on having these absurd exchanges with him, but he couldn't find the right way of putting it.

"I'm very happy for you," he said at last with a sigh, and made his way toward the house.

Murray and the two women were having an animated conversation while waiting for him in the doorway. Seeing him approach, they all smiled at him knowingly.

"What?" said Wells, trying unsuccessfully to hide his unease.

"Is it those shoes again, George?" Murray chortled. "Goodness, they've been pinching your feet for two years now. Isn't it about time you got rid of them?"

"Stop making fun of him, dear," Emma scolded, "and tell him the good news."

"Er, yes, dear . . . Listen, George: Emma's father has made a full recovery, and so we've finally decided on a date for the wedding. We are to be married on the first Sunday in March. Her parents will soon set sail for London and will arrive a few days before the ceremony. And, well . . ." An excited grin appeared on Murray's face as he clutched Wells's shoulder with his huge paw. "I'd be delighted if you would be my best man."

"It will be a true honor," replied Wells as Jane looked on, smiling.

"After all," Murray resumed, "it is thanks to you that we are together. If in your letter you hadn't advised me to—"

"Damn it, man, I never replied to any letter!"

They all laughed quietly, nodding as if this were a private joke between them.

"But, George, aren't you tired of playing this game?"

"How many times do I have to tell you that isn't my handwriting? Anyway, let's drop the subject, shall we?" Wells said, terminating the discussion with a sigh. "Today I have a surprise for you."

"A surprise?"

"That's right. This afternoon we have a very special visitor: your pet author," Wells announced with a mischievous grin.

Before Murray had a chance to react, Wells ushered him and the women into the sitting room, where a man was standing with his back to them, warming himself by the fire. Murray observed the fellow, increasingly intrigued: he was broad shouldered, robust, almost as tall as Murray himself, and seemed to be planted on the ground with the incontestable weightiness of a menhir. His posture, hands clasped behind his back, stooping slightly, gave the impression of a ship's captain issuing the order to steer his vessel clear of the rocks. Hearing them come in, the man swiveled round and walked over to them with an exaggerated briskness. He had a stern, soldierly face, as though chiseled in stone, and dark, twinkling eyes that betrayed his fiery nature. His hair was starting to thin at the temples, but this was compensated for by a splendid handlebar mustache that flowed over his lips and narrowed into sharp points.

Murray gasped. "Well, I never . . ."

"Clearly no introductions are necessary," Wells said with a grin, "Even so, allow me to stick to the usual protocol. Montgomery, this is Arthur Conan Doyle, creator of your beloved detective, Sherlock Holmes. Arthur, these are my friends, Montgomery Gilmore and his charming fiancée Emma Harlow."

With the vigor characteristic of all his gestures, Doyle bowed politely and kissed Emma's hand, then extended his arm in greeting to Murray, who first stared at him, dumbfounded. After all, it wasn't every day one ran into Britain's best-known author, and creator of one of the icons of literature, in your best friend's living room. In the days when Murray's ambition was to become a writer, he had greedily devoured all the Sherlock Holmes adventures, a captive to his charm, but he had also studied Doyle's life for clues as to his success, in a bid to understand how a young medical practitioner struggling to make a living in Portsmouth could have produced the mythical detective out of nowhere.

That had been in 1886, when the twenty-seven-year-old Doyle had already spent three years in a medical practice, had killed time between visits from his meager list of patients by writing stories and novels. He had published a few short pieces in local periodicals, but his first attempt at a novel had aroused no interest among publishers. Very well, he told himself, he would return to the drawing board. But what if, instead of writing ambitious novels no one seemed interested in, he tried to come up with something original and surprising? What would he like to discover in a bookshop? What would arouse his own interest? Recalling his early life, as though consulting the child he once was in order to discover the true preferences of the adult he had become, he dredged up a name: Auguste Dupin, Edgar Allan Poe's masterful detective. No detail was too trivial for Dupin, and the fictional sleuth was on the right track, for it was enough to read the newspapers in the real world to understand that the smallest detail contained in a piece of evidence might send a defendant to the gallows or save his life. Poe had only written three Auguste Dupin stories, but the character of the detective had continued to make discreet appearances in the novels of successive authors. For several decades Dupin seemed to have been trying tentatively to come back into the world. What if he, Doyle, gave birth to him by making him the protagonist of a novel? He only had to invent a detective whom readers would find sufficiently fascinating.

He remembered Joseph Bell, a surgeon and lecturer at the University of Edinburgh medical school for whom Doyle had worked as a clerk while he was studying there. It was his job to shepherd patients into the remarkable doctor's lecture theater, where something would take place that was more like a conjuring trick than anything Doyle had seen before: Bell would receive them, with his aquiline nose and penetrating grey eyes, seated amid his cohort of assistants, and sometimes, before proceeding to examine them using traditional methods, would play at guessing a patient's profession and character through silent, intense scrutiny. Thus he would pronounce, for example, that a fellow had served in the army, had recently been discharged, and even had been stationed in Barbados. And despite Bell's explaining to his rapt audience that he had deduced all this because the man hadn't removed his hat, suggesting that he hadn't yet adapted to the customs of civil society, and that he suffered from elephantiasis, a disease prevalent in the Antilles, for the first few minutes the effect was tremendous. Doyle told himself that if he could invent a forensic sleuth who applied Bell's methods to solve crimes using his own skills and not because of a villain's mistakes or follies, he could reduce the muddled problem of criminal investigation to something approaching an exact science.

Doyle thought his detective could be an amateur sleuth who collaborated with Scotland Yard, even though he despised their methods, the same way Dupin was scornful of those of the Sûreté. He picked up his notebook and jotted down a few possible names: Sheridan Hope, Sherringford Holmes, Sherlock Holmes. The last name, which belonged to his uncle Henry's mother-in-law's father, who was head curator at the National Gallery in Dublin, had the best ring to it. Sherlock Holmes, Doyle whispered to himself in his deserted consulting room, unaware that for the first time he was uttering that nonexistent name that would soon be on everybody's lips and would be talked about even after he was dead. Doyle was pleased he had resolved the matter of his character's name so swiftly, but then it occurred to him that readers might find his Sherlock objectionable if he tried to enthrall them by gloating over his own exploits. He therefore needed someone to boast for him, perhaps a fellow sleuth, a man who lived in a state of perpetual wonderment at the detective's deductive skills, who lavished praise on him, placed him on a pedestal, so that readers, infected by his admiration, would do so as well. And Holmes's sidekick, to whom Doyle would give the bland name Watson, must be a man of action who could join in Holmes's exploits but who was sufficiently literary to recount them afterward: perhaps an ex–army doctor, a straightforward man of integrity.

Doyle proceeded to write his first Sherlock Holmes adventure, *The Scarlet Skein,* and eagerly sent it to a few publishers. But, rejected by all of them, the manuscript kept coming back like a boomerang. Disillusioned, Doyle sent it to a publishing house specializing in popular fiction, and they offered him twenty-five guineas for it. The first Sherlock Holmes novel, renamed *A Study in Scarlet,* appeared a year later, but contrary to Doyle's expectations it did not make any splash in the literary pond. Nor did his next, *The Sign of Four.*

What had he done wrong? Doyle didn't know, but since it seemed he would never make a living from literature, he moved to London and opened an ophthalmologist's consulting room in Devonshire Place, round the corner from 221B Baker Street, where in the parallel world of fiction his amateur detective Sherlock Holmes resided. And there, too, he sat waiting from ten in the morning until four in the afternoon, until once again he took up his pen. But what should he write this time? Not another serialized historical novel, he reflected, eyeing the heap of weekly magazines he had brought to his consulting room to occupy patients while they waited. They already published too many of them in England, and their disadvantages outweighed their advantages: a reader who missed one issue, for example, would lose the thread of the story and, consequently, all interest in the tale. Why did no one write short fiction? Doyle sat bolt upright in his chair. Why didn't *he*? What if, instead of proposing yet another serialized novel, he offered those magazines stories featuring the same character? He searched through his repertory for a character who would lend himself easily to a series of short stories, and—as if he could hear through the cracks between dimensions the strains of a violin playing in 221B Baker Street—Doyle resurrected Sherlock Holmes.

Doyle's first detective story, "A Scandal in Bohemia," was published in *The Strand Magazine,* and within months Sherlock Holmes and Conan Doyle had become household names. Even Doyle's mother wrote to her son to tell him how much she admired his amateur detective. At last the miracle seemed to be happening, and Doyle decided to shut down his failed ophthalmology practice, betting all his money on his fictional character. And while Doyle was pleased that Sherlock Holmes seemed to grow more popular with each issue, even catching on in America, he soon realized the idea he had initially thought would change his life was fast becoming a bane. He had fallen into a trap of his own making, because the challenge of Sherlock Holmes was that each short story required a plot as well outlined and original as that of any longer work. And one thing Doyle refused to do was contrive plots he as a reader would find dissatisfying.

After finishing the twelve stories he had been commissioned to write for *The Strand*, Doyle was exhausted. The magazine, whose circulation had risen considerably thanks to him, asked for a second series, but Doyle suspected that his winning streak with the detective was reaching an end. But, more important, he was afraid that if he continued writing Sherlock Holmes adventures, his readers would identify him with what he considered not his best writing. He thought that demanding a thousand pounds for a half-dozen stories would be a polite way of ending the matter, but the magazine accepted without demur, and Doyle was obliged to write six more stories, which made him the most highly paid author in England. However, he soon realized that no amount of money was enough to compensate the prodigious exertions Holmes demanded of him. "I think of slaying Holmes in the sixth and winding him up for good and all. He takes my mind from better things," he wrote to his mother, who promised to dig up fresh intrigues for him to solve to prevent him from ending the life of that guardian angel from London, the only man capable of fighting the crime and injustice menacing the city. She would scour the newspapers, consult her neighbors, and send him any cases she thought could inspire him. Doyle accepted grudgingly, and Holmes was given a stay of execution. When *The Strand* commissioned another series, Doyle again demanded an exorbitant sum, and again, to his astonishment, the magazine agreed. He realized then that the only way to rid himself of Holmes was to kill him off. And, regardless of his mother's protestations, he would do exactly that at the end of the new series. During a brief holiday in Switzerland, at the formidable Reichenbach Falls, the author found a perfect resting place for poor Holmes. He would pitch him into the unfathomable depths of that daunting abyss where the waters plummeted with a terrifying, thunderous roar. "It is with a heavy heart that I take up my pen to write these the last words in which I shall ever record the singular gifts by which my friend Sherlock Homes was distinguished," Watson began, while Doyle smiled sardonically on the other side of the page as though in a two-way mirror. And in "The Final Problem," the last adventure in the series, published in 1893, that character who had attained unimaginable heights, that inveterate collector of clippings from the crime sections of newspapers who made no secret of his admiration for a well-conceived, ingeniously executed crime, who was well versed in anatomy and chemistry yet unaware that the Earth turned around the sun, who could distinguish between 140 different types of cigarette ash and guess a man's profession from the calluses on his hands or from the condition of his fingernails, fell into the Reichenbach Falls clutching Professor Moriarty, Holmes's archenemy and intellectual equal. And at the bottom of that churning cauldron of water and seething foam was where the detective had been languishing for the past seven years, without Doyle's having the slightest intention of bringing him back to life, despite constant offers from publishers and the endless exhortations of his many readers. Doyle was happy to have the time to write other things, or simply to accept the invitations of his friends, like the get-together Wells had arranged so that he could meet the millionaire Montgomery Gilmore, who by now had regained his composure.

"I have always wanted to meet you, Mr. Gilmore," Doyle told him. "Your extravagant declarations of love are famous all over England. It is thanks to you that every young lady in the kingdom expects something more from her suitor than a simple ring."

"Well, I didn't mean to make things difficult for others. I just wanted to prove to a headstrong young lady that I would go to any lengths to win her heart," said Murray, smiling significantly at Emma. "In any event, whilst I am flattered that you wished to meet me, I can assure you that my desire to meet you was greater still. My humble exploit will soon be forgotten. But you . . . you are the creator of Sherlock Holmes. Who could ever forget that?"

"I can vouch for Monty's sincerity," Emma spoke up. "He is positively bewitched by the adventures of Sherlock Holmes, Mr. Doyle. I am convinced no other woman will ever steal his affection, but that detective of yours has already succeeded."

"Then I rejoice all the more for having pitched him into the Reichenbach Falls. I consider it a crime for any man to ignore such beautiful ladies as yourselves even for a minute," Doyle replied gallantly, also smiling at Jane.

And while the two women thanked him for the compliment, Wells smiled to himself contentedly at this cheerful bandying among his friends. As he had suspected, two men as alike as Murray and Doyle couldn't help but get along from the first.

"You are right, it is unforgivable," Murray agreed. "A beautiful lady should be refused nothing, don't you agree?"

"Quite so," Doyle hurriedly concurred.

"Even if she asked you to bring Sherlock Holmes back to life?"

Doyle laughed at Murray's retort.

"I'm afraid I couldn't oblige her there," he lamented. "Holmes is dead and gone. Nobody could survive such a fall without undermining the plausibility of the story."

"I wouldn't be so sure about that," replied Murray. "It might be possible."

"Really? How?" Doyle asked with an amused curiosity. "How would you go about convincing readers that Holmes could survive a fall of over eight hundred feet?"

"Oh, there is no way anyone could survive such a fall," replied Murray. "In fact, ever since I read 'The Final Problem' I have been pondering how Holmes might have avoided his tragic fate, for I didn't want to believe you had killed him off. An extraordinary man like Holmes couldn't die. And, believe it or not, during the past seven years I've turned my search for a solution into something of a hobby. I've even visited the falls to see the scene for myself. And, much to my regret, as I stood flattened against the rocks, arms folded, watching the water tumble into the chasm below, as if I wanted to re-create Watson's last image of Holmes, I had to admit nobody could survive such a terrifying drop. Until I realized that Holmes hadn't plunged into the falls."

Doyle, who up until then had been nodding with quiet amusement at each of Murray's words, suddenly raised his eyebrows.

"What do you mean? Of course he plunged into the falls!"

Murray wagged his head with a mischievous grin.

"That's what Watson believes," he explained. "But what if he didn't? Remember, there were no witnesses. When Watson goes back to the falls after realizing Moriarty had deceived him, all he found was Holmes's walking stick, a farewell note, and two sets of footprints leading up to the edge of the abyss, which led him to deduce that both the detective and his archenemy had plunged to their deaths. But suppose that during the struggle Holmes, using his knowledge of jujitsu or Japanese wrestling, had managed to prize himself loose, so that Professor Moriarty alone fell into the chasm? Then, realizing fate had given him the opportunity to stage his own death and hunt down his remaining enemies, Holmes scrambled up the rock face to avoid leaving any tracks that might make Watson suspect that the best and wisest man it had been his honor to know had cheated Death."

Doyle's face appeared to crumple.

"An excellent solution, Mr. Gilmore," he admitted, once he had overcome his astonishment. "I have to confess that would be a fairly realistic way of saving Holmes, although the Japanese wrestling doesn't convince me much."

"I'm glad to hear it," Murray rejoiced. "Now you can correct the big mistake you made when you killed him off and carry on writing his adventures."

"I wouldn't call it a big mistake. As I'm sure you realize, I didn't slay Holmes so I could bring him back to life, but to rid myself of him once and for all. That accursed detective eclipsed the rest of my work, preventing it from achieving greater literary recognition."

Even as he spoke, Doyle did his best not to show his annoyance, although Wells, who had noticed his efforts, was beginning to worry about the turn the conversation was taking. It seemed Murray had finally met an author who was unimpressed by his unbridled honesty, and his millionaire status, and what would have made Wells rejoice under different circumstances now had the opposite effect on him.

"I always thought that it was the readers who decided what place an author should occupy in literature rather than the author himself." Murray grinned. "You have deprived them of their monthly enjoyment, and in some cases possibly their sole reason for getting up in the morning, apparently without the slightest remorse. Not that I don't blame you: writers tend to be oblivious to the spell they create, and I am sure you thought that what you were hurling into the falls was no more than a fictional creature, a handful of words, not a person who for many readers had become as real as their own brother or cousin."

"You don't blame me . . . ?" Doyle shook his head in disbelief. "Holmes was mine! I created him from nothing, and therefore I had the right to do whatever I wanted with him, whether slaying him or turning him into a Carthusian monk."

Murray laughed aloud as Wells glanced in alarm at Jane, who in turn looked toward Emma.

"That would have been an even worse fate than death," remarked Murray. "But I fear you are mistaken, Mr. Doyle: the moment you published Holmes's first adventure, he no longer belonged exclusively to you, but also to his readers."

"I see. So I should consult them before killing off my own character. And what do you propose to do about it, Mr. Gilmore? Are you going to offer me money if I bring him back to life? Is that why you arranged this meeting, George?" he said, turning to Wells, who was about to deny it when Doyle hushed him up with an abrupt gesture. "Very well, go ahead and make me an offer, Mr. Gilmore, but I warn you, you'll have difficulty surpassing that of my publishers."

Murray looked at him in amusement for a few moments.

"Believe me, I could multiply their offer by a hundred, but I won't. It would be an insult to you as an author and to me as a reader, although I doubt whether somebody who shows no respect for his own characters could understand that."

Wells made as if to intervene, but again Doyle prevented him with a wave of his hand.

"Wait a moment, George. This conversation is becoming more and more interesting," he said, taking what could only be described as an intimidating step toward Murray. "So you think I'm disrespectful toward my character, Mr. Gilmore?"

"Yes," said Murray undeterred. "In my opinion, you pay far more attention to detail in your chivalresque novels than in your detective stories."

Doyle contemplated him for a moment in silence, then he glanced at the two women, and at Wells, wondering whether he should unleash the anger boiling inside him or try to control the ferocious temper he had inherited from his Irish ancestors.

"You're quite right, Mr. Gilmore," he acknowledged at last, having decided on a conciliatory tone, much to Wells's relief. "But it doesn't follow that I disrespect Holmes."

"Oh, but it does," insisted Murray.

Doyle gave a forced laugh, as though wanting them all to believe he found the whole thing terribly amusing.

"Can you back up your claims?" he asked almost indifferently.

"Of course," replied Murray. "I have read every single one of Sherlock Holmes's adventures a hundred times over. And have jotted every error and imprecise piece of information I came across in a notebook, on the off chance I might one day discuss them with you."

"What a shame you didn't bring your notebook with you, Monty," Wells interposed. "Never mind, you can send it to Doyle tomorrow; that way he can read it in his own time. Now let's . . ."

"I certainly will, George, don't worry," Murray assured him. "But luckily I can remember a few. For example, the place where they discover Drebber's poisoned corpse in *A Study in Scarlet* doesn't exist. There is no number three Lauriston Gardens, is there, Emma?"

Everyone looked at Emma, in particular Doyle, who was no longer making any effort to smile.

"It's true. One night he took me out looking for it and we traipsed up and down the street without finding any house resembling the one in your novel," Emma said, rather ashamedly, in a tone that seemed at once to be apologetic toward Doyle and to recall the tedium of an evening spent pursuing her fiancé's obsession after he was suddenly transformed into Sherlock Holmes himself.

"And in that very same novel," Murray went on, oblivious to Doyle's increasing irritation, "Watson comments on a bullet wound he received in his shoulder during the Afghan war, whereas in *The Sign of the Four* he mentions a wounded leg. Where do they make these fiendish bullets that can cause two separate wounds, Mr. Doyle? I'd like to buy some."

"The bullet simply bounced off his shoulder bone, grazed the subclavian artery, left his body following a curved trajectory, then reentered his leg," explained Doyle gruffly.

"I see." Murray grinned. "Or perhaps poor Watson was shot while relieving himself behind a bush, and the bullet simply passed through his shoulder and into his leg."

Murray's loud guffaw shook the air, even though he was laughing alone. When he finally stopped, a strained silence descended slowly on the group. No one seemed to know what to say. Luckily, Jane took the situation in hand and invited them to sit at the table, as if the quarrel they had just witnessed had been no more than an unpleasant hallucination.

Five minutes later, Jane was serving tea, assisted by Emma, who passed the biscuits round and tried to fend off the looming silence by remarking on how delicious they tasted. Jane took the opportunity of admitting that because of their perfect blend of butter and aniseed, Kemp's biscuits were her favorites. Unfortunately, there wasn't much more to say on the subject of biscuits, and so the silence soon settled on them again like a film of dust.

Wells absentmindedly munched on what his spouse considered a miracle of baking, increasingly regretting he had ever arranged the meeting. He was well aware of the loathing Doyle professed for his character, a loathing Wells understood perfectly, for he didn't much care for the detective who had brought his friend so much fame either. For him the Sherlock Holmes stories were ingenious sleights of hand in which Doyle was less a writer than a performer, and any magician, however great, stopped impressing his audience once he revealed his tricks. Wells preferred the other Doyle, the one who admired Walter Scott and had written splendid historical novels like *Micah Clarke*, or the ambitious *White Company*, a somewhat idealized depiction of English knights. That giant of a man appeared to Wells as nothing other than one of those athletic, brave knights of old, someone too honorable and selfless for the times he lived in and who went through life as though in a suit of armor, adhering to an outmoded code of chivalry. Doyle had been born with one of those daunting physiques that seemed destined for gritty, heroic adventures, and that together with his lively, intrepid spirit had enabled him to emerge unscathed from many a scrape in life, but he had also been blessed with a passionate temperament he had difficulty controlling. He sighed as he watched Doyle now, sitting stiffly in his chair, trying not to let his face betray how insulted he felt. Wells realized it was only Doyle's good manners that prevented him from getting up and leaving, and he racked his brains for a topic that might initiate a more relaxed and—why not say it?—profound conversation than that about biscuits. Just then, a loud crash upstairs made everyone jump.

"Oh, it's the attic window again!" exclaimed Jane. "The catch came loose, and ever since . . . I'm sorry it made you start, my dear," she said to Emma, who had nearly spilled her tea down the front of her dress. "Bertie promised he'd fix it," and then, looking aslant at Wells, she added: "Two months ago."

"My promise still stands, Jane," protested Wells. "I told you I'd fix it, and I will . . . Just as soon as I've finished my novel."

"Just as soon as you've finished your novel . . . ," Jane repeated with a sigh. "You writers think life grinds to a halt while you are writing your books."

Another, even louder crash came from upstairs.

"If I were you, I wouldn't wait to fix that window, George, or your guests will start spreading the word that your house is haunted," Murray jested. "Luckily for you none of us believes in such nonsense."

Everyone fell silent again. Murray cast his eye over the group, unable to fathom what had caused Wells and Jane suddenly to turn pale and Doyle's eyes to flash with anger. It was Doyle who offered the explanation.

"This awkward silence is due to the fact that for the past seven months, Mr. Gilmore, I have been a member of the Society for Psychical Research," he said with a mixture of pride and bitterness. "I also subscribe to the psychic journal *Light,* to which I have contributed several articles . . . In brief, what I am trying to explain to you is that I take the subject of spiritualism rather seriously. Although that doesn't mean I can't enjoy a good joke," he added, without clarifying whether or not he included Murray's quip in that category.

Murray stared at him in surprise. He didn't consider himself an expert in the matter but would read with great interest any articles on spiritualism that appeared in the newspapers.

"Do you mean to say that you believe when someone dies his soul leaves his body and wanders about like a tortoise without a shell?"

"Monty, please . . . ," Wells began, but Doyle raised his hand, signaling to him to be quiet.

"If by that peculiar analogy you are referring to life after death, you could say that I am increasingly convinced of it, Mr. Gilmore," Doyle replied.

Murray smiled benevolently.

"Forgive me, Mr. Doyle, but I find it hard to believe that the creator of a man as rational as Sherlock Holmes—"

"I assure you my approach to spiritualism is entirely rational," interrupted Doyle, who did not need Murray to finish a sentence he had heard a hundred times. "George will doubtless back me up when I say I never affirm anything I am not completely convinced is true, even when it goes against my own interests or, as in the case of spiritualism, it means having to endure ridicule. Since it was established, many eminent men have been converted to the cause of spiritualism, and several of our leading scientists have testified to paranormal phenomena. Unfortunately," he lamented almost in a whisper, "this long list of prominent men has only increased the virulence of the cause's detractors, who realize they aren't contending with a handful of lunatics or idiots but rather with important people who can sway the masses."

"I'm not surprised. The masses are easily swayed. But can you convince one man, Mr. Doyle?" said Murray with an amused expression, thus offering himself as a guinea pig.

"This isn't why Arthur came here, Monty," said Wells, increasingly vexed at his friend's attitude.

"I suppose not, George. But since he's here, perhaps he won't want to pass up the opportunity to persuade the famous millionaire Montgomery Gilmore to join his cause. What do you say, Doyle? Do you have the guts to try? No religion satisfies me! Save me from the valley of shadows in which I find myself! Please, I beg you. Think of all the money I could donate to your society if only you succeed in convincing me," he concluded with a grin.

"That's enough, Monty!" Emma said disapprovingly. "Mr. Doyle isn't obliged to play your little games."

"Here, here," Wells agreed.

Murray protested, and the three began squabbling. Then Doyle's voice rang out loud and clear.

"Imagine someone close to you dies, Mr. Gilmore." His booming voice made them all sit up in their chairs, especially Murray. "Imagine burying that person and mourning for her." Almost instinctively, Murray took Emma's hand in his as he listened uneasily to Doyle's words. "Imagine if after several weeks of terrible grief over her loss, of trying to accept that you will never speak to that person again, her spirit made contact with you. And imagine that she spoke to you and told you something only you knew about, a detail so intimate no trickster could ever have discovered it. Wouldn't you believe in spirits then, Mr. Gilmore?"

Murray, who was still clasping Emma's hand, swallowed for a few seconds, as though discreetly trying to force down a cricket ball. He replied, trying to look calm:

"It's possible, providing that she communicated directly with me, Mr. Doyle, but certainly not if her words were relayed to me by one of those charlatans who call themselves mediums."

"I confess I agree with you there," said Doyle, "the majority of them are impostors, unscrupulous swindlers who resort to all kinds of trickery to convince unsuspecting people they possess supernatural powers, generally for criminal ends. As is often the case, the false prophets outnumber the legitimate ones. But discovering one genuine medium would be enough to prove that the spirit lives on after death. Then it wouldn't matter how many hundreds or thousands of false ones there were, don't you agree?"

"I suppose so," Murray conceded.

"Has that ever happened to you, Mr. Doyle?" Emma asked. "Have you come across a medium you were convinced was genuine?"

"I have, Miss Harlow, more than once, although of course not the first one turned to." Doyle settled back in his chair and appeared to reflect. "If I remember correctly, I first became interested in psychic phenomena before I left Plymouth, about twelve or thirteen years ago, although at the time I was no more than an informed novice who felt an amused curiosity for these miracles that purportedly breached the laws of science. And it was with that skeptical attitude that I attended various séances, but no spirit ever appeared to me . . . until one did."

Emma remained silent for a few moments, a tightness in her throat.

"And what did it tell you?" she ventured at last.

"Not to read Leigh Hunt's book."

Confronted by the young woman's bewilderment, Doyle explained that for several days he had been debating whether or not to read Hunt's Restoration comedies.

"Well, that's not a very dramatic example," Murray interjected.

"You may not think so, Mr. Gilmore, but I hadn't mentioned it to a living soul, so you can imagine my astonishment. I even wrote an article about it in *Light.* On the other hand, it could be that this episode simply proves that telepathy exists. Here's another example that—"

"Wait! Telepathy?" said Murray.

"Yes. Telepathy. The transmission of one person's thoughts to another. It was around that time that I was practicing it with Stanley Ball, my architect, with remarkable results."

"You've practiced telepathy?" Murray made no effort to hide his disbelief. "I think you have your work cut out for you, Mr. Doyle: now you'll have to convince me of that as well."

"We can practice together transmitting our thoughts whenever you like," replied Doyle.

"Well, yes, possibly . . . But, going back to the question of spiritualism, I think when you said you had proof of the existence of spirits we all expected something a little more dramatic, as I already said. For instance, have you ever come across one of those, what do they call them . . . ectoplasms? I mean a real one, not some crude trick."

"No," Doyle sighed. "But that doesn't mean I rule out the possibility that some mediums are able to create them. Many can exude from their bodies those luminescent clouds, which they themselves shape into a vaguely human form. And some, admittedly fewer, are able to generate materializations that are indistinguishable from a human being. The Eddy brothers, a couple of dirt farmers from Vermont, could make a gigantic Red Indian appear, together with his squaw, Honto, who was weighed one evening eleven times by the witnesses, her weight gradually diminishing, as if her body were no more than an image that could vary its density at will." Murray smiled skeptically, and Doyle added, "Naturally, I have no doubt whatsoever that a high percentage of these mediums resort to trickery, but many of them have been examined by our leading scientists, the majority of whom declare in their reports that there was no deception in those miracles. I may have my reservations about the judgment of some of them, but I cannot doubt them all. It would be illogical. One doesn't always need to see in order to believe."

"Quite so. But what if I were to offer you the possibility of *seeing*?" said Murray, with a mischievous grin. "Would you accept?"

Doyle looked at Murray suspiciously, trying to work out whether he was mocking him or not, but finally he replied to the offer as if it were genuine: "Without a doubt."

"Even if the spirit in question was a dog?"

"A dog?"

"A bloodhound, to be precise," Murray replied.

"Is that the best you can do? I thought with all your wealth you might pull something more . . . dramatic out of your hat," Doyle retorted.

"Oh, I assure you this bloodhound is very dramatic. Are you familiar with Dartmoor?"

"Yes," said Doyle. "That's where the prison is, in Princetown."

"Well, there's a house on Dartmoor called Brook Manor, which the local inhabitants say is haunted. It seems a fellow called Richard Cabell, a local squire from Buckfastleigh, lived there about two hundred years ago. Cabell had a passion for hunting and was reputed to be a monstrously evil man, among other things because he sold his soul to the devil. One night, suspecting his wife was cuckolding him, he flew at her in a jealous rage. She fled across the moor, and Cabell gave chase with his hunting dog, which he made pick up her scent from some of her clothing. Finally he caught up with her and slew her. But the dog turned on its master, ripping Cabell's throat out before he was able to stab the creature to death. On July fifth, 1677, the remains of the man who had defamed everything he could possibly defame were buried, but that was only the beginning of the story. That night, a ghost appeared in the form of a dog howling on his grave and roaming the moor. This all happened a long time ago, but local people still claim that on some nights a ghostly dog can be seen prowling around the house. They say it looks like a bloodhound, only much bigger than any seen by mortal eyes. They say the dog breathes fire, its eyes burn like embers, and an eerie glow envelops it."

There was a stunned silence, and everyone was secretly thankful that the window Wells resisted fixing hadn't rounded off Murray's tale with another untimely crash.

"Do you want to see the hound?" Murray then asked Doyle.

"Naturally, though I fear we must persuade the owner of the house to let us go there, and these things are delicate. In my experience—"

"You needn't worry about that, Mr. Doyle," Murray interrupted, "because the house is mine. I bought it this very morning."

"You bought a haunted house?" said Wells, astonished.

"That's right, George, and a couple of others besides. No one dared to buy them because of the strange phenomena that have been happening in those parts over the past few years, so they were going for a song. But, as you can see, where others see nothing but ghosts, I see a good business deal. Emma and I are thinking of going to visit the houses next week to see about renovations. You can come with us if you like, Mr. Doyle. And you, too, of course," he said to Wells and Jane. "In fact, we could organize a jaunt. What do you say, Mr. Doyle? With any luck we'll bump into the phantom bloodhound."

"I suspect those are mere folktales," replied Doyle. "I shan't deny that I enjoy visiting haunted houses. Unfortunately, most of them turn out to be nothing more than lugubrious places. There are atmospheres that are very conducive to the power of suggestion, Mr. Gilmore, which make it easy to see strange phenomena where there are none."

"Come with us, please!" Murray insisted. "And if we don't find any ghosts, you and I can still practice a bit of telepathy."

"That's an offer I can't refuse, Mr. Gilmore," replied Doyle, beaming at Murray.

Emma shook her head resignedly, then addressed Doyle.

"I'm so glad you've agreed to come, Mr. Doyle. It will be a pleasure for us to have you as our guest. And don't worry: I assure you my future husband means no offense with his boorishness. In fact, it is simply his irrepressible bluntness. Monty is the most genuine person I know. Of all his qualities, that is the one that made me fall in love with him," she confessed with a charming smile, "though I quite understand that it doesn't have the same effect on you."

For the first time since he had arrived at Arnold House, Doyle burst out laughing. A jovial rumble of stones rolling down a hillside, which caused Wells to sigh with relief. Doyle had laughed, and the atmosphere seemed to lighten up. Things might go more smoothly now, he reflected. Yes, perhaps Murray and Doyle would finally be able to enjoy a conversation free of tension, and possibly even get along. Just then, Jane noticed that the biscuits were finished and made ready to get up and bring some more, but Murray stood up first and politely offered to fetch the biscuit tin from the kitchen. And while Murray disappeared down the corridor, Doyle began to regale the two women with the fabulous arctic adventures he had been on when he had barely turned twenty. Wells slumped back in his chair almost voluptuously, content that the afternoon finally seemed to be taking the right turn. The wind was howling outside, whipping up the waves in the distance, and from time to time the attic window creaked menacingly, reminding everyone of Wells's laziness; the fire in the hearth spread its comforting warmth through the room, and everyone seemed to enjoy that unexpected moment of calm.

Unfortunately for Wells, this oasis of happiness lasted scarcely a few moments, because through the window, to which the others had their backs turned, Wells saw a despondent-looking Murray wandering around the garden, as if he had been told to play the most wretched man on Earth.

"Er . . . Murray seems to be having difficulty finding the biscuits. I'll go and lend him a hand," Wells told Jane.

Jane nodded absentmindedly, engrossed in Doyle's adventures, while Wells headed for the corridor.

"But if that adventure taught me anything, it was that in order truly to appreciate a woman, a man must be separated from her for six months," Wells heard Doyle say as he ducked out of the corridor and into the garden, making sure none of the others saw him.

14

$\mathcal{I}$F AT THAT MOMENT SOMEONE HAD SAT DOWN IN the chair Wells had just vacated, they would have seen the author, whom everyone assumed was in the kitchen, crossing the lawn with his jacket wrapped tightly around him. And if the sight of Wells intrigued him enough to make him get up out of his chair, go over to the window, and crane his neck at the right angle, he would also have seen him approach the burly man who was busy contemplating the hibiscus bush and pat him gingerly on the back a couple of times. Like you, dear readers, I, too, suspect that the conversation about to take place out in the garden promises to be far more interesting than Doyle's monologue, and so while he is busy describing the vast gatherings of seals that congregate on the icebergs to give birth en masse, let us go over and spy on Wells and Murray.

"You're quite mistaken if you think we keep the biscuit tin under the hibiscus bushes, Monty," Wells jested.

Murray smiled glumly.

"I know you keep it in the basket in the kitchen. That's not why I came out here, George."

"In that case, why did you decide to expose yourself to this wretched cold? What's the matter with you? A moment ago you were the world's most impudent impostor, and now you look like a ghost."

" 'Monty is the most genuine person I know.' Didn't you hear what she said?" Murray replied without looking up from the shrubs.

"Yes, of course I did," murmured Wells.

"Good, then you'll know how mistaken she is."

So that was what was tormenting Murray. Yet again. Wells sighed, realizing they were about to become embroiled in another of their endless discussions about the convenience or not of revealing Murray's true identity to Emma. Those conversations the two men were obliged to have behind the women's backs never resolved anything; they simply allowed Murray to let off steam. Wells glanced over his shoulder toward the sitting room window and saw Doyle waving his arms in the air, as if he were making a couple of marionettes dance. For the moment no one seemed about to come looking for them.

"But, Monty," he said, "we've been over this a hundred times. If you want to tell Emma who you really are, do it now, because the longer you stall, the more difficult it will become. Remember, it's been two years since you stepped out of that silly balloon. On the other hand, if you decide not to tell her, you must convince yourself it is the best thing for you both, so you can stop being affected by that kind of remark."

"I know, George, but the problem is I can't decide. Part of me thinks I should come clean with her. Find the right moment and explain it to her as best I can. I'm sure she'll understand . . . Or at least I like to think so."

"Then do it."

"But the other part of me doesn't want to risk spoiling our happiness. If I lose Emma . . . if I lose her, George, I don't know what I'd do . . . I'm afraid I would lose the will to live."

"Then don't do it."

"You aren't much help, George," Murray muttered.

"Damn it, Monty, it's for you to decide, not me!" exclaimed Wells, "And the sooner the better, because if you keep dragging this burden around with you, it will end up driving you crazy."

Murray nodded, pursing his lips until they resembled a freshly stitched wound.

"It almost has, George. I spend half the time racked with guilt when I remember that she doesn't know who I am and the other half worrying that she might find out. Do you remember that Scotland Yard detective who kept hounding me a while back? The arrogant, lanky fellow to whom you revealed my identity so as to save your own skin . . ."

"Yes, yes, I remember," Wells replied uncomfortably. "I already told you I was sorry. What was I supposed to do? At the time you and I were—"

"I know, George, I know, and I don't blame you. But the fact remains that during those few months when he was pursuing me I had a dreadful time. I spent a fortune thwarting his various attempts to unmask me. He was like a dog with a bone. It got to the point where I ran out of ideas. I had bribed half of London, but that arrogant devil was still intent upon exposing me. I tell you, it was a veritable war of attrition, but the most difficult part was trying to hide my alarm from Emma. And then one day, out of the blue, when he all but had me cornered, he stopped chasing me."

"Really?"

"Yes, he suddenly seemed to lose all interest in the investigation, and he hasn't troubled me since."

"And you never discovered why he gave up?"

"I imagine some superior of his whom I bribed must have called him off, but I find it hard to believe that a fellow like that wouldn't kick up a fuss. It could be that he gave up of his own accord, unaware that his quarry was about to surrender. Who knows, perhaps he isn't as dogged as I thought. Then I calmed down, you see. And I began to toy with the idea that after this no one could ever discover my secret. Until this afternoon."

"This afternoon?" Wells was surprised.

"Yes, all my old fears came flooding back when I saw Doyle. I was afraid he might recognize me, that he'd use his powers of deduction, and in no time he'd be calling me by my real name."

Wells laughed.

"Oh, come now, why on earth would Doyle connect you to Gilliam Murray? That would be like thinking I have a time machine in my attic."

Murray shrugged.

"I imagine that like most of his readers I have always assumed he was as shrewd as his detective." He paused and seemed to reflect. "In fact, when Murray's Time Travel still existed, Doyle was one of my most passionate defenders. Did you know he wrote several articles attacking those who accused me of being an impostor? We even exchanged correspondence, in which I described in great detail how I had discovered the hole leading to the fourth dimension during a trip to Africa. When he showed an interest in traveling to the year 2000, I even wrote to tell him that, as a sign of my appreciation for his vindication of me, I would organize an expedition especially for him, just as I had for the queen. But unfortunately, while I was organizing it . . . well, you know . . . the hole disappeared."

"Hmm. A real pity. Doyle would have loved your future."

"And so when I saw him here . . . ," Murray went on, ignoring Wells's remark, "Good God, George, I thought one glimpse of me and he would give the game away. And what's more, in front of Emma. And yet he didn't recognize me, and the fact that not even the creator of Sherlock Holmes himself was able to do so makes me think my secret is safe. Everyone seems to have forgotten all about the Master of Time. Emma need never know my secret, unless I reveal it to her myself."

Murray's head started to droop, as if his thoughts weighed him down like lead, until finally he was staring at his shoes. Wells waited patiently for him to continue.

"I could let sleeping dogs lie, of course," he said at length. "That way I would run no risks; I would only have to struggle with my remorse. But you can't imagine the terrible bitterness I feel knowing that I'm deceiving her! And I have no idea what to do. What advice can you give me, George?"

"I'm not qualified to give you any advice, Monty."

"Oh, come. You gave me the best advice anyone has ever given me in your letter. Please tell me what to do."

"I never wrote that damned— Oh, it doesn't matter." Wells gave a weary sigh. "Very well, Monty, I'll tell you what I would do."

But for several moments Wells said nothing. He felt incapable of deciding which of the two options was the best, since there were arguments in favor of both. He could advise Murray to confess, insisting Emma deserved to know his true identity. But he could just as well recommend he keep quiet, insisting that she was blissful in her ignorance and it didn't matter what he might have done in the past because he had changed so radically, it was as if someone else had done them. But the worst thing of all, Wells told himself, wasn't that he couldn't help Murray choose between the two options, but rather that he couldn't see what all the fuss was about. Try as he might (and he had been trying for two years) he couldn't understand what the problem was. As he saw it, there was no reason for Emma to be angry about something like that. If Jane had told him that prior to meeting him she had been the famous sword swallower Selma Cavalieri, would he have left her? Of course not. Nor did he understand why Murray was plagued with remorse by the thought that Emma didn't know who he really was. Wells was sure that, in his case, if he had decided that the best way to hold on to what he had was to keep a secret, he would have done so without hesitation. Why did Murray find that so difficult? He had no idea, but he sensed that wasn't the right question, and that he should be asking himself why he found it so easy. Because he lacked empathy, he told himself, that deficiency Jane so often referred to in order to explain his behavior. If he was empathic, he could have put himself in Murray's shoes and told him what the best course of action was for him. But that ability, instinctive in most people, was refused him. Murray had asked for his advice, and in order not to disappoint him, Wells could only choose one of those two options, however arbitrarily, and by means of that friendly gesture hide the fact that the lives of others were of no consequence to him.

"Well, George?" Murray asked in response to his lengthy silence.

"You should tell her," replied Wells, who might just as well have said the opposite.

"Do you really think so?"

"Definitely."

"Why?" Murray asked wretchedly.

Wells had to stifle a shrug.

"Because otherwise your happiness will be built on a lie," he improvised. "Is that what Emma deserves? I don't think so. She trusts you, Monty. It would never occur to her that you had secrets, much less that you are the Master of Time. If one day she discovered the truth, wouldn't she feel betrayed by the only person in the world from whom she would never expect a betrayal? And does her not being able to discover it make you any less of a traitor? You claim you love her. If that's true, how can you allow your love to be anything but completely honest?"

Murray reflected on what Wells had said, while for his part Wells mulled over how common it was for people to seek advice from others, to allow somebody else to decide for them, somebody who could examine the problem objectively, theoretically, safe from any ramifications.

"I suppose you are right, George," Murray said at last. "I take pride in loving her, and yet my love is flawed. It contains an impurity, a stain I must expunge. Emma doesn't deserve a love that isn't completely truthful. I shall tell her, George. I shall be brave and I'll do it. Before the wedding."

After making that promise, Murray flung his arms around Wells, who felt as if a grizzly bear were embracing him. The pair of them went back inside the cottage and took up their respective places at the table. No one asked about the biscuits. For a time, Doyle went on talking of seals, and oceans bristling with icebergs, while Murray was content to nod occasionally, visibly distracted. It was clear he was mulling over what Wells had just said to him, but Wells knew that no matter how intent Murray was upon following his advice, as always, the days would go by and he would fail to confess his true identity to Emma. Finally, even Doyle's adventures proved not to be inexhaustible, and after he ended his monologue with the usual moral he had drawn from the story, the conversation languished without anyone making any effort to stimulate it. It was already late, and the journey back was a long one, and so they decided to bid one another good-bye, setting a date for their excursion to Dartmoor the following week. However, judging from the look of determination on Murray's face, Wells had the sudden suspicion that on this occasion time might fail to weaken his resolve. It was quite possible that when they next met, Murray would have confessed to Emma that she was about to marry the Master of Time.

That night, Wells found it hard to fall asleep. He was fretting about what consequences his advice might bring if this time Murray was bold enough to follow it. Emma struck him as both sufficiently intelligent and in love for Murray's confession only to strengthen their bond. But what if it didn't? What if Emma was incapable of forgiving him and abandoned him? Should he feel guilty? Was it possible that in a part of his brain he rarely visited, the flame of his old hatred toward Murray was still burning and that the advice he had given him was designed to destroy his happiness, that dazzling, hypnotic happiness he perhaps secretly envied? No, Wells was certain that no remnants of his old animosity had survived. Otherwise he would never have gone to talk to Inspector Clayton two years before.

Wells only knew the inspector briefly from their excursion to Horsell Common on the morning the Martian cylinder had appeared, but something told him that this arrogant, meticulous fellow's determination to unmask Montgomery Gilmore would never wane, no matter how much money the millionaire threw at the situation. And so, one morning Wells had turned up at Clayton's office and supplied the answers he was looking for: after all, it was only a matter of time before the inspector discovered them for himself. He did so secretly, hoping that the inspector's need for truth outweighed his desire for glory, and once he had confirmed this to be the case, he used all his rhetorical skill to try to persuade the inspector to abandon the case: assuring him that this man was nothing like his former self, that everyone deserved a second chance, and much more besides. Sadly, none of his arguments succeeded in swaying Clayton. Finally, out of desperation, he had even appealed to the love story between Murray and Emma, which was the toast of all England, which had begun with the appearance of the Martian cylinder, and which Clayton had no right to destroy, even though it might pin another medal on his chest. If he made public everything he knew about Murray, Emma would probably abandon him and they would never be together again. Do you think you can persuade me with an argument like that? Clayton had exclaimed with a sardonic smile, to which Wells, cringing at his own words, had replied that he didn't, because to have done so, the inspector would have had to have known the torment of being condemned to go on living after hurting the person he loved most. The inspector had remained silent for a few moments, after which he asked Wells politely to leave his office, which he did, cursing his lamentable performance. Because of Murray, he had championed love, only to make himself look ridiculous in front of that stuck-up young man. However, during the following weeks, Murray made no more mention of Inspector Clayton, and Wells gradually realized that whilst he considered it an overrated emotion, love was a sentiment many others valued, and so when they came across it would step respectfully around it, as they might a flowerbed.

And so, in brief, Wells had prevented Emma from discovering her fiancé's secret. Then why the devil had he just advised Murray to tell her, when he could have done the exact opposite? In order to discover the answer to that, Wells would have to delve too deeply into his soul, and so he preferred to let it slide.

And yet Wells was struck by the parallels between that scene and the afternoon when Murray went to his house to ask his opinion about his shoddy little novel. Then, also, Wells could have chosen between two options. He had held the dreams of that complete stranger in his hands while Murray awaited his verdict pathetically ensconced in the armchair in his living room. And this afternoon someone had arranged the pieces in exactly the same way beside the hibiscus bush, so that Wells had the same feeling as five years ago of being able to set Murray's life on the course he chose, no matter that he was now Wells's best friend.

With a shudder, Wells wondered what Murray might find at the end of the path he had chosen for him this time.

15

ESPITE FINDING HERSELF ON HER AUNT'S front step, sheltered from an overcast sky, Emma Harlow gave a sigh, opened her parasol, and began twirling it above her head. It was the day of the trip to Dartmoor, and Monty was already half an hour late. He had promised her the day before that he would be on time. On the dot! he had said solemnly, as though reciting a family motto. He had even asked her to start waiting on the front step a few minutes early, because he had a surprise he wanted to show her, something to do with the way they would travel to Dartmoor, which was worth beholding in all its splendor. And Emma had deigned to accept, concealing a delighted smile, for secretly there was nothing she liked more than the theatricality with which her fiancé celebrated every occasion, which made her feel like a little girl who had stumbled into a great magician's secret lair. But after standing there for half an hour, bored and cold, she was beginning to regret having indulged him. Narrowing her eyes, Emma surveyed the driveway that crossed the gardens of her aunt's town house, then looked up at the leaden sky, unable to rule out the possibility that Monty might emerge from the clouds sitting on some preposterous flying machine.

"Goodness me! Are you still here?"

Emma wheeled round angrily, preparing to take out her frustration on her aunt, but seeing the old lady planted in the doorway, bundled up in various shawls, some of her irritation vanished.

"Yes, Aunt Dorothy," she sighed. "As you have so cleverly perceived, I am still here."

"I told you so," the old lady muttered, ignoring her niece's irony. "There was no need to go out so early to wait for him. I don't know why you still haven't realized that punctuality is not your fiancé's strong point. Although, heaven forgive me for offering my unsolicited opinion, I would be hard-pressed to say what his other strong points might be."

"Please, Auntie . . . not now."

"Oh, don't worry, I didn't come outside in this infernal weather to talk about your beloved Gilmore. I have little or nothing more to say about him. Quite frankly, for the past two years the subject bores me. I only came out to implore you to step inside, my girl. It is freezing out here! The servants will inform you when he arrives."

"No, Auntie. Monty specifically asked me to wait on the front step. Apparently, he has a surprise for me, and—"

"He can give it to you when he gets here!" her aunt interrupted. "It's far too damp out here. You'll catch your death! I can't imagine what would happen if you fell ill weeks before your wedding. It would be a complete disaster! What would I say to your wretched parents, who will arrive any day now? After their shock at your unusual engagement and your subsequent refusal to have the wedding in New York, not to mention the recriminations I have had to endure because of it all . . ."

"Come, now, Auntie, nobody who knows me—and I assure you my parents know me very well—could possibly hold you responsible for my actions."

"Well, they do! And your mother, my *beloved* sister-in-law, has made it her business to tell me as much in all her delightful letters, in that subtle, insinuating way of hers. I'm sure they think I didn't protect you enough when, two years ago, they placed you in my care so that you could enjoy a nice, safe holiday on the old continent. But how could I have suspected such contempt for the rules of etiquette in a young lady of your upbringing? Anyway, for better or for worse," she went on with the resigned tone of a martyr, "you will be Mrs. Gilmore in a few weeks' time and will no longer be my responsibility. But there is one last thing I will say, dear niece: notwithstanding my horror at the idea of a distinguished Harlow marrying an adventurer of uncertain origin, who made his fortune as a common merchant, I confess that after living with you for two years I can't imagine any other man who would put up with you."

"And I, dear Auntie, couldn't agree with you more. In fact, before I met Monty, I had decided not to get married at all, for I doubted any man was capable of making me happy."

The old lady sighed.

"Happiness is utterly overrated, my dear girl, and obviously it isn't something that should be entrusted to incompetent men. A woman has to find her own happiness and as far as possible avoid involving her husband in the search."

"Is that why you never married, Auntie?" Emma asked softly. "So that no man would ever spoil your happiness?"

"I didn't marry because I didn't want to! But if I had, I wouldn't have chosen an amiable buffoon for a husband. Breeding and money are the two most important things in a man, for they frame a woman's beauty and intelligence. A frame can embellish a painting, but if the frame is vulgar, then the painting is better without one. Anyway, at least it reassures me that with your future husband's fortune and your dowry you won't be short of money. But tell me, are you planning on spoiling everything by catching pneumonia? Would you like me to meet your parents off the boat bearing the tragic news that they have crossed the ocean to bid you farewell on your deathbed?"

Emma rolled her eyes.

"Don't be so dramatic, Auntie. I assure you a bit of cold air isn't going to leave me on any deathbed, and besides," Emma said, smiling inwardly, "I have sufficient reason to suspect that my future life with Monty will be anything but conventional. We share such an intense fear of boredom that I am sure neither of us will die in a mere bed. I daresay we shall meet our end in the jaws of a plesiosaurus at the center of the Earth, or fighting off a Martian invasion . . ."

"Young lady!" the old woman exclaimed. "Don't make fun of Death. Everyone knows Death has no sense of humor."

"Let me remind you that you started it." Emma grinned, softening her tone as she noticed the old lady's pallor. "But don't worry, Auntie. I've never felt better. Besides, I'm all wrapped up. And I'm sure Monty will arrive any moment . . . ," she added, scanning the driveway without much conviction.

After sensing her niece's doubts with the eagerness of a bloodhound, Lady Harlow returned to the subject of what she considered to be Montgomery Gilmore's faults—starting, of course, with his apparent fondness for being late. Emma knew the old lady's refrain by heart, after hearing it endlessly repeated for two years, and I have to confess, dear reader, that she agreed with every word: her fiancé possessed each of those exasperating, unfortunate, wearisome faults, and several others that her aunt had overlooked. But taken together they created a whole that was so stimulating and dynamic that anyone who came into contact with it had no choice but to be crushed or to reinvent herself. Two years ago, Montgomery Gilmore had entered her life like a train passing through a glass station, leaving her little choice but to climb aboard or spend the rest of her life on a platform smashed to smithereens. And Emma had jumped aboard without a second thought. Just as she had jumped aboard the hot-air balloon, where, to Monty's horror, she had laughed so much she had almost made the basket capsize. She would even climb on the back of an orange-plumed heron and fly to the stars if he asked her.

With a sense of joy, Emma realized that the more she listened to her aunt's diatribe, the less annoyed she felt about her fiancé's lateness. After all, he was bound to appear sooner or later. She had no doubt about that. She knew she could count on him the way she had never been able to count on anyone. And nothing else mattered to her. Monty would arrive inventing the most hilarious excuse, tying himself up in such knots with his apologies that instead of justifying himself, he would condemn himself hopelessly, and she would have no choice but to burst out laughing. Emma gave her aunt a sidelong, almost affectionate glance. She surprised herself thinking she would miss her, a little, and the old lady would doubtless miss her, too, when she left her all alone again, when she went to settle in her new house after the wedding. She promised herself that, amid all her happiness, she wouldn't forget her aunt and resolved to visit her as often as her duties as a newlywed would allow. A newlywed . . . the idea gave her butterflies in her stomach, a feeling that spread through the rest of her body.

"I hope that foolish smile doesn't mean you are laughing at me, Emma. And will you stop twirling that umbrella! You're making me dizzy."

The girl blinked a couple of times before realizing that her aunt had, for the moment anyway, stopped her ruthless dissection of her fiancé and was addressing her.

"Forgive me, Auntie. I was . . . remembering something funny that happened to me the other day."

"Something funny? I can't think what that might be. Perhaps the sight of Gilmore trying to eat properly with a knife and fork."

And then, to her own amazement, Emma lost her temper.

"That's enough, Auntie! That's enough! Can't you see I love him!" Emma paused, confronted with her aunt's wounded expression as she gaped at her openmouthed, and she fumbled around for a less clichéd way of telling her aunt how she felt. If only there were some magic formula to describe exactly what someone would see pulsating inside her if right then she were stretched out on a table and sliced open. But there wasn't. "I love him . . ." She gave in and simply repeated the same three words again very slowly: "I love him . . . I don't care how he holds a knife and fork. I don't care if he made his money by selling shoelaces or cleaning sewers. I don't care if he always arrives late, if he talks too loudly or always treads on my toes when we dance. Before I met him, I didn't know how to laugh . . . I never knew how, not even when I was small. I had the most absurd, pathetic childhood in the world: an unhappy little girl who didn't know how to laugh!"

"I always thought you were a most interesting child," the old lady protested. "I could never understand how my weak-willed sister-in-law managed to give birth to such a precocious little devil. I was convinced you would grow up free from all the frivolities of love and sentimentality, and I felt proud. At last, a Harlow woman with grit! I confess you even reminded me a little of myself when I was young. And now here you are, prattling on to me about true love! If you wanted to laugh, you could have gone to a zoo. Monkeys are very funny. They always made me laugh, but I never eloped with one."

Emma sighed and bit her lip impatiently: How could she make her aunt see why she loved Gilmore? How could she explain to her why she couldn't help loving him? How could she sum it up in one sentence, a few words? Suddenly, she knew.

"Monty is genuine."

"'Genuine'?" her aunt repeated.

"Yes, genuine," Emma insisted. "He is genuine. Look around you. All of us go through life wearing a mask. But not Monty. He doesn't hide beneath a mask. He is real, not two-faced. You can take him or leave him. But if you take him . . ." Emma smiled, her eyes moist with tears. "Oh, if you take him, then you can be sure he won't deceive you, that what he offers is all there is. I don't know whether Monty is the most marvelous man in the world, but I do know that he's the only man who would never lie to me to *pretend* that he is. And that is exactly what makes him so mar—"

"Stop right there, my dear," the old lady interrupted brusquely. "I can't abide romantic drivel. In my opinion, novelists who write that sort of twaddle should be shot at dawn. Of course, next you'll tell me you don't want to live in a world without him in it, or some such nonsense . . ."

Emma took a deep breath. She had nothing more to say, she knew she had found the right words, and all of a sudden she realized she no longer cared whether she had managed to convince her aunt or not.

"A world without him in it . . . ," she murmured with a faint smile. "Auntie dear, the whole world is nothing more than the precise length of each moment that separates us."

Just then, a distant rumble, which had been audible for a couple of minutes, but to which Emma and her aunt had not paid much attention, began to grow louder, suggesting that whatever was causing it was approaching the house at speed. Vaguely alarmed, the two women glanced at the wall separating the garden from the road, beyond which the din resounded as it approached the front gates. All of a sudden, there was a wail like a ship's siren, and an instant later a strange-looking horseless carriage burst into the driveway amid a cacophony of clatters and bangs, leaving a trail of thick smoke behind it. At a speed that could only be described as breakneck, the vehicle rolled up outside the front steps, where the two astonished women watched it come to a halt, gasping like a dying animal. Emma had never seen an automobile like that before. She had glimpsed a few illustrations of those early carriages that had substituted engine power for horsepower, but they hadn't looked very different from the ordinary horse-drawn ones. In addition, according to what she had read, the new automobiles barely reached speeds of twelve miles an hour, which any cyclist with strong legs could easily equal. Yet the impressive machine wheezing before her had sped through the front gates like greased lightning, covered the fifty yards between them, and pulled up outside the front steps in the time it took to draw breath. Moreover, the shape of it was unlike anything she had ever seen: the bodywork, which was cream colored and trimmed in gold, was long and sleek, and it was so low that the space between the ground and running boards was easily surmounted; the front was shaped like a big metal box with a grille, to either side of which two ostentatious lamps were attached, like a pair of elaborate horns; the back wheels were slightly bigger than the front ones, and above them was a roof, which at present was folded like an accordion; underneath the automobile, a mass of cranks and cogs was visible, seemingly operated by a tall lever to the right of the seat, which looked like a double throne; in front of the seat was the short shaft supporting the enormous steering wheel, which was adorned with a horn that was curled like a pig's tail. And plumb in the middle of that extraordinary carriage, sitting bolt upright and clutching the wheel as if he were afraid that at any moment the machine might start moving of its own accord, was Montgomery Gilmore. He was wearing a pair of huge goggles that covered half his face and a leather cap with flaps down over his ears, giving him the look of a giant insect. In spite of this, Gilmore managed to smile radiantly at Emma.

"Goodness gracious me . . . ," murmured Lady Harlow. "I'm afraid, dear girl, that your fiancé has decided to abandon his admirable habit of going through life without wearing a mask."

Ignoring her aunt, Emma descended the front steps, coming to a halt at what felt like a safe distance from the machine. Gilmore gazed at her, spellbound. She looked so enchanting with that astonished expression in her dark eyes that he could only give thanks once more to whoever had made possible the miracle of a woman such as she being in love with him.

"Emma, my darling! What do you think?" he shouted eagerly as he struggled to open the door so he could run over and fling his arms around her before the magic of the moment faded. But the handle was stuck fast. "I told you I had a surprise for you! It's a Mercedes, the first modern automobile! It's only a prototype, so it isn't even on sale yet. I had to wait while they made a few last minor adjustments in the workshop, that's why I'm so late. But it was worth it, don't you think? Just imagine! It can go up to fifty miles an hour almost without shaking! You'll see how comfortable it is, my love: like drifting on a silent cloud!" Gilmore tried desperately to force the handle, than stood on his seat to clamber over the door. But when he lifted one of his long legs, his shoe became stuck in the steering wheel, and there he stood, as though caught in a trap, his heel pressing on the horn, its deafening blast making Emma recoil. Gilmore fell back onto the seat in an ungainly posture, and the racket continued as he wriggled about trying to free his shoe from the unfortunate snare. Only when he had succeeded did the pitiful wail cease so that Gilmore could leap out of the vehicle. He stood gazing at his fiancé, tongue-tied, his face bright pink, his jacket crumpled, and his goggles askew. Emma raised an eyebrow.

"Did you say a silent cloud?"

The two of them burst out laughing.

Six months later, Lady Harlow would declare on her deathbed that the air around them had sparkled as the couple laughed. But there would be no one there to hear her, for she would die alone, her only companion an impassive nurse who came and went without paying much attention to the dying old woman's babblings. Yes, Lady Harlow would repeat those words to herself over and over. She had seen it with her own eyes as she stood on the front step: at first, she had thought it was an optical illusion caused by the mist, or possibly the lamps of that monstrous machine, but after the couple had left, and during the weeks that followed, as the now incurable solitude of that empty home gradually poisoned her soul, nourishing the tumor that six months later would deliver her into the arms of grim Death, she became convinced that she had witnessed a true miracle that morning.

"The whole world," Lady Harlow mumbled with her last breath before the stone-faced nurse, "was no more than the precise length of each moment that separated them."

AND JUST AS EMMA clambered aboard her fiancé's automobile and gave a little gasp of excitement, several miles away, Wells gasped, too, but out of boredom. He had started off feigning a polite interest, but as the carriage rattled toward Dartmoor, Doyle's tedious descriptions of his latest sporting exploit had increasingly plunged Wells into a slough of despond, finally convincing him that the jaunt wasn't going to be as enjoyable as they all imagined.

But how could things have gone so awry? In the days leading up to the trip, he had made all the arrangements, convinced that Murray's idea would not only be a pleasant change for everyone but would also allow him to resolve, at a stroke, the twin problems that had been worrying him lately. The first concerned Murray and Doyle, whose initial encounter at Arnold House hadn't gone as smoothly as Wells had hoped. Since Murray and Emma were making their own way to Devon, the Wellses had arranged to travel in the same carriage as Doyle. That would give Wells the chance to mollify him before his second encounter with

Murray. He didn't think that would be too difficult, for although Doyle had a fiery nature, which he himself admitted, blaming it freely on his Irish blood, he was also incapable of bearing a grudge. In that sense he differed greatly from Wells, who possessed the dubious ability to protect the smallest seed of hatred against the winds of time. As for Murray . . . well, what could he say about the new, lovesick Murray, who seemed willing to be friends even with the devil himself? Despite having gotten off on the wrong foot, Wells felt sure the two men were destined to get along, for they had more in common than either was prepared to admit. Given a second chance, it would only be a matter of time before they would end up the best of friends, which was precisely what Wells planned to intimate to Doyle on their way to Dartmoor.

The second problem was the one that most concerned Wells. Since both he and Murray had been otherwise engaged, this would be the first time they would meet since that fateful day when Wells had told him he should reveal his true identity to Emma. Wells had begun to fret over the disastrous possible consequences for Murray if he were to follow such foolhardy advice and had inquired about the matter in some of the notes they had exchanged confirming details of the forthcoming trip; but since Murray had warned Wells never to put anything relating to his true identity into writing, he had been forced to use all sorts of euphemisms and innuendos, and he very much doubted that he had correctly interpreted Murray's equally cryptic replies. However, as the days went by, the absence of any other news had put Wells's mind at rest. The planned excursion was to take place and, more important, so it seemed was the wedding. And that could only mean one of two things: that Murray had confessed to Emma without any major falling-out, or that he still hadn't told her. In the first case, Wells would simply undertake to congratulate his friend and rejoice with him over the success of his shrewd piece of advice; in the second case, Wells would have to find the right moment during the trip to take Murray aside and confess his qualms about the recommendation he had made in front of the hibiscus bush, thus absolving himself from any responsibility.

The idea of settling both issues had made Wells await the excursion with impatience, even though in the end they had to make the journey in Murray's carriage (for different reasons neither Doyle nor Wells had the use of their respective carriages that day), thus exposing themselves to the eccentric interrogations of Murray's coachman. Still, it was a small price to pay for the happy prospect of the trip, and Wells had been in an excellent frame of mind when he awoke that day. He had gone down to the kitchen to enjoy a cup of tea and browse through the newspaper while he waited for Murray's coach, which was stopping off on the way to pick up Doyle, unaware that his festive spirit would soon be crushed.

The first shock came from the newspaper itself: "The Invisible Man Is Coming!" the headline proclaimed. Wells had to blink several times, as if he had gotten lemon juice in his eyes. It seemed that the person responsible for the news item, one of many journalists reporting on the series of paranormal occurrences on Dartmoor, had thought it would be funny to use as his title the warning cry Wells's characters uttered as they fled in terror from the Invisible Man in his eponymous novel. As you may imagine, dear reader, Wells was not amused, for he did not like people appropriating his ideas. His aim when writing those words had been to shock the reader, dredging up his most primeval fears—the horror of what can be imagined but not seen—and so it vexed him that this disrespectful hack should use his words to make his readers laugh. But the article itself he found even less amusing, because after the *original* title, the second-rate reporter went on to describe disdainfully the recent spate of strange phenomena that had occurred on Dartmoor. It seemed as if the place had become the favorite haunt of spirits—although, perhaps, Wells speculated sarcastically, it was there that the Invisible Man had met the woman of his dreams, a creature as ethereal as he, and the two of them had given birth to a large ghost family that had infiltrated the local population of "visibles" and was trying to take over the county by instigating a reign of terror. Why not? he had concluded with an airy shrug: judging from the numerous chairs that moved by their own volition and plates that suddenly flew through the air in that sinister place, any explanation could be as or more compelling than the absurd notion that half of England's ghosts had chosen that barren area as a holiday destination.

Wells stopped reading. He felt a growing queasiness in the pit of his stomach. Wasn't it too much of a coincidence that, precisely that morning, the papers had borrowed a sentence from his novel as a title for an article, which also spoke of the very place they were going to on their outing? Much as he tried, Wells could not overlook this coincidence. Why, some of the terrifying events described had even occurred at Brook Manor, the first of the houses they were to visit! The locals swore they had seen a candle flame dancing like a wayward firefly from window to window in the supposedly deserted house, and a host of caretakers who had worked there had handed in their notice, they told the papers, unable to bear the continuous noise of voices, footsteps, and howls that echoed through the gloomy corridors of the mansion day and night.

And this was the house they would be visiting in a few hours' time? thought Wells uneasily, not because of the rumored ghosts, which didn't bother him much, but because of his disquiet at the hidden meaning he always read into every coincidence. Why had they published the article on that particular day and not the day before or after? Was this a mysterious warning? Perhaps it wasn't such a good idea to visit the place where his tormented creation appeared to be concealed after stepping out of the pages in which Wells had imprisoned him . . . Wells tried to curb his feverish imagination and think rationally. Yes, he told himself, he objected to anyone blurring the line between his novels and reality—even as a joke. But however childish his misgivings might appear, they were understandable, for whenever that happened, his life was always affected in one way or another. After he wrote *The Time Machine,* the appearance of Murray's Time Travel had given him a lot of headaches as well as an archenemy. Although, to be fair, the re-creation of the Martian invasion from his book *The War of the Worlds* had converted that same enemy into one of his closest friends. He found it difficult to imagine what a possible encounter with the invisible man of his novel might bestow on him. A new pet? Triplets?

But Wells had scarcely had time to laugh at his own joke when he heard the sound of horses' hooves announcing the arrival of the carriage with the pompous "G" emblazoned on its side. Through the kitchen window, he saw Doyle step out of the coach and then watched with irritation as he helped Miss Jean Leckie down. That put him in a bad mood. Not that Wells had anything against the young woman, who possessed the kind of exquisite, ethereal beauty (hazel eyes, ash-blond hair, and slender, petite figure) found in the illustrations of fairies Doyle was so fond of. On the contrary, he admired her shrewd intelligence and her straightforward sense of humor, and both couples tried to meet up whenever they could, as this wasn't the first time Doyle and Jean had been seen together in mixed company, although hitherto for the sake of appearances Jean had invariably been accompanied by her brother Malcolm or some female chaperone. But although Wells liked Jean, he couldn't help considering her presence that morning a hindrance to his plans. He cursed Doyle under his breath for having invited her along, for he knew the author well enough to be aware that never in the presence of his lady friend would he allow anyone to tell him how he should treat the impertinent Montgomery Gilmore.

And the fact was Wells had not been mistaken. He had tried several times during the long journey to Dartmoor to bring the topic up but had failed miserably. Fortunately, Jane had managed to lighten things up by asking Doyle about the match he had played at Lord's with the Marylebone Cricket Club a few days earlier, an epic game that was the talk of the town, and Doyle had launched into a blow-by-blow account of bats hitting balls according to some whimsical rules only he appeared to understand. To cap it all, they were moving so ludicrously slowly that Wells was expecting the slumbering figure of the coachman to fall off his perch at any moment.

Dejected, he ignored Doyle's exploits and glanced out of the window. Although they were still driving through pretty countryside, and the road was flanked with green meadows dotted with neat thatched cottages, Wells could feel a sadness descending on the landscape: the moor announced its presence like a brewing storm. If he pressed his forehead against the glass, he could make out an ominous line of hills in the distance, silhouetted against a sky so dark it resembled a swamp. And that desolate, gloomy place was where they were headed . . . Wells was no longer in any doubt: it was going to be an awful day.

After half an hour of negotiating narrow lanes bordered with ever more sinister pines and oaks, the carriage reached the top of a small knoll and came wearily to a halt. Doyle finally broke off his interminable story, and they all looked out of the windows. The ground sloped away into a deep hollow, and the dreamlike moor stretched before them like a threadbare carpet, a barren, endless expanse with only three or four buildings several miles apart and dotted with clusters of reddish rock and the odd crooked tree bent by the prevailing wind. The moor was solitude in earthly form, so to speak. Death had laid down its mantle here and was roaming the world naked.

"Brook Manor," the coachman said in a somber voice, pointing with his whip at the first of the houses.

As they made their way down to the mansion, a gloomy silence descended on them, broken only by the sound of the horses' hooves and the creak of the carriage wheels as they contemplated the colossal shape of the house towering before them: an impressive mass of stone from which two identical crenellated towers rose up into the darkening sky. To the right, the desolate moor stretched out, marked in the distance by what looked like a tiny hamlet and a couple of farms. Wells remembered that they were only four or five miles from Dartmoor prison, renowned throughout the land for its harsh regime. Moments later, the carriage ground to a halt outside the mansion's impressive wrought-iron gate, flecked with rust and flanked by two dilapidated stone pillars.

The travelers stepped out of the carriage to take a closer look and to stretch their legs, but no sooner had their feet touched the ground than an icy gust of wind forced them to wrap their cloaks and coats around them. They approached the bars, shivering, and nervously contemplated the tree-lined driveway that stretched beyond the gates, at the end of which, enveloped in mist, was the mansion. It seemed to pulsate imperceptibly, like some malevolent creature brought back to life by an evil spell. For a few moments, they all remained silent, clutching the bars of the gate as if that gloomy hole were threatening to suck out their very souls. The wind buffeted them, whipping their clothes before sweeping down the driveway, transforming the fallen leaves into a flock of demented crows.

"If the devil himself wanted to meddle in the affairs of men, he couldn't wish for a more perfect setting," sighed Wells.

"I couldn't agree with you more!" Doyle boomed, turning toward him. "Admit it, George: in spite of all your skepticism, if a gruesome hound were to appear on that driveway and come charging toward us, baring its teeth, wouldn't you think it came directly from hell?"

"I expect so . . ."

Wells scanned the driveway nervously and couldn't help remembering the Norfolk legend of Black Shuck, the big hairy dog that killed people with its eyes. Murray would need to spend a fortune on electric lightbulbs before Wells agreed to set foot in that dreadful house.

"Forgive me for butting in," said the coachman, who had climbed down off his perch and approached them quietly, "but I tell you, if I saw an evil dog running toward me, the last thing I'd care about is where it came from. I'd run like a man possessed by the devil and hide behind the nearest door."

They all looked at the coachman, slightly puzzled.

"Don't you like dogs?" Jean inquired politely.

The old man shook his head vigorously.

"You wouldn't believe how much I detest them, Miss Leckie. I'm afraid that anyone who was bitten by one as a child can never trust the perfidious creatures again."

"It is true that a lot of people have an aversion to them," Jane butted in, smiling sympathetically at the coachman. "But you have to admit some breeds are absolutely adorable, and harmless."

The old man gazed at her for a few seconds in silence, smiling with a strange tenderness.

He chuckled at last. "They all have teeth, Mrs. Wells."

"You're quite right," replied Jane, joining in his laughter.

"It's too cold out here!" Wells then muttered, annoyed by his wife's apparent empathy with Murray's coachman. All of a sudden, he wondered what the devil they were doing in the middle of that godforsaken moor, enduring that icy cold as they discussed with the old fellow his fear of dogs. "I think we'd better wait for Emma and Montgomery inside the carriage."

The others agreed and, bundled up in their coats, walked toward the supposed shelter offered by the coach.

"I hate dogs and you hate the stairs at Edwin Hyde's drapery, isn't that so?" the coachman whispered to Wells as he walked past.

Wells looked at him in astonishment while he tried to recall when he had told the old man that the stairs he had fallen down as a youth were the ones in the draper's at Southsea. The old fellow grinned to himself, pointing to the tiny scar on Wells's chin. Just then, a loud din caused everyone to look over toward the brow of the hill. Gleaming through the mist, a peculiar-looking vehicle was rolling down the hill toward them at an alarming speed, announcing its arrival with a sort of bellow that echoed across the moor, vying with the howl of the wind.

16

$\mathcal{T}$HE SOUND OF THE DOOR CREAKING SHUT BE-
hind them echoed off the walls of the vast entrance hall for
several minutes, and the small group that had dared disturb the silence
of that place huddled even closer together. They glanced about uneasily, mesmerized by those walls steeped in a thousand gloomy winters
and crammed with weapons and emblazoned shields. Murray, who had
organized that expedition into the heart of darkness and therefore felt
responsible for the mood of its members, decided to speak first.

"I plan to install a handful of Edison's electric lightbulbs there, there,
and there," he said resolutely, pointing randomly into the murkiness. "I
shall also get rid of all the shields and weapons and replace them with
beautiful paintings."

"Get rid of the weapons?" Doyle protested. "That would be madness, Gilmore. Why, this collection is worthy of a knight of old. Look
at that mace, for example!" He pointed to one of the walls where a club
with a big, rusty ball studded with spikes had been mounted. "The
perfect weapon for use in man-to-man combat, every bit as noble as
the sword, while clearly requiring less skill and more brute force. And
what about that crossbow? I'd say it's probably twelfth-century," Doyle
added, referring to a wooden device resting on the wall like a monstrous dragonfly. "Although the fact is I've always considered crossbows
to be despicable weapons, allowing any oaf to kill from a safe distance
a knight trained in the art of war. They are a test of marksmanship, not
manliness. And terribly difficult to reload so that during a battle every

crossbowman needed a shield bearer to protect him while he reloaded the damn thing."

And Doyle instantly launched into a detailed description of how to load a crossbow, accompanying his lesson with a pantomime of the movements. Murray interrupted him before everybody started to yawn.

"I'm glad you find them so interesting, Doyle. But in my view all these weapons merely illustrate man's ingenuity for dreaming up fresh ways to kill his fellow man, and I will get rid of them at the first opportunity," he said, inventing scruples he did not possess, or at least not in his old life, Wells reflected, when he had doubtless been skilled at handling weapons. "We'll hang up a few works by Leighton instead. What do you reckon, Emma?"

He took his betrothed by the arm and, without giving Doyle a chance to reply, began a tour of his recently acquired mansion while he chatted about the various improvements he was planning to make. The others had little choice but to tag along behind them. From the hallway, they passed into the main reception room, which seemed slightly more welcoming due to the enormous fireplace gaping in one corner and the tall stained-glass windows, which, despite the dull grey light filtering through them that day, promised rainbow colors when the sun shone. However, the smoke-blackened oak-beamed ceilings evoked the leaden skies that hung over the moor, and the dozens of deer heads mounted on the walls seemed to observe the passing group through glassy eyes tinged with death. Next, the group entered an enormous dining hall that offered no respite from the somber atmosphere pervading the house; on the contrary, it was a windowless, gloomy room that gave off a powerful smell of mustiness and despair. When Murray lit one of the few lamps there and placed it in the middle of the long central table, a feeble pool of light spilled from it onto the dusty wood. But it was enough for them to make out through the surrounding thicket of shadows a ring of pale phantoms spying on them. After the initial shock, Murray lifted the lamp and drew closer to one of the walls. A sigh of relief spread through the group as they realized that the ghostly faces belonged to a row of portraits, doubtless ancestors of the Cabell family. Regarded in descending order, these gentlemen, with their alternately stern or stoical expressions, exchanged dress coats for frock coats and prior to that the more sober tailcoats of the Regency era, illustrating the passage of time more entertainingly than rings on a tree ever did. Apart from the dozen portraits, there was a second door located just opposite the one they had come in through, as well as some rusty shields crossed with swords, a couple of faded tapestries depicting mythological scenes, and an enormous mirror that enclosed the whole room in an ornate gold frame.

"Heavens," Doyle murmured, pointing toward the portraits, "I don't think I'd be able to dine easily in their company."

Ignoring Doyle's commentary, Murray began pacing round the table, rubbing his hands together excitedly.

"Think how beautiful this room will look, Emma, when we, when we"—he glanced around, trying to imagine what refurbishments could miraculously embellish the room—"change it completely."

She chuckled. "Why, I think it's charming as it is, Monty. What is there to change? It's perfect . . . If you don't manage to sell the house, we could throw parties here. We could invite all the people we don't like and make them sit in this dining room eating interminable meals, and at night, when they are asleep, we could drag chains along the corridors and let out bloodcurdling howls. That way we'd be sure they'd never accept another invitation, and we wouldn't have to accept theirs either, assuming they ever invited us anywhere after such an experience."

"Oh, that's a brilliant idea, darling," Murray said enthusiastically.

"Actually it would be rather good to have somewhere like that," added Wells, who could think of dozens of people he would invite to such dinners.

"Very well, perhaps we'll keep it just as it is," Murray went on jovially. "On second thought, it could be put to other similar uses. We could even"—he grinned mischievously—"hire it out for séances."

"Oh, no, Monty, not that again . . . ," Emma began, suddenly growing serious.

"But, darling, feel the *atmosphere*!" Murray interrupted, signaling the room around them with feigned admiration. "I imagine this is what Mr. Doyle would call . . . what was it again? An atmosphere conducive to the power of suggestion."

Doyle only scowled at Murray.

"Why, yes," Murray said, spreading his arms, as though wanting to clasp all that darkness to him, "I think I've just found another perfect idea for a business. Any medium would happily pay whatever we asked to hold his séances here. With such a *conducive* atmosphere, he would scarcely need to employ his usual tricks—"

"That's enough, Monty," Emma cut in. "Arthur, I beg you to forgive us once more: we didn't mean to offend you by mocking your beliefs; we were only teasing." She looked sternly at Murray. "Isn't that right, darling?"

"Of course, it was just teasing, Doyle," Murray confirmed with a shrug.

"I appreciate your concern, Miss Harlow," said Doyle, ignoring Murray and addressing his fiancée with a look of injured pride. "As I already said when we first met, I know how to enjoy a good joke."

"Oh, I'm sure you do," Emma replied, without clarifying either whether or not Murray's remarks fell into that category. "Although, speaking of sinister atmospheres, it has to be said there is something very intimidating about this house."

"Well, it doesn't intimidate me in the slightest," Murray declared.

"Oh, come now, Monty," said Wells, who was praying Murray and Doyle weren't going to get into another unpleasant argument, "you must admit the place gives you the shivers, regardless of whether we came here expecting that or not."

"Well, I'd say the house is contaminated with energies beyond our understanding," Doyle announced with an authoritative air, casting an eye slowly around the room. "I don't think it is simply a matter of suggestion, George. We all perceive it, even if some of us daren't admit it."

"Who dares not admit it?" asked Murray.

"You, of course, darling," Emma replied.

"Really? And what exactly is it I'm meant to perceive? That the souls of this jolly lot are watching us to make sure we don't make fun of their whiskers?" Murray argued, pointing at the portraits.

"That's not what I meant, darling," replied Emma, maintaining her composure. "But, like Arthur, I, too, believe there is something in this house that our senses perceive without understanding. Maybe not the souls of the departed, or the idea we have of souls. But perhaps everything these people experienced"—she pointed at the portraits lining the walls, and pivoted slowly round—"what made them suffer, and what they loved, has somehow outlived them . . ." She walked over to the table and ran her finger gently along the back of one of the chairs while she went on dreamily. "Imagine all the scenes that have taken place in this dining room: the dinners, the family dramas, the news of war, the joyous tidings . . . Perhaps it is all still here, eternally taking place, somehow vibrating in the air, even though we neither hear nor see it, because our minds are only able to perceive the present . . . There could be places, like this, that are like backwaters in a river, places where the flow of time stagnates and experiences accumulate in layers over the centuries to form a unique, complex present, and that this . . . existential sedimentation, so to speak, is what we perceive. Perhaps the shiver you felt, George, was because at that very moment a butler walked through you carrying a tray of glasses"—at which Wells looked at Emma, startled, and took a discreet step to one side—"and you, Jane, right this minute, you might be standing in the sight line of two rivals who will fight a duel at dawn. And in this chair I am leaning against, perhaps a man is caressing his lover's foot under the table, while she is writing their initials on the table with her finger"—and with this, Emma's own slender forefinger traced in the dust an "M" and an "E." Then Emma contemplated the two letters with a pensive smile, probably wondering whether a hundred years from then, when those letters were long gone, and she herself wasn't even alive, some visitor would sense her making that gesture, until she realized they had all fallen silent. She looked up, her cheeks turning a delightful shade of pink. "Oh, please forgive my silly daydreams. I was born in a very young country, where the buildings have no memories, so that places like this seem completely magical to me . . ."

"There's no need to apologize, my dear," said Jane. "It was a truly beautiful description."

Everyone agreed except for Murray, who simply gazed at Emma in admiration.

"And not only that," Doyle chipped in excitedly. "It is also another way of expressing what I have always said: that part of what we are survives the death of our bodies. And why not? Perhaps death is a mere repetition of our lives on a higher plane, a sort of Hinton's cube where we experience every instant of our lives simultaneously . . . And anyway, mediums have relayed numerous messages from spirits who describe the Hereafter as a carbon copy of their former lives."

"I don't think you understood a single word that my fiancée said, Doyle!" exclaimed Murray.

"Of course I did," Doyle replied indignantly. "I am simply pointing out that there are many ways of expressing the same idea. Something transcends us, transcends our will, our perception of time and space—in other words, our death. Yes, even though our bodies turn to dust, part of us lives on forever. And I agree completely, Emma, that there must be places, as well as people, that serve as conduits for all that energy. Perhaps this house is one of those places, for there is no doubt that we all sense something now. You feel it, Emma, and George and I also feel it. And so do you, don't you, Jean?"

The young woman nodded, her expression reflecting her unease.

"It must be the damp," said Murray, wrinkling his nose and staring up at the ceiling.

"Oh, Monty, you are the limit," sighed Emma. "I promise that if I die before you, I will come back to haunt you every night."

"Well, you'll need to find a *proper conduit*," he reminded her with a grin.

"Well," she retorted, "with your great fortune, I have no doubt that you would hire the best medium there is."

"You can be sure of that, my darling."

Emma's eyes twinkled with amusement.

"And the séance would have to be held here at Brook Manor," she demanded, tapping her foot on the floor. "If I were a spirit, I couldn't possibly appear anywhere else. It is too delightfully sinister!"

"As always, my love, you show an exquisite taste in—"

Worried that the couple were about to initiate one of those conversations others find embarrassing, Jane hurriedly interrupted, asking Murray whether the house really suffered from damp.

"I'm afraid so, my dear," Murray told her. "We have found serious damp problems throughout the house. Some of the floorboards are completely rotten, but nothing that can't be fixed."

With that, Murray motioned to the others to follow him through the second door. Heaving a sigh, Wells prepared to join them, but a big cobweb hanging from the ceiling became tangled in his hair, and he frantically brushed it away. Fearing the creature responsible for such a colossal web might be proportionate in size to its architectural feat and could now be running about on his back, Wells went up to the mirror and, performing various risky contortions, began to examine himself carefully. Then something he saw reflected in the mirror made him pause. The others were filing out of the room, not through the second door, but rather through the one they had entered moments before. Wells wheeled round, only to find himself even more flabbergasted. There they were, still walking through the second door, Murray at the fore, listing the different ways of combating damp, followed by Emma and Jane, who appeared rapt, and behind them Jean and Doyle, who at that moment whispered something in his companion's ear that made her chuckle. Wells turned back to the mirror and felt his heart jump. There they were again, faithfully reflected, but filing through the wrong door. Unable to believe his own eyes, Wells turned his head from the real world to the reflected world and back again, watching his friends leaving the dining room through two different doors.

When they had all gone out, Wells stood mutely in front of the mirror, which now reflected a room that was empty except for one terrified man. He turned around and, although he could hear his friends' voices clearly coming from beyond the doorway they had just gone through in the real world, ran across to the one they had stepped through in the mirror. As he expected, the room with the big fireplace was deserted. Wells stood for a moment staring awkwardly at the mounted deer heads, which were gazing at one another with the idiotic expression guests have when they have exhausted all possible conversations. Then he ran over to the other door, leading to the vast entrance hall, at the far end of which he discovered his companions climbing up to the first floor via the magnificent marble staircase. Wells opened his mouth, ready to call out, but closed it instantly. What on earth was he going to say to them? He returned to the dining room and walked back over to the mirror. Trying to think rationally, he told himself that, due to the way it was positioned or to some distortion in the glass, he must have experienced a strange optical illusion. He spent several minutes examining the mirror and the frame from every possible angle. He even lifted it slightly away from the wall but found nothing behind it. He stood facing it once more and examined the reflected image of the deserted dining room, which seemed identical now to the real one. The same portraits adorned the walls, the same crossed swords, the same lamp spilling its tentative pool of light onto the dusty table . . . the dusty table . . . Wells breathed in sharply. Resting his hands on the mirror, he narrowed his eyes and drew closer until the tip of his nose was almost touching the glass.

In the reflected dust on the reflected table, where Emma had written the two initials, there was nothing. Wells glanced over his shoulder, and he could see them even through the gloom. They were still there, illuminated by the lamplight, an "M" and an "E" clearly traced in the thick layer of real dust. Of course they were still there; why wouldn't they be?

He was alone in the room, and they couldn't have erased themselves. Wells looked into the mirror again and confirmed once more that the initials weren't reflected there. His head started to spin. Was this still an optical illusion he couldn't account for? He tapped the cold surface gently with his splayed hands, as if to satisfy himself that it existed, that it had the consistency of a real object, that it wasn't a figment of his imagination as well. And then he noticed that, on the side of his chin where he had the tiny scar that gave him such a complex, his reflection showed nothing. As he stood gaping at himself, a wave of sheer terror began to crawl up his spine and spread around the base of his skull like a hungry snake, ready to feed on his sanity. Because there was no other possible explanation for that horror except insanity! Wells ran his fingers over the familiar roughness of his scar, while his reflection stroked his pristine skin with what must have been the same terrified expression.

He staggered backward, and his reflection did the same, both of them covering their corresponding chins with their hands. And then, just as he was about to start screaming, the light in the room changed. Wells looked around him, puzzled, trying to perceive the nature of that change, for it wasn't that there was any more or any less light but rather that a subtle variation in the same light had made everything seem suddenly less scary. He went back to the mirror with bated breath, and the Wells who lived in the mirror stared back at him with the same expectation, the same startled eyes, the same tension seizing his body . . . and the same scar on his chin.

Wells let out the breath he been holding in a whoosh as a growing sense of peace invaded him. Then he noticed the letters Emma had written in the dust, and he wanted to laugh, but he stopped himself, fearing he might succumb to a fit of hysterics. The sensation of normality was so overwhelming now that Wells couldn't help but feel slightly ridiculous at being so terrified by a mere trick of the light. How could the atmosphere of that place have made him so suggestive? He stood for a long minute in front of the mirror, examining his face from every possible angle, without the illusion happening again. Finally he realized he couldn't stay there forever, watching his reflection grow old, and he resolved to find his friends.

Wells went out to the hall through the same door the others had used and walked up the marble staircase leading to the first floor, until he reached a kind of gallery that, like an interior balcony, overlooked the entrance on each side of the staircase. Opposite the gallery was a tall window framing a leaden sky, with a long corridor on either side. Unsure which one to take, Wells listened out for a voice that might indicate where his companions were, but a dense silence enveloped him, punctuated only by the occasional creaks with which the wood announced its senescence. He decided to approach the window, in case something outside might give him a clue. It offered a splendid view of the moor, brooding gloomily beneath an ashen light. In the distance, beyond a band of rocks and heath, Wells glimpsed the swamp, where he understood several wretched ponies had drowned, and still farther away, dotted along the rolling hills, he saw a cluster of standing stones, ruined huts, and other relics of the ancient Britons. Wells realized, looking down, that he was above the curved driveway where the carriages were parked, and he contemplated the gloomy avenue bordered by two rows of trees, whose tops the wind continued to stir sensually. Then, on a jagged outcrop, Wells made out a dark, looming figure, outlined against the sky like a statue. It belonged to a very tall man who was leaning on a walking stick (or possibly a rifle, he was too far away for Wells to see) and appeared to be surveying the moor as though the place, and any soul brave enough to venture there, belonged to him. He was enveloped in a flowing cloak, which billowed in the wind so that it looked as if his body had gigantic wings, and he wore a wide-brimmed hat. Everything about him felt so familiar that Wells kept staring at him in astonishment, until a curious scene unfolding below caught his attention. Murray's coachman was on the driveway and appeared to be behaving in an even odder and more alarming way than usual: he had crouched down behind Murray's carriage and was peering out, apparently watching the watcher on the moor while simultaneously hiding from him. Astonished, Wells observed the old man as he glanced nervously a few times before making his way over to the Mercedes, stooping even more than his old back demanded, and ducked behind it before repeating the same ritual. Wells felt the urge to open the window and ask him in a very loud voice what on earth he was doing, purely out of a perverse desire to make the old boy jump out of his skin, but at that very moment a huge paw descended on his shoulder, almost causing him to leap out of his own.

"George! Where the devil have you been?"

Wells, exceedingly pale and clutching his chest, spun round to confront Murray.

"For goodness' sake, Monty, are you trying to scare me out of my wits?"

"Are you joking? *We're* the ones who got frightened when we realized you'd disappeared!"

"Well, you took your time," muttered Wells.

"But I've been searching all over the house for you! Doyle was convinced some evil force had detained you, and so he sent me to search while he stayed behind to watch over the ladies in the north gallery. Good heavens, you even had Emma worried. But where the devil have you been?"

"I, er . . ." Wells hesitated to mention the mirror episode for fear of seeming like a madman or a fool. "Where do you think?" he said at last. "I've been here, watching your coachman. Monty, as I've told you many times, there's something very peculiar about that old fellow's behavior. And here you have another example," he said pointing toward the window. "You can see for yourself. In my opinion he's either hiding something or he's off his rocker."

Murray took a look outside.

"I can't see anything, George."

"What?" Wells also looked out. The coachman had gone, the driveway was deserted, and on the craggy rock beyond there was no one either. "Well, he was down there all right," Wells said crossly, "apparently hiding from a strange figure on the moor. A man enveloped in a—"

"Yes, we all saw him!" Murray cut in. "Doyle says it was probably one of the prison guards from Princetown. Apparently whenever an inmate escapes they are often seen watching the roads and railway stations."

"Well, your coachman doesn't seem to be on such good terms with the prison guards. Don't you find that a bit strange?"

Murray chuckled.

"Do you think he's an escaped convict? The poor fellow is over eighty, George! How unforgiving you are when you take a dislike to someone. What must my villainous coachman do for you to give him a second chance?" He grinned ironically. "Save Jane's life?"

"Don't joke about such things, Monty. But speaking of second chances . . . ," said Wells, realizing this might be his only opportunity to speak to Murray alone that day. "Don't you think *you* might make an effort to give Doyle a second chance? I don't know whether you've noticed that he doesn't care much for your jokes . . . Damn it, Monty, Arthur is a friend of mine, and I only introduced you to him because I knew he was one of your favorite authors! I thought you two would get on so well. I don't understand why you insist on riling him all the time."

"I do nothing of the kind!" protested Murray. "At least, not intentionally. Frankly, I've never met anyone as thin-skinned. Except for you, of course."

"Have it your own way, Monty. But in a few weeks' time Doyle will be setting sail for the war in Africa."

"Did he manage to enlist? But he's no longer a young man!"

"No, but a friend has hired him as an assistant doctor in his field hospital. So he'll be leaving soon, which is why I think you ought to be nicer to him, don't you think? You know, men often don't return from wars."

"Oh, I have no doubt that Doyle is the sort who does. And if not, he'll doubtless come back as an irascible ectoplasm." Murray chortled. "But you're right, George. I'll try to be a bit nicer to our fastidious friend . . ."

"I don't know whether 'a bit' will suffice, though I suspect that's all you're capable of . . . But let's change the subject," said Wells, adding in a hushed voice, "What about that other thing?"

"What other thing?"

"You know . . . Emma and you."

"You mean the wedding? Oh, it's all going splendidly. I think the first rehearsal will be—"

"Don't try to bamboozle me, Monty! I'm asking you whether you have told Emma yet that you are the Master of Time!" Wells exploded, angrily stamping his foot.

Murray looked at him, taken aback.

"Would you mind awfully venting your frustration in some other way, George? This floor is particularly badly affected by damp. Another blow like that and we'll both end up in the dining room."

"Don't change the subject!"

Murray contemplated him in silence for a few moments, grunted, and then darted down the right-hand corridor, leaving Wells alone in the empty gallery. Wells followed him into the corridor, pausing at the doorway where he had seen Murray slip through. It led to a small room, which the builders appeared to be using, as it was scattered with sacks of plaster and various tools. Wells discovered Murray pacing round the room like a caged animal. He observed with dismay as each step his friend took kicked up clouds of white dust that formed into pretty swirls in the air before settling on his polished shoes and his immaculate suit.

"Will you stand still for a moment, Monty?" he exclaimed, brushing off the sleeves of his jacket. "Otherwise we soon won't be able to breathe in here! And tell me once and for all whether you've told Emma your secret."

Murray came to a halt and looked at Wells with anguish.

"Since you mention it, George . . . There's something I've been meaning to tell to you about that . . . ," he began, and then fell silent, gazing at his hands, as if the remainder of his speech were written on them.

Wells sighed. It was just as he had thought. Murray still hadn't said a word about it to Emma! He had suspected as much when he saw them climb out of the automobile, and now Murray had confirmed it. Good, good, Wells told himself; Murray hadn't burned any bridges yet, and so he could still retract the advice he had given him. He had found the perfect opportunity, and when he had done so, he would finally be able to stop tormenting himself.

"Don't imagine I haven't thought a great deal about the advice you gave me," Murray resumed at last while Wells nodded with a paternal smile. "In fact, I have pondered it at length and have reached the conclusion that . . . er, how can I put this without sounding rude . . . I think it is one of the stupidest pieces of advice I have ever been given in my life."

The smile vanished from Wells's lips.

"I beg your pardon?"

"I said it was a stupid piece of advice, George, and I'm sure you'd agree with me if you thought about it for a second. I shan't deny that two years ago it would have been an excellent idea to confess everything to Emma, but not now . . . In any case, all couples have their secrets, don't they? Look at your beloved Doyle . . . Not to mention you yourself! Yes, you, too, George. I understand your not wanting to admit to me that you replied to my letter, but I think it is terrible that you are incapable of confessing the truth to Jane . . . your own wife, George!" Murray wagged his head disapprovingly. "Come to think of it, compared to you two, I'm not so bad as all that . . . a tiny secret from my past that has nothing to do with the man I am today. So I have decided not to tell Emma anything." Murray folded his arms as a sign of his determination. "And nothing you say, George, will make me change my mind."

Then Wells took a deep breath and . . . Ah, but what can I tell you, dear readers, that you don't already know about man's irresistible need to defend his most misguided and outmoded beliefs when someone else questions them! I am sure that you have found yourselves more than once justifying absurd notions you no longer believed in simply because someone doubted your ability to do so. And so, in order to spare you the lengthy and tedious conversation that ensued, in which both men put forward arguments those of you who have been paying attention will be only too familiar with, suffice it to say that Wells's discourse was never more brilliant, lucid, and convincing, more ruthless and irrefutable in his reasoning and responses than in that debate that took place in the intimacy of the small room, amid clouds of plaster dust floating in the air like snowflakes in a storm. So that by the time the two friends heard Doyle's booming voice as he came looking for them, concerned about how long they were taking, Murray left the room transformed once more into a man overcome with remorse, more eager than ever to atone for the unforgivable sin weighing on his conscience, whereas Wells did so puffed up with pride, triumphant and exhilarated, at least until the moment when it occurred to him what he had done.

When the group gathered in the driveway to organize their departure for the second house they were to visit, Murray went over to Doyle, apparently keen to start honoring the pledge he had made to Wells that day.

"I'm so glad you enjoyed the tour, Arthur." Murray smiled, clapping Doyle on the back, to which the latter responded with a look of disbelief at his host's sudden preoccupation with his well-being. "I say, the tale of the Cabells and the curse of the bloodhound would make an excellent idea for a novel, don't you think?"

"Possibly," Doyle conceded reluctantly.

"I knew you'd agree!" Murray rejoiced. "After all, we share the same taste in literature . . ."

"Really, then why don't you write it yourself?"

"I would. But don't forget: there has to be a logical explanation behind the ghostly dog the locals claim to have seen, and who better to discover it than Sherlock Holmes, the champion of reason? Wouldn't a case with a supernatural twist challenge the mind of the greatest detective of all time and thrill your readers at the same time? Anyway, Arthur, you're welcome to use my idea. Think of it as a gift. Only an immense talent such as yours could do it justice—even if that does mean rescuing poor Holmes from his watery grave. Don't you agree?" Murray laughed and clapped Doyle on the back again. "But I've already explained to you how to do that."

"Yes, you have. But as I keep telling you, like it or not, Holmes is going to remain at the bottom of the Reichenbach Falls, where he plunged together with Professor Moriarty, from whose embrace he was unable to free himself because he had never practiced jujitsu or *wushu* or . . ."

"Of course, of course, splendid . . . ," murmured Murray, who had just spied Emma waiting for him in the Mercedes and was no longer listening.

She was perched in the driver's seat, playing at steering the automobile. Murray swallowed. She looked so lovely, she trusted him so much, and he was going to hurt her so dreadfully . . .

"Montgomery!" Wells shouted at his side. "Did you hear me?"

"What?" Murray blinked.

"I asked you where your coachman is hiding," Wells replied, trying to conceal his annoyance.

Murray looked about absentmindedly.

"Oh, well . . . I don't expect he can have gone very far at his age . . ."

"I daresay he's back in his prison cell . . ."

Murray sighed.

"Oh, damnation! I'll go and find him. But not another word, George! I warn you, I'm not in the mood."

Wells snorted and climbed into the carriage, where Doyle and the two ladies were already settling into their seats.

"But why are you resistant, darling?" Jean was saying to Doyle. "Montgomery's idea is wonderful."

"Really? I don't think it's that good."

"Oh, but it would be so exciting . . . A new Sherlock Holmes adventure!" Jean declared eagerly. "Perhaps you could call it *The Curse of the Hound*."

"Don't insist, my dear . . . ," said Doyle. "Besides, that's a terrible title."

"All right, what about . . . *The Hound of Dartmoor*?"

"Please, Jean, leave it . . ."

"Or *Holmes Hounds a Hound*?" Wells suggested.

"Very amusing, Wells," Doyle muttered. "Very amusing."

"*The Hound of the Cabells?*" Jane proposed.

Doyle sighed and, finally surrendering, thought about it for a moment: "Hmm, *The Hound of the Cabells* isn't bad at all. *The Hound of the . . .*"

"Baskervilles!" Murray thundered, making the passengers in the carriage jump.

"What the blazes is going on now?" Wells grumbled, leaning his head out of the window.

"Baskervilles!" Murray boomed again, as if his coachman were several miles away, and at that very moment the old man emerged from the side house. "Damn it, Baskervilles!" he cried. "Where the devil have you been?"

Wells watched with distaste as the old man made his way slowly over to the carriage while continuing to cast furtive glances toward the moor. Good heavens, was he really the only one who suspected that the old fellow was hiding something? In any event, since his and Murray's stupid conversation in the room with the sacks of plaster, the man's peculiar behavior had become the least of Wells's worries. He sank back in his seat, annoyed at himself, sad, irritable, and depressed, while the old fellow scrambled onto the driver's perch with surprising alacrity. The two women began a leisurely conversation about the latest Paris fashions, and Doyle shut his eyes. Wells wondered whether he was mulling over Murray's idea for a novel but thought it far more likely that he was attempting to participate in the bubbling energies of the place. Wells sighed and let his gaze wander out of the window as he reflected about their excursion. So far it had been a disaster, although at least he had not had to confront any invisible men, he consoled himself darkly.

After the carriage had gone, Murray took a deep breath, and putting on a smile, he turned toward where Emma was waiting for him in the automobile.

She pointed a menacing finger at him. "Stay right there, Mr. Gilmore! You will be traveling in the passenger seat, for I am pleased to inform you that your future wife will be piloting this old wreck to the next port of call."

"I won't hear of it, Emma," protested Murray. "Driving this thing isn't like steering a little two-horse buggy in the park. It's difficult to control and very dangerous . . ."

"So you don't think I'm clever enough to do it? If I put my mind to it, I can do anything just as well as you, if not better."

"I wouldn't dream of denying it, my darling. In fact, I'd say it is one of the few certainties in life. But driving, well . . . it's not ladylike."

"What do you mean?" Emma retorted, ignoring the implied compliment. "Remember, you were the one who told me, on our way here, that the first long-distance journey in an automobile was made by Bertha Benz, a woman. And if I'm not mistaken, you said that she drove sixty-six miles, stopping off at pharmacies en route to fill the gasoline tank. So . . . why won't you let me drive?"

"Change places, please, Miss Mournful."

Emma had opened her mouth to protest but instantly closed it. Monty had addressed her by the nickname they used in private. Each had given the other a secret pet name, which they promised never to pronounce in front of anyone else, for by mutual agreement they had imbued it with the highest power any word could possess. They could spend all day larking about and making little digs at each other, but when one of them called the other by his or her nickname, it meant that the frivolous, delightful game they were playing must wait while something more serious took over. Emma's nickname had come about the day that she had shown her fiancé a beautiful drawing she had brought with her from New York, a kind of map depicting an imaginary sky filled with wonderful creatures and fantastical marvels. Her great-grandfather had drawn the map especially for his daughter, and it spoke of other worlds where everything was possible. Perhaps that was why it had been such a comfort to her throughout her childhood, when she was a sad, mournful little girl who was convinced nothing would ever make her happy. But that little girl still hadn't met Montgomery Gilmore, the most infuriating of her future suitors, the one who would assure her that he could make any of her wishes come true, however impossible that might seem.

"What's wrong, Mr. Impossible?"

Murray contemplated his fiancée, a lump in his throat, trying to commit to memory the light in her eyes, which were, perhaps for the last time, gazing at him with such tenderness. He pursed his lips until he felt he could speak without his voice faltering.

"I don't want you to drive. There is something I have to tell you that . . . might upset you a little. In fact, I'm sure it will upset you a lot; you might even be angry with me. Although right now I'd give anything if an angry outburst were the only consequence I had to suffer. In any case, I'd better drive." He opened the door and extended his arm to Emma, who looked at him, wondering whether she should ask him to be more specific about this mysterious subject or change seats obediently. "Please, Emma," Murray insisted, thrusting his arm more forcefully at her as his eyes began to fill with tears. "Trust me."

Emma needed no more persuading. She took her fiancé's hand and stepped out of the automobile, looking uneasily into the glinting eyes of that big man she had never seen weep.

"It's all right, darling," she said, stroking his cheek. "I don't know what it is you have to tell me, but I'm sure it can't be all that bad. You know I trust you implicitly."

17

TEN-YEAR-OLD TOMMY DAWKINS PEDALED AS hard as he could down the path from his back garden to the Hexworthy Road as he tried to outrun the wind. He could feel his ears buzzing and his hair blowing, and he was almost sure that right then nothing in the whole world was faster than he and his bike. When Benjamin Barrie saw him ride up to his door on that amazing machine, he would have to eat his words. That idiot was always making fun of him, saying he couldn't walk without tripping over his own feet. Well, that morning Barrie would discover that walking and tripping over weren't all he could do. Barrie was about to discover that Tommy Dawkins could fly.

When he saw the junction ahead of him, he began to pedal even harder, getting ready to swerve into the road with one of those sharp turns he had practiced so often toward dawn, before the servants were even up, and unbeknownst to his brother. He felt a pang of anxiety at the thought of the drubbing his brother Jim would give him if he ever found out he had been riding his precious bike without asking and had even gone to the village on it. Luckily, Tommy's brother had just gone to the war in South Africa, and by the time he came back, if he ever did, Tommy didn't think he would be upset over something so trivial. Tommy narrowed his eyes and leaned over the handlebars. So lost was he in dreams of glory, and so loud was the wind in his ears, that he didn't hear the roar of the automobile coming along the road he was about to ride out into, hidden from view behind a bend. And if Tommy had been five seconds slower spreading honey on his toast that morning or tying his shoelaces, then that day would certainly have been his last on earth. But fortunately for him he wasn't meant to die until fifteen years later in a train crash and so, seconds before Tommy swerved into the road, he was forced to slam on his brakes because of a miracle on wheels that suddenly appeared from round the bend. The bike skidded and came to a halt at the end of the path, so that Tommy could fling one foot to the ground.

And from there, the bike twisted between his legs, his eyes on stalks, Tommy watched the extraordinary machine hurtle by, leaving a thick cloud of dust in its wake. He had never seen anything like it, and he marveled at the shiny, cream-colored bodywork and the gigantic wheels spinning like mad, although he only caught a fleeting glimpse of the two people sitting inside it before the black plume of smoke gave him a coughing fit. By the time the fumes had subsided, the miraculous carriage had vanished round the next corner. Tommy wasted no time. He picked up his bike and began pedaling furiously, following the tracks the tires had left on the road. He had to see it again! He knew he would never catch up with it, but he needed to see it again even if only from afar: he wanted to remember every important detail when describing the amazing machine to that know-it-all Barrie, who would never believe his story otherwise. Several more bends in the road prevented him from attaining his goal for a while, but finally, after one of them, the ground suddenly sloped steeply down, giving Tommy a perfect view of the road ahead as it snaked along a shallow gorge. And there, several yards away, he spotted the machine and its telltale cloud of dust and fumes. Tommy stopped on the brow of the hill, sweating and out of breath, and gazed at it in astonishment. How beautiful it was! And how shiny! And now that it was going downhill, it seemed even faster. What would it be like to travel at that speed? Tommy wondered, intensely jealous of the couple inside. All at once, the smile froze on his lips. The vehicle had suddenly veered off the road and was rolling down a steep slope, bouncing over the rutted ground like a horse that has bolted; the man at the wheel seemed to have lost control. Tommy shuddered as he thought he heard the couple's desperate screams, and he was seized with panic as he realized the machine and its two occupants were careering hopelessly toward the edge of the gorge, into which they would plunge in a few seconds if someone didn't do something.

THE HANDFUL OF LOCALS who found themselves in the Hexworthy Inn that morning tried not to stare at the two strangers sitting in front of the fireplace at the back of the room, speaking in hushed voices, oblivious to the curiosity they were arousing. Neither had removed his flowing cloak or wide-brimmed hat, hats they wore pulled down over their faces, and both had peculiar-looking canes between their knees, longer and thicker than the average walking stick, on whose handles an identical symbol shone: an eight-pointed star inside a circle. That wasn't the first time the regulars at the tavern had seen the two men there; in fact, they had appeared several times over the past few years, or if not exactly those two men, as some claimed, then two others very like them. In those heavy cloaks and those hats they never took off, they were almost impossible to tell apart, and the few words they deigned to exchange with others—if you could even call them words—resembled more a kind of metallic rattle, like the sound a tin bucket falling down a well would make. The fact was that little or nothing was known about them, or why they would appear only to disappear again for months, with no apparent rhyme or reason to their comings and goings. Some claimed to have seen them on the moor, posted on the hilltops like sinister sentries. On other occasions, as now, they would turn up without warning at the inn, always in pairs, and take a seat by the fire. They would order two tankards of ale, which they left untouched, and sit facing each other like statues, their unnerving stillness broken only by the slight tremor of their lips, an almost imperceptible vibration that suggested some form of communication, although, rather than talking or whispering, they seemed to be feeding, like fish, off the thoughts each dispersed through the air. No one had ever dared to ask them who they were or what they were doing there. In fact, everybody steered clear of them if they could and complained of the same disturbing feeling whenever they were close: as though an unbearable weight were crushing them, overwhelming them with all the misery and loneliness in the world. That very morning, Mr. Hall, the innkeeper, who, much to Mrs. Hall's despair, fancied himself a poet, had described it thus: it was, he said, akin to having a vast, immeasurable void in a starless universe suddenly expand inside you. And at that precise moment, Mrs. Hall had gone over to him to express her unease in far less poetic terms.

"Those two give me the creeps, George. And what's more, they're scaring away the customers. Why don't you go and ask them if they'll be wanting anything else while I see about laying the tables for lunch. Maybe they'll take the hint . . ."

"They'll be gone soon, woman," Mr. Hall replied with feigned indifference. "You know they never stay very long. Besides, they tip well."

"I don't want their money, George. I dread to think what sinister methods they use to get it . . . God, they're horrible . . . Lulu is under our bed, trembling," she told him, as if the image of their little dog scared half to death might stir him. "Can't you hear the horses whinnying outside? They scare the animals and they scare me, too! I want them out of here, and I hope they never come back. I insist you go and talk to them, George Hall!"

"But they haven't done anything to you, Janny, have they?" Mr. Hall swallowed hard. He was as keen to see them leave as his wife, but he had no desire to approach them. "Besides, it would be rude of me to ask two gentlemen with perfect manners to—"

"I don't care if it makes you look rude, George!" his wife interrupted. Then she added in hushed tones, "I'll tell you one thing: I'm not often wrong about people, as you know, and I wouldn't be surprised if either of those two would hesitate for a second to butcher a child or a defenseless old woman . . ."

As though Mrs. Hall's words, although faintly whispered, had reached the ears of the two strangers, one of them forced his lips into a taut smile and in voice devoid of any inflection, he murmured to his companion: "Old women and children. They are what I'm always afraid I'll find when I pick up a scent."

His companion did not reply; he simply contemplated him at length while the first man held his gaze, neither of them moving a muscle. But allow me to add, dear reader, just for the record, that despite their disquieting stillness the two men's faces, illuminated faintly by the glow from the fire, weren't altogether unpleasant: both had strong, symmetrical features that could even be considered handsome. And yet the exquisite paleness of their skin did not seem human and was moreover tarnished by a kind of dark tint that somehow seemed not to belong to it, like the shadow a cloud casts on the snow. At last, after the prolonged silence, the second man's lips began to vibrate imperceptibly: "You are suffering from a serious fault in your peptidogenesis, my friend. Perhaps a guilt neutralizer would minimize the unwanted effects of your remorse."

"I feel what you say is truth. But remember, we are no longer receiving any consignments from the Other Side."

"I feel what you say is truth."

There was another silence.

"What is the feeling of guilt like?" the second stranger asked.

His question elicited an even longer silence.

"How can I explain it? Imagine taking a huge dose of neuropeptides AB3003 and AZ001," the first stranger finally replied, "that canceled out all your connective mutation neutralizers."

The other raised his eyebrows slightly. "I feel surprised! Then . . . I suppose it is very similar to the sensation of pity."

"So they say. Although I've heard that guilt is more addictive." The first stranger stroked the handle of his cane with his forefinger. It was an extremely slow, almost imperceptible movement. "So . . . you've experienced pity."

"I have: I suffered a slight mutation soon after arriving here. That is why I feel sympathy for what you are going through. My bio-cells developed their own connections based on segments of my AZ model, producing their own neuropeptide chains. For a while I experienced the feeling of pity. Thank goodness it was quickly diagnosed, and in those days there was no problem with the consignments. Even so, it took three types of neutralizers to solve the problem."

"As I understand it," said the man who was afraid of finding old women or children when he followed his next trail, "years ago they discovered that the AZ model was responsible for nearly all those random mutations, and the Scientists decided to phase it out. That's why the last group of Executioners sent two years ago doesn't have it."

"Then they are lucky."

"They aren't aware of it: the feeling of satisfaction was a feature of the AZ model."

The two men's shoulders trembled for a few seconds, in what for them was presumably a moment of shared amusement. Another lengthy silence followed.

"Two years . . . It's been two years since the Other Side sent anything or anyone," remarked the first stranger.

"They are nearing the end. The temperature is almost zero and there are hardly any black holes left. Everything there is slow and dark now. They are saving their last, feeble strength in the event the Great Exodus might still be possible . . ."

"Then they're saving it in vain," his companion pronounced. "They'll never be reborn here: this world is doomed. I feel frustration. I feel impotence. We've carried out a senseless slaughter."

"We have done our job and have done it well. They needed more time and we gave it to them. We even provided two years more than they expected from their worst predictions. Remember that twelve years ago the Scientists calculated that this world had only a decade left . . ."

"Yes, but we, the Executioners, managed to claw back another two years."

The man who did not want to encounter old women or children rapped the floor with his cane. The gesture was so out of character that his companion raised his eyebrows several millimeters in surprise. "Yes, we did our job," the first stranger went on, ignoring the other man's silent disapproval. "And we did it well. That's why they created us, isn't it?" The stranger's voice, still inaudible to anyone who didn't press his ear to his lips, was slightly raised, or perhaps it wasn't, perhaps it had simply acquired a few nuances, like sarcasm or resentment, that the human ear could hear. "Even so, I insist it has been senseless." He rapped his cane on the floor again as his face began to flush. "The Scientists haven't managed to find a cure for the epidemic. They haven't even come close. And exterminating the carriers . . . well, it was always a crude solution, as chaotic as the malady itself. The epidemic is uncontainable, it always was. All those deaths for nothing!"

"Return to a state of calm, my friend. Return to . . ."

"They boast of possessing Supreme Knowledge and look down on us; they refer to us as killers. It enrages me just to think about it. They have no idea what it means to look into a child's eyes, to show him in your pupils the chaos for which he must die, and then put him to death . . . I could tell them a thing or two about their famous Supreme Knowledge!"

"Return to a state of calm!" The second stranger leaned forward and placed a hand on his companion's cane. It was an extremely swift, imperceptible movement. "The end is near," he reminded him in an expressionless voice. "What does it matter how many of them you have slain? They are all going to die. What does it matter what the Scientists think of us? We are all going to die."

With those words, both men sat up straight in their chairs again and remained silent. The one who had rapped the floor with his cane several times seemed gradually to regain his composure. After a while, he spoke again.

"I'm sorry. It's the effects of the remorse. If I don't get hold of a guilt neutralizer soon it will be the death of me. But as you so rightly said, what does it matter? What does anything matter now? Chaos is inevitable."

"Chaos is inevitable," the other man repeated. "And so is our mission,

my friend. That is why we were created, and we must go on accomplish-
ing it until the bitter end. Otherwise, what is the point of our existence?"

"If only one more death were needed. A single death that would put
a stop to it all . . ."

"And if that one death were the death of an old woman or a child?"

The Executioner who suffered from guilt closed his eyes and smiled.

"I feel what you say is truth. And if it's true that I need a guilt neutralizer"—he looked at his companion—"you could do with one for sarcasm, my friend."

Perhaps what made both men shake gently for a few moments was
another fit of laughter. Or perhaps not.

"Go on until the bitter end . . ." The one whom guilt was destroying
shrugged slowly. "Why not? After all, it won't be long now. The fabric
of the universe is as riddled with holes as a moth-eaten sweater. The
molecular traces of the carriers have become as jumbled as the roads on
a crumpled map; their trails are growing so faint that it's almost impossible to distinguish between the terminal molecules of a Destructor of
whatever rank and those of a natural Jumper. Our tunnels are no longer
infallible; our searches have become random, intuitive . . . This world
is coming apart at the seams. Any day could be the last. And when that
day comes, men will get out of bed and look out of the window on a
world inhabited by horrific, unimaginable phenomena, a world invaded
by their worst nightmares. And I promise you that all those we haven't
killed will wish they were dead."

"The background molecular nebula has increased a hundredfold in
the past few months," his companion remarked. "Only today, on the
moor, I sensed a very high concentration of it. I suspect that in one of the
nearby houses a window onto another world must have opened momentarily, but I was unable to detect whether anyone had jumped through it
or not. And yet, only four or five years ago, catching our prey was a daily
event, do you remember? What rich pickings we found in this sector!
Almost as valuable as the ones at that famous haunted house in Berkeley
Square. Not a day went by in one of those hyperproximity points where

whoever was on duty didn't capture a couple of level 6 Destructors at least. But those days are over. All I managed to detect today—more by accident than anything else, I suspect—was a potential aura. My cane picked it up. It was an old level 3 Destructor whom I had trailed before; the last time was two years ago, at the entrance to the Royal Opera House. That evening I almost caught him, but he was lucky, I let him go because I came across a level 6 *plus* Destructor. Luck was on his side again today, for as soon as I perceived him I lost him again. His aura simply dissolved into the background mist."

"Their aura is very faint when they haven't jumped for a while," his companion sympathized. "In any case, a Latent isn't such a big haul . . ."

"It is better than nothing."

"I feel what you say is truth. But tell me . . . that level six *plus* detector you just mentioned, it wasn't . . . ?"

There was a fresh silence. The Executioner who had lost the trail of the quarry he had let go two years before followed a drop of moisture trickling slowly down the side of his beer tankard, until he saw it merge with a small pool forming on the table. A few seconds later, he spoke.

"No, it was not the legendary M. That night I caught a big one, it is true, but it was not M. M's trail is unmistakable and was still being detected until relatively recently. It seems the legendary M is still jumping."

"I feel astonishment. I don't understand why he hasn't already disintegrated. Other far less active Destructors than he have already lost all their molecules . . . He should have been classified as terminal a long time ago."

"A six *plus* is never classified as terminal, my friend. They are considered Destructors down to their last surviving molecule. And M is the most powerful and fearsome Destructor of any we have ever come across since we started fighting this epidemic. His talents are as astonishing and formidable as his lunacy. Indeed, if M has become invisible, which I am sure he has, he is still as powerful as a hundred level 6 Destructors."

"I was on his trail for a while; there was even a time when I thought I might actually be able to catch him," said the man who felt guilty about his terrible task.

"And who has not? We have all dreamt of catching him. We have all tried to fish that legendary fifteen-pound salmon that snatches all our bait and avoids all our hooks. Oh, yes, dear friend, whenever I go to Lake Windermere, I pray the legendary fish is still alive and kicking and will end up dangling from my rod."

Mr. Hall, who had finally been forced by his wife's nagging to approach the two men, cleared his throat timidly.

"Gentlemen . . . forgive me for interrupting, but . . ." When the men looked up at him, Mr. Hall felt that terrible emptiness inside, which made him recoil. "Er, will you be wanting another drink?"

Before either of them could reply, the inn door swung open, and a small figure stumbled in, coming to a halt in the middle of the room. He stood motionless for a few seconds, gasping for air and casting his glazed eyes around the room. He was shivering from head to toe, and beads of sweat mixed with tears rolled down his face. Mrs. Hall went over to the boy and gently placed her hand on his bony shoulder.

"Whatever's the matter, lad?" she whispered

And at that point, little Tommy Dawkins began to scream.

18

OYLE SET SAIL FOR SOUTH AFRICA ON THE
Oriental surrounded by flowers. Jean Leckie, who did
not wish to see him off at the Port of Tilbury, had filled his cabin with
roses, hibiscus, and lilies, so that Doyle and his valet, sitting on their
bunks and besieged by that riot of color, undertook the voyage like a
couple of lovebirds in a floating greenhouse. If Doyle had been given the
choice, he would have preferred to see Jean in person, but she had made
it very clear she did not wish to be part of the joyous crowd that would
see off the ship, as if the man who every year on the fifteenth of March
sent her an edelweiss, that flower whose whiteness rivaled that of snow,
were going on a picnic and not to a war from which he might return in
a box after receiving a Boer bullet in his stomach. Fortunately, Doyle
would return six months later on his own two feet, if enveloped in quite
a different odor than on the outward journey. The long weeks he had
spent as a doctor in his friend's hospital, sewing up the guts of dying soldiers and amputating their limbs, including those of Jim Dawkins, who
would never ride his bicycle again, had impregnated him with the indelible perfume of death—a death devoid of heroism or glamour, foul and
dirty, covered in flies and noxious odors, a death that belonged more to
the Middle Ages than to the new century dawning.

But as he climbed the stairs at Undershaw, all of that seemed like a
dream. He had scarcely been home a week, and already the peaceful idyll
had begun to make him doubt he had ever been in the war in Africa—
that was, until he visited the bathroom, for his guts had still not recov-

ered from the bouts of dysentery he had suffered. He paused in front of the door to the room with the best views in the house. Stanley Ball, the architect with whom he had once practiced telepathy, had built it on the three and a half acres of land Doyle had purchased in Hindhead, which was referred to as Little Switzerland because of its clean air and spectacular hills. However, Ball hadn't needed to rack his brains to get some idea of what he wanted, as Doyle had made a sketch for him on a piece of paper. He had a very clear idea of how he wanted Undershaw to be: an imposing mansion worthy of an author of his stature, but also a cozy family home, practical for an invalid.

After considering whether to knock or not, Doyle decided to open the door without a sound. Lately, his wife would have a snooze when she went upstairs to read, and that morning was no exception: Louise, whom Doyle had affectionately nicknamed Touie back in the far-off days when they first knew each other in Portsmouth, was reclining in an armchair, her head tilted to one side, her eyes closed. She had been proving Sir Richard Douglas Powell, one of the country's leading TB specialists, wrong for many years now, so it was no wonder she felt exhausted. From their trip to Switzerland, Doyle had brought back the idea of how to finish off Holmes, whereas Touie had brought back in her lungs *Mycobacterium tuberculosis*. The doctors had given her no more than three months to live, and yet eight years had passed since that unfavorable prognosis and Touie was still alive, thanks undoubtedly to the ministrations of Doyle, who no sooner did he receive the news than he whisked her away on a therapeutic pilgrimage to Davos, Caux, and Cairo, and finally he built the house in Hindhead with all the comforts an invalid such as she could possibly need. However, although his ministrations appeared to have kept the gentle Touie's condition stable, everyone knew that it was only a matter of time before Death, which Doyle had so long kept at bay, finally took his wife, without his being able to prevent it.

However, as if Touie's tragic lot were not enough, in a flourish of inventiveness, fate had arranged matters so that Doyle would wish for her demise to come as soon as possible. And to that end, three years after the doctors had declared his wife terminally ill, it had placed in his path Jean Leckie, whom Doyle would not hesitate to describe as the woman of his life from their very first conversation, and whom you, dear readers, had the pleasure of meeting during the excursion to Dartmoor. Thus Doyle had been forced to live on the horns of a painful dilemma: on the one hand he longed for Touie to die so that he could express his love for Jean; on the other he strove more than ever to take care of his wife lest his feelings of guilt lead him to view any slackness in his ministrations as a desire to hasten her death. In the meantime, the love professed by Doyle and Jean, who were incapable of any shameful act that might stain Touie's honor, had earned them the respect of their closest friends and even their respective families. The couple maintained a friendship as platonic as it was tragic, repressing their burning passion for each other, and behaving as discreetly as possible so as not to threaten Touie's blissful ignorance. They had no choice but to wait, with a mixture of yearning and sorrow, for the sick woman to lose her life so that her husband could recover his.

The Imitation of Christ, the book Touie read over and over again, lay propped open on the floor, like a miniature sloping roof. Doyle placed it on the table next to the armchair and contemplated his wife as she slept. With her curls falling over the pillow and her slow breathing, Touie resembled a trusting child in repose. She knew her husband was watching over her, that there was no other place in the world where she would be as safe as at the center of that comfortable life he had built around her. And once more Doyle lamented his inability to love his wife. For if only he had been able, everything would have been so much easier for all concerned in that immutable situation in which he found himself. But that emotion had only blossomed in his heart when he met Jean. Doyle had only ever felt a cordial affection toward Touie, which had never developed into love, as he had assumed it would, given time. When he learned of her terminal illness, his inadequate affection changed into a sense of infinite pity. But above all, what Doyle felt each time he contemplated his wife was his terrible impotence at not having been able to protect her.

Standing over his sick wife, he recalled the stories his mother would tell him of knights rescuing kidnapped princesses, replete with challenges, duels, and tournaments, where the noise of swords clashing on armor rang out like pealing bells and honor was always saved. It was thanks to those tales that the most appealing ideals of chivalry (a knight errant must always protect the weak, defy the strong, and be gallant with ladies) had imprinted themselves on Doyle's young heart, and although in his own era chivalry had been reduced to mere sportsmanship, throughout his life Doyle had tried to put those ideals into practice whenever he could: firstly with his own mother, then at school, where he always protected the weaker boys, and finally with Touie, who one fine day had appeared, only to become his damsel—every knight's most prized possession. And as he pronounced the words "I will' in that Yorkshire church, so that everyone there knew he loved her, privately he was making a far more sacred pledge: to protect her from villainous black knights who would try to abduct her, or from their modern equivalent, whatever they might be: drunken scoundrels, crooks, fortune hunters . . . And for many years Doyle had with remarkable success dutifully fulfilled his pledge, until the appearance of that invisible foe whose steps were silent, who had no flesh for his sword to smite, who had come gliding through the air, evil and intangible, only to make his nest in his damsel's lungs, destroying her from the inside.

Doyle gave a rueful sigh and walked over to the window, gazing with satisfaction over the narrow valley where the woods converged, like a monarch appreciating the peace that enveloped his domain. Then he heard Touie stretch behind him.

"I love the view from this window, Arthur," she said, as if in his zeal to surround her with comfort and beauty her husband had also been responsible for ordering Nature (which had unquestioningly obeyed his booming voice) to rearrange her valleys and mountains to create that idyllic landscape. "And nothing makes me happier than the thought that I will continue enjoying it in the Hereafter, for as you once told me, there everything will be exactly as it is here."

"That's right, my dear," Doyle assured her. "Everything will be exactly the same."

He said this without turning, so that she couldn't see the corners of his mouth turn down in despair as he realized that the word "everything" comprised much more than that landscape. If after death everything stayed the same, then Touie, Jean, and he would remain trapped in an eternal triangle. There was no doubt that one day Touie would die in this world, after which Jean and he would be free to love each other openly, but that love would be no more than a leafy glade in the forest of life, a brief respite whose duration would be determined by how valiant their hearts were, for as soon as they entered the Hereafter the broken triangle would be reestablished. And then, perhaps, Doyle would be accountable to Touie, who through some peephole in that other world might have caught sight of him loving another woman the way he had never been able to love her.

Doyle made a supreme effort to replace that look of despair with the cheerfully optimistic one he always wore in the face of Touie's illness, so that she would forget the sword of Damocles hanging over her, and he turned toward his wife.

"Keep resting," he told her. "You need to get your strength back. I'll go down and do some work before lunch."

She nodded, smiling meekly, and Doyle was able to flee downstairs, pondering the Hereafter whose existence he never tired of predicting but that might be his damnation, unless Touie forgave him in death for what he dared not confess to her in life.

Seated at the desk in the comfortable study he had installed on the ground floor, Doyle lit his pipe and tried to relax. As he puffed away distractedly, he glanced around at the furniture and the shelves where his favorite books jostled for space with his numerous sporting trophies. Instead of the persistent sound of cannon and rifle fire accompanied by the rumble of mortars that he was used to hearing in South Africa, the laughter of his children, Kingsley and Mary Louise, filtered in through the window, together with the clatter of the miniature railway he had built shortly after the house was finished, so that his children could enjoy an exhilarating ride around the piece of land their father had managed to wrest from the world. Any other man would have let himself rock contentedly amid that benign calm, but Doyle was a man of action, and he knew that it was only a matter of time before he became more exhausted by all that peacefulness than by the chaos of the war. Although there were many things he could do—on the homeward journey he had considered standing for the Edinburgh elections, starting a gun club in order to make better marksmen of the English, and even writing an essay about the war he had just survived—he was sure he would soon be longing for some adventure that would provide him with another opportunity to prove his manliness. He had no doubt that war was mankind's most foolish mistake, and yet he believed that for any decent man it could also be an exciting journey capable of stirring his noblest virtues, which might otherwise have gone with him to the grave. Doyle had sent all his friends telegrams announcing his return, so that they knew they could once more depend on him, although he very much doubted any of them (for the most part other authors, agents, and publishers) would write back proposing he join them on some death-defying adventure. But at that stage, after less than a week of idleness, his demands were not quite so high: a simple luncheon invitation would suffice.

He banished these thoughts with a resigned shake of his head and told himself it was time to go back to his old routine after six months away. He decided to start with one of the most thankless of all the tasks he had to deal with whenever he returned from a trip: answering the backlog of correspondence. He stood up and called Wood, his secretary, who seconds later came into the study bearing a bag of letters. Alfred Wood was a primary-school teacher whom Doyle had employed whilst living in Portsmouth, not so much for his discretion, efficiency, and trustworthiness as for his cricketing skills. To begin with, Doyle had employed him as a simple secretary, but as time went on, almost unawares, he had started allotting him other tasks, such as that of messenger, driver, and typist. Occasionally, after Wood had beaten him at billiards or golf, Doyle had even sent him on some patently absurd errand simply out of revenge. Since his assistant had carried these tasks out without demur, pretending not to notice the odd nature of the request—or, worse, giving to understand from his gallant acceptance that he expected nothing less from his employer—this game of preposterous requests had become for both of them a diversion that enriched their relationship, or so Doyle liked to imagine, as they had never discussed the matter.

When Wood diligently emptied the bag of letters onto the desk, Doyle gazed at the large pile despondently.

"This is almost worse than war," he groaned. "Much more tedious, in any case. War may be bad in many ways, Woodie, but it is never boring, that's for sure."

"You should know, sir, having been in more than one yourself . . ."

Both men gave a loud sigh and began the laborious task of sifting through Doyle's correspondence. Much of it was addressed to Doyle from people convinced that anyone who could invent such complicated fictional crimes must obviously possess the necessary skills to solve real ones, and they therefore asked for his help in solving all kinds of cases. But much of it was also addressed to Sherlock Holmes himself at his nonexistent address of 221B Baker Street, which the sub–post office in London, with its habitual cooperativeness, had sent on to Undershaw. Before drowning in the Reichenbach Falls, the sleuth would receive all kinds of eccentric challenges from places as far afield as San Francisco and Moscow: complicated family mysteries, elaborate puzzles, and mathematical equations. But following Holmes's tragic disappearance, only a handful of scatterbrains insisted on testing his intelligence. Nowadays, the vast majority of letters were from women wanting to clean Holmes's rooms, and adventurers offering to organize expeditions to search for his remains; generally speaking, rather than demonstrate their affection for his creation, Doyle's readers seemed to betray their own lack of reason. After reading the letters, the two men divided them into piles: those that deserved a reply and those that, on account of being deranged, preposterous, or downright unanswerable, deserved only to be used to light a fire.

"It would never have occurred to me that life could contain so many mysteries," Doyle sighed after reading a letter containing the map of a supposed treasure buried on the South African coast by the crew of a shipwrecked vessel.

"Is that why you decided to invent a few more?" Wood inquired, plucking another letter from the pile. He opened it with the swiftness and elegance of someone with years of practice. "Ah, a Mrs. Emily Payne, recently widowed, offers to clean Holmes's rooms. Well, that's nothing new. But there's an interesting difference: she also proposes to alleviate Watson's grief, should Holmes's devoted companion be in need."

"On the fire pile," grunted Doyle.

Woodie obeyed, even though it was the first letter they had received expressing concern for poor Watson. A few moments' silence followed, broken only by the sound of envelopes being torn open.

"Well, listen to this," said Doyle after a cursory glance, "a William Sharp claims he is the real Sherlock Holmes and declares that he will soon astonish the world with his exploits."

Wood raised his eyebrows in a gesture of dutiful surprise as he perused another missive.

"And in this letter a Polish family insists you go to their country to solve the disappearance of a valuable necklace."

Just then Cleeve the butler, who had also returned from South Africa without any Boer bullet embedded in his body, opened the study door to inform Doyle he had a visitor.

"Forgive me for disturbing you, sir, but the author H. G. Wells is waiting for you in the library."

"Thank you, Cleeve." Doyle stood up from his desk without trying to conceal his relief at this timely interruption. "Sorry, Woodie, I'm sure you can manage the rest on your own. And when you've finished classifying them, start replying to them yourself. After all, your writing is far more beautiful and legible than mine."

"I appreciate the compliment, sir," Wood replied, lamenting all the hours he had spent as a child perfecting his penmanship. "But where do I put the Polish letter? They're willing to pay all your travel expenses, and you can name your reward. You must admit it's a very tempting offer."

Doyle grunted. "On the fire pile, Woodie, unless you want to go in my place."

"And risk having you drown in correspondence during my absence, sir?" Doyle heard him retort. "Why, I should never forgive myself."

Doyle strode off toward the library, at which point Cleeve gave up trying to follow him. He had spent enough time running after his master in South Africa, and so he strayed in the direction of the kitchen on the pretext of giving orders to the cook. Doyle hadn't clapped eyes on Wells for six months, not since Montgomery Gilmore's automobile drove into that gorge on the moor. He had regretted abandoning him in mid-tragedy but was loath to give up the medical posting he had fought so hard to obtain, nor was he close enough to the couple even to entertain the idea. Entering the study, he found Wells sitting on one of his custom-made, hand-carved Viking chairs, with the same forlorn air as a fly caught in the jaws of a carnivorous plant. As soon as Wells saw him, he leapt to his feet, and the two friends came together in one of those masculine embraces that are a perfect balance of affection and virility.

"My dear Arthur, I'm so glad you came back in one piece!" exclaimed Wells.

"Likewise, George. And I assure you it was no easy feat," Doyle said with a grin that suggested all manner of death-defying adventures.

With a commanding gesture that was doubtless a carryover from his days in the army, Doyle signaled to Wells to sit down again while he went over to the drinks table to serve them a couple of glasses of port. He did so with such agility that Wells had the impression he had received the drink even before it was poured. In any event, he promptly found himself clutching a glass, with Doyle sitting opposite him on an identical chair.

"Well, Arthur," he began, "I expect you have much to tell me."

"You are quite right, my dear fellow. The return voyage on the *Briton* was so entertaining I could write several novels about it. I was traveling with the Duke of Norfolk and his brother Lord Edward Talbot, you know? An amusing pair. There were also several prominent army chaps, with whom I spent the crossing exchanging war stories into the small hours. Unfortunately, were joined along the way by a journalist called Bertram Fletcher Robinson, a terrible bore who almost ruined the entire journey."

"How awful for you!" remarked Wells.

"It was, although not nearly as awful as whatever made you come here desperately seeking my help."

Wells looked at him in astonishment.

"H-How did you know?" he stammered.

"Elementary, my dear Wells, elementary." Doyle grinned. "You came here unannounced, when, as a stickler for etiquette, you usually send a telegram the day before, and furthermore, you look as if you've been dragged through a hedge backward: you are unkempt, you have bags under your eyes, and your suit is crumpled. But the most significant clue is the polite interest you showed while I recounted my adventures, which were no more than the chronicle of a tedious, banal ocean crossing. The old Wells would have interrupted me to say he had no interest in hearing about a cruise for retired people, yet you remained silent, nodding as I droned on, which proves you weren't listening to a word I said but were waiting for the best moment to broach your request. I don't have to be Sherlock Holmes to deduce that! Even my young son would have noticed. There is something seriously worrying you, my dear George, and the moment you knew I had returned from Africa, you came here because you think I can help . . . Am I wrong?"

Wells paused before running his hand across his brow. "Damn it, Arthur, you're right! I . . . Well, I apologize for not announcing my visit, but—"

"Oh, there's no need. I'm the one who should apologize. I regret having left . . . under those circumstances. I would have liked to attend the funeral at least."

Wells waved a hand in the air. "Don't fret," he said. "We all understood perfectly."

"How are you?" Doyle asked gently.

Wells grunted, as though wanting to make it clear that this was not an easy question to answer.

"You know, when one half of a couple dies in such circumstances, the survivor always feels guilty for not having died in his or her place," he said, as if this were something he knew from his own bitter experience.

"Quite so." Doyle nodded, as if he, too, had firsthand knowledge of it.

"Except that Montgomery isn't only racked with guilt because he was driving, Arthur. Above all it is because Emma died before he was able to confess his secret to her," Wells explained.

"His secret?"

"Yes, a secret very few know about. And that I am about to tell you."

Like a cat about to pounce, a tense silence hung over the two men. It was finally broken by Doyle.

"Wait a moment, George! Whatever Gilmore's secret is, I don't think it's right that you tell me. I hardly know the fellow, and besides—"

"You have to know, Arthur. Because, as you said earlier, I need your help. And unless you know the whole story you won't be able to help me."

"Very well, George. Whatever you say," replied Doyle a little uneasily.

"Good, now listen: Montgomery Gilmore is actually an assumed name. Gilmore's real name is—"

Wells broke off in mid-sentence, not for dramatic effect, but rather because he wasn't even convinced that revealing Murray's true identity to Doyle would not simply make matters worse. All of a sudden, the plan he had spent the past few weeks dreaming up seemed unrealistic and absurd. But it was the only one he had.

"Well?" said Doyle expectantly.

"His real name is Gilliam Murray," Wells declared at last, "better known as the Master of Time."

Doyle contemplated him, dumbfounded.

"B-But . . . the Master of Time died," he finally stammered.

"No, Arthur, he didn't die. He staged his own death and started a new life in New York under the assumed name of Montgomery Gilmore."

"Good heavens!" Doyle exclaimed, then fell silent for a moment as he attempted to digest the revelation. Wells waited rather warily for him to say something else. "Now that you mention it, George, his face always seemed familiar. Well, I'll be darned: here am I, the creator of the most famous detective in the world, and yet it never occurred to me that—"

"How could it have?" Wells hastened to reassure him.

"Gilmore is Murray . . . Gilmore is Murray," Doyle repeated, unable to overcome his astonishment. "Were you aware that I wrote several letters in his defense, George?"

Wells nodded quietly, allowing his friend to recover gradually from the shock before continuing.

"But . . . why stage his own death?" asked Doyle.

Wells realized Doyle had overcome his initial surprise and was now asking the appropriate questions. However, he wasn't sure Doyle would swallow the only reply Wells could give him.

"Well," he said calmly, as though he himself believed what he was saying, "the hole in the year 2000 suddenly closed up without any warning, and nobody knew why. But Murray suspected that people wouldn't be satisfied with that explanation. He feared they might think he had made it up so as to avoid sharing his discovery with the world, and he decided the best thing to do was, well . . . pretend he'd been eaten by a dragon in the fourth dimension."

Wells felt his pulse racing as for almost a whole minute Doyle contemplated him, pondering his reply.

"Carry on," he said at last, in the tone of someone who knows he is being lied to but also understands that he has no right to dig any deeper.

Wells hurriedly changed the subject. "The fact is he met Emma as

Montgomery Gilmore. And for the past two and a half years he has been debating whether or not to confess to her his true identity. The last time we discussed the subject was at Brook Manor, on the day of the accident. Monty told me he had decided not to say anything to her about it, but I, er . . . I convinced him he should." Wells shrugged, pulling an awkward face. "And it seems he was trying to do that while driving the car. He was so nervous he lost control of the wheel. The result is that I, too, feel partly responsible for Emma's death. In fact, I feel almost wholly to blame," he added in a strangled voice.

"I see," Doyle sighed, astonished by this wave of guilt that had washed over everyone.

His voice increasingly choked with sorrow, Wells began to relate everything that had happened during the six months Doyle had been away—not only to inform him, but also to vent all the frustration and remorse that had begun to engulf him, and that, with his tendency to feel victimized, he could not help exaggerating. For the first few days, Murray had seemed numb, incapable of reacting, as though unconsciously he had decided that if he refused to accept his beloved's death it would miraculously no longer be true. But acceptance finally came, bringing with it grief—an intense grief that seemed to spill out from his insides in an inconsolable, almost inhuman weeping. Several weeks passed during which Murray was reduced to a broken creature for whom simply being alive was painful, as if someone had covered everything around him with thorns. Then, when the weeping finished, leaving his body a dried-out husk, rage rushed in, a rage directed at the world, the universe, and even at the God he did not believe in, a God who, unbeknownst to the happy couple, had plotted to snatch Emma away from him in an act of cosmic conspiracy. But his blind rage also gradually subsided, giving way to a phase of exalted promises (Wells had heard Murray propose a none-too-altruistic pact with Death, vowing to destroy everything of value in the world if only it would bring back his beloved Emma), philosophical ramblings, and macabre poetry. Sprawled on the sofa, a perennially topped-up drink in his hand, Murray would ramble on about the precariousness of existence and how impossible it was for him to accept that Emma had vanished forever, never to return, that she had left the world of the living, when he knew that she was still there, buried in Highgate Cemetery, only a few hours' carriage ride away, her beauty wilting, silent as a rose in the darkness of her coffin. And finally, the guilt that had been stalking him all that time, and which he had perhaps not wanted to yield to until he had reflected all he could on his beloved's death: guilt at failing to protect her, guilt at not loving her even more than he had, and above all guilt at not having confessed to her the truth about who he was. Because of the fear that had prevented him from doing so, all he had left was a handful of poisoned memories, for their love affair had been nothing but a great big lie. And Wells, who also felt guilty because of what had happened, even though Murray had never reproached him for it, realized with horror that his friend was preparing to take his own life. Wells's suspicions were soon confirmed when Murray announced that he had gone through the obligatory mourning period, and all he had to do now was decide how he would kill himself. And kill himself he would, regardless of anything Wells might have to say on the matter, for he couldn't go on living with the knowledge that he had deceived the person he loved most, that he would never be able to beg her for forgiveness.

"I tried to dissuade him, Arthur, I assure you. I used every argument under the sun. But it was useless. I could persuade him to confess his secret to Emma, but I can't persuade him to go on living, doubtless because what I say no longer means anything to him," Wells lamented. "And so Murray is liable to kill himself at any moment. Jane and I have been watching over him day and night these past few months, but we can't go on like this forever, Arthur. We're exhausted. At some point we'll turn our backs and Murray will carry out his threat. I don't know when exactly, but I assure you he will do it, unless someone can convince him not to."

"But if you, his closest friend, haven't been able to, then who?" said Doyle.

Wells gave what Doyle thought was a slightly demented smile.

"Emma," he replied. "Emma can convince him."

"Emma? But she's . . ."

Doyle didn't have the heart to finish the sentence, as though he feared killing her a second time. Wells finished it for him.

"Dead. Yes, Arthur, Emma is dead. Dead and buried. And yet she is the only person who can convince him. Murray needs to end the conversation they started in the automobile. He needs to tell her who he is and beg her for forgiveness. And we all know that there's only one way to contact the dead, don't we?"

Doyle raised his eyebrows.

"You mean . . . ?"

Wells looked straight at Doyle, attempting to convey the urgency of what he was about to ask him.

"Yes, a séance. I need Emma to contact Murray. I need her to forgive him in death for what he was unable to confess to her in life. And to do that, Arthur, I need your help."

By then Wood had read a dozen more letters, and for a further twenty minutes continued to wade despondently through his employer's correspondence, until Cleeve came into the study and interrupted him.

"Major Wood, the master requires you in the library."

"Did he say why?" asked Wood a little uneasily.

"No, but he's still with Mr. Wells. And the two of them seem very . . . agitated. When I saw him in that state I feared the worst . . . but luckily all he wanted was for me to fetch you."

"Oh, no." Wood turned pale, with the same discretion that characterized his whole existence. "Tell me, Cleeve: he doesn't have that look, does he?"

The butler sighed regretfully.

"I'm afraid so, Major Wood."

Doyle's secretary heaved such a sigh of despair that it relegated the butler to the level of simple apprentice in the art of outwardly expressing inner regret. In common with Cleeve, Wood feared nothing more than when his employer summoned him with that *look* in his eyes. It could mean many things, none of which boded well: an invitation to spend a few months at the battlefront, lessons in flying a hot-air balloon, or a madcap scheme to fight against some injustice that would doubt-less involve treading a thin line between ridiculousness and illegality. What could it be this time? After exchanging a look of commiseration with Cleeve, Wood walked swiftly toward the library, straightening his impeccable jacket, smoothing his impeccable hair, and rehearsing the expression of placid indifference with which he habitually received his employer's most eccentric requests. And yet, underneath, he was far from being calm, which might explain why, when he reached the library door, he remained rather longer than was appropriate, knuckles poised, before rapping gently to announce his arrival. Wood could hear very clearly everything the two men were saying inside the room as they con-versed with audible excitement.

"He'll accept because he's desperate!" Wells was saying. "Especially if the suggestion comes from you, Arthur. I saw the expression on his face when you explained to him about spiritualism the day I introduced you. I assure you, very few succeed in shutting him up the way you did, even if it was only for a moment . . . Besides, he has nothing to lose . . ."

"Of course he has nothing to lose, George! And much to gain!" Doyle bellowed. "The chance to speak to his beloved one last time . . . who in their right mind wouldn't attempt it? He'll accept, of course he will. Especially when I tell him I've found an authentic medium hidden in one of South Africa's lost tribes, a medium with unquestionable pow-ers, waiting to be discovered."

"A genuine medium, who will make all the bogus ones pale into in-significance . . . Just as you predicted that day!" said Wells excitedly.

"It's true! That conversation . . . It was fate, I'm sure of it!" agreed Doyle with equal enthusiasm. "And Murray will think so, too."

"All we have to do now is bring your medium over to England as soon as possible!" Wood heard a festive clink suggesting a toast. "Inci-dentally, where the devil is your secretary?"

Behind the door, Wood gave a start. What were the two men thinking? Were they planning to send him to South Africa to fetch this medium? Well, they had another think coming if they thought that . . .

Doyle's booming voice interrupted his reverie. "Stop eavesdropping, Wood, and come in, damn it!"

"How the devil did he know . . ." Wood started to mutter, but he left his sentence unfinished as he pushed open the door, adopting his most unctuous smile.

"I beg your pardon, sir, I heard raised voices and I thought that, er . . . it might be an inopportune moment."

"Nonsense; I sent for you, didn't I?" Doyle cut in. "Woodie, I need your services."

"Yes, sir . . . ," Wood replied, preparing for the worst.

"Don't pull that face, my dear fellow. I assure you I'm not going to ask you to do anything complicated. At least, nothing for which you aren't fully prepared."

Doyle remained silent for a few moments, seeing through his secretary's nonchalant exterior and taking pleasure in prolonging the fearful anticipation it doubtless concealed.

"I think I'm going to need your wonderful penmanship again," he said, grinning at his employee's bewilderment. Yes, there was nothing he enjoyed more than testing the limits of Woodie's courteous behavior. "I need you to write a few lines on my behalf."

19

ERY EARLY THE NEXT MORNING, WELLS AND Doyle arrived at Murray's house, keen to relay the good news. They were convinced their proposal would have an instantaneous effect on the inconsolable fiancé, sweeping away the cobwebs of his despair, or at least giving him enough hope to refrain from killing himself before the medium from South Africa arrived in a few days' time.

"But he isn't just any medium . . . He is a *genuine* medium!" exclaimed Doyle, trying to instill some enthusiasm into the limp figure sprawled in the armchair smelling of liquor and musty clothes. "His powers are beyond question. I can vouch for that myself, and I assure you the miracles I witnessed are indescribable. The man who performed them has no interest in fame or fortune. Those words mean nothing to him."

And while Murray gazed at him listlessly through bloodshot eyes, Doyle began to pace up and down the room, narrating the tale of the extraordinary medium. Doyle had come across him in a village in Bakongo during his stay in South Africa. He was born to English parents and at the age of two or three had gotten lost in the veldt, that vast, wild southern African plain. A Bantu tribe had adopted him, and the village elders had given him the name Ankoma, which meant "the last child to be born." As time passed, Ankoma had assimilated the customs of his Bantu parents and behaved no differently from any other tribal member, despite standing out among them like a cream pudding in a coal bunker. But with the arrival of adolescence, his powers began to awaken. These were so formidable that, by the age of twelve, he had already ousted the tribe's shaman, who only knew how to make it rain, and even then only if a storm was brewing. When Doyle passed through the village of Bakongo after the bloody battle of Brandfort and heard about the legend of the Great Ankoma, the white man who made bowls and utensils levitate and who could speak to the dead, he immediately asked the Bantu chiefs if he could witness their pale-skinned shaman's powers for himself. They agreed in exchange for a handful of baubles, and inside a miserable hovel Doyle at last saw a genuine medium in action. The scope of Ankoma's powers was so astonishing that Doyle swore he would remember it as long as he lived. So that when Wells had come to his house the day before to ask for his help, Doyle had realized that despite his and Gilmore's unfortunate first encounter, their paths had crossed so that he, Arthur Conan Doyle, could go to the aid of Gilliam Murray, the Master of Time. And, utterly convinced of the truth of this, Doyle had spent the whole night dictating a raft of letters addressed to senior members of the armed forces and the South African government, promising so many favors in return for the one he was asking that he would doubtless have to spend the rest of his days endeavoring to honor them. But he knew it would be worthwhile: the Great Ankoma would come to England and summon Emma's spirit, so that Murray could speak to her and beg her for forgiveness.

Doyle ended his speech persuaded that tears of gratitude would soon start to flow from Murray's bloodshot eyes, and he even got ready for a possible embrace from that malodorous ruin of a man. But Murray simply contemplated him in silence for a few moments; then he stood up, grabbed the bottle of whisky he carried around with him everywhere, and, stumbling but dignified, left the room before the astonished eyes of his friends and went back to the bed they had dragged him from at dawn.

Both Doyle and Wells realized that it was not going to be as easy as they had thought to persuade Murray to attend a séance given by the Great Ankoma. Over the next few days, they discovered that Murray's views on spiritualism hadn't changed, despite his brokenhearted, semi-alcoholic state. Each time they tried to persuade him, he would refuse, doing so in various imaginative ways: he would laugh in their faces, or hurl drunken insults at them before vomiting on their shoes, or he would order them to leave the house with a dismissive gesture, even though most of the time they were at Wells's residence. There were even occasions when he would hurl whatever object was at hand at them, in general an empty whisky bottle . . . Nothing could breach Murray's stubborn refusal: not Wells's entreaties, nor Doyle's threats, nor even the gentle cajoling of Jane, who went as far as to remind Murray that he had once saved her life and that she could not bear to be unable to save his in return. Until the eve of the Great Ankoma's arrival in England.

Doyle, Wells, and Jane turned up at Murray's town house to announce the news, only to find Baskerville in a state of extreme agitation. It seemed his master had spent all day locked in his room, drinking, sobbing, and hurling a stream of blasphemous abuse at his servants. Even more alarmingly, for the past hour or so he had gone quiet. Wells and Doyle exchanged nervous glances and ran upstairs to Murray's room. His door was locked, but that didn't stop Doyle. After several attempts, he managed to break it down, splintering the frame and almost tearing the door off its hinges. Much to their relief, Murray had not hanged himself from the rafters, nor had he taken his life by any other means. He had simply passed out. A couple of jugs and a bowlful of water later, he was sitting in an armchair, listening to what they had to say.

"Tomorrow the Great Ankoma arrives, Gilmore," Doyle announced curtly. "And I don't need to remind you that in order for that to happen I have had to pledge my word and use all my influence, so that I hope all my efforts won't have been in vain."

Murray merely shrugged. "I didn't ask him to come."

"Well, he's coming!" Doyle lost his temper. "What the devil do expect me to do, send him back with a thank-you note hanging round his neck?"

"All I ask is that you pay for the damage to my bedroom door."

Doyle gave a bull-like snort, walked over to one of the windows, and looked out, trying to calm down.

"You are pigheaded and selfish, Monty," Wells said crossly. "You couldn't care less about the misery you're putting us through, could you? What skin is it off your nose if you attend a séance? What in heaven's name do you have to lose?"

"Please, Monty," Jane implored for the umpteenth time. "All we're asking is that you give it a try."

Murray looked at her with a pained expression.

"I can't do it, Jane," he murmured. "I won't allow Emma's spirit to be defiled now that she is dead. Every day when I lied to her while she was alive was an act of disrespect, and I refuse to let that happen again by agreeing to some stupid *sideshow*.

"But no one is going to defile her!" Wells cried, exasperated. "I assure you again, the Great Ankoma is a *genuine* medium."

"What are you scared of, Gilmore?" Doyle asked, wheeling round, hands clasped behind his back.

"Scared?" Murray looked puzzled. "I'm not scared of anything."

"Oh, yes you are," Doyle assured him harshly. "You're scared of talking to Emma and discovering that she won't forgive you, aren't you? Because what would be left then? You wouldn't even have the luxury of killing yourself . . . Why die and risk being confronted with an angry woman for all eternity? You prefer to carry on as you are, tormenting us with your asinine threats of suicide, threats you will never carry out because you're too much of a coward. And that is why you haven't already taken your life, and why you don't want to talk to Emma, and why you were incapable of telling her the truth when she was still alive."

"What! I was going to tell her!" Murray roared, almost keeling over as he leapt from his chair. "I was going to tell her before the damned automobile veered off the road. And of course I'm going to kill myself! I don't want to go on living! I don't care what's on the Other Side, I don't care if there's only a horrible void, or if Emma is there and she is angry with me for all eternity . . . Nothing could be worse than this, nothing . . ."

"You're going to kill yourself? Then do it!" Doyle flung open the windows behind him, and a soft, cool breeze like a lover's breath invaded the room. "Go on, jump! We're at least four floors up; you'll almost certainly die . . . Jump right now and end it all!"

Wells and Jane looked at Doyle, aghast.

"Arthur, please, I don't think this is the way to . . ." Wells hesitated.

But before he could finish his sentence, Murray strode over to the window, thrusting Wells aside.

"Don't do it, Monty!" Jane exclaimed in anguish, standing in his path.

Gently but firmly, Murray also pushed her to one side.

"For heaven's sake, Arthur, stop him!" Jane cried.

But Doyle took no notice. Instead, he stepped away from the window with a grin, politely extending his arm as if to let him through. Murray gave Doyle a black look as he walked past him and leapt up onto the windowsill, holding on to the frame with both hands.

"Monty, come down from there, I implore you," Wells said, approaching him with timid steps.

"Stay where you are, George!" Murray commanded.

Doyle, who was standing right next to Murray, signaled to Wells to do as he said. Stifling the urge to run and grab Murray, Wells stood stock-still, anxiously contemplating his bulky figure, silhouetted against the moonlight, almost filling the entire window.

His hands clasping the window frame and his feet balancing on the narrow sill, Murray took a deep breath. As they had been talking, the afternoon had faded amid glowing purples, giving way to a perfect summer's evening crowned by a full moon. A beautiful evening to die, he told himself, as the warm night breeze caressed his hair and brought with it the scent of jasmine. Why not end his suffering once and for all? Was he a coward, as Doyle maintained? He edged his right foot forward, eliciting a stifled shriek from Jane. He felt for her, and for George, and even for Doyle. He was sorry his friends would have to witness his demise, but Wells was right. He was putting them through a lot of misery. It was best to put an end once and for all to the sorry spectacle of his grief. And that was what he was going to do. He looked down. The gardens where he had so often strolled with Emma stretched out beneath him. In each of its nooks and crannies, the memory of a kiss, a caress, a joke that had made her laugh, lingered on like bits of fabric snagged on a bush. The silvery light of the moon delicately traced the outlines of the trees, made the dewdrops on the roses glisten like sequins, and shimmered on the pond where the lilies rocked gently, performing a slow waltz for themselves. At the end of the garden, rising like a new moon above the treetops of a small leafy forest, was the dome of the tiny, exquisite conservatory—in the shape of the Taj Mahal—that Murray had built with his own hands as a surprise gift for his bride-to-be. Then the yawning gap between him and the ground made him feel a sudden irrational fear, which reminded him of the day he had landed in a balloon to win Emma's heart. He had been forced to struggle against his fear of heights then, too, only it had been worth it because his beloved was waiting for him on Horsell Common. Murray closed his eyes and saw her once more as he had seen her that day, standing below him in a white dress, half-obscured by her parasol, which she twirled nervously as she waited . . . and, mustering the last of his courage, he told himself he must join her, and soon, because she liked him to be punctual, and he was already several months late . . . He opened his eyes, ready to leap into the void.

And then he saw her. On the path beside the rosebushes, where she used to pause during their strolls and delicately breathe in the scent of one of the roses. A woman was there now, her white dress gleaming in the moonlight, her face obscured by a parasol that twirled restlessly. An image as clear and terrifying as an unexpected laugh in the dead of night. Murray stood up straight and blinked several times as he felt her name tumble out of his mouth.

"Emma . . . ," he spluttered.

"No, Monty, please," implored Jane, horrified. "Don't jump. Emma wouldn't have wanted it—"

"Emma!" cried Murray.

He wheeled round, and leapt back into the room.

"I knew it!" Doyle exclaimed triumphantly. "I knew he wouldn't jump."

Taking no notice of him, Murray ran toward Wells and, grabbing his arm, dragged him over to the window.

"Look, George, look!" he said, his eyes flashing. "It's Emma, she's there . . ."

"What?"

They all rushed over to the window and poked their heads out expectantly.

"I don't see anything," Wells murmured.

"Nor do I," said Jane, screwing up her eyes. "What exactly did you see, Monty?"

Murray didn't answer. He spun round and darted out of the room. Alarmed, the others pursued him, almost stumbling over one another on the stairs. When Murray reached the spot where he had seen Emma, he halted and looked around, anxious and confused. The others arrived, gasping for breath, but before they could ask him to explain, Murray took off again across the lawn. His friends watched with pitiful faces as he ran up and down the pathways and around the lily ponds calling Emma's name, pausing occasionally, as if to listen, before resuming his mad, pointless race. At last he fell to his knees, exhausted, crooning his beloved's name amid loud sobs. Wells went over to Murray, knelt down beside him, and placed a hand on his shoulder. Murray looked at him, his eyes ravaged by the most devastating grief imaginable.

"I saw her, George, I tell you I saw her," he whispered between sobs. "It was her. She was there . . . Why did she vanish?"

Doyle also knelt beside Murray and smiled benevolently at him.

"She's trying to get in touch with you, my friend," he explained almost affectionately, like a father consoling his child, "but she can't find a way. Perhaps she simply wants to remind you of your assignation at Brook Manor. She herself prearranged it the day she died. As I once told you, spirits need a conduit in order to communicate with us. They need mediums . . ."

20

*T*HREE DAYS AFTER THE GREAT ANKOMA ARRIVED in England, Murray was at the door of Brook Manor just as evening was beginning to blur the contours of the landscape. He was accompanied by Jane, who had been watching over him that day. Waiting for them inside the house were Wells and Doyle, who had arrived in a hired carriage that morning with the medium. The Great Ankoma wanted to spend a few hours in the spot where the séance was to be held, allowing the spiritual forces there to scent him, like someone letting a strange dog sniff him before stroking it.

"I still don't know how I let myself be talked into coming all the way here," Murray snapped at Wells when he came to open the door to them.

Murray kept muttering to himself as he strode into the hallway, and Wells and Jane exchanged knowing looks. After a perfunctory embrace, Wells shepherded Murray into the dining room, where the séance was to take place. At a glance, he saw that his friend had at least spruced himself up a bit and wasn't wearing his clothes inside out, something for which he doubtless had Jane to thank.

"I promise you won't regret it, Monty. Just try to relax so that the mysterious forces of the Hereafter don't feel rejected by you, and—"

"That's enough, George, please," interrupted Murray, waving his hand impatiently. "I came here to see Emma, not to listen to your spiritualist nonsense."

Wells nodded with a sigh as the two of them, followed by Jane, entered the main reception room adjacent to the hallway. The room felt warmer, thanks to the last of the afternoon light, which was shining on the hearth. The mounted deer heads continued to challenge one another, caught in a duel that would never take place. At the far end of the room, Doyle was waiting for them, firmly planted in front of the door leading to the dining room, like a sentry guarding the entrance to the Hereafter.

"Good evening, Gilmore," Doyle greeted Murray. "I'm glad you came. I am sure that not only will you not regret this, but that you will also—"

"If you don't mind, Doyle," Murray cut in sharply, "let's get started, shall we?"

"Of course, of course, we can begin at once," said Doyle, who was not prepared to skip any part of the ceremony simply because of Murray's impetuosity. "However, before I introduce you to the Great Ankoma, who is busy concentrating in the dining room, let me remind you that he has traveled all the way from South Africa just to help you, that he has never taken part in this kind of séance before, and that he isn't motivated by greed. All of that is to his credit, as I'm sure you will appreciate, and I hope you demonstrate that by behaving with the due respect." He looked straight at Murray, doing his best not to appear threatening and, ironically, achieving the opposite effect. "The Great Ankoma only speaks the Bakongo dialect, but I shall interpret for him. I managed to pick up quite a few words during my stay in his village." With this, Doyle turned around and, opening the door ceremoniously, pronounced: "I hope you are prepared, Gilmore. Your idea of the world will change as of tonight."

The spacious, windowless room was dimly lit by rows of candles, their flames glinting off the rusty metal swords and making the faces of the Cabell ancestors look even more spectral, as if the artist had painted their portraits after their deaths from drowning. At one end of the table, a figure sat half in the shadow, head tilted, arms outstretched, palms facedown on the linen tablecloth in front of him. The meager light from the lamp placed in the middle of the table scarcely penetrated the gloom enveloping him. Doyle led the group a few paces to the opposite end of the table. Leaving them there, he approached the medium with reverential steps and whispered something to him, presumably to awaken him from his trance. The medium moved his head very slowly, as though emerging from a long snooze or a heavy bout of drinking, and looked at the others without seeing them. Ankoma was a skinny fellow whose age was difficult to judge, owing to his flowing beard and no less bushy hair, which all but swallowed up his features. Only his beady eyes twinkled intriguingly amid the cascade of grey locks that fell over his brow. He was wearing a sort of loose-fitting dark tunic, and around his neck hung colorful necklaces and strings of beads, among which Wells thought he glimpsed the tooth of some unknown animal. Speaking to no one in particular, the medium began to utter a series of guttural noises, which sounded as if he were choking on a chicken bone.

"He says there are many spirits here," Doyle translated dutifully.

"Hmm," grunted Murray, who refused to be easily impressed.

Doyle looked at him sternly in admonishment, then proceeded to the introductions. Once these were over, he invited Murray to take the seat facing the Great Ankoma, while he sat on the medium's right and Wells and Jane on his left. Once they had all settled in their chairs, Doyle resumed his role as master of ceremonies.

"Excellent. Now, Ankoma is a specialist in automatic writing," he explained to Murray, "and so is going to communicate with Emma's spirit, and if she agrees, he will try to make her talk to you by writing on this slate."

"But I don't want Emma to write on some stupid slate!" Murray protested. "I want to see her. I want her to appear to me as she did in the garden!"

Doyle wagged his head, genuinely dismayed by Murray's stubborn attitude.

"Look, Gilmore . . . ," he explained patiently. "Every medium has a method or a special talent for communicating with spirits; you can't just oblige them to do it another way. Besides, the main thing is for you to talk to her, isn't it? The way you do it is secondary."

Murray looked suspiciously at the slate on the table, next to the gas lamp.

"Did he communicate with his Bantu ancestors using slates?" he inquired coldly.

"Obviously not," replied Doyle, who was becoming irritated by Murray's insolence. "He used palm leaves. But we are a bit more civilized over here . . ."

"Palm leaves . . . ," sighed Murray. "Very well. Carry on, Amoka."

"Ankoma," Doyle corrected.

"Ankoma, Ankoma . . . ," Murray repeated, spreading his hands to encourage the medium to proceed.

Ankoma nodded almost indifferently, as if his orders came from a higher power unknown to men, and certainly to Murray. His body seemed to slacken, losing its previous rigidity, his eyes closed, and a sort of beatific calm relaxed what was visible of his face almost to the point of imbecility. Then he began a gentle rocking movement, which grew more and more intense, until soon he was writhing around on his seat as if someone had stuffed it with stinging nettles. Moments later, he began to jerk and make ridiculous gurgling noises, like a boiling kettle, which made Doyle sit up in his chair. Everyone sensed that something important was happening or was about to happen. And they were right, for just then a lengthy, spine-tingling sound, like grinding teeth, rent the air. They all peered into the surrounding shadows, trying to see where the screeching was coming from, until they realized it could only have been made by the rusty hinges on one of the doors. They examined them through the thick gloom, but both were closed. Then the floorboards began to emit faint, intermittent creaks, warning them that someone was walking toward them across the room. Murray arched his eyebrows as the steps came closer and closer before seemingly moving away again, as though whatever it might be had begun circling the table with sinister slowness and was scrutinizing them. Murray looked first at Doyle, then at Wells, but the two men ignored him, busy as they were exchanging uneasy glances. For his part, the Great Ankoma remained silent, staring apprehensively into the darkness enveloping the dining room. After several moments during which they looked at one another in bewilderment, Doyle drew the medium's attention with a subtle gesture and then pointed to the slate, as if to remind him that this was his usual way of communicating with spirits. The Great Ankoma picked it up with his scrawny hands, where the crisscrossed veins beneath his pale flesh stood out like snow-covered roots, and held it for a few moments as though unsure what to do next. At that moment, Wells squeezed Murray's shoulder abruptly, a gesture that was meant to encourage him, but in spite of the distraction, Murray noticed Ankoma make a suspicious movement under the table. When Murray caught his eye, the medium placed the slate facedown on a piece of chalk as his body seemed to go into brief convulsions, and a nonsensical refrain spewed from his mouth. A few seconds later, he turned the slate over with the nonchalance of someone removing a cake from the oven and pushed it toward Murray. On the side that had been clean, he recognized his beloved Emma's scrawl: "Hello, I'm Miss Mournful," he read in disbelief.

"Oh, dear, it looks as if the Great Ankoma has contacted the wrong spirit," Doyle remarked, disillusioned.

Wells and Jane nodded, also disappointed, though still glancing about warily.

"No, no," Murray hastened to explain. "Miss Mournful is the private nickname I used for Emma."

He contemplated the message on the slate with a puzzled expression. He could have sworn he saw the medium up to some trick, probably exchanging slates under the table, but that wouldn't explain the creaking door or the footsteps pacing round them. Above all, it didn't alter the fact that no one knew the nickname he had used with Emma in private. No one but her.

"Then . . . good God, he's contacted Emma!" Wells exclaimed, overcome with emotion.

"Yes, dear George! We did it!" Doyle bellowed excitedly. Then he turned toward Murray and barked, "Remember what I said to you, Gilmore, about believing in spirits if a loved one speaks to you using words only you and she were aware of?"

Murray looked at Doyle askance and then nodded slowly.

"Go on, Gilmore, the channel is open," Doyle urged, exalted. "Speak to Emma. Ask her anything you like. For instance, why don't you ask her if—"

Murray cut Doyle short with a gesture, contemplating him with a mixture of unease and indignation before raising his eyes to the ceiling.

"Emma, my love, are you really there?" he asked tentatively, unable to keep a tone of optimism from creeping into his voice.

"She already told you she's here, Monty," Wells remonstrated. "Why not ask her if—"

But before he was able to finish his sentence, Murray gave a start and sat bolt upright in his chair. The others looked at him, bewildered, not understanding what was the matter. For a few moments, Murray remained stiff and pale, a stupefied look on his face as he held his breath.

"Oh, God . . . ," he howled. "Oh, God . . ."

A few seconds later, still flattened against the back of the chair, he heaved a deep sigh, letting out all the air he had been keeping in, then raised his left hand to his face and gently stroked his own cheek, as though touching it for the first time, his lips breaking into a smile of dizzy joy.

"She caressed me!" he declared, filled with emotion as he clasped Wells's arm. "It's all true, George. Emma is here. She caressed me—I felt her fingers touch my cheek!"

"Calm down, Monty," Wells implored, looking inquiringly at Doyle.

"Calm down! Didn't you hear what I said? Emma is here!" Murray leapt out of his chair, casting his gaze anxiously around the room, unsure where to look. At last, his eyes alighted on the medium, and he commanded, "I want to see her!"

Alarmed, the Great Ankoma made a little grunt that seemed to express doubt.

"Make her appear, I beg you!" Murray implored, seized by an almost childlike excitement. "I'll give you anything you want!"

As he was pleading with the medium to make Emma materialize, even if only in the form of a vaporous ectoplasm, Murray could feel the blood throbbing so hard in his temples that he seemed to be on the point of passing out. Or perhaps it wasn't that, but the fact was that the light in the room, made up of the flames from all the candles and the oil lamp, seemed suddenly to grow dimmer.

"Er . . . I'm afraid that is beyond good old Ankoma's powers," Doyle lamented. "But perhaps you could ask Emma if—"

"I don't want to ask her a damn thing!" Murray roared in desperation. "All I want is to see her!"

He went quiet, gazing into the huge mirror that was in the room. The others also fixed their eyes on the mirror, trying to identify what it was that had silenced Murray. It took them a few seconds, because the glass appeared to reflect faithfully the scene in the dining room. They were all sitting in the same places at the table presided over by the Great Ankoma: on the right of the medium was Doyle, gazing over his shoulder at the mirror in an attempt to fathom its mysteries; on the medium's left sat Wells and Jane, wearing equally disconcerted expressions. However, it wasn't Murray who was standing opposite the Great Ankoma. His reflection had been replaced by that of a young woman in black, who, just as the others noticed her, stood up from the table and walked toward them with hesitant steps. They all stared dumbfounded as the sinister image approached the mirror. A moment later, she was close enough for them to make out her face in the candlelight.

"Emma!" exclaimed Murray.

He was so overcome by the discovery that he almost fell over. Quickly regaining his balance, Murray also walked toward the mirror, through which Emma was now peering, as if through a window, her hands resting on the glass. The young woman was studying the world on Murray's side with a look of surprise, as if she could see Murray as clearly as he saw her.

"Darling, I felt your caress . . . !" he cried as he approached the mirror, distraught.

Emma watched him move toward her while her eyes expressed a frenzied look of horror, confusion, and excitement. As he drew closer,

Murray reached out to touch his beloved's face, to feel once more the softness of her skin, her hair; but when his hand encountered the mirror's smooth surface, he realized that although she was there in front of him, she remained unreachable. Meanwhile, the others had risen from the table to take a closer look at the miracle that was occurring, and as they stood a few feet behind Murray, they saw themselves reflected on the other side in a silent huddle behind Emma.

"Emma, my love!" Murray cried, running his hands over the mirror's icy surface, which froze his fingertips with the coldness of dead things.

Once she had absorbed the strange phenomenon, Emma also tried to intertwine her fingers with Murray's, only to be prevented by the smooth glass. For almost a minute, they both clawed at their side of the mirror, as though desperately trying to scratch through its surface, to tear away the seemingly fine veil separating them, enclosing them in identical prisons. Until Murray finally lost his temper and began to strike the mirror with the heels of his hands. On the far side, Emma, who had a greater capacity for understanding (or perhaps for acceptance), was content to gaze at Murray, whispering "Monty," her eyes filled with tears. She had tilted her lovely face, moved by the immensity of his love for her, made evident by his desperate pounding on the mirror, increasingly angry yet restrained, for he knew that if he broke the glass he might lose forever the cherished image contained in it. They all understood that the mirror reflected a shared suffering. When Murray finally accepted that he would never be able to tunnel his way into Emma's arms, he moved back a few inches and gazed at her helplessly, noticing for the first time the air of weariness clouding her beauty: she had huge shadows under her eyes and her skin had lost its glow, as if something had been tormenting her for months, and it had begun to undermine her health. Murray's fingers trembled as he caressed her lips without being able to touch them. At that moment, through the tears welling up in his eyes, Murray noticed the light in the room grow brighter as the peculiar gloom that seemed to have distorted it for the past few minutes lifted, and then he blinked and found himself touching his own reflection. He stepped back with a mixture of surprise and irritation.

"No, no! Emma, don't leave! Come back!" Murray gave a loud bellow that gradually subsided as the relentless passing of the seconds threatened to transform Emma's reflection into a hallucination or a dream, until it was reduced to a pitiful wail.

Grief stricken and exhausted, he pressed his forehead against the mirror and began sobbing louder and louder. Images of the accident, which plagued him day and night, began to flash through his mind once more: his perspiring hands clutching the steering wheel of his shiny new automobile, his heart pounding in his chest as he tried to think of how to start his confession; Emma's smile, at once curious and amused; that sharp bend appearing out of nowhere; the car veering off the road and plunging into the gorge; his attempts to control the machine, which had started to bounce across the ground; the violent jolt that had sent him flying through the air; the world shattering into a thousand pieces, and Emma's voice, ever more remote, shouting his name even as the world went dark. And then, he never knew how long after, the slow awakening, the fog of his unconscious revealing snatches of hellish images: people running and shouting, concerned faces staring at him, the heels of his boots making a furrow in the ground as they dragged him away from the scene, and a voice ringing out with infernal clarity amid the din of orders being hurled left and right, the gruff voice of a stranger whose face Murray would never see, echoing in his head above the clatter of the carriage taking him to the hospital, above the questions of those accompanying him, above any other sound. Those words he would never manage to forget, those words that announced the end of everything: "We'll have to cut through the metal to get the body out."

"What the devil happened?" he heard Doyle ask behind him.

Wells opened his mouth to reply. He no longer had any doubt that his experience in front of the mirror the fateful day of the excursion hadn't been the result of an optical illusion. While the others had been busy looking at Emma and Murray, Wells had taken the opportunity to study his own reflection, which was also ignoring the lovers and staring straight at him, with an identical expression of terror, but without the scar across his chin. Wells hadn't a clue what any of it meant, although obviously both phenomena were closely related. But before he could utter a word, he heard Jane say, "Emma was wearing black. As if she were in mourning."

"That's true," Doyle said. "And I had a different suit on. The one I'd be wearing now if I hadn't spilled coffee down it this morning."

"And I—" Wells attempted to add.

But Murray didn't let him. He wheeled round, pointing his finger at the medium.

"Do it again!" he cried. "Bring her back!"

The Great Ankoma recoiled, waving his arms in front of his chest.

"Wait, Gilmore, let me explain," Doyle said, placing a hand on his shoulder.

Murray brushed it away and strode over to the medium.

"Makoma, or whatever your name is, make her come back, or I swear I'll strangle you with my bare hands!"

"I can't!" The Great Ankoma protested in perfect English, looking imploringly at Doyle.

Doyle tried once more to restrain Murray, this time gripping his arm hard.

"Listen to me, Gilmore: none of what happened here tonight has anything to do with Ankoma."

"It's true, Monty," Wells admitted, placing himself between Murray and the medium. "I'm afraid Ankoma has no special powers."

"It's true, Mr. Gilmore," the alleged medium said apologetically, trying to regain his composure. "I know exactly who my parents are, I speak perfect English, as you can see, and I've never been in a Bakongo village making bowls levitate, simply because I don't have the power to lift objects . . . It seems my only talent, in Mr. Doyle's worthy opinion, is my handwriting, which is more beautiful and more legible than his. At least, that is what he tells me whenever he asks me to write a few lines for him. And if I may say so, I don't think I deserve to be strangled for it."

"You say you can't lift objects. So how do you explain that?" Murray declared, pointing to the slate, which had risen off the table and was now floating in midair.

They gazed at the hovering object, openmouthed. They had scarcely recovered from their shock when the chalk also took to the air, moving toward the slate to write something on it. Having done so, it landed on the table again, like a strange insect, and then the slate drifted over to them, pausing in front of Murray. On it he was able to read the words "Would you like me to caress you once more, my love?"

"Oh, Emma," Murray gasped, gazing with infinite tenderness at the space above the slate where the face of his beloved should have been. "Of course, my love, I need to feel your hands . . ."

The message was swiftly erased from the slate, which returned to the table, where the chalk wrote a fresh message on it. Then it floated back over to Murray.

"I think killing you all would be much more fun," Murray read aloud.

At that moment, the slate suddenly fell on the ground, as if whoever was holding it had hurled it to the floor with contempt, and a man's bloodcurdling laughter rent the air. Everyone exchanged alarmed looks.

"What the devil . . . ?" Murray exclaimed. Realizing this was not Emma's spirit, he instinctively wiped his cheek with his jacket sleeve, a look of indignant disgust on his face. Then, addressing the place where the slate had fallen, he roared, "Who are you, you son of a bitch?"

The laughter grew louder and more deranged.

"Let me, Gilmore. I have more experience with spirits," said Doyle, pushing Murray aside and addressing an indeterminate spot in the dining room. "Who are you, you son of a bitch?"

A sharp voice cut the air like a scalpel.

"Shall I tell you who I am, Mr. Doyle? I am the purest form of evil! The most heinous villain you could ever imagine! But I assure you, your horror at my crimes, if you knew them, would be lost in your admiration at my skill."

Doyle looked puzzled while those familiar words fluttered around in his head.

"It is easy to write about evil," the voice went on, "but less amusing to confront it when it steps out of one of your stories, isn't that so, Mr. Doyle?"

"Steps out of one of my stories? What the devil do you mean?" Then it struck him why the words were familiar: they were almost the very ones he had written in "The Final Problem." "Oh, good grief . . . but that can't be . . . Are you . . . Moriarty?"

"Oh, no . . . ," the voice replied with a malevolent chuckle, "although my name does begin with M. Perhaps George would like to try his luck."

Wells raised his eyebrows when he heard the creature utter his name. The voice fell silent for a few moments, and when it spoke again, Wells sensed it was in front of him and even thought he caught a whiff of its sour breath.

"Go on, George, who am I?"

A pair of invisible fingers tweaked Wells's nose, causing him to stagger backward, taking with him Jane, who had been clutching him. Then, staring uneasily into the air, he ventured to pose the absurd and terrifying question that had been forming in his mind since the creature first began talking.

"Are you . . . the Invisible Man?"

"That doesn't begin with 'M,' George," whispered Doyle, who had positioned himself beside Wells.

"No, but 'Man' does," Wells replied weakly.

"What is wrong with you authors? Does your vanity know no bounds?" the voice exclaimed sarcastically. "Moriarty! The Invisible Man! I am simply someone who has come here to take back what belongs to me, what the old lady stole from me. Does that story ring a bell with you, George?"

"And what is it that I am supposed to have that belongs to you?"

"No, no, George. Don't pretend with me." The voice had begun to circle round the company so noiselessly that the darkness itself seemed to be speaking. "The book, that's what I'm after! *The Map of Chaos!* Give it to me, or I swear you will all die!"

"But I don't have your book!" Wells protested.

He instantly regretted having raised his voice, for the creature responded with a furious scream.

"You asked for it, George!"

Thereupon there was a din of laughter and footsteps that seemed to come from every direction, as if the spirit were rampaging around the dining room. The candle flames sputtered one after another, mapping out the creature's erratic path.

"The lovesick millionaire, the charming young lady, the Great Ankoma, the zealous Scotsman . . . Which would you like to see die first, George?"

Doyle broke away from the group.

"Start with me, you fiend—that is, if you are man enough!"

Scarcely had Doyle thrown down his challenge than there was a high-pitched whistle, and they all turned toward where the sound had emanated from—including Doyle himself, who managed to glimpse a silvery glint before he felt a stabbing pain in his right ear. He cursed, lifting his hand to his head, which felt as if it had suddenly burst into flames, while at his back he heard a dull thud. The group stared horror-struck at the wall directly behind Doyle, where, protruding from the forehead of an elegant gentleman in a ruff, was a sword, its blade still quivering. Doyle staggered back toward the others, suddenly pale as he realized it had been aimed at his head.

"Good God, Arthur!" Jane cried as she saw the blood seeping through Doyle's fingers. "Are you all right?"

"Yes, it's only a scratch," said Doyle, narrowing his eyes and looking around him. "But clearly that thing was intending something worse."

Shaken by this clear attempt on Doyle's life, the group remained huddled in the center of the room.

"Where the devil is it?" said Murray, his eyes darting round the room.

"Look, over there!" cried the petrified Great Ankoma, whose bushy beard had become unstuck and was dangling from his face.

They all saw one of the swords being unhooked from the shield he was pointing to. For a few seconds it remained suspended in the air, twisting slowly, the adjacent candles twinkling ominously along its blade, as if the creature had paused to marvel at its sharp edge before using it on them; then they looked on in terror as it cleaved the air with a couple of two-handed swishes. There was an evil threat implicit in those preparatory movements, but they also revealed the creature's position. Doyle and Murray understood this at the same time. Murray grabbed a chair and, raising it above his head, hurled it at the sword. There was a grunt of pain as the weapon dropped to the floor, and then an angry roar split the air. Meanwhile, Doyle had plucked the sword from the painting and was advancing toward where the creature supposedly was, swinging the blade furiously with both hands as he shouted, "George, keep Jane safe! Woodie, Gilmore, grab a weapon! Surround the table and—"

Before he could finish his sentence, he doubled over, crying out in agony. A second later, he straightened up abruptly, his face toward the ceiling, as if he had received a powerful uppercut, and tottered for a moment before collapsing. Almost instantaneously, the Great Ankoma felt a violent shove propel him toward the dining room table. As though swept up by a tornado, he landed on it with a terrifying crunch of splintered bones and wood, while the oil lamp rolled onto the floor, depriving them of the main source of light in the room. Jane gave a bloodcurdling scream that was quickly eclipsed by the creature's evil laugh.

"Give me the book, George!" the voice insisted. "Hand over *The Map of Chaos* and all this can end!"

He began to howl like an angry beast, and several of the portraits on the walls came crashing to the floor.

"Grab as many weapons as you can and defend yourselves!" Doyle spluttered, standing up and trying to make himself heard above the creature's spine-chilling cries.

Murray obeyed. He unhooked a sword from the nearest wall and threw it to Wells, who, paralyzed by the hellish scene before his eyes, failed to catch it. The haft hit him on the head, and that seemed to rouse him. Sluggishly, he retrieved the weapon from the floor and looked at Murray, visibly dazed.

"Get Jane out of here!" Murray ordered, grabbing another sword from the wall.

Wells nodded but remained rooted to the spot. Jane took his arm and dragged him toward one of the doors. Murray looked around for Doyle. He was tracing broad circles with his sword as he made his way over to the table where Wood lay a heap. Murray followed him, also repeatedly lunging at the air around him. The creature's yells had subsided, making it impossible to locate him. He could be anywhere. As soon as they reached Wood, Doyle felt for his pulse.

"Is he alive?" asked Murray, who had positioned himself behind Doyle and was still cleaving the air with his sword.

"Yes, he's only unconscious, but we must get him out of here, Gilmore. Help me to—"

"We're locked in!" Wells shouted from across the room, he and Jane having just tried both doors.

"What!" Murray exclaimed. "Where are the keys?"

"Damn! I left them in one of the doors," replied Doyle. "Are you sure they're not there, George?"

"Of course, Arthur, otherwise I wouldn't have said we were locked in!" yelled Wells impatiently. He had sandwiched Jane between himself and the wall and was brandishing his weapon with more energy than dexterity, ready to protect her against any possible attack.

"Haven't you a duplicate key on you, Gilmore?" Doyle whispered to Murray, listening for the slightest sound that might betray the creature's position.

"No, but there's a set in the hall, hanging on a hook by the main door," Murray whispered back. "We could all try shouting to alert Baskerville, though I doubt the old fellow will hear us from outside . . . but, what the devil . . . ?"

Doyle swung round, feeling a burst of heat on his face as he saw what had shocked Murray: the flame from a fallen candle had set alight the oil from the lamp, and a tongue of fire was climbing up one of the faded wall hangings.

"Damnation! We have to put out the flames!" exclaimed Doyle, tossing Murray his sword. "Keep him away from me!"

Murray positioned himself behind Doyle, flourishing both swords vigorously while Doyle took off his jacket and used it to beat at the hangings, causing a flurry of sparks to rise with each blow. But his efforts were in vain. The barely smothered flames quickly spread to an adjacent portrait, and from there to the next, greedily devouring the ancient canvases and wooden frames. With a gesture of defeat, Doyle gave up trying to fight the fire. Plumes of dusky smoke, like a gigantic ectoplasm, had begun to materialize in the room, spreading with extraordinary speed, the tentacles reaching up to the ceiling. Both Doyle and Murray started to choke. Across the room, Wells and Jane were also watching the fire spread with a look of terror.

"We're trapped in here with that thing!" Wells muttered, utterly defeated by the situation.

Just then Wells felt the air stir beside him, and before he could grasp what it meant, a sharp rap on his knuckles made him let go of his sword. Nervously, he watched it slide across the floor even as he felt Jane being wrenched from his side with the force of a punch that would break a jaw.

"Jane!" he yelled, stepping toward her.

"Stay where you are or I'll kill her, George!" commanded the voice, coming now from behind Jane. "And you," he added, addressing Murray and Doyle, "don't move an inch or I'll snap her scrawny neck before you can count to two!"

Uttering a cry of despair, Wells remained motionless. Murray and Doyle also froze, and for a long moment the three men watched helplessly as Jane, on tiptoes, remained almost suspended in the air, her face turning an ever darker shade of red. A tapestry engulfed in flames slipped off the wall with a quiet crackle, like rain falling on the ocean.

"Good, that's better. Now hand over the book, George, or your little wife will die," said the voice.

"Please don't hurt her!" Wells implored. Then he swallowed hard and, with a calm that belied his anguish, added: "Listen: I don't have a book called *The Map of Chaos,* but I'll give you whatever you ask for, I swear. I'll give you anything. Anything . . ."

The creature grew impatient. "I don't want anything from you, only my book!"

"Please, let her go, she can't breathe, please . . . I tell you, she can't breathe!" Wells cried, his voice cracking before it turned into a crazed howl: "Damn you, don't you dare hurt her, or else . . ."

"Or else what?" the voice gloated.

Wells shook his head, his eyes blurry with tears, overwhelmed by the senselessness of it all. The fire had started spreading to the ceiling, and tiny red-hot splinters rained from above, scores of burning lights gently rocking as they floated down before dying out when they touched the floor. Sensing Wells's helplessness, Murray began to edge his way around the table, but the voice brought him up short.

"Stop right there! I said nobody move or I'll kill her!"

To prove this was no empty threat, he hoisted Jane another inch from the floor. Her toes were scarcely touching the ground now, and Wells, the tears streaming down his face, watched Jane's hands claw at her neck as her face began to go purple. He saw her raise her arm, desperately groping the air with her fingers, as though fumbling for something behind her, but she only managed to loosen her hair.

But while Wells impotently contemplated Jane thrashing around, Doyle, his neck and shoulder drenched in blood, had focused his attention elsewhere: unbeknownst to the others, the handle of the door leading out into the hall had slowly started to turn. Murray's coachman was coming to the rescue, possibly alerted by their cries; but this was of little comfort to Doyle, not just because of the old man's lack of physical prowess, but because when he opened the door and looked inside, he would be unable to see any enemy, or to understand what was going on, and if Doyle tried to alert him, the creature would certainly kill Jane. Giddy from the fumes, Doyle struggled to think of a solution, but he was too late. The door swung open and the coachman's head appeared. Seeing the flames, he declared: "Good heavens!" And that sufficed. Jane's body jerked round like a rag doll, revealing that the creature had heard him, too. But then something unexpected happened: Jane, who seemed to be clasping something in her hand, thrust one arm back over her head, and the creature let out a terrible cry of pain and dropped her on the floor.

"My eye!" the voice howled as one of the long hairpins Jane used to fasten her bun shook violently from side to side, hanging in midair. "My eye!"

Wells rushed over to Jane, who was on her knees, retching and gasping for breath while her hairpin flailed around a few feet above their heads. All of a sudden, it swooped to the floor, then rose again, together with the sword Wells had dropped. Both floated toward the hallway door.

"Baskerville, get away from the door!" screamed Murray, realizing what was about to happen.

He leapt onto the table, tossing a sword to Doyle, who caught it in mid-flight as he, too, clambered onto the table. The two men bounded across it, brandishing their swords and spurring themselves on with simultaneous unintelligible cries. But the invisible creature reached the door before them, and the befuddled old man watched, paralyzed with shock, as the sword floated through the air toward him. The blade plunged effortlessly into his stomach like a knife through butter. The old man opened his eyes wide as he felt the sword slice open his guts, but he didn't utter a single cry. His body, still pierced by the sword, was sent flying at Doyle and Murray as they sprinted toward him, and the three men collapsed in a heap of flesh and metal.

Doyle rose to his feet quickly and ran out into the hallway while Murray held Baskerville in his arms. Narrowing his eyes, Doyle was able to make out Jane's hairpin floating up the stairs before it was flung violently to the ground, as if the Invisible Man had yanked it out in a desperate gesture. Doyle turned round and went back into the dining room, where the heat was by now unbearable.

"He's on his way upstairs!" he declared, covering his nose and mouth with his sleeve to protect himself from the fumes. There's no escape up there! Let's go after him, Gilmore!" Then, glancing at Wells, who was helping Jane to her feet, he commanded, "You two, carry the wounded out to the carriage! Take them to the hospital and then inform the police!"

"Have you lost your mind, Arthur?" Wells protested. "Forget about the creature! We must get out of here immediately!"

"It's true, the fire is spreading fast," Murray added.

Doyle studied the progress of the flames, which had now enveloped an entire wall and were making their way across the ceiling, curling around the supporting beams.

"I realize that, damn it!" he bellowed, trying to make himself heard above the noise of the crackling flames. "But listen to me: that monster will stop at nothing, don't you see? If he had wanted to flee, he would have left through the front door and disappeared onto the moor. Yet he remained in the house, clearly because he means to kill us before we can get away. If we don't stop him now that he is at a disadvantage, half-blind and unarmed, none of us will ever sleep easily again, especially not you, George."

"But in case you hadn't noticed, that thing is invisible!" Wells shouted frantically. "How the devil do you intend to find him if he doesn't want you to?"

"We'll find him!" exclaimed Murray before Doyle had a chance to reply. "Look, he's showing us the way!"

Before their astonished eyes, spots of blood began to appear as if by magic on the floor. The reddish trail ran between Doyle's feet, across the hall, and up the staircase.

"He's leaving a trail of blood!" Doyle exclaimed, scarcely able to believe their luck. "We must move quickly!"

He strode over to Wood, who was still lying crumpled on the table, took him by the shoulders, and began to drag him toward the door. Infected by Doyle's sudden burst of energy, the others picked up the old man, who groaned softly, as though not wishing to inconvenience them with his suffering. When they laid him on the hall floor, he looked feverishly at Jane.

"Are you all right, my dear?" he stammered, summoning every ounce of his waning strength to force a smile. "I couldn't bear anything to happen to you . . ."

Moved by the words of this old man whom she barely knew, Jane assured him that she was perfectly well.

"The poor fellow's delirious . . . ," Wells muttered, slightly wary of the coachman's excessive concern for his wife.

Doyle placed Wood next to Baskerville, who was gazing at the ceiling, gasping like a fish out of water. Blood trickled slowly from the corner of the old man's mouth. After casting a professional eye over his wound, Doyle gave him a look of infinite sorrow, and they all knew there was no hope for him.

"George, carry them out to the coach. And try to stanch the bleeding with . . . well, I'm sure you'll find something you can use." Doyle sighed helplessly before looking straight at Wells. "Now listen carefully: Gilmore and I are going after that thing." He glanced toward the staircase. "If we haven't come out after fifteen minutes, go for help. Fifteen minutes, do you hear? Not a moment longer!"

Wells nodded resignedly. He still considered Doyle's plan to hunt the creature down an act of folly, but he didn't have the strength to argue about it. Doyle had ordered him to evacuate the wounded, which, compared to the task he had allotted himself, was incredibly simple, and so the best thing to do was obey. Doyle looked across at Murray.

"Are you with me, Gilmore?"

"Of course." Murray grinned. "But if we are going to die together, Arthur, I think you should call me Gilliam—at least for this evening."

21

HILE JANE AND WELLS CARRIED THE OLD man out of the house, Murray and Doyle headed toward the staircase. Wells feared for their lives, though less for that of Doyle, whom he had always considered quite indestructible—immune to the everyday events that killed off ordinary folk. He was more concerned about Gilliam, whom Death had begun stalking lately, disgruntled perhaps by the irreverent disappearing act he had performed in the fourth dimension.

"Wait, Arthur!" Murray exclaimed at that very instant. "Why limit ourselves to a pair of swords?" He approached one of the walls in the hallway, took down the enormous iron mace, and handed it ceremoniously to Doyle. "This admirable weapon was apparently made for you. Besides, I hear you're a talented batsman, isn't that right?"

Doyle hung his sword from his belt, gripped the mace in both hands, and felt the weight of it with satisfaction.

"What a splendid weapon!" he declared, striking the air with a couple of almighty blows. "What about you, Gilliam? Which weapon will you choose?"

Murray wheeled round. He was holding the big crossbow, which he had loaded with an arrow; Doyle had explained its complicated mechanism to them on the day of the excursion.

"The truth is, I've never considered myself a very honorable man," he apologized with a half grin.

Despite the gloom, the trail of blood was quite visible against the marble steps. Doyle started the ascent, with Murray close behind, trying to fasten a second arrow to his belt. After hesitating a moment, he had finally taken it down off the wall. Two were better than one, he had thought, though he dearly hoped he wouldn't have to reload the crossbow. Doyle located Jane's hairpin on one of the stairs and stooped to pick it up carefully by one end. Noticing that it felt heavier than it should, he ran his finger slowly along it until he encountered an obstruction, something soft and viscous. He pulled a face.

"Good God, I think that's his eye . . . I'll be hanged if I understand what is going on here."

With a look of disgust, he replaced the pin on the stair and continued his ascent. Murray followed, making sure he didn't step on the invisible eyeball.

"Well, if you don't understand, and you're the expert . . . Oh, why don't we ask that *genuine* medium you brought over from Africa?" he suggested, feigning a burst of enthusiasm. "What did you call him just now? Oh, yes . . . Woodie. It doesn't sound quite as impressive as Amonka, does it?"

Doyle walked on, focusing on the trail of glittering rubies that seemed to sprout from the ground like evil flowers. He studied each stair closely, afraid the Invisible Man might have veered off suddenly, or even silently retraced his steps.

"I don't think now is the right time to bring that up, Gilliam," he muttered.

"Really? But there might not be another time, my dear Arthur," said Murray, almost glued to Doyle's back, pointing his crossbow at any shadow that seemed to move. "And I don't want to die without knowing where you got hold of the poor wretch and, more important, how the devil he knew Emma's nickname."

"He's my secretary."

"What!"

"Don't raise your voice!" Doyle commanded in a whisper. "Woodie is my secretary. There's no such person as the Great Ankoma. George and I invented him." Doyle continued climbing the stairs without turning round to contemplate Murray's astonished face. "As for Emma's nickname, the day I first mentioned the medium to you at your house, George slipped out of the room for a few moments. I imagine that, due to the state you were in, you don't remember, but the truth is he took the opportunity to search your study for anything we might be able to use. He came across your and Emma's correspondence in a drawer of your desk. That's where he discovered your nicknames . . . *Mr. Impossible.*"

Murray tried to choose one of the many questions buzzing round in his head while they climbed a few more steps in silence.

"But what the devil made you want to hold a phony séance in the first place?" he finally asked.

"To stop you from killing yourself," Doyle replied. "George was desperate . . . He felt he was to blame for the accident and for Emma's death. It was he who advised you to come clean with her, remember? And he considered it his duty to help you finish what you had started. He thought it was the only way you would find any peace. When George came to my house and told me that the only way to save you was to let you communicate with Emma during a séance, I assumed he meant a real one, but he soon disabused me. George wanted you to talk to her, but he didn't want to take any risks. He wanted to be in control of all the variables: the medium, Emma's responses, her forgiveness of you . . . everything. He wanted her to command you to go on living, even to force you to be happy, insofar as you could be . . ." Doyle shook his head and gave a wry grin. "I don't know how he managed to convince me to take part in one of those phony séances I have spoken out against so strongly . . . But damn it all, you know, I almost ended up enjoying it! You must admit we managed to build up a fairly compelling tale: the mysterious medium, the hand of fate . . ."

"But I saw Emma in the garden!" Murray interrupted.

"Oh, yes, that . . . ," said Doyle, pausing to examine the trail of blood with a frown, like a housekeeper finding fault with the housemaid's work. "The Emma in the garden was also our doing," he confessed, resuming his ascent. "That was Miss Leckie, who kindly offered to help us out. With the aid of some of your servants, we got hold of one of Emma's dresses and a parasol. It was all we could think of. We were desperate! Time was passing, and we had failed to persuade you to attend the séance with the Great Ankoma . . ."

"So, when you challenged me to jump out of the window . . ." Murray reflected. "What you really wanted was for me to see Miss Leckie!"

"Elementary, my dear Gilliam." Doyle grinned at him.

"Good heavens! . . . But what if I hadn't seen her? What if I'd jumped?"

"She was clearly visible," Doyle said with a shrug. "Besides, I knew you wouldn't do it."

"Good heavens . . . ," Murray repeated, incapable of saying anything more.

When they reached the top of the stairs, Doyle carefully examined the floor once more.

"The trail heads toward the right wing," he announced, signaling with his chin the long corridor receding into the darkness.

"That corridor is a dead end . . . ," Murray murmured with a distracted air. "All the rooms on that side are locked, apart from the one the builders use to store their plaster and tools."

"Then it won't be so difficult to hunt him down," said Doyle. "Though we could do with a bit more . . . energy."

From his pocket he plucked a small box of cocaine tablets with an image on the lid of two children playing innocently, and he offered one to Murray.

"No, thanks, Arthur," Murray said. "I think the rage I feel will suffice."

"As you wish." Doyle shrugged. He took a tablet, put the box away, and with a show of bravado lifted his mace. "Let's find that son of a bitch!"

But before he could step forward Murray restrained him, clasping his arm.

"Wait a moment, Arthur . . . I realize that this invisible monster isn't another of your little hoaxes." He reflected for a moment about what he was going to say. "No, of course it isn't. Running poor Baskerville through with a sword would have been going too far, even for you. But"—he looked straight at Doyle—"what about what happened with the mirror?"

"That wasn't our doing either," said Doyle. "We insisted on holding the séance at Brook Manor in order to practice the slate trick without anyone seeing; that would have been impossible at your house, and you spent much of your time at the Wellses', and as for my place . . . well, I could never have forgiven myself if my wife or children had found out that I was helping to organize a fraudulent séance. But what happened with the mirror . . . how could we have managed a stunt like that?" he gasped, betraying his own unease at the memory of it. "What we saw in the mirror was truly incredible, a mystery we need to look into dispassionately. But first we must get out of here alive, don't you agree?"

Murray nodded but made no attempt to move.

"And what exactly did we see, Arthur? Where was Emma?"

"I can't tell you that, my friend," Doyle confessed, shaking his head in perplexity.

"Was that the Hereafter you so often talk about?"

Doyle lowered the mace to the floor and sighed wearily.

"I don't believe it was, Gilliam. I think what we saw in the mirror was . . . another world."

"Another world?"

"Yes, another world. And the mirror must be an entry point, a sort of portal . . ." Doyle paused to reflect. "I was reminded of the hole the Reed People made in the air, weren't you?"

"Why, yes, of course." Murray nodded with a knowing air.

"If I'm not mistaken, that magic hole was also a portal, only it led to the fourth dimension, a vast pink plain filled with other portals to other moments in our past and future. But what if it wasn't true? What if that plain wasn't the fourth dimension but rather a sort of antechamber to other worlds? And what if mirrors are shortcuts, portals that lead directly into other realities, without passing through the great antechamber?"

"Other realities?"

"Yes, things that might have happened but for some reason didn't, or vice versa." Doyle was speaking hesitantly, as though thinking aloud. "I don't know whether you noticed that in the reflection I was wearing a different suit." Murray shook his head slowly. "Well, I was. The one I put on this morning, and that I changed for this one after spilling coffee on it. Do you realize what that means? It is as if we had seen a parallel world where things happened differently. I didn't spill coffee down my front, and Emma . . ."

"And Emma didn't die!" Murray finished Doyle's sentence, more perplexed than elated.

"No, in that parallel world *she* wasn't the one who died in the accident," Doyle corrected Murray, staring hard at him. He watched Murray's bewilderment give way to alarm as he gradually understood what that implied. But Doyle didn't give him a chance to carry on thinking, for he needed Murray to be as alert as possible. He lifted the mace and peered into the shifting darkness at the end of the corridor. "But let's put that to one side now, Gilliam. We have to catch an accursed ghost."

"And what does the invisible creature have to do with all this?" murmured Murray, not moving a muscle.

"I don't know."

"Does it come from one of those other realities?"

Doyle exploded. "I don't know that either, damn it!" For a few seconds, he peered anxiously into the corridor they were about to venture down, where an unimaginable horror was lurking, and then he turned to Murray. "But I can promise you one thing, Gilliam . . ." He took a deep breath, suddenly aware that this was the moment he had so longed for in his childhood dreams, the moment when he would behave like an authentic medieval knight. His hair was disheveled, he was wielding a ridiculous, rusty mace, and he wore a pitted sword hanging from his belt that could mutilate him permanently at the slightest wrong move; but despite all this, he was smiling the way only the heroes of old could. "I, Arthur Conan Doyle, father of Sherlock Holmes, swear to you, Gilliam

Murray, Master of Time, that if we come out of this alive, I will spend the rest of my days trying to unravel that mystery, and if there is a portal somewhere that leads to your damsel, I assure you I will find it."

Murray nodded, touched and at the same time daunted by Doyle's heroic attitude.

"Then what are we waiting for, Arthur?" he exclaimed, filled with an almost childlike excitement. "Let's go after the Invisible Man!"

But before they could make a move, they were startled by a rumbling noise from below. They both stared at the floor, which had begun to shake with growing intensity, and before the two men knew it, the floorboards had split asunder and everything collapsed with a deafening roar. Groping in the dark, Murray managed miraculously to grab hold of the banister on the balcony with one hand while with the other he hung on to the crossbow. He felt a terrible cramp in his left arm, and a wave of blistering heat scorched his face. He cried out as he felt the pain wrap round his body like barbed wire. When it abated slightly, he realized that he had torn away part of the banister as he fell and was dangling in midair, his body pressed against the jagged edge of an enormous hole, like the mouth of a volcano, spewing plumes of thick black smoke and searing heat. He was relieved to discover that between the crater and the banister a flimsy, narrow strip of floor had survived. He set down the crossbow as far from the edge as possible and made a supreme effort to haul himself up, scaling the piece of banister that had come away under his own weight. Each time he leaned his elbows or knees on the strip of floor, bits of it broke away, plunging into the flames below like a dreadful omen. Murray was terrified of falling, but with one last almighty heave he managed to reach the ledge, where he lay sprawled on his back, gasping for breath, his arms and legs covered in gashes. He discovered that the sword was gone, but he still had the second arrow. He would have preferred it to be the other way round, but clearly his opinion didn't count for much in this situation. At least for the moment he was out of danger, though he could not afford to rest. He retrieved the crossbow, and, standing up as straight as he could on that ledge, which was little more than a foot and a half wide, he tried to glimpse something through the smoke. The gallery floor was now a gaping hole, although, fortunately, the strip of floor under him stretched as far as the stairs, assuming it would hold up under his weight so that he could reach them.

His situation did not look very promising. But the worst thing was that there was no sign of Doyle. Murray had seen him fall like a lead weight, a stunned look on his otherwise stern face. He wondered whether he had been swallowed by the hole, vanishing into the voracious inferno, but something inside him refused to accept that the father of Sherlock Holmes could have met with such a fate. Perhaps he had also managed to cling on to something. Murray leaned tentatively over the hole, but at that precise moment a huge tongue of fire shot up from the floor below, forcing him to recoil from the edge. He resolved not to attempt that again.

"Arthur!" he shouted, between splutters. "Arthur!"

He continued calling Doyle's name until he felt he was going to choke. He rummaged around in his jacket pocket, pulled out a handkerchief, and covered his mouth and nose as waves of dizziness and nausea threatened to overcome him. His throat was gripped with convulsive sobs. Surely it wasn't possible. He couldn't be dead . . . Mustering the last of his strength, he called out Doyle's name one last time, feeling his scorched lungs beginning to fail. But no one replied. All he could hear was the fire's insatiable roar, that voracious, wild clamor, that ghastly, interminable crackle, as if a monstrous creature were chewing up the whole planet. All of a sudden, a familiar chuckle rang out a few yards from where he was on the ledge, between him and the stairs.

"So, your friend is dead . . . ," the voice said, oozing a jubilant rage. "Then it's just you and me. And you can't see me . . . Now who is the hunter and who the hunted?" Murray heard the deranged laugh again, and it occurred to him that if he went on hearing it much longer, he would be infected by its madness. "I am Invisible Death, you fool! I warned you: you are all going to die . . ."

"Damn you!" Murray shouted, aiming his crossbow toward where the laughter was coming from, though without daring to fire it, for he knew if he missed he would not have time to reload.

The laughter fell silent as unexpectedly as it had burst out. Murray hesitated, pointing the crossbow nervously in every direction. He listened, trying not to cough, blinking furiously as tears streamed down his cheeks only to dry almost instantly with a faint hiss. He couldn't tell whether the invisible man was standing or crouching, whether he had moved away or, on the contrary, had drawn closer, so close that he could reach out and touch him. Nor was there any way of knowing whether he was still bleeding, as the floor was now stained with his own blood and covered in soot and ash, making it impossible to perceive any trail. It occurred to Murray that he could aim at where the creature's legs ought to be, but what if the creature was on the other side of the banister, the hallway side, possibly edging his way silently toward him, slotting his invisible feet between the bars? Then all he would have to do when he reached him was to push him into the hole, still clutching his stupid crossbow. Murray hurriedly slipped one of his feet between the banister bars and began sweeping the air furiously with his weapon, realizing that it was only a question of time before the dreadful push came. Any moment now his feet would slip from the floor, he would feel a sudden hollow in the pit of his stomach, and his body would plunge straight into the flames. But he did not want to die, he told himself angrily, not now that he knew Emma was alive in some parallel world and all he had to do was to find a way of reaching her.

"Where are you, you coward?" he swore at the creature, waving the crossbow in the air. "Go on, keep talking! Let me hear your loathsome voice!"

Murray peered carefully around him but was unable to see anything. If, as Wells described in his novel, the smoke the creature inhaled was revealing his breathing apparatus somewhere, it would be indistinguishable from the thick fumes obscuring everything. So, what could betray his whereabouts? Certainly not the soot and ash settling on his skin: that swine could be covered from head to toe in them and he would be just another shadow in the gallery, among the thousands created by the flames. To be visible, he must be covered with something reflective, like water or snow . . . With a sudden flash of hope, Murray remembered the sacks of plaster stored in the first room along the corridor. Yes, that was what he needed. If he could only get to them . . . But, alas, they were beyond his reach, because the moment he made a move, lowering his guard, the push would come that would send him plunging into the void.

Then something very peculiar occurred. A word formed in his mind, or rather intruded into his thoughts, as if it had come from somewhere outside his own consciousness: Reichenbach.

Murray's body tensed. He fixed his gaze on the corridor beyond the flaming pit, where, after few seconds, he made out an indistinct figure charging toward him with what appeared to be a bulky object on its shoulders. Murray's jaw dropped in astonishment.

For a few seconds he couldn't think who it might be, but when the figure reached the edge of the hole, with a mixture of astonishment and joy, he recognized Doyle. Doyle spun round several times, lifting the object from his shoulders like a hammer thrower and hurling it aloft with a great roar. Murray realized then that it was a sack of plaster. Before Murray had completely understood Doyle's intentions, he raised the crossbow and fired at the sack. And as Doyle teetered on the edge of the precipice, flailing his arms comically in a frantic attempt to regain his balance, Murray's arrow shot clean through the sack of plaster and a silent white explosion spread out in all directions. Doyle toppled over but at the last minute managed to cling on to the edge of the hole with both hands.

"Arthur!" cried Murray.

"Find him, Gilliam! Find the creature!" Doyle commanded, his legs swinging in the air as he tried to scramble back up.

Murray screwed up his eyes and looked around. And then he saw him. The plaster, descending from the sky like a fine snowfall, had begun to settle on the creature, outlining his head and part of his shoulders against the sooty air, revealing a shape that although still hazy was clearly human . . . As Murray had suspected, the spirit, or whatever it was, stood only a few yards from him, clutching the banister on the other side. He realized it must have been there all the time, just far enough away so that Murray's lunges with the crossbow did not send him plummeting down to the hallway, waiting for Murray to tire himself out before pushing him over the edge.

But now the rat was visible, and like a typical rat was fleeing, scuttling along the banister toward the staircase. Murray was afraid he would escape without anyone being able to stop him. Then he looked at the crossbow he was still clutching. From where he stood he had a clear view of the stairs and almost the whole hallway. Peering through the billowing smoke, he could see that Doyle was still struggling to clamber up onto the edge of the hole. Trusting that Doyle's strength would not fail him, Murray began to tighten the string. Doyle had described the loading of a crossbow as difficult and time-consuming, but he had also assured them that the power of a crossbow's arrow was unrivaled by that of any other type of bow, as it was almost impossible to miss a target with it, and that encouraged him. He placed his foot on the metal stirrup and, using all his strength, tightened the string, which moved up the shaft with exasperating slowness. He glanced again at the position of the creature, who had just leapt over a small gap between the ledge and the top steps and was beginning his descent. Murray had no time to lose.

To his astonishment, the creature then stopped in his tracks and studied Doyle, who was still dangling pathetically above the hole; after a few moments, instead of continuing his escape, he retraced his steps and began to walk slowly over toward the author. Murray watched with horror as he realized that the monster, spurred on by the rage and the evil that possessed him, had decided that, before escaping to continue spreading his reign of terror through the world, he would take Doyle's life. Murray swore. There was no way for him to reach his friend before the creature did. He could only finish loading the crossbow and fire it as quickly as possible. With a rasping cry, he tugged harder on the string, baring his teeth in a ferocious gesture. He could feel his neck bulging, and a sharp pain shot up his back, as if his spinal cord were also a string about to snap. Tiny lights started dancing before his eyes, but he managed not to flag. The bowstring moved slowly up the shaft. An inch or two more and it would slot into the notch on the revolving nut. With a mixture of despair and impotence, he watched the Invisible Man, whose outline was becoming gradually clearer as more plaster dust settled on him, pause beside Doyle, his chalky head moving from side to side, searching for something on the ground. Terrified, Murray saw him crouch down and pick up a heavy stone in his ghostly hands and raise it above his head. Then he dropped it angrily onto Doyle's left hand. Doyle let out a fearful yowl as his fingers slipped from the edge. The creature picked up another stone, making ready to crush Doyle's other hand, cackling like a madman. The outline of his mouth resembled a gash in the smooth white sheet that seemed to cover his head. Murray, too, gave a cry of pain as the bowstring finally slotted into the nut. Raising the crossbow, he aimed at the creature's unfinished creamy silhouette, and before the monster could hurl the second stone at Doyle, he fired.

The arrow cleaved the air at an astonishing speed and plunged into the creature's shoulder, propelling him several yards before slamming him against the wall. There he remained impaled, like a big pale butterfly pinned to a piece of cloth. Seeing he had hit a bull's-eye, Murray expelled all the air from his lungs. He had done it! He had shot the Invisible Man! However, now wasn't the time to revel in his exploit, when Doyle was holding on like grim Death to the edge of the hole with one hand. Murray discarded the now-useless crossbow and, after taking a deep breath, ran as fast as he dared along the ledge, feeling the floor break up beneath his feet like flakes of pastry. Reaching the end of the narrow strip of floor, he took a running jump and landed on the other side of the gallery. He was amazed to have emerged unscathed from his ordeal, but without wasting a second he ran toward Doyle, flung himself to the floor, and managed to grasp Doyle's hand just as his fingers were starting to slip disastrously off the edge, his last reserves of strength finally drained.

"I've got you, Arthur!"

IT WAS A GRUELING task, but nothing compared to loading a crossbow. With Murray's help, Doyle managed to clamber up over the edge of the hole. For a few moments they both lay sprawled on the floor, utterly exhausted, almost unconscious. Realizing they had no time to waste, they quickly got to their feet. Doyle coughed a couple of times, examining his bloody hand with the stoicism of a soldier accepting his wounds, and then contemplated the figure half-outlined in white pinned against the wall.

"We must take him with us," he said.

"What!" Murray exclaimed.

"He's an exceptional creature and should be the subject of a scientific study."

Just then the creature's head, which had been slumped on his chest, began to lift. One-eyed as he was, he contrived to look straight at them, as if he were the very essence of loathing or madness itself. A moment later, he vanished. He simply ceased to be there. All that was left was the arrow driven into the wall, no longer impaling anything but the air. From its wooden shaft a trickle of red blood appeared.

"No! Damn and blast it!" cried Doyle.

He took a step forward, but Murray stopped him.

"Where the hell do you think you're going? The house is about to fall down," he said, pointing toward the stairwell.

Doyle swung round and saw that the fire had spread to the walls adjoining the stairs. The crashes and thuds they could hear coming from different corners of the house told them that parts of it were already collapsing.

"The hallway is in flames . . . ," Doyle said unnecessarily.

"Getting across it is going to be difficult," Murray added.

"But not impossible," the other man grunted, undaunted by the situation. "Our only chance is to cover ourselves with some thick, resistant material and run through the flames."

They looked at each other.

"The sacks of plaster!" they exclaimed as one.

The two men hurried to the storeroom, where Murray tore open a couple of the sacks and emptied the contents on the floor. He felt mildly euphoric. They might get out of there alive after all. Doyle seemed to think so, and he'd had many lucky escapes.

"Damn it, Arthur, I thought you were dead!" he cried, almost jubilantly, as he helped Doyle protect himself with one of the bags, pulling it down over his head like a medieval monk's hood.

"The truth is I remember little of what happened to me," Doyle said, pressing his injured hand to his chest to make Murray's job easier. "I think I managed to grab hold of something when the floor gave way, but I must have banged my head and passed out. Your cries brought me round, and I was about to reply when I heard the creature's voice. I realized he assumed I was dead, and I decided it was best he go on believing that, for a while at least. Then, just as I was thinking how to help you . . ." Doyle looked solemnly at Murray. "I had the impression that . . . I could hear your thoughts."

"My thoughts?"

"Yes, as clearly as if you'd been whispering in my ear, I heard the words: 'If only I could get to the sacks of plaster.' That's why I went to fetch one, Gilliam."

Taken aback, Murray stared at him but said nothing. He took the opportunity of covering himself with the sacking to avoid Doyle's gaze.

"That's what you were thinking, isn't it?" he heard Doyle say as he protected his head and as much of his exposed skin as possible.

"Yes," Murray admitted at last. Then, after a long pause, he added: "Something similar happened to me. I thought . . . I heard you too."

"What did you hear?" Doyle asked, increasingly excited.

"Well, I . . ." Murray faltered.

"For God's sake, Gilliam, tell me what you heard!"

"'Reichenbach.' I heard the name 'Reichenbach,'" Murray said at length, ashamed not to have picked up a more significant thought than a single foreign name.

Doyle burst out laughing.

"My God, it worked. It worked!" Calming down a little, he looked at Murray, who still could not believe it. "That's exactly what I was thinking, Gilliam: that I hadn't fallen into the abyss—that I'd escaped the way you wanted me to have Holmes escape from the Reichenbach Falls. And you heard me! My God! Do you know what this means? We have communicated telepathically!"

Murray sighed as he replaced the sacking Doyle had dislodged with all his gesticulating. When he thought they were as ready as they would ever be, he clapped Doyle on the shoulder.

"My dear Arthur, I once challenged you to make me believe in all the things I didn't believe in," he said, wheeling round and heading for the door. "Well, I promise I won't ever challenge you to do anything again."

"Well, Gilliam, perhaps one last challenge would be good . . ." Doyle grinned. "What do you reckon? Can we can get out of a burning building alive?"

22

I'M GOING IN AFTER THEM!" CRIED WELLS.
He moved away from Jane and took two steps toward
the front door, but once again the sinister fronds of flames visible behind
the windows made him pause.

"Please don't go in there, Bertie," Jane implored. "How could you
possibly help two strapping men like Arthur and Monty?"

"I don't know! I don't even know what's going on in there. Perhaps
the Invisible Man has killed our friends and is coming for us," said Wells,
glancing around them, a look of fear and shame on his face. "We should
have done what Doyle said! If we had left fifteen minutes ago, we would
have reached the village by now and help would be on its way! But by
now it's probably too late. And all because of me."

"Don't torment yourself for carrying out a dying man's last wish,
Bertie," whispered Jane, looking out of the corner of her eye at the
coachman, who lay sprawled on the gravel driveway. "You aren't to
blame if—"

"But if he is to blame, then I am to blame, aren't I?" Wells interrupted, pointing at the old man and letting out a hysterical guffaw that
caused his wife to recoil. "Of course I am!"

He strode over to Baskerville, but when he knelt at the old man's side,
his childish fury gave way to deep sorrow. The coachman's eyes were
closed and had sunk back into his head, which was resting on Wells's
overcoat, From his ashen-colored face, his nose, suddenly sharper, stood
out, pointing up at the sky like the prow of a sinking ship. Wells lifted

the rug they had covered him with, which now had a big dark stain on it, and, after peering beneath, replaced it again.

"He's still breathing, albeit very faintly. I don't think it will be long before . . ." His words hung in the air as he stood up. Jane began to sob quietly. "Don't cry, my dear, he is no longer suffering, and he'll soon be at peace. He was able to tell us what he wanted. There is nothing more we can do for him. We must think of ourselves now, and of our friends and . . . God, I wish we hadn't heard what he had to say!"

"Do you mean that?" Jane exclaimed, astonished. "Would you honestly have preferred not to know?"

"Yes! No! I suppose . . . Oh, Jane, of course I prefer to know! It is so incredible . . . But what if the price of knowing turns out to be the lives of Arthur and Monty?"

"They are all right, Bertie, I am sure of it," Jane said, looking toward the house and striving to lend her voice a certainty she was far from feeling. "Any moment now they will come rushing through that door."

"How can you be so sure?" asked Wells. He gave a sigh of despair, took his wife by the arms, and announced firmly: "Jane, I think you should go for help while I . . . go inside the house." His perfect imitation of an assertive husband lost some of its plausibility as his voice quavered on his last words.

"Don't even consider it, Herbert George Wells!" Jane was adamant. "I won't have you burned alive in some stupid haunted house! Do you want me to be the only woman in the world to be widowed twice in the same day?"

Before Wells could reply, the front door swung open and two bodies enveloped in flames burst upon the night, rending the darkness like two wavering human torches.

"Well, I never!" exclaimed Wells.

As if in a choreographed routine, Murray and Doyle tore off the flaming sacks and flung themselves on the ground, where they rolled around amid cries of pain and whoops of joy. After recovering from their shock, Wells and Jane hurried to help their two friends, unsure of what they might find. But by the time they reached Murray and Doyle, the two men were already struggling to their feet, joking as if they had just come back from a sleigh ride instead of having escaped from an inferno. Their hair was singed and whiffs of smoke rose from their clothes, but apart from Doyle's ear, his hand, which was covered in blood, and a few superficial burns, they seemed unscathed. For several minutes, the four of them exchanged emotional embraces, clapping one another on the back so excitedly that Murray even went as far as to plant a kiss on Jane's lips. Amid all the rejoicing, Wells approved of the gesture, although he made sure that Doyle did not express his excitement in a similar manner. After the embraces came the explanations, somewhat disjointed due to the two men's euphoria at being alive: the Invisible Man had been hit probably by the best crossbowman those ancient walls had ever known, but unfortunately, before they could apprehend him, the creature had vanished, taking with him the mystery of his unimaginable wickedness.

"But have no fear, George, I doubt your invisible man will be bothering you again in a hurry," Murray declared theatrically as a series of random explosions inside the house solemnly underlined his pronouncements.

Doyle begged to differ: "I wouldn't be so sure if I were you. I don't think the story ends there. I suspect we shall be hearing from him again very soon . . . and I shan't deny how eagerly I await that day! I want to find out who that evil creature is who knows you so well, George, and what the devil he wants from you . . . I refuse to add another mystery to the world!"

Wells and Jane exchanged looks, which did not escape Doyle's eagle eye.

"What's going on?" he asked suspiciously. The couple opened their mouths, but neither spoke. Doyle became alarmed. "Did something happen while we were in there? Why didn't you go for help? And how is Woodie?"

"Oh, don't worry, he is fine," Wells replied, content to be able to provide a straightforward answer to at least one of Doyle's questions. "He's in the carriage. He hasn't come round yet, but his pulse and breathing are normal. I think he is severely concussed, that's all."

"What about Baskerville?" Murray asked sadly. "Is he . . . ?"

Jane let out a cry that made everyone jump.

"Oh, no! I forgot all about my beloved Bertie!" she exclaimed, hurrying toward the body sprawled under the rug.

They all watched as she knelt down beside the old man and clasped his hand with infinite tenderness.

"Is he still alive?" asked Murray.

"I think so . . . ," replied Wells.

Doyle looked at Wells askance.

"Just a moment," he said. "Why did Jane call Baskerville 'my beloved Bertie'? And why the devil didn't you evacuate the wounded and go for help? My orders were clear, George," Doyle barked as he fashioned a makeshift bandage for his injured hand with his handkerchief.

"I didn't realize we were in the army, Arthur," Wells retorted, with more weariness than sarcasm. "Besides, we were going to, but Baskerville refused to let us put him in the carriage."

"And you listened to an old man's ravings, George?" said Murray, taken aback.

"I assure you he wasn't raving," protested Wells. "He implored us not to take him anywhere, because he doubted he would survive the journey, and he had something to tell us before he died, something terribly important, for us and for . . . the whole of humanity. And so we laid him on the ground, covered him with a rug, and . . . well, we let him tell us his . . . extraordinary story."

Doyle and Murray gazed at him intently while Wells wondered where to begin that rambling tale.

"Arthur, Gilliam," he said at last, "I know you will have difficulty believing this, but that dying old man over there . . . well, he is me."

There was an astonished silence.

"Baskerville is you?" Murray exclaimed, at a loss.

"Yes, although not exactly."

"Not *exactly* . . . What the devil does that mean?"

"He is a Wells from another world."

Murray shook his head doubtfully, while Doyle remained silent, casting a skeptical eye over first Wells and then the coachman.

"That Wells comes from a world that exists parallel to ours," Wells explained, and before Murray was able to express his unease anew, he traced two parallel lines on the ground with the toe of his shoe. "A world that is almost an exact replica of ours, identical in many ways, but different in others. And each of the inhabitants of that world has his or her twin in ours, or, if you prefer, each of us has an exact copy in that world: a twin who lives the same life we live, sometimes with tiny variations, sometimes not, and who is as oblivious to our existence as we are to his or hers." He paused for a moment, and then, looking at each of his friends in turn, he went on: "In that other world there is a Gilliam Murray, and certainly an Arthur Conan Doyle . . . unless of course," he reflected, addressing Doyle, who was listening quietly to Wells's explanation, "your mother in the other world had a miscarriage and your twin was never born. Or if he was, he died from malaria during that trip to Africa you made when you were young. But, like you, he could also have escaped death and become a writer, although his famous detective might be called Sherringford Holmes. Or perhaps in that other world Arthur Conan Doyle is simply an honest medic, a dreamer who is addicted to books of chivalry and hopeless at cricket. As you can see, the possibilities are endless."

"I doubt any twin of mine could lack my talent for cricket," Doyle solemnly interjected.

"Who knows, Arthur, who knows?" Wells grinned. "But one thing is for sure: my twin and I have lived almost identical lives, at least up until the moment when the path he was on came to an abrupt end." To emphasize what he was saying, Wells made another line with his foot through one of those he had traced in the dirt. "Just like me, he wrote *The Time Machine, The Invisible Man,* and *The War of the Worlds* . . . and he married Jane, or should I say, Jane's adorable twin. And yet there are a few minor differences between our two lives: as a child he was bitten by a dog, but I wasn't; he traveled to the Antarctic and lost two of his fingers, but I didn't; he is gifted, or cursed, depending on how you look at it, with the ability to jump between worlds, and I . . . well, clearly I don't possess that talent."

"But you do have an undeniable gift for making us believe far-fetched stories," said Murray.

"And how do you know these aren't simply the ravings of a dying man?" Doyle asked with almost professional interest, ignoring Murray's remark.

"Because he told me things only I could know: thoughts, dreams, youthful longings I never shared with anyone, not even with Jane, and that only someone who had . . . lived the same life as I could know about." Wells sighed, motioning with his chin toward where the old man lay. "That man is me. He is my self from another world. You have to believe me."

Doyle contemplated the crestfallen Wells and, after reflecting for a few moments, said, "All right, George, supposing he is. You said he came here because of a gift he has for, er . . . jumping between worlds?"

Wells nodded, slightly encouraged by the attitude Doyle had chosen to adopt.

"Yes. But he doesn't seem to have any control over it," he added. "It is more like a sort of latent ability he possessed without knowing it, until it was triggered by some calamity that occurred in his world. And that is how he crossed over to our world. Except that when he arrived here it was 1829, and he was almost as old as I am now, which explains why he is an old Wells, and why I didn't recognize him the first time we met."

"You two had met before?" Doyle exclaimed.

"Yes, when I was fifteen, on the pier at Southsea. It was he who came to me . . . In fact, since I was born he had been secretly watching over me from a distance. Bear in mind that when he arrived in this world, none of the people he loved had been born yet . . . and it would be thirty-seven years before my birth! As a result, this man spent most of his life as an exile, alone and lost. Can you imagine what he must have gone through? In the beginning, he tried to forge a new life for himself here that was as serene as possible, afraid that another intense emotion might provoke a fresh jump. It seems that is what triggers them. And, naturally, not wishing to encroach in any way on my legitimate future, he changed his name and his profession. After all, in this world I was the genuine Wells. And when finally I was born, he promised himself he would resist any temptation to interfere in my life, because the consequences that would have were inestimable. But when I reached the age of fifteen, he couldn't help breaking his promise. Back then, my mother had sent me to work as an apprentice at a confounded draper's shop in Southsea, and I felt so wretched with my lot in life that each afternoon I would go down to the pier with the intention of jumping into the sea and ending it all."

"Good heavens!" exclaimed Doyle, who was too indomitable ever to have considered giving up on life.

"In fact I was just striking an attitude, Arthur," Wells explained. "But it was on one of those afternoons that my twin approached me, and there, gazing into the murky depths, the strangest conversation I had ever had in my life took place. The reason why he jeopardized the universe by speaking to me was purely literary. He had already written *The War of the Worlds* in his world, but he wasn't very happy with the ending, in which the Martians conquered the world. And so he made me a gift of the plot, on the condition that if one day I wrote it, I would give it an ending that held out more hope for the human race. And that is precisely what I did. I gave it an ending in which the human race triumphed. I suppose that my other self realized that one of the few advantages of his unfortunate situation was that he could improve his work."

Doyle let out a guffaw that sounded more like a horse whinnying.

"You amaze me, George! Your whole life has been destroyed, and all you can think about is improving one of your novels! That alone would be enough for me to recognize you!"

Wells shrugged, annoyed because Doyle was reproaching him for something that the old man and not he had done, despite the fact that for a good few minutes now he had been trying to convince them that they were, in some sense, one and the same person.

"The fact is, when I first met your scruffy, eccentric old coachman, Gilliam, I never identified him as that stranger," Wells went on, "although whenever I went near him I was beset by a curious unease, a sort of vague anguish that was completely incongruous . . . And today I realized why. Perhaps because of the peculiarity of coming face-to-face with myself, or because his presence reminded me of the constant anxiety I suffered as an adolescent . . . All I know is that this acute sadness only afflicts me when I go near him, and that is proof enough for me: the old coachman is my twin from another world . . ." Wells gave a tired sigh. He knew he was right, but no matter how convinced he was, part of his brain could not help finding it absurd. "I never met him again after that. He carried on watching over me from afar, making sure everything that happened to me was also engraved on his memory. But he soon realized that not all the details corresponded. And that brought him to an important discovery. It was several years before he understood the reason for those differences, before he worked out that his initial assumption was incorrect; he hadn't traveled to—"

"His own past, but to another world!" Doyle interrupted.

"Why, those were his exact words. How the devil did you—"

"Elementary, my dear George! When your twin first arrived here, he assumed he had gone back in time. He had no way of knowing he was in another universe. How could he have? Before he started to notice the differences between your two lives, he must have believed he had only jumped through *time,* that is, he had traveled back into a past that preceded his birth . . . It was only later on that he realized he was in another world, a different world, where events didn't occur in the *exact* same way."

Once again, Doyle surprised Wells with his swift powers of deduction.

"The same mistake you made when you crossed the pink plain, Gilliam," Doyle said, turning to Murray. "You thought you were traveling through the fourth dimension into the future, when in fact you were approaching a portal that led to another world . . ." Murray flashed a surly look at Doyle. "Oh, don't be offended, Gilliam, apparently it is a common mistake nowadays to think one is time traveling when in fact one is jumping between worlds. So Baskerville's world and our world move in tandem," Doyle summed up, taking a couple of steps sideways, eyes shining as he cradled his injured hand. "Doubtless with an infinitesimal distance between them, as you described in *The Wonderful Visit,* George."

Wells realized with a shudder that yet again this was something he had already written about. He thrust the thought aside with a shake of his head and returned to the conversation with Doyle.

"I'm afraid so. Although I believe there aren't only two worlds. There are at least three: ours, the coachman's, and the one we glimpsed in the mirror, because what we saw there *was* another world. A world almost identical to ours, apart from a few differences, such as, for example, that there Emma is still alive. However, the other Wells doesn't come from that world. He told me so when I described it to him, and for some reason, he seemed genuinely convinced of that. So we are talking about three worlds," he concluded with a shrug.

"Why three?" said Doyle. "Wouldn't it make more sense if the number were . . . infinite? I am sure there are many more worlds, George, as many as there are portals on the pink plain, possibly even more . . ."

Then Murray, who up until then had been following the conversation without a word, asked, "What are the differences between the world in the mirror and the world your twin comes from, George?"

"I beg your pardon?"

"Your twin is adamant that he doesn't come from the world in the mirror, so he must have noticed something that didn't correspond to your description. What is it? Does it concern Emma?"

"Er . . . the truth is we didn't talk about it much, Gilliam," Wells faltered.

Murray looked at him askance.

"I know you well enough to be able to tell when you are fibbing,

George! What is it you aren't telling me? How does Baskerville know that the world in the mirror isn't his? Why is Emma still alive? Is it possible that in his world there was no accident and she and I are still together?" Murray had seized Wells by the shoulders and was shaking him with each question, but after the final one his energy seemed to drain away. "No, that can't be true, can it? Otherwise you would have told me the good news. So . . . ," he surmised, stifling a sob, "there are infinite worlds, but Emma and I aren't happy in any of them, damn it!"

"I didn't say that, Gilliam," Wells hastened to reassure him, feeling a lump rise in his throat. "All I meant was that I had a lot of questions to ask, and your coachman was fading so fast that—"

"Of course you had a lot of questions! I can think of several myself," said Doyle, who didn't consider it an opportune moment for anguish or melodrama. "For example, who is this invisible man? Did you ask him that, George? Perhaps he comes from another dimension as well."

"Of course I did, Arthur!" Wells retorted, peeved that Doyle doubted him even as he noticed Murray move away from them slightly, a forlorn expression on his face. Clearly he was no longer interested in their conversation. "But he told me that he didn't know him. That as far as he knows he has never come across an invisible man before today. However, he is convinced that there is a link between that creature and the mysterious men who have been pursuing him for the past two years, apparently with the intention of killing him."

"Good Lord, and I thought *my* life was full of excitement!" Doyle exclaimed.

"He calls them the Hunters," Wells went on. "And we saw them, too. Do you remember the incident at the opera house, Gilliam, when you saved Jane's life?"

"Naturally: How could I forget the day our friendship began?" Murray replied sullenly.

Wells sighed.

"Then you will also remember the strange man dressed in a cloak and hat who startled the horses before quickly vanishing down a side street." Murray nodded disdainfully. "Well, he was one of those Hunters. And guess whom he was pursuing? Baskerville! Because Baskerville was there, right behind us, eavesdropping on our conversation. That was how he found out that you intended to dismiss your coachman, and so he applied for the job. As I already told you, one of his greatest consolations was to watch over Jane and me from afar, but also over you and Emma, because in his world you were two of his closest friends. He knew you called yourself Montgomery Gilmore now, and he even watched your theatrical proposal of marriage from the top of a hill. And do you remember the figure we saw on the moor the day we went to Brook Manor, which we all assumed was a prison guard?"

"It was another Hunter," deduced Murray, who seemed to have laid aside his annoyance. "That explains why Baskerville was behaving so oddly that morning."

"Precisely. For the past two years, the Hunters have been tightening the net around him, forcing him to change names and jobs, although he has always eluded them, mostly through luck."

"And what is the connection between his pursuers and the monster that attacked us this evening?" Doyle wanted to know.

"*The Map of Chaos*," said Wells. "When Baskerville was alerted to our cries and came running, he heard the creature demanding I hand over that book, a book he is familiar with and that bears an eight-pointed star on the cover, identical to the one on the Hunters' weapons."

"Baskerville knows about the book! Then he must know its whereabouts as well as what it is for," Doyle exclaimed excitedly.

"Er . . . I suppose he must," Wells said gravely, "only he lost consciousness before he was able to tell me,"

"I don't believe it!" cried Doyle. "So you are saying that all we have is a long list of facts that are apparently meaningless?" Wells shrugged, avoiding Doyle's flashing eyes until he seemed to calm down. "Good. Let's not get agitated. We have two Wellses from two different worlds, both of whose lives are in danger, for reasons unknown to us, and the only thing linking their strange pursuers is a mysterious book whose whereabouts are also unknown . . . It is obvious which piece of the puzzle is missing. And it is regrettable, dear George, that you didn't manage to wheedle it out of Baskerville during your little chat."

"Let me remind you that his words were those of a dying man, *dear* Arthur. He kept losing the thread, or simply repeating himself . . ."

"All the more reason for you to have reflected a bit more about what you were going to ask him. A good investigator must always make the person questioned discover that he knows more than he thinks he knows."

"I agree with Arthur entirely, George: I don't think you asked the right questions either," Murray chipped in. "If it had been me, I would have remembered to ask about my best friend's fate in whatever world."

"Oh, I beg your pardon! Forgive me for being such a disappointment!" Wells exploded, raising his arms to heaven. "I am sure any one of you would have done much better in my place. Oh, yes, I can just see you: confronted by your twin from another world, discovering the true nature of the universe, while your two closest friends do battle with an invisible villain inside a burning house, and yet perfectly able to ponder each question calmly."

At that moment, a terrible crash from the house shook the night, and they turned as one just in time to see the roof begin to cave in. As the house gradually collapsed in on itself, it seemed to cower, like a bludgeoned animal. Then, from among the rubble, flames appeared, reaching up to the sky as though intending to burn that, too. The din slowly began to die away, and they heard Jane's cries.

"Bertie, he has come round!"

The three men hastened to where the old fellow was lying. Reaching him, they paused uneasily, less because of the extraordinary miracle of knowing they were in the presence of a man from another world than because they were confronted by the solemn, distressing spectacle of death. The old man had opened his eyes and was gazing at them as if he could see right through them.

"George, is that you . . . ?" whispered Murray, who had knelt down beside Jane.

The old man nodded, smiling at him weakly, his eyes suddenly lighting up.

"Gilliam, my dear friend," he said in a croaky voice, "how happy it made me to find you again! Despite how bothersome it has been calling you 'sir' for the past two years—"

He broke off, a brief coughing fit obliging him to turn his head and spit out a gobbet of blood; then, wearily, he closed his eyes. Murray hurriedly shook his arm, which earned him a disapproving look from Jane.

"George, George, don't you dare die . . . I beg you, there is something I need to ask you."

The old man opened his eyes with great difficulty.

"You always were a pain in the neck, Gilliam . . ." His voice sounded distant, as if he were already speaking to them from the Hereafter. "As an employer, as an enemy . . . I think I can only tolerate you when you are my closest friend."

"You are also a better friend than you are a coachman, George," Murray chuckled, relieved that the old man had opened his eyes again. "But there is one thing I do need to know . . . Were Emma and I happy in your world? Tell me the truth . . ."

"Gilliam, please," Wells interjected behind him, "there are more urgent matters to—"

The dying old man and his younger twin exchanged a glance. A glance so subtle and swift that Murray, who was waiting for the least sign that his coachman was fading to shake him to life again, didn't notice it. But Doyle did, and his heart sank as he also saw the young Wells shake his head imperceptibly in response.

"My dear Gilliam . . . ," the old fellow murmured with visible difficulty, "Emma and you were terribly happy in my world. In order to be together you had to overcome many things—too many things—but in the end you succeeded. Although I am ashamed to confess that it was no thanks to me . . . That is why, when I arrived here, I resolved to make every effort to bring you two together . . . And so I allowed myself to reply to the letter you sent to my twin, afraid that he would be as embittered as I was and decide to ignore it."

When Wells, who had been watching the scene with a beatific smile, heard the old man's last words, his jaw dropped.

"So it was you!" he cried, unable to restrain himself. "You replied to that accursed letter in my place! I told you all that it wasn't me! But . . . but . . . surely you and I must have the same handwriting!"

Feebly, the old man raised the hand with the two fingers missing.

"I never did learn to write properly with my left hand . . . ," he murmured apologetically. All at once, he screwed up his face, as if he were trying to swallow a huge, burning ember stuck in his gullet. He opened his mouth and inhaled a few meager mouthfuls of air, which scarcely filled his lungs. His next words, spoken between gasps, were barely intelligible. "Gilliam, I'm so sorry your love affair ended so tragically in this world. But believe me when I tell you that in the world I come from, nothing came between you . . . Please, cherish that thought as long as you live."

Murray lowered his head, his eyes brimming with tears. Jane began to sob loudly. Wells knelt down beside them and contemplated the old man, bewildered, trying to assimilate the fact that he was witnessing his own death.

"George, please," he implored. "We need to know where *The Map of Chaos* is."

Doyle, who had remained standing, and had been doing his best to stay silent, stepped forward. The old man's mouth was gaping open, and his chest was shaking convulsively as he contemplated Jane, trying to convey with his eyes how much he loved her. His eyelids fluttered momentarily and his gaze finally alighted on the younger Wells.

"Look for Inspector Cornelius Clayton, of the Special Branch at Scotland Yard," he managed to whisper. "He has the book. And please, George, be extremely careful. I am afraid my curse is also latent in . . ."

The old man was unable to finish the sentence. His eyes opened very wide, and his chest arched upward. Jane let out a stifled scream. For a few seconds, the old man struggled to breathe in air that had suddenly grown immensely thick, but almost immediately his body collapsed and his eyes, staring vacantly, gradually clouded, until the brightness illuminating them went out. Doyle said a silent prayer, fully aware of the miracle he had just witnessed, of those bonds of love and friendship that had breached infinity to join two whole universes. The young Wells placed his fingers on the wrinkled eyelids that would one day be his, and with a gentle movement, as though he were turning a page of a missal, he closed them forever. At that precise moment, the old man's body vanished from view.

For a long time, in that place on the moor, the only sound to be heard was the crackle of the flames daubing the trees in the driveway with golden reflections. The glow dimly illuminated the four silent figures and the emptiness where the coachman had lain, an emptiness that spoke of other worlds besides the one they knew. Perhaps three worlds. Or hundreds, or thousands, or millions of worlds. Perhaps an infinity. And in one of them, on a moor similar to this one, the body of an old man suddenly appeared, as though emerging from the dark night, adding another mystery to that world.

PART THREE

*I*S THAT THE SOUND OF BREATHING
YOU HEAR BEHIND YOU? COULD IT BE
THAT SOMEONE IS READING THIS TALE
OVER YOUR SHOULDER . . . ?

DO NOT LET THAT DETER YOU, VALIANT
READER, FOR WE HAVE REACHED THE POINT
IN OUR STORY WHERE YOU WILL DISCOVER
WHETHER OUR HEROES ARE ABLE TO
SAVE THE WORLD, AND WHERE ALL YOUR
QUESTIONS WILL FINALLY BE ANSWERED,
INCLUDING THE MYSTERY OF MY IDENTITY.

POSSIBLY YOUR CONCEPTION OF THE UNIVERSE
WILL CHANGE. AND YOUR NIGHTMARES WON'T
SEEM QUITE SO HARMLESS ON WAKING. PERHAPS
YOU WILL NO LONGER BE ABLE TO LOOK IN
A MIRROR WITH THE SAME EQUANIMITY.

23

*E*XECUTIONER 2087V WOULD HAVE PREFERRED not to suffer from the feeling of guilt that raged inside him, or to experience it acutely enough to force him to sabotage his own existence. If that were to happen—if he were audacious enough to disengage, to give up that dreadful mission for which he had been created—he would finally be able to rest in an eternal, guiltless peace. But, alas, his feelings weren't controlled by him, but rather by those who had implanted deep in the most inaccessible part of his memory that molecular code expressly designed to create the personality of the perfect killer. The Executioner had to acknowledge that the Scientists had done an excellent job, even in cases like his, where something went awry, where life prospered among the thicket of circuitry, and the orderly chains of neuropeptides rooted themselves in some cell or other, possibly in a hidden strand of soul, where they began to produce their own connections. And so, as with humans, when some emotion spilled over uncontrollably, the perfect programming implanted in his entrails would dutifully respond, attempting in some way to compensate for the malfunction. Thus his feeling of guilt at slaying innocents would be superseded by an even more intense feeling of guilt at the thought of not slaying them, of failing in his duty. Yes, those Machiavellian minds, worshippers of the Supreme Knowledge, had certainly done a first-rate job on them, a job as admirable as it was futile.

The Executioner smiled sadly, although it might be better to say that his mouth curled up gloomily. Keep calm, he told himself, nothing matters now, everything is about to end, we're all going to die . . . He felt reassurance, even a touch of serenity, and he gradually forced his vital signs to slow, to the point where when he slid like the ghost of a ghost past a cat dozing on a windowsill, the animal's ears didn't even twitch. It was something the Executioner was good at. Aware that when animals sensed them they became frantic, he knew the only way to prevent that was to attain a state close to hibernation, which rendered their movements imperceptible. That was the ideal emotional state to be in when stalking. Later, when the actual hunt was on, it was necessary to give way to other feelings: tension, longing, hatred, pleasure, melancholy, and guilt, above all guilt . . . But by that stage it would no longer matter if all the dogs and cats in the area began to howl and meow like mad, proclaiming his monstrous presence to the moon. When the victim was there with him, looking into his eyes, unable to understand why he or she had to die, it was already too late.

He reached the house and slipped across the tiny garden encircling it. Had the night not been so dark, and had the Executioner not blended so perfectly with it, I would be able to describe his movements to you, dear reader, but I can only imagine them: a series of silent, almost feline steps, followed by a fluttering cloak. He had no difficulty opening one of the downstairs windows and climbing into a small dark sitting room. The Executioner lifted his cane, and the eight-pointed star adorning its handle vibrated slightly, informing him that at present the house was empty. Even so, he decided to inspect the rooms one by one, partly because he did not trust his detectors, which were in a deplorable state, and partly due to an unhealthy need to know about the lives he was about to cut short. Who lived there? What were they like? What kind of carefree, tumultuous, or humdrum existence was he preparing to destroy? He didn't know. He only knew that whoever lived there had jumped at some point, although it was possible that his detectors had finally gone completely haywire and he wasn't just about to slay an innocent—for weren't they all in the end?—but an innocent who was perfectly healthy . . . That afternoon, while he was trailing a level 2 Destructor, he had thought he detected the residual aura of a Latent at the center of this house and had made a note of the coordinates in order to return there later. In fact, Latents weren't much of a catch for any Executioner, for they were former Destructors in whom, for some reason, the sickness had entered a dormant phase. That didn't mean they couldn't reactivate at any moment, but, compared to an active Destructor, trailing them was not a priority. However, gone were the days when the priorities of the hunt were clear. In the past, Executioners were fitted with perfectly calibrated detectors, so that in a single day they could locate an infinite number of trails whose coordinates were clearly traceable, easy to follow and to classify. But nowadays . . . nowadays they simply did the best they could.

Without the need for any light to see where he was going, the Executioner searched the downstairs until he was satisfied that it was indeed empty; then he went upstairs. There he entered the first room he came to, a small, cozy study that had a distinctly feminine atmosphere to it. He leaned over the bunch of roses sitting on a corner of the desk and inhaled deeply, letting the delicate fragrance flood his nostrils. Then he ran his hand gently over some of the objects on the table while he thought about all the times their owner must have handled them, whether with affection, indifference, or some other emotion, imbuing them with part of her soul. Wasn't he, too, like those objects? Hadn't his victims, before breathing their last, passed on part of their humanity to him? Yes, for as they dwindled before him he couldn't help looking in their eyes, and that was when he discovered whether their lives had been fulfilling or cruelly unsatisfactory; whether they left behind a trail of bitterness and misunderstanding or had known true love; whether they left that world filled with rage, fear, or a melancholy acceptance. And in that instant of absolute communication, like an object steeped in the soul of the other, the Executioner was overwhelmed by the ecstasy of Supreme Knowledge, but also by the devastating power of guilt.

Then his hand collided with what appeared to be three manuscripts. The first two were entitled, respectively, *The Map of Time* and *The Map of the Sky*, but it was the third that caught his attention. It was entitled *The*

Map of Chaos, and on its cover the author had carefully traced in ink an eight-pointed star. The Executioner propped his cane against the table and seized the third manuscript, standing there in the darkness, reading with growing absorption what appeared to be a novel whose plot soon began to appear oddly familiar. He read without stopping up to the page where Mr. and Mrs. Wells, together with their dog, Newton, leapt through a wormhole in the laboratory of their deceased friend Charles Dodgson toward an unknown destination, leaving behind them the evil Gilliam Murray and his henchmen. When he reached that part, the Executioner paused. Raising his eyes, still clutching the pages, he stared into the distance. He remained so still that the darkness began to settle over him like a shroud of black butterflies, until he all but vanished. Then, pulling up the desk chair, he sat down and gathered up the remainder of the manuscript with what might have been a sigh. After all, he had to amuse himself somehow until his victim arrived.

And now allow me, dear readers, to tell you what the Executioner read in those pages, as if you yourselves were in that darkened room, reading over his shoulder—or, better still, through those very eyes that thought they had witnessed things beyond any of their victims' wildest imaginings.

A BLINDING LIGHT SEEMED to envelop the couple as they leapt through the hole, as though a circular ray were spinning around at breakneck speed, while a mass of contradictory sensations struck them: they felt that they were plunging headlong into a void, floating in zero gravity, and that a monstrous force was pressing down on them, flattening them until they believed they had been reduced to the ridiculous thickness of a hair . . . Then everything stopped abruptly, as if the river of time had suddenly frozen over.

Wells opened his eyes, which he had instinctively closed when he entered the tunnel, and he found himself falling down some kind of well, although he didn't have the sensation of falling, perhaps because the walls were going up, or possibly down, so that he was *falling* upward. In any event, he was moving (whether he in relation to the well or the well in relation to him it didn't matter) as the various objects rushing past him confirmed. Wells noticed several shelves lined with books (he even had time to take one out, leaf through it, and then leave it afterward on a subsequent shelf), his favorite armchair, several lamps and clocks, a sarcophagus, a gigantic deck of cards, the crown of Queen Victoria herself . . . And yet, among all that junk, he didn't see Jane, which might have worried him had he not felt so sleepy: his eyelids kept closing and he couldn't stop yawning. He thought perhaps he had been falling through that well for hundreds or thousands of years, but if that was so, then nothing mattered, and he might as well have a little nap while he continued his descent. But scarcely had he begun to snore when all of a sudden, *thump!*—down he came on something hard and cold. And he understood that this absurd, extraordinarily lengthy fall was over.

Wells kept his eyes closed, vaguely aware that he was lying on a solid surface. Resisting the desire to carry on sleeping, he tried to open his eyes, although he was afraid of confronting some nameless, or nameable, horror—or, worse still, of seeing nothing, having been blinded by the intense light at the beginning and having lost consciousness, so that everything that had happened afterward had been no more than an absurd dream woven by his unconscious. Then a couple of vigorous licks stoked his fears, forcing him to open his eyes. The horror confronting him was none other than Newton's cold, wet nose looming over him. When he managed to push the dog aside feebly, he discovered Jane sprawled beside him on the floor, whose black and white tiles resembled a checkerboard. Wells pulled himself up, overwhelmed by an unpleasant dizziness, and shook Jane's shoulder. After blinking a few times, she looked at him, somewhat bewildered, then flung her arms round Newton, glancing about uneasily.

"Bertie . . . Where are we?"

But her husband didn't reply. He was staring intently at the tile beneath his right hand, and he had such a strange expression on his face that Jane felt more scared by that than anything that had happened to them so far.

"What is it, my dear?"

"I—I . . . ," Wells stammered, "I can't tell whether the tile my hand is resting on . . . is black or white."

Jane contemplated him in silence for a few seconds, without understanding what he was talking about, until she followed her husband's astonished gaze toward the tile beneath his hand.

"It's black," she assured him, but a moment later she blinked, confused. "No, wait . . ." She examined the tile with a frown. "It's white! . . . No, no, it's definitely black, but . . . how strange: it keeps changing to white . . ."

Closely scrutinized by Jane, Wells raised his hand and lowered it again, placing it very carefully on the same tile.

"I put my right hand down on the black tile. That is what I did, nothing else. You saw me, didn't you, Jane?" Wells asked anxiously.

"I think so," she replied uneasily, "and yet . . . oh, goodness me, Bertie, I don't know. Perhaps not. After all, you could also have placed your hand on the white tile. Why did you choose the black one? And . . . wait, are you sure that is your right hand? You could also be leaning on your left hand."

Wells looked at her in amazement and raised his left hand level with his eyes, scrutinizing at it as though he were seeing it for the first time.

"This is my left hand, and I am leaning on the floor with my right hand . . . Although, indeed, it could be the other way around . . ."

"Or you could be standing up . . ."

"Or unconscious . . ."

A singsong voice interrupted their fascinating debate: "Who are you?"

Wells and Jane stopped examining the tile whose color they were unable to agree upon and lifted their respective heads only to discover a charming little girl a few feet from where they were kneeling. She was about six years old, dressed in a ragged tunic and barefoot. They were instantly struck by her casual beauty: a mop of dark chestnut hair framed her heart-shaped face, and bangs fell over her keen, inquisitive eyes, and her lips, set in a pout, held the promise of a radiant smile for anyone sufficiently deserving. Newton scampered over to her, wagging his tail, and lay down, splaying his tummy, which she stroked with her bare foot.

"Are you sprites?" she asked.

While she waited for an answer, she took a sip from the glass she was holding, which appeared to contain lemonade. Wells rose to his feet, helping Jane up, and tried not to think that the girl could be drinking milk, not lemonade, or playing with a spinning top or juggling while she waited for them to answer.

"Er . . . why should we be sprites?" asked Wells.

"There's no reason why you *should* be sprites. I only thought you *might* be because of the way you appeared, though I hope my question didn't offend you." Clearly, despite being dressed in rags, the little girl had impeccable manners. "You came out of nowhere," she explained sententiously, with a touch of impatience, like a diminutive schoolmarm addressing a couple of not-very-bright pupils. "A hole suddenly opened in the air and a very, very, very bright light came out of it, so bright I had to close my eyes. When I opened them again, there you were on the floor, staring at a tile as if you had never seen one before in your lives. You are very funny sprites," she added earnestly.

Wells and Jane exchanged glances. So Dodgson's hole had brought them here . . . but where were they? Had they landed in another universe? They examined their surroundings more closely and saw that they were in a room that seemed familiar, despite looking old and fusty. The flowery wallpaper, the music boxes, the children's drawings—all gave them a clue as to where they might be. And yet there were a few details missing from the picture, which made it not quite recognizable. Hard as they looked, they found no trace of a communication screen, or a food warmer, or any other sort of technical device. It was as if the room had been divested of every artifact man had invented over the past hundred years, including dust-eating mice. But before either of them could express those thoughts, a voice somewhere behind them rang out.

"Come along, Alice! I am ready to take the photograph now . . . What is keeping you?"

Wells and Jane turned around just as a young man entered the room, cradling what looked like a metal tube, the end of which he was polishing carefully with a piece of cloth. When he caught sight of the two strangers, and the dog suddenly barking at him frantically, he stood stock-still in the doorway. Alice put her glass of lemonade down on the table and ran over to him, passing like a ghost between the two intruders.

"Charles, Charles, these two sprites appeared through a hole in the air!" she announced excitedly.

She flung her arms possessively around one of the young man's legs, and he instantly placed a protective hand on her shoulder while examining with trepidation the supposed pair of sprites who had just materialized in his house, as if he were wondering whether sprites would also interpret human greetings as a gesture of welcome. For their part, the supposed fairy couple contemplated the newcomer with bulging eyes, as though unwilling to accept that he really was who he appeared to be . . . And doubtless, dear reader, you will wish to know exactly what the young man was like. Well, he was approximately twenty-five years old, tall and as thin as a stick insect, and he possessed one of those faces whose features seem to take pleasure in contradicting one another: if his pronounced forehead and receding chin gave him a bovine air, this was belied by eyes brimming with intelligence and his nobly proportioned skull; and if his eyebrows, like two horizontal sea horses above his drooping eyelids, gave the impression of a man prone to melancholia, the mocking expression on his lips betrayed both a keen sense of humor and the spirit of a dreamer. As for his clothes, he wore an elegant velvet jacket, a pair of overly tight trousers, a hat with a turned-up brim, and a dazzlingly white bow tie. However, in spite of his eccentric attire, he gave the overall impression of extreme neatness, as extreme as the overpowering perfume enveloping him. The young man opened his mouth, but for a few moments no sound emerged. Then the words came out in a rush, tumbling over one another, in a stammer that was as familiar to the Wellses as the room. They had no choice, then, but to accept the impossible.

"F-F-Forgive me, but, w-w-who are you and w-w-what are you doing in my h-house?"

"It's him . . . ," Wells whispered to Jane, who nodded vehemently, holding on to Newton to try to calm him down. "Well, I'll be damned, it's him all right. Only he's much younger . . ."

"But how is that possible? Have we traveled back to . . . the past?"

"Time travel is impossible, Jane. It has been proven . . . and for God's sake, hold on to that dog and make him shut up!"

"But I am!

"Well, then let go of him."

"But I already have, haven't I?"

"F-F-Forgive me . . . ," the young man interrupted timidly.

"Oh, no . . . ," Jane wailed, ignoring the young man and looking at Newton, bewildered. "In fact I've been holding him all along. By the Atlantic Codex! Have we lost our minds? Is it an effect of time travel?"

"Jane, I told you we haven't traveled in time!"

"But it's him, Bertie, it's him!" she protested, pointing at the young man while Newton started barking again. "And he can't be older than thirty . . . And yet when we jumped through the hole he was sixty-six. Moreover, he was . . ."

Unable to finish her sentence, Jane buried her face in Newton's fur to muffle her sobs, at which the dog instantly stopped barking, surprised at this new role as a pillow.

"F-F-Forgive me . . . ," the young man ventured again.

"One moment!" Wells interrupted him, slightly irritated. The young man raised his hand in a sign of peace. Wells turned to Jane, endeavoring to sound as composed as possible: "Jane, I implore you, regain your composure. We won't be able to understand anything if we allow our emotions to get the better of us. We must calm our minds to allow knowledge to flourish in them."

Jane nodded, her sobs beginning to subside. Wells rubbed the bridge of his nose and turned to face the young man, doing his best to appear as cordial and unthreatening as possible.

"Please forgive the inexcusable manner in which my wife and I have turned up in your home. I assure you there are reasons for it that are beyond our control, and we will gladly explain them to you. But, in order to do so, firstly I must beg you to answer a couple of questions. Preferably"—he gestured subtly toward the little girl—"*alone*. You have my word that it is absolutely necessary and that afterward we will be only too happy to answer any questions you may wish to ask us, Mr. . . . Dodgson. For you are Charles Lutwidge Dodgson . . ."

The young man looked at them inquiringly.

"D-Do I k-know you?"

Wells did not know how to reply. If all the current theories were incorrect, and they had in fact traveled back in time, then that twenty-something-year-old Charles still did not know them, because neither of them had been born yet . . . But time travel *was not possible*. Wells observed the young man attentively, studying his clothes, his hairstyle, and the tube he was clasping . . . Then, in a flash, what might have been the correct answer suddenly occurred to him. The young man would doubtless find it most odd, but if this Charles was anything like the Charles he knew (and Wells prayed he was), he was convinced he would accept it, because as well as strange it was also beautiful.

"Not in this world, Mr. Dodgson. But in the world we come from, another Dodgson identical to you taught me how to enjoy a golden evening."

Jane looked at her husband, wide-eyed, as a spark of comprehension lit up her face. Wells smiled at her lovingly, proud of her quick mind, of having her as a companion on the long journey toward Supreme Knowledge. Dodgson cleared his throat.

"P-P-Please excuse me for a m-moment, if you would be so k-k-kind, er . . . Mr. and Mrs. Sprite," he said, and then turned to Alice, prizing her gently from his leg. "My dear girl, I am afraid you must join your governess and your sisters in the garden and, er . . . ask them to take you home. We won't be able to take any photographs today, because, as you can see, I must attend to these unexpected guests." He spoke to her in a hushed tone, not in the way adults habitually speak to children, but with the more intimate manner they use among themselves and, oddly enough, with no trace of any stammer. "Is that all right?"

"No, it is not all right," the girl protested rather crossly. "Look . . . I've dressed up as an urchin! I've even been practicing the pose you told me." She ran to the nearest wall, which she leaned against, propping up one of her legs and extending a cupped hand before staring defiantly at the young man. "I might forget it by tomorrow," she threatened gently.

"I am sure you will remember it perfectly tomorrow," the young man replied, taking her by the shoulders and steering her gently toward the door. "Although I think you ought to sleep in that position all night just to be on the safe side."

"But, but . . . you promised you'd take me into the darkroom to develop the plates!"

"A promise that will still be valid tomorrow. Providing it doesn't rain starfish tonight. If that happens, I am afraid I shall be forced to break my promise, for as everyone knows—"

"But I want to stay and talk to the fairies! They're so amusing . . ."

"Oh, I don't think that's a very good idea . . ." The young man glanced uneasily at the couple and lowered his voice. "Sprites are very particular, Alice, and there are few things they find more vexatious than naughty little girls. Except perhaps for the sight of human feet . . . Yes, now I remember, they can't abide bare feet! It gives them insomnia, tinnitus, and terrible stomach cramps. Ah, and another thing they detest is orange marmalade; they only have to look at it and they come out in bumps . . . Luckily we didn't eat orange marmalade for breakfast this morning and you aren't a naughty little girl!"

"But, Charles . . . ," the child whispered, "I've got bare feet!"

"Goodness gracious! Alice Liddell! Why didn't you say so before?" The young man looked aghast at the girl's feet. "Hurry, hurry!" He propelled her out of the room. "Run home and ask your mother to smother the soles of your feet in orange marmalade . . . tell her it's a matter of life or death! I promise I will come to fetch you tomorrow . . ." And closing the door abruptly, he wheeled round, leaning his whole weight against it, as though afraid the little girl might break it down at any moment.

"W-W-Would you like a cup of tea?" he managed to ask. "Or p-p-perhaps some l-lemonade, or even some f-f-f—"

"Anything will do, thank you," Wells cut in, too impatient to wait to discover what it was that started with "f." "The journey here was rather long."

"Er, yes, well . . . please, h-h-have a seat," the young man said, pointing at the exquisite carved wooden table in the center of the room, accompanied by four Chippendale chairs. "I shall put the kettle on to boil," he added. Before leaving the room, he rested the tube and the piece of cloth he was still holding on a corner of the table.

"Thank you," Jane said, taking a seat.

Wells slumped onto the chair next to her, and they both sank into a determined silence, trying hard not to think about the infinite places where the young man could have left the tube and the piece of cloth, until he came back into the room.

"Allow us to introduce ourselves," Wells said when the young man was standing before him. "My name is Herbert George Wells, and this is my wife, Catherine. As I already mentioned, for our tale to be credible as possible, first you must agree to resolve some of the doubts that are plaguing us, although I ought to warn you that many of our questions might surprise you, and I daresay you will find our own explanations somewhat . . . incredible."

"Don't w-worry," said Dodgson, sitting down on one of the empty chairs opposite them. "Why, sometimes I've believed in six impossible things before breakfast."

Wells smiled hesitantly, then exclaimed, "Oh . . . I see you have taken the chair on the right. Yes, I am almost sure of it . . . Although you might have taken the one on the left. What do you think, Jane?" Wells's wife nodded, perplexed. "Anyway, let's drop the subject . . . Where do I begin?"

"It is m-m-most usual to begin at the beginning," Dodgson said encouragingly, "after which you carry on until you reach the end. And then you stop."

"And yet," Wells replied pensively, "an end can also be a beginning—"

"What year are we in? And where are we?" Jane asked abruptly, cutting short her husband's circumlocutions.

Dodgson looked at her, slightly bemused.

"This is the year of our Lord 1858, and we are in Oxford, England, in the reign of H-H-Her Gracious Majesty Queen Victoria."

"And what is your date of birth?" Jane asked again.

"The twenty-seventh of January 1832."

"And your profession?"

"I apply myself to the thankless t-task of teaching ill-disposed young men who have no appreciation of knowledge: in other words, I am a p-professor of m-mathematics here at Christ Church, Oxford."

"What mathematical research are you engaged in?"

"I am c-currently working on *A Syllabus of Plane Algebraic Geometry.*"

"I think that is enough, my dear . . . ," Wells chipped in.

"Do you write poems and children's books?" she asked, ignoring him.

"Y-Yes, I have been published in several magazines."

"Do you ever use a pseudonym?"

"My most recent poems in *The Train* appeared under the name Lewis Carroll . . ."

Jane looked significantly at Wells while Newton, who had decided that the man was not only harmless but also a terminal bore, jumped down off his mistress's lap and began to explore the room.

"It's incredible," Wells whispered to Jane. "This universe is almost identical to ours . . . Dodgson has a twin here, as does Queen Victoria herself . . . I suppose everyone in our world must have a replica on this side. And so must we, of course! However, since we have arrived in 1858, our twins haven't been born yet. And yet, scientifically speaking, our 1858 was far in advance of this world: this room, Charles's mathematical studies . . . and have you seen that lens?" He pointed to the tube Dodgson had left on a corner of the table.

Jane nodded.

"Why, it's positively prehistoric," she declared.

"P-P-Prehistoric?" Dodgson said, completely taken aback. "But it belongs to the latest Sanderson camera . . ."

"Don't be offended, Mr. Dodgson," Wells said reassuringly. "I fear my wife was exaggerating slightly when she referred to it in those terms, though I confess that in our world that way of taking photographs is completely obsolete. You see, my wife and I come from . . . another world. It was 1898 when we left. I admit that I have no idea why we landed here forty years earlier, although I intend to reflect about that as soon as I can; but while I am no expert in history, I can assure you that in 1858 our photographers had long since stopped using the collodion wet plate, nor were they forced to carry out lengthy exposures or arduous developing processes . . . For over a century now we have been capturing images of the world around us using a matrix made up of thousands of tiny photosensitive elements that transform light into an electrical signal, storing it numerically so that . . ." Seeing the young man's astonished face, Wells paused in midflow. "Never mind, I will tell you all about it when we have a quiet moment. What I am trying to say is that your world is very similar to ours . . ."

"So similar, in fact, that we feel quite at home here," Jane went on. "The clothes, the furniture, you with the same age and appearance our Dodgson would have had in 1858 . . . all that made us believe for a moment that we had traveled back in time . . ."

"But time travel isn't possible. And seeing that lens, which you don't treat as an antique, but rather as an everyday object . . ."

"And seeing that there isn't a single mechanical servant in here . . ."

"And that you are working with mathematical theories that have been obsolete in our world for a lot longer than forty years—for centuries, in fact . . ."

"In brief, seeing all that made us realize that we haven't traveled back in time, but rather to another universe. A world very similar to ours, but with a few differences."

The young man's mouth opened and closed a couple of times before he managed to ask, "And h-how am I to know that you aren't simply s-s-stark staring mad?"

"Mr. Dodgson . . ." Jane looked at him with infinite tenderness. "Does the poem *The Hunting of the Snark* mean anything to you?"

The professor went pale.

"I . . . well, I never. It's an idea I've been mulling over for a poem, but I haven't mentioned it to anyone yet . . . How can you . . . ?"

"You will write that poem," Jane confirmed. "You will write it in a few years' time, and it will be truly wonderful. It has always been my favorite. Our Charles once confided in me that the idea came to him when he was very young . . ."

Dodgson, whose pallor was taking on a greenish hue, leapt to his feet, although he immediately had to hold on to the back of his chair. He ran a trembling hand across his noble brow.

"Am I to u-understand that you come from . . . a-another universe?" he reiterated. "A world that is the same as this, aesthetically at least, b-but much more, er . . . evolved?"

Wells and Jane nodded as one.

"And h-how did you get here?"

"That is rather difficult to explain, Mr. . . . Charles, may I call you Charles?" Wells asked. "It feels more normal." The young man nodded. "Oh, thank you . . . Perhaps it would help if you could imagine a kind of . . . rabbit hole that connects two different universes across hyperspace."

"And where is that hole now?" asked Dodgson, gesturing toward their surroundings.

"It must have imploded after we came through it," replied Wells, recalling the deafening noise he had heard shortly before he jumped. "I fear this was a one-way journey."

He shot Jane a worried look, but she pressed his hand. After a brief silence, Dodgson ventured another question.

"And on the other side of that rabbit hole someone identical to me, w-with my name, is living a p-parallel life to mine?"

"That's right, Charles," said Wells proudly. "He was my teacher. A brilliant scientist. He created the hole that brought us here."

"And why hasn't he come with you?"

Wells and Jane looked at each other, this time with deep sadness.

"Well, you see . . . ," Wells began.

"Because they killed him before he had the chance," interrupted Jane.

She gave a brief summary of what had happened in his laboratory on the Other Side before they managed to jump. By the time she finished, Dodgson was looking at her aghast. Just then the kettle started whistling in the kitchen. Bobbing his head politely, the young man left the room swaying like a drunkard, moving his lips and shaking his head, as if he were talking to himself. And while he was away, the couple held the following hurried conversation in hushed tones:

"Why did you tell him he had died, Jane?" Wells asked. "Do you think that was a good idea?"

"Why should he care?" Jane said, surprised. "After all, *he* didn't die, his *other* self did . . ."

"Yes, but if the two Charleses were born on the same day and have so many other things in common . . . don't you think they might also die on the same day? And who wants to know the possible date of his own death?"

"You could be right . . . And yet, as you can see for yourself, they aren't *that* similar. As far as I recall, our Charles was never keen on photography, nor do I think he cultivated the friendship of little girls when he was young . . . Wait a moment!" Jane squeezed Wells's arm. "What name did he call that little girl?"

"Alice . . ." Wells searched his memory. "That's all I remember."

"Liddell," Jane declared, her eyes flashing with excitement. "Alice Liddell. And what is our Charles's wife called?"

"You know perfectly well, my dear, she was your friend: Pleasance Dodgson . . ."

"Yes, yes." Jane nodded impatiently. "But her maiden name is Liddell! And can you guess what her middle name is?"

Wells, who was flabbergasted, didn't reply.

"Her full name is Pleasance *Alice* Liddell . . . ," Jane explained. "Do you see? Our Pleasance is that little girl! Although here it seems her parents have changed her names around. Lie down, Newton! Now it all makes sense . . . Our Charles was twenty years older than his wife, do you remember, and neither of them liked talking much about how and where they met. It was rumored that during his wedding preparations there were more inspections than usual, and that Charles had to make countless visits to his relationship advisor as well as go through his prenuptial reports several times . . ."

"Good grief! If the Church knew that Charles had spent years waiting for that little girl to grow up just so that he could marry her, it must have been terribly difficult to persuade the vicar that such an excessive love wouldn't cause him to stray from the path towards Knowl—"

A timid cough made them look up. They had been so absorbed in their tête-à-tête that they hadn't heard Dodgson come in. He was standing beside the table, holding the tea tray, and the expression on his face left them in no doubt that he had heard the end of their conversation.

"We English always manage to turn up in time for tea, even when traveling between universes," Wells tried to jest.

But that didn't distract the young Dodgson, who murmured, his cheeks turning bright pink, "In your world, my twin married his Alice . . ." He placed the tea tray abruptly on the table and sat down as if he felt suddenly dizzy. He took several minutes to compose himself before asking, "Tell me, w-what was Alice like as a grown-up? What sort of w-woman did she turn into?"

"This time you sat down in the chair on the left . . . ," Wells ventured.

"Why didn't you sit on the same chair as before?" Jane asked.

"Well . . . I c-can change seats if you like," Dodgson said solicitously, moving to the other chair with unexpected alacrity. "Very well," he proposed, once he was ensconced, "now, t-tell me your story, and that of the o-other Charles . . ."

"Of course, of course . . . Now, in our world—" Wells began, but instantly broke off. "Forgive me, Charles, but did you actually change seats, or did you only have the intention of doing so?"

"For heaven's sake!" the young man exclaimed. "What is your problem with the chairs? You appear to have a peculiar obsession with randomness . . ."

The couple looked at him in astonishment.

"What problem could we possibly have with a concept that is so completely theoretical and unreal?" Wells asked.

Now it was Dodgson's turn in that improvised contest of flabbergasted expressions, and I must say he came out of it rather well.

"Do you m-mean that e-everything in your w-world is predetermined?"

"Predetermined? What the deuce does that mean?" Wells replied crossly. "In our world things simply happen the only way they *can* happen. It would never have occurred to me that it could be any other way . . . And yet, objects in this world have the tiresome habit of never staying still . . . It is like wanting to take something off a shelf only to find that it has moved to another shelf out of reach . . . And every decision is so . . ."

"So impossible, so uncertain . . . ," murmured Jane.

"It is a peculiar and frustrating sensation . . . ," Wells added, genuinely despondent.

"So we c-could say that everything is *impocertain* and at the s-same time *pecuriating*." Dodgson smiled with a dreamy air.

The couple gaped at him while Dodgson gazed back at them, apparently lost in thought.

"I have an idea," he said at last, with sudden excitement, or rather with *sudditement*. "Each time you have a d-doubt about which ch-chair I am sitting on, why don't you shout 'Change seats!' and the three of us will move up one, do you agree? I imagine that this circular movement might ease your anxiety, at least long enough for us to carry on a quiet conversation . . ."

Wells and Jane exchanged looks and cried, "Change seats!"

"Oh . . . v-very well." And all three of them stood up and moved to the chair on their right. Then, smiling politely, Dodgson said, "Good, now that we are all in our proper places . . . for the time being, George, Catherine, would you kindly tell me all those incredible things I have to believe in before breakfast tomorrow, assuming there are more to tell?"

And this was how the mad tea party that would mark the beginning of their friendship commenced. Had anyone been spying on them through the window, he would have never suspected that, although what he was seeing looked very like a game for children without any children, a miracle was taking place in that room, because amid the heated debates, theorizing, and hypothesizing, as the teacups piled up on the table, three exceptional minds had begun to stumble upon what until then no one else had ever grasped: the true nature of the universe.

24

URING THE DAYS THAT FOLLOWED, WELLS and Jane were heartened to be able to count on Dodgson in what they would soon consider to be the greatest adventure of their lives. They couldn't imagine what would have become of them had they been set adrift in that universe so similar and yet so different from their own without the help of the young mathematician, who was not only good at resolving practical problems, such as finding a way of earning a living or inventing an identity with which to be able to integrate into society, but also at other equally important things, such as staying sane. It was clear that only someone like Dodgson could have accepted their unbelievable tale almost without turning a hair, for the young professor saw the world through a child's eyes, and, as everyone knows, children respond perfectly to nonsense: only they allow strange things to remain strange, refusing to apply to them the rules of any rational system. And it was thanks to this method that Wells, Jane, and Dodgson discovered many answers to their questions.

The most important answer of all they arrived at that first evening when, after much speculation veering inevitably between clearheadedness and nonsensicality, they succeeded in establishing the main difference between their two universes, which would be the basis for all their future deliberations. Dodgson, inspired by his keen love of the theater, stumbled on the metaphor that would be the origin of what they later referred to as the Theory of Theaters. And the main difference had to be connected to the Wellses' obsession with randomness.

After considering the matter in great depth, the three of them concluded that the only way to determine whether an event occurred one way and not another was through observation. That way, the infinite possibilities of how an event occurred condensed into a single truth: that witnessed by the observer. Thus, the Wellses' universe resembled a theater where life's drama was being played out before an audience, and their intense observation precluded any other possible version of the play, so that only the performance they were watching existed with absolute certainty. That would explain why randomness did not exist in that distant universe.

In contrast, the young Dodgson's universe was a theater with no audience, where the only spectators were the actors themselves. Yet they were observing "from the inside," while they were performing, and so their point of view was necessarily limited, partial, and yet infinite, for it depended upon the infinite decisions each actor took at any given moment. It was as if in that empty auditorium infinite versions of the same play were being performed on infinite parallel stages, superimposed upon one another, and the infinite number of different theater troupes were oblivious to their twins' existence. All of them believed they were the only ones, because there was no spectator to determine which of them *was* the only one. Perhaps young Dodgson's universe was no more than that: the sum of the infinite possibilities of what his universe could be, all somehow existing simultaneously.

The idea was too beautiful not to be true, the three of them agreed, almost with tears in their eyes. That explained the Wellses' problem with randomness, their feeling of being assailed by a deafening clamor when confronted with the most trivial decisions . . . They had spent their entire lives within the four walls of a theater where the audience's respectful silence allowed no possibility of randomness. And, thanks to the other Dodgson's magic hole, they had crossed the street to the theater opposite, where the terrible cacophony coming from the other stages was a murmur only they perceived.

For all the other inhabitants of this young Dodgson's world, accustomed as they were to it from birth, the infinite possibilities created by free will were imperceptible.

"But who is the spectator who watches the play in the theater on the Other Side, compressing the infinite possibilities into one?" remarked Wells. "Is it God sitting in the stalls?"

"Why would God choose some theaters and not others?" said Dodgson. "And if he were in all of them, or none of them, the differences we have found between them wouldn't exist, because all the theaters would be the same. Rather than consider God as the audience, I think we should see him as the director, the playwright who follows the performance from behind the scenes or even from the prompting box . . . Someone who is too involved with the work to be able to compress the infinite stages into one."

"And yet in the theater we come from there is only one play," Jane added, "which means *someone* must be watching it. For whom are we acting out our lives?"

There was a pensive silence. And then Wells said excitedly, "What if the power to compress all the different possibilities into one came from the actors themselves?" Jane and Dodgson looked at him, baffled. "Imagine a troupe of actors with an exceptional gift for observation, an extraordinary capacity to watch the play from inside and outside simultaneously, as if part of their minds could sit in the stalls while they declaim their lines onstage. The universes whose inhabitants possessed that amazing gift would exist as a single, predetermined reality that wouldn't disintegrate into a set of infinite possibilities the way this one does."

"Are you saying that we possess that gift?" Jane asked, surprised. "If so, why were we never aware of it?"

"Because you had nothing to compare yourselves with," replied Dodgson, after pausing to reflect. "Would a man who could see through walls be aware of his gift if he lived in a world where all the buildings were made of glass?"

From that moment on, Dodgson dubbed the inhabitants of the Other Side "Observers." He referred thereafter to "Observer Dodgson" or "Observer Queen Victoria" so as to differentiate between them and their twins who lived in the theater on Dodgson's side of the street. And in the days that followed, the Theory of Theaters came into its own, for they soon discovered they could use it to explain any doubts they had. It also fitted in well with the mathematical theories Dodgson and Wells delighted in elaborating, as a pastime more than anything else, even though this obliged Dodgson to grapple with the terribly advanced mathematics of the future and Wells to dust off his knowledge of one of the subjects he had found most boring at university. Nonetheless, with cheerful diligence they began to trace intricate mathematical maps that aimed to chart, the way ordinary maps did, the various highways and byways a traveler could take to go from one world to another, inventing formulas allowing them to work out the coordinates of any corner of the universe from its opposite end, as if the entire cosmos could be reduced to a single, formidable equation.

Alas, the first empirical proof of the Theory of Theaters came about because of an incident that left Jane very distraught. It happened five months after their arrival. Wells, Jane, and Dodgson had gone on an excursion to the meadows at Godstow with the daughters of the college dean, the young Liddell sisters, as was their custom after the good weather started. That day in particular was a golden afternoon in late spring. The sun was baking hot, the flowing waters made the reeds on the riverbanks rustle, and the three little girls were playing hide-and-seek while the grown-ups laid the picnic things out on a rug on the grass, chatting about this and that. Newton meanwhile rushed about chasing butterflies and, when he had grown tired of that, sniffed around the picnic baskets, trying to filch a cold cut, until Jane half jokingly shouted, "Shoo, disappear, greedy dog!" Upon which, as if he hoped to earn the title of most obedient pet in the world, Newton literally vanished. One moment he was there, his four paws planted on a corner of the rug, and the next he was gone. All that was left of him was the imprint of his four paws in the cloth. Jane had the impression she had magicked him away. She screamed. There followed an absurd, desperate search of the surrounding area, until finally they had to accept what they had at first been reluctant to believe: Newton had indeed disappeared before their eyes. After consoling Jane as best they could and making up a convincing excuse for the little girls, they returned to Christ Church with the aim of rethinking what had happened. Aided by several pots of strongly brewed tea, they arrived at the only possible conclusion: the cronotemia virus worked. And whilst for Jane this was no great consolation, Wells felt a surge of satisfaction.

Their research had not been so misguided after all. Newton's disappearance proved that those infected with the virus could indeed jump, but only between the stages of a single theater. Apparently, what they couldn't do, to employ Dodgson's metaphor, was cross the street to the theater opposite.

That was why Newton hadn't jumped when they injected him with the serum on the Other Side, because there was no other stage to jump to in their theater. Perhaps the virus only made it possible to jump between parallel worlds that together formed a single theater, reflected Wells. Good heavens! If only he had known, he wouldn't have regarded the lack of results on the Other Side as a failure. He would have pursued his investigations, he would have made the necessary modifications to the serum in order to obtain that movement between theaters, he would have . . . But there was no point worrying about that now. There was nothing he could do in that primitive world where they had only just discovered fire. His moment had passed. He had done what he could, and so had the other Dodgson, and now he knew they had both of them been partly right . . . His world would simply have to get by without him, he told himself. However, the discovery that both branches of research had been on the right track made him more hopeful that in the future one of their successors might be able to perfect one of them.

And so, amid astonishing discoveries and golden afternoons, the Wellses gradually adapted to their new existence. The most difficult part was undoubtedly learning to live with the cacophony caused by randomness, that constant, irritating murmur in their heads whenever they had to make a decision: in other words, at every waking moment. But they soon devised a few strategies and mental techniques to help them put up with that continuous drone, and when either of them felt they were flagging, they could always count on the other's support, or that of Dodgson, who never stopped watching over them. Fortunately, as the days went by, they found it easier to ignore that agonizing sensation. To their surprise, one of the activities that most helped them to control it was photography. That laborious process, with its antiquated alchemy that impregnated them with mysterious odors, became an unexpected balm for their exhausted brains. It was not uncommon for students and teachers alike coming out of an afternoon lecture to bump into Professor Dodgson and his two new friends lugging the heavy apparatus from one place to another, planted opposite Christ Church Cathedral's imposing spire or the little sweet shop nearby, operating the gleaming camera, grappling with its various joints and hinges, like hunters laying a complicated trap with which to capture a fleeting glimpse of beauty before it faded.

The Wellses took several remarkably skilled photographs of the environs, in the words of Dodgson, who would marvel over the appearance on the light-sensitive plates impregnated with silver nitrate of herds of deer, the rectilinear courtyards of the colleges, the illustrious silence of their libraries, or the beautiful tree-lined pathway along the Cherwell, perpetually overrun by groups of idling students. It was an inexhaustible source of pleasure for Dodgson to try to appreciate his ordinary everyday reality from those fresh angles that gave it a magical air. But more than the surrounding world, Dodgson liked photographing the dean's adorable daughters: the charming Lorina, little Edith, and Alice, the prettiest and most intelligent of the three, his favorite, and the one he would end up marrying in the world the Wellses came from. The photograph sessions with the girls were always a joy. Dodgson would open his costume box and take snapshots of them dressed as Chinamen, Indians, princes, or beggar girls, sprawling on divans or acting out complicated scenes from mythology, always aware that he was capturing for eternity a brief instant, a moment in their lives never to be repeated, a memory they would always return to when they were grown women. The Wellses soon realized that, apart from them, Dodgson did not cultivate many adult friendships. He appeared to feel at ease only in the company of little girls, perhaps due to his shyness, his stammer, or his dreamy nature. Boys terrified him, for they invariably poked fun at him, and he could never get along with them, but with girls it was different. Girls were sweet natured and thoughtful, they possessed a fragility that moved him to tears, and they aroused in him feelings of affection and protectiveness. But, above all, he knew what tone to use with them. It was so obvious to him that he was amazed no one else could see it, that the other adults, whether parents or teachers, spoke to girls the same way they spoke to boys, as if they belonged to one and the same race, a race of little people, when this was so clearly not the case. Girls required different treatment, and to any adult who provided that, the girls would not hesitate to give them their affection, astonished and grateful at having won the support of an older person. Consequently, Dodgson never seemed so happy to the Wellses as when he was surrounded by the Liddell sisters. With them he could spend hours chatting about a hundred and one nonsensical things. One afternoon, for example, during a boating trip, Wells and Jane heard him explain to the girls that they couldn't sign off a letter "millions of kisses," because at twenty kisses a minute, and if they were generous and fixed such an imprecise quantity at two million, it would take twenty-three weeks of hard work to be true to their word. Like the Charles from their universe, Dodgson seemed allergic to exaggeration.

And whenever they could, Wells and Jane were delighted to join those outings, in which Dodgson proved the most charming playmate imaginable; he shared the girls' innocent pleasures, was hopelessly infected by their childish woes, and above all he told them made-up stories, which drifted idly on the summer breeze like shimmering soap bubbles. He narrated them with such ease and enthusiasm that when he finished, the girls, oblivious to how tired they were, would invariably exclaim, "Tell us another!" For the Wellses, those afternoons filled with laughter and games became another perfect way of silencing the persistent clamor inside their heads.

Ah, those were happy times—who could deny it?—despite the numerous difficulties the couple came up against in their daily lives, in particular Jane, who faced a further obstacle to her adaptation to that new world: the sorry role women were relegated to in society. At first she could scarcely believe the things Dodgson told her, or what she saw with her own eyes, for she could never have imagined anything like it. For hundreds of years, the Observers on the Other Side had made no distinction between men's and women's minds. Naturally, the two sexes saw the world differently, but that didn't imply superiority or inferiority. On this side, in contrast, the only thing expected of Jane was that she be the new biology professor's charming wife, that she occasionally invite the other wives to tea at their rooms in Merton College, or, at the very most, that she organize a women's reading circle. Understandably, at the outset Jane rebelled against inevitably being cast in an inferior role, convinced she would never be able to resign herself to it. She even went to speak in person to some of the deacons at the various colleges in an attempt to persuade them to let her join one of the science departments, if only as a simple assistant. However, after their initial shock at her unusual request, they fobbed her off with polite excuses. One of them, while accompanying her to the door with paternal concern, even remarked, "My dear girl, I understand that you feel lonely—it is common among women—but if you are so keen on science, perhaps you would like to draw pictures of animals?" And his words, which an indignant Jane later repeated to her husband and the young Dodgson, became their catchphrase: whenever Jane argued against one of Dodgson's or Wells's theories during the course of a golden afternoon, they would respond with a mocking smile: "My dear girl, perhaps you would like to go and draw pictures of animals?" But this was harmless banter, which always amused Jane, and the days they spent together seemed to be filled with their intermingled laughter. And yet, as summer wilts beneath the onset of autumn, so that radiant joy was doomed to fade.

Three years after the Wellses arrived in that world, Dodgson was ordained deacon. He had done everything in his power to delay that first step toward his inexorable future, which was none other than to become a priest a year later, given that ordination into the ranks of the Church was obligatory for any professor at Christ Church. Yet, in his heart of hearts, Dodgson considered himself a layman. Naturally, he believed in God, and even went to church twice on Sundays, but he wasn't convinced that his God was the same silent deity who inhabited the cold, dark cathedral and whose fearful rage must be appeased by tedious, plaintive, never-ending rituals. His difference of opinion with Dean Liddell on that point fueled the reservations of Mrs. Liddell, who no longer approved of the burgeoning friendship between her three daughters and that strange professor and his eccentric friends, whose mysterious past accompanied them everywhere. Her pretexts for sabotaging their boating trips, which had become something of a tradition, grew more frequent and more blatant, and the helpless Dodgson realized how increasingly difficult it was for him to maintain his friendship with the three little girls, and in particular with Alice. Even so, he refused to believe that this could be the beginning of the end. And yet so it proved. The golden afternoons were almost over, and that summer of 1862 was to be the beautiful swan song of those happy times.

On the afternoon of July fourth, a rowing boat manned by a clergyman, a married couple, and three small girls glided down a tributary of the Thames on the way to the village of Godstow. The sky was such a glorious blue it seemed to color the whole world, the boat slid gently over the tremulous mirror of the water, while the landscape seemed to be slumbering, so intense was the stillness, disturbed only by the splash of oars and three childish voices imploring, in ever more imperious tones, "Tell us a story, Charles, please." And when he considered it convenient, Dodgson, who had been pretending to be asleep simply to infuriate them, stretched his limbs slowly and decided to indulge them. Accompanied by the sleepy buzzing of insects, he started to tell them the story of a girl called Alice who fell down a rabbit hole, and ended up in a wonderful world where the only rule seemed to be if you can imagine it, then it could exist. "Is that one of your made-up stories, Charles?" Wells, who was rowing at the stern, inquired with a mischievous grin. "O-Of course, George. I am m-making it up as we go along," Dodgson replied, winking at him. And all day long, as they made their way downstream, and in the meadow where they picnicked in the shade of a golden haystack, Dodgson held both the little girls and the Wellses spell-bound with his tale. The couple would grin at each other whenever they recognized one of their own adventures through the filter of Dodgson's imagination. Wells couldn't have been provided with a better example of a man using his imagination without the need to inhale fairy dust. Yes, Dodgson's imagination took wing with only a golden light and three en-raptured girls to help him. Later on, when they headed back to drop the children off at the deacon's residence, Alice, the real Alice, the ten-year-old girl for whom Dodgson had invented that tale, took his hand in hers, and, gazing with unusual solemnity into his eyes, she said, as if for the last time, "I would like you to write down Alice's adventures for me, Charles."

And if there was one man in the world incapable of refusing a little girl's request, that man was Charles Dodgson. He stayed up all night consigning to the page the weird and wonderful images with which he had tried to hypnotize Alice that afternoon, as though hoping to capture her attention forever. A few days later, he went to deliver the fruits of his wakeful night to her: a bundle of folios covered in the black scrawls of his long, curvy handwriting and sprinkled with his own illustrations, but Mrs. Liddell was having none of it. She was so adamant that from then on his meetings with the girls became as fleeting as they were in-tense, and so tinged with guilt, that, when they were over, Dodgson in-variably sank into a depression. Wells and Jane did their best to console him, assuring him that Alice would one day grow into a woman, and if they knew her as well as they thought, she wouldn't give tuppence about her parents' opinion. All he had to do was remain in Christ Church, close to the girl, and wait until she turned into the uncomplicated, passionate woman they knew she would become. He must wait. Wait until he could marry her.

However, being able to see Alice for only a few fleeting moments each day tormented Dodgson, and, after grappling with his secret pain for a year, Christmas 1863 seemed to give him the perfect pretext to present her with the manuscript he had written for her, provisionally entitled *Alice's Adventures Under Ground*. At the insistence of the girls, above all Alice, who threatened to stop eating until she was a hundred if they didn't let her accept her present, the Liddells were obliged to relent, although there was nothing to prevent them from receiving the young professor with unimaginable coldness. But Dodgson would not let himself be deterred by such an inauspicious beginning. He had gone to the Liddells' house with a definite aim, and he was determined to carry it through. And so, at some point during the afternoon, between pitiful stammers and nervous digressions, he posed the following question to the self-righteous Mr. Liddell and the horrified Mrs. Liddell: "Might it be p-possible, s-seven or eight years from now, when Alice is a woman, and assuming she reciprocates my feelings, for you to consider, er . . . a u-union between us?" Despite Dodgson's good intentions and the genuineness of his feelings, the effect was the same as if he had collected a barrow of cow dung and emptied it over them. And so the Liddells, who dreamed of marrying their pretty daughters into the aristocracy, if possible to someone of royal descent, replied without even conferring: "Never." It was clear that never before had they agreed so firmly about anything.

Everyone acknowledged that, of all the blunders Dodgson had made in his life, this was undoubtedly his greatest. After Dodgson's outrageous proposal of marriage, Mrs. Liddell resolutely forbade any more communal boat trips, or indeed any meeting that didn't take place under her strict surveillance. Even so, during the months that followed, Dodgson remained hopeful that things would go back to normal. With childlike naïveté, he was convinced their golden afternoons would return, that summer would survive the onset of autumn, and he clung to those ideas, continuing to impart his lectures as best he could, yet increasingly prey to resentment and apathy. And where five years before the Wellses had wondered what they would have done without their young friend, now it was Dodgson's turn to wonder what would have become of him without his friends from the Other Side. Wells and Jane strove to watch over him and, to cheer him up, reminded him that in the world they came from his love for Alice had overcome far greater obstacles. However, Dodgson would listen with a rueful smile before saying, "My dear sprites, I fear that in this theater the play will end very differently for me." Fortunately, his revision of the manuscript of Alice's adventures, and his search for a publisher, kept him occupied for a time. At last, on July 4, 1865, the third anniversary of the golden afternoon on which it was invented, *The Adventures of Alice in Wonderland* was published by Macmillan under the pseudonym Lewis Carroll. On that same day, Alice Liddell received her copy. And Dodgson waited anxiously for a thank-you letter that never came.

However, he scarcely had time to feel sorry for himself, for he was swept away by the overnight success of his book by a tide of literary events and public receptions, which once again kept him busy. It also allowed the Wellses to reflect further about the matter that for the past few weeks had been occupying their minds, and about which they had said nothing to Dodgson for fear it would plunge him even deeper into despair. If the roles they were acting out on that stage coincided in time with the world they came from, the following year, on September 21, 1866, to be precise, a baby boy named Herbert George Wells would be born in Bromley, and six years later a baby girl called Amy Catherine Robbins, who would be Wells's pupil and then his wife. And for some reason they were still unable to fathom, the Wellses felt duty-bound to remain as close as they could to their twins, who would soon take to the stage. They could find no logical justification for such a profound conviction, unless their gift for observation, which had so far served the sole purpose of driving them crazy, was warning them about something their conscious minds were unaware of. Taking advantage of the fact that the queen herself had sent a letter congratulating Dodgson on his

wonderful book, and that this had perked him up a bit, the Wellses resolved to tell him their plans, a little nervous that he might not respond
well to being abandoned. But once more their friend surprised them. He
encouraged them to move to London at the first opportunity and even
declared that he might go with them. "Yes, w-why not?" he said, a flash
of excitement in his eyes. "I've had enough of all this, of teaching math
to a lot of impudent young men, of being pressured by Liddell . . . Why,
I'm the famous Lewis Carroll! I can devote myself to writing. And you,
George, might try to find a post at the Normal School of Science, where
your young twin will study, assuming he follows in your footsteps . . .
Just imagine that! You his teacher, a witness to or even the architect of
his intellectual coming-of-age! . . . London, the great capital, far away
from the meadows and our golden afternoons . . . Yes, I b-believe that
would be for the best . . ."

The Wellses also believed it would, but their belief was genuine.

This being the case, the three friends concurred that when Dodgson
returned from a trip to Europe and Russia, which he had promised to go
on with his friend the Reverend Henry Liddon, they would arrange his
move to London without delay.

But Dodgson never returned.

One windy November evening, two months after baby Wells came
into the world, Professor Dodgson informed Reverend Liddon, with
whom he had just had supper in the sumptuous dining room aboard
the ship that was ferrying them home to England, that he needed to
take a little air before retiring to his cabin. Liddon warned him that
this might not be such a good idea, as the sea was quite rough. "Oh, I
have very good reasons to think that my death won't occur for another
thirty-two years, my friend," said Dodgson; he grinned at him mysteriously and began to leave the dining room. "Not that way," Liddon told
him, "the other way." Dodgson observed both exits, and then his blue
eyes settled on the reverend once more. "When you don't know where
you are going, any path will do," he said with bitterness, before walking
out of the dining room, leaving behind his notebook, which had been

with him throughout the trip. Shaking his head, Liddon picked up the notebook to leaf through it while he finished his coffee. In it Dodgson had described, with a child's enchanted gaze, all the palaces, museums, theaters, churches, and synagogues they had seen over the past months. Reading those words, Liddon felt as though he had spent the entire trip blindfolded. He slipped the notebook into his pocket, meaning to return it to his friend the following morning; only Dodgson did not show up at breakfast time. After a thorough search of the entire ship, it was concluded he must have fallen overboard. Reverend Liddon stood for a long while on deck, staring at the grey waters, imagining Dodgson on the seabed, telling stories to fish and enchanting mermaids with his syllogisms.

When the news reached Oxford that Charles Lutwidge Dodgson, better known as Lewis Carroll, had disappeared, swallowed up by the ocean, the whole university mourned his passing, as did all of England and the rest of the world: Who could begin to imagine the great works of literature humanity would lose because of that untimely tragedy! But, unquestionably, those who suffered his loss the most were the Wellses, from whom Dodgson had twice been taken. The wreath of flowers that the couple laid on his grave the day of his crowded funeral was much remarked upon by the other mourners, for no one could make sense of the words inscribed on the satin ribbon:

CHARLES LUTWIDGE DODGSON
(1832–1898–1866)

OUR DEAR FRIEND, WE MOURN YOU
IN MORE THAN ONE WORLD.
GEORGE AND CATHERINE LANSBURY

25

PROFESSOR LANSBURY WOKE UP IN THE MID-
dle of the night, his heart pounding, drenched in
sweat, clutching his wife's arm as if it were the only thing preventing
him from falling off the edge of the world, and cried out the same words
his mother was yelling at that very moment in other universes with
equal terror: I'm dying!

Let me explain, dear reader, that despite their deafening howls,
most of the Sarah Neal Wellses scattered throughout the many universes were hardened women, accustomed to confronting the trials and tribulations of life with heroic fortitude, and furthermore, in
most cases, this child who would be named Herbert George was not
their firstborn. However, they were all terrified of childbirth. Labor
pains horrified them, and since, to put it mildly, they weren't exactly
paragons of self-control, each time the dreaded contractions ripped
through them, their screams woke half of Bromley and the neighboring villages of the habitually quiet county of Kent. And while the supposedly moribund Mrs. Wellses lay on their beds, their backs arched
and their eyes bulging, Professor Lansbury remained curled up on his,
also insisting between groans that he was dying, as well as other still
more terrifying nonsense, which his alarmed spouse found hard to
understand.

"For God's sake, Bertie . . . What's happening to you?" Jane sobbed.
"Tell me what to do."

"Jane . . . I can't breathe," her husband gasped.

"Shall I open the window?

"No, water . . . I need water," Wells implored, just as his infinite mothers broke their waters.

Jane ran to the kitchen and returned with a glass full to the brim.

"Here, my dear, drink this . . ."

"No!" Wells cried, snatching the glass from her and pouring the contents over his face. "I need water to breathe. My lungs are dry, they hurt!"

"Bertie . . ."

The dousing seemed to calm her husband, but after a while he began howling again, perching on the edge of the bed and glancing about in terror.

"The walls! They're closing in on me, they're crushing me!" He tried to halt their nonexistent advance, arms outstretched, only to fall back on to the bed seconds later, almost unconscious. For a few minutes he lay gasping for air, like a fish out of water. Then it all started again: "My head!" he cried, clutching his skull with both hands even as his infinite mothers pushed downward, the veins on their necks bulging, their faces distorted, gripping the heads of their infinite beds. "They're squeezing my head! It's going to burst!"

"Bertie, no one is . . ."

"Why are you shouting, woman?"

"I'm not shouting, dear . . . ," Jane assured him, her eyes filled with tears.

"I can hear a woman shouting. No, lots of them . . . all shouting . . . Make them stop! Please, Jane, I beg you, make them stop. I can't breathe . . ."

This wailing went on for many, many hours, and at no point did Jane rush off to fetch a doctor, because, after her initial shock, she quickly realized what was happening to her husband. When, the next afternoon, Wells finally stopped shouting and burst into tears, amid cries of joy, unable to express in words the immeasurable feeling of relief that spread through his whole body, relaxing him to the point where he even thought his bones had shaken loose, Jane remained by his side, stroking his hair, sticky with sweat, until he fell asleep.

"You weren't dying, my dear . . . ," she whispered gently. "You were being born."

In fact, had he not been overwhelmed by that tumult of sensations, Wells would also have known instantly what was happening to him. Not for nothing had he been experiencing the most peculiar, beautiful dreams during the past few months. Dreams where he was floating in a warm, pink liquid. Bobbing contentedly in this kind of magical elixir, he occasionally drank from it and could feel the fluid filling all his cavities. He was lulled by a pounding heart, which seemed to have been echoing in that chamber from the beginning of time like some primordial drum, drowning out the other mysterious, soporific noises absorbed by the silence. In this gentle, warm place, Wells felt blessed, safe from all harm. There was no such thing as cold, pain, loneliness, fear, and anger . . . He was filled with a sense of boundless peace and a foolish, inexplicable happiness, but above all a stubborn desire to remain there forever. When he told Jane of these incredibly vivid recurring dreams, they both concluded that Wells was perceiving the sensations all his twins were experiencing as they prepared to be born in their different worlds, sleeping a dreamless sleep in their mothers' wombs. Wells and Jane realized with amazement that they were possibly the only beings in all creation who had been given the privilege of witnessing such a miracle: of going back to their mothers' wombs and feeling afresh all those sensations, forgotten by the rest of humanity. They were the recipients of an unexpected slice of the Supreme Knowledge. And yet, inevitably, they were filled with niggling doubts: if the connection with their twins in this universe was going to be as intense as Wells's dreams suggested, what would happen once they were born? Would the vague murmur they constantly heard at the back of their minds turn into something even worse? Perhaps a deafening clamor of sensations and images, so strong and intense that they would be cast forever into the abyss of madness?

Their gloomy predictions came true two months sooner than expected, because several of Wells's twins decided to bring forward their arrival in this world. It was clear that the different clocks in the different theaters, and even on the different stages, weren't synchronized but kept different times, which meant that some performances started before others. The following months were a complete torment for Wells, who experienced the same horrific seizures each time the miracle of life occurred in another universe. It seemed as if his twins lacked the most basic organizational skills, because, far from arranging to be born all at the same time, they had decided to come out each according to his whim, causing a series of staggered births that threatened to undermine Wells's sanity. There were days when the attacks were less ferocious, probably because fewer twins were being born, and Wells managed to grin and bear them, curling up on his bed in the dark, clasping Jane's hand in his, a vinegar compress on his forehead, as if he were suffering from a common migraine. He was reminded of the regular headaches he used to get and concluded that they must be due to random births of twins in universes where time moved at a quicker pace. He also recalled the strange visions that had assailed him, and that he had assumed were hallucinations caused by the relentless sensation of randomness. Now it dawned on him, not without some trepidation, that he must have been connecting with twins who had already been born. It felt as if he was in a stretch of universal time where the worlds were in a state of effervescence, and his twins were bursting onto the stage like a rowdy horde while all the sensations he had were multiplying infinitely. Often the rate of these births would peak so intensely that Wells could only bear the pain by taking laudanum, which Jane administered in such large doses that he almost lost consciousness. The worst day of all was September 21, 1866, his own birthday. It seemed as if most of his twins had decided to follow their elder brother's example after all, and everything that had occurred before then had been no more than a quick rehearsal before the main event. That day, Jane was convinced that the terror would cause her husband's mind to snap, that his body would be unable to endure the massive doses of laudanum, that he would either die or go insane, and that she would be powerless to prevent it. But Wells's mind did not snap, and although the agony continued for several months while the stragglers were being born, it gradually became less intense, until the day finally came when everything appeared to be over. After two weeks without a single attack, Wells and Jane concluded that almost all his infinite twins had appeared on their respective stages. However, this apparent hiatus brought no respite, because when Wells managed to sweep away the lingering cobwebs in which the laudanum had shrouded his brain, he realized with horror that everything had changed inexorably, and for the worse.

The familiar harmless background noise no longer echoed in his head. Instead, he was plagued by a constant stream of painfully clear images, of violent sensations he could no longer regard as occasional hallucinations. He would suddenly be invaded by a voracious hunger, an insatiable thirst, or the opposite: a fullness that would make him drowsy, or in the worst case he would vomit uncontrollably. For no reason, an animal fear would grip his insides, or he would be crushed by a terrible, savage loneliness. Faces would sometimes appear out of nowhere and lean over him, smiling grotesquely, or he would feel a humiliating wetness between his buttocks, or be overwhelmed by deep sleep, inconsolable crying, or paroxysms of laughter, which would end up infecting Jane . . . Wells was powerless to stop himself, at any moment, from feeling and seeing everything a baby felt and saw from his cradle, or from his mother's arms, magnified and repeated ad infinitum. It was as if he had suddenly been locked in a room filled with bats wheeling round and screeching as they tried to escape. This was nothing like the unsettling sense of fragmentation the two of them had experienced when they first landed in this world, or the pleasant, pink dreams of the previous months . . . This was the insanity of looking at oneself in a hall of a thousand mirrors, if you will forgive the oblique reference, dear reader.

Fortunately, their late lamented friend Dodgson, as a timely precaution they only discovered a month after his death, had named them sole heirs to the copyright of all his works "as a just reward for the inspired ideas they gave me during all those unforgettable golden afternoons." Charles's reasons for doing this just before he set sail for Europe gave them much food for thought, but regardless of his intentions, the money allowed the Wellses to endure their terrible ordeal safe in the knowledge that they were relatively financially secure. Reduced to a gibbering, incapable, whining wreck, Wells had to give up the teaching post he had secured at an academy in Bromley, the town of his birth, and place himself in the hands of his wife, and it was Dodgson's bequest that enabled them to keep paying the rent on the cottage they had taken in the nearby village of Sevenoaks. During this period, Jane was everything to Wells: mother, friend, and wife to her husband, and the hand he clung to desperately as he dangled by a thread over the abyss. And they both realized how lucky they were that Jane was six years younger than he and so would not have to suffer that torment until sometime in the future. And thanks to this fortunate circumstance, when it did happen, it was Wells's hand that held tightly to hers, preventing her from plummeting into the abyss he knew so well. Neither liked to think what would have become of them if they had been forced to go through that hell at the same time.

But even though they knew they had their economic needs covered, and could count on each other, to begin with they thought they would not be able to bear it, that this really was the end, a fitting punishment for having broken the rules of the game. Did they really believe they could challenge the established order without suffering the consequences? They had fled the square the Creator had placed them on before he rolled the dice. And now they were paying the price. That gift for observation, which had made the universe they came from into a unique, indivisible, unambiguous place, a temple of knowledge, was now their Achilles' heel. Their observational skills didn't seem to work in the same way in their new theater, and instead of condensing all the possible realities into one, it enabled them to see each and every one of the infinite stages through the eyes of all their twins, with whom they appeared to be closely connected. All of a sudden, whether they wanted to or not, they were all-knowing and all-seeing. And that seemed to them like a fate worse than the one suffered by their own dying universe. A fate from which there was no escape this time.

At first, the brutal onslaught of images and sensations that plagued them daily left them in pain and bewildered, with no time to reflect on what was happening to them or to elaborate any kind of response. Once again, they had to resort to laudanum in order to sleep, and the days turned into a long succession of indescribable torments. It was like living inside an iron maiden, feeling the sharp spikes piercing their bodies without touching any vital organs. I can't bear it any longer! Chop off my head! they would cry out to each other. And yet, gradually, as they had done with the sensation of randomness, they managed to contain the deluge of multiple perceptions that threatened to overwhelm them. How? You may ask, dear reader. Well, that is not easy to explain without resorting to metaphors: Imagine that an immense cosmos lives inside every skull, a cosmos largely uncharted, and that Wells and Jane were able to create a magic hole in their consciousness, a kind of conduit through which they transmitted that vast amount of information to the farthest reaches of their minds. Naturally, that information bubbled ceaselessly inside their brains, like an infinite cluster of meteorites hurtling toward a vortex of darkness; but, depending on the day, they were more or less able to habituate themselves to it. And so, ten years later, both were able to state categorically that they had at last managed to control this gift, which they would never have known they possessed had they not left their own world.

Not only did they become accustomed to it, they also succeeded in perfecting their technique. If they concentrated hard enough, they could momentarily close the magic hole pulsating at the center of their mind and capture one of the infinite worlds careering toward it. For a brief moment that world rescued at the last moment floated gently in their consciousness, blotting out all other perceptions. The Observer couple were thus able to spy on the lives of the twins in that world, as if through their own eyes, before the image dissolved. They realized immediately that, ironically, this curious game brought them relief from the intense concentration they had to maintain at all times, because while the hazy world they had ensnared bobbed placidly inside their heads, the deafening roar created by the other worlds subsided.

Once they had discovered this, the couple started to spend the end of their almost invariably exhausting day sitting beside the fire, trying to connect with the mind of one of their twins. They would pour themselves a liqueur and, sipping it slowly, close their eyes. After a few moments' concentration, voilà, they found themselves inside the head of another Wells or Jane, seeing his or her world through his or her eyes and ensconced in his or her most intimate thoughts. It was like setting anchor in someone else's soul, except that this someone was him or her, or a *possible* version of him or her. After the spell had worn off, when the image of that world dissipated and they opened their eyes again, each would tell the other about the lives he or she had glimpsed, like making up stories round the fire, beautiful bedtime stories. And as each tried to captivate the other with the astonishing twists and turns in the story of their lives, they also revealed the secret universes their twins had hidden inside them, that private realm no one else can ever fully penetrate. And so, besides bringing them precious moments of calm, those stories allowed Wells and Jane to get to know each other in a way no couple ever had in any of the possible worlds.

As you will doubtless appreciate, dear reader, for the first few years, when the majority of their twins were still very young, the stories they told each other were little more than amusing, childish anecdotes, like when Wells told Jane that one of his twins would steal his father's cricket bat and use it to have swordfights with his brothers, or that most of them had decided to practice their handwriting by scrawling the word "butter" on the kitchen window. However, the timepieces on some of the stages were running slightly faster, and as many of Wells's twins grew up, fell in love with one of their students (invariably the same frail young girl called Amy Catherine Robbins), and married her, their thoughts and innermost desires gave rise to absurd arguments between the Wellses.

Observer Jane wasn't pleased to discover that several of her husband's twins had decided to win her over simply because they thought her liberal ideas and lack of inhibitions would make her a passionate bedfellow. Indeed, she was so upset by it that Wells had to remind her that he wasn't responsible for his twins' actions. Notwithstanding, Jane had stopped talking to him for nearly two whole days, and she was aware of a delicious burning sensation in her guts, something every angry lover invariably felt, but which she was experiencing for the first time.

It was while trying to describe those new emotions more precisely that the miracle occurred: without realizing it, they were taking the opposite path to the one they had been following in their world. Thus they ended up feeling the powerful emotions they were exposed to. They loved each other in infinite different ways, with infinite different results, only to discover that there was only one true way of loving: when two hearts beat as one. When that happened, nothing else mattered, Jane finally admitted, having discovered to her astonishment that many of her twins accepted that their respective husbands took lovers, provided the women they chose pleased them—in other words, that they posed no threat to their marriages. Her only request (which he fulfilled out of a respect for the truth?) was that he didn't fall in love with them. Afterward, when Wells left them, in some of the universes she herself wrote them long letters of condolence.

In the meantime, in this universe it was Observer Wells who had to take the blame for his dissolute twins.

"But, my dear," he had protested timidly, in an effort to stop his wife from decimating the rosebushes, "you must admit that intellectually speaking at least it was a brilliant idea. I'm not saying I agree with it, but if you think about it from a logical point of view, in a world dominated by passions, monogamy doesn't reflect man's natural state. In my humble opinion the approach a few of our twins have taken is highly intelligent. After all, provided there is no emotional attachment and both sides consent, what is the harm in an occasional extramarital affair?"

"Would you like to put your theory into practice and verify it empirically, *my dear*?" Jane replied, spinning round with an icy smile as she brandished a pair of pruning shears, which seemed to Wells bigger and more pointed than usual.

"Er . . . I already told you I don't agree with that approach, my dear. I was simply analyzing the, er . . . the logic behind it." Despite the dangerous proximity of the pruning shears, Wells couldn't help ending his apology with a gibe: "But have no fear. I shall follow the example of those twins of mine who have decided to repress their instincts to promote through their wholesome example a system of virtue and integrity they have no belief in."

"I think that is the most *intelligent* approach you could possibly adopt, my dear, in my *humble opinion*" was Jane's retort.

But those quarrels were part of their new way of loving each other, and both of them discovered that their ensuing reconciliations, habitually enveloped in a pungent aroma of freshly cut roses, made them worthwhile.

Their minor differences resolved, those were happy times again. Wells was delighted to learn that many of his twins had found success as authors, and moreover with the same books he had thrown on the fire in his universe. He was also very relieved to be able to share that old secret with Jane at last, though even more amazed to discover that she already knew. She had crept into his study one day with the aim of finding out why he shut himself away in there every evening and had been unable to resist reading them.

"I thought they were so wonderful, Bertie, that I was mortified when you condemned them to the flames," she confessed. "Why don't you go back to writing stories like that? You could do it openly in this world."

"I don't know, Jane . . ." He hesitated. "I used to be so . . . miserable. I didn't realize it, but I was. And I suppose those stories were my way of escaping, a kind of liberation . . ." He took his wife's hand and kissed it tenderly. "If you want the truth, I no longer feel any need to write."

"But we are what we imagine," she said, remembering what the Dodgson from their world had once told her.

"No, my dear," corrected Wells, smiling suggestively. "We are what we love."

Jane smiled back at him, and for a few seconds they were content to make eyes at each other, the way they had only recently learned to do. Suddenly, Jane asked, "What if I were to write?"

Wells looked at her, surprised.

"You, write . . . ?" He hesitated, "Well, if that's what you want . . . But why? And what about?"

"Oh, I don't know. And I probably won't even bother," she replied with a nonchalant air. "I was only thinking aloud . . . Besides, if I did, I would keep it from you, the way you kept yours from me. I have been thinking, and I came to the conclusion that, knowing your twins' 'urges' as well as I do, the only way I can keep you interested is by making sure you don't know everything about me. I am afraid that if you did, you would get bored and start looking for other . . . *mysteries.*"

"My dear . . . ," Wells said, his voice choked with desire as he leaned toward his wife's mouth, which parted sensually to receive his kiss, "I assure you that in none of the infinite worlds in which you exist could you be considered a boring woman."

Jane knew he meant it. Much to her relief, she had seen for herself that, in one way or another, all her twins had managed to escape the fate normally reserved for women in their adopted universes. They were without exception brilliant young women who had avoided humdrum existences by pursuing serious intellectual activities, or a wide array of artistic disciplines, and although that meant they were shunned by society, none of them seemed to care. Those infinite Janes enjoyed being part of their husbands' cultural and political circles, not merely as companions, but as valued and admired colleagues. In fact, none of them fulfilled the roles expected of women in their respective worlds, and Observer Jane felt as proud of that as if she had instructed each of them herself.

And yet it made her equally sad to observe that they all voiced the same complaint: their husbands didn't love them enough. They all thought, as they pruned their rosebushes with a vengeance, filling their respective houses with reproaches that reeked of freshly cut roses, that their husbands would never understand them or realize how far they were from making their wives happy. But they were mistaken. All of them were mistaken. Observer Jane wished she could tell them everything she knew, about what her Wells had described to her in so much detail, about what all of their husbands felt deep inside, safe from prying eyes: how much they admired and respected their wives, how profound their love for them was, and the terrible impotence they experienced in not being able to show it. Perhaps Wells was incapable of grand romantic gestures in any of the infinite universes, but Observer Jane knew that somewhere deep down he possessed that ability, and it was only a matter of time before it burst forth in one of those worlds, before some Wells showed his Jane what he was capable of doing for love. Indeed, Observer Wells was a case in point: no doubt intimidated by a universe full of discontented Janes, he had developed an unexpectedly amorous nature that would have made Casanova himself turn green with envy. And if her Wells could do it . . . Although he wasn't just any Wells, Jane reflected proudly, he was a unique Wells. Different from any other Wells. And he was hers.

When his twin went off to London to study at the Normal School of Science, Wells decided it was time to resume his old plan and try to become part of the lives of that Wells and his future wife. Curiously, no matter how hard they concentrated, the minds of these two were the only ones Observer Wells and Observer Jane were unable to inhabit. Although that made some sense: the stage on which their twins were performing must have been a sort of observatory from which to contemplate the other stages in the theater, and perhaps that was why it was more difficult for them to observe it. As a result, the only way for them to discover more about their lives was through the traditional method of spying, watching from a distance their movements, which didn't seem to differ much from those of their other twins. Thus far, nothing in that couple's placid existence seemed to justify the urgent need that had driven Wells and Jane to move to Sevenoaks, although, now that Wells's double had moved to the biggest city in the world, that might all change. With the aim of keeping as close an eye on his twin as possible, Observer Wells requested references from his former dean at Oxford and managed to obtain a teaching post at the Normal School of Science. It was the second time the Wellses had moved since they fell down a rabbit hole into Dodgson's sitting room, in front of Alice's startled little eyes, and they couldn't help wondering whether that change might also herald the beginning of another Dark Era. Having found happiness again, having turned their lives into a prolongation of those golden afternoons by learning to love each other with utter devotion, neither wanted that to end. They did not believe fate could be so cruel.

But it was, as they discovered a week after they moved to London. The couple were sitting in front of the fire, after what for Wells had been a particularly grueling day. He had taught his first lessons at the school, and although he had been quite satisfied with the experience, he came home exhausted. After almost twenty years of not teaching and relating to practically nobody apart from Jane, it had taken a Herculean effort for Wells to control his talents and avoid giving his pupils the impression that he was a madman. Perhaps that was why he had spent longer than usual with his eyes shut, a weary smile on his lips, barely holding on to his forgotten glass, whose contents threatened to slosh onto the carpet. He looked so shattered that Jane decided not to trouble him. There would be no story that night, she said to herself resignedly, standing up to find a book with which to pass the time. Then her husband cried out, opening his eyes abruptly as he clutched his left hand, finally spilling half his drink. He had an expression of genuine bewilderment on his face.

"What's the matter, Bertie?" asked Jane, alarmed.

Wells allowed reality to settle around him for a few moments before stammering, "I just saw Newton . . . and he . . . he bit my hand."

"Our dog bit you?"

"Naturally, my dear, I would scarcely be referring to Newton the scientist."

Jane ignored the retort.

"What do you mean he bit you?"

"Well . . . he didn't bite me, of course; he bit the Wells whom I was observing," he explained, rubbing his left hand absentmindedly. "He was a very young Wells, almost a child, out strolling in the countryside, on a lovely, sunny day, when suddenly Newton leapt out of a bush. The dog seemed jumpy. Perhaps because he recognized my scent on that young Wells but at the same time he realized it wasn't me. I suppose that must have confused him . . . . In any case, he sprang at my twin and bit his hand."

"Are you sure it was *our* Newton?" asked Jane, still unwilling to believe it.

Wells nodded sadly.

"It was definitely him, my dear. He had that white heart-shaped patch on his head."

"Oh, God . . . And what did your twin do?"

"Er . . . he kicked him."

"Bertie, how could you?"

"It wasn't me, Jane!" protested Wells. Then he cleared his throat before adding: "Newton ran off yelping and . . ."

"And what? For goodness' sake, Bertie, what happened to—"

Wells clasped her hands in his and gazed at her forlornly.

"I'm awfully sorry, my dear, but a carriage was going past at that moment, and Newton—"

"No!" Jane buried her face in her hands and began to sob loudly.

Wells attempted to console her. "Don't cry, my dear. At least he had a happy life."

"You can't be sure of that," Jane spluttered.

"Oh, I can," replied Wells. "After the, er . . . tragedy, a woman came running over and held Newton in her arms."

"A woman?"

"His mistress. According to what she told my twin, the dog had run off while she was taking him for a walk. When she noticed the boy's bloody hand she was horrified. She said she couldn't understand what had come over Bobbie, that he was a docile, affectionate creature who had never bitten anyone in all the years he had been with her family, ever since they found him wandering around a field in Oxford." Wells stroked his wife's hair. "My dear, she really seemed to love Newton. I saw for myself how she wept inconsolably and held him tight, as if she thought that warming him with her body might bring him back to life . . . Our puppy immediately found a good home, and he has been very happy all this time."

But Wells's words didn't seem to console his wife, and so he remained silent and let her weep. Not a single day had passed when Jane didn't think about Newton, hoping that wherever he was he was safe and sound, and if possible in a happy home. But discovering that was the case didn't diminish her terrible grief over his gruesome death: crushed under the wheels of a carriage after being kicked by the person he had possibly just recognized as his previous owner. When she looked up, her face puffy from crying, she was furious to see her husband staring off into space, without so much as a tear in his eye.

"Herbert George Wells, how can you be so callous!" Jane scolded. "Don't you care what happened to Newton? We are to blame, or more precisely *you* are to blame! You injected him with that accursed virus! You made him—"

"Return to a state of calm, my dear."

That old proverb, spoken in a tone long forgotten by them both, caused Jane to stop crying instantaneously, and she stared at her husband in astonishment.

"Listen, Jane," Wells resumed before she had a chance to interrupt, "I'm sorry you are so beset by grief, and I wish I could do something to stop that, for two reasons: because I don't like to see you suffering, and because it is clouding your mind. And I need your cleverness, Jane. I need it now. Think, dear, think . . . As you so rightly said, I injected the dog with the virus. A virus we didn't know worked until we arrived here . . . Now, what do you think will happen if Newton has infected my twin with that virus? It could be more contagious now: it may have mutated and be active in humans . . ."

"But . . . heaven help us!" Jane opened her eyes wide as the implication of his words penetrated her mind. "If the virus begins to spread among humans, and those infected begin jumping between parallel worlds . . . what will happen then, Bertie?"

Wells looked at her gravely.

"I don't know, my dear . . . But I fear I shall be responsible for something more than the sad demise of a dog."

26

OWEVER, FOR A WHILE, NOTHING HAPPENED. Wells's twin who had been bitten by Newton did not begin jumping merrily between universes the way one might hop across a river on a row of stepping-stones. He was content to live his life, following in the dull footsteps of the majority of his twins, of whose existence he was in any case unaware. Nor, of course, did he suspect that the scar on his left hand made him unique, different from all the other Wellses, because the dog responsible was also unique and hadn't leapt out of a bush, as though according to a preestablished plan, and attacked any other lad.

For months, Wells devoted himself to watching over this twin, for whom he now felt a special attachment, for he had become almost as unique as Wells himself. He delved into the lad's mind in search of something (he wasn't sure what: strange dreams, unusual feelings) that might betray the presence of the virus in his body. However, he had found nothing significant, except for the feverish cold his twin caught shortly after Newton attacked him, from which he recovered normally. And after two more years during which nothing out of the ordinary happened to him, Wells finally dismissed the idea that this fever was a reaction to the virus—a virus that appeared not to spread between animals and humans, and if it did, it failed to trigger any hidden mechanism in the human brain, enabling the carrier to remain oblivious to the fact that a microorganism synthesized on a distant universe was flowing calmly through his bloodstream. In any case, it made perfect sense, Wells thought with a sense of relief, because when he had injected Newton, the cronotemia virus was still in an experimental phase. It would doubtless have needed a lot of modifying before it could work on humans.

Despite everything, the Wellses kept up their anxious surveillance of the twin who had been bitten, who lived out his life in a universe where time went by more quickly than in their adopted world, exactly as it was meant to, apparently with no major disruptions. Finally, they had to acknowledge that, besides his curious scar and his phobia of dogs, the bite itself didn't seem to have had any effect on Wells's twin, or on the parallel worlds that made up the universe in which they had been stranded.

Relieved that was the case, they were gradually able to relax, and, as they had done prior to poor Newton's sudden appearance, went back to their old habit of sitting by the fire and spying on other worlds purely for pleasure. With practice, they found they were able to move farther from the neighboring universes, that infinite pentagram of parallel worlds, and from the lives most similar to their own. This enabled them to connect with twins who were completely dissimilar to them. They infiltrated the ice-cold mind of a Wells who killed prostitutes by ripping their guts out, the harmonious brain of a Wells who was a pianist, the enlightened soul of a Jane who was a nun, and the farther they traveled from their adopted universe, the more unlikely their twins' personalities became. Filled with awe, they discovered that those distant worlds contained the most miraculous notes in the universal melody. They glimpsed worlds as strange as they were wonderful, where humans had merged with the rest of Nature to create bat-men, wolf-women, and rain-girls; as well as worlds where automatons had conquered the planet, almost wiping out the human race, except for a small band of rebels who resisted valiantly under their leader, the brave Captain Shackleton; and still others where there were more colors than usual, or where men had only one eye in the middle of their foreheads, or where they could float and walk on water because the physical laws that controlled that universe were completely different from the ones they knew. A brilliant kaleidoscope of fantastical worlds Wells and Jane could describe to each other solely through metaphors and similes that only diminished the miracles they had seen.

And, very occasionally, they would watch over the Wells with the scar again, the Wells who had a fear of dogs, which none of the other Wellses suffered from in any of their parallel lives. However, in his world, everything appeared to be running smoothly: he had just published his first novel, *The Time Machine,* which had enabled him to live off his writing but had also embroiled him, as it had many of his twins, in an absurd rivalry with Gilliam Murray, who was as corpulent as the murderous thug who had forced them to jump through the magic hole in their own world, except that here his nickname was the Master of Time, because he had opened a time-travel company.

Meanwhile, life in their adopted universe was also unfolding, although at a somewhat slower pace. It was 1887, and Wells's twin was no longer Professor Lansbury's pupil. Having just turned twenty-one, he had graduated from university and was now teaching at the Holt Academy in Wrexham. Fortunately, however, the Wellses kept in touch with him thanks to the friendship that Observer Wells had managed to forge with his youthful doppelgänger, a friendship very similar to the one he had enjoyed with the Dodgson who existed back in his own universe, only he had exchanged the role of novice disciple for that of decrepit professor. Did I say "decrepit," dear reader? Indeed, because despite being only fifty-nine, Observer Wells increasingly resembled a doddering old wreck. Alas, Jane, who was six years his junior, was not far behind. Both were aging more quickly than they should, possibly due to the jump they had made between universes. It was something they had been slow to notice because it had not announced itself so suddenly or with such fanfare as their gift for observing. Possibly time in their world was going so much more quickly than in their adopted world, and the inertia of that acceleration had stayed in their bodies, driving them into a rapid physical decline. For the moment those around them, who had no idea how old they were, had not noticed anything, and, besides their twin, they had scarcely bothered to cultivate any friendships in that alternative London. They preferred to spend their evenings at home, discussing in front of the fire all the possible and impossible universes, rather than mingling with the natives of that world, who were incapable of seeing beyond their own noses. Thus it did not bother them greatly. Besides, they had escaped Death so often they almost felt obliged out of politeness to allow it to come sooner.

They decided not to waste what little time they had left worrying about something about which they could do nothing. However, before putting the matter aside, they spared a few wistful thoughts for their old world, for if time was passing at such a vertiginous pace there, even the stars had probably begun to die.

"Do you suppose our universe has already entered the Dark Era, Bertie?" Jane asked Wells one evening.

"I expect so," he replied forlornly.

"And do you think they might have found a way to avoid their terrible fate?"

"I would like to think so, my dear. The generations after ours will have carried on doing research, just as we did, and it is possible they have succeeded in opening another tunnel to one of the many worlds in this universe. For all we know the Great Exodus has already taken place."

"But if that were the case, wouldn't we have found out about it through our twins?" Jane said, surprised. "How could we not notice one of their worlds being invaded by an entire civilization?"

"My dear, there must be plenty of universes where we have no twins, and if our old, dying civilization had moved to one of them, we would never know about it. Besides, just as there are many universes that move at a faster pace than this, there are others that do so more slowly, which means there must be worlds where the first scenes of the play are taking place, just as the curtain is lifting, before anyone has come out on-stage. Any one of them would be a perfect place for our civilization to be reborn."

"And we wouldn't be able to see that either because our twins won't be born for millions of years . . . ," Jane concluded. "So it could be that we have already succeeded, that our world has been saved."

Wells nodded with a cheerful smile, although they both knew it might be untrue, that their marvelous, brilliant civilization might be dying even as they spoke, plunged into eternal darkness, watching helplessly as the end approached . . . And yet neither of them acknowledged it, preferring not to dwell on such thoughts. There was little they could do for the world they had left behind. Besides, they wanted to spend what little time they had left on each other. Contrary to what many believe, dear reader, love makes people tremendously selfish and insensitive to others, and Wells and Jane loved each other with increasing devotion. Very soon the problem they had once dedicated their lives to trying to solve seemed as alien as it was remote. They believed it no longer had anything to do with them.

Unfortunately, they were wrong.

Another five years went by in their adopted world before they received the first sign that the fate of their old universe was still inextricably linked to their own. It happened one evening in March 1892. Wells and Jane were still recovering from a feverish cold that had kept them in bed for several weeks. They assumed they had caught it from their twins, who had organized a picnic so that the young Wells could introduce them to Amy Catherine Robbins, the charming girl for whom he had left his cousin Isabel. The Wellses had arrived only to find their doubles with watery eyes, runny noses, and flushed faces, and so the meeting had been brief, though long enough for Mrs. Lansbury later to confess to her husband that Jane seemed no less intelligent and brilliant than all the others and would doubtless very soon become frustrated by the way her inexperienced husband made love to her. The following day, the Wellses developed the same symptoms as their twins, although, owing to their declining bodies, it took them longer to recover. That evening in March was the first time they had ventured out of bed to enjoy their favorite secret ceremony in front of the fire. But they had only been distracted for a few minutes when they both opened their eyes with a start, looked at each other aghast, and exclaimed as one:

"I saw a Wells jump!"

"I saw a Jane jump!"

They spent the next few minutes shouting and gesticulating to each other to calm down, though neither appeared to be listening to the other. When they finally composed themselves, they decided that they had to trawl through other worlds, as many of them as possible, to find out whether the same thing was happening in the rest of the universe. It was essential they weigh up the true significance of what they had just seen, and if they wanted to proceed in the most scientific way possible they must stay calm. And so each set off on a frantic search that lasted several hours and left them exhausted and shaking. Alas, the results of their search were as revealing as they were terrifying. Of the three thousand or so twins Wells had been able to connect with that night, five had jumped into a parallel universe at some point during the past few weeks and were wandering around in their new worlds scared out of their wits, unable to understand what was happening to them. Two thought they had traveled in time, and of the three who didn't know what to think, one appeared to have gone mad. Jane had also connected with thousands of her twins and like Wells had come across several of her doubles who had strayed onto stages they should not be on, as if they had fallen through hidden trapdoors no one had warned them about. The couple looked at each other uneasily. Wells was the first to express in words what they both already knew.

"It's the virus . . . ," he murmured.

"It's *our* virus . . . ," Jane corrected, rubbing her temples. "Newton must have transmitted the virus to the Wells he attacked . . . Your twin didn't develop the disease himself, but he became a carrier and has infected others . . . in parallel worlds! How can that be?"

"The virus may have mutated and is now highly contagious," Wells suggested. "Perhaps, after the first case of infection, everyone in that London rapidly become carriers, and it would only take one carrier to develop the disease and jump into a parallel world for the virus to spread in that universe as well. And so on . . . until it became an epidemic, which is now ravaging all the possible universes," Wells said, unable to conceal his horror.

Jane cried out, shaking her head. "How could we have been so reckless, so . . . foolish? We were content to watch over that Wells for a few years, and when he showed no symptoms, we decided not to worry . . . The fact is we so were so eager to live a quiet life that we convinced ourselves everything was all right. And in the meantime a universal epidemic was unfolding right under our noses."

"How could we have possibly known?" protested Wells, who refused to take the blame for everything. "Take into account that the first person to jump might not have been one of our twins, in which case we couldn't possibly have sensed it, since we are only able to establish a connection with our doubles." He paused for a moment to reflect. "It must have been a while before our infected twins developed the disease and started jumping. And as we have just seen, the percentage is still relatively small. In fact, it was only by chance that we connected with some of them today. We could have found out before, it's true, but also much later . . . We can hardly blame ourselves for that, Jane . . ."

"Oh, can't we? Then who is to blame?" she erupted. "We are scientists! We should have considered all the variables, and we didn't. This epidemic is our doing," she declared harshly. "We brought the virus with us; *our* dog infected the first patient. Everything that happens as of now will weigh on our consciences."

"Let's try to look on the bright side," Wells protested feebly. "What is the worst thing that could happen? A few poor wretches will jump into parallel worlds and be forced to rebuild their lives there. No easy feat, I admit, but not insurmountable either. *We* managed it, didn't we?"

"Yes, but what if it isn't as simple as that? What if that affected . . . the fabric of the universe? What if we were all carrying the virus, and it was only a matter of time before everyone started jumping uncontrollably? Heaven help us if that happened . . . It would be chaos."

"But it needn't be like that, Jane . . . For example, the first patient never developed the disease. This could mean that the number of cases in which the virus becomes active is small. Granted, it might spread fast, but the majority of those infected may never develop the disease. Besides, there is no way of knowing whether we have all been infected. So let's not jump to conclusions, my dear . . ."

"I don't know why, but something tells me we have been," Jane whispered. "Goodness me! The colds we had!"

"What? People catch colds all the time, Jane. That doesn't mean anything."

"Or perhaps it means everything."

Wells looked at her uneasily.

"Think back, Bertie: since the first infection, all the twins we have connected with were either suffering from or recovering from that strange cold we caught, or their relatives were . . . and they all showed identical symptoms: the sudden onset of the illness, a fever, followed by a swift and complete recovery . . . Your fellow teachers at the school all came down with that same cold last term . . . And our twins in this world had a cold when we went to see them last month!"

"But, Jane, it is winter. Lots of people get colds!"

"And do lots of people get colds after being bitten by a dog from another world?" she asked ironically.

"We don't know whether *that* cold was caused by the virus, damn it!" cried Wells, springing out of his chair.

He went over to the fireplace and, turning his back to his wife, leaned on the mantelpiece and buried his face in his hands. But Jane was not about to back down.

"While we're on the subject, you say the first patient hasn't developed the disease . . . ," she went on, adopting a falsely sweet tone. "But how can you be sure? Have you connected with him this evening?"

"No, Jane," murmured Wells wearily through his fingers. "I didn't connect with him this evening because . . . well, I really don't know why."

Jane smiled wistfully. She stood up slowly and wrapped her arms around her husband's waist, resting her head on his beloved back, stooped now like an old man's.

"Is it because deep down you are as afraid as I am?" she asked gently. "He is the first patient, and if he has developed the disease and started jumping . . . then the chances of controlling this epidemic would be almost nonexistent. You know that, don't you? You know . . . ," she repeated in a whisper.

Wells remained motionless for a moment, feeling his wife's warm body pressed against his. Finally, he turned round and, very slowly, moved his forehead toward hers until they were touching. The couple abandoned themselves willingly to that ancient, symbolic gesture from their old world that honored the mind of the other. Their fingers intertwined but afterward, obeying the urges they had developed in their adopted universe, moved tremblingly up each other's arms, turning into a cascade of caresses down the other's curved back. Wells cupped his wife's face, kissing with a sudden fervor her lips, now salty from her tears, which still seemed to him like a genetic miracle.

"What have we done, Jane?" he asked, burying his face in the warm crook of her neck like a frightened child. "What have we done? And what are we going to do? We wanted to save one world and now we are going to destroy them all . . ."

For a few moments, Jane stroked his wispy hair. Then she dried the tears running down her cheeks and stepped away from her husband with gentle determination.

"You have to find the first patient," she insisted with renewed vigor. "Do it, Bertie. Find him and connect with him. I want to know what he is doing right this minute . . ."

Wells sighed. The woman was indefatigable. He sat down again in the armchair and closed his eyes while Jane stared at him intently from the fireplace, rubbing her hands impatiently. After five long minutes, her husband opened his eyes.

"Did you find him?" Jane asked. "Has he jumped?"

"Er . . . no, he hasn't jumped. He is still in his universe . . ."

"That's wonderful news! . . . So why are you pulling that face?"

"I . . . I don't know what to think."

"Why?" Jane demanded. "What is your twin doing now?"

Wells looked confused.

"He is fleeing a Martian invasion."

THIS ASTONISHING STORY DISTRACTED them for a while from the threat posed by the epidemic they themselves had caused, which, after all, was equally extraordinary, if not more so. In the world of the Wells with the scar, the Martians were razing London, and there was nothing the empire's crude weaponry could do to stop them—exactly as the author himself, together with many of his twins, had described in one of their novels. And over several evenings, instead of spying on the other universes to check on the spread of the epidemic, the couple couldn't help following with amazement the adventures of that Wells, who, besides being the first patient, was currently being forced to confront the terrifying fantasy he himself had concocted in *The War of the Worlds*. Until the thing he and Jane most feared took place. One day, pursued by Martians through the sewers of London together with a motley group of survivors, Wells's twin had jumped into a parallel universe. And this, apart from depriving them of the end of the spine-chilling tale, had also destroyed any hopes that the consequences of the epidemic would be less catastrophic than they feared. Apparently, all those infected ended up jumping sooner or later.

From then on, they made it their duty to seek out and watch over other twins who had also developed the disease, to measure the effect their jumps might have on the fabric of the universe. And so, every night, they became privy to dozens of fantastical adventures. But as we all know, every good adventure must have a villain. And that was how they came across Marcus Rhys.

The name may possibly be familiar to some of you, dear readers, as he made a brief appearance in my first tale. He was a ruthless killer who had developed the disease of cronotemia almost from the moment the virus entered his body, as if his evil blood were greedy for power. And, unlike other sufferers, due to a natural talent, which was as unique as it was sinister, he had learned to master where his jumps took him. Naturally, Rhys had no understanding of the nature of his disease. In the world he came from, which was in a relatively advanced future, governments were aware of the epidemic, but, as in a lot of the other parallel universes, they had confused it with a mysterious mutation that created time travelers. To combat the obvious threat this posed, they had banned time travel, hunting down anyone in breach of the law. Rhys, of course, was one of those. He considered himself the most prominent specimen of *Homo temporalis,* of that evolutionary link he believed was destined to rule the world. But rather than putting his amazing talent to good use, he had squandered it wandering through the centuries like a mischievous tourist: he blasted the Vikings with machine guns, sacked the tombs of the pharaohs, appeared in the guise of the devil at the Salem witch trials, bedded Marie Antoinette . . . When he grew bored of subverting History at his whim, he decided to steal his favorite authors' most celebrated novels before they had time to publish them, and to kill them, in this way creating a unique library for himself of famous works of literature, whose pages he alone could read, because for the rest of the world they had never existed. The Observer Wellses knew Rhys precisely because the Wells from whom he tried to steal the manuscript of *The Invisible Man* had luckily managed to escape by jumping into another universe, for he, too, had developed the disease. There began a frenzied chase across many parallel worlds, which the Observer Wellses followed with bated breath, clapping their hands like children every time Wells's twin managed to escape from his evil pursuer . . . Or did he? Because in fact dozens of Rhyses were chasing dozens of Wellses through dozens of parallel worlds, all of them believing they were unique, all of them believing they were traveling in time, galloping through the centuries, and persecutor and persecuted had crossed paths and interchanged so many times without knowing it that even the Observer Wellses were no longer sure who the first Wells was who had started that infernal relay race.

The one thing they knew for sure was which of those Marcus Rhyses deserved the title of Villain. You will know him by his wickedness,

Wells told Jane each time they lost track of him in the chaos of the multiverse. And by his cunning, Jane added, unable to conceal the fear his attributes instilled in her. With good reason: the Villain was the only one among his evil twins who never gave up the chase; he was so obsessed with finding the wretched scribbler who had slipped through his fingers that he had sworn he would not stop until he had caught him. He went on searching tirelessly, and whenever he found one of Wells's twins he would brutally murder him, convinced he had killed the only Wells that existed. However, each time he returned to what he mistakenly believed was the future or the past in his own world, eager to contemplate the fruits of his vengeance and to savor a world where the only trace of the exasperating H. G. Wells was a forgotten grave, he would bump into a live version of the author again. Unable to comprehend how this was possible, he would kill him again. Thus, many Wellses died in many parallel worlds at the hands of the Villain, who was growing increasingly angry and disturbed. Not only that: he was becoming transparent.

By following the trail of that deranged killer through the unfortunate Wellses whom he killed, the couple discovered that another side effect of jumping between universes was molecular loss: Marcus Rhys was becoming more and more translucent in what appeared to be a one-way journey toward invisibility. This could only mean that each time one of the cronotemics jumped, he left some of his molecules in hyperspace, causing his body mass to realign, eventually giving him that extraordinary see-through quality. The molecular loss resulting from one jump was negligible, so that the cronotemics who had jumped only two or three times in their lives barely noticed it. In contrast, those firmly in the grip of the disease, who were subjected to an unending succession of leaps, could only watch in horror as first their skin and eventually their muscles, their organs, and finally their blood became more and more transparent, until the light pierced their bodies like a lance. Fortunately, by that time, the majority had already lost their minds and no longer remembered who they were or where they came from.

The Villain, however, never forgot who he was or whom he was chasing. And if he had any inkling of the terrible havoc his burning desire for vengeance was wreaking on his body, it did not seem to bother him in the slightest. On the contrary, he appeared to welcome his progressive invisibility as an unexpected boon, which made him feel even more powerful and intimidating. That accursed Wells would have nowhere left to hide once Rhys attained complete invisibility. What other tricks could he resort to in order to escape from him? None. When Rhys became Invisible Death, Wells would finally be trapped.

ALL THESE FRESH PERILS lying in wait for their twins had cast a pall over the wonderful stories the Wellses exchanged by the hearth as they took an increasingly sinister turn. The couple could not help shuddering at the thought of the as-yet-unknown effects the epidemic might have on the fabric of the universe, or simply when contemplating the travails of those cronotemics forced to rebuild their lives in parallel worlds, without any clue as to what was happening to them. They could consider themselves fortunate in comparison to those whom the virus forced to jump endlessly from universe to universe, their minds and bodies unraveling until, in the most extreme cases, they ended up dissolving in hyperspace like the vague memory of some deranged universal consciousness.

Many of those poor wretches spent their final days prey to a phenomenon that was related to the nature of parallel worlds, which Wells referred to as the Maelstrom Coordinates. He had discovered that in many universes there were certain places that acted like gigantic ocean sinkholes that sucked toward the centers of their powerful vortexes any strange elements that fell into them from other worlds. So, when a cronotemic jumped, instead of reappearing in the same spot, or wherever the equivalent coordinates might be, one of those cosmic whirlpools often dragged him to a different place. The Maelstrom Coordinates might be located somewhere specific like a house, a moor, or a cave, but also could be in a person. A cronotemic might leap from a snowy peak in the Himalayas or the scorching dunes of the Sahara Desert and reappear in a parallel London through a haunted house or the body of a medium conducting a séance.

Wells could not help smiling to himself when he discovered that this epidemic of leaping through worlds was responsible for the obsession with spiritualism and the hordes of mediums blighting so many parallel worlds in that multiple universe. Those worlds, which were so removed from the Supreme Knowledge, did their best to make sense of the strange plague, whether by designating those infected as *Homo temporalis*, as in Rhys's world, or mistaking them for lost souls, spirits doomed to haunt bewitched places and communicate with the living through mediums until they laid to rest their unfinished business. In actual fact, all those haunted houses and those remarkable people with an apparent gift for speaking to the dead were simply each universe's Maelstrom Coordinates sucking up the cronotemics in mid-leap only to regurgitate them later as terrifying apparitions, whether in the form of a woman in black suddenly appearing at the top of a tower in a deserted house or a nebulous ectoplasm emerging from the body of a medium in a trance.

The Wellses also discovered that once a cronotemic had been sucked up by a Maelstrom he would remain bound in some way to that universe, doomed to return there again and again, and always through the same portal. As a result, some cronotemics became trapped in a crazed vicious circle made up of a few worlds, forced to appear in the same haunted houses, or through the same mediums, shedding with every jump an increasing number of molecules and memories. Many ended up in the thrall of the mediums, their virtual slaves, pathetic puppets who believed blindly everything the mediums said: that they were dead, and that their hazy memories were merely visions of the Hereafter, where they now belonged, and that was no doubt an exact replica of the world of the living. Until one day, during a jump, their delicate molecular structure would fragment into a million scattered apparitions. When that happened, the curse of the haunted house would be lifted, until another cronotemic took up the vacant post of resident ghost or a medium would lose contact with her enslaved spirit, believing that he or she had at last found the path into the light.

For five long years, the Wellses watched the epidemic spread, tormented by the terrible fate of their twins who had developed the disease and wondering anxiously how it would all end. Occasionally, eager to retain some hope amid that madness, they told themselves the situation might resolve itself: the day might dawn when those actively infected would end up disintegrating, including the evil Villain himself, leaving only the harmless carriers, who would develop some kind of immunity that they would then pass on to their offspring, and the universe would heal itself. But on the days when they were plagued with guilt, all they could tell each other was that Chaos, always inevitable, might come to that universe as predicted, but not for thousands of millennia, thanks to H. G. Wells and his wife.

27

THE ANSWER TO THEIR OMINOUS MUSINGS CAME A few weeks later, when Wells infiltrated the mind of a twin who had just jumped for the fourth time in less than two months. His first jump had interrupted a peaceful stroll through the streets of London, leaving him stranded in the middle of a deserted plain, where, trembling behind a rock, he had heard the distant blast of hunting horns and the thunderous gallop of a hundred horses. But before he could take a look, he had been dragged back to London scarcely two years before his own birth. There he had stayed for almost two months before being plucked afresh, this time while crossing Grosvenor Square, and transplanted to a London reduced to a heap of rubble from which plumes of hot vapor rose. He was expecting any moment to be devoured by one of the monstrous creatures resembling giant crabs that were scuttling amid the ruins, when another jump had sent him back to Grosvenor Square. And that was where Observer Wells connected with him, just as he was wondering when that crazy journey through time would end.

The square had changed a lot—a few of the houses surrounding the garden in the middle had been replaced by more functional-looking buildings—but at least it was still standing. At that moment it was filled with people. A large crowd had gathered in the square, mostly youngsters sitting in rows on the grass or huddled in the corners, singing and playing the guitar and waving banners bearing the slogan "Make Love Not War' and other expressions Wells didn't understand. The youngsters' harangues were directed at an exceptionally ugly building on the west side of the square, in front of which was posted an army of police-men, many of them on horseback, who were observing the youths hos-tilely. For several minutes, Wells's twin was content to wander, dazed, through the noisy crowd, staring in astonishment at the youths' garish clothes and the flowers that seemed to blossom from their long, scruffy locks. Vaguely intoxicated by the sweet aroma of the cigarettes they were smoking, he accidentally bumped into one young lad.

"Hey, look where you're going, Teddy Boy!" shouted the youth, who was wearing a suede jacket, his hair almost down to his waist.

"I'm terribly sorry," Wells hurriedly apologized, slightly intimidated.

The youth appeared to calm down and stared at him in silence, a vaporous smile clinging to his lips. Taking advantage of this inadvertent contact with one of the natives of that era, Wells asked the youth what year it was, but before he could reply, several anguished cries rang out from the far end of the square followed by gunshots. In the distance, the crowd rose to its feet, and Wells saw a tide of alarmed youths hurtling toward him like a wave rolling toward the shore, and before he had time to react he was swept away. He only just managed to glimpse at the far end of the square a dozen or more mounted policeman riding through the crowd without a care. Suddenly, there was a deafening explosion, and the human tide became a raging sea. A cloud of thick black smoke floated up over the terrified crowd. Pandemonium reigned as people started scattering in all directions. The mounted policemen lashed out indiscriminately, while the youngsters fought back with stones, which bounced off the policemen's helmets with an ominous crunching sound. Afraid of being trapped in the midst of that spontaneous battle royal whose logic he neither understood nor cared to understand, Wells tried to slip away through a gap in the crowd. He had no idea which way he was running, but he didn't care, providing he managed to get away from the heat of the skirmish. He passed several dazed youths with bloodied faces, crying and pleading for help, but he kept on running.

All of a sudden, an explosion went off dangerously close, and Wells fell to the ground, entangled in an unseemly heap of bodies. For a few seconds, he thought he couldn't hear, for the world seemed enclosed in a quilted cocoon of silence. He sat up as best he could and glanced about: through the smoke he saw some youths being helped up and starting to run about aimlessly. He felt an immense relief as the familiar dizziness came over him, heralding a jump. In a few seconds, he would be traversing the universe to another era, which, however inhospitable, could not be worse than this.

But before the giddiness intensified, Wells saw a huge figure wrapped in a black cape striding toward him through the smoke, apparently unperturbed by the uproar. With his cape billowing behind him, brandishing a cane with a glowing handle, his hat pulled down over his face, the figure seemed like something out of a dream. And yet he was more real to Wells than anything else around him. Was this Death coming for him? he wondered, petrified amid the turmoil. When the figure reached Wells, it took him by the arm, lifting him with a strength that could only be described as superhuman. Taken aback by the sinister apparition, the tide of youths seemed to part before him like the sea before Moses while the policemen's horses whinnied and reared up in terror.

When at last they came to a deserted alleyway, the stranger flattened him against a wall. Wells scarcely had time to rub his arm, which felt as if it had been clamped in a pair of blacksmith's tongs, when the figure seized his neck with a gloved hand, immobilizing him. Realizing with horror that a team of oxen couldn't drag him away from that powerful grip, Wells made no attempt to struggle free. He simply confronted the stranger's face, half-obscured by his huge, wide-brimmed hat. Swathed in shadows, barely illuminated by the strange bluish light seeping from his cane, the stranger's pale features resembled those of a beautiful, terrible deity. All at once, his lips seemed to vibrate faintly, and Wells heard a voice, distant and metallic, as if it were traveling through a long tube.

"I am Executioner 2087V and I've come to kill you. I feel pity for you, but I'm powerless to prevent your fate. Although if you want to know why you must die, you can find the answer by looking deep into my eyes." Half-dazed, Wells instinctively sought out the stranger's gaze.

"Look deep into my eyes! Don't stop looking, even if you feel fear or despair, even if you want to surrender. Keep looking into my eyes, until the last moment of your life in this world is over."

Wells did as he was told, and while chaos reigned beyond the alleyway, he submerged himself in his executioner's eyes, where two eight-pointed stars shone with an increasingly blinding light before they finally exploded, shooting past him, expanding into infinity and breaking up into the millions of galaxies in a universe. Wells saw all the stars die, and he saw the most absolute darkness envelop the world. He saw a vanishing civilization curled up around the frozen embers of a black hole, waiting to escape its deadly fate, and he saw the face of Chaos and understood why his death was justified and necessary. He discovered that the Executioner felt guilt, and although he was unable to utter a word, Wells tried to tell him he forgave him, and he knew that his killer had heard him, and that in that instant of absolute communication each belonged to the other, and they were both overwhelmed by the ecstasy of the Supreme Knowledge. Despite the intensity of that final thought, Wells managed to keep staring into the eyes of his executioner until the last moment of his life in this world came to an end.

At the precise moment in which Observer Wells saw his twin expire, he opened his eyes and desperately gulped air into his lungs. His heart was hammering so hard against his chest he thought it would bore a hole through it, and his back was bathed in a cold sweat. Glancing about, wild-eyed, he discovered Jane kneeling beside him with a worried look on her face.

"They succeeded, my dear." His voice was a faint whisper. She looked at him, confused. "They are here, they are here . . ."

"Who?"

Wells slumped back into his chair.

"The twin I connected with this evening . . . he met someone from our world."

"Someone from our world is here!" exclaimed Jane.

"Well, actually, not so much as some*one*—some*thing* . . . I mean, not a human, but not an automaton either. And . . . it killed my twin."

Jane looked at him, aghast.

"Good Lord, Bertie. But . . . why?"

"Because that is his job," sighed Wells. "Because that is why the Scientists from the Other Side created him: to exterminate all those infected with the virus. There are hundreds like him throughout the different worlds. They call themselves Executioners, and their mission is to detect the molecular trails left by cronotemics, hunt them down, and kill them."

Jane raised her hands to her mouth to stifle a cry. Wells waited a few seconds for her to absorb the information before continuing.

"They classify cronotemics according to how infectious they are, and they call them Destructors: level 1 Destructors, level 2 Destructors, and so on . . . *Destructors,* Jane! Do you realize what that means? Cronotemics are destroying the universe!"

Jane nodded, increasingly pale. Her husband ran a trembling hand over his face as he tried to order the jumble of images the Executioner had transmitted to him through his dying twin, but it wasn't easy to express in words the thoughts of a creature that wasn't human. How could he begin to describe that madness? Begin at the beginning, then carry on until you reach the end, he told himself, harking back to the words of his old friend Dodgson all those years ago. And so he began at the beginning . . .

After the Wellses' mysterious disappearance, scientists of that and subsequent generations had continued to do research. But it would be hundreds of years before they achieved any notable results. And perhaps hundreds of years too late. Just as the Wellses had always suspected, their old world was moving at a faster pace than their adopted world, and the stars on the Other Side had already started to die, heralding the Dark Era. Time was running out, and in the distant future in which their world found itself, Chaos was imminent. That was why, when the Scientists succeeded in opening and stabilizing a magic hole, everyone understood that this was their final hope: they had used up their last reserves of strength on that achievement; they were exhausted, dying, and hadn't the energy needed to open another. And so they were relieved and delighted to find out that the tunnel led them straight into a young world during the Stelliferous Age, a world made up of infinite parallel worlds, many of which were capable of accommodating a homeless civilization. The same multiverse, the same theater with its infinite stages, that they, the Wellses, had ended up in. But, alas, when the Scientists began to scrutinize that multiverse in preparation for the Great Exodus, to their horror they discovered that it was desperately ill.

"The cronotemia epidemic . . . ," Jane murmured.

Wells nodded gloomily.

"Yes, my dear. The cronotemia epidemic . . . Even so, they didn't give in. They began studying the strange epidemic to try to understand how it had all started. But the worst part was when they discovered the effect it had. You were right, my dear. You always are. This disease is going to destroy the multiverse. The molecular footprint left by the cronotemics each time they jump causes scarring in hyperspace: they shrink it, making it increasingly brittle and bringing the parallel worlds that make up this multiverse gradually closer together. If that shrinkage continues, those worlds will end up colliding, setting off a series of apocalyptic explosions that will lead to mass extermination . . . The infinite stages will collapse into one another, bursting into a gigantic ball of cosmic fire, and this theater itself will disintegrate."

"Good God!" exclaimed Jane. Then, after a few seconds' silence, she added incredulously, "And is exterminating all the cronotemics the only solution they could come up with? I find that hard to believe. How could they be so cruel, Bertie?"

Wells shrugged wearily.

"They may simply be trying to gain time, dear. I expect they considered the death of a few innocents a small price to pay compared to saving two universes. For it isn't only about *this* universe, Jane. Unless they cure the disease in time for the Great Exodus—"

"The Other Side will also perish," Jane concluded in a horrified whisper.

They both remained silent. For several moments the only sound in the tiny sitting room was the crackle of the fire and the elderly couple's labored breathing.

"Do you remember the day of the Great Debate, Jane?" Wells asked suddenly, his voice choked with anguish. "How everyone admired me! Shouting my name in adulation. If I close my eyes I can still hear them. They trusted in me; they put themselves in my hands. They thought I possessed the truth, and so did I, but . . . Oh, Jane!" Wells sighed, and gazed at his wife. "I lied to you! I was only motivated by vanity! And you knew that, didn't you? I wanted to go down in history as the Savior of Humanity. And yet . . . can you imagine what they must think of me now, back in our world? Can you imagine our colleagues' surprise when at last they reached the promised land only to discover it was doomed because of a stupid failed experiment in their Victorian era? All their hopes destroyed by a tiny virus synthesized by H. G. Wells, the biggest catastrophe in the history of the Church of Knowledge, the eternally cursed Destroyer of Universes . . ."

Jane stood up almost abruptly and leaned against the mantelpiece. Wells remained in his chair, lost without her, sobbing with his head sunk between his shoulders, overwhelmed by self-pity. Finally, his wife's silence forced him to look up timidly. She was watching him weep with that look of fierce determination he knew so well.

"Well, Bertie, if that is what they think of you . . ." She grinned. "Then we'll just have to make them change their minds."

28

OVER THE DAYS THAT FOLLOWED, THE WELLSES set about elaborating a plan to save the two universes while at the same time changing the disastrous opinion the inhabitants of their world must have of H. G. Wells. Or vice versa. They began with a detailed study of all the information and images Wells had gleaned from the mind of the Executioner, or at any rate everything he could remember or express in words. Apparently, that sinister slaughter had been going on for some time (the equivalent of ten years in their adoptive universe, they calculated). That it had taken them so long to come across an Executioner only made obvious—whether they liked it or not—the infinite nature of the universe. How could scientists from the Other Side eradicate an epidemic that affected so many other worlds? They couldn't unless someone guided them to the original source of the infection so that they could eradicate it at the root.

While scanning the Executioner's mind, Wells had discovered that those killers were able to jump between worlds thanks to the canes they carried, whose handles bore the eight-pointed Star of Chaos. Apparently these devices helped them chase cronotemics from stage to stage, burrowing tunnels through hyperspace without leaving any scars in the fabric of the universe, guiding them by working out complex coordinates based on the molecular trails left by the cronotemics. In other words, the Executioners could travel anywhere in the universe providing their diseased quarry left a big enough trail of bread crumbs. And probably also if someone drew a map with mathematical coordinates their canes could interpret.

"Such a map could guide any Executioner, from whichever world he is in, to the exact place and time of the first infection!" Wells exclaimed excitedly. "Or more precisely, to one minute before, so that he could prevent it from happening."

"And who, may I ask, could draw that map?" Jane asked innocently.

She knew perfectly well who, but she wanted her husband to have the pleasure of pronouncing it. Wells gave his first smile in a very long time. A dazzling smile, brimming with optimism—a touch ingenuous, perhaps, but what did that matter?

"Why, someone with sufficient mathematical knowledge," he replied proudly.

And so, oozing enthusiasm, Wells dusted off the old maps he and Dodgson had dabbled with in Oxford and spread them out on the table. But one look at those pages filled with formulas, equations, and diagrams was enough to make his heart sink. Those pretentious scribblings were mere intellectual games, ornamentations as brilliant as they were empty, totally theoretical, and never meant to be taken seriously . . . Now, however, it was up to him to find out whether they contained a shred of truth by applying them to a real-life problem of unimaginable magnitude. He had to draw a map, the biggest map of all time and all worlds, a map that would shrink infinity to a calculation of coordinates, a map that would reduce the entire universe to a simple equation . . . He didn't know whether such an undertaking was possible. And if it was, whether he wanted to reveal life as a mirage woven from the ethereal threads of mathematics, one of his least favorite subjects. But he didn't appear to have many alternatives, and so he had to try.

He began working day and night on the map, which he decided to call the Great Mathematical Map of Inexorable Chaos. Jane thought the name sounded rather pompous, but Wells was adamant: if this was to be his magnum opus, one that would enable him to go down in history as the Savior of Humanity, the title should reflect that importance. He soon became absorbed in the Herculean task, and once more it was Jane's task to look after him, as she had during the dark days: making sure he ate, washed, and had enough sleep, besides bolstering his enthusiasm each time he started to flag. Such commitment forced them to sacrifice their beloved sessions in front of the fire as well, for by the time evening came Wells was so exhausted he scarcely had the strength to drag himself to bed.

And while he was shut away in his study, grappling with contradictory formulas, reaching conclusions that rendered all previous ones void, and lamenting bitterly that Dodgson wasn't there to help him, Jane would take refuge, in her quiet moments, in the cozy little study she had made for herself in one of the spare rooms. Sitting at her desk, where there was always a vase of freshly cut roses, she would spend a few hours every day trying to alleviate her loneliness. She and Wells had decided that she would help revise each chapter, which would require the fresh insight of a mind uncontaminated by the tortuous process of calculating and writing. Otherwise, she would devote herself to solving the no less important domestic aspects of life, so that Wells could work on his magnum opus without interruption. For the first time in many years, this division of labor forced them to remain sadly apart for several hours a day, although I would be lying, dear reader, if I didn't tell you that, during those hours of solitude, Jane also felt contentment. True, she missed her husband dreadfully, despite their being separated only by a partition wall, for the bond between them was so close they had ended up becoming a single entity. Jane experienced her husband's absence in every fiber of her being as an unpleasant sensation, like leaving her coat and hat at home on a particularly breezy day. And yet, that discomfort would occasionally turn into an exhilarating feeling of freedom, as if, once she had accepted the inevitable oversight, she had no choice but to brace herself against the wind as she felt it freeze her face and tousle her hair.

However, her husband did not appear to cope so well with those forced separations. Ever since his wife had told him she was planning to make a study for herself in one of their spare rooms, Wells had resolved to spend part of his very limited and valuable spare time trying to discover exactly what his wife was doing in there. Direct questioning had failed, because she merely replied with a shrug. Joshing hadn't worked either. "Are you drawing pictures of animals in there?" he had once asked, but Jane hadn't laughed the way she usually did when he said that. Her silence was tomb-like, and since torture was not an option, Wells had been forced to resort to surprise incursions. And so he had discovered that Jane went into her study to write. In fact, this wasn't much of a discovery, as he could almost have worked it out without having to go in there. She was hardly likely to use the room for breeding rabbits, practicing devil worship, or dancing naked. Besides, she had half jokingly threatened him with it. Now all he had to do was find out *what* she was writing.

"Oh, nothing of any interest," Jane replied, quickly hiding the sheets of paper in her desk drawer, the lock of which Wells had unsuccessfully tried to force open. "I'll let you read it once it's finished."

Once it was finished . . . That meant nothing. What if it was never finished? What if for some reason she decided not to finish it? What if the world came to an end first? If it did, he would never know what Jane had been doing during the three or four hours she spent in her study every day. Was she writing a diary? Or perhaps a recipe book? But why be so cagey about a recipe book?

"One of the things I most hate in life is couples who keep secrets from each other," Wells said, being deliberately dramatic.

"I thought what you most hated was the fact that no one has invented an electric razor yet," Jane chuckled. She went on talking to him as she took his arm and led him toward the door, trying not to give the impression she was getting rid of him. "But don't be such a grouch. What does it matter what I write? Your work is the important thing, Bertie, so stop wasting your time spying on me and get writing."

After shrugging a few times, Wells went down to the ground floor, where he hid away in *his* study. There he contemplated the sheaf of blank pages before him, where he had proposed to record all his hard-earned wisdom, everything he had seen. He reached for his pen, ready to begin his "crowning work," as Jane had called it, while the sounds from the street and the neighboring park seeped in through his window, noises from a world that went by immersed in the smug satisfaction of believing it was unique . . . and safe from harm.

It took Wells almost a year to finish the book, which—after several prunings that extended even to the pretentious title—ended up being called simply *The Map of Chaos*. By the time Jane had revised the final pages and given her husband's mathematical extravaganza her approval, the year was 1897 in their adopted world. They had arrived there four decades ago, and a lot had changed since then. The two sprites now looked like an elderly couple approaching a hundred (although Wells had just turned seventy and Jane sixty-five), and indeed that is what they felt like: extremely old and tired. The past year had been very difficult for them both. Neither had connected with any of their twins during those many months, for nearly all their time and energy had been devoted to the colossal task of creating *The Map of Chaos*. Besides, neither Wells nor Jane wanted to see how the epidemic and the cruel extermination of those infected was running its course. It would only have made them more anxious. If the end of the world took place before they finished the map, they would soon know about it, for they doubted whether the cosmic explosions caused by infinite worlds colliding would go unnoticed. But finish it they had. And, for the time being at least, the universe was still in one piece.

Wells then decided that the completion of the work that contained the key to saving that and all other possible worlds called for a celebration, and that they both deserved a rest. And so they lit the fire, poured themselves a drink—only a drop, as alcohol no longer agreed with them very well—and slumped into their respective armchairs with a contented sigh and a creaking of elderly joints. It was time to enjoy one of their soothing, magical sessions by the fire that they had so missed. But before starting they agreed they would connect with only happy twins that evening, not with those poor wretches who had developed the disease, or those fleeing Martians, or the Invisible Man, or any other equally

THE MAP OF CHAOS

disturbing threat. No, they had had enough thrills and shocks. That evening they would savor the dull but peaceful existences of those twins who were simply minding their own business, because fortunately, in a universe made up of infinite parallel worlds, it was still possible to live a normal life.

But Wells cheated. He could not resist the temptation to take a peek at the first person infected. He wanted to know what had been going on in his life since he had stopped watching him, although what he might find was as daunting as Jane discovering his small deception. At first, he had difficulty locating his twin, because after not using his gift for a year he was somewhat out of practice. But at last he found him: that Wells was now an old man, and by leafing back through the pages of his memory he discovered everything that had happened to him since he last ventured into his mind. He was pleased to see that at the end of an eventful life his twin had attained a measure of peace. After an exciting adventure in the Antarctic, where he had lost a couple of fingers on his right hand, he had jumped into the universe in which he currently found himself, where his disease had entered a dormant phase, allowing him to rebuild his shattered life as best he could. Alas, just when he thought that his last days would be spent calmly preparing for death, an Executioner had picked up his trail, and for months he had been forced to live in hiding, escaping only narrowly and by sheer luck on a couple of occasions, like that time in front of the Royal Opera House. He had moved residences, changed his name to Baskerville, and adopted a different profession . . . Wells couldn't help smiling when he saw that he had ended up as coachman to Gilliam Murray, who in that universe called himself Montgomery Gilmore. Just as Wells infiltrated his mind, the twin with the scar was holding a conversation with the original Wells from that universe.

"So you have no scar on your left hand . . . ," Baskerville was saying to him. "But you do have one on your chin, whereas I don't . . ."

"When I was fifteen I fell down some stairs," replied the other Wells.

"I see. Whereas I didn't. I was always very careful with stairs."

"I'm very happy for you," his young twin sighed.

Observer Wells chuckled to himself in his armchair in front of the fire, his eyes still closed. He felt tremendously proud of Baskerville, who was no less unique than he, not merely because he had succeeded in defeating a Martian invasion single-handedly, but because it seemed that he, too, had worked out the true nature of the universe, and of his disease, all by himself . . . Contented, he silently bade him farewell and let that world vanish slowly into the magic hole at the center of his mind. Then he opened his eyes.

Jane's eyes were still half-closed, and so he sat gazing at her affectionately as he waited for her to wake up. He had no idea what his wife was seeing, but, judging from the sweet smile on her face, she must have been enjoying it. Ten minutes or so later, Jane opened her eyes to find Wells observing her with a rapt smile.

"Where have you been, my dear? You were grinning like a little girl on a merry-go-round."

"Oh, I connected with a young twin of mine who was about to fall in love with her biology teacher." She smiled significantly as she remembered. "As in many parallel worlds, they, too, were in the habit of walking to Charing Cross station together to catch their respective trains. But if the majority of your twins used the time to impress mine with their sparkling wit, this Wells was much . . . bolder. As we walked past a little gated garden, we slipped inside, and there, hiding behind a hedge in the moonlight we . . . Oh, Bertie, it was wonderful . . ." Jane noticed her husband gaping at her and thought it best not to go into any more detail. "And what about you, dear?"

"Er . . . well, I'm afraid the twin I connected with wasn't up to such exploits."

BUT THE FACT THEY had finished *The Map of Chaos* did not mean their work was done. On the contrary, the most difficult part remained: to make sure the book found its way into the hands of one of the Executioners. But how? Those ruthless killers weren't in the habit of strolling through the city, smelling flowers in the park, or traveling by tram, nor did they leave a visiting card after eliminating cronotemics. The only way Wells and Jane could see Executioners was when they were hunting down one of their twins, and even then they couldn't communicate with them. Nor could they wait for one to come looking for them, since they weren't Destructors. They might develop the disease in the future, but equally they might not. However, they were convinced there had to be at least one Executioner on their adopted stage who was pursuing a cronotemic, or there would be at some point. And a book called *The Map of Chaos,* especially if it had the same eight-pointed star on its cover that adorned their cane, was bound to catch the attention of any Executioner. Therefore, all they had to do was to ensure that the book became popular enough to appear in every bookshop window and newspaper in England for as long as possible. Yes, it had to enjoy the same success as Dodgson's *Alice's Adventures in Wonderland* or the novels of Wells's own twin or, better still, the adventures of that pompous detective Sherlock Holmes.

However, after two weeks traipsing round London, knocking on every publisher's door, they were forced to admit defeat. Regardless of whether it contained the key to saving the world, no one wanted to publish a complicated mathematical treatise entitled *The Map of Chaos* that was impossible to make head or tail of. Wells had to be satisfied to have his rejected manuscript bound in fine leather with the silver Star of Chaos embossed on its cover. He had devoted a year of his life to the absurd task of writing an indecipherable book, a map that would only make sense if a pair of inhuman eyes alighted on its pages, which seemed most unlikely.

Back home, they placed the one existing copy of *The Map of Chaos* on the table and sat down in their armchairs to try to think up some other way of making sure it reached an Executioner. But the problem seemed insoluble.

"Maybe we should turn the search on its head," Jane suggested after a few moments' reflection.

"What do you mean?" asked Wells.

"Instead of trying to find an Executioner in order to give him the book, we should let them come to us. We could find a twin who has become a Destructor and give him the book."

Wells looked at her in astonishment.

"You mean . . . entrust our mission to them?"

Jane nodded, although she didn't seem all that convinced either.

"Yes, I suppose we could . . . ," Wells mused. "But it would have to be a cronotemic who is active enough to attract the Executioners but whose mental and molecular decline hasn't set in and who is young and healthy enough to pass the mission on to another twin when the initial symptoms of degeneration start. In short: we would have to find the Perfect Twin. He or she would be the only one to whom we could safely entrust the book."

They both agreed they needed to find the Perfect Twin, but how? They could look for as many as they wanted without moving from their chairs, but that would be of no use. They had no way of communicating with them, and if they accidentally jumped into their world, they would lose all trace of them immediately, because they were incapable of infiltrating the mind of any double occupying the same stage as they. That would mean searching all over London, as they doubted the poor wretch would stay put wherever they appeared, waiting for them to turn up. And that was assuming they arrived at the same place they had left from, for there was always the possibility they might be sucked up by a Maelstrom Coordinate and spat out in the Himalayas or the Sahara Desert or some other equally remote corner of the universe . . . It was then that the Supreme Knowledge illuminated their minds as one.

"The Maelstrom Coordinates!" they exclaimed.

Why hadn't they thought of it before? There was no need for them to tramp blindly around the city. They only had to wait beside one of those whirlpools for a cronotemic twin to land in their world and hope that he or she was the Perfect Twin. Then they would hand him or her the book, explaining that it contained the key to saving the universe. They trusted they could convince him or her without too much difficulty.

After all, they should know their own doubles better than they knew anyone. It would be like convincing themselves, or so they hoped. But they would worry about that later. First of all they had to find a Perfect Twin.

"I'm afraid, my dear, that we will have to become devotees of spiritualism," said Wells.

They both smiled at that, remembering how they had pitied people who went to séances to communicate with their dead relatives.

Throughout the following year, Wells and Jane visited every medium practicing in England at the time, as well as with any who included the British Isles in their European tours. They attended séances conducted by C. H. Foster, Madame d'Esperance, William Eglinton, and the Reverend Stainton Moses, to name but a few. In rooms plunged into a reddish gloom, they sat around tables touching fingers with those next to them while the medium of the day levitated above their heads, held up by wires concealed beneath his or her tunic or conjured some ectoplasmic materialization made from a painted chiffon veil. They also visited several supposedly haunted houses in England. But the results of their exhaustive search were less than encouraging. Among all those charlatans it was hard to discover a genuine medium who also contained a Maelstrom Coordinate, and on the rare occasions that they did, none of the cronotemics that emerged from their bodies were the Wellses' twins, but instead some half-translucent wretches whose minds had gone and who simply recited pathetically whatever the medium had told them. Only once they thought they recognized a boy of six or seven who materialized in the middle of a séance looking sadly neglected and grubby, like an Oliver Twist of the multiverse, and crying out that he wanted his mummy. At Borley Rectory they also found a demented eighty-year-old twin of Jane's whose appearances were responsible for the rector's daughters' claims that the house was haunted. Those futile encounters were all they had managed to achieve with their desperate plan.

And so it was no wonder that, as the months went by, each became secretly convinced that this strategy wasn't going to work either. However, neither of them dared to put it into words, so as not to demoralize the other completely. But then, one afternoon, events took over. They were on their way home after attending a séance conducted by a medium who had turned out to be a fake, and as they walked Wells railed continuously against that bunch of charlatans who used their cheap tricks to take advantage of other people's unhappiness.

"They are wasting our precious time!" he fumed. "Not to mention our money!"

Jane felt equally angry, but as they entered Charing Cross station she told her husband to keep his voice down.

"Return to a state of calm, Bertie, unless you want to draw attention to yourself with your shouting."

But that only incensed Wells more, and he repeated his vociferations as they descended the stairs to the concourse. All of a sudden, Wells came to a halt, pallid and stiff as a snowman. After struggling for breath for a few seconds, he raised a clawed hand to his chest and fell in a heap on the steps, on the exact same spot where dozens of his consumptive twins had collapsed in various parallel worlds. However, Wells's diagnosis was very different: his frustration and rage over their fruitless search had formed a ball of anguish that had blocked one of the arteries in his heart.

Had he had access to drugs from his own universe, Wells would have made an instant recovery. However, medicine was still in its infancy in his adopted world, and he was prescribed only an extract of the herbaceous perennial digitalis and several weeks' rest. Laid up in bed, stymied by that rudimentary medicine, Wells felt more powerless than ever. What further could he and Jane do? They had found the solution to the problem, but that didn't seem to be enough to atone for his sins.

For her part, Jane momentarily forgot the fate of the universe, as she was far more concerned with that of her husband. Seeing him collapse like that while walking along, she had feared the worst, and afterward she devoted herself to caring for him as tenderly as ever, infinitely grateful that her husband had resisted death's first approach. She prepared vinegar compresses for him and occasionally in the afternoons she would read him adventure novels by authors from their adopted universe who simply invented things with words, such as Stevenson, Swift, or Verne. When he had fallen asleep, she would begin to weep silently. Jane knew that this first attack was only a stab in the dark and that very soon another, possibly fatal thrust would come. And although she had often thought about death, it had never crossed her mind that she and her husband might die separately. They had always done everything together, by mutual agreement; why change things now? But Bertie apparently planned to precede her in that final adventure, and she found it inconceivable, shameful almost, that she should carry on living in a world without him. She found devastating not only the pain but above all the shock of no longer being two. She and Bertie had been together for longer than she could remember, and she did not think she could go on living with such a wound to her heart. But she would have no choice, for if that happened, then, frail and diminished as she was, there would be no one else standing between the universe and its annihilation.

Fortunately, as the days went by, Wells appeared to recover. His cough was gradually abating, and some color returned to his cheeks. However feebly, he still clung to life. One afternoon, when he was feeling stronger, he called out to Jane. She entered that room reeking of old age, medicaments, and deferred death and sat down in the armchair beside his bed. Wells tried to speak but instead began to whoop joyously, as though ascending the musical scale. Jane took his hand and waited for the coughing fit to subside, contemplating him with a tenderness that time had smoothed, as water polishes pebbles on the riverbed. She couldn't bear to see the man with whom she had shared her life so vulnerable, so exposed to death, that man who had loved her with the rationality decreed by the Church of Knowledge and with the passion dictated by his heart, and who had been responsible for offering her whatever happiness life had allotted her.

"I've been thinking, my dear," she heard Wells say in a reedy, almost childlike voice when she had regained her composure, "and in my opinion we shouldn't go to any more séances. It is getting us nowhere."

Jane was taken aback. She had assumed that when her husband recovered they would resume their search, no matter how unpleasant they both found it, incapable of shirking the responsibility they had taken on.

"What other options are there?" Jane asked, aware that giving up wasn't one of them.

Wells took a deep breath before replying. "I think the only thing left to do is . . . give the book to them."

"To *them*? But, Bertie, we decided not to involve them in this, to let them get on with their lives, remember?"

"Of course I remember, my dear. But I fear we have no choice. Look at the two of us. We don't have much time left. You and I will soon . . . disappear, and if before then we haven't given the book to an Executioner, or entrusted someone else with that mission, we might as well never have written it. And the entire universe will die without ever knowing it had a tiny chance of being saved."

"Even so, Bertie, I don't think we should make them shoulder this terrible burden," Jane stammered. "They are still young; it will ruin their . . ."

"Their lives?" Wells said gloomily. "What lives? If we do nothing, no twin of ours in this multiverse will live to be old and decrepit like us."

Jane nodded, and they both smiled sadly. Then Jane laid her head on her husband's chest and let herself be lulled by his slow but tenacious heartbeat. It was the sound of a worn-out drum, but she didn't want to go on dancing if it ever stopped. Presently, she heard Wells's voice.

"Have you never wondered what was behind that feeling of urgency that made us move away from Oxford to be near them when they were born, that mysterious certainty we sensed that we had to be part of their lives?"

"Every day," she admitted.

"And what conclusion have you come to?"

Jane sighed.

"That it was probably our instinct as Observers telling us that sooner or later they would be the ones to take over our mission," she said with resignation.

"That is the same conclusion I reached, my dear."

Neither of them uttered another word, content to remain silent, embracing each other with what they knew to be the last of their strength, feeling more marooned than ever as the sky darkened through the windowpanes.

29

$\mathcal{A}$ND SO, ONE WINDSWEPT AFTERNOON IN LATE February 1900, when Wells was feeling strong enough to be able to walk without feeling dizzy, the Wellses went to Arnold House with the aim of entrusting the book to their twins in that world. Jane was carrying it in a small embroidered silk purse, which she clasped to her chest with one hand, while with the other she held on to her cloak to stop the wind from blowing it away. Standing at the tall entrance gate, they rang the bell several times, but no one came to let them in. Squashing his hat against his skull, Wells let out a curse. The journey by coach had almost pulverized their bones, and all for nothing. Where were their twins? They had stated very clearly in their message the time of their arrival. They were about to go back the way they had come when they saw the couple's carriage approach.

"Professor Lansbury, Mrs. Lansbury, please forgive the delay!" the young Wells exclaimed as he stepped out of the coach and found them at the gate.

The four of them greeted one another effusively, for they had not met since the twins moved to Sandgate for the sea air, which was more invigorating.

"I'm so sorry we are late. Our excursion to Dartmoor took longer than we had expected, because on the way back we had a bit of a shock," Wells's twin explained. "Our friend Montgomery Gilmore and his fiancée had a slight accident when their Mercedes, one of those newfangled automobiles, veered off the road . . . Thank goodness, Gilmore managed to regain control of the fiendish vehicle."

"I'm so glad to hear it," replied Jane, somewhat shaken.

The Wellses asked their coachman to wait, with the vague promise of a mug of broth, and the two couples walked down the garden path leading up to the house. On the way, Wells noticed his twin glancing sideways at him and recalled how difficult it had been to befriend him back when he was still his teacher. Each time he tried to engage the lad in conversation, he seemed to shrink into himself, as though afflicted by a sudden colic, and, after exchanging a few pleasantries, he would hurry off under some pretext or other. Perhaps the poor boy had been suffering the effects of meeting himself. Fortunately, over time the inevitable kinship between them had developed into a mutual affection, which had eased the young man's awkwardness with his eccentric teacher. Now his double was watching him surreptitiously, trying to hide the pity his doddering gait instilled in him. It was clear he was shocked at the dramatic changes that the past six years had wreaked on Wells's body. But what did he expect? He, too, would grow old one day. His face would be lined with the same furrows he was now contemplating so wistfully, and his erect back would develop the same stoop, until finally he would leave the stage like everyone else, amid boos or applause.

After they entered the house, Jane's twin went to the kitchen to prepare tea while her husband ushered them into the sitting room. He invited them to take a seat at the table while he lit the fire. Soon, Jane brought in the tea. As she began pouring it briskly, the old lady was filled with melancholy: How long had it been since she went about her chores with that familiar vigor? However, a deafening crash interrupted her musings. They all gave a start.

"How strange, I thought you told me you had fixed that attic window, Bertie," Jane said, gazing up at the ceiling apprehensively.

"Why, yes, dear. I did it only last week. But clearly I have more of a flair for writing novels than fixing windows," he jested, but as no one laughed, he quickly went on: "So . . . Professor, what is the urgent matter that brought you here on this inclement afternoon?"

Wells exchanged a meaningful look with Jane before clearing his throat. The moment had come when they must destroy their twins' peaceful existence.

"Well, it is something we had hoped to keep from you, because we are aware that it will change your lives forever. And for the worse, I am afraid," he added gravely. "But, alas, we have no choice."

"You certainly know how to capture the attention of your audience, Professor," the young Wells remarked wryly. "You would have made an excellent novelist."

The old man responded to the compliment with a grim look and then sipped his cup of tea to buy a little time. Since he and Jane had resolved to go and see them, he hadn't stopped thinking about where best to begin their story and had concluded that they must first tell them who they were. If they didn't believe that, there would be no point in going on, and so he sat up as straight as possible and showed them his best side.

"Look at my face, George, and you, too, Jane. Take a good look. Try to see beneath all these wrinkles and this beard. Look at my eyes, especially, the expression in my eyes. And don't rule out any possibility."

Bewildered by his request, the couple leaned forward and peered into the old man's face, screwing up their eyes exaggeratedly, like a jeweler examining a stone. After a few seconds, Wells's twin lost his patience.

"What are you driving at, Professor?" he asked with a sardonic smile.

Disappointed at his double's lack of observational skills, Wells shook his head and turned his attention to the young woman.

"What do you see, Jane? How do you imagine I looked when I was thirty-three?" he asked, alluding to his twin's current age.

The young woman put on a serious face and tried to do what the old man had asked: she brushed away his wrinkles, shaved off his beard, covered his balding temples with hair, and replaced his weary expression with that of a young man brimming with belief in life. The result made her frown. Seeing her face, the old man smiled softly.

"Yes, Jane," he told her, "don't reject what your mind is trying to tell you. What you are thinking is exactly right."

"But what I am thinking is absurd!" she exclaimed, almost amused.

"No, my dear girl," the professor contradicted her. "It is exactly right."

"*What* is absurd? What the devil are you thinking, Jane?" Wells's twin demanded, puzzled.

"Henry Lansbury is an assumed name," Wells said suddenly, looking at the young man solemnly. "My real name is Herbert George Wells. I am you, only a good few years older, as you can see. Then he pointed to his wife. "And this is Amy Catherine Robbins. My wife and yours. Because we are you."

The young twins stared at each other in bewilderment, then examined the old couple again while they held hands as though posing for a portrait. A few seconds later, the younger woman mumbled, "Good heavens . . . But that's impossible!"

"Not if you believe what I am about to tell you," said Wells. And in a calm voice, aware of how bizarre his tale would sound to their twins, he began to narrate the story, a story with which, dear reader, you are more than familiar. He described in broad brushstrokes the world they had come from; he told them about the inevitable destruction of that universe, of how he and Jane had traveled to their adopted world in 1858 through a magic hole, about the years they had spent in Oxford with Dodgson, the disappearance of their dog, Newton, and the subsequent spread of the virus he was carrying. He told them about their gift for observing, the extermination of the cronotemics, and their reasons for writing *The Map of Chaos,* the book that contained the key to saving that and all other possible worlds. Their twins listened intently, with a mixture of wonder and dread. When Wells had finished, a heavy silence descended on the little sitting room.

Finally, after clearing his throat noisily, Wells's twin declared, "Goodness me: cronotemics, Executioners, parallel worlds . . . It sounds just like one of my fantasy novels!"

"I wish it were," sighed Wells. "But I assure you, George, everything I have told you is very real."

Wells's twin looked at his wife, then bit his lip before adding, "Don't take offense, Professor, but you are asking us to believe a lot of implausible things based on the sole evidence of a . . . vague resemblance between us."

Wells gave a sigh of disappointment, even though he had known convincing them wouldn't be easy, especially his own twin, who, as was to be expected, was as stubborn as he. He was about to reply when a voice rank with Evil roared behind him, "Would a genuine cronotemic be proof enough?"

The two couples turned as one toward the entrance to the sitting room, from where the voice had emanated. And what they saw caused them to leap from their seats. Standing in the doorway, watching them with a baleful grimace, was a semitransparent man. He was dressed in a dark suit and had an athletic build, but the disturbing thing about him was that they could see through the veil of his flesh to what was behind him: the doorframe, the gloomy corridor, the pictures on the walls . . . The stranger let them admire him for a moment, a mocking expression on his face, before walking over to them with the supple, self-assured movements of a predator approaching its prey. Wells and Jane recognized him immediately and instinctively clung to each other. As the apparition drew closer, they all noticed with alarm that he was carrying a strange-looking pistol. Apart from the wooden grip, it was made entirely of metal, and although the barrel seemed very narrow in relation to the rest, it was undoubtedly a deadly weapon.

"Who the devil are you, and what are you doing in my house?" inquired the young Wells, trying to conceal the tremor in his voice.

The creature clicked his tongue, demonstrating his disappointment.

"My dear George, under any other circumstances, tired of hearing the same old greeting, I would have said to you, 'Don't you recognize

me? My name is Marcus Rhys, and I have come to kill you—again,'"
he replied with a tone of reproach. The young Wells's face turned pale.
"However, now I know why you never remember me. Now I know *everything*." He grinned ferociously at his terrified audience. Then, addressing the old man, he added, "And so, correct me if I am wrong, Professor,
I am not *Homo temporalis* after all but rather a poor wretch infected with
a virus you created in a parallel universe. Therefore, it would be more
appropriate for me to say, 'My name is Marcus Rhys, and I have come to
kill you, as I have many of your twins in parallel worlds.' Isn't that right,
Professor?"

Observer Wells remained silent. Clearly, Marcus Rhys had been listening to their whole conversation from behind the door (he remembered the noise of the attic window and concluded he must have been
there awhile), and now he knew everything there was to know about his
own nature and the secrets of the universe. But that information didn't
seem to have altered in the slightest his diabolical intentions. The creature had positioned himself strategically at the head of the table, cornering them against the wall, and as he pointed his strange-looking pistol
at them, he cast a wild eye over the panic-stricken group until he came
to a halt at the unfortunate Jane, who happened to be standing closest to
him.

"I am so glad I brought along this semiautomatic Walther, which I
kept as a souvenir of my last trip," he declared suddenly, brandishing
the weapon proudly and causing them all to jump. "It is a standard-issue
Wehrmacht pistol used in the Second World War, a rather crude weapon
compared to my heat-ray gun, which I lost while fighting a *Tyrannosaurus
rex*. And although there is nothing I enjoy more than killing you with
my bare hands, George, it seems this afternoon I have my work cut out
for me. Because, you see, I am afraid I am going to have to kill all of
you . . . ," he said with feigned regret. "After I have destroyed that book
you wrote, Professor, which might take away my powers."

"You don't *have* any powers, Mr. Rhys. What you have is a terrible
disease," replied the old man, trying to make his voice sound as calm and

convincing as possible. "And if we don't find a cure, it is you who will end up being destroyed, the same as all the other cronotemics. Sooner or later, your molecules will disappear into the void without a trace. Unless, that is, the universe explodes first."

"I see," said Rhys rather wistfully. He thought about it for a few moments and then replied, "But, do you know something, Professor? I don't believe it will destroy me. On the contrary . . . That may happen to those other poor wretches, but, you see, I think the virus has made me immortal . . . It has made me into a kind of god, a being beyond the existence of any universe. Actually, I couldn't care less if I am a superior being or a common invalid. I want to continue to be whatever I am. My powers are astonishing! And now that I understand them fully, and, thanks to you, I have discovered that we live in a multiverse where anything is possible, imagine all the things I could do! I could seduce Madame Bovary, drink Doctor Jekyll's potion, sink Noah's ark with a missile! I am sure I could travel to distant, fantastical worlds . . . Or even jump into neighboring multiverses, before this one explodes . . . And very soon I will become the most powerful being in all Creation! I will be Invisible Death! The God of Chaos! And I will not allow some stupid book to stand in my way!" he finished with a brutal, savage roar.

For a few seconds, the Villain stood panting, a faraway look in his eyes, lost, perhaps, in the labyrinth of his own folly. Suddenly he looked straight at the old man.

"Give me the book, Professor," he ordered with surprising calm, "so that I can throw it on the fire as though it had never existed."

Wells shook his head and squeezed Jane's hand hard. He had no intention of giving Rhys the book. It contained the key to saving the world, and besides . . . it was a whole year's work.

"Really?" said Rhys, with theatrical disappointment. "I am sure I can make you change your mind."

With an incredibly swift movement, he seized Jane's twin by the hair, slammed her head against the table, and pressed the muzzle of his pistol to her temple. Wells's young twin made as if to intervene, but the creature's scowling face stopped him in his tracks, and he simply contemplated the scene as helplessly as the old couple.

"Don't be foolish, George: we both know you are no hero. Why not help me persuade your old teacher instead. Tell him to hand over the damned book or I'll kill her."

The young Wells obeyed instantly. Turning to the old man, he implored, "Give it to him, Professor, for the love of God!"

Wells looked at him with infinite sorrow. That would not save the girl, or them. He knew this better than anyone; true to his name, the Villain would kill them all and destroy the book, or destroy the book and kill them all—it mattered little in what order.

"Right now, that book is the most valuable thing that exists in the entire universe. Do you really think I would be foolish enough to carry it around with me?" Wells improvised.

"Then take me to where the damn thing is before I lose my temper. Perhaps we could all do with some fresh air," muttered the Villain, hissing like a snake preparing to strike its prey.

Wells glanced at Jane's twin, her face still brutally crushed against the table by the creature's translucent hand, and he tried to gain some time.

"Mr. Rhys, listen to me! You and I can come to an agreement. If you allow me to save the universe, I promise I will find the way to make the virus not go beyond your body. After all, I created it. That way, you would be the only one in the entire multiverse with the power to—"

The Villain pointed his weapon at the young Wells, who suddenly found himself staring down the barrel of a pistol; he pulled the trigger without even looking at him. Wells's twin fell to the floor, his head blown off. Rhys smiled and released the girl, who, half-dazed by what had just happened, knelt down and took her beloved's lifeless body in her arms. Fortunately, from where they were standing, the old couple couldn't see this tragic scene. All they glimpsed was the back of the girl's head, which began to shake with her sobs. That was where the Villain aimed his pistol.

"Do you take me for a fool, Professor?" he said wearily, as though bored of the whole affair. "I'll shoot her this time unless you tell me where the book is."

Wells squeezed Jane's hand firmly as he muttered to himself, "Forgive me, forgive me . . ."

The Villain shook his head, visibly displeased by Wells's stubbornness, and pulled the trigger. A blue flash spewed from the barrel. They did not see where the bullet struck, but the girl's sobs stopped abruptly. Rhys glanced casually at the fruits of his wickedness and then grinned at the old couple.

"And then there were three."

"Damn you, you son of a bitch," Wells spluttered, feeling his rage burning in his throat. "I hope you pay for all your crimes."

"I very much doubt it, Professor." The creature grinned. "Well, the time has come to hit you where it hurts most," he said, training the pistol on Jane.

Seeing his wife threatened was enough to make Wells lose any semblance of calm, and the book's destruction and that of the multiverse itself paled into insignificance. He made as if to grab Jane's bag, but she clasped it to her chest. The Villain understood.

"Ah, so that is where it is. Then you are no longer of any use to me, Professor." His pistol swept through the air until it was pointing at Wells. "This is between your charming wife and me."

Wells looked at the muzzle of the pistol trained on him and then at Jane. It broke his heart to see her face contorted with fear, her cheeks damp with tears. He gave her a tender smile, to which her lips responded instantly. There was no need for words. During their many years together, they had learned to communicate with their eyes, and so Wells let all his feelings for Jane flow out from them. Their life had been extraordinary, an adventure worth telling, and he had enjoyed sharing it with her—the best possible traveling companion he could have had on the path toward Supreme Knowledge. I love you, he said to her silently, I love you in all the possible and impossible ways imaginable, and she replied the same . . . but Wells felt that she was speaking to him from very far away. He gazed intently at her beloved face, and he had the impression it was no longer there in front of him but was more like a memory. Then he saw that Jane's eyes were clouded by a kind of giddiness and instantly realized what was happening to her: he knew those symptoms well. He knew that she, too, had understood, and with one final smile, brimming with pride and encouragement, he bade her farewell, wishing her all the luck in the world. Then he turned to face the Villain, who at that precise moment (only a second after Wells had turned to his wife, because a second was all they had needed to tell each other everything I have just told you, dear reader) pulled the trigger. The bullet ripped through Wells's heart, where he kept his love for Jane, as she started to fade, and everything went black.

Jane had to stifle a cry when the man she loved collapsed at her feet. She was grateful not to be able to see the expression on his face because the giddiness was clouding her vision. She wanted to cling to that last look Bertie had given her, the memory of which she would need in order to confront the sinister fate threatening her. She straightened up, turning to face the Villain's pistol. She clutched the bag to her as tightly as she could, so she would not lose it during the jump. Her gesture appeared to amuse Rhys: he was not expecting to have any difficulty wrenching it from her.

"Good-bye, Marcus," said the old lady.

"Good-bye, Mrs. Lansbury." The Villain smiled politely.

He pulled the trigger. But the bullet never hit her. With nothing to hinder it, it flew through the air, slamming into one of the framed photographs on the wall at the level of Jane's heart. The impact caused the glass to shatter into a dozen pieces. It was no longer so easy to identify Wells and his wife in that little boat, he rowing cheerfully while she sat behind, gazing at him with infinite tenderness, as if reality were no more than what they could see and touch and they had all the time in the world to enjoy it together, always together.

30

$\mathcal{E}$XECUTIONER 2087V FINISHED READING AND LEFT
the bundle of papers on the desk. He remained motionless, and
his sphinx-like figure, modeled from the first darkness that enveloped
the world, merged into the shadows.

After a while, he heard a key being inserted clumsily into the front
door, but he did not stir. He was content to trace the movements with his
auditory sensors: he heard his victim open the door, light the oil lamp in
the hall, hobble through to the kitchen, open the pantry door, and put
away a meager bag of groceries. Finally he heard the sound of footsteps
slowly climbing the stairs to where bedroom was, and the tiny study, inside which Death lay in wait. When the footsteps reached the top of the
stairs, they turned toward the bedroom before halting abruptly. The Executioner understood that the Latent had just noticed that the study door
was ajar. There followed a moment's silence, in which the ruthless killer
could feel his victim's fear firing through his circuits. Had someone
opened the study door, his victim must have been wondering, petrified
in the middle of the corridor. Then he heard the footsteps moving cautiously toward where he sat, wrapped in darkness. A shaft of light seeped
into the study as his victim stood in the doorway. Although the sound
it made was barely audible, the Executioner could hear his victim's hand
resting on the door, pushing it open gently, letting the lamplight trace
the contours of the furniture in the study, including the huge shadow
waiting for his victim in the chair. The Executioner rose to his feet, tall
and dark, like an archangel of death, and victim and slayer exchanged

looks for a moment, recognizing each other. The Executioner fingered his cane almost imperceptibly, but Mrs. Lansbury said, "Since you have invited yourself in, I hope you will at least be kind enough to share a cup of tea with me before killing me."

"ER . . . DO YOU TAKE milk?"

The Executioner and Mrs. Lansbury were sitting at the tiny kitchen table, lit only by the flickering flame of the oil lamp. On the table sat a chipped teapot, two steaming cups, and the little porcelain jug, which the old lady had just picked up with trembling fingers.

Executioner 2087V's lips quivered slightly.

"Will I feel more pleasure?"

"Oh . . . well, I think there are differing opinions about that. Personally, I prefer it without, but, alas, this cheap brew is all I can afford, and since I have no biscuits to offer you as an accompaniment, I suggest you take a drop of milk."

There was silence. Followed by more silence.

"All right." The Executioner focused on the diminutive old lady, and she saw something fleeting in his eyes that made them seem for a few moments less terrifying. "Thank you very much, Mrs. Lansbury . . . or should I call you Mrs. Wells?"

The old lady smiled.

"Call me Jane. And I suppose that because I am still alive you must be Executioner . . . 2087V."

The air around the killer nodded imperceptibly. Jane also nodded, serving herself milk after pouring some into the Executioner's steaming cup. Her movements were quick and efficient, despite her hands shaking with old age. She closed her eyes and sipped her tea. As the hot liquid scalded her lips and ran down her throat, she felt her strength renewed. She was alive, she told herself, she was still alive . . . She had succeeded. Her broken old body had survived the onslaught of the years, the torments of loneliness, and here she was at the meeting she and her husband had eagerly awaited for so long. She had only jumped twice, but some deity had heard her prayers, it seemed, and her level of infection had been enough to attract one of those ruthless killers. And not just any one: the one who had opened his mind to Bertie, the one riddled with guilt because of his ghastly mission, the perfect Executioner to whom to entrust *The Map of Chaos* and the salvation of the world. If it weren't for the fact that she no longer had it, of course . . . Jane cursed to herself, then, with a sigh, replaced the cup on the saucer and opened her eyes, only to find the Executioner staring at her fixedly. She couldn't help thinking, despite the immense sadness she felt, that her former world had created one of the most beautiful deaths imaginable. With scientific curiosity she observed the pale hands of that phenomenon, lying inert on the table like two mythical birds left there by some hunter, and then she regarded his face, whose features seemed to have been shaped out of the soft light of dawn and the primeval darkness of night. Well, I never! she reflected, fascinated. And to think we marveled at the automatons created by Prometheus Industries!

"Can you eat and drink?" she inquired with interest, pointing at the cup of tea she had poured for him, which was still untouched.

The Executioner smiled, although it would be more precise to say that his mouth curved like the neck of a dying swan.

"I don't need to, but I can."

The old lady extended a trembling hand toward one of his and caressed it gently, marveling like a child.

"Oh, it is warm . . . I don't think I could tell the difference between that and real skin . . ."

"It *is* skin," the Executioner informed her. "Most of my body is made of synthetic bio-cells."

"But, then . . . what are you?"

"I'm a cybernetic organism. I was made by the best bio-robotic engineers on the Other Side." He paused. "There was a time when I felt proud to say that . . . But not any longer."

"Well, you should try to recapture that feeling," Jane said, looking straight at him. "You are a wonderful . . . creation. I would have given my right arm if we had possessed the technology capable of creating something like you in my generation! Besides, pride is a good thing. It keeps guilt and despair at bay. Believe me, I know. Sometimes, when you have lost everything, pride is the only thing you have left—" The old lady's voice snapped like a dry twig. She raised a wrinkled hand to her lips and blinked a few times until she took hold of herself. "The day my husband was . . . *murdered*," she went on with sudden vehemence, "I jumped into a parallel world, as I assume you must have read in my manuscript . . . There I was, washed up on a strange shore, only this time I was alone, widowed, racked by grief and persecuted by a deranged killer . . . I imagine the easiest thing would have been to admit defeat, to take my own life in the most painless way possible, to let the eternal night of Chaos descend on the universe without caring in the slightest . . . But I realized that not only was the fate of all possible worlds in my hands, but also that of my husband's magnum opus, for which he had sacrificed his life, and for which he should be remembered. And so I swore to myself that one day humanity would be as proud of H. G. Wells as I am." She sighed, smiling sadly at the ruthless killer. "You see, it was pride that made me decide to carry on."

For several seconds another silence fell upon them. Then Jane nodded absentmindedly.

"Bio-robotic engineers . . . ," she said, savoring those words, which evoked the exquisite, distant pleasures of scientific research. "I'd like to know what they would have done, faced with the same terrible circumstances as I . . ."

"And what *did* you do, Jane?"

The old lady looked at him in astonishment. She thought she had perceived in that metallic murmur a curiosity that was so . . . human, almost childlike; she even thought the Executioner's cheeks had turned a subtle shade of pink. Or perhaps they hadn't. Possibly that creature merely reflected his victim's feelings. And *she was his victim,* she reminded herself.

"Oh, you want to know what happened next in the story you read.

Well, after escaping with the book, I carried on with our original plan; what else could I do? True, as an active cronotemic, I could have simply waited for an Executioner to pick up my trail. But I had to bear in mind that I had only jumped once, and there was too much at stake for everything to depend on that, so I saw no harm in continuing to go to séances. At least until I came up with a better idea. I won't go into how I managed to survive in that new world; suffice it to say I didn't fare too badly. In less than a year I had amassed a small fortune thanks to the Mechanical Servant, an invention that revolutionized the wealthiest households in London. It was more of a clever contraption than a serious scientific innovation, and I tried to play it down so as not to draw too much attention to myself, because I hadn't forgotten that the Villain was trailing me. Even so, it made me the richest, most mysterious widow in all London . . ."

Jane smiled as she recalled those days, but something in the Executioner's face—a flicker of impatience, perhaps—made her continue quickly.

"Well, I might tell you that amazing story some other time. The main thing is that money allowed me to spend nearly two years attending hundreds of séances and visiting dozens of haunted houses. Alas, I never bumped into any of our cronotemic twins. I saw a Jane roaming round a graveyard once, but she was in the final stages of the disease, so almost invisible and utterly mad, and therefore of no use to me. The months flew by, and I felt increasingly weak and tired. I began to think that by the time I found a Perfect Twin to whom I could entrust *The Map of Chaos* it would be too late, and yet, even so, I was reluctant to seek out our twins in that world. I couldn't forget the charming couple who had died because of us. I didn't want any more deaths on my conscience . . . And so I decided to revert to my original plan and publish *The Map of Chaos*—not the one my husband had written, but rather my own version. The story I had started writing as a gift for Bertie, in which I narrated in detail how H. G. Wells saved the world, tried at the same time to redeem him from the fact that in order to do so it was necessary for him to first put it in mortal danger. It had begun as a simple pastime in the first world I washed up in, where I experienced the pleasure of boating on the river with the author of *Alice's Adventures in Wonderland* himself. But when the Villain murdered Bertie, forcing me to leap, I was unable to take my manuscript with me and had to start over again. However, this time my intention was to publish it; I thought that if an Executioner were to see my book in a shop window with the Star of Chaos embossed on the cover, he would undoubtedly read it and instantly begin searching for the author. Then, at last, I would be able to give him the real, the genuine *Map of Chaos.* That is why I chose a male author to narrate my story, because in the backward society I was living in, it would have been much more difficult to publish a book written by a woman (even if she was the inventor of the Mechanical Servant) and I needed that to happen as quickly as possible and in as many different countries as possible. I even thought of publishing it under the pseudonym Miles Dyson—the bioscientist who designed the original prototype of the Executioner. My idea was as ingenuous as attending séances in search of the perfect twin, but I could not think of a better one. Unfortunately, before any of my plans bore fruit, the Villain caught up with me again. That happened on 12 September 1888. At the residence of the famous medium known as Lady Amber, the evil Rhys materialized and recognized me instantly. Naturally, he demanded I hand over *The Map of Chaos.* Then he tried to strangle me. Thanks to the intrepid Inspector Cornelius Clayton of Scotland Yard's Special Branch, I managed to escape his clutches. But I no longer had any doubt about what I must do. The Villain had caught up with me. Out of all those infinite parallel universes, he had found the one I was hiding in. And he wouldn't leave until he succeeded in taking from me what he believed was his, and so the moment I arrived home, I wrote a note to the Wells from that world—I chose him because my own twin was still only sixteen at the time—and I can tell you those were the most difficult few lines I have ever written in my life. I had to redraft the note several times, because in my excitement I couldn't find the right words to convince a young man of twenty-two that he must come urgently to the house of a strange old woman in the middle of the night, as a matter of life and death . . . Finally, I finished the note and sent it with my faithful maid, Doris, to Fitzroy Road, where Wells was living with his aunt. Even though I knew there were no walls or doors that could keep the Villain out, I locked myself in my study and waited up all night, shivering with fear and clutching my beloved book, which was all I had left of Ber—"

"I am aware of M's strength," the Executioner interrupted. "He is a powerful level 6 Destructor. None of us has ever been able to catch him."

Jane nodded sadly and continued: "The Wells from that world didn't answer my cry for help. And Doris never returned. I don't know what became of her, or whether my note ever reached its destination . . . In any event, whether it did or not, the Villain found me first. Thankfully, the young Inspector Clayton was with me again when he attacked a second time . . . The detective had come to my house at dawn to ask me about the mysterious events at Madame Amber's the previous evening . . ." Jane smiled almost tenderly. "As soon as I opened the door and saw his pale, solemn face, it struck me that this eccentric young man was the answer I had been waiting for all night. Why not? I told myself. I could trust him. I knew him well . . . or I knew one of his twins, at least. I had seen him fighting off the Martians, and he had seemed like an honest, brave young man . . ." The Executioner's eyebrows arched subtly in what would have been an ironical gesture had it materialized. "Besides, I was desperate!" the old lady defended herself furiously. "And people were not exactly queuing up outside my door to save the world . . . However, I had just begun to explain the situation to Clayton when Rhys broke into my house. I scarcely had time to entrust the inspector with *The Map of Chaos* and beg him to guard it with his life. Clayton slipped the book into his pocket, ordered me to lock myself in my study, and went out to confront the Villain. Soon afterward, I heard crashing from upstairs, followed by the monster's roars, his violent pounding on my study door, and finally a gunshot. Then, for the second time in my life . . . I jumped. Thanks to the fact that I was in my own study, I was able to take the manuscript of *The Map of Chaos* with me. However, as you can see, publishing it in this backward world was impossible. The printing press hadn't yet been invented, and to all appearances wouldn't be for several more centuries. If I went on writing, it was only to stop me from taking my own life. As you can imagine, life here hasn't been exactly easy for me. I was forced to earn my crust by working in arduous, insecure jobs that undermined my already frail health. In this world of lanterns and superstitions, inventing the Mechanical Servant would have been tantamount to an act of witchcraft. And, needless to say, no one held séances. And so, when I reached the point in *The Map of Chaos* where I could no longer go on writing, because I didn't know how the adventure Bertie and I had embarked upon when we leapt through the magic hole ended, I decided to narrate those experienced by my husband's favorite twins. I entitled them respectively *The Map of Time* and *The Map of the Sky*, and I assure you they have been a true balm for my—"

"You don't have the book," the Executioner interrupted again.

The weight of that solitary sentence was sufficient to flatten an anvil.

The old lady looked at him in silence.

"No, I don't," she said at last, a tear rolling down her wizened cheek, tracing the path of her wrinkles. "I jumped into this universe, having left it in the hands of a stranger, to whom I was barely able to explain its importance or what he had to do with it . . . And I swear I have been tormenting myself about it ever since! For the longest time I shed bitter tears and my sleep was haunted by nightmares in which my husband scolded me for not keeping his work safe. Believe me, not a day has gone by when I haven't thought of ending it all. A thousand times I have asked myself what sense there was in continuing . . . But I always came up with the same answer: up until the very moment before Chaos, there is still hope. However slight. Perhaps one day an Executioner would find me, I told myself, and I could explain to him where the book was . . . And now here you are, taking tea with me in my kitchen."

"But you don't know where the book is."

"Of course I do," the old lady replied. "I told you who has it: Cornelius Clayton, from the Special—"

"No. *One of his infinite twins* has it," the Executioner corrected. "And I need to know which."

Jane looked at him imploringly.

"How could I possibly know that? Every night I trawl the multiverse using my twins' minds to try to find the Clayton to whom I gave the book. But so far I have come up with nothing. All I know is that he had a metal hand, a broken heart, and—"

The Executioner swept the air with a movement of his hand that Jane only intuited, unable to discern whether it had been too fast or too slow for her to see.

"Many of his twins will share those same characteristics," he said in a toneless voice. "But only one Clayton has the book. Assuming he has kept his promise and it is still in his possession."

"He *must* have! I told you, the inspector is honest and—"

"Then, to be able to find it, I need to know the coordinates of that universe. That is how my detector works in the multiverse," he said, pointing to his cane. "It calculates the coordinates from the trails left behind by the cronotemics. A mathematical map like the one your husband made would also suffice. But I need something. Possibly something unique to that universe. A single detail that would help me to differentiate it from all the other parallel worlds. If I have been there before, the coordinates will be recorded in my detector's memory."

"Something unique to that universe?" the old lady reflected. "Me! I am unique!" she exclaimed eagerly. "There is only one Observer Jane in the whole multiverse, and I have been in that world . . ."

The Executioner shook his head.

"That's no good. You and I clearly never met in that universe . . . It has to be something that helps me identify that particular universe."

"Hmm . . ." Jane chewed thoughtfully of one of her nails. "Something unique . . . Wait a moment! I invented the Mechanical Servant, so that has to be a unique invention and can therefore only exist in that world! Perhaps you saw it in one of the houses where you went to . . . er, carry out your mission." The Executioner shook his head again, and Jane sighed, discouraged. "All right . . ." She went on thinking. "Let me see . . . They had some delicious biscuits there. Kemp's biscuits, they were called. I have never tasted anything so exquisite! They did not exist in the first world my husband and I traveled to, and they don't have them here either, so . . . well, perhaps they are unique." The old lady observed the Executioner's face. Was it sarcasm she saw there? "Oh, forgive me, you don't usually eat, so that detail would not mean much to you . . . Well, I am sorry, but I can't think of anything else that might be unique to that world . . . Buckingham Palace was in the same spot, the sun rose in the east, the river Thames flowed through the same places, fire burned if you touched it, and there were seven notes in the musical scale . . . Saints alive!" cried the old lady, exasperated. "We are in a multiverse, in case you hadn't noticed," she snapped at the Executioner. "Everything has a copy somewhere! Only you and I are unique. As Doctor Ramsey said, in that accursed séance where the Villain found me: every reality is an imitation of itself . . ."

The Executioner rose abruptly from his chair. His immense silhouette stood out against the wall, accompanied by an even bigger shadow.

"Did you say Doctor Ramsey?"

"Yes, I think that was his name."

"Was he a professor at the Faculty of Medicine, a surgeon, chemist, biologist, a tall man with an infuriating habit of cracking his knuckles?"

"Yes, how did you know that?"

The Executioner was seized by a series of convulsive spasms. The old lady stood up, withdrawing a few paces, afraid he was suffering from some kind of short circuit and might explode at any moment.

"Are you all right?" she whispered.

"I feel mirth," replied the Executioner, who after a couple more spasms seemed to calm down. "Doctor Ramsey is as unique as you and I, Jane. He's a Scientist from the Other Side who is conducting field studies in this multiverse."

Jane's mouth was agape.

"There are Scientists here?" she managed to stammer. "Bertie and I thought that you kill . . . you Executioners . . . were the only ones."

"And to begin with we were. When the Scientists opened the first wormhole, they sent us ahead. In those days, we weren't killers, we were explorers. We arrived here, discovered the nature of this multiverse, set up communication antennae, recorded images, took all manner of samples back to the Other Side; we even designed our own canes . . . All so that the Scientists could study this universe from the Other Side in comfort and safety. However, when they discovered the epidemic, they modified us. They reprogrammed us to turn us into . . . ruthless killers. And finally, when they realized that studying from a distance wasn't providing satisfactory results, they decided to send a few men and women to this multiverse to carry out field studies. It was a difficult decision, but they had no choice. For hundreds of years on the Other Side, humans had been genetically modified to withstand extremely low temperatures, and those chosen had to undergo urgent adjustments so they wouldn't melt from the heat in this world. They received refrigeration implants and electro-neuronal circuits to inhibit the anguish of randomness. Only those with the most brilliant minds and resilient bodies were sent out to different worlds, but none of them obtained any results. The Scientists came from such a distant future that none of them had a twin in this multiverse. And so they never developed the miraculous gift you and your husband possessed, thanks to which you discovered where the first infection took place. Only you were able to see and know everything."

"And yet we never saw them!"

"Don't be angry, Jane. It is logical. There are only a few Scientists in this infinite multiverse, and their work is clandestine. They are extremely careful not to give themselves away. They don't get their hands dirty. They leave that to us."

Jane looked frantically around the room. Suddenly, she pummeled the table with every ounce of strength her feeble body possessed.

"Are you saying that during that séance I was sitting next to a Scientist from the Other Side, someone to whom I could have entrusted *The Map of Chaos*? Are you saying I could have ended that whole nightmare there and then and prevented all that suffering, all those deaths?"

"Yes."

Jane opened her mouth to reply but instead slumped in her chair and, burying her face in her hands, started to cry.

The Executioner took a step toward her.

"Jane."

The old lady shook her head weakly.

"Jane."

"What, for goodness' sake?" she said, looking up.

A bluish light had begun to emanate from the eight-pointed star on the Executioner's cane, illuminating the entire kitchen. Jane looked around in awe. It felt as though they were at the bottom of an ocean from which all the fish had been banished.

"My detector is connected to the minds of all the Scientists from the Other Side in this multiverse," the Executioner informed her in his distant, metallic voice. "It is part of my job. I can locate them and go to wherever they are. Generally speaking, they don't like to have anything to do with us. They despise us. But occasionally one of them needs us to take him to another world to carry on his research there. Ramsey, however, has never moved from the first world he appeared in."

For a few seconds Jane simply stared at him. Then the Supreme Knowledge sparked an idea. She summoned all her remaining strength and smiled.

The air around the Executioner smiled back at her.

31

ND SO, LADIES AND GENTLEMEN, THE dreaded Day of Chaos has finally arrived! The day when your world and all other possible worlds will end! But how can I begin to describe such an extraordinary day, especially when most of what I have to tell you will be happening simultaneously? Is it possible to explain Chaos in an orderly fashion? I doubt it, but despite my limited skills as a storyteller, I shall do my best. Allow me to disappear through the hidden trapdoor in Mrs. Lansbury's kitchen and return to a stage with which you are more familiar, to the world where old Baskerville died, to a few days after the fire that burned Brook Manor to the ground. It is September 23 in this universe, a brisk wind announces the arrival of autumn, and dawn trembles before the night like an awkward young lover, afraid to divest her of her darkness, if you will excuse my purple prose.

Good, then it only remains for me to choose with which of the many actors who will take part in this performance to begin my tale. Although, for the moment, only three of them are awake, so that shouldn't be too difficult. Wells is in the kitchen putting a kettle on the fire. A few seconds later, Inspector Clayton hurries down the corridor to take his kettle, which is whistling like mad, off the fire. Before long, the whistle of a third kettle begins to sound at Captain Sinclair's house, causing his beloved wife, Marcia, to give a start in bed. Which of these tea-loving early risers should I decide upon?

I choose Wells, for no other reason than the fondness I have developed for him after narrating his adventures for so long. As I said before, although dawn has not yet broken, our author is already in the kitchen, having been woken by a loud bang from somewhere in the house. The window, the accursed attic window, he had muttered after recovering from the shock, and, still half-asleep, he had gotten out of bed to close it before the chorus of crashes woke up his wife. It was too early yet to listen to Jane nagging him again about his sheer idleness when it came to addressing minor domestic problems. However, when he reached the attic, he had found the window closed. He stood gaping at it for a few seconds. Then, as if one thing led inevitably to the other, he went down to the kitchen to put the kettle on.

Next, he headed for the sitting room, which he surveyed carefully from the doorway. Everything seemed in its place. Puzzled, he walked over to the window, where the garden was timidly revealing itself in the first light of day. Perhaps he had merely imagined the noise. Lately, he had been more nervous than usual, which was hardly surprising given that, only a few days before, his world had been turned completely upside down. He had encountered a twin of his from a parallel universe, in a state of surprising decrepitude, and had watched him die at the hands of an invisible man at Brook Manor. This had all obliged him to believe in more things than his brain seemed willing to accept in such a short space of time.

The whistling kettle interrupted his thoughts. He hurriedly removed it from the hob, praying this fresh uproar wouldn't wake his wife. That cup of tea no longer seemed so urgent . . . It was then he noticed that on the kitchen table there were three cups, which he hadn't put there. He stood gaping at them, wondering whether, for some absurd reason, Jane had put them out before going to bed. And yet, he could have sworn they weren't there when he came in to put the kettle on. And there were three of them. Then one of the drawers in the dresser slid open slowly, and three teaspoons floated toward the table, landing gracefully next to the cups.

"Bertie?" his wife's voice rang out from upstairs.

"Jane, whatever you do, don't—"

But before Wells could finish his sentence, a knife rose from the draining board, arced through the air like a salmon leaping upstream, and pressed itself against his neck. This didn't surprise him. Clayton had warned them that sooner or later they would all be forced to resume their duel with the Invisible Man.

"Oh, let's invite your charming wife to join us for breakfast, George," said the voice that for nights on end had plagued his dreams. "Why do you think I put out three cups?"

With the knife at his throat and his back arched over the stove, Wells heard his wife padding down the stairs. She walked into the kitchen, still half-asleep, wearing her nightdress, and with her hair hanging down her face.

"What are you doing, dear? Why don't you go come back to bed?" she asked before noticing her husband's strange posture, the pallor of his face, and the knife pressing against his throat, apparently with no one holding it. "Oh, B-Bertie . . . ," she stammered. "He is here . . ."

"Good morning, Mrs. Wells," said the knife, moving away from her husband's neck and floating toward her. "What a pleasure to meet you again."

Jane swallowed, unable to take her eyes off the hovering knife.

"And how considerate of you to come down without your hairpins; you've no idea how glad I am." A chair slid out from under the table. "Be so good as to sit down, Mrs. Wells."

Jane obeyed, and Wells saw an invisible hand gather up her hair, revealing her graceful neck and, in a flash, the knife pressing against it. The sharp blade made her shudder.

"Don't hurt her, you son of a . . . ," Wells cried, making as if to hasten toward her.

"Stay right there!" the voice commanded. "Don't force me to kill you both again, George. I've done it so many times now that, quite frankly, it is starting to bore me."

Wells looked anxiously at his wife, who was pursing her lips with the forced determination of someone trying desperately not to give way to panic. He tried to speak calmly, but the voice that came out sounded more like a pitiful howl.

"Please . . . I beg you. You are making a dreadful mistake. We don't have what you want."

"A dreadful mistake, you say?" A dark guffaw spread like a drop of ink through the air, darkening it. "No, George. I know you have the book somewhere. The old woman gave it to you. I am absolutely certain of that. H. G. Wells wrote *The Map of Chaos*. His wife took it away with her when I killed him and then gave it back to H. G. Wells, ingeniously completing the circle! I'll grant her that, at least."

"What?" Wells looked nonplussed.

"Don't make me lose my patience, George," the voice snapped. "I warn you, it is running out fast."

"I haven't the faintest idea what you are talking about!" Wells yelled, red with rage.

"You're lying," hissed the Villain. "And you don't know how sad that makes me."

The tip of the knife suddenly broke Jane's skin, causing her to squeal. A shiny drop of blood began to trickle down her neck, like a stream meandering down a hillside.

"Please, no, please . . . ," Wells implored. "I swear I don't have the accursed book . . ."

"Really?" The tip of the knife crept up his wife's neck and began circling her right eye menacingly. "Good. I've been looking forward to inflicting on your little wife the excruciating pain of having an eye plucked out."

"Stop, stop!" cried Wells. "All right, you win! I'll tell you where the book is!"

"Don't, Bertie," whispered Jane. "He'll kill us anyway . . ."

"You are as intelligent as you are beautiful, my dear lady," the Invisible Man hissed in her ear. "Yes, I might kill you anyway. But, Jane, let me tell you that there are many different ways to die . . ."

Wells took a step forward, his hands raised in a gesture of surrender.

"The book is in the Chamber of Marvels!"

The knife paused.

"And where the devil is that?" growled the voice.

"I'll take you there . . . ," said Wells, "when you tell me who you are and why the book is so important."

Behind Jane's head, the silence hesitated for a few moments.

"Didn't the old lady explain that when she gave it to you?" the Villain asked suspiciously. "I find that hard to believe, George . . ."

Wells looked with infinite weariness at the empty space looming behind his wife. Then he shrugged.

"I wasn't given the book by any old lady . . . Why would I insist on lying to you? However, I know where it is. That is all I know, apart from the fact that you, once you have the book, will kill us. Which is why I don't intend to plead for our lives. All I ask is that you do it quickly and that you grant us the right to know why we are going to die . . ."

The knife appeared to reflect.

"Very well, George," the voice purred. "But I warn you, if you are trying to buy time, it won't do you any good. I have all the time in all the worlds at my disposal!" Suddenly the knife moved away from Jane's face, slicing through the air as if the creature had spread his arms in a theatrical gesture. "So . . . you want to know who I am!" the voice roared. "Are you sure you want to know? I am the most powerful being in all creation! I am the epilogue of mankind! When the universe comes to an end, only I will remain . . . presiding over all your accursed graves. My name is Marcus Rhys, and I am the God of Chaos!"

And he began to tell his story.

32

OWEVER, DEAR READER, UNLIKE THE
Wellses, you already know Rhys's story, and so in the
meantime I will take the opportunity to scan the board in search of one
of the other pieces in this game. What would you say if we jumped forward to dawn and took a look at Doyle, whose carriage has just this minute dropped him off outside Murray's London town house? Despite the
early hour, Doyle already has his habitual air of contained energy, like a
cup of coffee about to spill over. After taking a few deep breaths to allow
the cold morning air to purify his lungs, he stepped through the ornate
entrance gates. But he had scarcely taken a few steps when something
made him come to an abrupt halt. He glanced uneasily down the drive
leading to the house, as though unable to believe his own eyes. Yet they
weren't mistaken: hanging from the branches of every tree bordering the
path were hundreds of mirrors of all shapes and sizes, swaying in the
breeze like a new species of fruit, stretching the boundaries of the world
they reflected and creating fresh, dizzying perspectives. Doyle stood
for several minutes, shaking his head in disbelief, before heaving a sigh
and carrying on walking. So that was how Murray intended to find the
Emma that existed on the other side of the looking glass. And it also explained why he hadn't attended the meeting with Inspector Clayton or
returned any of Doyle's calls . . . How could he, if since their return from
Brook Manor he had been trawling through all the stores and antique
emporiums in London in search of that colorful assortment of mirrors.
And that wasn't all. He had ordered his army of servants to keep watch

over them, too, as Doyle discovered when he saw the maids, footmen, and other domestic staff dotted along the drive, sitting on chairs in front of their assigned trees, each holding a bell in his or her hand. No doubt they had been ordered to ring if Emma Harlow, their master's hapless fiancée, appeared before them in defiance of every law of physics. It was no surprise that their expressions alternated between bewilderment, tedium, and even superstitious fear. Unsure whether to be amazed or alarmed at this foolishness, Doyle continued down the path, his burly frame reflected from every conceivable angle.

When he reached the house, he discovered that the front was also plastered with mirrors, glittering in the sun like the scales of some enormous dragon. The front door was wide-open, so he walked in without ringing the bell. Doyle wandered round the hallway and the spacious main reception room, which were also infested with mirrors, calling out to Murray in his booming ogre's voice. In one of the rooms, he came across Murray's dog, Buzz, sitting very still in front of a huge mirror leaning against the wall, as if he, too, were convinced that sooner or later his mistress would appear there. Doyle snorted. This was ludicrous. He patted the dog's head resignedly.

"Mr. Doyle, we weren't expecting you today!" a voice behind him rang out.

Doyle wheeled round to find Elmer, Murray's valet.

"Well, in fact, we weren't expecting anyone," the young man added with a shrug, as though apologizing for having been unable to stop the house from being turned into a fairground attraction. Elmer was accustomed to his master's eccentricities, but this was beyond even him.

"Yes, I see, Elmer," Doyle said, sympathizing. "Where is he?"

"In the garden next to the conservatory, sir."

Doyle left the sitting room almost at a march, determined to put a stop to this madness. The gardens to the right of the house were also overrun with looking glasses. Leaning against fountains, tied to hedgerows, and even floating in ponds, hundreds of them reproduced the world around them, amplifying it and endowing it with secret corners.

The leaves were beginning to turn, and the fiery red of autumn multiplied by the mirrors gave the impression that some lunatic had set the garden on fire. Doyle shook his head as he walked toward the conservatory, an impressive glass replica of the Taj Mahal. He spotted Murray standing in front of it in his shirtsleeves, busy arranging what looked like a Stonehenge of mirrors around an armchair, from which he would be able to survey twenty at once simply by turning his head. At that moment, he was trying to prop up a gigantic Venetian mirror with the aid of several stones.

"Good morning, Gilliam," Doyle announced as he approached.

Murray glanced up at him absentmindedly. "Well, well, look who we have here," he murmured. "What happened to the time-honored tradition of informing people you are coming?"

"I sent you a telepathic message; didn't you hear me?" Doyle jested.

Murray smiled grudgingly. "No. Clearly I am only receptive during a fire. In any case, Arthur, you and I are probably the only two people in England who possess a telephone. You should use it more often; it is easier than it looks."

"I telephoned several times, Gilliam! But your servants are clearly too busy to answer."

Murray shrugged, as if he had no say over what his servants did. He made sure the Venetian mirror was firmly secured, then stood upright and looked Doyle up and down, examining his injuries.

"You're in a sorry state . . . ," he muttered as he contemplated Doyle's ear, his bandaged hand, and his face covered in tiny burns. "Though I imagine the soldier in you is proud of his battle scars. And how is the Great Ankoma?"

"Oh, Woodie has almost fully recovered from his concussion. Although, after what happened at Brook Manor, he seems convinced he is a genuine medium and goes round capturing mysterious presences all over the house."

"Why don't you tell him the truth?" Murray asked casually.

"I shall when it ceases to amuse me," Doyle replied sardonically.

Then it was his turn to look Murray up and down. "You're in a sorry state yourself, Gilliam. How long is it since you slept?"

"I have no time to sleep, Arthur! As you see, I'm very busy."

"Yes, I can see," Doyle sighed, contemplating the circle of mirrors. "And what are you hoping to achieve with all this?"

Murray looked at him, irritated.

"What am I hoping to achieve? Why, I am hoping to find Emma, of course."

"Yes, but, Gilliam . . ."

Murray swung round abruptly and walked over to where a load of mirrors lay in piles or leaned haphazardly against one another next to the conservatory.

Doyle had no choice but to follow him. "Don't you think this is all rather unscientific?"

"Is that what you came here to tell me, Arthur?"

"No," Doyle replied in a placatory tone. "I came here to tell you about the meeting George and I had with Inspector Clayton after we got back from the moor, which incidentally you didn't attend . . ."

"Inspector Clayton . . . Ah, yes, I remember." Murray scanned the pile of mirrors and seized one with a frame that seemed to be made of solid gold. "A rather awkward one," he added with a sigh, so that Doyle was unsure whether he was referring to the inspector or the mirror.

Making a huge effort, he resolved to maintain a friendly tone, at least for the moment. "Well, I won't deny that this Clayton fellow is a little . . . impertinent. And I understand that you didn't want to see him . . . Wells told me about how determined he was to investigate your time-travel company, and how he even accused Wells of orchestrating a Martian invasion at some point. But wasn't Inspector Clayton the person Baskerville said we should see before he died, because he had *The Map of Chaos*? Who else could we have consulted regarding invisible killers, universal travelers, and mirrors that are portals between worlds? We had no choice, Gilliam. And, regardless of all that, you should have come, as it was an extremely interesting meeting," he added mysteriously.

Murray indicated with a nod that he should pick up the other end of the mirror and help him carry it. Doyle gritted his teeth and did as Murray asked.

"After we had given him a summary of what happened at Brook Manor," Doyle went on, gasping as they inched their way over to the circle of mirrors, "Clayton admitted that he had *The Map of Chaos* and told us he had already come across the creature at a fake séance in 1888."

"Really?" Murray said, signaling with his chin the place where he wanted the mirror to go.

After resting it on the ground, Doyle, out of breath, explained to Murray that the Invisible Man had tried to steal the book from an old lady who had also been at the séance, but that Clayton had managed to stop him. However, he had failed to arrest the creature because he had vanished into thin air, exactly the way he did at Brook Manor when he, Murray, shot him with the crossbow. The old lady had also disappeared, but not before she gave Clayton the book, although she managed only to tell him it contained the key to saving this and all other possible worlds and that he must protect it with his life, for she was certain the creature would come back to destroy it.

"Do you realize what I am saying, Gilliam? The book has been in Clayton's possession all this time, but for some reason the monster believes Wells has it . . ."

"Yes." Murray nodded thoughtfully.

Encouraged, Doyle went on. "Good, good . . . So, if what the old lady said is true and the book contains the key to saving all the worlds, and the creature finds it, or if he finds Wells . . ."

"Yes." Murray nodded again, directing his gaze at his circle of mirrors. "There: I think every corner is reflected now, and that is the most important thing, because she could be anywhere."

"You aren't listening to me, damn it!" exclaimed Doyle. "What I am trying to tell you is that your beloved friend George is in mortal danger, and possibly the entire universe to boot!"

Murray stared at him blankly for a few moments.

"Let's go to the conservatory," he said.

Once again, Doyle was forced to follow him. When they went in, he was surprised to find the place empty.

"Emma used to spend a lot of time in here tending her flowers," Murray explained. "So I have taken everything out in order to fill it with mirrors. I am expecting another delivery from Bristol this afternoon, which Elmer ordered."

"Splendid," Doyle retorted. "Look, Murray, I sympathize with your obsess—I mean, your *interest* in finding Emma, but what I am telling you ought to interest you as well. If what the old lady predicted twelve years ago is true, and the end of the world is upon us, you won't have much chance of finding Emma, will you? The quicker we sort out this mess, the better, because we don't know how much time we have left. So, listen carefully: I think the key to it all lies in the story Baskerville told Clayton . . ."

"Baskerville?" Murray asked, looking at him in astonishment.

"Yes, Baskerville, Baskerville," Doyle replied, trying not to lose his patience. "Apparently, your coachman went to see Clayton about six or seven months ago. It seems the old man had met one of Clayton's twins in another world, and together they had tried to defeat a . . . Martian invasion. And so, when the Hunters came after him, he considered turning to Clayton. Wells hoped the Clayton in this world would be able to help him, the way his twin had in the other universe. Even so, for a while he refrained from going to see him—after all, he had been fairly successful in avoiding the Hunters for two years, and during the previous couple of months he thought he had finally given them the slip. But when Wells saw the watcher on the moor, he realized they had caught up with him again, and, too worn-out by then to continue facing the situation alone, he resolved to turn to Clayton, praying he would believe him and, more important, that he would offer some solution . . . *Our* Clayton did believe him, though he knew nothing about those killers. But when Baskerville described the symbol on their canes, he recognized it as the same eight-pointed star adorning the cover of *The Map of Chaos*! That is why he showed Baskerville the book, in the hope he might be able to give him some information about it, but the old man knew nothing . . . Although clearly the Hunters, the book, the invisible creature, and the journeys between worlds are all connected . . . We just have to find out how!"

Murray nodded as he glanced about thoughtfully.

"Hmm . . . how many mirrors do you reckon will fit in here, Arthur?" he said.

Doyle could contain himself no longer.

"But what the devil is the matter with you, Gilliam?" he exploded. "Do you care so little about what might happen to George and Jane? For God's sake, man, they are your friends! And what about the universe? Don't you care about the end of the world?"

Murray looked at him resentfully. "And what could I possibly do for the universe that you, our most eminent thinkers, aren't already doing?" he said sarcastically. "Arthur Conan Doyle, Inspector Clayton, H. G. Wells, and his brilliant wife . . . With all of you working to solve the problem, I can sleep easily in the knowledge that the universe is in good hands. But meanwhile . . . who is bothering to look for Emma? No one!" he roared suddenly, pointing accusingly at Doyle, who contemplated him in astonishment. "And yet you promised you would help me find her! You swore to me at Brook Manor, before confronting the invisible creature, that if we came out of there alive, you would devote the rest of your life to solving that riddle. You told me if there was some way of getting to Emma, you would find it! And I believed you! I took you at your word! I believed your damnable chivalrous posturing!"

Doyle waited for Murray to calm down, looking at him sorrowfully, and then he said, "And I meant it, Gilliam. Otherwise, why would I be doing this? Or do you honestly believe this method of yours is going to work?" he exclaimed crossly, pointing at all the mirrors. "I am absolutely convinced that the only way to discover the path that leads to your beloved Emma is by understanding what is going on all around us. As I said before: everything is connected. Everything. If I manage to solve the case of this mysterious book, not only will I save Wells and probably the entire universe, I will also discover the underlying nature of things . . . Do you realize what that means, Gilliam? I used to toy with the idea of writing a book about Spiritualism, but what is that compared to a theory that explains everything we are and all that is around us? I shall call it the theory of manifold worlds. And, you see, Gilliam, once I have truly grasped reality, I will also understand how to travel between worlds and will be able to guide you to the Emma in the mirror, just as I promised."

Murray looked skeptically at his friend, hesitating to show any enthusiasm. He was still angry, although he had to admit there was some sense in what Doyle was saying.

"Very well . . . ," he muttered, "how can I help you?"

"In lots of ways. We have devised a plan, which I will explain later . . . but first of all, I need you tell me everything you discovered on your trips to the fourth dimension in the *Cronotilus,* because in light of what we know now, it seems increasingly clear that the pink plain is an antechamber between those parallel worlds. I am convinced it contains many clues, possibly even the solution of how to reach Emma."

Murray looked at Doyle in disbelief and then smiled ruefully.

"Is that your plan for finding Emma?" he said, visibly disappointed. "Then I fear we never shall."

"What makes you say that?" Doyle said, surprised. "I feel sure there is a doorway leading to her on the pink plain—probably very similar to the hole that you thought took you to the year 2000, and much easier to pass through than a mirror."

Murray sighed.

"Do you want to know the whole truth about the fourth dimension?"

"Of course." Doyle nodded excitedly.

"Very well." Murray breathed another sigh. "Then I think you are in for a greater surprise than you bargained for."

But wait a moment, dear reader! Whilst Murray and Doyle are embroiled in their discussion, oblivious to all that is happening around them, I can see everything willy-nilly, and I have just noticed that the hundreds of mirrors with which Murray has adorned his property have stopped reflecting what is in front of them. Instead of contemplating their own bored expressions in the looking glasses Murray had told them to watch over, the maids and footmen were seeing quite different images, strange worlds they could never have conjured in their own imaginations. One mirror revealed a valley of silky grass through which a herd of centaurs was galloping; another a huge amphibious creature, its back bristling with spikes as it bobbed on a greenish ocean; another a grey wilderness with thick, driving rain and dazzling lightning bolts, where enormous metallic beetles fought to survive; another a landscape of toadstools as tall as trees, on which caterpillars wearing waistcoats and frock coats conversed with one another; another a cluster of floating castles drifting through lilac clouds, with waterfalls flowing from them like fringes made of foam; another the dome of St. Paul's, over which at that very moment flew a magnificent pterodactyl.

Of course, none of the servants were aware that these were the infinite stages of the theater collapsing and colliding, the myriad different worlds crashing against one another. The end of the world had begun, ladies and gentlemen. But instead of trumpets, it was heralded by the frenzied tinkle of a hundred bells.

33

*F*IFTEEN MINUTES EARLIER, DR. RAMSEY HAD gotten out of bed, unaware that this was the last day of the universe. He liked rising at a quarter to eight in order to perform his ablutions, which included, among other things, a perilous shave with the rudimentary razor from that world. Unlike his colleagues, who had brought electric shavers with them in their trousseaus of microscopic and sundry devices from the Other Side, Ramsey felt a sentimental attachment to that relic from the past. He considered that the slow, measured rhythm it required of him was the best way to help him adapt to the unhurried pace of that world. After managing to finish his conventional shave without slitting his throat, he went down to the dining room, unaware that behind him in the bathroom mirror an intricate maze had appeared, in the midst of which stood a bored-looking Minotaur. With his customary punctuality, Ramsey's servant had just laid out his peculiar breakfast: a cup of coffee swimming in ice cubes, different types of fruit arranged on a thick bed of crushed ice, and assorted flavors of ice cream. After casting a doleful glance through the window at the sunny autumn day outside, Ramsey sat down at the table with a faint sigh, cracked his knuckles, picked up the newspaper, and began to read the headlines on that ordinary September 23, 1900, unaware that, as I have already told you, dear reader, in the world he inhabited at least, this was the dreaded Day of Chaos.

He turned the pages wearily, no news items drawing his attention, since most of the articles were still reporting on the powerful hurricane that had razed the city of Galveston, Texas, to the ground on September 8, with the loss of approximately eight thousand souls. Ramsey looked with vague curiosity at some of the photographs showing dozens of carts brimming with dead bodies and endless funeral pyres dotted along the beach, where they were incinerating the hideously bloated corpses that the ocean continued to disgorge onto the sand. Ramsey pulled a face and carried on thumbing nonchalantly through the newspaper. After all these years, he still couldn't help being surprised at the dreadful fuss the humans on this side made whenever Nature flexed her muscles, as if they had never heard of the second law of thermodynamics. Chaos is inevitable, he muttered to himself. The same law had been discovered in the majority of worlds in that multiverse, and yet its inhabitants seemed to take great pains to ignore it. Tornados, earthquakes, meteorites, ice ages . . . such phenomena terrified and astonished them in equal measure, despite being as insignificant as a couple of mosquito bites that only affected their minuscule planet, nothing compared to the Dark Era, the frozen, black, irreversible end that awaited the entirety of the universes . . . and that he had seen with his own eyes.

He set the newspaper aside wearily, dropped a couple more ice cubes into his coffee, and, leaning back in his chair, began to stare into the distance, beyond the encircling walls, beyond the universe he found himself in at present, beyond all the worlds that coexisted in that room, recalling with sorrow the protracted war his civilization had decided to wage on chaos, which still wasn't over.

Ever since the Victorian age, long before he was born, the inhabitants of the Other Side had been trying to find a way to flee their doomed universe. For thousands of years they had been trying, even as the stars gradually began to die out and the firmament grew darker every night, but without success. And currently they had to confront another, more urgent problem of an almost domestic nature: the extinction of their own Sun, which had gradually turned into a red giant star, filling the sky and forcing the Earth's inhabitants to seek refuge beneath the sea. There they had built splendid underwater cities where the Church continued to guide the minds and hearts of its flock toward the Supreme Knowledge. Ramsey had no trouble imagining the giant squid that dwelled in the ocean's depths, where they had implanted their new Palace of Knowledge, yawning at the innumerable debates they had to have before deciding what to do next, while above them the oceans boiled and the mountains melted. Fortunately, they reached a decision in time: by drawing a couple of asteroids into the Earth's orbit, they managed slowly to steer the planet safely away from the raging ball of fire that had already swallowed Mercury and Venus. This ingenious solution bought them a little more time in which to carry on working on the only solution they considered ultimately viable: the Great Exodus to a different universe through a wormhole. However, successive generations failed to stabilize one of these holes, and after several more millennia as a red giant, the Sun finally exhausted its store of nuclear energy and cooled down, shrinking until it became a white dwarf, a tiny, pale speck that the cosmic winds eventually snuffed out, like a god blowing out a match. By that time, the universe had taken on a desolate air: most of the stars had burned out, and the planets orbiting around them had frozen over. The only surviving source of light and heat were the red dwarfs, tiny stars whose nuclear energy burned very slowly, giving off a weak, sickly light. The remarkable QIII civilization once more found a way of relocating the Earth's orbit around one of those dying fireflies, the Proxima Centauri, only 4.2 light-years away, and in its meager glow, mankind continued its research, impervious to discouragement. Even so, there were many who started to lose hope. They thought they would never succeed, that they would never escape the cold, dingy vault they had been confined to since the Creator had shut out the last rays of light, plunging them into eternal darkness. But they did. When Proxima Centauri's energy was almost expended, nearly all the other red dwarfs in the universe had expired. Mankind had remodeled the human body through genetic mutation, replacing most of the organs with mechanical parts in order to endure the freezing temperatures. Then they succeeded, managing to open a stable two-way wormhole, perfectly suitable for transmitting vast quantities of complex data, a passageway they could open and close at will and that led to a new universe, in a mid-stelliferous era, brimming with stars, trillions upon trillions of glistening bright lights illuminating the heavens from one side to the other. When they discovered that this was a multiple universe, consisting of infinite parallel universes, their joy was even greater, for it seemed that in a sudden gesture of magnanimity the Creator had given them the possibility of choosing, from among infinite worlds, which one they considered most suitable to be reborn in. The celebrations lasted for days and days. The Church of Knowledge declared holidays and bestowed praise and honors. Until, that is, they discovered that the multiverse was ailing, that the wormhole had taken them to a polluted paradise.

Ramsey placed his coffee cup on the table with a sigh and cracked his knuckles one by one. That awful discovery had been made three generations before, by his very own great-grandfather, the famous Scientist Timothy Ramsey. He was part of the team that had identified the epidemic after isolating the virus in the blood of a cronotemic the Executioners had captured and sent back to the Other Side for them to study. Of course, those poor wretches had lost their minds and died hours after their arrival in a world that must have seemed nightmarish to them, enveloped by a pitch-black sky, on whose horizon the only thing visible was an immense, terrifying vortex, darker than darkness itself, churning slowly and menacingly. Everything there seemed frozen, even time itself, and they had perished from exposure and from fear, clueless as to why they were dying or indeed where they were. But at least their warm blood had provided a few, albeit extremely discouraging, answers for that QIII civilization, which was almost out of options. When Proxima Centauri died, the inhabitants of the Other Side had used up all their remaining energy dragging the Earth into the orbit of a black hole, whose slow evaporation was one of the last, meager energy sources in the universe. This was another clever move, yet everyone knew there was nowhere else to go. When that source was extinguished forever, the temperature would reach absolute zero, the atoms would stop moving, the protons would disintegrate, and all intelligent life would be irremediably wiped out. Under such circumstances, the discovery of the epidemic was devastating. They no longer had the time or the energy to open up another magic hole to another universe. They realized then that there was only one possible solution: to try to cure the multiverse they had found, however small their hope of success.

Ramsey stood up, went over to the window, and contemplated the street, noticing with sadness how eternal and beautiful everything appeared when viewed from behind glass: in the distance the shiny dome of St. Paul's Cathedral stood out against the deep-blue sky, two men were chatting beneath his window, a couple were stepping out of a carriage, a pair of ragamuffins were sprinting along the pavement as if they had just stolen something, and the flower girl was arranging her blooms with the same care as every morning, all of them oblivious to the fact that they were living in a world that would soon come to an end. Would they carry on strolling beneath that autumn sun if an enormous ship suddenly appeared in the middle of the street, its cannons roaring, or if the earth spewed out a plague of giant ants? When the myriad parallel worlds started to collide, freakish visions such as these would surely appear before the Great Annihilation. The different universes and their realities would become jumbled up, the inhabitants of the infinite worlds thrown together before being shaken by the hand of an inebriated God and tossed onto the same board. And none of them would have a clue to what was happening. The only ones who knew would be Ramsey himself and a few other fortunate souls, if indeed they could consider themselves as such.

He clicked his tongue and walked back to the table to pour himself another cup of iced coffee before beginning his working day, which promised to be a particularly exhausting one. Fortunately, he told himself, the efforts made by those generations were finally about to bear fruit, or so it seemed. For the past twelve years, various scientists had been working on the blood sample Dr. Higgins had taken from Inspector Cornelius Clayton, and after countless experimental serums they had succeeded in synthesizing an effective vaccine. What a stroke of luck to have been able to obtain a blood sample from such a unique subject, Ramsey reflected. After exhaustive studies using the most advanced microscopes both there and on the Other Side, the CoCla cells, named in honor of their donor, had soon revealed that they were capable of isolating the virus and, in time, destroying it. When a natural Jumper had infected a suitable receptor, a miraculous combination had occurred, giving rise to a mutation that appeared to contain the definitive cure for the disease.

It made Ramsey sad to think of Armand de Bompard, the original champion of the theory, who had not lived to see the results of the line of research he himself had initiated. Bompard had always maintained that the key to combating the epidemic of cronotemics probably resided in the nature of the Jumpers, whose existence Scientists from the Other Side had become aware of when carrying out more in-depth studies of that multiverse. These were individuals who might have been sucked through specific hyperproximity points and who could jump between worlds naturally, with no need to be infected by a virus. The first known jumps dated back to long before the first appearance of that confounded epidemic, and so it was safe to suppose that the phenomenon had always existed. In any event, unlike the cronotemics, who traveled through the multiverse like cancerous cells, growing malignantly and destroying the healthy fabric of the universe, which hadn't the time or space to regenerate itself, the natural Jumpers wrought no such havoc, so that by studying them they might find answers. Convinced that his theory was correct, Armand de Bompard had been one of the first to volunteer to do fieldwork on this side. Although, according to what Ramsey had heard, after several years of fruitless research, Bompard had been on the verge of abandoning that line of investigation and would doubtless have done so if one morning he had not come across a pretty little girl lost and alone in a forest.

Bompard had been unable to resist taking her under his wing, suspecting almost from the beginning that she was not of this world. He gave her the appropriate tests, but, to his surprise, he found no trace of the cronotemia virus in her blood. He realized then that he had a natural Jumper living in his castle, and no ordinary one at that, as he would soon discover to his horror, but one who came from a very distant world. Bompard had heard rumors about such specimens but had never come across any, let alone been able to examine one. Very few beings managed to jump between such distinct worlds, and when they did, their strange natures inevitably turned them into monsters in the eyes of their new neighbors. Bompard realized that this little girl, whom he called Valerie, must have come from one of the most remote sectors of that multiverse, where, according to reports, vegetable, mineral, and animal were fused into one; where sentient and nonsentient beings lived together in harmony, like a single, miraculous entity. Nature made one species that flowed between various states, creating wolf-women, bat-men, flower-children, mist-elders, and wind-boys. And inevitably, when one of those beings jumped into a parallel world governed by different laws of physics, their organisms suffered abnormal mutations in an attempt to adapt themselves to their new surroundings. Many became tormented, crazed creatures, hungry for blood, their most savage instincts exacerbated by fear and a desire to survive. And so they lived like freaks amid the human population, feeding on the nightmares of men, who, at a loss to understand the true essence of these creatures, had invented a thousand names to describe that horror: werewolves, vampires, hobgoblins . . .

But Armand understood their nature. And he couldn't help but see past the monster Valerie became under the influence of her animal self to the scared little girl who had clung to him after he lifted her onto his horse. Nor could he help falling in love with her. For Ramsey and many other of Bompard's colleagues, that had been his mistake: to attempt to suppress the young girl's instinct to kill, to deprive her of human flesh, unaware that her corrupted bodily fluids had to infiltrate the blood of a receptor in order to create the immunity everyone was so desperately searching for. Persuaded by the Church of Knowledge to continue his research in another world, Bompard was forced to abandon Valerie, whom he had made his wife, and, despite fulfilling his duties in his new posting, he could never forget her. He grew embittered, taciturn, given to depression, and even overbearing; he started to drink too much, he disobeyed orders, and finally, when it was rumored that it wouldn't be long before the Other Side sent an Executioner to deal with him, Bompard saved them the trouble. He took his own life barely a week after Higgins managed to obtain a blood sample from Clayton, the same day on which he, and all the other Scientists scattered through the multiverse, received a delivery with instructions to make it their research priority. It contained a preparation of the CoCla cells, the legendary cells born of the sacrifice his beloved made for the sake of another man.

Bompard had killed himself for love, Ramsey said aloud as he sat alone in his sitting room. And although that act of rebellion seemed to vindicate the Church of Knowledge's view that intense emotions were fatal, it was also true that the multiverse was about to be saved thanks to a lovesick policeman and a tormented woman abandoning themselves to them. Furthermore: if that multiverse deserved to be saved, it wasn't only so that a stale, dying civilization could find a new home. No, Ramsey told himself, glancing about cautiously, as though fearing someone might read his blasphemous thoughts. That world was worth saving because of its wealth of feelings, which hadn't yet been sacrificed on the altar of some Supreme Knowledge. Of course, everything there was mistaken, misguided, and divorced from the truth, but that was precisely why people's imaginations were so fertile, their art so stimulating, their emotions so intoxicating . . .

Yes, Ramsey understood very well why Bompard had been on the verge of betraying their world for love. Had he not been tempted to do so himself out of a simple sense of friendship? He smiled sadly as he recalled Crookes, that passionate enthusiast, as brilliant as he was naïve, for whom he had felt a deep fondness and whom he had nevertheless betrayed. When his friend had fallen desperately in love with that wretched cronotemic called Katie King, who thought she was the dead daughter of a pirate, Ramsey had seriously considered telling him the whole truth, sharing the Supreme Knowledge with him. Did Crookes not deserve this token of his trust? Wasn't that the mark of true friendship? But Ramsey had done nothing of the kind. On the contrary, he had joined in the scientific community's ridicule of Crookes's research, publicly renouncing his disgraced friend. And not content with that, he had reported to the Executioners so that they could hunt down the Destructor Katie King. Afterward, he had eased his conscience by telling himself he had simply been doing his duty. After all, the fate of two universes was at stake. But that thought hadn't consoled him any more than it would have consoled Bompard. And although many years had passed since then, whenever he remembered Crookes, or heard his name come up (there was a rumor going round that Crookes had installed some mysterious columns in his garden that glowed and flashed at night, scaring his neighbors out of their wits), Ramsey would feel a pang in his chest, as if someone had ignited a flame too close to his heart.

But this wasn't the time for such thoughts, he reproached himself, or for questioning whether his world might not be mistaken. Not now that they had reached the final effort. Higgins had just returned from the Other Side, and after the hibernation period to recover from the extreme conditions to which he had been exposed, he would bring round the latest serum approved by the Church, the most effective of all the prototypes they had synthesized. They must go to work on it immediately, because, although the vaccine had been perfected, the problem remained of how to administer it. For the moment, the patient had to be inoculated via injection and then given three booster shots to ensure the vaccine's full effectiveness. Naturally, it would be impossible to inject the entire population of the multiverse one by one, so they had to find another way of doing it. If only they knew where and when the first infection had occurred, Ramsey thought, then they could inoculate the primary source of contagion, and the shock wave of inverse causality would probably neutralize the epidemic, although they could not be absolutely certain of that. In any event, they didn't know, and so they could only attempt to change the route of administration of the serum.

Perhaps if they could make it airborne, it would simply spread through hyperspace like a fine dew, pollinating all the atmospheres in the multiverse, and everyone would breathe it in without even realizing. There was a slim chance it could work! Ramsey said to himself, leaping up from the table with a burst of enthusiasm. And they might manage it in time . . .

Just then, he felt something vibrate in his pocket. He took out his fob watch and opened the lid, which was engraved with a Star of Chaos. He turned the glowing dial to the wall, where it threw a beam of light that traced his colleague's flickering face in the air.

"What is it, Higgins?" he asked. "Are you still at home?"

Higgins replied with another question. "Have you looked out of your window recently?"

For a few seconds, Ramsey gazed uneasily at his colleague, who was tugging furiously at his little black beard.

"Yes, a moment ago. Why?"

"And you didn't notice anything . . . odd?" Higgins inquired nervously.

Ramsey shook his head.

"Then take another look," Higgins almost commanded him.

Ramsey lowered the hand in which he was clasping the fob and made his way tentatively over to the window, dragging Higgins's face across the floor as if it were a dirty rag. He had no idea what he would find, but he was aware of what it would mean. His heart in his throat, he peered out, surveying the street from end to end: the two gentlemen were still calmly chatting, and at that moment a couple of mounted policemen were passing below his window, a nursemaid with a perambulator was buying a bunch of roses . . . It looked no different from any other morning, the same scenes as every day. What was it Higgins wanted him to see? Then, just when he was about to turn away, a deafening squawk tore through the air like a hacksaw. Everyone in the street raised his or her head to the sky, as did Ramsey. To his astonishment, he saw the silhouette of a gigantic pterodactyl, its membranous wings spread imposingly, circling the dome of St. Paul's Cathedral.

"Can you see it, Ramsey?" he heard Higgins ask in a frantic voice. "It has started! We must leave this multiverse immediately! I have summoned an Executioner, and Melford, too . . . We must go back to the Other Side. At least there we will enjoy an easy death . . . This multiverse is going to explode . . . Ramsey, can you hear me?"

Ramsey's watch slipped out of his fingers and fell to the floor. He stepped on it, crushing its cogs under his shoe. Higgins's puzzled face vanished abruptly. Ramsey leaned against the window frame and watched through eyes brimming with tears the policemen take off at a gallop, the nursemaid shriek, the two gentlemen wave their arms about and point up at the sky . . . "It has arrived," he said. The Day of Chaos has finally arrived, as it had been written. And they had been unable to prevent it. All those worlds would vanish in the Great Annihilation, and the Other Side would freeze over. All their sacrifices, the attainment of the Supreme Knowledge, the terrible slaughter of innocents ordered by their superior civilization, had been in vain. They would all disappear, the learned and the ignorant, those who had known love and those who had not, victims and Executioners, and their only legacy would be their atoms floating in the endless void, tracing the symbol of barbarism for all eternity and for no one . . .

"Chaos is inevitable," he whispered sadly.

"Chaos is inevitable," a metallic voice rang out behind him.

Ramsey swung round knowing exactly what he would find. There, in the middle of the room, stood an Executioner, dark and shiny like a black flame. He recognized him.

"Why are you here, 2087V?" he snapped. "Did Higgins send you? Tell him I am not leaving. Go without me. Get out! I am tired. And in any case . . ." He shook his head, almost in despair. "What difference does it make dying in one world or another? What difference . . . ?"

Ramsey broke off his sad soliloquy. The Executioner was slowly spreading his arms, his cape rising like a curtain to reveal a cowering figure. When the light filtering through the window illuminated her, Ramsey saw an old lady, so frail she seemed to be made of fossilized tears. The woman stepped forward, rubbing her hands together nervously and gazing solemnly at Ramsey.

"Good morning, Doctor Ramsey. Do you remember me? I see you don't . . ." She smiled at Ramsey's unease. "We met a long time ago at Madame Amber's house."

Ramsey screwed up his eyes.

"Mrs. Lansbury . . . ?"

Jane nodded. "That was what I called myself, but my real name is Amy Catherine Wells. I am the widow of H. G. Wells, the famous biologist from the Other Side who synthesized the cronotemia virus."

Ramsey stood gaping at her, fascinated and dumbfounded. He managed to nod. Then Jane took a deep breath. Here I go, Bertie, she said to herself.

"I am truly ashamed to admit that we were the ones who caused this epidemic. We brought the virus to this world, dooming it to destruction. However, fortunately, before he died, my husband . . . left a written account of how to save it."

34

ND NOW, THE TIME HAS FINALLY ARRIVED for Cornelius Clayton to resume his prominent role in our story. We find him at the moment in a place he goes to whenever he does not want to be found, brooding over *The Map of Chaos,* which is lying on the table next to a cold teapot. He runs his fingers over the eight-pointed star embossed on its cover and then leans back in his chair, his eyes roaming sadly over the array of magic objects hidden in the Chamber of Marvels, that damp, dusty room that has served as his refuge over the years.

He sighed, glancing back at the book. It remained a mystery to him. A mystery that only grew, he thought, recalling Baskerville. A few months ago, the eccentric old man had turned up at his office and told him he came from a parallel world, a world where everyone had a twin, a potential variant of oneself. The old man himself, for example, was a variant of the author H. G. Wells, although rather more doddering than the one in Clayton's world, as he could see, and that in the world he came from he and Clayton's double had been friends. Any other police officer would have called him crazy and sent him packing, but the inspector's job was to listen to people like him, and so he had told Baskerville to sit down, had closed the door, and within ten minutes he was persuaded that the old man was speaking the truth. How could he not have been, when Baskerville had told him that his twin from another world had lost his hand in a ferocious duel with the woman he loved, whose portrait was hanging in his cellar? For over half an hour, the inspector had listened spellbound to the adventures of the old man, who had sought his help because for the past two years he had been pursued by strange killers. Something about his description of them had made Clayton sit up in his chair: the weapons those Hunters carried bore the same star as the one on the cover of *The Map of Chaos*. Clayton had shown the old man the book, anxious that someone might finally be able to shed some light on that mystery. However, although they both recognized the symbol and acknowledged there must be some link between the book and the Hunters, neither could offer any fresh information.

After he had left, Clayton sent a patrol to scour the moor for anyone fitting the description the old man had given of his pursuers—impossibly tall men swathed in flowing capes, with broad-brimmed hats and peculiar-looking canes—while he himself resolved to pursue that alleged Wells from another world. Just as he had told Clayton, he worked for the famously wealthy Montgomery Gilmore, who at the time was plunged into deep despair after his fiancée died in a car accident. A tragic fact that had not only caused Clayton to view more leniently that man whom he couldn't abide, and whom he had stopped investigating in the name of something as foolish as love (he still flushed when he remembered the arguments Wells had used to persuade him), but had also made his surveillance extremely tedious. Murray spent the entire time drinking himself into a stupor either at his house or that of the Wellses, obliging his coachman to sit around twiddling his thumbs most of the day. And so, after several months of fruitless surveillance, Clayton decided to stop shadowing the old man. He couldn't keep putting his other inquiries on hold due to a case his superiors had long since filed away.

This was a great shame, for had he persisted just a few days longer, as many of his twins in other worlds did, he would have seen Arthur Conan Doyle show up at Murray's house in the early hours, accompanied by Wells and his wife, and, intrigued by this untimely meeting, would have tailed the two famous authors for several days afterward. Increasingly bemused, he would have seen them visiting fancy dress shops, purchasing slates, and making secret excursions to Brook Manor.

Finally, he would have followed them on the day of the fake séance with the Great Ankoma, during which the Invisible Man had appeared, and thus prevented Baskerville's death, causing events to take a very different turn.

But alas, dear readers, I am not telling you the story of any of those worlds, but rather of this one, in which events took place the way I have already described. And so, a few days after Clayton stopped following Baskerville, Wells and Doyle went to Clayton's office to inform him that Baskerville had been slain with a rusty sword wielded by an invisible man. Needless to say, the news left Clayton reeling. The old man was dead, and although Doyle and Wells described his killer as completely invisible, it was clearly the Villain. Just as Mrs. Lansbury had predicted twelve years before, he had come back for the book, although for some reason he thought Wells had it.

In short, those days had brought a flurry of revelations, each more surprising than the last. Yet they had only added to the list of questions Clayton had been asking himself for the past twelve years: Had the old lady been referring to those Hunters when she told him to give the book to those who came from the Other Side? And if so, how was he supposed to find them? And what if, like the Villain, they wanted to destroy the book as well? After all, they were killers, too. Moreover, if what Baskerville had said was true and they were living in a multiple universe, there might be more than one Villain, just as there was more than one Wells and more than one Clayton . . . The inspector heaved a sigh. The threats to the book were multiplying, and he still had no idea whom he ought to give it to.

All these musings led him back to Valerie de Bompard. How could he not think about her? How could he not wonder whether in this universe brimming with fantastical worlds taking shape before him, there might not be more than one Countess de Bompard? Was the Valerie he knew a traveler from another world? That would have accounted for her strange nature, he reflected, remembering what he had experienced the first time he met her: that unnerving feeling of being in the presence of something extraordinary, a creature so fascinating she couldn't possibly belong to the humdrum universe that surrounded her. He felt a pang in his heart as he imagined the torment of that lost little girl, alone in a world that must have seemed terrifyingly strange to her, abandoned by the only man who had truly understood her. And as if that weren't enough, years later she had fallen in love with him, an arrogant fool, who only wanted to understand her because, as she herself had pointed out, it was the closest he could come to possessing her. But at least there was one world among that cluster of possible worlds where they were happy, where Valerie was still alive and was not a monster but rather part of a world that was as miraculous and sublime as her own spirit, even if he could only visit her there during his fainting fits.

A sound of frantic knocking on the door brought him back to reality. The inspector breathed a sigh and went to open it, wending his way through the piles of junk filling the room and negotiating peculiar columns draped with wires and lightbulbs, sprouting from them like tree limbs in a mechanical forest. When he reached the door, he took a deep breath and opened it to discover Wells and his wife, both in their nightclothes, as if they had just gotten out of bed.

"Mr. and Mrs. Wells . . . what the devil . . . ?"

"Inspector Clayton," Wells gasped, "how glad we are to find you here! We needed to see you, and as you told us you spent a lot of time in this chamber, we decided to try our luck before going to your office, given how early it is."

Clayton nodded suspiciously.

"What brings you here? It must be something very urgent if you haven't even had time to get dressed," he remarked sarcastically.

"Indeed, indeed. You see . . . ," Wells began, a note of alarm in his voice, "my wife and I wanted to talk to you about a very important matter, relating to the . . . um . . . the . . ."

"Oh, the *book*," replied Clayton cautiously. "Yes, yes. Let us talk about the *book*. Please, follow me."

The inspector guided them toward his desk through the sea of objects. As they walked behind him, Wells glanced fleetingly at some of the marvels they passed—a mermaid's skeleton, a Minotaur's head, the skin of a gigantic werewolf—but all the while his eyes returned again and again to the knife hovering at Jane's back, the tip of the blade almost touching the nape of her neck.

"I would offer you some tea," Clayton remarked as they reached his desk, "but I am afraid it has gone cold. I doubt it is drinkable . . ."

"Oh, don't worry, Inspector, we have had our breakfast," Wells said, and then, pointing timidly at the book on the table, he added, "Er . . . isn't that *The Map of Chaos*?"

"Yes, it is," replied Clayton.

All at once, Wells was propelled toward the inspector, as if he had been seized by a sudden urge to embrace him. Then a knife appeared from behind Jane and its sharp tip pressed into her neck.

"Good morning, Inspector Clayton," a voice said. "We meet again. It has been a long time."

Clayton, who had just dodged Wells's hurtling body, contemplated the knife no one was holding with a look of revulsion but said nothing.

"George, while the inspector is recovering from the shock," the creature went on, "relieve him of his pistol, would you? And don't try anything, or I shall trace a pretty smile on your wife's neck!"

Clenching his jaw, Clayton opened his jacket to enable Wells to take his pistol.

"Forgive me, forgive me," Wells implored. "What could I do? He was going to wound my wife."

Clayton looked at him scornfully. Wells hung his head and turned round, but he had scarcely taken a step toward the creature when the voice made him stop in his tracks.

"Oh, I am sorry, George, I forgot . . . I don't wish to abuse your kindness, but while you are at it, bring me the book, would you? Remember, I came here to destroy it."

35

EANWHILE, IN A CONSERVATORY CREATED in the image and likeness of the Taj Mahal, Arthur Conan Doyle was listening to the feeblest defense he had heard in his entire life.

"Actually, I was only making them dream, Arthur," Murray was saying. "And dreams are necessary. They are humanity's pick-me-up!"

"'Making them dream'! Is that what how you would describe it?" Doyle said indignantly, his booming voice echoing through the empty conservatory.

"You did the same with Sherlock Holmes," Murray protested. "You provided your readers with the balm they needed to be able to bear their wretched lives. And then you snatched it from them!"

"Holmes was a character in a book, damn it," Doyle objected, increasingly irritated. "I never tried to pass him off as a real person."

Murray snorted and tried a fresh approach. "True. But what about the Great Ankoma? Didn't you and George pass him off as a genuine medium capable of putting me in touch with Emma? You thought if I believed your charade I would forget about killing myself."

"That lie was meant to save your life, which is why I agreed to be part of it. But the aim of Murray's Time Travel was very different. And to think I defended you! I wrote dozens of articles pleading your cause!"

"And didn't I thank you for it at the time? It is hardly my fault if you are gullible!"

"I am not gullible!" Doyle roared, beside himself with rage.

Murray raised his eyes to heaven, but before he had time to let out the chortle rising up his throat, a speck in the sky drew his attention. He narrowed his eyes in an attempt to focus on it, and as the shape grew clearer, his jaw began to drop. When he realized what it was, he said with a splutter, "And would you believe me if I told you a pterodactyl is about to fly overhead?"

"A pterodactyl? For God's sake, Gilliam!" Doyle said, incensed. "What do you take me for! Of course I wouldn't!"

He had scarcely finished speaking when a sound like sheets whipped by a gale began to grow steadily louder. Then the sky suddenly clouded over as an enormous shadow passed overhead. Taken aback, Doyle looked up, and, through the roof of the conservatory, witnessed an enormous pterodactyl flying over their heads. Identical to the reconstructions he had seen in engravings, it had a narrow skull and an elongated jaw bristling with teeth, while its greenish-grey wings must have measured over six feet.

When the creature had vanished into the distance, Doyle asked in a trembling voice, "How the devil did you do that?"

Murray shrugged, the blood draining from his face. "Would you believe me if I tell you it isn't my doing?"

Doyle concealed his astonishment. So, what had just crossed the sky was real? They had seen a flying reptile extinct for millions of years? It was then the two men heard the sound that their heated argument and the subsequent noise of the creature's flapping wings had drowned out: the frenzied tinkling of a hundred bells. They rushed out of the conservatory, only to find Elmer running toward them.

"Mr. Gilmore, sir!" cried the butler as he reached them. "The mirrors . . . the servants . . . fantastical things . . . centaurs . . . dragons."

"Elmer, my good man, try to speak properly. Otherwise, how do you expect Mr. Doyle and me to understand you?" Murray said good-naturedly.

"Er, forgive me, sir," replied Elmer, attempting to summon the unflappable composure befitting his station. "I shall do my best, sir, though

I fear I still may not make any sense. It is the servants, sir: they have just informed me that the mirrors have stopped reflecting, er . . . reality."

"And what are they reflecting?" asked Murray.

"Well . . . I am not sure I can tell you, sir. There seems to be some disagreement: Billy, the stable boy, assures me that his mirror shows a knight slaying a dragon, while Mrs. Fisher, the cook, claims to have seen a group of hoofed children playing panpipes. For his part, Ned, the assistant butler, glimpsed a man with a falcon's head, while Mrs. Donner, the housekeeper, says she saw a sinister vehicle driving round a snow-covered field, blowing flames out of an enormous tube . . ."

Murray and Doyle exchanged glances, then hurried toward the circle of mirrors. Once they got there, they could see for themselves that it was true: none of the mirrors reflected the banal reality in front of them; they all seemed to be dreaming of other worlds, each more incredible than the last.

"My God . . . ," whispered Murray. Then he turned to the butler and commanded: "Elmer, go back to the house and calm the servants."

"Calm them? Why, of course. At once, sir," Elmer retorted, and he went off to carry out his master's simple command.

After he had gone, Murray and Doyle took a closer look at the miraculous reflections, but they soon realized that the phenomenon wasn't confined only to the mirrors. Outside the circle, a few yards away, translucent trees had started sprouting from the lawn. They emitted a faint glow, as if the light were passing through them.

"What the devil is going on, Arthur?" exclaimed Murray. "I ordered those trees to be cut down when I bought the house."

"Then in some other world you decided to leave them there," Doyle mused, gazing in astonishment at the horizon, where two red moons were now hovering. "Good God . . . the infinite worlds in the universe seem to be closing in on one another, or even overlapping . . . Is this the end of the world that the old lady predicted?"

"What old lady?" Murray asked.

"What do you mean, 'What old lady?'?" Doyle snapped. "The old lady who gave the book to Inspector Clayton, of course. Damn it, Gilliam, didn't you hear a word I said? When Wells and I went to see Clayton, he told us that . . ."

But Murray was no longer listening. One of the mirrors had caught his attention. The glass had misted up suddenly, turning into a bright, silvery haze that instantly evaporated to reveal the bedroom of a house, where a woman was frantically packing a suitcase while a man stared in horror out of the window. Murray moved closer to the mirror until his face was almost touching the glass.

"I know those people," he murmured, somewhat startled. "It is Mr. and Mrs. Harlow, Emma's parents."

Doyle glanced over his shoulder at the image. Judging from the horrified expression of the man looking out of the window, the end of the world, or whatever the hell it was, was happening there, too. Their voices were distorted yet audible.

"What is going on, dear?" the woman was saying as she grabbed more clothes out of the wardrobe.

The man did not answer immediately, as if he was having difficulty interpreting what he was seeing.

"I think . . . they are attacking New York," he said at last, in a somber voice.

"My God. But who?"

"I don't know, Catherine." The man paused. "The buildings are . . . going hazy. And our garden . . . oh, God, it's like someone is drawing another garden on top of it."

The woman looked at him, trying to understand what he was saying, and then she shouted, "Emma, if you're done packing, come and give me a hand!"

Doyle felt Murray shudder. At that moment, Emma entered the room.

"Oh, my God . . . ," Murray whispered.

The girl began to help her mother squeeze all the clothes she was rescuing from the wardrobe into the suitcase, from time to time casting worried glances at her father, who remained transfixed by the scenes outside. She was dressed in black, her face still stricken with grief.

"Do you think we need take all this with us, Mother? And where are we supposed to be going, anyway?" they heard her protest.

"We'll follow the Brittons down to the sewers," her father replied without looking at her. "We'll be safe down there."

Then Murray breathed in, cleared his throat, and called her name: "Emma!"

And his voice must have reached her, for she instantly raised her head and turned very slowly toward the mirror in the room and opened her mouth in astonishment. Her parents also looked at the mirror, bemused. For a few seconds, none of them spoke or did anything. Then, very slowly, the girl began to approach the mirror. Murray watched her walk toward him with faltering steps, her face reflecting a tumult of emotions. When at last she reached the mirror, the two of them stared into each other's eyes.

"Monty . . . ," she whispered in a muffled voice. "I knew you'd come back, I just knew it . . ."

"Yes," said Murray, unsure whether to laugh or cry. "I always do, you know that, although sometimes I arrive late."

"And now I can hear you!" said Emma with childlike glee.

"Then hear this: I love you and I will never stop loving you."

She beamed with joy, choking back her tears as she placed her hands on the surface of the glass. Murray did the same, and the two lovers realized despairingly that they couldn't touch each other this time either. They were close enough to embrace, and yet once more they were locked inside their separate prisons.

"I am so sorry about what happened," she said in voice choked with tears. "If only I hadn't insisted on driving, like a spoilt child . . . you would still be alive."

Murray shook his head, unable to utter a word. Is that what Emma believed? That he was the spirit of a dead man with a penchant for appearing to her in mirrors? For an instant, he was tempted to tell her the truth, to explain that he was alive, even though he was a different Gilliam who had watched a different Emma die. But he thrust the idea aside. It would probably confuse her, and besides, there wasn't time for lengthy explanations. If I hadn't let you drive, he said to himself, smiling at her tenderly, it would have been you who died.

"Where are you?" he heard Emma ask.

Murray breathed a sigh.

"Worlds away," he replied. "But I promise I will come for you. I will find a way to get to your world."

"The whole world is nothing more than the precise length of each moment that separates us," she whispered.

At that moment, Emma's father approached the mirror.

"What's going on, Montgomery? Can you help us?"

But before Murray could speak, the image began to fade. The figures of Emma and her father slowly dissolved, and a different image began to invade the mirror. It looked as though someone had set fire to the throne room of a castle. Murray and Doyle watched two empty thrones on a dais go up in flames as Emma became more and more nebulous.

"Emma!"

"Come for me!" she cried before her figure disappeared completely.

"I will, Emma! I promise!" cried Murray. "The word 'impossible' doesn't exist in my vocabulary!"

But his voice was scarcely audible above the raging fire in the castle. Murray cursed, clenching his fists, ready to strike the mirror that was mocking him now, showing him some stupid castle in flames. But Doyle placed a hand on his shoulder.

"We must go, Gilliam."

"Go? Where?" replied Murray, bewildered.

"Listen to me." Doyle stood squarely in front of him and looked him in the eye. "If you want to see Emma again, you must trust me. We have to save the world! And I know where to find the key that will help us do so . . ."

"The key? But what the devil are you—"

Without letting him finish, Doyle grabbed hold of Murray's arm and, dragging him from the mirror circle, ordered him to run to the house, breaking into a sprint himself. Murray snorted and followed after him. As they crossed the lawn, one by one the hundreds of mirrors Murray had installed there began to shatter as though bombarded by invisible projectiles, smashing to smithereens and filling the air with broken glass. Doyle and Murray shielded their heads with their arms just as a shower of splinters fell on them. When the din stopped, Doyle looked around for a way out that was free from mirrors, but Murray had covered every corner. They would have to chance it. He dragged Murray down a path bordered by hedges while the mirrors on either side continued to shatter at random.

"Damn and blast . . . ," Murray cursed, stumbling behind Doyle.

Doyle tried to spur him on. "Come on, Gilliam, stop complaining. What are a few bits of broken glass compared to a burning house?"

They managed to escape relatively unharmed from the death trap the gardens had suddenly become. Despite having used their arms for protection, their faces were covered in tiny cuts. Reaching the side of the house, now lined with broken mirrors, they saw the servants fleeing down the driveway and scattering into the gardens on either side, alarmed by the exploding mirrors and the bizarre images they had seen in them. Just then Elmer, who was clearly overwhelmed by events, emerged from the house and spoke to Doyle.

"Mr. Doyle, sir, thank goodness I have found you! Your secretary called. Apparently the telephone was ringing for some time, but with all this racket going on no one took much notice of it. I offer you my sincerest apologies, sir, and furthermore . . ."

"Cut out the excuses and get to the point, Elmer!" interrupted Doyle. "What did he want? Are all the mirrors at Undershaw shattering, too?"

"Er, yes, sir . . . But he wanted you to know that, despite being anxious, your wife, children, and servants are safe and sound."

"Thank God . . . ," Doyle sighed.

"There is one other thing, sir," said Elmer. "It seems the kettle in your study started whistling shortly after you left and hasn't stopped since. Your secretary can't seem to make it stop and has asked for permission to silence it with a hammer, sir."

"Curses!" Doyle exclaimed, visibly upset. "My kettle . . . Why does everything have to happen on the same day? Who the devil wrote this infernal script!"

Far from taking that remark personally, dear reader, I shall continue telling my story. Murray looked at him in astonishment:

"What the devil does a blasted kettle matter with all this going on!" he protested.

Ignoring Murray, Doyle commanded: "Elmer, call Miss Leckie. Tell her not to leave the house and not to worry; I will get to the bottom of this!" Then he seized Murray's arm once more and dragged him toward the drive. "Come on, my carriage is waiting outside! We might still be in time . . ."

MURRAY AND DOYLE PUFFED and panted as they ran down the driveway, proving that neither was any longer in the flush of youth. Here, too, the mirrors had shattered, strewing the fallen leaves with shards of glass. Naturally, the servants had all abandoned their posts, leaving a row of empty chairs, many of them upturned. But then, as they got halfway down the path, they saw an army of horsemen appear in the distance. The two men stopped dead in their tracks, transfixed for a few seconds as a troop of cavalry bristling with pennants galloped toward them. As the riders drew closer, they could make out the horses, their flanks protected with engraved barding, their heads in sinister helmets that gave them a grotesque appearance. The riders were strange humanoid creatures with long, angular faces, pointed ears, and white hair, also sheathed in shining armor with spiked shoulder plates. Most were brandishing swords and lances, and three or four of them carried pennants bearing strange symbols. When he finally managed to rouse himself from this mesmerizing sight, Doyle turned and fled back toward the house.

"Run, for your life, Gilliam, or you'll be trampled!"

Doyle's booming voice stirred Murray, and he sprinted after Doyle. He gritted his teeth as the horsemen's fierce battle cries, the clank of armor, the horses' snorts, and the din of hooves on the trodden earth drew closer. He instantly realized there was no escape: run as hard as they might, the house was too far away. In a few seconds they would be crushed. They would die a ridiculous death, trampled by a ferocious army that wouldn't even notice as they galloped over them. He prepared to be knocked down by the first horse and then trampled pitilessly by the rest.

"Forgive me, Emma," he whispered as he felt the horses' breath on the back of his neck.

However, the expected collision did not happen. Astonished, he looked on as the first rider passed straight through him as if he were made of smoke. First the horse's forelegs emerged from his stomach, turning him fleetingly into a centaur, then its body carrying the rider, and finally its hindquarters. He felt no pain, only a slight shiver. A second afterward, the same thing occurred with the next rider, and the next. Yet he kept running and, glancing sideways, saw that Doyle did, too. Only when the army had finished going through them did the two men come to a halt, both astonished that they hadn't fallen under the hooves. Murray's lips broke into an uneasy smile. To his astonishment, he was still alive. At his side, Doyle was looking at him, his face glowing with a similar expression of bemused relief.

"I can't believe they went straight through us!" Murray exclaimed. "They are like mirages!"

Doyle nodded, still panting for breath, and they both watched the alien army ride into the distance, leaving a cloud of translucent dust in its wake.

"But who were they?" asked Murray.

"An army from another world, it would appear. A world that at this very moment seems to be superimposing itself on ours," Doyle reflected. "But I fear this is only the beginning."

"The beginning?"

Doyle nodded solemnly. "At Brook Manor we glimpsed another world through the mirror. It was close, but not close enough, since our voices couldn't even reach it."

"But today I was able to speak to Emma . . ."

"That means the parallel worlds are now brushing against one another. And if that continues, we can assume that those seemingly harmless transparencies . . . will end up becoming flesh and blood."

"Good God . . . ," Murray whispered, terrified.

"There's no time to lose, Gilliam," said Doyle, striding back toward the main gate. "We must get to the city center as quickly as possible. I fear the whole universe—everything we know and everything we imagine—is about to explode. And only Inspector Clayton can prevent it."

"Clayton?" Murray raised his eyebrows. "Why him?"

"That is what I have been trying to tell you since I got here. *The Map of Chaos* contains the key to saving the world, and Clayton has it . . ." Then Doyle remembered the accursed kettle whistling in his study. "Or at least I hope he does."

36

At that very moment, Doctor Ramsey, Mrs. Lansbury, and Executioner 2087V were emerging onto the street, which was filled with a throng of people seized with panic and running frantically from something. They did not need to look far to see what the crowd was fleeing from. In the distance, St. Paul's Cathedral looked as if it had been buried under layers of gauze veils. Ramsey supposed that this meant that other cathedrals from other parallel Londons were superimposing themselves on it. Everything that had occupied that space over the centuries was occupying it once more at that very instant, creating the illusion that the cathedral was encased in a gleaming chrysalis and had become a building with manifold hazy contours. Among the myriad layers, the doctor thought he caught a glimpse of the medieval cathedral that had been consumed by flames in 1666 and even the tiny wooden church built in 604, which was reputed to have been the first in England. The effect seemed to be spreading to the adjacent buildings, which were slowly vanishing beneath a similar misty veil. Amid the panic-stricken crowd, Ramsey also made out a handful of translucent people and carriages, escaped from another world, who were now colliding with their doubles in this frenzied escape. Ramsey sighed. There was no time to lose.

"We must head for Great George Street immediately," he announced, looking at the Executioner, "to the headquarters of Scotland Yard."

"Well, I fear we shall have to use more conventional means of transport, Doctor. If we try to go there via another world, I doubt my cane will find the right coordinates to return us to this one, amid all these colliding universes."

"I see," sighed Ramsey, "although finding a carriage for hire in London will be even more difficult, especially in these circumstances."

They decided to head for the river Thames, trusting they would come across some means of transport that would spare them having to make the long journey on foot. Ramsey had offered his arm to the old lady, and the two of them were walking close together while the Executioner led the way. Amid all that chaos, no one gave them a second glance. Presently, in the next street, which was oddly deserted, they spotted a coachman sitting atop his carriage, transfixed by a diaphanous figure limping toward him.

"Hey, driver!" Ramsey cried when he saw the man.

His voice made the driver tear his eyes away from the apparition, and he gazed at them blankly.

"Could you take us to Great George Street?"

The man nodded silently, without giving it a moment's thought, as if he sensed that the only way to keep his sanity amid the surrounding chaos was to stick to his routine. The Executioner lowered his energy potential so as not to alarm the horses and climbed into the carriage with the old lady. However, Ramsey paused for a few seconds to observe more closely the blurred figure about to walk past them. The creature seemed to be made up of bits of dead body sewn together, and when it came alongside him, the doctor thought he glimpsed a flash of lightning in the terrifying darkness of its eyes. When he reached his hand toward its face, which was crisscrossed with seams, he saw it pass straight through the creature's head and come out at the back of its neck. He stepped aside so that the figure would not walk through him and watched it continue on its way with a swinging gait.

"Fascinating . . . ," he whispered, examining the hand that had passed through the monster's brain.

He climbed aboard the carriage and told the coachman to drive on. The whip gave a resounding crack, and they soon found themselves bowling along by the river on the Victoria Embankment. Through the carriage windows, they saw rows of buildings covered in that translucent shell and streams of shimmering ghosts darting this way and that. On the Thames, at Cleopatra's Needle, Ramsey contemplated what looked like a scene from the Battle of Lepanto, in which one of the Holy League's frigates was under attack by a Turkish galleon. A group of onlookers gazed, transfixed, at an event they only knew from the *Encyclopædia Britannica*.

When at last the carriage reached Great George Street, Ramsey felt as if they had journeyed through the mind of a madman. They climbed down and made their way to Scotland Yard, where similar scenes of chaos awaited them. Policemen were wandering around aimlessly, shouting contradictory orders at one another. Nobody paid any attention to the strange trio, and, after briefly assessing the situation, Ramsey was about to order the Executioner to accost one of the passing bobbies, when all of a sudden, a skinny, pasty-faced detective, striding purposefully toward them, bumped straight into the Executioner, who appeared not to notice the impact. The young man looked up at him uneasily, rubbing his sore chin.

"Er . . . I am afraid our friend here is no apparition, Inspector," said Ramsey.

The young man glanced curiously at the doctor and the old lady and then, raising his head toward the Executioner, tried to make out his face, which was in the shadow of the brim of his hat.

"And what is he?" he asked suspiciously.

"He is . . . a foreigner," replied Ramsey.

"I see," said the inspector, visibly suspicious. Then he turned toward Ramsey, whose appearance was much less troubling. "And what brings you here? What strange miracle have you witnessed? I assure you we have received all kinds of reports." And as if to prove it, he waved the bundle of papers he was holding in the air. "The world and his wife are bumping into characters from novels, fairy tales, and children's stories." He glanced at his notes. "One man says he saw Captain Nemo's *Nauti-*

lus on the Thames, and a woman claims there is a lion in her yard with the head of a man and the tail of a scorpion. As far as I know, that's a manticore! There are several creatures we are unable to identify. Have you heard anyone mention a giant gorilla? We've been told there is one climbing up Big Ben . . ."

Just then, a phantom copy of the inspector walked toward them, also waving a bundle of papers, and passed straight through his double without flinching. In despair, the inspector raised his eyes to heaven.

"Not again . . . It's impossible to work in these conditions!"

"If you please, young man," the old lady's sweet voice chimed in before he had time to resume his complaints, "we came here to see Special Inspector Cornelius Clayton. Could you kindly tell us where he is?"

The young inspector looked at her, astonished.

"I only wish I knew, dear lady!" he exclaimed. "Inspector Clayton has devoted half his life to chasing magical creatures, and the day they decide to throw a party, it seems the earth has swallowed him up!"

"Inspector Garrett!" someone yelled from the other side of the huge room.

"I'm coming!" he yelled back. Then, turning toward the old lady, he added, "I'm sorry, but I have no idea where Clayton is, or Captain Sinclair for that matter. In fact, everyone from the Special Branch seems to have vanished! Now, if you'll excuse me . . ." And he made his way toward the officer who had called him.

"I fear it isn't going to be easy finding him," the old lady said despondently.

"Hmm . . . There might be a way," Ramsey reflected. "Let's find somewhere a bit quieter."

He opened a nearby door, which happened to lead to an empty office, and they took refuge in there. After blocking the door with a chair so that no one—from that world anyway—could disturb them, Ramsey turned to the Executioner.

"Special Inspector Cornelius Clayton is a mental jumper," he told him.

If this was a revelation to the Executioner or a simple affirmation, no one could have guessed.

"What is a mental jumper, Doctor?" the old lady asked.

"An individual who is infected by the virus, but for some as-yet-unknown reason cannot jump physically, only mentally," explained Ramsey. "Until now, we haven't detected any other jumper of this type, even among Clayton's twins. The majority of them, including those bitten by the creature he had the misfortune to fall in love with, suffer from simple narcolepsy, which is completely unrelated to the incident in which they lost their hand. The symptoms appear sooner in some than in others, and some even die without ever developing them . . . However, the appearance of the disease in the Clayton existing in our world coincided with the attack by the natural jumper. And for some reason, which we still don't understand—perhaps because his emotions were the strongest emotions possible, or due to some other peculiarity of his—his mind uses his disease to visit his beloved. In other words, he has become a mental jumper. Whenever he travels, his body is left behind like an abandoned shell, but his mind is able to reach her. And it so happens that his trail is the most luminous of all. Our Executioners have never hunted him down because he doesn't cause any damage to the universal fabric and is therefore harmless. But they know his trail well. It resembles a shiny, golden flash of lightning . . ." His face took on a dreamy expression. "It is the molecules of the imagination, the ability to dream . . . those qualities that make this multiverse so special and that may be its only hope of salvation. After all, it was thanks to the blood of this mental jumper that we succeeded in synthesizing an effective vaccine! And his gift might help us to locate him now and so find your husband's book. Do you think that would be possible, 2087V?"

"I feel hope," murmured the Executioner without moving his lips. "His trail is very clear and powerful. It's possible that, despite the chaos, I might be able to follow Clayton to the world he visits and then retrace his trail to where he has left his body."

"Good, then all we need is for Clayton to suffer one of his fainting fits, although there is no guarantee that will happen before the universe—"

"Excuse me, Doctor Ramsey," the old lady broke in, her face lit up with excitement. "Did I hear you say they had found an effective vaccine?"

"Yes. Except that we won't need it now: thanks to your husband's map, we could arrive a minute before the first infection and simply prevent it—"

"And use the vaccine on Newton!" the old lady interjected. "Then he wouldn't need to be killed . . . would he?"

Ramsey smiled benevolently.

"We can try . . . ," he replied cautiously. "The serum is certainly very effective. But you must understand, Mrs. Lansbury, that if there is the slightest sign that the virus has remained in the animal's body . . . well, we wouldn't be able to risk a repetition of all this."

"Oh, of course not, I quite understand . . . but it would make a wonderful ending for my book," said the old lady, and then, turning to the Executioner, she added, "And you could leave me, and my beloved Newton, in some tranquil world where I could finish it in my own time."

After a moment, the Executioner nodded imperceptibly.

"Well, what are we waiting for?" said the old lady. "We must find the lovesick inspector."

Ramsey nodded and asked the Executioner to proceed. Placing himself at the center of the cramped office, 2087V waited for Ramsey to pull down the blinds and then raised his cane aloft with the solemnity of a king showing his scepter to his subjects. A moment later, a faint bluish spark flickered up and down the cane, growing in intensity, and the sapphire glow finally began to illumine the encircling darkness, spreading round the room inch by inch, like a piece of paper unfolding, until it enveloped them all. Then, when it had filled almost the entire office, red lines began to emerge on its surface, like a network of veins, mapping out the geography of the multiverse. Before the Day of Chaos, those crimson lines, which represented each of the infinite worlds, had been arranged in parallel, like the strings of a harp, but now they were rippling and bending toward those next to them, touching in places or becoming entangled or even fusing together, producing continuous explosions and purple-tinged rents in the seemingly smooth blue surface that was the fabric of the universe. That chaotic tangle was a faithful replica of what was going on outside, a blueprint of devastation. But among the mass of lines were also hundreds of greenish trails hopping between them, pulling them together like the strings of a corset. Those were the cronotemics, jumping desperately between worlds, as if they thought they could flee that ferocious, unexpected Chaos. But Chaos was inevitable. There was no escape from it. And all the cronotemics achieved with their demented leaps was to make more holes in the beleaguered tapestry of life.

"This is the true map of Chaos," whispered the old lady.

Ramsey nodded. "If Clayton were to fall asleep right now, somewhere on it a golden trail would appear," he told her, pointing at the glorious haze of light and color, which nevertheless represented the greatest cataclysm the universe had ever known.

"Then we can only wait," said Mrs. Lansbury, "and hope that he falls asleep soon . . ."

37

LEASE, GOD, DON'T LET ME FALL ASLEEP now, Clayton was thinking at that precise moment. The Villain had snatched Clayton's pistol and the book from Wells, and both were floating in the air a few yards in front of the inspector.

"Well, dear friends!" came the Villain's honeyed voice from behind the weapon, which was pointing first at the couple, then at Clayton. "I'm afraid this pleasant reunion has come to an end. Much as I enjoy your company, there are countless worlds out there that I have yet to explore, and so, regretfully, I must take my leave. George, I promised you I would kill you painlessly, and I am a man of my word. Of all the methods I have used so far, a bullet in the head is the most civilized one, I think. But, of course," he whispered as the black muzzle of the pistol spun round toward Jane, "ladies first."

Wells placed himself in front of his wife, his face deathly pale, but then Clayton guffawed loudly. The pistol paused for a few seconds before whirling round toward the inspector, who was convulsed with laughter.

"What is it you find so amusing, Inspector?" the creature snapped.

Clayton took a few deep breaths, trying to compose himself.

"Oh, forgive me . . . I just couldn't help remembering the day I shot you in the leg at Mrs. Lansbury's house . . . That trail of blood appearing out of nowhere, and then vanishing, as if by magic . . . one last drop and then *puff!* gone."

"Believe me, I haven't forgotten it either, Inspector," the Invisible

Man snarled. "That bullet forced me to jump and leave the book behind . . . after all the trouble I went to, finding the old woman among all the possible worlds!" The pistol drifted toward Clayton, like some menacing insect. "So it was you . . . ," hissed the voice, oozing hatred. "I didn't get a good look at you because it was dark on the stairs. I assumed one of the old woman's stupid servants had shot me . . ."

"What a shame"—Clayton shrugged—"because if you had known there was a police officer in the house that day, it might have occurred to you that I was the custodian of the book, and you wouldn't have wasted all that time chasing Wells . . . That was your big mistake!"

"A trivial one, as it turns out, now that I have it!" roared the creature, waving the book in the air. "Although you are right: if I hadn't believed it was in George's possession, we would all have been spared a lot of unpleasantness. But it never occurred to me that the old woman could have entrusted it to anyone else. When I went back to her house to finish what I had started, I realized she had jumped, thanks to some of the remarks made by the policemen searching her house. Once more I was forced to chase her to another world, although I found her more easily that time. My powers were being enhanced, and now I could *smell* the fresh trail of a jumper. And so, after wandering through a few similar worlds, I managed to track her down. She was living in a humble dwelling, which I entered one night with the aim of stealing the book. The old woman was sleeping, though not very soundly. The tears seeped from her closed eyelids and rolled down her cheeks as she murmured, '*Forgive me, Bertie, dear . . . I had to do it, I had to give him the book and jump, forgive me . . .*'" The Villain imitated the old lady's quavering speech in a reedy voice before resuming his angry tone. "Damnation! I should have woken her up and tortured her until she told me who she was talking about . . . but I just assumed it was the Wells from this world. After all, the note she gave her stupid maid was addressed to him. That was how I first got wind of her plan, and when I overheard those policemen, I assumed she must have somehow got the book to him before she jumped. The book had remained in this world, and Wells had it! I tried for several years to find my way back to this universe, but, believe me, returning to the same world isn't as easy as it sounds," he boasted. "Only someone with my immense talent could pull it off . . . I had done it a few days after you shot me by following my own trail! But after I heard the old woman talking in her sleep, my last trail had gone cold, or at least I couldn't find it, and my search for this world turned into something of an odyssey. But I found it. Not just once, but twice! The first time I appeared at Brook Manor, where I was forced to jump again, this time with a bolt in my shoulder and an eye missing . . ." The pistol seemed to glance sideways at Jane, who shivered in her husband's arms. "By that time, all of me was invisible—even my clothes, which were shedding molecules at the same rate as my body, and that only increased my power . . . Though I have to admit, George and his friends won that battle. But my peculiar molecular structure not only gives me invisibility, it also causes my wounds, however serious, to heal more quickly than normal. And so, as soon as I had recovered, and before the tracks from my last jump vanished, I came back here. I appeared early this morning at my dear friend George's house, still believing he had *The Map of Chaos*. But George was kind enough to tell me who its true guardian was and even offered to bring me here . . . for which I intend to thank him by giving him a swift and painless death. However, I see no reason why your death should be so merciful, Inspector Clayton. Perhaps I shall blow your kneecaps off and let you bleed to death, as payment for that bullet that brought me so many problems . . . What do you think?"

Clayton looked at him in surprise and then burst into even louder guffaws than before.

"Stop that cackling!" yelled the Villain.

"Oh, forgive me, forgive me . . . I just can't help laughing when I think of the way you describe as an immense, unique gift a simple disease caused by a tiny virus accidentally brought into this universe . . ." The inspector dried his eyes. "I confess I admire your unwavering belief in yourself. I think we should all take a lesson from your irrepressible optimism, Mr. Rhys . . ."

"I see you know my name and everything about the cronotemia virus . . . ," the voice hissed. "The old woman had time to tell you a lot before she jumped."

"Oh, no. Alas, Mrs. Lansbury scarcely had time to tell me anything. Actually, it was you who told me everything I know . . ."

Beaming, Clayton turned around, picked up the kettle sitting on the table, and flicked a small switch on its side. Instantly, the Villain's voice boomed out, crossing time and space:

"Very well, George. But I warn you, if you are trying to buy time, it won't do you any good. I have all the time in all the worlds at my disposal! So, you want to know who I am! Are you sure you want to know? I am the most powerful being in all creation! I am the epilogue of mankind! When the universe comes to an end, only I will remain . . . presiding over all your accursed graves. My name is Marcus Rhys, and I am the God of Chaos!"

Clayton flicked the switch back and the kettle went quiet. He patted it lightly, as one would a dog that has just performed a trick, before turning to the Villain, smiling.

"We are very proud of these little gadgets at Scotland Yard's Special Branch. They can record any conversation and transmit it to a similar terminal on the other side of the city, and they work as remote alarms . . ." Clayton clucked his tongue in admiration. "Thanks to the fact that, courtesy of the Division, Mr. Wells also has one of these kettles, he was able to warn me this morning when he sensed danger. And not just me. As soon as Wells placed his *special* kettle on the fire, another kettle started whistling in my boss's house . . . Isn't that so, Captain Sinclair?" he addressed the air, hands clasped behind his back.

At this, several police officers popped up from behind the piles of wonders kept in the Chamber, silently aiming their weapons at the empty space where the book and the pistol were floating. Finally, the plump Captain Sinclair stepped out from behind one of the strange columns, his false eye glowing red in the dark, like an infernal lighthouse beacon. He placed one hand on a lever to the side of the column and raised the other slowly, also aiming his pistol at the invisible man.

"Quite right, lad," he said to Clayton. "Only, next time, remind me to adjust the volume on that damned thing. My wife is threatening to leave me next time that unbearable whistling wakes her up . . ."

"Oh, I am sure Marcia would never do such a thing."

"Be quiet! Be quiet, both of you!" the voice roared, the book and the pistol gyrating in the air, as if the Villain was spinning round, observing the ring of police officers now surrounding him. "What is this farce? Do you really think you have caught me in your silly trap?" He let out a menacing guffaw and the pistol and the book instantly dropped to the floor. "I am the Invisible Man! You can't see me, and you can't stop me from escaping. I can leap into another world! And when I come back for what is mine, you will never know when I am behind you. You will never see me coming!"

Clayton contemplated him with the weary expression of someone realizing that the most boring guest is still at the party.

"Invisible, really?" he retorted scornfully. "Take a good look at yourself. Do you still think we can't see you?"

At that moment, the captain pressed down the lever on which his hand had been resting, and the strange columns dotted about the Chamber lit up with a subdued hum, emitting a ghostly bluish light. Before everyone's eyes, clearly traced in the air was the gelatinous outline of a hand, slowly extending to an arm, a rounded shoulder, and part of a chest and neck, as if someone were blowing up a blue bubble in the shape of a human.

"What the devil is happening to me?" the Villain stammered, his watery hand opening and closing in front of his still-invisible face.

"I don't wish to bore you with complex chemical explanations," replied Clayton amiably, "so I shall try to sum up the most important facts: that book isn't *The Map of Chaos,* it is an amusing novella I wrote when I was younger. I had it bound to look like the original, and then our scientists impregnated the cover with a substance you have been absorbing through your skin for the last few minutes, which reacts to a certain kind of light . . . It is now in your bloodstream and, as you can see, is already coloring your cells . . . irreversibly. Soon your body will be visible even in daylight. Congratulations, Mr. Rhys, you have ceased to be a monster! At least in appearance . . ."

The Villain's lower jaw and mouth had started to appear, and a savage cry of rage issued from his lips. Then the outline of his body, which was gradually becoming whole, began to flicker, as though intermittent pulses of forgetfulness were racing through it.

"He is going to jump to another world!" Wells cried out.

Just then, Captain Sinclair lowered the lever to a second position. The gentle hum of the columns gave way to a deafening roar, and hundreds of lights flashed through the encircling cables at an incredible speed. A blinding light filled the room, forcing everyone to screw up their eyes. Marcus Rhys's body stopped hovering between the real and the imaginary and resumed its solid shape, which was beginning to look more and more like an irate ice sculpture.

"I left out the most important part!" Clayton cried as he walked toward him, straining to make his voice heard above the roar of the columns. "These masts also give off a very special kind of radiation. We commissioned them from Sir William Crookes, one of the greatest scientists of our time . . . I met him at that séance at Madame Amber's and took an instant liking to him, which wasn't the case with you. I have a sixth sense that allows me to see people's true natures; it is a gift that has failed me only once in my life . . . but not with Sir William. When I went to see him a few days ago to tell him about an outlandish theory of parallel worlds, and to ask whether he could design some sort of machine to stop people from jumping between them, he didn't so much as raise an eyebrow. And yesterday he sent us these splendid columns. Just in the nick of time, it would seem. Obviously, he didn't have time to test them, but he thought there was a good chance they would work. And judging from your expression, Mr. Rhys, and more important from the fact that you are still here, I don't think Sir William was boasting." Clayton had walked right up to the Villain, who was roaring like a caged animal, baring his teeth and clenching his fists. The inspector knelt down, picked up his pistol, and put it back in his jacket. Then he took a book out of one of his pockets and dangled it in front of the watery silhouette into which the Villain had been transformed. "This is the real book, Mr. Rhys, *The Map of Chaos*! I have kept it safe from you for twelve years, knowing that one day you would come back for it! And now, finally, it is all over. You have lost, Mr. Rhys. You will spend the rest of your life in a miserable cell specially designed for you, from which you will never be able to escape. The book is no longer in danger, and all its mysteries have been unraveled," he said, almost to himself, unable to hide his satisfaction. "It only remains for me to find those for whom it was intended, those who come from the Other Side, and I will have fulfilled the promise I made to Mrs.—"

Inspector Clayton broke off suddenly, his eyes glazed, the blood draining from his face. He staggered back a few paces, murmuring softly, "No, please, not now . . ."

Then he fainted.

38

By this time, Gilliam Murray and Arthur Conan Doyle were hastening down Cromwell Road toward the Natural History Museum. They had passed through a Kensington in uproar, with streets overrun by transparent ghosts. Doyle was maneuvering the carriage with difficulty through the terrified crowd fleeing in all directions, trying not to be distracted by the translucent figures all around him. Murray wasn't helping much.

"Would you believe me if I told you I had just seen a white rabbit in a waistcoat looking at his watch?" he said with the same amazement he had been expressing ever since they left the house.

"In any other situation, no. But in this one I will believe anything you tell me, Gilliam," muttered Doyle.

He tried to concentrate on the road ahead, dodging the real carriages and letting the translucent ones pass through them with a shudder while Murray enumerated each preposterous apparition that popped up, like a child in a safari park.

"Good God, Arthur! Was that a Cyclops?"

Doyle ignored him. If, as he suspected, the troupe of fantastical creatures Murray was describing ceased to be harmless mirages and became flesh and bone, they would be in serious trouble. They had to reach the Chamber of Marvels before that happened, although he wasn't sure what awaited them there. If Clayton's idea of setting a trap had been successful, they would find the Invisible Man caught in the device Crookes had invented. Wells and Jane would also be there, and between them all they might come up with a solution. It was conceivable the creature knew how to use the book to put a stop to this mayhem and could be persuaded to reveal its secrets. Doyle knew how to help the creature overcome any reluctance he might have; all he needed was a few minutes alone with him and a heavy stone to crush his hands with. And if that got them nowhere, it was still possible they could find the solution on their own, in a flash of collective inspiration. Human beings rose to the occasion in moments of great crisis, and he doubted there could be a greater crisis than this . . . He breathed a sigh. Who was he trying to fool? According to Clayton, the most celebrated mathematicians in the land had pored over the book and had not been able to decipher a single page, so what chance did they have? They were doomed to perish along with the rest of the universe . . .

When they reached Marloes Road, they found the street blocked by a barricade of rubble. Doyle pulled up the carriage and observed with irritation the obstruction they would be forced to climb. The museum was not far, but this would certainly delay them. Stepping wearily down from the carriage, he began to scale the hillock, with Murray following him. When they reached the tiny summit, they saw that the rest of the street revealed the same devastation; as far as the eye could see it was littered with a layer of rubble and chunks of masonry. Treading gingerly, they started to make their way along it.

"How odd," Doyle murmured, noticing that the buildings along either side of the street were intact.

Where did all that rubble come from? It was as though someone had brought it there simply to pave that stretch of Cromwell Road. They had scarcely walked a few yards when, on the corner of Gloucester Road, they glimpsed the clock tower of Big Ben lying at the end of the street like a severed fish head, flattening several buildings. Murray contemplated it with a mixture of suspicion and melancholy, which Doyle couldn't help noticing. They proceeded to pick their way among the mounds of debris, and as they walked past the remains of a staircase sticking out of the rubble, a sound of clanking metal reached their ears on the breeze. The two men stopped in their tracks and squinted. Emerging from a cloud of black smoke at the end of the street, they saw a group of strange, vaguely human metallic creatures walking with a sinister swaying movement, propelled by what appeared to be miniature steam engines on their backs. Four of them were bearing a throne, on which another automaton sat stiffly, a crown on his iron head.

"My God . . . It can't be," murmured Murray: "It's Solomon!"

Doyle said nothing. He was speechless with shock. Then Murray began to walk with open arms toward the cortege, as if to greet them.

"I can't believe it!" he cried. "I can't believe it!"

The convoy came to a halt as it spotted the human being. The automaton heading the procession took one step forward, opened a little shutter in its chest from which a tiny cannon emerged, and opened fire at Murray. The shot glanced off his shoulder, causing him to howl in pain. Astonished that the apparitions were no longer harmless, Murray watched as the automaton prepared to fire a second time. Transfixed, Murray grinned uneasily before Doyle fell on top of him, flinging him to the ground. The projectile cleaved the air where a second before Murray's head had been.

"They hit me, Arthur!" wailed Murray, more out of resentment than pain.

Still sprawled on top of him, Doyle examined his wounded shoulder.

"Don't worry, Gilliam, it's only a scratch," he pronounced.

He surveyed the cortege. Two of the automatons, the one that had fired and one of his companions, were clanking slowly toward them with that unnerving sway of inebriated children, pointing the weapons in their chests at them.

"Curses, they're going to shoot us!" Doyle declared, having already worked out they wouldn't have time to get up and make a run for it.

He gritted his teeth, defying his killers, while Murray looked terrified. But before the automatons were able to fire, a shadow leapt over them. From where they lay, almost level with the ground, they saw a pair of black boots with bronze buckles planted on the ground. The shadow was between them and their killers, so they could only see him from behind, but he struck them as an impressive figure. Whoever it was, he was clad in an intricate suit of riveted armor and a complicated-looking helmet, beneath which only his powerful chin was visible. They watched him draw his sword from the scabbard round his waist with one swift movement. Then they heard a swish of metal, and one of the automaton's heads rolled across the ground. Doyle took the opportunity to sit up and to help Murray to his feet. He clutched his wounded shoulder, watching their savior execute a series of two-handed thrusts as he charged the second automaton.

Murray laughed nervously. "It's the brave Captain Shackleton!"

"Whoever he is, he's real, Gilliam. They're all real! And so are their weapons!" exclaimed Doyle, grabbing him by the arm. "We have to hide!"

He dragged Murray over to a mound of rubble large enough to shield them both. They reached it just as, in response to an order from their captain, four soldiers emerged from beneath the mound, encircling the startled automatons. They opened fire as one. Crouched behind the debris, Doyle and Murray were observing the skirmish in openmouthed astonishment, when all at once, a few yards away, the air seemed to rip open like a canvas slashed by a knife. The tear was accompanied by a deafening explosion that split their eardrums. Taken aback by that seemingly monstrous howl, the automatons and Shackleton stopped fighting. Then, with an equally earsplitting roar like a hurricane, the hole started sucking in everything around it. The reality around it crumpled like a bunched-up tablecloth. The bulky automatons quivered for a moment before being uprooted and dragged toward the tear by the suction force that had also overpowered the captain. Flabbergasted, Doyle and Murray saw them disappear inside the hole, which contained a throbbing, primeval blackness. From their hiding place, they seemed to be contemplating the first darkness—or rather, what was there before darkness was created, before any god appeared onstage to endow the world. Inside the hole was nothingness, nonexistence, whatever was there before the beginning, for which no one had invented a name. Then Solomon's support was torn abruptly off the ground and sucked through the orifice, too. The debris between them and the tear were gradually swept away as the suction field around the hole expanded. The air, and the reality painted on it, puckered into infinite folds around the opening. A few seconds later, the huge chunk of masonry they were crouched behind began to quake.

"My God!" exclaimed Doyle. "We have to get out of here!"

They started running back the way they had come but soon felt the suction power of the hole pulling them toward it, rolling up everything behind them. Doyle grunted with frustration. Running was like climbing an impossibly steep hill or swimming in a turbulent sea. Each step they took required a titanic effort, and they had the impression they were making less and less headway.

"We won't make it!" Murray declared, giving a strangled cry.

He was struggling forward, teeth clenched, face bright red, body tilted forward. Doyle realized that Murray was right. The greedy mouth of nothingness would soon swallow them up. Within seconds they would be pulled off the increasingly concave ground, following the captain and the automatons into the orifice, where a blackness awaited them that would obliterate their minds and shrivel their souls. With great difficulty, Doyle turned his head to the right and saw that they were only a few yards from Gloucester Road.

"Follow me, Gilliam!" he shouted, changing direction.

Murray obeyed, realizing that if they managed to veer off to one side they might free themselves from the force that was making their every movement an excruciating torment. Walking as though buried waist-deep in quicksand, and praying they wouldn't be hit by any of the smaller bits of rubble transformed into lethal projectiles by the terrible suction, they managed to gain a few agonizing yards. Finally, they reached the intersection and immediately noticed they could move more freely. It no longer felt as if they were sheathed in leaden armor. As soon as they were outside the suction field, they collapsed in an exhausted heap.

From the relative safety of Gloucester Road, they watched as the piece of masonry that had been their shield finally rose off the ground and flew toward the hole, into which the whole world seemed to be spiraling. The building on the corner of Gloucester Road and Cromwell Road was gradually beginning to tilt over, and Doyle and Murray realized that the strange fissure was not only sucking in whatever was around to it, but that its force was expanding, forming a semicircle in which everything was turning into an undulating carpet of bumps and hollows. Soon the street they were in wouldn't be safe either.

"What the devil is happening?" exclaimed Murray when he finally caught his breath.

Doyle gave a sigh of despair before replying. "I suppose we are witnessing the beginning of the end."

39

ND WHILE DOYLE WAS REACHING THAT OMI-
nous conclusion, in the vaults of the Natural History
Museum, Wells was gazing with astonishment at Clayton's tall, thin
body curled up in a ball on the floor after he had collapsed in front of
them. While Captain Sinclair rolled his eyes, Wells and the creature
fixed theirs on the book the inspector had dropped as he fainted, which
now lay on the floor a few steps from Wells. Thinking about it only for
the length of time a man as indecisive as he needed to think about anything, Wells took those few steps forward and snatched the book.

"I have it!" he announced unnecessarily, stepping back again until he
was once more standing beside Jane.

The watery bluish silhouette of the Invisible Man shook with rage,
trapped in his radiation prison.

"That book is mine! Mine! No one deserves to have it more than me!
I have crossed deserts of time to find it! I have waded through oceans of
blood! I have strewn the vast expanses of the void with the ashes of my
soul! You can't take it from me now! You can't!" he cried frantically, ending his torrent of words with a howl of pain that seemed to cleave the air.

After this angry outburst, he fell to his knees sobbing.

"Well, I think this has gone far enough," said Captain Sinclair, unimpressed, putting his gun away. "Summers, McCory, take Inspector
Clayton and leave him somewhere where he won't be in the way. And
you, Drake, tell them to bring round the carriage with Crookes's special
cage, and park in front of—"

An almighty crash drowned out the rest of what Sinclair was saying. A dozen or so yards behind the line of detectives, something tore the air as if it were a piece of paper. They turned as one toward where the earsplitting noise had come from, only to see a strange rent in the surface of reality reaching from the floor up to the high ceiling. A draft as cold as all the winters in the world issued from it, where a pristine darkness reigned. Before anyone had time to react, Professor Crookes's columns began to explode one by one amid a deafening hum, hurling lightning bolts in all directions. Horrified, Wells and Jane flattened themselves against the nearest wall as the lightning flashes zigzagged around the room, searing the air and striking many of the piles of objects. Sinclair and his men broke ranks, scattering in all directions, dazzled and half-deafened. Then the intense light filling the room was abruptly extinguished. Rhys stood up, took a few tentative steps, smiling triumphantly as he realized he was no longer a prisoner. His head, becoming visible around its one empty eye socket, swiveled round, searching for Wells. It found him pressed up against the wall a few yards away, pale and trembling.

Wells looked imploringly toward the police officers, but one glance was enough for him to see that none of them was in a fit state to help. Captain Sinclair was on his knees, momentarily blinded and dazed, and his men didn't look any better. The lightning bolts had done quite a lot of damage: the bones from the alleged mermaid's skeleton were strewn all over the floor, a werewolf costume was engulfed in flames, the Minotaur's head had been reduced to a handful of ashes, and everywhere crates had burst open, revealing their mysterious contents. Thick plumes of smoke and clouds of ages-old dust darkened the room. After casting an approving eye over all that destruction, Rhys approached the defenseless Wells, half a languid smile traced in the air.

"Hand over the book, George," he said, almost wearily, "and let's put an end to this. Can't you see that even the universe itself is on my side?"

Wells did not answer. Instead, clasping the book tightly to his chest, he grabbed Jane by the hand and started to run toward the Chamber door. Rhys breathed a sigh.

"All right," he muttered to himself resignedly, "let's play catch one last time."

However, scarcely had he taken two steps after them, when some of the objects around him began to vibrate, as though announcing an earthquake. Suddenly, the smallest and lightest ones rose into the air and flew toward the hole like a flock of birds released from a cage. Transfixed by the strange phenomenon, Rhys didn't notice the heavy bronze chalice, labeled "The Holy Grail," hurtling through the air toward his head. The impact knocked him to the ground, leaving him dazed. Still running, Wells looked back over his shoulder at the scene. On the far side of the room, he saw Captain Sinclair, who had just stood up, flailing around for a handhold as the sudden rush of air threatened to pull him toward the hole. The whirlwind was also starting to drag Inspector Clayton's inert body across the floor, toward the lethal opening. Alas, Wells couldn't help any of them. The book was now in his possession, and he had to protect it from the creature, who had already come round and was rising to his feet, shaking off his dizziness. Without losing any more time, he and Jane slipped out the Chamber into the maze of corridors before the mysterious force could reach them.

"What was that?" his wife asked between gasps for breath.

"I don't know, Jane. Possibly one of Crookes's columns short-circuited," he replied.

But he doubted it. He had only been able to glance fleetingly at the hole, but the darkness inside it, the icy cold exuding from it, and that suction power . . . He thrust the thought from this mind, quickening his pace as he tried to get his bearings in that labyrinth and listen for whether the creature was following them. He thought he heard the swift, angry pounding of his footsteps in the distance and his blood ran cold. It was definitely Rhys, and he was gaining on them. If they could only reach the street, they might stand a chance. He was sure someone would help them, or perhaps they could take a carriage and flee before he caught up with them . . . But Wells soon realized he was lost in those winding underground passages, which all of a sudden would end in a wall, forcing them to retrace their steps, or a door that would take them back to where they had started. It was as if the original maze of corridors had sprouted new offshoots that led nowhere or turned back on themselves. Some doors even had dozens of handles to choose from. With no time to stop and deliberate over this strange phenomenon, Wells and Jane ran haphazardly, with the sole aim of fleeing the footsteps resounding in the distance. When they came across the stairs leading up to the entrance hall, they bounded up them, grateful to chance for freeing them.

As soon as they reached the upper floor, they heard the sound of footsteps running toward them, and a young guard in uniform, with a look of panic on his face, emerged from one of the side galleries. Wells tried to stop him to ask for his assistance, but the young lad didn't seem to be in his right mind. He thrust Wells aside and carried on running as if all the demons in hell were on his heels. Wells and Jane exchanged glances, wondering what had given the young man such a fright. The only thing they knew capable of doing that was the creature chasing them. But they were mistaken.

First they heard their chant. It was coming from the room the guard had fled from and seemed to emanate from throats that were not human.

"His is the House of Pain. His is the Hand that makes. His is the Hand that wounds. His is the lightning flash . . ."

Wells and Jane looked at one another, aghast. They knew the words of that blood-chilling chant by heart, but it was impossible that . . . A cohort of grotesque figures emerged from the gloom of the gallery. This ragged mob walked with the rolling gait of the lame, and all of them, without exception, possessed bestial features: the creature heading the company had a silvery pelt and was faintly reminiscent of a satyr, the issue of a coupling between a monkey and a goat; behind him followed a creature that was a cross between a hyena and a pig, and a woman who was half fox and half bear, and a man with a black face in the middle of which was a protrusion dimly suggestive of a muzzle. Fortunately, Wells and Jane were able to duck into the shadow of the staircase just in time. Chanting their grotesque song, the horde of beasts disappeared inside the museum, a confusion of imaginatively antlered heads, fanged mouths, bulging eyes that shone in the dark . . . Wells shook his head with a mixture of disgust and hilarity. How was it possible they had just encountered the cast of characters he had imagined for his novel *The Island of Doctor Moreau*?

He had no time to answer his own question, for they soon saw Rhys's figure appear at the foot of the staircase. The couple started running again toward the entrance, which, fortunately, one of the guards had left wide-open. But as they reached the door, they were forced to come up short. From the top of the museum steps, Wells and Jane contemplated the scene before them, paralyzed with fear. It was as if someone had spilled all of mankind's nightmares onto South Kensington. Up in the sky, which looked like a web of blue, lilac, and purple hues, like sections of different skies tacked together, a huge flaming bird was tracing circles of fire. Below, a three-headed dog with a serpent's tail was careering down one of the streets, the ground quaking beneath its feet; ahead of it, trying to escape its ferocious jaws, a panic-stricken crowd was scattering in all directions. Farther away, toward Chelsea, a swarm of strange flying machines with propellers on their wings was dropping bombs on buildings, which blew up in an orgy of destruction. While they were trying to take in what they were seeing, a herd of unicorns, like a wave of shimmering beauty, galloped out of Brompton Road, passed before their astonished eyes, and then vanished down Cromwell Road.

"Look, Bertie!" Jane said suddenly, pointing toward one of the side streets.

Wells turned and saw a Martian tripod, identical to the one he had described in *The War of the Worlds,* walking on slender jointed legs and firing heat rays at people and buildings. He was horrified to see his invention playing its part in that madness and mayhem, but he had no time to lament the fact, for the sound of loud flapping caused them to raise their heads to the sky. At that instant, a dragon straight out of some medieval bestiary circled the buildings opposite, scattering the group of bat-men who appeared to be idling on the rooftops, oblivious to the devastation around them. Tipping its enormous membranous wings, the creature swooped down on a row of carriages clogging one of the nearby streets. With no Perseus or Siegfried at hand to confront it, the dragon spat out a tongue of fire that set alight the carriages one by one. The occupants leapt out, fleeing blindly in all directions. A small group of them noticed that the museum doors were open and made a dash for the steps, hoping to take refuge inside, but the dragon anticipated their movements and, wheeling round abruptly, flew over them, spraying them with horrific flames, setting the poor wretches alight in front of the horrified couple. The fireball had come so close that Wells and Jane could feel the heat scorching their cheeks. Terrified, they retreated a few steps backward into the museum. Some of those caught by the flames fell on the steps, but others managed to reach the door, only to collapse, writhing grotesquely on the ground before suddenly becoming still. The sickening stench of charred flesh filled the air. Wells and Jane stood observing the grisly scene, aghast, until they spotted Rhys crossing the entrance hall toward them. The way out blocked by the dragon, they grabbed each other by the hand once more and fled toward one of the side galleries. Rhys set off in pursuit, determined to kill them once and for all.

Meanwhile, the detective Sherlock Holmes and his archenemy Professor Moriarty were engaged in a violent struggle above the Reichenbach Falls. Although seen from below by untrained eyes they might have looked like a pair of clumsy dance partners on the narrow path beside the falls, the two men were exchanging well-aimed punches, each trying to throttle his opponent by means of surprise chokeholds, demonstrating their skills in the art of wrestling. At some point, the rivals gripped each other tight and a vigorous tussle ensued, which took them to the edge of the abyss, over which they finally toppled. It took Holmes and Moriarty seconds to fall into the deep well past the eight-hundred-foot black escarpment down which the mass of water plummeted. A continual spray drifted up like smoke from its craggy edges, making the air look like iridescent glass. A few droplets splashed onto Arthur Conan Doyle's face as he stood at the foot of the waterfall. He wiped them away with the back of his hand, his eyes fixed intently on the mighty cascade stretched like a gigantic liquid sheet between two buildings on Queen's Gate.

"Good heavens . . . I'll be damned if it isn't the Reichenbach Falls!" said Murray, who was standing right beside him. "And that was Holmes, who just perished in front of us exactly as he did in your story. What the devil does all this mean?"

Doyle made no reply. He was still in shock after seeing the scene he had pictured in his mind's eye seven years before acted out with a degree of realism that human imagination could never hope to create. Then, rousing himself from his stupor, he grabbed Murray by the arm and forced him to carry on running.

"Come on! It doesn't matter now. We can think about it later . . . assuming we manage to reach the museum and save the world, of course."

"Do you really think we can stop all this?" Murray said, panting loudly beside him.

"I don't know," Doyle admitted. "As I explained, Inspector Clayton has a book that can supposedly do so. But for all we know, the Invisible Man has already snatched it from him."

"What of the brilliant plan you mentioned? The one you didn't let me in on . . . ," Murray reminded him, unable to prevent a note of resentment from entering his voice.

"For the love of God, I told you I tried calling you a hundred times! And I only went to your house today because no one answered . . . Otherwise I would have stayed at home watching the kettle and would be taking part in the ambush right now!"

Doyle suddenly came to a halt. They had reached the back of the imposing Romanesque building, but instead of walking round to the front, Doyle went over to a small door hidden discreetly down a narrow alleyway. Murray followed him with a disconcerted look.

"Clayton gave George and me a set of keys to all the doors in the building, so that we could enter the museum even when it was closed to the public. I think this is the one closest to the Chamber," Doyle explained as he started trying all the keys in the tiny lock, cursing each time one didn't fit.

"Well, he might have labeled them for you," remarked Murray. "I don't mean to sound pessimistic, but I think I detect a distinct lack of organization in your plan."

"You aren't being very helpful, Gilliam," Doyle muttered, poking around angrily in the lock.

"What do you mean? May I remind you that I shot the Invisible Man with a bolt. Doesn't that inspire you with some confidence?"

"It would if you had your crossbow," grunted Doyle, just as one of the keys clicked in the lock, finally opening the accursed door.

On the other side, a maze of corridors awaited them. Doyle strode resolutely down one but had scarcely reached halfway when he spun round, walked back, and set off down another with equal determination. Murray tagged along, unconvinced it was the right way.

"This Chamber of Marvels seems rather hard to find . . . don't you have a map or something?" He snorted. "The Chamber of Marvels . . . Who the devil thinks up the names for these places?"

Just then, they heard a clamor coming from somewhere among the maze of corridors. Doyle stopped in his tracks and Murray bumped into him.

"Blast it . . . ," he muttered.

Doyle ordered him to be quiet and he pricked up his ears . . .

"It sounds like they are in trouble," he whispered.

Following the noises, he changed direction and walked down another corridor. Murray followed behind, rubbing his bruised nose. As they advanced, the din grew louder: it was made up of desperate cries, deafening thuds, and, almost drowning everything else out, a familiar hurricane roar. At the end of the passage, they saw the door to the Chamber of Marvels flung wide-open. They hastened toward it, rushing into the room without stopping to think what they might find. But as soon as they entered they came to a halt. A rent in the fabric of the air similar to the one that had ended the skirmish between Captain Shackleton and the automatons had opened up inside the Chamber and was threatening to devour everything in it. The tear reached almost from the floor to the ceiling, widening slightly in the middle like the iris of some gigantic reptile. Its force field was spreading relentlessly through the enormous room. Close to the hole, where reality had already started to warp, they saw a handful of police officers clinging to crates or other heavy objects, which the whirlwind was unable to drag toward it, at least not yet. A few yards in front of the police officers, they saw Captain Sinclair holding on like grim Death to one of Crookes's columns, the suction power pulling at him with such force that his stocky form was almost parallel to the floor. And finally they made out Inspector Clayton, sprawled unconscious on the floor, the whirlwind dragging his crumpled body along the ground, bringing it dangerously close to where the force field seemed strongest. If no one did anything, in a matter of seconds he would be sucked into the hole. Exchanging glances, Doyle and Murray rushed toward him with the admirable intention of grabbing him and dragging him away, but as soon as they entered the suction field they realized it would not be so easy. They immediately felt themselves pulled by a funnel of air, paltry in comparison to the one that had tried to suck them up on Cromwell Road, but strong enough to cause them to lose their balance. They fell on the floor and slid around as though riding on an invisible sleigh while Clayton's body suddenly gained momentum as it neared the center of the hole. Meanwhile, Captain Sinclair, who had calculated that Clayton's body would pass near him, extended his left arm as far as he could and managed to grab hold of Clayton's metal hand. But the suction was so great, he was left holding only the prosthesis. One-handed and unconscious, Clayton's body continued on its path toward the hole until it bumped into one of Crookes's columns and became momentarily entangled in its wires.

Doyle, who had been following everything as he slid around on the floor, cried out to Murray, "Grab hold of the captain! Let's form a chain!"

Murray, who at that moment was passing close to Sinclair, stretched out his arms and managed to seize Sinclair's legs even as he felt Doyle's viselike grip around his left ankle. Glancing over his shoulder, he saw Doyle grab hold of Clayton's collar just as the whirlwind wrenched him free from the tangle of wires. The four men remained like that, forming a kind of human snake of which Sinclair, clasping the column, was the head, and Clayton, unconscious and missing a hand, was the tail, while the hole pulled at them as if it were tightening the string on a guitar.

"The column is giving way!" Captain Sinclair announced, to their dismay.

A DRAGON WAS BLOCKING their way . . . He had never imagined that the course his life took might lead to any such situation, Wells told himself as they fled from the invisible creature. And yet it was true. The dragon was from another world, from a world in which dragons existed because in a universe made up of infinite worlds, everything was possible. Everything man could imagine already existed somewhere, like the myths and fairy tales full of captive princesses, brave knights, and angry dragons that breathed fire. That was why they had come across the beast folk, and why Martian tripods were razing London to the ground . . . It was the end of the world, of all possible worlds, of all the imaginable worlds. And the book he was clasping to his chest, the book he himself had written, contained the key to preventing that, even though for them it seemed like mumbo jumbo.

Still running, Wells and Jane entered one of the museum's side galleries. They felt worn-out, but the sound of the Villain's grunts behind them spurred them on. They ran through the whale room filled with skeletons and gigantic models of cetaceans, through another containing every species of plant, and finally they ventured into the fossil room, from which there was no exit. Gasping for breath, their faces bathed in sweat, the couple leaned against the end wall, too exhausted to regret their misfortune. The Villain's watery form entered the room, found them propped against the wall, and sauntered toward them. He looked tired as well and eager to bring to an end this prolonged chase across so many worlds, in which Wells and Jane were the last relay. As the creature approached, they could see that the bluish substance had almost completely defined his figure, although a few patches still needed coloring in—for example, his left arm and part of his chest. His face, in contrast, was complete, although most of his head was still missing, so that his expression seemed to be floating in the air, as though painted on a crumpled cloth. He stopped a few yards from them and gave a sigh of genuine dismay.

"Was this absurd chase really necessary, George? What good has it done you?" He contemplated Wells at length. "Give me the book. You have no choice, George. You can't fight me alone."

Rhys extended his one visible hand, which looked as if it were made of glass. Wells stared at it with a distracted air, as though thinking to himself. Then, when it seemed he was about to hand over the book, he held it even tighter to his chest, shut his eyes, and bowed his head slightly, as he were praying. Jane looked aghast at her husband's submissive posture, while the Villain contemplated his final eccentricity with amusement.

"As you wish . . . ," he said sadly, as though regretting that things had turned out that way. "Then I will just have to take it from you by force."

But before he could take a step, an unruly group of about a dozen men burst into the room from God knew where—among them a tram conductor and a couple of laborers.

"The Invisible Man!" one of them cried, pointing at the alarmed silhouette of the Villain.

A huge laborer stepped out from the group and, hurling abuse, lifted his spade and brought it crashing down on the creature's head. Rhys fell to the floor and was instantly surrounded by the men. His body started to flicker, but before he was able to jump, an angry torrent of kicks and punches rained down on him. Anyone coming into the room might have thought that an exceptionally vicious game of rugby was in progress. Despite the continuing blows, the Villain managed to drag himself to his feet, but the tram conductor grabbed him by the neck and shoulders and forced him to the floor again, where his companions gave him another savage kicking. Wells and Jane watched the scene from against the wall, appalled by the display of brutality. Then, when it was clear the Villain was not going to be able to get up or jump into a parallel world, Wells took his wife's hand and led her toward the exit, skirting around the group of men still engaged in that fearsome beating, until suddenly they all stopped. From the doorway, Wells and Jane saw the men step away with bloodied fists, panting for breath, and in the center of the circle they saw the inert figure of the Villain.

"G-Good God, B-Bertie, it happened exactly like . . . ," Jane stammered, too bewildered and horrified to finish her sentence.

"Yes, exactly as at the end of *The Invisible Man*. Rhys died in the same way at the hands of the same people as the deranged Griffin."

"But how can that be?"

"Because I imagined it," replied Wells.

Jane looked at him, puzzled.

"Haven't you seen everything that is going on around us? *The Island of Doctor Moreau*, *The War of the Worlds* . . . Those are my novels, Jane, but apparently they are also worlds that exist somewhere. And now they are colliding with ours, and I see that somehow my creations, if indeed they ever belonged to me, felt . . . drawn toward me."

"And you thought that if you concentrated hard enough you could conjure the death scene from *The Invisible Man*," Jane concluded admiringly.

Wells nodded and they both looked at Marcus Rhys's body, the man from the future who had killed them so many times. Crookes's substance had by now sketched his whole frame, which was gradually becoming more clouded and opaque. He resembled a normal man with an athletic build and harsh, rather crude features, half-obscured by a thick, unkempt beard. His clothes were spattered with blood and torn in several places. His bruised, battered face wore an expression of anger and dismay.

"*The Map of Chaos* is no longer in danger," said Wells.

But the world was still coming to an end. They hurried back to the

Chamber of Marvels, where they had been obliged to leave Inspector Clayton, Captain Sinclair, and his men at the mercy of the engulfing hole. As they passed the entrance, they avoided looking toward the main door. The cries and explosions from the street were enough to tell them that madness and mayhem were raging outside. Once they had reached the basement, they were guided to the Chamber by the roar of the black hole. They paused in the doorway, contemplating the human chain formed by Sinclair and Clayton, with the addition of Doyle and Murray, who must have arrived at some point. The relentless power of the hole was gradually squeezing reality, sucking up increasingly heavy objects, and tugging furiously at their friends. The only police officer who had so far escaped could hold on no longer: his fingers slipped from the crate they were clasping, and he went spinning toward the interior of the insatiable hole. At that moment, the column the captain was holding on to creaked threateningly.

"The column is giving way!" Sinclair cried.

"They are going to die, Bertie!" exclaimed Jane, clinging to the doorframe, her skirts and petticoats flapping in the air.

Wells nodded dejectedly and gazed wistfully at the book he was holding.

"Damn it! The key to stopping all this is supposed to be in here, but none of us knows how to use it," he said despairingly.

"I wouldn't be so sure, Bertie."

At first he thought it was Jane's voice. But his wife was standing next to him, looking at him imploringly and in silence. And the voice had come from outside the Chamber. Wells and Jane turned round. Halfway down the corridor they discovered a strange trio. A small, frail old lady was gazing at them in a kindly fashion. Beside her stood a lanky gentleman with a horsey face and the stuffy air of an academic. And finally, behind them stood a striking figure, over six feet tall, wearing a flowing black cape and a broad-brimmed hat that obscured his face. Stifling a shudder, Wells looked again at the old lady, who quickly smiled to put him at ease. And in a flash, he recognized those defiant, intelligent eyes.

"Jane . . ."

She nodded and gazed with sorrow at the book Wells was clutching.

"At last it is with you," she said softly.

Wells nodded, standing erect in a dismal attempt to appear worthy. After all, he was the last Wells in that long chain of doubles, the Wells who had been entrusted to guard it with his life, to prevent the Villain of the story from destroying it.

"If you will allow me, Mr. Wells," the well-dressed gentleman said, extending his hand to take the book. "We have to save the world and I don't think there is much time."

Wells gave it to him with a sense of relief rather than solemnity. The man began flicking through it with nimble fingers, nodding from time to time, which was more than anyone else had done and which led Wells to deduce that he might be a Scientist from the same universe as the old lady. Then he contemplated Jane's aged twin, who was gazing at him with a wistful smile, and he felt a sudden surge of admiration. It was clear that despite everything she had been through since the Villain killed her husband, she had never given in, and now, at last, she had succeeded in handing the book over to those who came from the Other Side.

"I am proud of you, Jane," said Wells, smiling back at her. "And I think I can speak for all the Wellses in the universe."

The old lady's smile grew a little broader. Then she stepped toward him and studied his face tenderly for a moment. Wells understood that she was simply contemplating the face of the man she loved, whom she had seen shot in the heart an eternity ago. Then she brought her face closer to his. Wells closed his eyes, expecting her to kiss him, preparing to become the depositary of that posthumous gesture, which, through the invisible threads that linked him to all the other Wellses, would reach the lips for which they were intended. But there was no kiss. Instead he felt the old lady press her forehead against his. She remained like that for a moment, as though listening to the sound of his thoughts, and then pulled away. Afterward, she clasped her twin's hands and performed the same solemn gesture with her. For a few seconds, the two women remained in that position, one leaning against the woman she would become, the other against the woman she had once been.

Just then, the man poring over the book broke the spell with a triumphant cry. He showed the page to the Executioner, who nodded almost imperceptibly. His fingers touched the handle of his cane, which lit up instantly.

"We must leave," he said without moving his lips. "I have a multiverse to save, and you a book with a happy ending to finish."

The old lady nodded, bade the couple farewell with a smile, and placed herself next to the Executioner, who enfolded her in his cape like a conjuror. The air quivered slightly, and Wells and Jane found themselves alone with the Scientist. Then a loud crack made them turn toward the inside of the Chamber, in time to see the column Captain Sinclair was holding on to break in half and their friends fly toward the hole.

"My God!" the couple cried as one.

But just as Inspector Clayton, who was at the front of the chain, was about to pass through the hole, it suddenly vanished as if it had never been there, and with it the whirlwind that was pulling them along. Now that nothing was holding them aloft, the four men dropped to the floor amid a shower of objects. From the doorway to the Chamber, Wells and Jane breathed a sigh of relief. Their friends stood up, groaning in pain and looked around them, bewildered, including Inspector Clayton, whom the crash to the floor appeared to have brought round.

"What happened?" he asked no one in particular.

Jane turned to her husband with a knowing smile and whispered, "You saved the world with your imagination, Bertie."

40

Every morning, the guard at the Natural History Museum, a young lad of eighteen called Eric, would climb the steps and unlock the magnificent door while he dreamed he was Goldry Bluszco, one of the chief lords of Demonland, at war with Gorice XII, the king of Witchland. The crafty sorcerer never went anywhere without his escort of evil magicians, each of them the personification of wickedness, and Eric could almost hear the clashing swords, see the crimson blood oozing from the charred earth during their ferocious battles. That had been his favorite fantasy for the past ten years, ever since he began sketching its scenes and characters in a notebook. And now he had turned to it again to enliven the lowly post of museum attendant that he had obtained, a job far removed from his old aspirations. He would amble through the deserted galleries, switching on the lights and making sure everything was in order before opening time, amusing himself by imagining the exploits Goldry carried out in that world so distant from his own, a world that existed only in his imagination, where sword fights, magic spells, and Machiavellian intrigues were the order of the day. Accompanying him on his stroll was the metallic clink of the cluster of keys on his belt, which opened all the doors but one. There was no doubt that this was the only time of the day when he felt at peace with himself, for, as far back as he could remember, he had always believed that something in his life was not quite right. He often suspected that his soul wasn't truly his own, that it belonged to a nobleman or an artistic genius—someone destined for greatness, in any case—and that due to some cosmic error it had been placed in this body that lived in a prosaic world where it was relegated to an insignificant role.

However, on the morning of September 23, the young man was too sleepy to escape into his fantasy world. He yawned several times as he climbed the museum steps, unable to understand what the matter was with him: he had gotten out of bed feeling as if he hadn't slept a wink, but also with the impression that the confused remains of a strange nightmare were trying unsuccessfully to percolate up to the surface of his mind, unable to reach the edges of his consciousness . . . A nightmare in which all he had done was to run, terrified. He shook his head to try to rouse himself while rummaging in his pocket for the keys. He had to stop inventing those stories all the time or he would end up going mad, he thought. And in the end, what good did they do him? He wasn't a writer, as he had dreamt of being when a child; he wasn't even a senior civil servant at the Board of Trade or some similar respectable position. He was a lowly museum attendant and would probably always be one. He should be grateful for that, as his mother would tell him whenever he dared mention his fantasies to her. Imagination is all very well if you have money, Eric, she would say, but it won't put food on the table . . .

Just as he was about to insert the key in the lock, the museum door swung open, almost knocking him over, and a man with a long, horsey face came striding out.

"Ah . . . look. The universe is saved!" he exclaimed, throwing his arms out wide. Then, winking at the strange couple behind him, he added, "And all thanks to the imagination!"

The couple, who to Eric's surprise were in their nightclothes, formed part of a tiny, eccentric procession that now emerged from the museum all wearing the same expression of amazement. The young man surveyed the group with interest. Besides the couple, who were gazing up at the sky in wonder, and the man with the horsey face, who was glancing about in raptures, there were two well-built men. One had a wispy blond beard and the other, who sported a bushy mustache, was the spitting image of the famous author Arthur Conan Doyle. Both of them also appeared to be celebrating the fact that the sky that morning was a radiant blue and kept clapping each other vigorously on the back and giggling like a pair of naughty schoolboys. Finally, a lanky fellow with a somber face emerged from the gloomy interior, dressed in black from head to toe, followed by a plump older man with a strange glass lens over one eye. The eye glared at Eric, who, plucking up his courage, decided it was time for him to intervene:

"Er . . ." He gave a timid cough. "Excuse me, ladies and gentlemen, but . . . may I ask what you were doing in the museum at this time of the morning? No one is allowed in here before opening time. I'm afraid I shall have to inform the police . . ."

The plump man and the lanky youth with the somber face, who was busy screwing a metal hand into one of his sleeves, exchanged faint smiles. The lens of the plump man gave a muffled buzz as it focused on him. Eric recoiled instinctively.

"What is your name and your position in this museum, lad?"

"Eric R-Rücker Eddison," he stammered. "I—I've only b-been working here a few days . . ."

"Ah, that explains why we have never met before. Still, I am sure you have already heard about the Guardians of the Chamber, isn't that so?"

The two men loosened their shirt collars slightly, and Eric could see the two little keys with angel's wings round their necks.

"Oh . . . are those keys to the . . . ?" he whispered. The two detectives nodded. "Well, I never . . . I was wondering what was in there . . ."

"Nothing much. Imagining it is more interesting than seeing it," the younger of the two replied with a wink that seemed to Eric more arrogant than friendly.

"Er, excuse me a moment, lad," the horsey-faced man piped up. "You didn't happen to have noticed anything out of the ordinary in the last couple of hours, did you?"

"Out of the ordinary? What exactly do you mean, sir?"

"Anything, for example . . ." The man looked hesitantly at his companions. "Well, I don't know . . . anything odd, *different*. An impression of multiple edges when looking at a building, or passersby with a translucent quality about them . . . Anything resembling a . . . mirage, or that gave you a feeling of . . . unreality."

Eric shook his head, puzzled.

"For the love of God! What sort of questions are these?" the burly man with the wispy beard exclaimed impatiently. "Now, listen, lad . . . have you seen a hole in the air that sucked in everything around it? Did an army of elves pass right through you? Has an automaton from the future fired at you?"

"No, sir. As you can see, everything is as it should be," replied Eric somewhat nervously, gesturing toward Cromwell Road with a sweep of his arm.

The big man snorted exasperatedly while the others contemplated the scene of a sunny autumn morning spreading across the street: a few early risers were strolling on the pavements while carriages rolled sleepily along the road and a couple of white clouds drifted over from the north . . .

"It is as if nothing had ever happened . . . ," murmured the man who looked like Arthur Conan Doyle. "And yet, only moments ago, I saw my own creation, Sherlock Holmes, fighting with Moriarty at the edge of the—"

Eric's eyes popped out of his head.

"Good Lord, then you are . . . Arthur Conan Doyle!"

"Yes, my boy, at least I think I am . . . ," Doyle replied, still staring intently at the nearby buildings.

"I can't believe it!" exclaimed the young lad excitedly. "I'm a great admirer of your work, Mr. Doyle! You see, I . . . this is just a temporary job. Actually, I'm a writer, too . . . Well, not a real one, of course," he added in a modest voice. "I'm only an amateur . . . I'm writing my first novel, although, now that I am only able to write in my spare time, I doubt I'll ever finish it—"

"Young man," Doyle interrupted in an authoritative voice, "it is up to you whether you invent excuses or stories. I created Sherlock Holmes at my medical practice, where I had no patients. A real writer!" he snorted. "I wish I knew what the devil that is. Why don't you think of yourself as a make-believe attendant?"

Eric's face broke into a smile.

"Yes . . ." He nodded thoughtfully. "In fact, that is precisely how I feel, as if everything that takes place in my life should be happening differently, as if this weren't my real life . . ." Then he stood squarely in front of Doyle. "Sir, may I send you the manuscript I am working on so that you can give me your opinion?"

Responding to Doyle's alarmed look, Murray came to the rescue.

"If you want a famous author's opinion about your work, lad, I suggest you send it to H. G. Wells here." He pointed a thumb at the diminutive gentleman in his nightclothes, to whom Eric had been too polite to pay much attention. "I've never known anyone more sincere in his opinions or more discreet when it comes to giving them."

"Oh . . . Mr. Wells," the guard exclaimed. "I . . . I beg your pardon, I didn't recognize you in your . . . ahem . . . Naturally, I am also a fervent admirer of yours . . . I have read all your novels several times, in particular *The Island of Doctor Moreau,* which is my favorite—" He broke off suddenly and screwed up his eyes exaggeratedly. "That's odd: I think I had a dream about it last night, though I don't remember what exactly . . ."

"Perhaps the beast folk were chasing you through the museum?" Wells suggested nonchalantly.

The attendant looked at him openmouthed.

"Yes, that's exactly right. H-How did you know?"

Wells played it down with a wave of his hand. "It is a fairly common dream among, er . . . budding writers and museum staff."

"Other parts of that dream are coming back to me . . . ," Eric went on, slurring his words as if he had just emerged from a long bout of drinking. "Ouroboros, my dragon, was in it, too, setting the whole neighborhood alight from the air, and . . ."

"Ouroboros?" the man with the horsey face inquired.

"Yes, that's the title of my novel: *The Worm Ouroboros.*" Eric grinned timidly. "It's a Scandinavian myth: a sort of dragon or snake that devours its own tail, symbolizing eternal rebirth. You see, I've always been fascinated by the Norse myths, and my novel is an attempt to imitate—"

"Yes, yes," the man with the metal hand cut in, exchanging a meaningful glance with the others, who nodded as one. "I think you should return to your post, lad. The museum will be opening soon, and I expect you have things to do . . ." He placed his prosthesis on the young man's shoulder and shepherded him gently inside while Eric observed his metal hand nervously. "Ah, and don't be alarmed if you come across a few officers from the Yard in the museum taking notes and samples . . . It is simply a routine inspection, nothing of any importance, though we trust we can count on you to be discreet. If you prove you are able keep quiet, I'll bring you Mr. Doyle's and Mr. Wells's details, so that you can send them your manuscript . . . all right?"

Eric nodded and, after one last dazed glance at the remarkable group, entered the museum.

"Remember, you are only living one of your many possible lives. There are others. An infinite number!" Doyle shouted after him.

"And for the love of God, if you want to be a writer, shorten your name!" added Wells.

When the doors closed, Murray remarked, "That's incredible! He doesn't remember anything. He thinks it was all a dream! And his writer's fantasies also appeared to him! Just like my Captain Shackleton!"

"And my Sherlock Holmes!" exclaimed Doyle.

"And I saw Martian tripods," Wells chimed in, "and, as I told you, when Rhys was chasing us, I even conjured—"

"Well, I'm damned," Doyle interrupted. "That means everything we imagine exists somewhere!"

"But . . . where are all those creatures now? And what happened to the damaged buildings? And the dead bodies?" said Jane. "Look at everyone: they are all strolling along calmly . . . no one seems to remember a thing!"

"It's true," said Murray. "Does that mean the end of the world didn't happen?"

"But we remember it," Jane reflected. "And that young man dreamt . . ."

Sinclair asked them to calm down and turned to Dr. Ramsey.

"Doctor, if I understood correctly what you were telling me on our way up from the Chamber, you come from the same world as Mrs. Lansbury, a world far in advance of ours. Perhaps you can shed some light on this matter."

"Yes, Doctor, what is going on?" Clayton interjected. "Clearly the Executioner managed to prevent the infection, and now everything is as it would have been had that dog never bitten Mr. Wells. And yet all of us remember perfectly what happened just now."

"And we also remember Baskerville, and the evil Rhys . . . ," said Wells. "But if the epidemic never took place, how could we have met them? And, more important, why are my wife and I still in our nightclothes?"

Ramsey gave them a paternal smile.

"Mrs. Wells, gentlemen . . . I don't think any of you fully appreciate what a wonderful, magical universe you live in. Although that is not your fault. In fact, the reason your universe is so special is precisely because none of its inhabitants understands it in its entirety. You live in a fascinating universe where everything is possible, where everything you dream or imagine exists somewhere . . . and perhaps at this very moment in another place, someone is also dreaming you or imagining you . . . Did the end of the world happen? Yes. Did it not happen? The answer is also yes."

"But both things can't be true at the same time!" protested Murray.

"Of course they can, Gilliam! Didn't you hear what the doctor said?" exclaimed Doyle, a feverish look in his eyes. "Everything is possible! Everything! That means somewhere all the realities we encountered and experienced exist exactly as we remember them, and because we remember them. All those lost worlds: the epidemic, Baskerville's adventures, Rhys's odyssey, the Day of Chaos . . . But the world we are living in now, where none of that happened, where we managed to prevent the epidemic and therefore its devastating consequences, could also be in the process of being remembered or recounted by someone at this very moment. It also *exists* . . . Perhaps we are all a memory of a memory of a memory, and so on until infinity."

"What the devil does that mean?" Murray muttered.

"Perhaps you are right, Mr. Doyle." Ramsey nodded with satisfaction. "Existence is no more than an endless, repeated imitation of itself, like that snake devouring its own tail . . ."

"Or one of those things that simply happens because it *can* happen . . ." Jane added with a mysterious smile.

Wells looked at her in bewilderment.

"And why are we the only ones who seem to remember anything?" asked Clayton.

"You have all been in contact with the Supreme Knowledge. You have understood the profound truth of what has been happening. You have become Observers and, as a result, in some sense foreigners in your own universe, at least for a short time. However, for them," said Ramsey, pointing at the passersby in front of the museum, "the Day of Chaos never existed, because they have never stopped belonging to this world, in which that day never actually happened. How could they remember something that never happened? But you have privileged minds, minds that are practiced in the art of imagination, minds that are open to every possibility, and that have allowed you, for a few moments, to become spectators and actors simultaneously. That is why you can't forget. You have seen what *didn't happen,* but also what *might have happened,* and for that very reason *it did happen* . . ." Ramsey looked at them one by one, his eyes radiant with joy, searching among their expressions of puzzlement and concentration for a glimmer of excitement that matched his own. He sighed, pointing vehemently toward the door of the museum. "Like that young attendant. He possesses a mind similar to yours, which is why he can sense that he has other lives. Who knows, perhaps deep down he is aware that there are parallel worlds where things have turned out differently for him. But clearly, thanks to having a mind capable of imagining other possible realities, he is able to remember what happened, though only in the form of a dream, because, unlike you, he hasn't been touched by the Supreme Knowledge. Do not attempt to understand this. Be content . . . simply to experience it. Therein lies the true beauty of your world. The supremacy of the emotions, magic, mystery . . . Today you were touched by the Supreme Knowledge . . . But tell me, can you say you feel happier than any of those people quietly strolling along? Of course not. The thirst for knowledge, the tyranny of reason . . . those are the viruses that destroyed my world and almost caused us to destroy yours. Since the dawn of our civilization, we on the Other Side tried so stubbornly to scrutinize every mystery around us that all we achieved was to speed up the disintegration of our universe . . . I am convinced that the true fabric of existence, the final layer below the subatomic level, is the imagination. And whoever tries to fathom its enigma destroys it forever. Some of us have finally learned this lesson, and we will have to teach it to our own civilization, now that we will be reborn in one of your worlds. Perhaps we will need your help, my friends. The help of those of you who have not forgotten . . ."

"You can always count on the help of Scotland Yard's Special Branch in this world, Doctor Ramsey," Sinclair assured him.

"Thank you, Captain. Inspector Clayton, you told me just now that Sir William Crookes designed those splendid columns you used to imprison Rhys." Clayton nodded. "Good. I believe I have some unfinished business with my old friend, whom I let down in the past, and to whom I have a great deal of explaining to do—a very great deal." Ramsey looked absentmindedly up at the sky. "There is so much to be done! The Church of Knowledge should change its name, perhaps to the Church of Dreams . . ."

Clayton cleared his throat.

"Speaking of dreams, Doctor. When I fainted in the Chamber of Marvels . . . well, perhaps I ought to tell you first that during my fainting fits I frequently dream about a world where . . . well, it is difficult to explain. The point is that in that world the Day of Chaos also took place today . . . and I, er . . . I told *someone* from there about everything that was happening here."

"I am aware of your dreams, Inspector." Ramsey grinned. "And believe me, there is much I have to tell you about the important part they played in the final victory. When I assert that the ability to dream is what saved your world, I assure you I am not simply using a poetic image . . . Rest assured I shall happily to explain it all to you, as well as the excellent use we made of an old blood sample of yours . . ." Clayton's bewilderment caused Ramsey's smile to broaden. "But there will be plenty of time for that . . . What do you want to know now, my dear chap? Whether that *someone* will remember everything because she had been in touch with the Supreme Knowledge? Whether the curse of your fainting fits is in some way related to the cronotemia virus? Whether you will be able to carry on jumping mentally to that other world now that there has been no epidemic?"

"I . . . well, I would be glad if you answered all those questions, but what I really wanted to know is . . . whether an Executioner could take me to the world of my dreams. In body as well as in mind, I mean."

Ramsey looked straight at Clayton for a moment and then shook his head regretfully.

"My dear chap, whatever world *she* ends up in, she will always be a monster; you know that. And I am afraid that if you went to any of her worlds, your own nature would become as monstrous as hers . . . I'm sorry, but I don't believe you can ever be happy together, because the worlds you come from are too different. Perhaps the love between you can exist only in dreams."

If what Ramsey said wounded Clayton, no one could have detected it from the slight flutter of his eyelids. All of a sudden, Doyle stepped forward.

"But it would be possible to take someone to another world that is similar to this one—isn't that so?" he said, grabbing Murray's arm and thrusting him forward.

Ramsey nodded. After another gentle prod from Doyle, Murray looked at him, puzzled, for a few moments before suddenly reacting.

"J-Just a minute . . . ," he stammered. "Are you saying that . . . if I asked one of those giants in black to take me to a world where my beloved is still alive . . . he would? Is that really possible?"

"We can try, Mr. Murray, we can try, although . . . ," Ramsey started to say.

"Did you hear that, George?" Murray interrupted, his face flushing. "And you, Jane? I can search for the Emma in the mirror . . . I can find her, Arthur!"

"First I must study the fabric of the multiverse," Ramsey explained calmly, "and find out if the Executioners have regained full use of their canes. In fact, I was thinking of going to my club right now, as I am sure some of my colleagues are already there, keen to have the first of what will be many meetings, since those of us who come from the Other Side have a Great Exodus to prepare. And so I think the time has come for me to bid you farewell. Mrs. Wells, gentlemen, we shall meet again soon, I am sure. Mr. Murray, if you would like to accompany me, perhaps we can discuss the details of your possible trip on the way."

For a moment, everyone thought Murray was going to fling his arms around the doctor and kiss him. Fortunately, he seemed to stop himself just in time.

"Certainly!" he declared excitedly. "Tell me, if everything is in order, could I leave immediately?"

"I don't see why not, if that is what you want."

"It is."

And never, in any of the infinite worlds, were two words spoken more sincerely. After that pronouncement, Murray turned to his friends to say his good-byes while Ramsey did the same with Sinclair and Clayton.

"Arthur . . . ," Murray murmured, eyes moist as he went over to his friend.

"I know, I know . . . you don't need to thank me. I promised you

I would find a way to reach the Emma in the mirror, and I have been as good as my word." Doyle beamed with satisfaction, thrusting his thumbs into his waistcoat pockets.

"Well, I don't think you deserve all the credit, but . . . bah, no matter." Murray seized Doyle's shoulders, as if he were trying to plump them up like cushions. "Thank you, Arthur. Thank you for everything. I don't know if I will have a telephone where I am going . . . but let me know how you are telepathically from time to time."

"That will be far more effective, given your servants' disinclination to answer the telephone," Doyle retorted.

Murray guffawed, and the two men shook hands cordially. Then Murray turned to Wells.

"George . . ." His voice failed him, and he gave a cough to mask it. "My dear George, I . . . I owe you so much. It is thanks to you that I won Emma over—"

Wells cut him short, exasperated, "Gilliam, you know perfectly well I didn't write that blasted—"

Before he could finish, Murray clasped him in a tight embrace, to which Wells instantly yielded. When they separated, Murray took Jane's face in his huge paws and planted a resounding kiss squarely on the young woman's lips, again before Wells could to do anything.

"Take care of him, Jane," he whispered to her, gesturing toward Wells with his chin. "And don't let that big head of his think too much."

"Don't worry, I won't. And give my love to Emma," she said, her eyes brimming with tears.

Finally, Murray turned to the two inspectors, who were speaking with Ramsey. He shook Sinclair's hand, bobbing his head, and then, after a moment's hesitation, he extended it to Clayton as well.

"I hope there is some other world where we will like each other more, Inspector Clayton." He smiled earnestly.

"Who knows, Mr. Murray?" the inspector replied, shaking his hand. "We have seen things more impossible happen."

Murray signaled to Ramsey that he was ready to leave, and the two men made their way down the steps while the others stood watching them. When he reached the bottom, Murray stopped abruptly, as if he had forgotten something, and shouted back to Doyle, "Arthur, remember you must write the story about the bloodhound! And I want you to dedicate it to Gilliam Murray, the greatest crossbowman in all the worlds!"

"We shall see, we shall see . . ." Doyle chuckled as he waved his friend good-bye.

At that very instant, a few feet behind Doyle and the Wellses, Sinclair glanced at Clayton, who was watching the two men start down the stairs with the dark, melancholy air of a drenched crow.

"Come on, my lad . . ." The captain sighed, clapping his former disciple on the shoulder. "Let's go back to the Yard and have a nice cup of coffee. Miss Barkin will be there by now, and you know she always makes yours—"

"Just the way I like it," Clayton cut in, rolling his eyes. "Do you really think the solution to all my problems is to be found in a cup of coffee?"

Sinclair shrugged.

"I don't know, lad, I don't know . . . But what I do know is that, despite all Ramsey's fine words, man cannot live by dreams alone, believe me. So, you decide."

Sinclair began descending the steps, whistling a jolly tune, hands in his pockets, nodding to Doyle and the Wellses as he went past them. A few seconds later, Inspector Cornelius Clayton of Scotland Yard's Special Branch came to the conclusion that the only thing to do if he wanted some peace, in this world at least, was to follow the captain and have that blasted cup of coffee.

As the two detectives walked down Brompton Road away from the museum, Doyle, who still seemed to have energy to spare, offered to go and retrieve his carriage, which he hoped was waiting for him where he and Murray had abandoned it during that morning of madness, and drive Wells and Jane home. The couple accepted, as they didn't fancy traipsing round London in their nightclothes. Doyle continued down the museum steps at a vigorous trot while Wells and Jane sank onto one of the steps, utterly exhausted.

"Jane, I don't feel like a dream, or someone's memory," Wells sighed, returning to the subject that was troubling him. "Do you really believe what Ramsey said is true? Do you think we are here now because someone is telling our story? Because if that is the truth, then I shan't write another word as long as I live . . ."

Jane chuckled.

"What do you find so funny? Go on, tell me; you know I don't like it when you keep your opinions to yourself."

"I am laughing because I can't think what else you would do if you didn't write."

Wells bridled. "Well, lots of things, actually. Teaching, for example. I was rather good at that, if you remember . . ."

"You hated it, dear."

Well . . . then I could devote myself to being the most romantic husband in the world. I could come home every day in a hot-air balloon, perform the most incredible feats . . ."

"You have already performed the most incredible feat of all, Bertie: you saved my life, and you saved the world. How could you improve on that?"

"Hmm, well . . . I suppose you are right. I have made it very difficult for myself. I don't think even Murray could improve on that, do you?"

Jane's face broke into an amused smile.

"Listen to me, dear," she said, resting her head on his shoulder. "If writing seems like a terrible thing to you now, it is only because you associate it with the traumatic experience we have just been through. But remember what I have always told you: you must ignore any disturbing factor. You like writing. You always have. And you will like it again. Why should you care if your creations come to life in other worlds? You will probably never see them again . . ."

"But supposing for instance I write about a mother whose child dies. Wouldn't I feel responsible for—"

"What does that matter?" Jane quickly interjected. "Doubtless another Wells will write about her not losing her child. And as for the idea that we might be someone else's creations . . ." Jane shrugged. "Well, I only hope our author has good taste in babies' names."

Wells looked at her, puzzled.

"Why do you say that?

"Because it would be terrible if our narrator called our firstborn Marmaduke or Wilhelmina, don't you think?"

So saying, she gently patted her belly. Wells leapt to his feet.

"Do you mean that . . . ? But how? Since when have you known?"

"I wouldn't have expected a biologist to ask how. As for your second, far more sensible question: I have known for a few days, but I didn't tell you because, well . . . I didn't want to worry you, what with the end of the world being just round the corner and everything."

"You didn't want to . . ."

Wells looked at her in astonishment, as if he were seeing her for the first time. This was the woman he loved, crouched on a dusty step, embracing her knees in an attempt to cover her legs with her thin white nightie, her chestnut hair falling over her eyes, eyes that had seen inconceivable horrors, tiny and fragile like a china figurine, and yet equally capable of plunging a hairpin into the eye of the most fearful Villain as she was of consoling her husband after some critic demolished one of his novels.

"My dear . . . ," he said with a lump in his throat, kneeling down beside her. "To think that you kept that secret to yourself all those days we were waiting for the Invisible Man to come. That you have you listened to me holding forth about Clayton, the book, the end of the world, the blasted ambush, and that you didn't tell me anything so as not to worry me. To think that you have endured the horror of the past few hours knowing that . . . Good heavens . . . You are the bravest woman in the world! And I am a . . . boor." He cupped Jane's face in his hands. "We are going to have a baby!" he exclaimed, as if he had only just realized, and she nodded, tears in her eyes. "This is the most wonderful thing that could happen to us; it is fantastic, incredible; it is . . ." Wells shook his head, at a loss for words. "You see? And besides being a boor, I am a dreadful writer. I can't even think of the proper adjective to describe this miracle . . ."

She grinned happily, abandoning herself to her husband's embraces. "Well, don't give it another thought, Bertie. Perhaps it is just one of those things that happen simply because they *can* happen."

41

STROLLING THROUGH THE GARDEN OF HER parents' home during the first days of autumn made Emma feel doubly sad. The trees were turning a tragically bright orange, fallen leaves blurred the contours of the paths, the ponds reflected leaden skies, and a cold breeze surprised her round every corner like a capricious child. Still, even though they only made her gloomier, Emma refused to give up her walks: it was the only way of airing out her soul, now that apathy had prompted her to reduce the world to her parents' house. She had no desire to walk in Central Park or go to the theater or opera, or pursue any activity that involved meeting people. She didn't want them looking at her pityingly, assessing her strength or fragility. Nor did she wish to receive the spurious condolences of those who had criticized her when she had announced her betrothal to the millionaire Montgomery Gilmore. New York had never interested her, and now the entire world and all its inhabitants didn't interest her either, because he was no longer among them. But at least she had the garden, which with all its secret corners was big enough for her to wander around, fleeing her mother's kindly gaze. It was her second refuge.

Her first was her dreams. Those curious, often-recurring dreams. When she awoke, she couldn't remember all the details, yet she felt a tiny spark ignite in her frozen heart, a sensation that lasted almost the entire day. And she had no doubt that this pleasant warmth was because she had spoken with him. The dream was always the same: she was in her room, doing something, when he called to her from the mirror.

She would go over to the glass where he was reflected, pale and gaunt, his hair disheveled, as if he were trapped in the kingdom of the dead. After smiling at each other for a long time, they would try to hold hands through the mirror, but they never could, and he would end up beating his fists against the glass in despair, furious that they were so close and yet so far away. When at last he calmed down, she would ask him to forgive her for having insisted that she drive, because if she hadn't he would still be alive, and he would shake his head and say it didn't matter, and, between sobs, he would promise to come back, to find the way to reach her world. Emma did not know what those dreams meant, but they were so vivid that the following day she could not help peering into all the mirrors in the house with a mixture of foreboding and anticipation, as though expecting to find something reflected there other than what was in front of them. On those days when the imprint of his voice warmed her heart, it felt as if he were less dead.

Lost in her thoughts, Emma walked down one of the paths leading to the pond. She studied her reflection in the grey water: a figure in mourning, a black, quivering teardrop. She breathed a sigh, folding her arms around herself, and rocking gently. She closed her eyes, trying to grasp the sensations the dreams aroused in her, that warm, pleasurable memory that made her glow inside.

"I'll come for you," he would tell her in her dreams. "I promise. I will find the way to reach your world. The word 'impossible' doesn't exist in my vocabulary!"

And she believed him, just as she had always done. Yes, he would find a way to reach her, to bridge the abyss separating them. How could she not believe in a man who had asked for her hand by planting a Martian cylinder on Horsell Common, who had created a world within a world only for her, who knew how to make her laugh? How could she not believe that this man, who alone had achieved the miracle of making her fall in love, would not come for her? That was why, whenever she was in the garden, she would make herself forget he had died, pretending he was simply keeping her waiting interminably the way he used to, and that she was putting up with it because she knew that sooner or later he would arrive. He would arrive inventing the most hilarious excuse, tying himself up in such knots with his apologies that, instead of justifying himself, he would condemn himself hopelessly. But he would arrive. She had never had the slightest doubt about that, so why should she doubt his promise now? Because he had only made it in her dreams? Because the man who had promised he would come back lay six feet under the ground?

She opened her eyes. Her reflection was still shimmering on the water, but behind her, a few feet away . . . His suit was torn in several places and had bloodstains on the shoulder, as though after dying in the accident his first thought had been to come and find her, without stopping to change. She didn't turn round. She doubted he was real, convinced that she had finally lost her mind. Until he spoke.

"Hello, Miss Mournful. I told you I'd be back."

Emma gritted her teeth and felt her heart leap.

"And I've been waiting for you, Mr. Impossible," she replied.

Then she wheeled round, and their eyes locked.

"You're late," she reproached him.

He raised his eyebrows.

"Er, forgive me, but . . . ," he stammered in apology. "I was helping to save the world."

She smiled and stepped forward, lips parted, those lips that believed they would never kiss anyone again. And the whole world was reduced to the precise length of each moment that separated them.

Acknowledgments

Little did I know that when I wrote the first word of this trilogy, more than six hundred thousand would follow. Seven years devoted to this project, including the latest book, dear reader, which you have just finished. If your patience allows, I would like to devote a few more words to thank you for having accompanied me on this long adventure. I hope you enjoyed it as much as I did.

This journey would not have been possible without the help of some wonderful people: my publisher, Judith Curr, and editor, Johanna Castillo, along with the entire team at Atria Books in New York, and my agents, Tom and Elaine Colchie, whose enthusiasm for my work is priceless.

As I've said before, only geniuses are capable of writing novels without help. The rest of us need someone who can look at it from the outside while we are writing, to let us know whenever we have lost sight of our goal. In my case, my friend and colleague Lorenzo Luengo acted as a lookout during this journey, and I can never thank him enough for his enthusiasm.

But this titanic project would not have come to fruition without the compass of my own discerning Jane, who hides behind the initials M.J. She has been my muse for all this time, and she took her job so seriously that she didn't just inspire me but whispered many of these pages in my ear. Without her, this book would not only have been a very different one, but it might not even exist. I can only thank her and put here in writing that I cannot imagine a more exciting adventure than loving her every day.

I also want to thank Alex for being the teenager and son I would have liked to be.

It would be impolite if I did not include in my thanks the master H. G. Wells, who started as one of my favorite writers and, after seven years of living together, ended up becoming a brother. Thank you, Bertie, for your novels that inspire the imagination of many readers, including one who now writes the last word of this trilogy and who owes you so much.

Cast of Characters

Given the many twists and turns of the plot and the numerous characters in this novel, I feel obliged to provide my kind readers with a list of those who are most important. In strict order of appearance, this is as follows:

Observer Wells: Eminent biologist, an alternative version of the author H. G. Wells in a parallel world.

Observer Jane: Observer Wells's spouse, project director in Wells's laboratory, an alternative version of Amy Catherine Robbins in a parallel world.

Observer Dodgson: Professor of mathematics, an alternative version of the author Lewis Carroll in a parallel world.

Newton: A Border Collie used by Observer Wells in his experiments.

Herbert George Wells: A British author more commonly known as H. G. Wells, considered the father of science fiction. Among other books, he wrote *The Time Machine, The War of the Worlds,* and *The Invisible Man.* For anyone who has read those three novels, I need add nothing more, except perhaps that in 1970 Wells had a lunar impact crater named after him.

Amy Catherine Robbins: The author H. G. Wells's spouse, whom he affectionately nicknamed "Jane."

Cornelius Clayton: An inspector with Scotland Yard's Special Branch, responsible for investigating the supernatural. Since losing his left hand on his first mission he has used an elaborate wood and metal prosthesis.

Angus Sinclair: Captain at Scotland Yard's Special Branch. No one knows how he lost his right eye, so an accident with a pair of tweezers cannot be ruled out.

Valerie de Bompard: A beautiful French countess residing in the accursed village of Blackmoor, and Inspector Clayton's love interest.

Armand de Bompard: Husband of the Countess de Bompard, a scientist ahead of his time.

Muscardinus avellanarius: Also known as the hazel dormouse, a species native to the British Isles.

Madame Amber: A famous medium from London, specialist in ectoplasmic materializations.

Sir Henry Blendell: Architect to Her Majesty Queen Victoria, creator of the most celebrated secret passageways and trick furniture in history, a man of outstanding moral virtue until proven otherwise.

Theodore Ramsey: Surgeon, chemist, and eminent biologist, given to cracking his knuckles.

Sir William Crookes: Well-known scientist and investigator of paranormal phenomena. Renowned for his defense of the medium Florence Cook, who communicated with the spirit of Katie King, daughter of the legendary pirate Henry Morgan.

Catherine Lansbury: An elderly lady with a mysterious past, a widow with an interest in spiritualism, inventor of the Mechanical Servant, who has a penchant for Kemp's biscuits.

Cast of Characters

The Invisible Man: The villain of the piece, a ruthless killer who is known as M.

Clive Higgins: Doctor of neurology, psychoanalysis, and other afflictions of the soul.

Gilliam Murray: Known as the Master of Time, who died in the fourth dimension. From then on poses as the millionaire Montgomery Gilmore, who suffers from vertigo.

Emma Harlow: A young lady from New York, engaged to Gilmore, who refuses to be wooed as other women are.

Dorothy Harlow: Emma's aunt, an embittered old maid, condemned to die alone.

Baskerville: Gilmore's coachman, who is at least eighty and has a phobia about dogs.

Arthur Conan Doyle: Scottish physician and author, adept of spiritualism and allegedly telepathic, famous for being the creator of Sherlock Holmes, the most renowned detective in the world.

Jean Leckie: Arthur Conan Doyle's lover.

Executioner 2087V: A cyber creature programmed to kill anyone who has the ability to jump between worlds. Efficient at his job but suffers from overwhelming feelings of guilt owing to a design defect.

Cleeve: Head butler at Undershaw. Nothing is known about his private life.

Alfred Wood: Alias "Woodie," stoic personal secretary to Arthur Conan Doyle and a more than decent cricketer.

The Great Ankoma: Also known as Amoka or Makoma; a fabulous medium brought up in South Africa by a Bantu tribe, and who specializes in automatic writing. His name, when pronounced correctly, translates as "last-born child," although we cannot be sure of this.

Alice Liddell: A six-year-old girl, one of Dean Liddell's three daughters, and the real-life inspiration for Alice in *Alice's Adventures in Wonderland*.

Lewis Carroll: Pseudonym of the British author Charles Dodgson, who wrote *Alice's Adventures in Wonderland* and its sequel, *Through the Looking Glass*. He also published numerous articles and books on mathematics under his real name, and was a prominent photographer and a harmless dreamer with a charming stutter. For reasons unknown, he refused to be ordained a priest while a professor at Christ Church, Oxford.

Elmer: Gilmore's butler, happily married to Daisy, who is addicted to blueberry muffins.

Eric Rücker Eddison: British author known chiefly for his first novel, *The Worm Ouroboros,* an homage to Norse mythology. Many scholars consider this work as paving the way for modern fantasy fiction.

The Map of Chaos: A book containing the key to saving this and all other worlds imaginable.